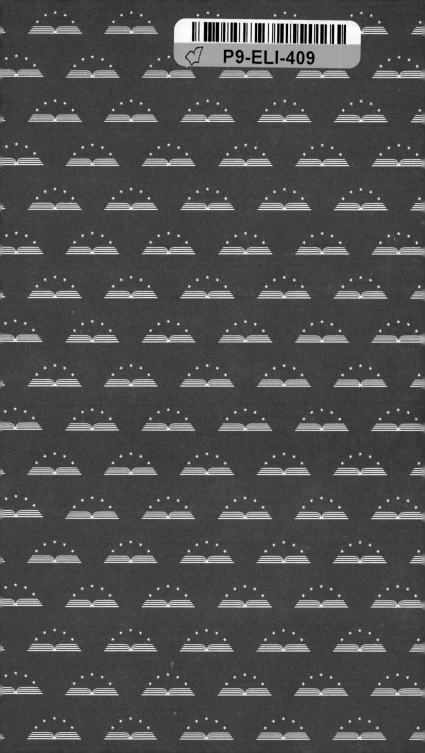

Library of America, a nonprofit organization,
champions our nation's cultural heritage
by publishing America's greatest writing in
authoritative new editions and providing resources
for readers to explore this rich, living legacy.

ELMORE LEONARD

ELMORE LEONARD

WESTERNS

Last Stand at Saber River
Hombre
Valdez is Coming
Forty Lashes Less One
Stories

Terrence Rafferty, *editor*

THE LIBRARY OF AMERICA

This paper meets the requirements of
ANSI/NISO Z39.48–1992 (Permanence of Paper).

Distributed to the trade in the United States
by Penguin Random House Inc.
and in Canada by Penguin Random House Canada Ltd.

Library of Congress Control Number: 2017951258
ISBN 978–1–59853–562–4

———

First Printing
The Library of America—308

Contents

LAST STAND AT SABER RIVER

1

PAUL CABLE sat hunched forward at the edge of the pine shade, his boots crossed and his elbows supported on his knees. He put the field glasses to his eyes again and, four hundred yards down the slope, the two-story adobe was brought suddenly, silently before him.

This was The Store. It was Denaman's. It was a plain, tan-pink southern Arizona adobe with a wooden loading platform, but no *ramada* to hold off the sun. It was the only general supply store from Hidalgo north to Fort Buchanan; and until the outbreak of the war it had been a Hatch & Hodges swing station.

The store was familiar and it was good to see, because it meant Cable and his family were almost home. Martha was next to him, the children were close by; they were anxious to be home after two and a half years away from it. But the sight of a man Cable had never seen before—a man with one arm—had stopped them.

He stood on the loading platform facing the empty sunlight of the yard, staring at the willow trees that screened the river close beyond the adobe, his right hand on his hip, his left sleeve tucked smoothly, tightly into his waist. Above him, the faded, red-lettered *Denaman's Store* inscription extended the full width of the adobe's double doors.

Cable studied the man. There was something about him.

Perhaps because he had only one arm. No, Cable thought then, that made you think of the war, the two and a half years of it, but you felt something before you saw he had only one arm.

Then he realized it was the habit of surviving formed during two and a half years of war. The habit of not trusting any movement he could not immediately identify. The habit of not walking into anything blindly. He had learned to use patience and weigh alternatives and to be sure of a situation before he acted. As sure as he could be in his own mind.

Now Cable's glasses moved over the wind-scarred face of the adobe, following the one-armed man's gaze to the grove of willows and the river hidden beyond the hanging screen of branches.

A girl came out of the trees carrying a bucket and Cable said, "There's Luz again. Here—" He handed the glasses to his wife who was kneeling, sitting back on her legs, one hand raised to shield her eyes from the sun glare.

Martha Cable raised the glasses. After a moment she said, "It's Luz Acaso. But still it doesn't seem like Luz."

"All of a sudden she's a grown-up woman," Cable said. "She'd be eighteen now."

"No," Martha said. "It's something else. Her expression. The way she moves."

Through the glasses, the girl crossed the yard leisurely. Her eyes were lowered and did not rise until she reached the platform and started up the steps. When she looked up her face was solemn and warm brown in the sunlight. Martha remembered Luz's knowing eyes and her lips that were always softly parted, ready to smile or break into laughter. But now she wore an expression of weariness. Her eyes went to the man on the platform, then away from him quickly as he glanced at her and she passed into the store.

She's tired, or ill, Martha thought. Or afraid.

"She went inside?" Cable asked.

The glasses lowered briefly and Martha nodded. "But he's still there. Cabe, for some reason I think she's afraid of him."

"Maybe." He watched Martha concentrating on the man on the platform. "But why, if Denaman's there?"

"If he's there," Martha said.

"Where else would he be?"

"I was going to ask the same question."

"Well, let's take it for granted he's inside."

"And Manuel?" She was referring to Luz's brother.

"Manuel could be anywhere."

Martha was still watching the man on the platform, studying him so that an impression of him would be left in her mind. He was a tall man, heavy boned, somewhat thin with dark hair and mustache. He was perhaps in his late thirties. His left arm was off between the shoulder and the elbow.

"I suppose he was in the war," Martha said.

"Probably." Cable nodded thoughtfully. "But which side?" That's something, Cable said to himself. You don't trust him. Any man seen from a distance you dislike and distrust. It's good to be careful, but you could be carrying it too far.

Briefly he thought of John Denaman, the man who had given him his start ten years before and talked him into settling in the Saber River valley. It would be good to see John again. And it would be good to see Luz, to talk to her, and Manuel. His good friend Manuel. Luz and Manuel's father had worked for Denaman until a sudden illness took his life. After that, John raised both of them as if they were his own children.

"Now he's going inside," Martha said.

Cable waited. After a moment he turned, pushing himself up, and saw his daughter standing only a few feet away. Clare was six, their oldest child: a quiet little girl with her mother's dark hair and eyes and showing signs of developing her mother's clean-lined, easily remembered features; resembling her mother just as the boys favored their father. She stood uncertainly with her hands clutched to her chest.

"Sister, you round up the boys."

"Are we going now?"

"In a minute."

He watched her run back into the trees and in a moment he heard a boy's shrill voice. That would be Davis, five years old. Sandy, not yet four, would be close behind his brother, following every move Davis made; almost every move.

Cable brought his sorrel gelding out of the trees and stepped into the saddle. "He'll come out again when he hears me," Cable said. "But wait till you see us talking before you come down. All right?"

Martha nodded. She smiled faintly, saying, "He'll probably turn out to be an old friend of John Denaman's."

"Probably."

Cable nudged the sorrel with his heels and rode off down the yellow sweep of hillside, sitting erect and tight to the saddle with his right knee touching the stock of a Spencer carbine, his right elbow feeling the Walker Colt on his hip, and keeping his eyes on the adobe now, thinking: This could be a scout. This could be the two and a half years still going on. . . .

As soon as he had made up his mind to enlist he had sold his stock, all of his cattle, all two hundred and fifty head, and all but three of his horses. He had put Martha and the children in the wagon and taken them to Sudan, Texas, to the home of Martha's parents. He did this because he believed deeply in the Confederacy, as he believed in his friends who had gone to fight for it.

Because of a principle he traveled from the Saber River, Arizona Territory, to Chattanooga, Tennessee, taking with him a shotgun, a revolving pistol and two horses; and there on June 21, 1862, he joined J. A. Wharton's 8th Texas Cavalry, part of Nathan Bedford Forrest's command.

Three weeks later Cable saw his first action and received his first wound during Forrest's raid on Murfreesboro. On September 3, Paul Cable was commissioned a captain and appointed to General Forrest's escort. From private to captain in less than three months; those things happened in Forrest's command. Wounded twice again after Murfreesboro; the third and final time on November 28, 1864, at a place called Huey's Mills—shot from his saddle as they crossed the Duck River to push Wilson's Union Cavalry back to Franklin, Tennessee. Cable, with gunshot wounds in his left hip and thigh, was taken to the hospital at Columbia. On December 8 he was told to go home "the best way you know how." There were more seriously wounded men who needed his cot; there would be a flood of them soon, with General Hood about to pounce on the Yankees at Nashville. Go home, he was told, and thank God for your gunshot wounds.

So for Cable the war was over, though it was still going on in the east and the feeling of it was still with him. He was not yet thirty, a lean-faced man above average height and appearing older after his service with Nathan Bedford Forrest: after Chickamauga, had come Fort Pillow, Bryce's Crossroads, Thompson's Station, three raids into West Tennessee and a hundred nameless skirmishes. He was a calm-appearing man and the war had not changed that. A clear-thinking kind of man who had taught himself to read and write, taught himself the basic rules and his wife had helped him from there.

Martha Sanford Cable was twenty-seven now. A West Texas

girl, though convent-educated in New Orleans. Seven years before she had left Sudan to come to the Saber River as Paul Cable's wife, to help him build a home and provide him with a family. . . .

Now they were returning to the home they had built with the family they had begun. They were before Denaman's Store, only four miles from their own land.

And Cable was entering the yard, still with his eyes on the loading platform and the double doors framed in the pale wall of the adobe, reining in his sorrel and approaching at a walk.

The right-hand door opened and the man with one arm stepped out to the platform. He walked to the edge of it and stood with his thumb in his belt looking down at Cable.

Cable came on. He kept his eyes on the man, but said nothing until he had pulled to a halt less than ten feet away. From the saddle, Cable's eyes were even with the man's knees.

"John Denaman inside?"

The man's expression did not change. "He's not here any more."

"He moved?"

"You could say that."

"Maybe I should talk to Luz," Cable said.

The man's sunken cheeks and the full mustache covering the line of his mouth gave his face a hard, bony expression, but it was not tensed. He said, "You know Luz?"

"Since she was eight years old," Cable answered. "Since the day I first set foot in this valley."

"Well, now—" The hint of a smile altered the man's gaunt expression. "You wouldn't be Cable, would you?"

Cable nodded.

"Home from the wars." The man still seemed to be smiling. "Luz's mentioned you and your family. Her brother too. He tells how you and him fought off Apaches when they raided your stock."

Cable nodded. "Where's Manuel now?"

"Off somewhere." The man paused. "You been to your place yet?"

"We're on our way."

"You've got a surprise coming."

Cable watched him, showing little curiosity. "What does that mean?"

"You'll find out."

"I think you're changing the subject," Cable said mildly. "I asked you what happened to John Denaman."

For a moment the man said nothing. He turned then and called through the open door, "Luz, come out here!"

Cable watched him. He saw the man's heavy-boned face turn to look down at him again, and almost immediately the Mexican girl appeared in the doorway. Cable's hand went to the curled brim of his hat.

"Luz, honey, you're a welcome sight." He said it warmly, and he wanted to jump up on the platform and kiss her but the presence of this man stopped him.

"Paul—"

He saw the surprise in the expression of her mouth and in her eyes, but it was momentary and she returned his gaze with a smile that was grave and without joy, a smile that vanished the instant the man with one arm spoke.

"Luz, tell him what happened to Denaman."

"You haven't told him?" She looked at Cable quickly, then seemed to hesitate. "Paul, he's dead. He died almost a year ago."

"Nine months," the man with one arm said. "I came here the end of August. He died the month before."

Cable's eyes were on the man, staring at him, feeling now that he had known Denaman was dead, had sensed it from the way the man had spoken—from the tone of his voice.

"You could have come right out and told me," Cable said.

"Well, you know now."

"Like you were making a game out of it."

The man stared down at Cable indifferently. "Why don't you just let it go?"

"Paul," Luz said, "it came unexpectedly. He wasn't sick."

"His heart?"

Luz nodded. "He collapsed shortly after noon and by that evening he was dead."

"And you happened to come a month later," Cable said, looking at the man again.

"Why don't you ask what I'm doing here?" The man looked up at the sound of the double team wagon on the grade, his eyes half closed in the sunlight, his gaze holding on the far slope now. "That your family?"

"Wife and three youngsters," Cable said.

The man's gaze came down. "You made a long trip for nothing." He seemed about to smile, though he was not smiling now.

"All right," Cable said. "Why?"

"Some men are living in your house."

"If there are, they're about to move."

The smile never came, but the man stared down at Cable intently. "Come inside and I'll tell you about it." Then he turned abruptly, though he glanced again at the approaching wagon before going into the store.

Cable could hear the jingling, creaking sound of the wagon closer now, but he kept his eyes on Luz until she looked at him.

"Luz, who is he?"

"His name is Edward Janroe."

"The man acts like he owns the place."

Her eyes rose briefly. "He does. Half of it."

"But why—"

"Are you coming?" Janroe was in the doorway. He was looking at Cable and with a nod of his head indicated Luz. "You got to drag things out of her. I've found it's more trouble than it's worth." He waited until Cable stirred in the saddle and began to dismount. "I'll be inside," he said, and stepped away from the door.

Cable dropped his reins, letting them trail. He swung down and mounted the steps to the platform. For a moment he watched Luz Acaso in silence.

"Are you married to him?"

"No."

"But he's been living here eight months and has a half interest in the store."

"You think what you like."

"I'm not thinking anything. I want to know what's going on."

"He'll tell you whatever you want to know."

"Luz, do you think I'm being nosy? I want to help you."

"I don't need help." She was looking beyond him, watching the wagon entering the yard.

All right, he thought, don't push her. It occurred to him then that Martha was the one to handle Luz. Why keep harping at her and get her nervous. Martha could soothe the details out of her in a matter of minutes.

Cable patted her shoulder and stepped past her into the abrupt dimness of the store.

He moved down the counter that lined the front wall, his hand gliding along the worn, shiny edge of it and his eyes roaming over the almost bare shelves. There were scattered rows of canned goods, bolts of material, work clothes, boxes that told nothing of their contents. Above, Rochester lamps hanging from a wooden beam, buckets and bridles and coils of rope. Most of the goods on the shelves had the appearance of age, as if they had been here a long time.

Cable's eyes lowered and he almost stopped, unexpectedly seeing Janroe beyond the end of the counter in the doorway to the next room. Janroe was watching him closely.

"You walk all right," Janroe said mildly. "Not a mark on you that shows; but they wouldn't have let you go without a wound."

"It shows if I walk far enough," Cable said. "Or if I stay mounted too long."

"That sounds like the kind of wound to have. Where'd you get it?"

"On the way to Nashville."

"With Hood?"

"In front of him. With Forrest."

"You're a lucky man. I mean to be in one piece."

"I suppose."

"Take another case. I was with Kirby Smith from the summer of sixty-one to a year later when we marched up the Kentucky River toward Lexington. Near Richmond we met a Yankee general named Bull Nelson." Janroe's eyes narrowed and he grinned faintly, remembering the time. "He just had recruits, a pick-up army, and I'll tell you we met them good. Cut clean the hell through them, and the ones we didn't kill ran like you never saw men run in your life. The cavalry people mopped up after that and we took over four thousand prisoners that one afternoon."

Janroe paused and the tone of his voice dropped. "But there was one battery of theirs on a ridge behind a stone fence. I was taking some men up there to get them . . . and the next day I woke up in a Richmond field hospital without an arm."

He was watching Cable closely. "You see what I mean? We'd licked them. The fight was over and put away. But because of this one battery not knowing enough to give up, or too scared to, I lost a good arm."

But you've got one left and you're out of the war, so why don't you forget about it, Cable thought, and almost said it; but instead he nodded, looking at the shelves.

"Maybe Luz told you I was in the army," Janroe said.

"No, only your name, and that you own part of the store."

"That's a start. What else do you want to know?"

"Why you're here."

"You just said it. Because I own part of the store."

"Then how you came to be here."

"You've got a suspicious mind."

"Look," Cable said quietly, "John Denaman was a friend of mine. He dies suddenly and you arrive to buy in."

"That's right. But you want to know what killed him?"

When Cable said nothing Janroe's eyes lifted to the almost bare shelves. "He didn't have enough goods to sell. He didn't have regular money coming in. He worried, not knowing what was going to happen to his business." Janroe's gaze lowered to Cable again. "He even worried about Luz and Vern Kidston. They were keeping company and, I'm told, the old man didn't see eye to eye with Vern. Because of different politics, you might say. So it was a combination of things that killed him. Worries along with old age. And if you think it was anything else, you're going on pure imagination."

"Let's go back to Vern Kidston," Cable said. "I never heard of him; so what you're saying doesn't mean a whole lot."

Janroe's faint smile appeared. "Vern came along about two years ago, I'm told. He makes his living supplying the Union cavalry with remounts. Delivers them up to Fort Buchanan."

"He lives near here?"

"In the old Toyopa place. How far's that from you?"

"About six miles."

"They say Vern's fixed it up."

"It'd take a lot of fixing. The house was half burned down."

"Vern's got the men."

"I'll have to meet him."

"You will. You'll meet him all right."

Cable's eyes held on Janroe. "It sounds like you can hardly wait."

"There's your suspicious mind again." Janroe straightened and stepped into the next room. "Come on. It's time I poured you a drink."

Cable followed, his gaze going from left to right around the well-remembered room: from the door that led to the kitchen to the roll-top desk to the Hatch & Hodges calendar to the corner fireplace and the leather-bottomed chairs, to the pictures of the Holy Family and the Sierra Madre landscapes on the wall, to the stairway leading to the second floor (four rooms up, Cable remembered), and finally to the round dining table between the front windows. He watched Janroe go into the kitchen and come out with a bottle of mescal and two glasses, holding the glasses in his fingers and the bottle pressed between his arm and his body.

Janroe nodded to the table. "Sit down. You're going to need this."

Cable pulled out a chair and stepped over it. He watched Janroe sit down and pour the clear, colorless liquor.

"Does my needing this have to do with Vern Kidston?"

Janroe sipped his mescal and put his glass down gently. "Vern's the one living in your house. Not Vern himself. Some of his men." Janroe leaned closer as if to absorb a reaction from Cable. "They're living in your house with part of Vern's horse herd grazing in your meadow."

"Well"—Cable raised the glass of mescal, studying it in the light of the window behind Janroe—"I don't blame him. It's good graze." He drank off some of the sweet-tasting liquor. "But now he'll move his men out. That's all."

"You think so?"

"If he doesn't vacate I'll get the law."

"What law?"

"Fort Buchanan. That's closest."

"And who do you think the Yankees would side with," Janroe asked, "the ex-Rebel or the mustanger supplying them with remounts?"

Janroe looked up and Cable turned in his chair as Luz entered from the store. Behind her came Martha holding Sandy's hand and moving Clare and Davis along in front of her.

"We'll see what happens," Cable said. He rose, holding out his hand as Davis ran to him and stood close against his leg.

"Mr. Janroe, this is my wife, Martha." He glanced at Janroe who had made no move to rise. "This boy here is Davis. The little one's Sanford and our big girl there is Clare, almost seven years old already." Cable winked at his daughter, but she was staring with open curiosity at Janroe's empty sleeve.

Martha's hand went to the little girl's shoulder and she smiled pleasantly at the man still hunched over the table.

"Mr. Janroe"—Martha spoke calmly—"you don't know how good it is to be back here again." She was worried one of the children might ask about Janroe's missing arm. Cable knew this. He could sense it watching her, though outwardly Martha was at ease.

Luz said, "I invited them for dinner."

Janroe was staring at Clare. She looked away and his eyes went to Davis, holding him, as if defying him to speak. Then, slowly, he sat back and looked up at Luz.

"Take the kids with you. They'll eat in the kitchen."

Luz hesitated, then nodded quickly and held out her hand to Sandy. The boy looked up at her and pressed closer into his mother's skirts.

"They're used to being with me," Martha said pleasantly. Gently she urged Clare forward, smiling at Luz now, though the Mexican woman did not return her smile. "While Cabe . . . while Paul was away the children didn't have the opportunity to meet many new people. I'm afraid they're just a little bit strange now."

"If they eat," Janroe said, "they still eat in the kitchen."

Martha's face colored. "Mr. Janroe, I was merely explaining—"

"The point is, Mrs. Cable, there's nothing to explain. In this house kids don't sit at the table with grownups."

Martha felt the heat on her face and she glanced at her

husband, at Cable who stood relaxed with the calm, tell-nothing expression she had learned to understand and respect. It isn't your place to answer him, she thought. But now the impulse was too strong and she could no longer hold back her words, though when she spoke her voice was calm and controlled.

"Now that you've said it three times, Mr. Janroe, we will always remember that in this house children do not eat with grownups."

"Mrs. Cable"—Janroe spoke quietly, sitting straight up and with his hand flat and unmoving on the table—"if your husband has one friend around here it's going to be me. Not because I'm pro-South or anti-Union. Not because I favor the man who's at a disadvantage. But because I don't have a reason not to befriend your husband. Now that's a pretty flimsy basis for a friendship."

"If you think I was rude," Martha said patiently, "I apologize. Perhaps I did—"

"Just wait a minute." Janroe brought up his hand to stop her. "I want you to realize something. I want you to understand that I don't have to smile at your husband for his business. If you don't trade with me you go to Fort Buchanan and that's a two-day trip. Add to that, I do business with the Kidstons. They buy most of the goods as fast as I receive them. And I'll tell you right now, once they learn I'm dealing with your husband they're going to come in here and yell for me to stop."

"Mr. Janroe—"

"But you know what I'll answer them? I'll tell them to go to Buchanan or hell with their business, either one. Because no man on earth comes into my house and tells me what I can do or what I can't do. Not Vern Kidston or his brother; not you or your husband here."

Janroe relaxed against the back of his chair. "That's how it is, Mrs. Cable. I'd suggest you think about it before you speak out the first thing that comes to your mind."

Again there was silence. Cable saw his wife tense, controlling herself with a fixed tightness about her nose and mouth. She stared at Janroe.

"Martha," Cable said mildly, "why don't you take the children to the kitchen? Maybe you could help Luz dish up."

Martha looked at him, but said nothing. She held out her hand to Davis, gathered her children about her, and followed the girl to the kitchen.

"Your wife looks like a woman of strong character," Janroe said as Cable sat down again.

"She sticks up for what she believes."

"Yes," Janroe said. "A strong-minded woman. I noticed you *asked* her when you told her to go to the kitchen. You said, 'Why don't you take the children? . . .'"

Cable stared at him. "I think I said that."

"I've found," Janroe said, "it works a sight better to *tell* women what to do. Never *ask* them. Especially a wife. You were away for a while and your wife took on some independence. Well, now you're back I'd suggest you assume your place as head of the family."

Cable leaned forward, resting his arms on the edge of the table. "Mr. Janroe, I'd suggest you mind your own business."

"I'm giving you good advice, whether you know it or not."

"All I know about you so far," Cable said quietly, "is that you like to talk. I've got no reason to respect your advice. I've got no reason to respect you or anything about you."

He saw Janroe about to speak. "Now wait a minute. You gave my wife a lecture on what she was supposed to understand. I stood by and watched you insult her. But now I'll tell you this, Mr. Janroe: if you didn't have the misfortune of being one-armed you never would have said those things. You might be a strong-minded, hard-nosed individual who doesn't care what anybody thinks and who won't stand for any kind of dependence. You might even be a man to admire. But if you had had both your arms when you said those things, I'd have broken your jaw."

Janroe stared at Cable, his chest rising and falling with his breathing. He remained silent.

"I'm sorry I had to say that," Cable told him after a moment. "But now we know where we stand. You've got your ideas and I've got mine. If they cross, then I guess you and I aren't going to get along."

Janroe sipped his mescal, taking his time, and set the glass down gently. "You were with Bedford Forrest," he said then. "Were you an officer?"

"I reached captain."

"That speaks well of you, doesn't it—an officer with Forrest?"

"It depends from which side you view it."

"How long were you with him?"

"Since June, sixty-two."

"In the saddle most every day. Living outside and fighting—" Janroe's head nodded slowly. He raised the glass again. "You might be able to break my jaw at that."

"Maybe I shouldn't have said that."

"Don't back off. I'm being realistic, not apologizing. I'm saying you *might*."

Cable stared at him. "Maybe we should start all over again."

"No, I think we've come a long way in a short time."

"Except," Cable said, "you know more about me than I do about you."

"You don't have to know anything about me," Janroe said. "The Kidstons are your problem."

"I'll talk to them."

"But why should they talk to you?" Janroe watched him intently. "You're one man against, say, fifteen. You're an ex-Confederate in Union territory. The Kidstons themselves are Yankees. They sell most of their cattle and all of their horses to the Union army. Vern's brother Duane even held a command, but now he's back and he's brought the war with him. Has everybody calling him 'The Major' and he orders Vern's riders about like they were his personal cavalry." Janroe shook his head. "They don't have to listen to you."

Cable shrugged. "We'll see what happens."

"How do you eat?" Janroe asked. "That's your first problem."

"For now," Cable said, "I plan to buy provisions and maybe shoot something. Pretty soon I'll start buying stock and build my herd again."

"Buy it from where?"

"South. Luz's brother has friends in Sonora. I sold my stock to them when I enlisted on the agreement they'd sell back whatever I could buy when I came home."

"Manuel's down that way right now," Janroe said.

Cable's eyes raised. "When will he be back?"

"In a few days, I suppose. But your problem is now. I said before, some of Vern's men are living at your place."

"I'll have a talk with them," Cable said.

"One of them was here this morning. Bill Dancey." Janroe paused as Luz approached the table. She put plates in front of them and a serving dish of meat stew between them. Janroe asked her, "Where's his wife?"

"With the children." Luz served them as she spoke.

"Was Dancey here this morning?"

"I saw no one else."

"Who's up there with him?"

"I think Royce and the one named Joe Bob Dodd."

"Tell Mr. Cable about them."

Luz looked off, as if picturing them, before her eyes lowered to Cable. "Bill Dancey is head. He is a large man and wears a beard and is perhaps ten years older than the others. This Royce and the one called Joe Bob look much alike with their thin faces and bodies and their hats worn straight and low over their eyes. They stand with their hands on their hips in a lazy fashion and say things to each other and laugh, though not genuinely. I think they are Texans."

"They are," Janroe said. "I'm not sure about Dancey. But it's said this Joe Bob and Royce, along with Joe Bob's two older brothers, that's Austin and Wynn, deserted from Sherrod Hunter's Texas Brigade when he came through here and Duane Kidston hired them. They say if Duane knew they'd been Rebel soldiers he'd have a fit." Janroe paused. "Royce and Joe Bob are the ones at your place. Austin and Wynn are probably at the main house."

Cable said, "You're telling me not to go home?"

"I'm telling you how it is. You do what you want."

"We'll leave as soon as we load up."

From the platform Janroe watched the wagon, with Cable's sorrel trailing, move off toward the willows. He watched intently, his right hand on the stump of his arm and massaging it gently, telling himself not to become excited or hasty or jump to conclusions.

But, my God, it was more than he could have hoped blind luck would provide—an ex-Rebel suddenly showing up here; coming home to find the Kidstons on his land.

He's your weapon, Janroe thought. Now it was right in front

of him after months of waiting and watching and wondering how he could make it happen and never be suspected. If necessary he would even apologize to Martha for what he'd said. It had come out too quickly, that was all. He would smooth it over if he had to, because Cable's presence could be far more important than where kids ate, or if they ate at all, for that matter. He would have to watch himself and not let his mind clutch at petty things just to be tearing something apart.

But think it out carefully, he thought, now that there could be a way. Don't stumble; he's right here waiting, but you have to use him properly.

Cable—Janroe could feel the certainty of it inside of him—was going to help him kill Vern and Duane Kidston. And then, thinking of Cable's wife, he decided that before it was all over, Cable would be as dead as the two men he would help kill.

Cable forded the river at the store and followed it north out into the open sunlight of the mile-wide valley, then gradually west, for the valley curved in that direction with the river following close along its left, or west, slope. The far side of the valley was rimmed by a low, curving line of hills. The near slope also rolled green-black with pines; but beyond these hills, chimneyed walls of sandstone towered silently against the sky. Beyond the rock country lay the Kidston place.

Sandy was asleep. Davis and Clare sat on the end-gate, Davis holding the reins of the sorrel. And Martha sat with Cable, listening in silence as he told her everything Janroe had said about the Kidstons.

When he had finished, Martha said, "What if they won't leave, Cabe? The ones in our house."

"Let's wait and see."

"I mean with the children to think of."

"The children and a lot of things," Cable said.

They talked about Luz then. Even in the kitchen, Martha said, Luz had acted strangely: tense and almost reluctant to talk even about everyday things. She did tell that the store had been left to them, to Manuel and herself, in John Denaman's will; and they would stay here. The grave of their mother in a Sonora village was the only tie they had with their birthplace; the store had been their home for a dozen years. Luz had been only six, Manuel twelve, when their father came here to work for John Denaman. The next year their father died of a sickness and John Denaman had cared for them from that day on.

But she related little more about Edward Janroe than what she had told Cable—the man's name, the fact that he owned a half interest in the store and had been here eight or nine months.

But if business was so poor, Cable asked, why would Janroe want to buy into the store?

Because of Luz? Martha offered.

Perhaps. Luz was a good-looking girl. Janroe could easily be attracted to her.

But Martha was sure that Luz still liked Vern Kidston. Luz mentioned that she used to see Vern frequently; but that was before Janroe came. Something else to wonder about. Though Janroe himself was the big question.

"What do you think of him?" Cable asked.

"All I'm sure of is that he has a low opinion of women," Martha said mildly, "judging from the lecture he gave me."

"He won't do that again," Cable said. "I talked to him."

Martha smiled. She moved closer to her husband and put her arm through his.

They rode in silence until they saw, through the willow and aspen along the river, horses grazing farther up the meadow. Martha handed her husband the field glasses and took the reins.

"About thirty, just mares and foals," Cable said after a moment. "And a man with them."

Martha kept the team moving. They were close to the base of the slope with the dark well of pines above them and the river close on their right. Their house was perhaps a quarter of a mile ahead, no more than that, set back a hundred feet from the river; but it was still out of sight, hidden by the pine stands that straggled down from the slope.

Through the glasses, Cable saw the rider come out of the trees on this side of the river. He noticed that the man was bearded and remembered Luz Acaso's description of the one named Bill Dancey: older by ten years than the other two; the one in charge.

"He must have seen us," Cable said. "He just crossed over."

"Waiting for us?" asked Martha.

"No, going for the house." He handed the glasses to Martha, feeling the children close behind him now.

Davis said, "Can I look?"

"Not right now." Cable half turned on the seat. "Listen, I want you children to stay right where you are. Even when we stop, stay there and don't jump off."

Clare's dark eyes were round and open wide. "Why?"

"Because we're not sure we're staying."

Cable looked at the boy again. "Davis, you hold on to Sandy. You won't let him jump out now, will you?"

The little boy shook his head solemnly. "No, sir."

Cable smiled at his children. His hand reached to the wagon bed, felt the short barrel of the Spencer carbine, then moved to the shotgun next to it and brought it out, placing it muzzle-down between them on the seat.

"Martha, this one's yours. Put your hand on it when I climb off, but don't lift it unless you see you have to."

He drew the Walker Colt from its holster, eased back the hammer, turned the cylinder carefully, feeling the oil-smoothness of the action, and lowered the hammer again on the empty chamber.

"There's the house," Martha said anxiously. "Part of it." She could see an adobe-colored shape through the pines close in front of them.

Then, coming out of the trees, the house was in full view: a one-story adobe with an addition made of pine logs, a shingled roof and a ramada that ran the length of the adobe section. Beyond, part of the barn could be seen.

Cable's eyes were on the bearded rider. He was near the house, still mounted but facing them now, watching them approach. A second man had come out of the house and stood near the mounted man.

"This is far enough," Cable said. They were less than fifty feet from the men now. As the wagon stopped a third man, thumbing a suspender strap up over his bare chest, appeared in the doorway of the adobe. All three men were armed. Even the one in the doorway, though half dressed, wore crossed belts holding two holstered revolvers.

"The one in the door," Cable said. "Keep a close eye on

him." Martha made no answer, but he didn't look at her now. He breathed in and out slowly, calming himself and putting it off still another moment, before he jumped down from the wagon, holding his holster to his leg, and moved toward the mounted man.

"You were a while getting here," Bill Dancey said. He dismounted, swinging his leg over carefully, and stood with his feet apart watching Cable coming toward him.

Within two strides Cable stopped. "You knew we were coming?"

"Janroe mentioned it." Dancey's short-clipped beard hid any change of expression. He nodded toward the man who stood near him. "Royce here went in for something I forgot this morning and Janroe told him."

Cable glanced at the one called Royce: a tall, thin-framed man who stood hip-cocked with his thumbs hooked into his belt. His hat was tilted forward, low over his eyes, and he returned Cable's stare confidently.

Royce must have taken the horse trail, a shorter route that followed the crest of the slope, to and from the store; that's why they hadn't seen him, Cable decided.

He looked at Dancey again. "Did Janroe tell him it's my land you're on?"

Dancey nodded. "He mentioned it."

"Then I don't have to explain anything."

"That's right," Royce said. "All you have to do is turn around and go back."

There it was. Cable gave himself time, feeling the tension through his body and the anger, not building, but suddenly there as this lounging, lazy-eyed poser told him very calmly to turn around and go back. At least there was no decision to make. And arguing with him or with Dancey would only waste time. Even with Martha and the children here he knew how far he would go if necessary. He wanted to feel the anger inside of him because it would make it easier; but he wanted also to control it and he let his breath out slowly, shaking his head.

"I was afraid this was going to happen."

"Then why did you come?" Dancey asked.

The back of Cable's hand moved across his mouth, then dropped heavily. "Well, since I own this place—"

Dancey shook his head. "Vern Kidston owns it."

"Just took it?"

"In the name of the United States Government," Dancey said. "Mister, you must've been dreaming. You ever hear of Rebel land in Union territory?"

"I'm not a soldier any more."

"You're not anything any more." Dancey glanced at the wagon. "Your wife's waiting for you. And the kids. You've got kids, haven't you?"

"Three."

"A man doesn't do anything crazy with three kids."

"Not very often," Cable said mildly. His eyes moved to Royce, then past him to the bare-chested man who had come out to the edge of the ramada shade. This would be Joe Bob Dodd. He stood with one hand on his hip, the other raised to a support post. He wore his hair long with sideburns to the angle of his jaw. This and the dark line of hair down the bony white-ness of his chest made him appear obscenely naked. He was somewhat shorter than Royce but had the same slim-hipped, slightly stoop-shouldered build.

Cable's eyes returned to Dancey. "I'll give you the rest of the afternoon to collect your gear and clear out. Fair enough?"

Royce looked over at Joe Bob, grinning. "You hear what he said?"

The man at the ramada nodded. "I heard him."

"You don't have the time to give," Dancey said. "I told you, you're going to turn around and go back."

"Bill," Joe Bob called, "tell him he can leave his woman."

Cable's eyes went to him, feeling the tingle of anger again. No, wait a little more, he thought. Take one thing at a time and don't make it harder than it already is. His gaze returned to Dancey.

"Go get Kidston and I'll talk to him," Cable said.

"He wouldn't waste his time."

"Maybe I would though," Joe Bob said easily. His hand came down from the post and both thumbs hooked into his crossed belts. "Reb, you want to argue over your land?"

"I'll talk to Kidston."

"You'll talk to me if I say so."

Watching him, seeing him beyond the lowered head of

Dancey's horse and feeling Dancey still close to him, Cable said, "I think that's all you are. Just talk."

"Bill," Joe Bob said, "get your horse out of the way."

Cable hesitated.

He sensed Dancey reaching for the reins, his body turning and his hands going to the horse's mane.

And for part of a moment Dancey was half turned from him with his hands raised and the horse was moving, side-stepping, hiding both Royce and Joe Bob, and that was the time.

It was then or not at all and Cable stepped into Dancey, seeing the man's expression change to sudden surprise the moment before his fist hooked into the bearded face. Dancey stumbled against his horse, trying to catch himself against the nervously side-stepping animal, but Cable was with him, clubbing him with both fists, again and again and again, until Dancey sagged, until he went down covering his head.

Cable glanced at the wagon and away from it with the sound of Martha's voice and with the sound of running steps on the hard-packed ground. He saw Joe Bob beyond Dancey's horse. Now a glimpse of Royce jerking the bridle, and a slapping sound and the horse bolted.

Both Joe Bob and Royce stood in front of him, their hands on their revolvers; though neither of them had pulled one clear of its holster. They stood rooted, staring at Cable, stopped suddenly in the act of rushing him. For in one brief moment, in the time it had taken Royce to slap the horse out of the way, they had missed their chance.

Cable stood over Dancey with the Walker Colt in his hand. It was cocked and pointing directly at Dancey's head. Joe Bob and Royce said nothing. Dancey had raised himself on an elbow and was staring at Cable dumbly.

"Now you take off your belts," Cable said. He brought Dancey to his feet and had to prompt them again before they unbuckled their gun belts and let them fall. Then he moved toward Joe Bob.

"You said something about my wife."

"Me?"

"About leaving her here."

Joe Bob shrugged. "That wasn't anything. Just something I felt like saying—"

Abruptly Cable stepped into Joe Bob, hitting him in the face before he could bring up his hands. Joe Bob went down, rolling to his side, and when he looked up at Cable his eyes showed stunned surprise.

"You won't say anything like that again," Cable said.

Dancey had not taken his eyes off Cable. "You didn't give him a chance. Hitting him with a gun in your hand."

Cable glanced at him. "You're in a poor position to argue it."

"In fact," Dancey said, "you didn't give me much of a chance either. Now if you want to put the gun away and go about it fair—"

"That would be something, wouldn't it?"

Dancey said, "You're not proving anything with that gun in your hand."

"I don't have anything to prove."

"All right, then we leave for a while." Dancey looked over at Royce. "Get the stuff out of the house."

"Not now." Cable's voice stopped Royce. "You had a chance. You didn't take it. Now you leave without anything," Cable said. "Don't come back for it either. What doesn't burn goes in the river."

Royce said, "You think we won't be back?"

Cable's gaze shifted. "You'll ride into a double load of buckshot if you do. You can tell Kidston the same."

Royce seemed to grin. "Man, you're made to order. Duane's going to have some fun with you."

Dancey's eyes held on Cable. "So one man's going to stand us off."

"That's all it's taken so far."

"You think Vern's going to put up with you?"

"I don't see he has a choice," Cable answered.

"Then you don't know him," Dancey said flatly.

2

With DAYLIGHT a wind came out of the valley and he could hear it in the pines above the house.

Cable lay on his back listening, staring at the ceiling rafters. There was no sound in the room. Next to him, Martha was asleep. In the crib, beyond Martha's side of the bed, Sandy slept with his thumb and the corner of the blanket in his mouth. Clare and Davis were in the next room, in the log section of the house, and it was still too early even for them.

Later they would follow him around offering to help. He would be patient and let them think they were helping and answer all of their questions. He would think about the two and a half years away from them and he would kiss them frequently and study them, holding their small faces gently in his hands.

The wind rose and with it came the distant, dry-creaking sound of the barn door.

Later on he would see about the barn. Perhaps in the afternoon, if they had not come by then. This morning he would run Kidston's horses out of the meadow. Then perhaps Martha would have something for him to do.

They had worked until long after dark, sweeping, scrubbing, moving in their belongings. There would always be something more to be done; but that was all right because it was their home, something they had built themselves.

Just make sure everything that belonged to Royce and Joe Bob and Bill Dancey was out of here. Make double sure of that. Then wait. No matter what he did, he would be waiting and listening for the sound of horses.

But there was nothing he could do about that. Don't worry about anything you can't do something about. When it's like that it just happens. It's like an act of God. Though don't blame God for sending Vern Kidston. Blame Vern himself for coming. If you can hate him it will be easier to fight him.

And there's always someone to fight, isn't there?

Ten years ago he had come here from Sudan, Texas—a nineteen-year-old boy seeking his future, working at the time for a

freight company that hauled between Hidalgo and Tucson—
and one night when they stopped at Denaman's Store he talked
to John Denaman.

They sat on the loading platform with their legs hanging over
the side, drinking coffee and now and then whisky, drinking
both from the same cups, looking north into the vast darkness
of the valley. John Denaman told him about the river and the
good meadow land and the timber—ponderosa pine and aspen
and willows, working timber and pretty-to-look-at timber. A
man starting here young and working hard would have himself
something in no time at all, Denaman had said.

But a man had to have money to buy stock with, Cable said.
Something to build with.

No, Denaman said, not necessarily. He told about his man
Acaso who'd died the winter before, leaving his two kids,
Manuel and Luz, here and leaving the few cattle Denaman
owned scattered through the hills. You're welcome to gather
and work the cattle, Denaman said. Not more than a hundred
head; but something to build on and you won't have to put up
money till you market them and take your share.

That was something to think about, and all the way to
Tucson Cable had pictured himself a rancher, a man with his
own land, with his own stock. He thought, too, about a girl
who lived in Sudan, Texas.

The first thing he did in Tucson was quit his job. The same
day he bought twenty head of yearling stock, spending every
last dollar he had, and drove his cattle the hundred and twenty
miles back to the Saber River.

In the summer of his second year he built his own adobe,
with the help of Manuel Acaso, four miles north of the store.
He sold some of his full-grown beef to the army at Fort
Buchanan and he continued to buy yearlings, buying them
cheap from people around Tubac who'd had enough of the
Apache and were willing to make a small profit or none at all
just to get shed of their stock and get out of southern Arizona.

The next year he left Manuel Acaso with his herd and traveled back to Sudan. The girl, Martha Sanford, was waiting for
him. They were married within the week and he brought her
home to the Saber without stopping for a honeymoon. Then he
worked harder than he ever imagined a man could work and he

remembered thinking during those days: nothing can budge you from this place. You are taking all there is to take and if you don't die you will make a success of it.

He was sure of it after living through the winter the Apaches came. They were Chiricahuas down out of the Dragoons and every few weeks they would raid his herd for meat. From November through April Cable lost over fifty head of cattle. But he made the Chiricahuas pay.

Lying prone high on the slope with a Sharps rifle, in the cover of the trees, he knocked two of them from their horses as they cut into his herd. The others came for him, squirming unseen through the pines, and when they rushed him he killed a third one with his revolver before they ran.

Another time that winter a war party attacked the house of Juan Toyopa, Cable's nearest neighbor to the west, killing Juan and his family and burning the house. They reached Cable's place at dawn—coming suddenly, screaming out of the grayness and battering against the door. He stood waiting with a revolver in each hand. Martha stood behind him with the shotgun. And when the door gave way he fired six rounds into them in half as many seconds. Two of the Apaches fell and Martha stepped over them to fire both shotgun loads at the Apaches running for the willows. One of them went down.

Then Cable rode to Denaman's to get Manuel Acaso. They returned to the willows, found the sign of six Chiricahuas and followed it all day, up into high desert country; and at dusk, deep in a high-walled canyon, they crept up to the dry camp of the six Apaches and shot three of them before they could reach their horses. The survivors fled, at least one of them wounded, Cable was sure of that, and they never bothered him again.

Perhaps they believed his life was charmed, that he was beyond killing, and for that reason they stopped trying to take him or his cattle. And perhaps it was charmed, Cable had thought. Or else his prayers were being answered. It was a good thing to believe; it made him feel stronger and made him work even harder. That was the time he first had the thought: nothing can budge you from this land. Nothing.

The next year their first child was born. Clare. And Manuel Acaso helped him build the log addition to the house. He remembered planning it, lying here in this bed with Martha next to him and Clare, a month-old baby, in the same crib Sandy was sleeping in now; lying awake staring at the ceiling and thinking how he would build a barn after they'd completed the log room.

And now thinking about that time and not thinking about the years in between, he felt comfortable and at peace. Until the murmur of Martha's voice, close to him, brought him fully awake.

"They'll come today, won't they?"

He turned to her. She was on her side, her eyes open and watching him. "I guess they will."

"Is that what you were thinking about?"

Cable smiled. "I was thinking about the barn."

"You're not even worried, are you?"

"It doesn't do any good to show it."

"I thought you might be trying out your principle of not worrying about anything you can't do something about."

"Well, I thought about it."

Martha smiled. "Cabe, I love you."

He rolled to his side, pulling her close to him and kissed her, brushing her cheek and her mouth. His face remained close to hers. "We'll come out of this."

"We have to," Martha whispered.

When Cable left the house the sun was barely above the line of trees at the river's edge. The willow branches moved in the breeze, swaying slowly against the pale morning sky. But soon, Cable knew, there would be sun glare and deep shadows, black against yellow, and the soft movement of the trees would be remembered from another time with another feeling.

With Davis and Clare he brought the four team horses out of the barn and put them on a picket line to graze. It wouldn't help to get them mixed with Kidston's herd. He saddled the sorrel gelding, but let the reins hang free so it could also graze. The sorrel wouldn't wander. After that he returned to the house.

Martha came out of the log room with Sandy. "What did you forget?"

"The Spencer," Cable said. He picked it up, then turned sharply, hearing Clare's voice.

The little girl ran in from the yard. "Somebody's coming!"

Cable stepped to the doorway. Behind him Martha called, "Davis— Clare, where is he?"

"He's all right." Cable lowered the Spencer looking out past Davis who was in the yard watching the rider just emerging from the trees. "It's Janroe."

The first thing Cable noticed about Janroe was that he wore two revolvers—one in a shoulder holster, the other on his hip—in addition to a shotgun in his saddle boot.

Then, as Janroe approached, he noticed the man's gaze. Taking it all in, Cable thought, seeing Janroe's eyes moving from the saddled gelding to the gear—cooking utensils, clothing, curl-toed boots, bedding and the three holstered revolvers on top—that was in a pile over by the barn.

Janroe reined in, his gaze returning to the adobe. "Well, you ran them, didn't you?" His hand touched his hat brim and he nodded to Martha, then fell away as Cable walked out to him. He made no move to dismount.

"I don't think you expected to see us," Cable said.

"I wasn't sure."

"But you were curious."

Janroe's gaze went to the pile of gear. "You took their guns," he said thoughtfully. I'd like to have seen that." His eyes returned to Cable. "Yes, I would have given something to see that. Was anybody hurt?"

Cable shook his head.

"No shooting?"

"Not a shot."

"What'll you do with their stuff?"

"Leave it. They'll come back."

"I think I'd burn it."

"I thought about that," Cable said. "But I don't guess it's a way to make friends."

"You don't owe them anything."

"No, but I have to live with them."

Janroe glanced at the saddled horse. "You're going somewhere?"

"Out to the meadow."

"I'll ride along," Janroe said.

They passed into the willows, jumping their horses down

the five-foot bank and crossed a sandy flat before entering the brown water of the river. At midstream the water swirled chest high on the horses, then receded gradually until they again came up onto a stretch of sand before mounting the bank.

"Now you're going to run his horses?" Janroe asked.

"I'll move them around the meadow," Cable said. "Toward his land."

"He'll move them right back."

"We'll see."

"You've got a fight on your hands. You know that, don't you?"

They were moving out into the meadow toward Kidston's horse herd, walking their horses side by side, but now Cable reined to a halt.

"Look, I haven't even met Vern or Duane Kidston. First I'll talk to them. Then we'll see what happens."

Janroe shook his head. "They'll try to run you. If you don't budge, they'll shoot you out."

Cable said, "Are you going back now?"

Janroe looked at him with surprise. "I have time."

"And I've got work to do."

"Well," Janroe said easily, "I was going to try to talk you into going back to the store with me. I've got a proposition you ought to be interested in."

"Go ahead and make it."

"I've got to show you something along with it, and that's at the store."

"Then it'll have to wait," Cable said.

"Well"—Janroe shrugged—"it's up to you. I'll tell you this much, it would end your problem all at once."

Cable watched him closely. "What would I have to do?"

"Kill Vern," Janroe said mildly. "Kill him and his brother."

Cable had felt himself tensed, but now he relaxed. "Just like that."

"You can do it. You proved that the way you handled those three yesterday."

"And why are you so anxious to see the Kidstons dead?"

"I'm looking at it from your side."

"Like hell."

"All right." Janroe paused. "You were pretty close to John Denaman, weren't you?"

"He gave me my start here."

"Did you know Denaman was running guns for the South?"

Cable was watching Janroe closely. "You're sure?"

"He was just part of it," Janroe continued. "They're Enfield rifles shipped into Mexico by the British. Confederate agents bring them up over the border and the store is one of the relay points. It was Denaman's job to hide the rifles until another group picked them up for shipment east."

"And where do you come in?"

"When Denaman died I was sent out to take his place."

Cable's eyes remained on Janroe. So the man was a Confederate agent. And John Denaman had been one. That was hard to picture, because you didn't think of the war reaching out this far. But it was here. Fifteen hundred miles from the fighting, almost another world, but it was here.

"I told you," Janroe said, "I was with Kirby Smith. I lost my arm fighting the Yankees. When they said I wasn't any more use as a soldier I worked my way into this kind of a job. Eight months ago they sent me out here to take Denaman's place."

"And Manuel," Cable said. "Is he in it?"

Janroe nodded. "He scouts for the party that brings up the rifles. That's where he is now."

"When's he due back?"

"What do you want to do, check my story?"

"I was thinking of Manuel. I haven't seen him in a long time."

"He'll be back in a day or so."

"Does Luz know about the guns?"

"You can't live in the same house and not know about them."

"So that's what's bothering her."

Janroe looked at him curiously. "She said something to your wife?"

Cable shrugged off the question. "It doesn't matter. You started out with me killing Vern and Duane Kidston."

Janroe nodded. "How does it look to you now?"

"You're telling me to go after them. To shoot them down like you would an animal."

"Exactly."

"That's called murder."

"It's also called war."

Cable shook his head. "As far as I'm concerned the war's over."

Janroe watched him closely. "You don't stop believing in a cause just because you've stopped fighting."

"I've got problems of my own now."

"But what if there's a relation between the two? Between your problems and the war?"

"I don't see it."

"Open your eyes," Janroe said. "Vern supplies remounts to the Union army. He's doing as much to help them as any Yankee soldier in the line. Duane's organized a twelve-man militia. That doesn't sound like anything; but what if he found out about the guns? Good rifles that Confederate soldiers are waiting for, crying for. But even without that danger, once you see Duane you'll *want* to kill him. I'll testify before God to that."

Janroe leaned closer to Cable. "This is what I'm getting at. Shooting those two would be like aiming your rifle at Yankee soldiers. The only difference is you know their names."

Cable shook his head. "I'm not a soldier any more. That's the difference."

"You have to have a uniform on to kill?"

"You know what I mean."

"I know exactly what you mean," Janroe said. "You need an excuse. You need something to block off your conscience while you're pulling the trigger. Something like a license, so killing them won't be called murder."

Cable said nothing. He was listening, but staring off at the horse herd now.

Janroe watched him. "That's your problem. You want Vern and Duane off your land, but you don't have the license to hunt them. You don't have an excuse your conscience will accept." Janroe paused. He waited until Cable's gaze returned and he was looking directly into his eyes.

"I can give you that excuse, Mr. Cable. I can fix you up with the damnedest hunting license you ever saw, and your conscience will just sit back and laugh."

For a moment Cable was silent, letting Janroe's words run through his mind. All at once it was clear and he knew what the man was driving at. "If I worked for you," Cable said, "if I was an agent, I could kill them as part of my duty."

Janroe seemed to smile. "I could even order you to do it."

"Why me? If it's so important to you, why haven't you tried?"

"Because I can't afford to fool with something like that. If I'm caught, what happens to the gun running?"

"And if I fail," Cable said, "what happens to my family?"

"You don't have anything to lose," Janroe said easily. "What happens to them if Vern kills you? What happens to all of you if he runs you off your land?"

Cable shook his head. "I've never even seen these people and you want me to kill them."

"It will come to that," Janroe said confidently. "I'm giving you an opportunity to hit first."

"I appreciate that," Cable said. "But from now on, how would you like to keep out of my business? You stop worrying about me and I won't say anything about you. How will that be?" He saw the relaxed confidence drain from Janroe's face leaving an expressionless mask and a tight line beneath his mustache.

"I think you're a fool," Janroe said quietly. "But you won't realize it yourself until it's too late."

"All right," Cable said. He spoke calmly, not raising his voice, but he was impatient now, anxious for Janroe to leave. "That's about all I've got time for right now. You come out again some time, how's that?"

"If you're still around." Janroe flicked his reins and moved off.

Let him go, Cable thought, watching Janroe taking his time, just beginning to canter. He's waiting for you to call him. But he'll have a long wait, because you can do without Mr. Janroe. There was something about the man that was wrong. Cable could believe that Janroe had been a soldier and was now a Confederate agent; but his wanting the Kidstons killed—as if he would enjoy seeing it happen—that was something else. There was the feeling he wanted to kill them just for the sake of killing them, not for the reasons he brought up at all. Maybe it would be best to keep out of Janroe's way. There was enough to think about as it was.

Cable swung the sorrel in a wide circle across the meadow and came at the horse herd up wind, counting thirty-six, all mares and foals; seeing their heads rise as they heard him and caught his scent. And now they were moving, carefully at first, only to keep out of his way, then at a run as he spurred the sorrel toward them. Some tried to double back around him, but the sorrel answered his rein and swerved right and left to keep them bunched and moving.

Where the Saber crossed the valley, curving over to the east side of the meadow, he splashed the herd across with little trouble, then closed on them again and ran them as fast as the foals could move, up the narrowing, left-curving corridor of the valley. After what he judged to be four or five miles farther on, he came in sight of grazing cattle and there Cable swung away from the horse herd. This would be Kidston land.

Now he did not follow the valley back but angled for the near slope, crossed the open sweep of it to a gully which climbed up through shadowed caverns of ponderosa pine. At the crest of the hill he looked west out over tangled rock and brush country and beyond it to a towering near horizon of creviced, coldly silent stone. Close beyond this barrier was the Toyopa place, where Kidston now lived.

Cable followed the crest of the hill for almost a mile before he found a trail that descended the east slope. He moved along the narrowness of it, feeling the gradual slant beneath the sorrel, and seeing the valley again, down through open swatches in the trees. Soon he would be almost above the house. A few yards farther on he stopped.

Ahead of him, a young woman stood at the edge of the path looking down through the trees. Luz Acaso, Cable thought. No.

Luz came to his mind with the first glimpse of this girl in white. But Luz vanished as he saw blond hair—hair that was tied back with a ribbon and swirled suddenly over her shoulder as she turned and saw him.

This movement was abrupt, but now she stood watching him calmly. Her hand closed around the riding quirt suspended from her wrist and she raised it to hold it in front of her with both hands, not defensively, but as if striking a pose.

"I expected you to be older," the girl said. She studied him calmly, as if trying to guess his age or what he was thinking or what had brought him to this ridge.

Cable swung down from the saddle, his eyes on the girl. She was at ease—he could see that—and was still watching him attentively: a strikingly handsome girl, tall, though not as tall as Martha, and younger by at least six years, Cable judged.

He said, "You know who I am?"

"Bill Dancey told us about you." She smiled then. "With help from Royce and Joe Bob."

"Then you're a Kidston," Cable said.

"You'll go far," the girl said easily.

Cable frowned. "You're Vern's—daughter?"

"Duane's. I'm Lorraine, if that means anything to you."

"I don't know why," Cable said, "but I didn't picture your dad married."

Her eyebrows rose with sudden interest. "How did you picture him?"

"I don't know. Just average appearing."

Lorraine smiled. "You'll find him average, all right."

Cable stared at her. "You don't seem to hold much respect for him."

"I have no reason to."

"Isn't just because he's your father reason enough?"

Lorraine's all-knowing smile returned. "I knew you were going to say that."

"You did, huh? . . . How old are you?"

"Almost nineteen."

Cable nodded. That would explain some of it. "And you've been to school. You're above average pretty, which you'll probably swear to. And you've probably had your own way as long as you can remember."

"And if all that's true," Lorraine said. "Then what?"

Cable shook his head. "I don't know."

"What point are you trying to make?"

Cable smiled now. "You didn't react the way I thought you would."

"At least you're honest about it," Lorraine said. "Most men would have tried to bluster their way out. Usually they say, 'Well'—with what passes for a wise chuckle—'you'll see things differently when you're a bit older.'" Lorraine's eyebrows rose. "Unfortunately, there isn't the least shred of evidence that wisdom necessarily comes with age."

"Uh-huh," Cable nodded. This girl could probably talk circles around him if he let her. But if she pulled that on Martha—

Cable smiled. "Why don't you come down and meet my wife?"

Lorraine hesitated. "I don't think I should put myself in the way."

"You wouldn't be in Martha's way. She'd be glad of the chance to sit down and talk."

"I wasn't referring to your wife. I meant my father. He's coming, you know." She saw Cable's expression change. "Didn't you think he would?"

"Coming now?"

"As soon as he gathers his company," Lorraine answered. "Not Vern. Vern went up to Fort Buchanan yesterday on horse business." She looked away from Cable. "You know you can see your house right down there through the trees. I came here to watch."

She stepped back quickly as Cable moved past her, already urging his sorrel down the path as he mounted. She called out to him to wait, but he kept going and did not look back. Soon he was out of sight, following the long, gradual switchbacks that descended through the pines.

Martha had cleaned the stove for the second time. She came out of the house carrying a pail and at the end of the ramada she lifted it and threw the dirty water out into the sunlight. She watched it flatten and hang glistening gray before splattering against the hard-packed ground. She turned back to the house, hearing the sound of the horse then.

"Clare!" Her gaze flashed to the children playing in the aspen shade. They looked up and she called, not as loud, "Clare, bring the boys in for a while."

"Why do we have to—" Davis's voice trailed off. He made no move to rise from his hands and knees.

Martha looked back at the stable shed, then to the children. "Dave, I'm not going to call again." The children rose and came out of the trees.

She heard the horse again and with it a rustling, twig-snapping sound. She waved the children toward the house; but Clare hesitated, looking up toward the pines. "What's that noise?"

"Probably not anything," Martha said. "Inside now."

As they filed in, Cable turned the corner of the house. Martha let her breath out slowly and stood watching him as he dismounted and came toward her.

She wanted to say: Cabe, it's not worth it. One alarm after another, running the children inside every time there's a sound! But she looked at Cable's face and the words vanished.

"What is it?"

"They're on the way."

Martha glanced at the house, at the three children standing in the ramada shade watching them. "Clare, fix the boys a biscuit and jelly."

As she turned back, she again heard the rustling, muffled horse sound. She saw her husband's hand go to the Walker Colt a moment before Lorraine Kidston rounded the adobe.

"I decided," Lorraine said as she approached, "it would be more fun to watch from right here." She dropped her reins then, extending her arms to Cable. When he hesitated, she said, "Aren't you going to help me?"

Cable lifted her down from the side saddle, feeling her press against him, and he stepped back the moment her feet touched the ground. "Martha, this is Lorraine Kidston. Duane's girl."

Martha recognized his uneasiness. He wanted to appear calm, she knew, but he was thinking of other things. And she was aware of Lorraine's confidence. Lorraine was enjoying this, whatever it was, and for some reason she had Cable at a disadvantage. Martha nodded to Lorraine, listened as Cable explained their meeting on the ridge, and she couldn't help thinking: Soon we could be thrown to the lions and Lorraine has dressed in clean white linen to come watch.

"Come inside," Martha said pleasantly. "We can give you a chair at the window if you'd like."

Lorraine hesitated, but only for a moment. She nodded to Martha and said easily, "You're very kind."

At the door, the children stood staring at Lorraine. Martha named them as they entered the ramada shade, and reaching them, brushed Sandy's hair from his forehead. "The little Cables are about to have biscuits and jelly. Will you join them?"

"No, thank you," Lorraine said. She nodded politely to the children, but showed no interest in them, edging through the doorway now as if not wanting to touch them. Martha followed, moving the children to the table and sitting them down. Cable came in a moment later carrying the Spencer.

As he propped it against the wall between the two front windows, Lorraine said pleasantly, "I hope you're not going to shoot my father."

Cable closed both shutters of the right window, but only one shutter of the window nearer to the door. He turned then. "I hope not either."

"Oh, don't be so solemn," Lorraine said lightly. "If Duane does the talking you can be pretty sure he'll mess it up."

Cable saw Martha's momentary look of surprise. She placed a pan of biscuits on the table, watching Lorraine. "Miss Kidston," Cable said mildly, "doesn't have a very high regard for her father."

Martha straightened, wiping her hands on her apron. "That's nice."

Lorraine regarded her suspiciously. Then, as if feeling a compulsion to defend herself, she said, "If there is nothing about him personally to deserve respect, I don't see why it's due him just because he's a parent."

Cable was leaving it up to Martha now. He watched her, expecting her to reply, but Martha said nothing. The silence lengthened, weakening Lorraine's statement, demanding more from her.

"I don't suppose you can understand that," Lorraine said defensively.

"Hardly," Martha said, "since I've never met your father."

"You've met him," Lorraine said, glancing at Cable. "He's the kind who can say nothing but the obvious." Cable was looking out the window, paying no attention to her, and her gaze returned quickly to Martha.

"I know exactly what he's going to answer to every single thing I say," Lorraine went on. "One time it's empty wisdom, the next time wit. Now Vern, he's the other extreme. Vern sits like a grizzled stone, and at first you think it's pure patience. Then, after a few sessions of this, you realize Vern simply hasn't anything to say. I haven't yet decided which is worse, listening to Duane, or not listening to Vern."

"It sounds," Martha prompted, "as if you haven't been with them very long."

That brought it out. Lorraine recited a relaxed account of her life, using a tone bordering on indifference, though Martha knew Lorraine was enjoying it.

Her mother and father had separated when Lorraine was seven, and she had gone with her mother. That didn't mean it had taken her mother seven or eight years to learn what a monumental bore Duane was. She had simply sacrificed her best years on the small chance he might change. But finally, beyond the point of endurance, she left him, and left Gallipolis too, because that Ohio town seemed so typical of Duane. Wonderful years followed, almost ten of them. Then her mother died unexpectedly and she was forced to go to her father who was then in Washington. In the army. That was two or three years ago and she remained in Washington while Duane was off campaigning. Then he was relieved of his duty—though Duane claimed he "resigned his active commission"—and, unfortunately, she agreed to come out here with him. Now, after over a year with Duane and Vern, Lorraine was convinced that neither had ever had an original thought in his life.

Cable listened, his gaze going out across the yard and through the trees to the meadow beyond. You could believe only so much of that about Vern and Duane. Even if they were dull, boring old men to an eighteen-year-old girl, they could still run you or burn your house down or kill you or whatever the hell else they wanted. So don't misjudge them, Cable thought.

He heard Martha ask where they had lived and Lorraine answered Boston, New York City. Philadelphia for one season. They had found it more fun to move about.

Even with that tone, Martha will feel sorry for her, Cable thought, watching the stillness of the yard and the line of trees with their full branches hanging motionless over empty shade.

He tried to visualize the girl's mother and he pictured them—Lorraine and her mother—in a well-furnished drawing room filled with people. The girl moved from one group to another, nodding with her head tilted to one side, smiling now, saying something; then everyone in the group returning her smile at the same time.

Cable saw himself in the room—not intending it—but suddenly there he was; and he thought: That would be all right about now. Even though you wouldn't have anything to say and you'd just stand there—

He saw the first rider when he was midway across the river, moving steadily, V-ing the water toward the near bank. Now there were three more in the water and—Cable waited to make sure—two still on the other side. They came down off the meadow; and beyond them now, over their heads, Cable saw the grazing horse herd. They had returned the mares and foals.

As each man crossed the river, he dismounted quickly, handed off his horse and ran hunch-shouldered to the protection of the five-foot cutbank. One man was serving as horse holder, taking them farther down the bank where the trees grew more thickly.

Out of the line of fire, Cable thought. Behind him he heard Lorraine's voice. Then Martha's. But he wasn't listening to them now. This could be nine months ago, he thought, watching the trees and the river and the open meadow beyond. That could be Tishomingo Creek if you were looking down across a cornfield, and beyond it, a half mile beyond through the trees and briars, would be Bryce's Crossroads. But you're not standing in a group of eighty-five men now.

No, a hundred and thirty-five then, he thought. Forrest had Gatrel's Georgia Company serving with the escort.

How many of them would you like?

About four. That's all. Shotguns and pistols and the Kidstons wouldn't know what hit them. But now you're out-Forresting Forrest. He had two to one against him at Bryce's. And won. You've got six to one.

He could just see their heads now above the bank, spaced a few feet apart. He was still aware of Lorraine's voice, thinking now as he watched them: What are they waiting for?

A rifle barrel rose above the bank, pointed almost straight up, went off with a whining report and Lorraine stopped talking.

Cable turned from the window. "Martha, take the children into the other room." They watched him; the children, Martha, and Lorraine all watched him expectantly, but he turned back to the window.

He heard Lorraine say, "He's going to die when he finds out I'm here."

"He already knows," Cable said, not turning. "Your horse is outside."

Her voice brightened. "That's right!" She moved to Cable's side. "Now he won't know what to do."

"He's doing something," Cable said.

The rifle came up again, now with a white cloth tied to the end of the barrel, and began waving slowly back and forth.

"Surrender," Lorraine said mockingly, "or Major Kidston will storm the redoubts. This is too much."

Cable asked, "Is that him?"

Lorraine looked past his shoulder. Four men had climbed the bank and now came out of the trees, one a few paces ahead. He motioned the others to stop, then came on until he'd reached the middle of the yard. This one, the one Cable asked about, wore a beard, a Kossuth army hat adorned with a yellow, double-looped cord, and a brass eagle that pinned the right side of the brim to the crown; he wore cavalry boots and a flap-top holster on his left side, butt to the front and unfastened.

He glanced back at the three men standing just out from the trees, saw they had not advanced, then turned his attention again to the house, planting his boots wide and fisting his hands on his hips.

"Sometimes," Lorraine said, "Duane leaves me speechless."

"The first one's your father?" asked Cable, making sure.

"My God, who else?"

"That's Royce with the flag," Cable said.

"And Joe Bob and Bill Dancey in reserve," Lorraine said. "I think Bill looks uncomfortable."

Cable's eyes remained on her father. "Where's Vern?"

"I told you, he went to Fort Buchanan," Lorraine answered.

Her attention returned to her father. "He loves to pose. I think right now he's being Sheridan before Missionary Ridge. Wasn't it Sheridan?"

"Cable!"

"Now he speaks," Lorraine said gravely, mockingly.

"Cable—show yourself!"

Cable moved past Lorraine into the open doorway. He looked out at Duane. "I'm right here."

Duane's fist came off his hips. For a moment before he spoke, his eyes measured Cable sternly. "Where do you have my daughter?"

"She's here," Cable said.

Again Duane stared in silence, his eyes narrowed and his jaw set firmly. The look is for your benefit, Cable thought. He's not concentrating as much as he's acting. He saw Duane then take a watch from his vest pocket, thumb it open and glance at the face.

Duane looked up. "You have three minutes by the clock to release my daughter. If you don't, I will not be responsible for what happens to you."

"I'm not holding her."

"You have three minutes, Mr. Cable."

"Listen, she came on her own. She can walk out any time she wants." Behind him he heard Lorraine laugh.

Cable looked at her. "You'd better go out to him."

"No, not yet," she said. "Call his bluff and let's see what he does."

"Listen, while you're being entertained my wife and children are likely to get shot."

"He wouldn't shoot while I'm in here."

"That's something we're not going to find out." Cable's hand closed on her arm. Lorraine pulled back; but he held her firmly and drew her into the doorway. He saw Duane return the watch to his pocket, and saw a smile of confidence form under the man's neatly trimmed beard.

"All of a sudden, Mr. Cable, you seem a bit anxious," Duane said. His hands went to his hips again.

Close to him, as Cable urged her through the door, Lorraine gasped theatrically, "Would you believe it!"

"Go on now," Cable whispered. To Duane he said, "I told you once I wasn't holding your daughter. What do I have to do to convince you?"

Duane's expression tightened. "You keep quiet till I'm ready for you!" His gaze shifted to Lorraine who now stood under the ramada a few steps from Cable and half turned toward him. She stood patiently with her arms folded. "Lorraine, take your horse and go home."

"I'd rather stay." She glanced at Cable, winking at him.

"This is not something for you to see," Duane said gravely.

"I don't want to miss your big scene," Lorraine said. "I can feel it coming."

"Lorraine—I'm warning you!"

"Oh, stop it. You aren't warning anyone."

Duane's voice rose. "I'm not going to tell you again!"

Smiling, Lorraine shook her head. "If you could only see yourself."

"Lorraine—"

"All right." She stopped him, raising her hands. "I surrender." She laughed again, shaking her head, then moved unhurriedly to her horse, mounted and walked it slowly across the yard, smiling pleasantly at her father, her head turning to watch him until she was beyond his line of vision. She passed into the willow trees.

She's had her fun, Cable thought, watching her. But now the old man is mad and he'll take it out on you. Cable's gaze returned to Duane. You mean he'll try. At this moment he did not feel sorry for Duane; even after Duane had been made to look ridiculous by his own daughter. No, if Duane pushed him he would push him back. There was not time to laugh at this pompous little man with the General Grant beard; because beyond his theatrics this was still a matter of principle, of pride, of protecting his family, of protecting his land. A matter of staying alive too.

Cable said bluntly, "Now what?"

"Now," Duane answered, drawing his watch again, "you have until twelve o'clock noon to pack your belongings and get out." He looked down at the watch. "A little less than three hours."

There it is, Cable thought wearily. You expected it and there it is. He looked over his shoulder, glancing back at his wife, then turned back to Duane.

"Mr. Kidston, I'm going to talk to my wife first. You just hang on for a minute." He stepped back, swinging the door closed.

"Well?" he asked.

"This is yesterday," Martha said, "with the places reversed."

Cable smiled thinly. "We don't make friends very easy, do we?"

"I don't think it matters," Martha said quietly, "whether Mr. Kidston likes us or not."

"Then we're staying," Cable said.

"Did you think we wouldn't?"

"I wasn't sure."

Martha went to the bedroom. She looked in at the children before coming to Cable. "Clare's doing her letters for the boys."

"Martha, make them stay in there."

"I will."

"Then stand by the window with the shotgun, but don't shove the barrel out until I'm out there and they're looking at me."

"What will you do?"

"Talk to him. See how reasonable he is."

"Do you think Vern is there?"

"No. I guess Vern does the work while Duane plays war."

Martha's lips parted to speak, but she smiled then and said nothing.

"What were you going to say?" Cable asked.

She was still smiling, a faint smile that was for Cable, not for herself. "I was going to tell you to be careful, but it sounded too typical."

He smiled with her for a moment, then said, "Ready?" She nodded and Cable turned to the door. He opened it, closed it behind him, and stepped out to the shade of the ramada.

Duane Kidston had not moved; but Royce, holding the carbine with the white cloth, had come up on his right. Bill Dancey and Joe Bob remained fifteen to twenty feet behind them, though they had moved well apart.

"You have exactly"—Duane studied his watch—"two hours and forty-three minutes to pack and get out. Not a minute more."

Cable moved from shade to sunlight. He approached Duane, seeing him shift his feet and pocket his watch, and he heard Royce say, "Don't let him get too close."

Then Duane: "That's far enough!"

Cable ignored this. He came on until less than six feet separated him from Duane.

"I thought if we didn't have to shout," Cable said, "we could straighten this out."

"There's nothing to straighten," Duane said stiffly.

"Except you're trying to run me from my own land."

"That assumption is the cause of your trouble," Duane said. "This doesn't happen to be your land."

"It has been for ten years now."

"This property belonged to a Confederate sympathizer," Duane said. "I confiscated it in the name of the United States government, and until a court decides legal ownership, it remains ours."

"And if we don't leave?"

"I will not be responsible for what happens."

"That includes my family?"

"Man, this is a time of war! Often the innocent must suffer. But that is something I can do nothing to prevent."

"You make it pretty easy for yourself," Cable said.

"I'm making it easy for *you*!" Duane paused, as if to control the rage that had colored his face. "Listen, the easy way is for you to load your wagon and get out. I'm giving you this chance because you have a family. If you were alone, I'd take you to Fort Buchanan as a prisoner of war." Duane snapped his fingers. "Like that and without any talk."

"Even though I'm no longer a soldier?"

"You're still a Rebel. You fought for an enemy of the United States. You likely even killed some fine boys working for that bushwhacker of a Bedford Forrest and I'll tell you this, whether you're wearing a uniform or not, if it wasn't for your family, I'd do everything in my power to destroy you."

Joe Bob shifted his weight from one leg to the other. "That's tellin' him, Major." He winked, grinning at Bill Dancey.

Duane glanced over his shoulder, but now Joe Bob's face showed nothing. He stood lazily, with his hip cocked, and only nodded as Duane said, "I'll do the talking here."

Like yesterday, Cable thought. They're waiting to eat you up. His gaze shifted from Royce and Duane to Joe Bob.

Just like yesterday—

And the time comes and you can't put it off.

Cable's gaze swung back to Duane, though Joe Bob was still in his vision, and abruptly he said, "There's a shotgun dead on you." He waited for the reaction, waited for Joe Bob's mind to snap awake and realize what he meant. And the moment the man's eyes shifted to the house, Cable acted. He drew the Walker Colt, thumbed back the hammer and leveled it at Duane's chest. It happened quickly, unexpectedly; and now there was nothing Duane or any of his men could do about it.

"Now get off my land," Cable said. "Call a retreat, Major, or *I* won't be responsible for what happens."

An expression of shocked surprise showed in Duane's eyes and his mouth came open even before he spoke. "We're here under a flag of truce!"

"Take your flag with you."

"You can't pull a gun during a truce!"

"It's against the rules?"

Duane controlled his voice. "It is a question of honor. Something far beyond your understanding."

Royce stood with the truce-flag carbine cradled over one arm, holding it as if he'd forgotten it was there. "He makes it worthwhile. You got to give him that."

"Major"—Joe Bob's voice—"are you a chance-taking man? I was thinking, if you were quick on your feet—"

"I told you to keep out of this!" Duane snapped the words at him.

Looking at Duane as he spoke, at him and past him, Cable saw the horse and rider coming up out of the river, crossing the sand flat, climbing the bank now.

"I was just asking," Joe Bob said lazily. "If you thought you could flatten quick enough, we'd cut him in two pieces."

The rider approached them now, walking his horse out of the willows. A moment before they heard the hoof sounds, Cable said, "Tell your man to stay where he is."

Joe Bob saw him first and called out, "Vern, you're missing it!" Royce and Dancey turned as Joe Bob spoke, but Duane's eyes held on Cable.

"You've waited too long," Duane said.

Cable backed off a half step, still holding the Walker on Duane; but now he watched Vern Kidston as he approached from beyond Dancey, passing him now, sitting heavily and slightly stooped in the saddle, his eyes on Cable as he came unhurriedly toward him. A few yards away he stopped but made no move to dismount.

With his hat forward and low over his eyes, the upper half of his face was in shadow, and a full mustache covering the corners of his mouth gave him a serious, solemn look. He was younger than Duane—perhaps in his late thirties—and had none of Duane's physical characteristics. Vern was considerably taller, but that was not apparent now. The contrast was in their bearing and Cable noticed it at once. Vern was Vern, without being conscious of himself. Thoughts could be in his mind, but he did not give them away. You were aware of only the man, an iron-willed man whose authority no one here questioned. In contrast, Duane could be anyone disguised as a man.

Vern Kidston sat with his hands crossed limply over the saddle horn. He sat relaxed, obviously at ease, staring down at this man with the Walker Colt. Then, unexpectedly, his eyes moved to Bill Dancey.

"You were supposed to meet me this morning. Coming back I stopped up on the summer meadow and waited two hours for you."

"Duane says come with him else I was through," Dancey said calmly, though a hint of anger showed in his bearded face. "Maybe we ought to clear this up, just who I take orders from."

Vern Kidston looked at his brother then. "I go up to Buchanan for one day and you start taking over."

"I'd say running this man off your land is considerably more important than selling a few horses," Duane said coldly.

"You would, uh?" Vern's gaze shifted. His eyes went to the house, then lowered. "So you're Cable."

Cable looked up at him. "I've been waiting for you."

"I guess you have."

"Vern"—it was Duane's voice—"he pulled his gun under a sign of truce!"

Kidston looked at his brother. "I'd say the issue is he's still holding it." His eyes returned to Cable. "One man standing off four." He paused thoughtfully. "His Colt gun doesn't look that big to me."

Cable moved the Walker from Duane to Vern. "How does it look now?"

Vern seemed almost to smile. "There's seven miles of nerve between pointing a gun and pulling the trigger."

Cable stared at him, feeling his hope of reasoning with Kidston dissolve. But it was momentary. It was there with the thought: He's like the rest of them. His mind's made up and there's no arguing with him. Then the feeling was gone and the cold rage crept back into him, through him, and he told himself: But you don't budge. You know that, don't you? Not one inch of ground.

"Mr. Kidston," Cable said flatly, "I've fought for this land before. I've even had to kill for it. I'm not proud of saying that, but it's a fact. And if I have to, I'll kill for it again. Now if you don't think this land belongs to me, do something about it."

"I understand you have a family," Kidston said.

"I'll worry about my family."

"They wouldn't want to see you killed right before their eyes."

Cable cocked his wrist and the Walker was pointed directly at Vern's face. "It's your move, Mr. Kidston."

Vern sat relaxed, his hands still crossed on the saddle horn. "You know you wouldn't have one chance of coming out of this alive."

"How good are your chances?"

"Maybe you wouldn't have time to pull the trigger."

"If you think they can shoot me before I do, give the word."

Twenty feet to Cable's right, Joe Bob said, "Wait him out, Vern. He can't stand like that all day. Soon as his arm comes down I'll put one clean through him."

Dancey said, "And the second you move the shotgun cuts you in two."

Vern's eyes went to the house. "His wife?"

"Look close," Dancey said. "You see twin barrels peeking

out the window. I'd say she could hold it resting on the ledge longer than we can stand here."

Vern studied the house for some moments before his gaze returned to Cable. "You'd bring your wife into it? Risk her life for a piece of land?"

"My wife killed a Chiricahua Apache ten feet from where you're standing," Cable said bluntly. "They came like you've come and she killed to defend our home. Maybe you understand that. If you don't, I'll say only this. My wife will kill again if she has to, and so will I."

Thoughtfully, slowly, Kidston said, "Maybe you would." A silence followed until his eyes moved to Duane. "Go on home. Take your cavalry and get."

"I'm going," Duane said coldly. "I'm going to Fort Buchanan. If you can't handle this man, the army can."

"Duane, you're going home."

"I have your word you'll attend to him?"

"Go on, get out of here."

Duane hesitated, as if thinking of a way to salvage his self-respect, then turned without a word and walked off.

Kidston looked at his three riders. None of them had moved. "Go with him. And take your gear."

They stood lingeringly until Vern's gaze returned to Cable. That dismissed them and they moved away, picked up the gear Cable had piled by the barn and followed Duane to the willows.

"Well," Cable said, "are we going to live together?"

"I don't think you'll last."

"Why?"

"Because," Kidston said quietly, "you're one man; because you've got a family; because your stomach's going to be tied in a knot wondering when I'm coming. You won't sleep. And every time there's a sound you'll jump out of your skin. . . . Your wife will tell you it isn't worth it; and after a while, after her nerves are worn raw, she'll stop speaking to you and acting like a wife to you, and you won't see a spark of life in her."

Cable's gaze went to the house and he called out, "Martha!" After a moment the door opened and Martha came out with the shotgun under her arm. Kidston watched her, removing his hat as she neared them and holding it in his hand. He stood with the sun shining in his face and on his hair that was dark and straight and pressed tightly to his skull with perspiration. He nodded as Cable introduced them and put on his hat again.

"Mr. Kidston says we'll leave because we won't be able to stand it," Cable said now. "He says the waiting and not knowing will wear our nerves raw and in the end we'll leave of our own accord."

"What did you say?" Martha asked.

"I didn't say anything."

"I don't suppose there's much you could." She looked off toward the willows, seeing the men there mounting and starting across the river, then looked at her husband again. "Well, Cabe," she said, "are you going to throw Mr. Kidston out or ask him in for coffee?"

"I don't know. What do you think?"

"Perhaps Mr. Kidston will come back," Martha answered, "when we're more settled."

"Perhaps I will," Kidston said. His eyes remained on Martha: a woman who could carry a shotgun gracefully and whose eyes were dark and clear, warmly clear, and who stared back at him calmly and with confidence. He recalled the way she had walked out to meet him, with the sun on her dark hair, coming tall and unhurried with the faint movement of her legs beneath the skirt.

"Maybe you'll stay at that," Vern said, still looking at Martha. "Maybe you're the kind that would."

Cable watched him walk off toward the willows, and he was trying to picture this solemn-faced man kissing Luz Acaso.

For the rest of the morning and through the afternoon, there was time to think about Kidston and wonder what he would do; but there was little time for Cable and Martha to talk about him.

Vern wanted the land and if Cable didn't move, if he couldn't be frightened off the place, he would be forced off at gun point. It was strange; Vern was straightforward and easy to talk to. You believed what he said and knew he wasn't scheming or trying to trick you. Still, he wanted the land; and if waiting wouldn't get it for him, he would take it. That was clear enough.

Cable chopped wood through the afternoon, stacking a good supply against the back wall of the adobe. Soon he'd be working cattle again and there would be little time for close to home chores.

Then, after supper, he heard the creaking barn door. If the wind rose in the night, the creaking sound would become worse and wake him up. He would lie in bed thinking and losing sleep. You could think too much about something like this; Cable knew that. You could picture too many possibilities of failure and in the end you could lose your nerve and run for it. Sometimes it was better to let things just happen, to be ready and try to do the right thing, but just not think about it so much.

So he went out into the dusk to see about the door. Carrying an unlit lantern, Cable opened the door and stepped into the dim stillness of the barn. He hung the lantern on a peg and was bringing his arms down when the gun barrel pushed into his back.

"Now we'll do it our way," Joe Bob said.

3

ROYCE LIFTED the Walker from Cable's holster. He stepped back and Joe Bob came in swinging, hooking his right hand hard into Cable's cheek. In the semidarkness there was a grunt and a sharp smacking sound and Cable was against the board wall. Joe Bob turned him, swinging again, and broke through Cable's guard. He waded in then, grunting, slashing at Cable's face with both fists, holding him pinned to the boards, now driving a mauling fist low into Cable's body, then crossing high with the other hand to Cable's face. Joe Bob worked methodically, his fists driving in one after the other, again and again and again, until Cable's legs buckled. He had not been able to return a blow or even cover himself and now his back eased slowly down the boards. Joe Bob waited, standing stoop-shouldered and with his hands hanging heavily. Then his elbows rose; he went back a half step, came in again and brought his knee up solidly into Cable's jaw.

Abruptly, Royce said, "Listen!"

There was no sound except for Joe Bob's heavy, open-mouthed breathing. The silence lengthened until Royce said, between a whisper and a normal tone, "I heard somebody."

"Where?"

"Shhh!" Royce eased toward the open door.

"Cabe?" It came from outside. Martha's voice.

Royce let his breath out slowly. He stepped into the doorway and saw Martha in the gray dusk. She was perhaps forty feet from him, near the corner of the house.

"Who is it?"

"Evening, Mrs. Cable."

"Who's there?"

"It's just me. Royce." He stepped outside.

"Where's my husband?"

"Inside. Me and Joe Bob came back for some stuff we left"—he was moving toward her now—"and your husband's helping us dig it out."

She called past Royce. "Cabe?"

No answer. Five seconds passed, no more than that, then

Martha had turned and was running—around the corner of
the log section to the dark shadow of the ramada, hearing him
behind her as she pushed the door open into bright lamplight
and swung it closed. She heard him slam against it, hesitated—
Hold the door or go for the shotgun!—saw Clare wide-eyed and
said, "Go to the other room!" Martha was near the stove, raising the shotgun when Royce burst into the room. His hand
was under the barrel as she pulled the trigger and the blast
exploded up into the ceiling.

Royce threw the shotgun aside. He stood breathing in and
out heavily. "You like to killed me."

"Where's my husband?"

"Old Joe Bob's straightening things out with him."

She was aware of the children crying then. Past Royce, she
saw them just inside the bedroom. Clare's face was red and
glistened with tears. And because she cried, Sandy was crying,
with his lower lip pouted and his eyes tightly closed. Davis was
staring at Royce. His eyes were round and large and showed
natural fear, but he stood with his fists balled and did not
move.

"There's nothing to cry about," Martha said. "Come kiss
me good night and go to bed." They stood in their flannel
nightshirts, afraid now to come into the room. Martha started
for them, but she stopped.

Cable stood in the doorway. Joe Bob pushed him from
behind and he lurched in, almost going to his knees, but
caught himself against the back of a chair. Davis watched his
father. His sister and brother were still crying, whimpering,
catching their breath.

Abruptly both children stopped, their eyes on Joe Bob as
he came toward them. He said nothing, and no more than
glanced at them before slamming the bedroom door in their
faces. Immediately their crying began again, though now the
sound was muffled by the heavy door.

Martha poured water from the kettle, saturating a dish
towel; she wrung the water from it and brought it to Cable
who was bent over the back of the chair, leaning heavily on it
with his arms supporting him stiffly.

"Cabe, are you all right?"

He took the towel from her, pressing it to his mouth, then

looked at the blood on the cloth and folded it over, touching it to his mouth again. His teeth throbbed with a dullness that reached up into his head. He could not feel his lips move when he spoke.

"It's not as bad as it looks."

Joe Bob said, "Then maybe I should give you some more."

Martha turned the chair around, helping her husband sit down.

Cable's eyes raised. "The children—?"

"They're all right. They're frightened, that's all."

"You better go talk to them."

"You better not," Joe Bob said. "They'll shut up after a while."

Martha looked at him now. "What do you want?"

"I'm not sure," Joe Bob said. "We're taking one step at a time." He glanced at Royce. "I wish Austin and Wynn were here." He was referring to his two brothers who also worked for Kidston. "They'd have some ideas. Man, would they!"

"Do you want us to leave?" asked Martha.

"Not right yet." Joe Bob glanced at Royce again, winking this time. "We might think of something." His gaze went beyond Royce, moving over the room and coming back to Martha. "You're such a fine housekeeper, maybe we'll keep you here." He winked at Royce again. "How'd you like to keep house for us?"

Martha did not speak, but she held Joe Bob's gaze until he grinned and moved away from her, going toward the kitchen cupboards.

"I don't know if I'd want her," Royce said. "She like to took my head off."

"I heard," Joe Bob said. He had opened a top cupboard and was reaching up into it. "Man, look at this." He took down an almost-full whisky bottle, smiling now and looking at Cable as he turned. "Would you've thought it of him?" Joe Bob uncorked the bottle and took a drink. "Man—"

Royce was next to him now, taking the bottle and drinking from it. He scowled happily, wiping his hand across his mouth. "Now this puts a different light on the subject."

Joe Bob took the bottle again, extending it to Martha. "Sweetie?"

"No, thank you."

"Just a little one."

Royce said, "Don't pour it away. If she doesn't want any, all right." He watched Joe Bob lift the bottle and snatched it from him as it came down. Now he took his time, smiling, looking at the label before he drank again.

"I think we ought to sit down," Royce said. "Like at a party."

"And talk to her about staying," Joe Bob said.

Royce grinned. "Wouldn't that be something."

"Man, picture it."

"Maybe we'd even pay her."

"Sure we would. With love and affection."

Cable said, "Does Vern know you're here?"

Royce looked at Cable. "Maybe I ought to take a turn on him."

"Help yourself," Joe Bob said.

"Vern and I agreed to settle this ourselves," Cable said.

Joe Bob looked at Royce. "He don't talk so loud now, does he?"

"He knows better," Royce said.

Joe Bob nodded thoughtfully. He drank from the bottle before saying, "You think we need him?"

"What for?" Royce took the bottle.

"That's the way I feel."

"Hell, throw him out."

"What about the kids—throw them out too?"

"Do you hear any kids? They're asleep already. Kids forget things a minute later." Royce lifted the bottle.

"Just throw him out, uh?"

"Sure. He'll lay out there like a hound. Else he'll crawl away. One way or the other, what difference does it make?"

Joe Bob considered this. "He can't go for help. Where'd he go, to Vern? To the one-arm man?"

Royce nodded. "Maybe to Janroe."

"So he does," Joe Bob said. "How's the one-arm man going to help him?" Joe Bob shook his head. "He's in a miserable way."

"Sure he is."

"Too miserable."

"Don't feel sorry for him."

"I mean, put him out of his misery."

Now Royce said nothing.

"Not us do it," Joe Bob said. "Him do it."

"I don't follow."

"You don't have to." Joe Bob drank from the bottle, then stood holding it, staring at Cable. "As long as he does." After a moment he handed Royce the bottle and walked over to Cable.

"You understand me, don't you?"

Cable straightened against the back of the chair. He shook his head.

"You will." Joe Bob stood close to him, looking down, and said then, "You're a miserable man, aren't you?"

Cable sat tensed. He could not fight Joe Bob now and there was nothing he could say. So he remained silent, his eyes going to Martha who stood with her hands knotted into slender fists. Still with his eyes on Martha, he felt the sudden, sharp pain in his scalp and in a moment he was looking up into Joe Bob's tight-jawed face.

Close to his belt, Joe Bob held Cable's head back, his hand fisted in Cable's hair. "I asked if you're a miserable man!"

Cable tried to swallow, but most of the blood-saliva remained in his mouth. He said, "I'd be a liar if I said I wasn't." The words came hesitantly, through swollen lips. But he stared up at Joe Bob calmly, breathing slowly, and only when he saw the man's expression change did he try to push up out of the chair. Then it was too late.

He went back with the chair as Joe Bob's fist slammed into his face. On the floor he rolled to his side, then raised himself slowly to his hands and knees. Joe Bob stood looking down at him with both fists balled and his jaw clenched in anger.

"I hate a man who thinks he's smart. God, I hate a man who does that."

Joe Bob was feeling the whisky. It showed in his face; and the cold, quiet edge was gone from the tone of his voice. On Royce, the whisky was having an opposite effect. He was grinning, watching Joe Bob with amusement; and now he said, "If he bothers you, throw him out. That's all you got to do."

"Better than that," Joe Bob said. He extended a hand to Royce though his eyes remained on Cable. "Give me his Colt."

"Sure." Royce pulled the revolver from his belt and put it in

Joe Bob's hand. He stepped back, watching with interest as Joe Bob turned the cylinder to check the loads.

"You're going to kill him?"

"You'll see." Joe Bob cocked the revolver. He pointed it at Cable and motioned to the door. "Walk outside."

Cable came to his feet. He looked at Martha, then away from her and walked toward the open door, seeing the dark square of it, then the deep shadow of the ramada as he neared the door, and beyond it, over the yard, a pale trace of early moonlight.

Now he was almost in the doorway, and the boot steps came quickly behind him. He was pushed violently through the opening, stumbled as he hit the ground and rolled out of the deep shadow of the ramada. He pushed himself to his knees, then fell flat again as Joe Bob began firing from the doorway. With the reports he heard Martha's scream. And as suddenly as the gunfire began, it was over. He heard Joe Bob say, "I wasn't aiming at him. If I was aiming he'd be dead. I got rid of four rounds is all."

Joe Bob leaned in the doorway looking out into the darkness, the whisky warm inside of him and feeling Royce and the woman watching him. He would make it good, all right. Something Royce would tell everybody about.

He called out to Cable, "One left, boy. Put yourself out of your misery and save Vern and me and everybody a lot of trouble. Pull the trigger and it's all over. Nobody worries any more."

He flipped the Walker in his hand, held it momentarily by the barrel, then threw it side-arm out to the yard. The revolver struck the ground, skidded past Cable, and the door slammed closed.

What would Forrest do?

That was a long time ago.

But what would he do? Cable thought.

He'd call on them to surrender. Not standing the way Duane stood, but with a confidence you could feel. The Yankees felt it and that part was real. He'd convince them he had more men and more artillery than they did—by having more buglers than companies and by having the same six field pieces come swinging down around the hill and into the woods, which was the reason the Yankee raider, Streight, surrendered—and only that part was unreal. And if they didn't surrender, he'd find their weak point and beat the living hell out of it.

But these two won't surrender. You're seven hundred miles away from that. So what's their weak point?

Almost a quarter of an hour had passed since the door slammed closed. Cable lay on his stomach, on the damp sand at the edge of the river. He bathed his face, working his jaw and feeling the soreness of it, and rinsed his mouth until the inside bleeding stopped. The Walker Colt, with one load in it, was in his holster. And now what?

Now you think it out and do it and maybe it will work. Whatever it is.

What would Forrest do?

Always back to him, because you know he'd do something. God, and Nathan Bedford Forrest, I need help. God's smile and Forrest's bag of tricks.

When too many things crowded into Cable's mind, he would stop thinking. He would calm himself, then tell himself to think very slowly and carefully. A little anger was good, but not rage; that hindered thinking. He tried not to think of Martha, because thinking of her and picturing her with them and wondering made it more difficult to take this coldly, to study it from all sides.

Two and a half years ago, he thought, you wouldn't be lying here. You'd be dead. You'd have done something foolish and you'd be dead. But you have to hurry. You still have to hurry.

But even thinking this, and not being able to keep the picture of them with Martha out of his mind, he kept himself calm.

He was thankful for having served with Forrest. You learned things watching Forrest and you learned things getting out of the situations Forrest got you into. There had been times like this—not the same because there was Martha and the children now—but there had been outnumbered times and one-bullet times and lying close to the ground in the moonlight times. And he had come through them.

Their weak point, Cable thought. Or their weakness.

Whisky . . . its effect on Joe Bob. His act of bravado, throwing the one-load revolver out after him, telling him to use it on himself.

What if he did?

What if they heard a shot and thought he did? Would they come outside? The one-load revolver could be Joe Bob's mistake. His weak point.

There it was. A possibility. Would one come out, or both? Or neither?

Just get them out, he thought. Stop thinking and get them out. He crawled on his hands and knees along the water's edge until he found a rock; one with smooth edges, heavy enough and almost twice the size of his fist. He rose now, moved back to the chest-high bank, climbed it and stood in the dark willow shadows. Drawing the revolver, cocking it, he moved closer to the trunk of the willow. Then, pointing the barrel directly at the ground, he squeezed the trigger.

The report was loud and close to him, then fading, fading and leaving a ringing that stretched quickly to silence; and now even the night sounds that had been in the trees and in the meadow across the river were gone.

Through the heavy-hanging branches he watched the house, picturing Joe Bob standing still in the room. Wonder about it, Cable thought. But not too long. Look at your friend who's looking at you and both of you wonder about it. Then decide. Come on, decide right now. Somebody has to come out and make sure. You don't believe it, but you'd like to believe it, so you have to come see. Decide that one of you has to watch Martha. So only one of you can come out. Come on, get it through your head! That's the way it has to be!

And finally the door opened.

He saw a man framed in the doorway with the light behind him. The man stood half turned, talking back into the room. Then he stepped outside, drawing his revolver. Another figure appeared in the doorway, but the man outside came on alone. Cable let his breath out slowly.

He stood close to the trunk of the tree now, holding the rock against his stomach, watching the man coming carefully across the yard. He was not coming directly toward Cable, but would enter the trees about twelve or fifteen feet from him.

Now he was nearing the trees, moving cautiously and listening. He came on and a moment later was in the willows, out of sight.

"I don't see him!" The voice came from the trees, shouted toward the house. It was Royce.

From the doorway, Joe Bob called back, "Look along the bank."

Cable waited. He heard Royce. Then saw him, moving along the bank, stepping carefully and looking down at the sand flat. Cable tightened against the tree, waiting. Now Royce was near, now ducking under the branches of Cable's tree—his revolver in his right hand, on the side away from Cable. Royce stepped past him and stopped.

"I don't see him!"

From the house: "Keep looking!"

Royce started off, looking down at the sand flat again. Cable was on him in two strides, bringing the rock back as he came, holding on to it and slamming it against the side of Royce's head as the man started to turn. Cable's momentum carried both of them over the bank. He landed on Royce with his hand on the revolver barrel and came up holding it, cocking it, not bothering with Royce now, but ducking down as he wheeled to climb out of the cutbank and into the trees again.

From the house: "Royce?"

Silence.

"Royce, what'd you do?"

Take him, Cable thought. Before he goes back inside. Before he has time to think about it.

He took the barrel of the revolver in his left hand. He wiped his right hand across the front of his shirt, stretched his fingers, opening and closing his hand, then gripped the revolver again and moved out of the trees.

Joe Bob saw him and called out, "Royce?"

Cable remembered thinking one thing: You should have taken Royce's hat. But now it was too late. He was in the open moving across the yard that was gray and shadow-streaked with moonlight.

"Royce, what's the matter with you!"

Cable was perhaps halfway across the yard when he stopped. He half turned, planting his feet and bringing up the revolver; he extended it straight out, even with his eyes, and said, "Joe Bob—" Only that.

And for a moment the man stood still. He knew it was Cable

and the knowing it held him in the light-framed doorway unable to move. But he had to move. He had to fall back into the room or go out or draw. And it had to be done *now*—

Cable was ready. He saw Joe Bob's right-hand revolver come out, saw him lunging for the darkness of the ramada and he squeezed the trigger on this suddenly moving target. Without hesitating he lowered the barrel, aiming at where Joe Bob would have to be and fired again; then a third time; and when the heavy, ringing sound died away there was only silence.

He walked through the fine smoke to where Joe Bob lay, face-down with his arms outstretched in front of him. Standing over him, he looked up to see Martha in the doorway.

"It's all right now," Cable said. "It's all over."

"Is he dead?"

Cable nodded.

And Royce was dead.

Now, remembering the way he had used the rock, swinging viciously because there was one chance and only one, Cable could see how it could have killed Royce. But he hadn't *intended* killing Joe Bob. He had wanted badly to hold a gun on him and fire it and see him go down, doing it thoroughly because with Joe Bob also he would have only one momentary chance; but that was not the same as wanting to kill.

Cable found their horses in the pines above the barn. He led them down to the yard and slung the two men face-down over the saddles, tying them on securely. After that he took the horses across the river and let them go to find their way home. Let Vern see them now, if he put them up to it. Even if he didn't, let him bury them; they were his men.

When Cable returned to the house he said, "In the morning we'll go see Janroe. We'll ask him if you and the children can board at the store."

Martha watched him. "And you?"

"I'll come back here."

Bill Dancey came in while the Kidstons were eating noon dinner. He appeared in the archway from the living room and removed his hat when he saw Lorraine at the table with the two men.

"It's done," Dancey said. "They're both under ground."

Vern looked up briefly. "All right."

"What about their gear?"

"Divvy it up."

"You could cast lots," Lorraine said.

Duane looked at her sternly. "That remark was in very poor taste."

Duane was looking at Vern now and not giving Lorraine time to reply.

"You mean to tell me you weren't present at their burial? Two men are murdered in your service and you don't even go out and read over their graves?"

"They were killed," Vern said. "Not in my service."

"All right." Duane couldn't hide his irritation. "No matter how it happened, it's proper for the commanding . . . for the head man to read Scripture over their graves."

"If the head man knows how to read," Lorraine said.

"I didn't know you were burying them right away." Duane's voice became grave. "Why didn't you tell me? I'd have read over them. I'd have considered it an honor. Two boys giving their lives defending—"

Vern's eyes stopped him. "That's enough of that. Duane, if I thought for a minute you sent those two over there—"

"I told you I didn't. They went on their own."

"Something else," Bill Dancey said. "Cable's moved his wife and kids into Denaman's."

Vern looked at him. "Who said so?"

"Man I sent to the store this morning. He saw the wagon and asked Luz about it. Luz says the woman and the kids are staying there, but Cable's going back to his place."

Vern rose from the table and walked around it toward Bill Dancey. He heard Duane say, "You'll run him out now; there's nothing to stop you. Vern, you hear me? You let me know when you're leaving because I want to be there." Vern did not reply or even look at Duane. Dancey turned and he followed him out through the long, beam-ceilinged, adobe-plastered living room, through the open double doors to the veranda that extended across the front of the house.

Dancey said, "What about their horses?"

"Put them in the remuda."

"Then what?"

"Then work for your money." As Dancey turned and started down the steps, Vern said, "Wait a minute." He moved against a support post and stood looking down at Dancey.

"How do you think he did it?"

"With a Colt and a rock," Dancey answered dryly.

"I asked you a question."

"And I don't know the answer you want." Dancey walked off, but he stopped within a few strides and looked back at Vern. "Why don't you ask Cable?"

"Maybe I will."

"With Joe Bob's brothers along?"

"He hit you, too, Bill. The first time you met him."

"Not that hard," Dancey said. He turned away.

Vern watched him continue on. So now it was even starting to bother Dancey, this fighting a lone man.

He was almost sure Cable had not murdered them. He was sure Joe Bob and Royce had gone to him with drawn guns, but somehow Cable had outwitted them and had been forced to kill them. And that was the difficult fact to accept. That Cable was capable of killing them. That he could think calmly enough to outsmart them, to do that while having a wife and children to worry about; and then kill them, one of them with his hands, a rock, yes, but with his hands.

What kind of a man was this Cable?

What was his breaking point? If he had one. That was it, some people didn't have a breaking point. They stayed or they died, but they didn't give up.

And now, because he had handled Joe Bob and Royce, Cable's confidence would be bolstered and it would take more patience or more prying or more of whatever the hell it was going to take to get him off the Saber.

Kidston had made up his mind that the river land would be his, regardless of Cable or anyone else who cared to contest it with him. This was a simple act of will. He wanted the land because he needed it. His horses had grazed the lush river meadow for two years and he had come to feel that this land was rightfully his.

The news of Cable's return had caused him little concern. A Confederate soldier had come home with his family. Well, that was too bad for the Rebel. Somehow Cable had outmaneuvered three men and made them run. Luck, probably. But the Rebel wasn't staying, Kidston was certain of that.

He had worked too hard for too many years: starting on his own as a mustanger, breaking wild horses and selling them half-green to whoever needed a mount. Then hiring White Mountain Apache boys and gathering more mustangs each spring. He began selling to the Hatch & Hodges stage-line people. His operation expanded and he hired more men; then the war put an end to the Hatch & Hodges business. The war almost ruined him; yet it was the war that put him back in business, with a contract to supply remounts to the Union cavalry. He had followed the wild herds to the Saber River country and here he settled, rebuilding the old Toyopa place. He employed fourteen riders—twelve now—and looked forward to spending the rest of his life here.

During the second year of the war his brother Duane had written to him—first from their home in Gallipolis, Ohio, then from Washington after he had marched his own command there to join the Army of the Potomac—pleading with Vern to come offer his services to the Union army. That was like Duane, Vern had thought. Dazzled by the glory of it, by the drums and the uniforms, and probably not even remotely aware of what was really at stake. But it was at this time that Vern received the government contract for remounts. After that, joining the army was out of the question.

The next December Duane arrived with his daughter. Duane had not wanted to return to Gallipolis after having been relieved of his command. They had made him resign his commission because of incompetence or poor judgment or whatever shelling your own troops was called.

It had happened at Chancellorsville, during Duane's first and only taste of battle. His artillery company was thrown in to support Von Gilsa's exposed flank, south of the town and in the path of Stonewall Jackson's advance. When Von Gilsa's brigade broke and came running back, Duane opened fire on them and killed more Union soldiers than Jackson had been able to in his attack.

Duane, of course, gave his version. It was an understandable mistake. There had been no communication with Von Gilsa.

They were running toward his position and he ordered the firing almost as a reflex action, the way a soldier is trained to react. It happened frequently; naturally mistakes were made in the heat of battle. It was expected. But Chancellorsville had been a Union defeat. That was why they forced him to resign his commission. A number of able commanders were relieved simply because the Army of the Potomac had suffered a setback.

Vern accepted his explanation and even felt somewhat sorry for him. But when Duane went on pretending he was a soldier and hired four new riders for his "scouts," as he called them, you could take just so much of that. What was it? Kidston's Guard, Scouts for Colonel J. H. Carleton, Military Department of Arizona. It was one thing to feel sympathy for Duane. It was another to let Duane assume so much importance just to soothe his injured pride.

And Lorraine, spoiled and bored and overly sure of herself. The worst combination you could find in a woman. Both she and her comic-opera officer of a father living under one roof. Still, it seemed there were some things you just had to put up with.

Though that didn't include a home-coming Confederate squeezing him off the river. Not after the years and the sweat, and breaking his back for every dollar he earned. . . .

That had been his reaction to Cable before he saw Cable face to face, before he talked to him. Since then, a gnawing doubt had crept into his mind. Cable had worked and sweated and fought, too. What about that?

Duane's logic at least simplified the question: Cable was an enemy of the Federal government in Federal territory. As such he had no rights. Take his land and good damn riddance.

"His family is *his* worry." Duane's words. "But in these times, Vern, and I'll testify to it, men with families are dying every day. We are a thousand miles from the fighting, but right here is an extension of the war. Sweep down on him! Drive him out! Burn him out if you have to!"

Still, Vern wished with all his strength that there was a way of driving Cable out without fighting him. He was not afraid of Cable. He respected him. And he respected his wife.

Vern found himself picturing the way Martha had walked out from the house with the shotgun under her arm. Cable was a lucky man to have a woman like that, a woman who could keep up with him and who had already given him three healthy children. A woman, Kidston felt, who thoroughly enjoyed being a woman and living with the man she loved.

He had thought that Luz Acaso was that kind exactly. In fact he had been sure of it. But ever since Janroe's coming she seemed a different person. That was something else to think about. Why would a woman as warm and openly affectionate as Luz change almost overnight? It concerned Janroe's presence, that much Kidston was sure of. But was Luz in love with him or mortally afraid of him? That was another question.

He heard steps behind him and looked over his shoulder to see Lorraine crossing the porch. She smiled at him pleasantly.

"Cabe makes you stop and think, doesn't he?"

"You're on familiar terms for only one meeting," Vern said.

"That's what his wife calls him." Lorraine watched her uncle lean against a support post. He looked away from her, out over the yard. "Don't you think that's unusual, a wife calling her husband by his last name?"

"Maybe that's what everybody calls him," Vern answered.

"Like calling you 'Kid.'" Lorraine smiled, then laughed. "No, I think she made up the name. I think it's her name for him. Hers only." Lorraine waited, letting the silence lengthen before asking, "What do you think of her?"

"I haven't thought."

"I thought you might have given Martha careful consideration."

"Why?"

"As a way of getting at her husband."

Vern looked at her now.

"What do you mean?"

Lorraine smiled. "You seem reluctant to use force. I doubt if you can buy him off. So what remains?"

"I'm listening."

"Strike at Cable from within."

"And what does that mean?"

Lorraine sighed. "Vern, you're never a surprise. You're as predictable as Duane, though you don't call nearly as much attention to yourself."

"Lorraine, if you have something to say—"

"I've said it. Go after him through Martha. Turn her against him. Break up his home. Then see how long he stays in that house."

"And if such a thing was possible—"

"It's very possible."

"How?"

"The other woman, Vern. How else?"

He watched her calmly. "And that's you."

She nodded once, politely. "Lorraine Kidston as"—she paused—"I need a more provocative name for this role."

Vern continued to watch her closely. "And if he happens to love his wife?"

"Of course he loves her. Martha's an attractive woman if you like them strong, capable and somewhat on the plain side. But that has nothing to do with it. He's a man, Vern. And right now he's in that place all alone."

"You've got a wild mind," Vern said quietly. "I'd hate to live with it inside me." He turned away from her and walked down the steps and across the yard.

You shocked him, Lorraine thought amusedly, watching him go. But wait until the shock wears off. Wait until his conscience stops choking him. Vern would agree. He would have it understood that such methods went against his grain; but in the end he would agree. Lorraine was sure of it and she was smiling now.

Cable passed through the store and climbed the stairs to the bedroom where Martha was unpacking. He watched her removing linens and towels from the trunk at the foot of the bed, turning to place them in the open dresser drawer an arm's length away.

"The children will be in here?"

Martha looked up. "Clare and Dave. Sandy will sleep with me."

"With Luz here, I think you'll get along with Janroe all right."

"As long as the children eat in the kitchen."

"Martha, I'm sorry."

She saw his frown deepen the tightly drawn lines of his bruised face. "Someday I'm going to bite my tongue off. I shouldn't have said that."

"I can't blame you," Cable said.

"But it doesn't make it any easier."

"If you weren't here," Cable said, "it wouldn't even be possible." He moved close to her and put his arms around her as she straightened.

"I want to say something like 'It'll be over soon,' or 'Soon we'll be going back and there won't be any more waiting, any more holding your breath not knowing what's going to happen.' But I can't. I can't promise anything."

"Cabe, I don't need promises. Just so long as you're here with us, that's all we need."

"Do you want to leave? Right this minute get in the wagon and go back to Sudan?"

"You don't mean that."

"I do. You say it and we'll leave."

For a moment Martha was silent, standing close to him, close to his bruised cheekbone and his lips that were swollen and cut. "If we went back," Martha said, "I don't think you'd be an easy man to live with. You'd be nice and sometimes you'd smile, but I don't think you'd ever say very much, and it would be as if your mind was always on something else." A smile touched her mouth and showed warmly in her eyes. "We'll stay, Cabe."

She lifted her face to be kissed and when they looked at each other again she saw his smile and he seemed more at ease.

"Are you going back right now?"

"I have to talk to Janroe first." He kissed her again before stepping away. "I'll be up in a little while."

Janroe was sitting in the kitchen, his chair half turned from the table so that he could look directly out through the screen door. He paid no attention to Luz who was clearing the table, carrying the dishes to the wooden sink. He was thinking of the war, seeing himself during that afternoon of August 30, in the fields near Richmond, Kentucky.

If that day had never happened, or if it had happened differently; if he had not lost his arm—no, losing his arm was only an indirect reason for his being here. But it had led to this. It had been the beginning of the end.

After his wound had healed, eight months later, with his sleeve in his belt and even somewhat proud of it but not showing his pride, he had returned to his unit and served almost another full year before they removed him from active duty. His discharge was sudden. It came shortly after he had had the Yankee prisoners shot. They said he would have to resign his commission because of his arm; but he knew that was not the reason and he had pleaded with them to let him stay, pestering General Kirby Smith's staff; but it came to nothing, and in the end he was sent home a civilian.

He had not told Cable about that year or about anything that had happened after August 30, after his arm was blown from his body. But Cable didn't have to know everything. Like soldiers before an engagement with the enemy—it was better not to tell them too much.

Stir them up, yes. Make them hate and be hungry to kill; but don't tell them things they didn't have to know, because that would start them thinking and soldiers in combat shouldn't think. You could scare them though. Sometimes that was all right. Get them scared for their own skins. Pour it into their heads that the enemy was ruthless and knew what he was doing and that he would kill them if they didn't kill him. Beat them if they wouldn't fight!

God knows he had done that. He remembered again the afternoon near Richmond, coming out of the brush and starting across the open field toward the Union battery dug in on the pine ridge that was dark against the sky. He remembered screaming at his men to follow him. He remembered this, seeing himself now apart from himself, seeing Captain Edward Janroe waving a Dragoon pistol and shouting at the men who were still crouched at the edge of the brush. He saw himself running back toward them, then swinging the barrel at a man's head. The man ducked and scrambled out into the field. Others followed him; but two men still remained, down on their knees and staring up at him wide-eyed with fear. He shot one of them from close range, cleanly through the head; and the second man was out of the brush before he could swing the Dragoon on him.

Yes, you could frighten a man into action, scare him so that he was more afraid of you than the enemy. Janroe stopped.

Could that apply to Cable? Could Cable be scared into direct action?

He eased his position, looking at Luz who was standing at the sink with her back to him, then at the screen door again and the open sunlight beyond. He had given his mind the opportunity to reject these questions, to answer them negatively.

But why not? Why couldn't Cable be forced into killing the Kidstons? He had been a soldier—used to taking orders. No, he couldn't be ordered. But perhaps now, with his wife and children staying here, he would be more easily persuaded. Perhaps he could be forced into doing it. Somehow.

In Janroe's mind it was clear, without qualifying shades of meaning, that Vern and Duane Kidston were the enemy. In uniform or not in uniform they were Yankees and this was a time of war and they had to be killed. A soldier killed. An officer ordered his men to kill. That was what it was all about and that was what Janroe knew best.

They could close their eyes to this fact and believe they were acting as human beings—whatever the hell that meant in time of war—and relieve him of his command for what he did to those Yankee prisoners. They could send him out here to die of boredom; but he could still remember what a Yankee field piece did to his arm. He was still a soldier and he could still think like a soldier and act like a soldier and if his job was to kill—whether or not on the surface it was called gun-running—then he would kill.

He felt his chest rising and falling with his breathing and he glanced at Luz, calming himself then, inhaling and letting his breath out slowly.

Still, an officer used strategy. He fought with his eyes open; not rushing blindly, unless there was no other way to do it. An officer studied a situation and used what means he had at hand. If the means was a brigade or only one man, he used that means to the best of his ability.

Janroe looked up as Cable entered the kitchen. He glanced at Luz then, catching her eye, and the girl dried her hands and stepped out through the back door.

"I've been waiting for you," Janroe said.

"I was with my wife." Cable hesitated. "We're grateful for what you're doing."

"I guess you are."

Cable sat down, removing his hat and wiping his forehead with the back of his hand. "Martha will be glad to help out with the housekeeping, and she'll keep the children out from under your feet."

"I took that for granted," Janroe said.

"We'll be out of your way as soon as I settle this business with the Kidstons."

"And how long will that take?"

"Look, we'll leave right now if you want."

"You lose your temper too easily," Janroe said. "I was asking you a simple question."

Cable looked at him, then at his own hand curling the brim of his hat. "I don't know; it's up to the Kidstons."

"It could be up to you, if you wanted it to be."

"If I kill them."

"You didn't have any trouble last night."

"Last night two men came to my home," Cable said. "My family was in danger and I didn't have any choice. Though I'll tell you this: I didn't mean to kill them. That just happened. If Vern and Duane come threatening my home, then I could kill them too because I wouldn't be trying to kill them; I'd be trying to protect my home and my family, and there's a difference. When you say kill them, just go out and do it; that's something else."

Janroe was sitting back in his chair, his hand idly rubbing the stump of his arm; but now he leaned forward. His hand went to the edge of the table and he pushed the chair back.

"We could argue that point for a long time." He stood up then. "Come on, I'll show you something."

Cable hesitated, then rose and followed Janroe through the store and out to the loading platform. The children were at one end, stopped in whatever they were playing or pretending by the sudden appearance of Janroe. They looked at their father, wanting to go to him, but they seemed to sense a threat in approaching Janroe and they remained where they were.

Janroe said, "Tell them to go around back."

"They're not bothering anything." Cable moved toward the children.

"Listen," Janroe said patiently, "just get rid of them for a while—all right?"

He waited while Cable talked to the three children. Finally they moved off, taking their time and looking back as they turned the corner of the adobe. When they were out of sight, Janroe went down the stairs and, to Cable's surprise, ducked under the loading platform.

Cable followed, lowering his head to step through the cross timbers into the confining dimness. He moved with hunched shoulders the few steps to where Janroe was removing the padlock from a door in the adobe foundation.

"This used to be a storeroom," Janroe muttered. He pushed the door open and moved aside. "Go on; there's a lantern in there."

Cable hesitated, then stepped past him, glancing back to make sure Janroe was coming.

Janroe followed, saying, "Feel along the wall, you'll find it."

Cable turned, raising his left hand. He heard the door swing closed and he was in abrupt total darkness.

He heard Janroe's steps and felt him move close behind him. Too close! Cable tried to turn, reaching for the Walker at the same time; but his hand twisted behind him and pulled painfully up between his shoulder blades. He tried to lunge forward, tried to twist himself free, but as he did Janroe's foot scissored about his ankles and Cable fell forward, landing heavily on the hard-packed floor with Janroe on top of him.

4

Now there was silence.

With Janroe's full weight on top of him and the cool hardness of the floor flat against his cheek, Cable did not move. He felt Janroe's chest pressing heavily against his back. His right arm, twisted and held between their bodies, sent tight, muscle-straining pain up into his shoulder. Janroe had pulled his own hand free as they struck the floor. It gripped the handle of Cable's revolver, then tightened on it as the boards creaked above them.

Faint footsteps moved through the store and faded again into silence. Cable waited, listening, and making his body relax even with the weight pressing against him. He was thinking: It could be Martha, gone out to call the children. Martha not twenty feet away.

He felt the Walker slide from its holster. Janroe's weight shifted, grinding heavily into his back. The cocking action of the Walker was loud and close to him before the barrel burrowed into the pit of his arm.

"Don't spoil it," Janroe whispered.

They waited. In the darkness, in the silence, neither spoke. Moments later the floor creaked again and the soft footsteps crossed back through the store. Cable let his breath out slowly.

Janroe murmured, "I could have pulled the trigger. A minute ago I was unarmed; but just then I could have killed you."

Cable said nothing. Janroe's elbow pressed into his back. The pressure eased and he felt Janroe push himself to his feet. Still Cable waited. He heard Janroe adjust a lantern. A match scratched down the wall. Its flare died almost to nothing, then abruptly the floor in front of Cable's face took form. His eyes raised from his own shadow and in the dull light he saw four oblong wooden cases stacked against the wall close in front of him.

"Now you can get up," Janroe said.

Cable rose. He stretched the stiffness from his body, working his shoulder to relieve the sharp muscle strain, his eyes returning to Janroe now and seeing the Walker in Janroe's belt, tight against his stomach.

"Did you prove something by that?"

"I want you to know," Janroe said, "that I'm not just passing the time of day."

"There's probably an easier way."

"No." Janroe shook his head slowly. "I want you to realize that I could have killed you. That I'd do it in a minute if I thought I had to. I want that to sink into your head."

"You wouldn't have a reason."

"The reason's behind you. Four cases of Enfield rifles. They're more important than any one man's life. More important than yours—"

Cable stopped him. "You're not making much sense."

"Or more important than the lives of Vern and Duane Kidston," Janroe finished. "Does that make sense?"

"My hunting license." Cable watched him thoughtfully. "Isn't that what you called it? If I was in the gun-running business, I could kill them with a clear conscience."

"I'll tell it to you again," Janroe said. "If you worked for me, I'd order you to kill them."

"I remember."

"But it still hasn't made any impression."

"I told you a little while ago, now it's up to the Kidstons."

"All right, what do you think they're doing right this minute?"

"Maybe burying their dead," Cable said. "And realizing something."

"And Joe Bob's brothers—do you think they're just going to bury him and forget all about it?"

"That's something else," Cable said.

"No it isn't, because Vern will use them. He'll sic them on you like a pair of mad dogs."

"I don't think so. I've got a feeling Vern's the kind of man who has to handle something like this himself, his own way."

"And you'd bet the lives of your family on it," Janroe said dryly.

"It's Vern's move, not mine."

"Like a chess game."

"Look," Cable said patiently. "You're asking me to shoot

the man down in cold blood and that's what I can't do. Not for any reason."

"Even though you left your family and rode a thousand miles to fight the Yankees." Janroe watched him closely, making sure he held Cable's attention.

"Now you're home and you got Yankees right in your front yard. But now, for some reason, it's different. They're supplying cavalry horses to use against the same boys you were in uniform with. They're using your land to graze those horses. But now it's different. Now you sit and wait because it's the Yankees' turn to move."

"A lot of things don't sound sensible," Cable said, "when you put them into words."

"Or when you cover one ear," Janroe said. "You don't hear the guns or the screams and the moans of the wounded. You even have yourself believing the war's over."

"I told you once, it's over as far as I'm concerned."

Janroe nodded. "Yes, you've told me and you've told yourself. Now go tell Vern Kidston and his brother."

End it, Cable thought. Tell him to shut up and mind his own business. But he thought of Martha and the children. They were here in the safety of this man's house, living here now because Janroe had agreed to it. He was obligated to Janroe, and the sudden awareness of it checked him, dissolving the bald, blunt words that were clear in his mind and almost on his tongue.

He said simply, "I don't think we're getting anywhere."

Janroe's expression remained coldly impassive; still his eyes clung to Cable. He watched him intently, almost as if he were trying to read Cable's thoughts.

"You might think about it though," Janroe said. His eyes dropped briefly. He pulled the Walker from his waist and handed it butt-forward to Cable.

"Within a few days, I'm told, Bill Dancey and the rest of them will start bringing all the horses in from pasture. That means Duane and maybe even Vern will be home alone. Just the two of them there." Janroe lifted the lantern from the wall. Before blowing it out, he added, "You might think about that, too."

They moved out of the cellar into the abrupt sun glare of

the yard, and there Janroe waited while Cable went inside to tell Martha good-by. Within a few minutes Cable reappeared. Janroe watched him kneel down to kiss his children; he watched him mount the sorrel and ride out. He watched him until he was out of sight, and still he lingered in the yard, staring out through the sun haze to the willows that lined the river.

He isn't mad enough, Janroe was thinking. And Vern seems to want to wait and sweat him out. If he waits, Cable waits and nothing happens. And it will go on like this until you bring them together. You know that, don't you? Somehow you have to knock their heads together.

Manuel Acaso reached Cable's house in the late evening. The sky was still light, with traces of sun reflection above the pine slope, but the glare was gone and the trees had darkened and seemed more silent.

Manuel moved through the streaked shadows of the aspen grove, through the scattered pale-white trees, hearing only the sound of his own horse in the leaves. He stopped at the edge of the trees, his eyes on the silent, empty-appearing adobe; then he moved on.

Halfway across the yard he called out, "Paul!"

Cable parted the hanging willow branches with the barrel of the Spencer and stepped into the open. Manuel was facing the house, sitting motionless in the saddle with his body in profile as Cable approached, his face turned away and his eyes on the door of the house.

He looks the same, Cable thought. Perhaps heavier, but not much; and he still looks as if he's part of the saddle and the horse, all three of them one, even when he just sits resting.

Softly he said, "Manuel—"

The dark lean face in the shadow of the straw hat turned to Cable without a trace of surprise, but with a smile that was real and warmly relaxed. His eyes raised to the willows, then dropped to Cable again.

"Still hiding in trees," Manuel said. "Like when the Apache would come. Never be where they think you are."

Cable was smiling. "We learned that, Manolo."

"Now to be used on a man named Kidston," Manuel said. "Did you think I was him coming?"

"You could have been."

"Always something, uh?"

"Why didn't you run him when he first came?"

Manuel shrugged. "Why? It's not my land."

"You skinny Mexican, you were too busy running something else."

The trace of a smile left Manuel's face. "I didn't think Janroe would have told you so soon."

"You haven't seen him this evening?"

"No, I didn't stop."

"But you knew I was here."

"A man I know visited the store yesterday. Luz told him," Manuel said. "I almost stopped to see Martha and the little kids, but I thought, no, talk to him first, about Janroe."

"He wants me to join you, but I told him I had my own troubles."

"He must see something in you." Manuel leaned forward, resting his arms one over the other on the saddle horn, watching Cable closely. "What do you think of him?"

Cable hesitated. "I'm not sure."

"He told you how he came and how he's helping with the guns?"

"That he was in the war before and wounded."

"Do you believe him?"

"I don't have a reason not to. But I don't understand him."

"That's the way I felt about him; and still do."

"Did you check on him?"

"Sure. I asked the people I work with. They said of course he's all right, or he wouldn't have been sent here."

Looking up at Manuel, Cable smiled. It was good to see him, good to talk to him again, in the open or anywhere, and for the first time in three days Cable felt more sure of himself. The feeling came over him quietly with the calm, unhurried look of this man who lounged easily in his saddle and seemed a part of it—this thin-faced, slim-bodied man who looked like a boy and always would, who had worked his cattle with him and fought the Apache with him and helped him build his home. They had learned to know each other well, and there was much between them that didn't have to be spoken.

"Do you feel someone watching you?"

"This standing in the open." Manuel nodded. "Like being naked."

"We'd better go somewhere else."

"In the trees." Manuel smiled.

He took his horse to the barn and came back, walking with a slow, stiff-legged stride, his hand lightly on the Colt that was holstered low on his right side, holding it to his leg. He followed Cable in to the willows. Then, sitting down next to him at the edge of the cutbank, Manuel noticed the horse herd far out in the meadow beyond the river.

"You let Vern's horses stay?"

"I ran them once," Cable said. "Duane brought them back."

"So you run them again."

"Tomorrow. You want to come?"

"Tonight I'm back to my gun business."

Denaman, Cable thought. The old man's face appeared suddenly in his mind with the mention of the gun-running. He told Manuel what Janroe had said about John Denaman's death. That he was worried about his business. "But I suppose that meant worried about the guns," Cable said. "Having to sit on them and act natural."

"I think the man was just old," Manuel said. "I think he would have died anyway. Perhaps this gun business caused him to die a little sooner, but not much sooner."

"I'm sorry—"

"Thank you," Manuel said, with understanding, as if Denaman had been his own father.

"At first," Cable said, "I couldn't picture John fooling with something like this—living out here, far away from the war."

"Why?" Manuel's eyebrows rose. "You lived here and you went to fight."

"It seems different."

"Because he was old? John could have had the same feeling you did."

"I suppose."

"Sure, and I think you going off to war, and the other people he knew who went, convinced him he had to do something to help. Since he couldn't become a soldier he did this with the guns."

"Did he talk to you about it first?"

Manuel shook his head. "There were already guns under the store when I found out. John got into it through some man he knew who lives in Hidalgo. He didn't want me to help, said I had no part in it. But I told him if he believed in what he was doing then so did I, so why waste our breath over it."

"Do you believe in it?"

"I believed in John; that's enough."

"But what about now?"

"He started it," Manuel said. "I'll finish it, with or without the help of this man who's so anxious to kill."

"Something else," Cable said. "Janroe told me that John was worried about Luz. That she was keeping company with Vern, and John didn't like it."

Manuel nodded. "She was seeing him often before Janroe came. Sometimes it bothered me, Vern being around; but John said, no, that was good, let him sit up there in the parlor with Luz. If we sneaked around and stayed to ourselves, John said, then people would suspect things. . . . So I don't think he was worried about Vern Kidston. If anything, John liked him. They talked well together; never about the war but about good things. . . . No, Janroe is wrong about that part. He figured it out himself and maybe it made sense to him, but he's wrong."

"Luz stopped seeing Vern?"

"Right after Janroe came."

"Do you know why?"

"I think because she was afraid Janroe would kill him, or try to, and if it happened at the store it would be because of her." Manuel paused. "Does that make sense?"

"I suppose. Since she knew Janroe and Vern were on opposite sides."

"Luz is afraid of him and admits it," Manuel said. "She says she has a feeling about him and sees him in dreams as a *nagual*, a man who is able to change himself into something else. A man who is two things at the same time."

"He could be two different people," Cable said, nodding. "He could be what he tells you and he could be what he is, or what he is thinking. I don't know. I don't even know how to talk to him. He wants me to work for him and kill Vern and Duane because of what they're doing."

Manuel stared. "He asked me to do that, months ago."

"What did you tell him?"

"To go to hell."

"That's what I wanted to say," Cable said. "But now Martha and the kids are living in his house and I have to go easy with him. But he keeps insisting and arguing it and after a while I run out of things to tell him."

In the dimness, Manuel leaned closer, putting his hand on Cable's arm. "Do you want to find out more about this Janroe?"

"How?"

"I'll take you to the man I work for. John's friend from Hidalgo. He can tell you things."

"I don't know—"

"You were at the war and you'd understand what he says about Janroe. You'd be able to ask questions."

"Maybe I'd better." Cable's tone was low, thoughtful.

"Listen, you're worried about your land; I know that. But after this I'll help you and we'll run these Kidstons straight to hell if you say it."

"All right." Cable nodded. "We'll talk to your man."

It was still sky-red twilight when they rode out, but full dark by the time they passed the store, keeping to the west side of the river and high up on the slope so they wouldn't be heard.

Martha stood at the sink, taking her time with the breakfast dishes, making it last because she wasn't sure what she would do after this. Perhaps ask Luz if she could help with something else. Luz, not Mr. Janroe. But even if there was something to be done, Luz would shake her head no, Martha was sure of that. So what would she do then? Perhaps go outside with the children.

Her gaze rose from the dishwater to the window and she saw her children playing in the back yard: Davis and Sandy pushing stick-trains over the hard-packed ground and making whistle sounds; Clare sitting on a stump, hunched over her slate with the tip of her tongue showing in the corner of her mouth.

They're used to not seeing him, Martha thought. But you're not used to it, not even after two and a half years. And now he seems farther away than before.

That was a strange thing. She had waited for Cable during the war knowing he would come home, knowing it and believing it, because she prayed hard and allowed herself to believe nothing else. Now he was within one hour's ride, but the distance between them seemed greater than when he had served with General Forrest. And now, too, there was an uncertainty inside of her. Because you haven't had time to think about it, she thought. Or not think about it. This time you haven't gotten used to not thinking anything will happen to him.

For a moment the thought angered her. She had things to do at home. She had a family to care for, husband and children, but she stood calmly waiting and washing dishes in another person's house, away from her husband again, and again faced with the tiring necessity of telling herself everything would be all right.

Was it worth it?

If it wasn't, was anything worth waiting or fighting for?

And she thought, If you don't have the desire to fight or wait for something, there's no reason for being on earth.

That's very easy to say. Now wash the dishes and live with it. Martha smiled then. No, she told herself, it was simply a question of stubbornness, or resignation. If you ran away from one trouble, you would probably run into another. So face the first one, the important one, and get used to it. She remembered Cable saying, years before, "We've taken all there is to take. Nothing will make us leave this place."

And perhaps you can believe that, just as you knew and believed he would come home from the war, Martha thought. So put on the big-smiling mask again. Even if it makes you gag.

But I'm tired, Martha thought, not smiling now. Perhaps you can keep the mask on only so long before it suffocates you.

She glanced over her shoulder as Luz entered the kitchen.

"I think Mr. Janroe is going out," Luz said. She pulled a towel from a hook above the sink and began drying dishes. "He's in the store, but dressed to go out."

"Where would he be going?" Martha asked.

"I don't know. Sometimes he just rides off."

"Would it have anything to do with the guns?"

Luz looked at her. "You know?"

"Of course. Don't you think Paul would have told me?"

"I wasn't sure."

"Luz, do you have anything to do with it?"

The girl nodded. "On the day the guns are to arrive, I ride down to Hidalgo in the afternoon. That night I return an hour ahead of them seeing that the way is clear. Manuel follows, doing the same. Then the guns come."

"Are you due to go again soon—or shouldn't I ask that?"

"It doesn't matter." The girl shrugged. "Tomorrow I go again."

"Aren't you afraid?"

"Not when I'm away from here."

"But you're afraid of Mr. Janroe," Martha said. "I'm sure of that. Why, Luz?"

"You don't know him or you wouldn't ask that."

"I know he's gruff. Hardly what you'd call a gentleman."

"No." Luz shook her head solemnly. She glanced at the doorway to the main room before saying, "It isn't something you see in him."

"Has he ever . . . made advances?"

"No, it isn't like that either," the girl said. "It's something you feel. Like an awareness of evil. As if his soul was so smeared with stains of sin you were aware of a foulness about him that could almost be smelled."

"Luz, to your knowledge the man hasn't done a thing wrong."

"The feeling is a kind of knowledge itself."

"But it isn't something you can prove, is it?" Martha stood with her hands motionless in the dishwater, her full attention on Luz. "What if suddenly you realize that all you've said couldn't possibly be true, that it's all something out of a dream or—"

"Listen, I did dream about him! A number of times before, then again last night." The girl's eyes went to the main room and back again.

"I saw an animal in the dream, like a small wolf or a coyote, and it was slinking along in the moonlight. Then, in front of it, there was a chicken. The chicken was feeding on the ground and before it could raise its head, the animal was on it and tearing it apart with its teeth and eating it even while the chicken was still alive. I watched, cold with fear, but unable to move. And as I watched, the animal began to change.

"It was still on its haunches facing me, still eating and smeared with the blood of the chicken. First its hind legs became human legs; then its body became the clothed body of a man. Then the face began to change, the jaw and the nose and the chin. The teeth were still those of an animal and he had no forehead and his eyes and head were still like an animal's. He was looking at me with blood on his mouth and on his hand . . . on the one hand that he had. And at that moment I ran from him screaming. I knew it was the face of Mr. Janroe."

"Luz, you admit it's a dream—"

"Listen, that isn't all of it." Luz glanced toward the main room again. "I awoke in a sweat and with a thirst burning the inside of my throat. So I left my bed and went down for a drink of water. The big room was dark, but at once I saw that a lamp was burning in here. I came to the door, I looked into this room, and I swear on my mother's grave that my heart stopped beating when I saw him."

"Mr. Janroe?"

Luz nodded quickly. "He was sitting at the table holding a piece of meat almost to his mouth and his eyes were on me, not as if he'd looked up as I appeared, but as if he'd been watching me for some time. I saw his eyes and the hand holding the meat, just as in the dream, and I ran. I don't know if I screamed, but I remember wanting to scream and running up the stairs and locking my door."

Martha dried her hands on her apron. She smiled at Luz gently and put her hand on the girl's arm.

"Luz, there isn't anything supernatural about a man eating with his fingers."

"You didn't see him." Luz stopped. Her eyes were on the doorway again and a moment later Janroe appeared. Martha glanced at him, then at Luz again as the girl suddenly turned and pushed through the screen door.

Janroe came into the kitchen. He was holding his hat and wearing a coat, but the coat was open and Martha noticed the butt of a Colt beneath one lapel in a shoulder holster. Another Colt was on his hip.

"Did I interrupt something?"

"Nothing important." Martha turned from the sink to face him. "You're going out?"

"I thought I would." He watched her with an expression of faint amusement. "Wondering if I'm going to see your husband?"

"Yes, I was."

"I might see him."

"If you're going that way, would you mind stopping by the house?"

"Why?"

"Why do you think, Mr. Janroe?"

"Maybe he's not so anxious to let you know what he's doing."

Now a new side of him, Martha thought wearily. She said nothing.

"I mean, considering how he dropped you here and ran off so quick." Janroe hooked his hat on the back of the nearest chair. Unhurriedly he started around the table, saying now, "A man is away from his wife for two years or more, then soon as he gets home he leaves her again. What kind of business is that?"

Martha watched him still coming toward her. "We know the reason, Mr. Janroe."

"The reason he gives. Worried about his wife and kids."

"What other reason is there?"

"It wouldn't be my business to know."

"You seem to be making it your business."

"I was just wondering if you believed him."

He was close to her now. Martha stood unmoving, feeling the wooden sink against her back. "I believe him," she said calmly. "I believe anything he tells me."

"Did he tell you he led a saintly life the years he was away?"

"I never questioned him about it."

"Want me to tell you what a man does when he's away from home?"

"And even if I said no—"

"They have a time for themselves," Janroe went on. "They carry on like young bucks with the first smell of spring. Though they expect their wives to sit home and be as good as gold."

"You know this from experience?"

"I've seen them." His voice was low and confiding. "Some of them come home with the habit of their wild ways still inside them, and they go wandering off again."

He watched her closely, his head lowered and within inches of hers. "Then there's some women who aren't fooled by it and they say, 'If he can fool around and have a time, then so can I.' Those women do it, too. They start having a time for themselves and it serves their husbands right."

Martha did not move. She was looking at him, at his heavy mustache and the hard, bony angles of his face, feeling the almost oppressive nearness of him. She said nothing.

Janroe asked, almost a whisper, "You know what I mean?"

"If I were to tell my husband what you just said," Martha answered quietly, "I honestly believe he would kill you."

Janroe's expression did not change. "I don't think so. Your husband needs me. He needs a place for you and the kids to stay."

"Are you telling me that I'm part of the agreement between you and my husband?"

"Well now, nothing so blunt as all that." Janroe smiled. "We're white men."

"We'll be out of here within an hour," Martha said coldly.

"Now wait a minute. You don't kid very well, do you?"

"Not about that."

He backed away from her, reaching for his hat. "I don't even think you know what I was talking about."

"Let's say that I didn't," Martha said. "For your sake."

Janroe shrugged. "You think whatever you want." He put his hat on and walked out. In front of the store, he mounted a saddled buckskin and rode off.

He could still see the calm expression of Martha Cable's face as he forded the shallow river, as he kicked the buckskin up the bank and started across the meadow that rolled gradually up into the pines that covered the crest of the slope. Then he was spurring, running the buckskin, crossing the sweep of meadow, in the open sunlight now with the hot breeze hissing past his face. But even then Martha was before him.

She stared at him coldly. And the harder he ran—holding the reins short to keep the buckskin climbing, feeling the brute strength of the horse's response, hearing the hoofs and the wind and trying to be aware of nothing else—the more he was aware of Martha's contempt for him.

Some time later, following the trail that ribboned through the pines, the irritating feeling that he had made a fool of himself began to subside. It was as if here in the silence, in the soft shadows of the pines, he was hidden from her eyes.

He told himself to forget about her. The incident in the kitchen had been a mistake. He had seen her and started talking and one thing had led to another; not planned, just something suddenly happening that moment. He would have to be more careful. She was an attractive woman and her husband was miles away, but there were matters at hand more important than Martha Cable. She would wait until later, when there were no Kidstons . . . and no Paul Cable.

Still, telling himself this, her calmness and indifference grated on his pride and he was sure that she had held him off because of his missing arm, because he was something repulsive to her. Only part of a man.

He jerked his mind back to the reason he was here. First, to talk to Cable, to hammer away at him until he consented to go after the Kidstons. Then, to scout around and see what was going on.

The latter had become a habit: riding this ridge trail, then bearing off toward the Kidston place and sometimes approaching within view of the house. He did this every few days and some times at night, because if you kept your eyes open you learned things. Like Duane's habit of sitting on the veranda at night—perhaps every night—for a last cigar. Or Vern visiting his grazes once a week and sometimes not returning until the next morning. But always there had been people around the house while Duane sat and smoked on the veranda; and almost invariably Vern made his inspections with Bill Dancey along. Knowing that Kidston's riders would be off on a horse gather in a few days was the same kind of useful intelligence to keep in mind. He had already told Cable about the riders being away. Perhaps he would tell him everything—every bit of information he knew about Vern and Duane Kidston. Lay it all out on the table and make it look easy.

High on the slope, but now even with Cable's house, Janroe reined in. There was no sign of life below. No sounds, no movement, no chimney smoke. But Cable could still be home, Janroe decided.

Then, descending the path, keeping his eyes on the shingled roof and the open area of the front yard, he began to think: But what if he isn't home?

Then you talk to him another time.

No, wait. What if he isn't home and isn't even close by?

Reaching the back of the adobe, he sat for a moment, listening thoughtfully to the silence.

And what if something happened to his house while he was away? Janroe began to feel the excitement of it building inside of him.

But be careful, he thought.

He rode around to the front and called Cable's name.

No answer.

He waited; called again, but still the house stood silent and showed no signs of life.

Janroe reined the buckskin around and crossed the yard to the willows. His gaze went to the horse herd out on the meadow and he studied the herd for some moments. No, Cable wasn't there. No one was.

He was about to turn back to the house, but he hesitated. No one anywhere. What does that say?

No, it's too good. When a thing looks too good there's something wrong with it. Still, he knew that all at once he was looking at an almost foolproof way to jab Cable into action. He sat motionless, looking at the horse herd, making sure no riders were out beyond the farthest grazing horses, and thinking it all over carefully.

Would he be suspected? No. He'd tell Martha and Luz he went to Fort Buchanan on business and no one was home when he passed here. He could even head up toward Buchanan, spend the night on the trail and double back to the store in the morning.

But what if someone came while he was in the house? What if Cable came home?

You either do it or you don't do it, but you don't think about it any more!

It was decided then. He returned to the adobe, swung down as he reached the ramada, and pushed open the front door.

Inside, in the dim closeness of the room, an urgency came over him and he told himself to hurry, to get it over with and get out.

From the stove he picked up a frying pan, went to the kitchen cupboards, opened them and swung the pan repeatedly into the shelves of dishes until not a cup or a plate remained in one piece. With a chair he smashed down the stove's chimney flue. A cloud of soot puffed out and filtered through the room as he dragged the comforter and blankets from the bed. He emptied the kitchen drawers then, turning them upside down; found a carving knife and used it to slash open the mattress and pillows still on the bed.

Enough?

He was breathing heavily from the exertion, from the violence of what had taken him no more than a minute. Hesitating now, his eyes going over the room, he again felt the urgent need to be out of here.

Enough.

He went out brushing soot from his coat, mounted and rode directly across the yard and forded the river. He stopped long enough to convince himself that no riders had joined the Kidston herd since his last look at it. Then he rode on, spurring across the meadow now, pointing for the east slope and not until he was in the piñon, beginning the steep climb up through the trees, did he look back and across to Cable's house. Not until then did he take the deep breath he had wanted to take in the house to make himself relax.

You've pushed him now, Janroe told himself, hearing the words calmly, but still feeling the excitement, the tension, tight through his body.

You just busted everything wide open.

It was evening, but not yet dark, a silent time with the trees standing black and thick-looking and the sky streaked with red shades of sun reflection. A whole day had passed and Cable was returning home.

He had already skirted the store, wanting to see Martha but wanting more to avoid Janroe, and now he was high up in the shadows and the silence of the pines, following the horse trail along the ridge.

He would talk to Janroe another time, after he had thought this out and was sure he knew what to say to him.

This morning he had talked to a man, a small old man who was perhaps in his sixties with a graying beard and a mustache that was tobacco-stained yellow about his mouth. Denaman's friend from Hidalgo. In the dimness of the adobe room, and with the early morning sounds of the village outside, the man seemed too old or too small or too fragile to do whatever he was doing.

But he asked Manuel Acaso questions about Cable, then looked at Cable and asked more questions; and it was his eyes that convinced Cable that the man was not too old or too thin or too frail. Brown eyes—Cable would remember them—that were gentle and perhaps kind; but they were not smiling eyes. They were the eyes of a patient, soft-spoken man who would show little more than mild interest at anything he saw or heard.

He was willing enough to talk about Janroe once he was sure of Cable, and he made no attempt to hide facts or try to justify Janroe's actions. He spoke slowly, carefully, as if he had memorized the things he was saying. . . .

Edward Janroe, Cable learned, was a native of Florida, born in St. Augustine a few years before the outbreak of the second Seminole war, and had lived there most of his early life. Almost nothing was known of Janroe during this period; not until he joined the army in 1854. From then on his life was on record.

In 1858, a sergeant by this time, Janroe was court-martialed for knifing a fellow soldier in a tavern fight. The man died and Janroe was sentenced to six years of hard labor at the Fort Marion military prison. He was well into his third year of it when the war broke out. It saved him from completing his sentence.

With a volunteer company from St. Augustine, Janroe traveled to Winchester, Virginia—this during the summer of 1861—and was assigned to the 10th Virginia Infantry, part of General Edmund Kirby Smith's forces. Strangely enough, despite his prison record, but undoubtedly because of his experience, Janroe was commissioned a full lieutenant of infantry.

A year later, and now a captain, Janroe lost his arm at the battle of Richmond, Kentucky. He was sent to the army hospital at Knoxville, spent seven months there, and was discharged sometime in March, 1863.

But Janroe didn't go home. He learned that Kirby Smith had been made commander of the Trans-Mississippi Department, headquartered at Shreveport, Louisiana, and that's where Janroe went. In the early part of April he was reinstated with the rank of lieutenant and served under Dick Taylor, one of Kirby Smith's field generals.

Up to this point Cable had listened in silence.

"He didn't tell me that."

"I don't care what he told you," the bearded man said. "He served under Taylor in the fighting around Alexandria and Opelousas."

But not for long. He was with Taylor less than two months when he was discharged for good. He was told that he had given enough of himself and deserved retirement. The real reason: his wild disregard for the safety of his men, throwing them into almost suicidal charges whenever he made contact with the enemy. This, and the fact that he refused to take a prisoner. During his time with Taylor, Janroe was responsible for having some one hundred and twenty Union prisoners lined up and shot.

Janroe pleaded his case all the way to Kirby Smith's general staff—he was a soldier and soldiering was his life; but as far as every one of them was concerned, Janroe was unfit for active duty and immediately relieved of his command.

Janroe returned to St. Augustine, then in the hands of Federal forces. Through a man he had known there before, he made contact with Confederate Intelligence agents and went to work for them. And eventually—in fact after well over a year in Florida—he was sent to Mexico. There he was given his present assignment.

"I can see why he didn't tell me everything," Cable said.

The bearded man nodded. "Naturally."

Cable watched him. "What do you think of Janroe?"

"He's a hard man to know."

"But what do you think?"

"I don't care for his kind, if that's what you mean."

"Yet you have him working for you."

"Mr. Cable," the bearded man said, "Janroe seems to have one aim in life. To see the South win the war."

"Or to see more Yankees killed."

"What's the difference?"

"You know what I mean."

"I know he's moved over two thousand rifles through the store since coming here," the bearded man said.

"And now he wants to kill two men who aren't even in the war."

"Well, I wonder if you can blame him," the bearded man said, somewhat wearily now. "A man is sent to war and taught how to kill; but after, the unlearning of it is left up to him."

"Except that Janroe knew how to kill before he went to war," Cable said. . . .

So you'll wait, Cable thought now, and wonder about Janroe and wonder when Vern will make his move, while you try to stay calm and keep yourself from running away.

He was perhaps a mile from his house, passing through a clearing in the pines, when he saw the two riders down in the meadow, saw them for one brief moment before they entered the willows at the river.

Cable waited. When the riders did not come out of the trees on this side of the river he dismounted, took his field glasses and Spencer from the saddle and made his way carefully down through the pines on foot. Between fifty and sixty yards from the base of the slope he reached an outcropping of rock that fell steeply, almost abruptly, the rest of the way down. Here Cable went on his stomach. He nosed the Spencer through a V in the warm, sand-colored rocks and put the field glasses to his eyes.

He recognized Lorraine Kidston at once. She stood by her horse, looking down at a stooped man drinking from the edge of the water. When he rose, turning to the girl, wiping his mouth with the back of his hand, Cable saw that it was Vern Kidston.

Two hundred yards away, but with them, close to them through the field glasses, Cable watched. He studied Vern standing heavily with his hands on his hips, his shoulders slightly stooped and his full mustache giving his face a solemn, almost sad expression. Vern spoke little. Lorraine seemed to be doing the talking. Lorraine smiling blandly, shrugging, standing with one hand on her hip and gesturing imperiously with the other.

She stopped. For a moment neither of them spoke: Vern thoughtful; Lorraine watching him. Then Vern nodded, slowly, resignedly, and Lorraine was smiling again. Now she moved to her horse. Vern helped her up. She rode off at once, heading north out into the meadow, and did not look back. Vern watched her, standing motionless with his hands hanging at his sides now.

He was close, his hat, his mustache, his shirt, his gun belt, his hands, all in detail. Then the glasses lowered and Vern Kidston was a small dark figure two hundred yards away.

There he is, Cable thought. Waiting for you.

He put the field glasses aside and took the solid, compact, balanced weight of the Spencer, his hands under it lightly and the stock snugly against the groove of his shoulder.

There he is.

It would be easy, Cable thought. He knew that most of the waiting and the wondering and the wanting to run would be over by just squeezing the trigger. Doing it justifiably, he told himself.

And it isn't something you haven't done before.

There had been the two Apaches he had knocked from their horses as they rode out of the river trees and raced for his cattle. He had been lying on this same slope, up farther, closer to the house and with a Sharps rifle, firing and loading and firing again and seeing the two Chiricahua Apaches pitch from their running horses, not even knowing what had killed them.

And there had been another time. More like this one, though he had not been alone then. Two years ago. Perhaps two years almost to the day. In northern Alabama. . . .

It had happened on the morning of the fifth day, after they had again located the Yankee raider Abel Streight and were closing with him, preparing to tear another bite out of his exhausted flank.

He lay in the tall grass, wet and chilled by the rain that had been falling almost all night; now in the gray mist of morning with a shivering trooper huddled next to him, not speaking, and the rest of the patrol back a few hundred yards with the horses, waiting for the word to be passed to them. For perhaps an hour he lay like this with his glasses on the Union picket, a 51st Indiana Infantryman. The Yankee had been closer than Vern Kidston was now: across a stream and somewhat below them, crouched down behind a log, his rifle straight up past his head and shoulder. He was in plain view, facing the stream, the peak of his forage cap wet-shining and low over his eyes; but his eyes were stretched wide open, Cable knew, because of the mist and the silence and because he was alone on picket duty a thousand miles from home. He's wondering if he will ever see Indiana again, Cable had thought. Wondering if he will ever see his home and his wife and his children. He's old enough to have a family. But he hasn't been in it long, or he wouldn't be showing himself.

I can tell you that you won't go home again, Cable remembered thinking. It's too bad. But I want to go home too, and the way it is now both of us won't be able to. They're going to cry and that's too bad. But everything's too bad. For one brief moment he had thought, remembering it clearly now: Get down, you fool! Stop showing yourself!

Then someone was shaking his foot. He looked back at a bearded face. The face nodded twice. Cable touched the trooper next to him and whispered, indicating the Yankee picket, "Take him."

The man next to him pressed his cheek to his Enfield, aiming, but taking too long, trying to hold the barrel steady, his whole body shivering convulsively from the long, rain-drenched hours. "Give me it," Cable whispered. He eased the long rifle out in front of him carefully and put the front sight just below the Indiana man's face. You shouldn't have looked at him through the glasses, he thought, and pulled the trigger and the picket across the stream was no more. They were up and moving after that. Not until evening did Cable have time to remember the man who had waited helplessly, unknowingly, to be killed. . . .

The way Vern Kidston is now, Cable thought.

There was no difference between the two men, he told himself. Vern was a Yankee; there was no question about that. The only difference, if you wanted to count it, was that Vern didn't have a blue coat or a flat forage cap with the bugle Infantry insignia pinned to the front of it.

What if the 51st Indiana man had had a different kind of hat on but you still knew what he was and what he was doing there?

You would have shot him.

So the uniform doesn't mean anything.

It's what the man believes in and what he's doing to you. What if Vern were here and you were down there, the places just switched?

The thumb of Cable's right hand flicked the trigger guard down and up, levering a cartridge into the breech. The thumb eased back the hammer. Cable brought his face close to the carbine and sighted down the short barrel with both eyes open, placing the front sight squarely on the small figure in the trees. Like the others, Cable thought. It would be quick and clean, and it would be over.

If you don't miss.

Cable raised his head slightly. No, he could take him from here. With the first one he would at least knock Vern down, he was sure of that. Then he could finish him. But if Vern reached cover?

Hit his horse. Then Vern wouldn't be going anywhere and he could take his time. He wondered then if he should have brought extra loading tubes with him. There were four of them in his saddle bag. Each loading tube, which you inserted through the stock of the Spencer, held seven thick .56-56 cartridges. The Spencer was loaded now, but after seven shots—if it took that many—he would have to use the Walker.

Vern Kidston moved out of line. Cable looked up, then down again and the Spencer followed Vern to his horse, hardly rising as Vern took up the reins and stepped into the saddle.

Now, Cable thought.

But he waited.

He watched Vern come out of the trees, still on the far side of the river, and head north, the same way Lorraine had gone. Going home probably. Either by way of the horse trail or by following the long curving meadow all the way around. But why weren't they together? It was strange that Vern would let her ride home alone at this time of day. In less than an hour it would be full dark. Cable doubted that she knew the country that well.

Another thing. Where had they been? Why would they stand there talking for a while, then ride off separately?

Instantly Cable thought: You're letting him go!

He shifted the Spencer, putting the front sight on Vern again. He held the carbine firmly, his finger crooked on the trigger and the tip of the barrel inching along with the slow-moving target. The distance between them lengthened.

You've got ten seconds, Cable thought. After that he wouldn't be sure of hitting Vern. His arms and shoulders tightened and for one shaded second his finger almost squeezed the trigger.

Then it was over. He let his body relax and eased the hammer down on the open breech.

No, you could have a hundred years and you wouldn't do it that way. There's a difference, isn't there? And you're sure of it now. You feel it, even if you can't define it.

Cable rose stiffly, watching Vern for another few moments, then trudged slowly back up through the pines.

Mounted again, he felt a deep weariness and he sat heavily in the saddle, closing his eyes time and again, letting the sorrel follow the path at a slow-walking pace. His body ached from the long all-day ride; but it was the experience of just a few minutes ago that had left the drained, drawn feeling in his mind. One thing he was sure of now, beyond any doubt. He couldn't kill Vern Kidston the way Janroe wanted it done. He couldn't kill Vern or Duane this way regardless of how logical or necessary the strange-acting, sly-talking man with one arm made it sound.

Knowing this, being sure of it now, was something. But it changed little else. The first move would still be Vern's. Cable would go home, not hurrying to an empty house, and he would hold on to his patience until he had either outwaited or outfought Vern once and for all.

He descended the slope behind the house, dismounted at the barn and led the sorrel inside. Within a few minutes he appeared again. Carrying the Spencer and the field glasses he walked across the yard, letting his gaze move out to the willows now dull gray and motionless against the fading sky. When he looked at the house he stopped abruptly. Lamplight showed in the open doorway.

His left hand, with the strap of the field glasses across the palm, took the Spencer. His right hand dropped to the Walker Colt and held it as he approached the house, passed through the semidarkness of the ramada and stepped into the doorway.

He stood rigid, seeing the strewn bedcovers, the slashed mattress, the soot filming the table and the caved-in stove chimney on the floor; seeing the scattered, broken ruin and Lorraine Kidston standing in the middle of it. She turned from the stove, sweeping aside fragments of china with her foot, and smiled at Cable. "I've been waiting for you."

5

CABLE SAID nothing, his eyes going to the shattered china still on the cupboard shelves, then to the stove again and to the battered chimney flue lying on the floor.

So Vern or Duane, or both of them, had become tired of waiting. Now they were doing something and this was a warning. Fix the house, Cable thought, then another time when you're away they tear it apart again. How much of that could you take? Do you run out of patience right now or later sometime?

He could release his anger and kick at the broken dishes or yell at Lorraine, threaten her, threaten her father and Vern. But what good would it do? That was undoubtedly their intention—to rile him, to make him start something. And once you did what the other man wanted you to, once you walked into his plan, you were finished.

Lorraine was watching him. "When the wife is away, the house just seems to go to ruin, doesn't it?"

He looked at her. "What do they expect me to do now?"

"I'm sure I don't know."

"Or care," Cable said.

"Well, I'm sorry; but there's nothing I can do about it, is there?"

"Did both of them have a hand in this?"

"I doubt if either of them did. They've been home all day."

"I just saw Vern."

"Alone?"

"You were with him."

"Do I have to explain what we were doing?"

"It doesn't matter."

"Vern and I went for a ride after supper. When we reached the meadow he said he wanted to look at his horses. I told him to go ahead, I was going home."

Cable said nothing.

"Well?" Lorraine looked at him inquiringly.

"All right. Then what?"

"Then I left him."

97

"And came to see what he did to the house."

Lorraine smiled, shaking her head. "Guess again."

"Some other time."

She caught the note of weariness in his tone. For a moment she said nothing, watching him stand the carbine next to the window and then move slowly to the table and place the field glasses there. "Did you see my horse outside?" she asked.

Cable glanced at her. "I didn't notice."

"No horse," Lorraine said lightly. "That's why I'm here." She watched Cable gather the blanket and comforter and pile them on the slashed mattress.

"I was going up the path behind your house, taking the short cut home, when something frightened my horse. It happened very suddenly; he lost his footing and started to slide back and that's when I fell off." Lorraine touched her hair lightly and frowned. "I hit my head."

Cable was looking at her again, sensing that she wasn't telling the truth. "Then what happened?"

"Then he ran off. I could hear him way up in the trees, but I couldn't very well chase after him, could I?"

"So you came to the house."

"Of course."

"You want me to look for your horse?"

"He's probably still running."

Cable paused. He was certain she was here for a reason and he was feeling his way along to find out what it was. "I've only got one horse here."

"I know," Lorraine said.

"You want me to ride you home?"

"The way my head hurts I don't know if I could stand it."

"Just for an hour? That's all it would take."

She was staring at Cable, not smiling now, holding him with the calm, knowing impudence of her gaze.

"We could wait until morning."

He almost knew she was going to say it; still, the shock, the surprise, was in hearing the words out loud. Cable's expression did not change. "What would your father say about that?"

"What could he say? I don't have a choice. I'm stranded."

Cable said nothing.

"Or I could tell him I spent the night outside." Lorraine smiled again. "Lost."

"You're serious, aren't you?"

"What do you think?"

"If you're ready, I'll saddle the horse."

"I told you, I couldn't bear the ride."

"You told me a lot of things."

The knowing, confident expression was in her eyes again. "I think you're afraid of me. Or afraid of yourself."

"Being alone with you?"

Lorraine nodded. "But I haven't decided which it is. The only thing I'm sure of is you don't know what to do. You can't take me home by force; and you can't throw me out. So?"

Momentarily, in his mind, he saw Lorraine at home sitting with Vern and her father evening after evening, looking up from her book and wanting to do something, anything, to break the monotony but having no choice but to sit there. Until she planned this, or somehow stumbled into it. Perhaps that was all there was to her being here. It was her idea of excitement, something to do; not part of a plan that involved Vern or Duane.

So, Cable thought, the hell with it. He was too tired to argue. Tired and hungry and her mind was made up, he could see that. He moved to the door of the next room, glanced in and saw that the two single beds had not been touched, then looked at Lorraine again.

"Take your pick."

She moved close to him in the doorway to look into the room. "It doesn't matter."

"Whichever one you want." He walked away from her and for the next few minutes concentrated on shaping and straightening the stove flue. He was able to put it up again, temporarily, but his hands and face were smudged with soot when he'd finished.

Lorraine waited until he started a fire in the stove, then told him to go outside and wash; she'd fix something to eat. Cable hesitated, doubting her ability at the stove; but finally he went out—washed up at the river, scrubbing his hands with sand and scooping the cool water into his face. He felt better being alone outside and he took his time at the river, then went to the barn and looked in at the sorrel again before returning to the house.

Coffee was on the fire; Cable smelled it as he came in. For a moment he watched Lorraine making pancakes in the iron frying pan and he thought: She wants you to be surprised. But he turned away from her and busied himself sweeping up the broken china. After that he turned the slashed mattress on the bed and spread the bedcovers over it. When it was time to sit down she served him the corn meal cakes in a pie plate and poured his coffee into a tin drinking cup. Lorraine sat down with him, watching him eat, waiting for him to say something; but Cable ate in silence.

"Well, what do you think?"

"Fine." He was finishing the last of his coffee.

"Surprised I know how to cook?"

"You're a woman, aren't you?" he answered, knowing she would react to it, but saying it anyway.

"Does that follow," Lorraine said peevishly. "Just because you're a woman all you're to be concerned with is cooking and keeping house?"

"I didn't say that."

"You're probably hopeless. You deserve to live out here with a wife and three kids."

"You make it sound like a sentence."

"You *are* hopeless."

"And tired," Cable said. He got up from the table, walked around to Lorraine's chair and pulled it out for her. "So are you."

She looked up at him. "Am I?" Her tone was mild now.

"Tired out from that long ride with Vern." He took Lorraine by the arm to the bedroom. "Have a good sleep and before you know it it'll be time to fix breakfast." He pushed her inside and closed the door before she could say a word.

Cable blew out the lamp, then walked to the open front door and stood looking out at the night, letting the stillness and the breeze that was coming off the meadow relax him. This was good. But it was a peace that lasted only as long as the night. Slowly Cable sat down in the doorway. Take advantage of the peace you can feel, he thought. Sleep was good, but it wasn't something you could enjoy each minute of and know you were enjoying it.

So he sat in the doorway, feeling the silence and the darkness about him, thinking of his wife and children, picturing them in bed in the rooms above the store; then picturing them here, seeing himself sitting with the children close to him and talking to them, answering their questions, being patient and answering the questions that were unrelated or imaginary along with the reasonable ones. Clare would ask the most questions and through her eyes that were wide with concentration he could almost see her picturing his answers. It was like the times she would relate a dream she had had and he would try to imagine how she saw it with her child's eyes and with her child's mind. While he was talking to Clare, Davis would become restless and jump on his back, Davis with enough energy for all of them and wanting to fight or be chased or swim in the river. Sandy, lying against him, listening to them contentedly with his thumb in his mouth, would scowl and yell at Davis to stop it. Then he would quiet them and they would talk about other things until Martha called.

And after the children were in bed they would sit here on the steps, watching the willows turn to silent black shapes against the sky, hearing the night sounds in the pines and far out on the meadow. They would talk in low murmurs, feeling the familiar nearness of one another. They talked about the children and the house and about things they had done and about things they would do someday; but not talking about the future, because if they accomplished or acquired nothing more than what they had, it would be enough and they would be satisfied; perhaps as happy as anyone, any family, could expect to be.

If you can hold on to what you have, Cable thought. Right now you would settle just for that and not hope for anything more.

He was certain that the Kidstons had damaged the house, as a warning. Maybe not Vern. It seemed more like something Duane would do. But regardless of who did it, the effect was the same.

He heard the sound behind him, the bedroom door opening

and closing. He turned, starting to push himself up, but Lorraine was already over him. Her hand went to his shoulder and she sank down beside him.

"I thought you were tired."

"I'm going to bed in a minute," Cable said. He saw that Lorraine was wearing one of Martha's flannel nightgowns. He had felt it as she brushed against him to sit down.

"What were you thinking about?"

"A lot of things at once, I suppose."

"Vern and Duane . . . the happiness boys?"

He looked at her. "I'd like to know what you're doing here."

"I explained all that."

"You didn't any more get thrown than I did."

Lorraine smiled. "But I had to tell you something."

"Did Vern send you?"

"Don't be silly."

"Then what are you doing here?"

"Keeping you company."

"I guess you are."

Lorraine moved, rising to her knees and turning to him. Her hands went to his shoulders, then to his face caressingly as she kissed him.

"You're not very responsive, are you?" She pressed close to him, kissing him again. "In fact you're rather cold. I'm surprised."

"You've got the wrong one, that's all."

"Oh, come now—"

"Or else the wrong time and place."

"Would you like to go somewhere else?"

Quietly, Cable said, "Lorraine, you're probably the pleasantest temptation I've ever had—but I've got enough things living in my mind the way it is."

Close to him her head moved slowly from side to side. "The only halfway decent looking man within fifty miles and he has to have a conscience." She felt his hands circle her waist and when they lingered, holding her, she said, "I'll give you one more chance."

But now he pushed her away and rose, lifting her with him. "I don't think this would do either of us any good."

In the darkness her eyes remained on him, but it was some

time before she said, "I suppose your wife is very fortunate. But I doubt if I'd want to be married to you. I can't help feeling there's such a thing as being too good."

The next morning Cable cleaned the main room and fixed the stove flue more securely. Later on, he decided, he would ride to Denaman's Store. He would buy plates and cups, probably tin ones if Janroe had any at all; and he would stay as long as he could with Martha and the children.

Cable was outside when the two Kidston riders came by. He saw them crossing the river, approaching cautiously, and he walked out from the ramada, the Walker on his leg. He waited then as the two riders came across the yard toward him. A vague memory of having seen them before made Cable study their faces closely. No, he was certain he didn't know them. Still—

The two riders looked somewhat alike, yet the features of one appeared more coarse and his coloring was freckled and lighter than the other man. It was as if both of their faces— both narrow and heavy boned—had been copied from the same model, but one had been formed less skillfully than the other. Both wore full mustaches and the darker of the two men showed a trace of heavy beard, at least a week's growth.

"If you're looking for Lorraine," Cable said, "you've found her."

The two riders were watching Cable, but now their eyes rose past him as Lorraine appeared.

She seemed a little surprised. "How did you know I was here?"

"Your daddy's got everybody looking everywhere," the dark man said. There was no trace of concern in his voice.

"Is he worried?"

"About out of his mind."

"I can just see him." Lorraine stepped down from the doorway and walked out to them. "You two will have to ride double," she said, looking up. Neither of the men made a move to dismount. Lorraine moved toward the dark rider's chestnut gelding. "This one." Still the man hesitated and Lorraine added, "If you don't mind."

"Where's yours?"

"I have no idea," Lorraine answered.

The dark rider's gaze moved to Cable. "Maybe we ought to use his then."

Lorraine's face showed sudden interest. "If he'll let you."

"He will."

"We can't do it while the girl's here," the other man said then. "Duane wouldn't have any part of that."

"I suppose we got time," the dark one grunted.

"All we want," the other rider said.

The dark one swung down. Not bothering to help Lorraine, he walked past her, raised his hand to the other rider and was pulled up behind him. He looked down at Cable again.

"Long as we got time."

They rode out, past the house to the horse trail that climbed the slope. In the saddle now, straddling it with her skirt draped low on both sides, Lorraine waited long enough to say, "That was Austin and Wynn Dodd."

Cable frowned. "I don't know them."

Lorraine smiled pleasantly. "You knew their brother. Joe Bob."

She rode off toward the slope, following the Dodd brothers. Before passing into the pines behind the house, Lorraine looked back and waved.

There were times when Janroe could feel his missing hand; times when he swore he had moved his fingers. He would be about to pick something up with his left hand, then catch himself in time. A moment before this Janroe had absently raised his missing arm to lean on the door frame. He fell against the timber with his full weight on the stump, and now he stood rubbing it, feeling a dull pain in the arm that wasn't there.

Luz Acaso appeared, coming from the back of the building. She was riding her dun-colored mare, sitting the saddle as a man would, her bare legs showing almost to her knees. Two of the Cable children, Clare and Davis, were following behind her as she crossed the yard toward the river.

Janroe stepped out to the loading platform.

"Luz!" The dun mare side-stepped as the girl reined in and looked back at him.

"Come over here."

She held the horse, standing almost forty feet from the platform. "I can hear you," she said.

"Maybe I don't want to shout."

"Then you come over here!"

Don't ruffle her, Janroe thought. Something was bothering her. He had first noticed it as she served him his breakfast. She seldom spoke unless he said something to her first, so her silence this morning wasn't unusual. Still, he had sensed a change in her. Her face was somber, without expression, yet he could feel a new tension between them. Even when she served him she avoided his eyes and seemed to reach out to place the coffee and food before him, as if afraid to come too close to him.

That was it. As if she was guarding something in her mind. As if she was so conscious of what she was thinking, she felt that if he looked in her eyes or even came too close to her, he would see it.

But while he was eating he would feel her eyes on him, watching him carefully, intently; although when he looked up from his plate she would be turning away or picking something up from the stove.

Now she was riding down to Hidalgo. Tonight there would be a gun shipment and Luz would lead it to the store, making sure the way was clear. Janroe said, "You're leaving a little early, aren't you?"

"I want to have time to see my brother."

"About what?"

"Nothing."

"You seem anxious enough over nothing."

"I want to see him, that's all." She waited a moment longer, watching Janroe, but when he said no more she flicked the reins and moved on across the yard. Janroe watched her pass into the willows and even after she was out of sight he continued to stare at the trees. What was it about her—was she more confident? More sure of herself since the Cables had come home. Afraid when she was alone with him, still somewhat more confident.

He noticed the Cable children then. Clare and Davis were still in the front yard, standing close to each other now and looking up at him on the platform.

"I told you once to play in the back," Janroe called out.

"I'm not going to tell you again. I'll get a stick next time, you understand?"

Clare stood rigid. Davis nodded with a small jerk of his head and reached for Clare's arm. They turned to go.

"Wait a minute." Janroe looked down at them sternly. "Where's your father? Is he still here?"

"Upstairs," the boy said.

"All right." Janroe waved them away and they ran, glancing back at him as they rounded the corner of the building.

What do you have to do to a man like that? Janroe thought. A man that finds his house wrecked and comes moping in to buy tin plates and sit with his wife. Cable had arrived about mid-morning and had been here ever since.

Janroe stood for some time holding the stump of his arm, rubbing it gently. He was looking above the willows now, to the hillside beyond the full roundness of the tree tops. But it was moments before he realized a file of riders had come down out of the pines and was descending the slope.

Perhaps because his hand still held the stump, or because he had jarred it and imagined the pain still present; because of this and then abruptly seeing the riders on the hillside and for the moment not caring who they were—his mind went back to another time, another place. . . .

There had been riders then on a hillside; directly across the cornfield and not more than eight hundred yards away, a line of riders appearing along the crest of the hill, then stopping and dismounting. He had seen that they were unhitching the horses from artillery pieces—three of them—and rolling the guns into position.

He had waited then, studying the position through his field glasses for at least ten minutes, or perhaps a quarter of an hour; so by the time he brought his men out of the pines, screaming at them, shooting one and seeing the other soldier who had been afraid suddenly run by him, the field pieces were ready and loaded and waiting for him.

Janroe himself was no more than a hundred yards out from the woods when the first shell exploded. The blast was loud in his ears and almost knocked him down; but he kept moving, seeing two, then three, men come stumbling, crawling out of the smoke and dust that seemed to hang motionless in the air.

One of the men fell face-down and didn't move. As he watched, a second and third shell exploded and he saw one of the crawling men lifted from the ground and thrown on his back. Close around him men were flattening themselves on the ground and covering their heads.

But the ones in front of him were still moving, and with the next explosion Janroe was running again. He saw the man who had been afraid a few moments before, running, breathing heavily, his head back as if he was looking up at the three artillery pieces. Janroe was close to the man, almost about to run past him and yell back at him to keep coming, and then the man was no more.

It was as if time suddenly stopped, for Janroe saw the man, or part of him, blown into the air and he could remember this clearly, the fraction of a moment caught and indelibly recorded in his mind. And it was the same sudden, ground-lifting, sound-smashing burst of smoke and iron that slammed Janroe senseless and cleanly severed his left arm. . . .

For some time the line of riders was out of sight, low on the slope now and beyond the bank of willow trees. Janroe waited, watching, judging where they would cross the river and appear out of the tree shadows. They would be Kidston riders, Janroe was certain of that. He wondered if he should call Cable. No, wait, Janroe decided. Act natural and just let things happen.

There were six of them. Janroe recognized Duane Kidston at once: Duane sitting a tall bay horse with one hand on his thigh, a riding quirt hanging from his wrist and his elbow extended rigidly. Duane wearing the stiff-crowned Kossuth hat squarely on his head, the brim pinned up on one side with the regimental insignia. Duane playing soldier, Janroe thought contemptuously. Pretending that he's a man.

Have your fun, Major, Janroe thought then, not taking his eyes from Duane. Have all the fun you can. Your time's about run out.

Briefly he noted the five men with Duane: Bill Dancey, the solemn, bearded one close to Duane's right; then the two Dodd brothers, Austin and Wynn. They had been here only once before but Janroe remembered them well, the brothers of one of the men Cable had killed. Austin and Wynn Dodd, one light, the other dark, but both with angular, expressionless faces. Janroe remembered their eyes; they watched you coldly, impersonally, as if you were a thing that couldn't look back at them.

Janroe was not sure if he had ever seen the two other riders before. He watched these two veer off midway across the yard and circle to the back of the store.

Moments later the two Cable children, Clare and Davis, came running around from the back yard. Then, seeing the four riders approaching the platform, they stopped and stood watching, their eyes wide with curiosity.

"Where is he?" Duane asked.

"Inside." Janroe moved nearer the edge of the platform.

"Get him out."

"What for?"

"That's my business."

"You want to kill him?"

"Duane's got things to say to him," Dancey said then.

Janroe's eyes moved to the bearded man. "I wouldn't want to think I fetched him to be killed."

"We're not going to kill him," Dancey said.

"That would be an awful thing to have on your conscience," Janroe said. "Calling a man to be killed in front of his children."

Dancey shook his head. "You've got my word."

"And with his wife here too," Janroe said. "I couldn't ever face her again."

"Mr. Janroe," Duane said, "if you don't get him out here, you can be assured we will."

Janroe looked past the men to the Cable children. His eyes settled on Clare.

"Honey, go tell your daddy there's some men here to see him."

Clare hesitated, but Davis pushed her and she ran up the steps to the platform, holding close to the wall as she ran by Janroe and into the store.

"Fine youngsters," Janroe said pleasantly. "He's got three of them." Duane wasn't listening. He glanced at Dancey. Then Dancey and the Dodd brothers dismounted and came up the steps to the loading platform. Duane remained in his saddle.

"Where is he?" Dancey asked.

"Upstairs a few minutes ago."

"He mention what happened last night?"

"Not a word." Janroe's tone indicated only mild interest. "What did?"

"About Lorraine—"

"No!" Janroe's face showed surprise, then an eager curiosity. "What happened?"

But Dancey's gaze moved beyond him. Janroe turned. He heard the steps on the plank floor then Cable, wearing his Walker Colt, was standing in the doorway. Janroe saw Martha and the little girl a few steps behind him.

"Take off that gun," Dancey said.

Cable looked from Dancey to the Dodd brothers—to Austin, the dark one, who was a step nearer than Wynn—then back to Dancey.

"What's this about?"

"Take it off," Dancey said again. "You're covered front and back."

Cable heard the quick steps behind him. He seemed about to turn, but he hesitated. The two riders who had circled the adobe had entered by the back door and had waited for Cable behind the counter. Now one of them pulled the Walker from its holster. Feeling it, Cable glanced over his shoulder. He saw the second man standing close to Martha.

As Cable turned back to Dancey, Austin Dodd moved. He stepped in bringing his balled left hand up from his side. Before Cable saw it coming the fist slammed into his face. He fell against the door frame, went to his hands and knees with his head down and close to the platform boards. Austin Dodd followed through. His right hand came up with his Colt, his thumb already hooking back the hammer.

"Hold on!" Dancey stepped in front of him. "We didn't come here for that." He looked out at Duane Kidston angrily. "You'd have let him, wouldn't you?"

"Austin has his own reason," Duane said. "Stopping him wouldn't be any of my business."

"We didn't come here to satisfy Austin," Dancey grunted.

Duane stared at the bearded foreman. "I'm beginning to wonder why I brought you."

"You wouldn't've if Vern had been around. You said you wanted to talk to this man. That's all."

"I'm going to."

"But you'd have let Austin kill him."

"It wasn't your brother Cable shot down," Duane said flatly. "That's the difference."

"He took him in a fair fight."

"We're not even sure of that. All we know is Joe Bob and Royce came home face-down over their saddles," Duane said. "And it wasn't your daughter he—"

Duane stopped. His eyes went to Cable who was still on one knee, but watching Duane now.

"Get him up."

Dancey moved aside. He said, "Go ahead," and stepped back to the edge of the platform near Janroe. The Dodd brothers pulled Cable to his feet. They planted themselves close to him, each holding an arm with both hands. Cable stood quietly, making no attempt to free himself. Behind them, Dancey could see Martha and the little girl in the square of light formed by the doorway. Martha seemed calm, Dancey judged. But you couldn't tell about women. The little girl was afraid. And the little boy—Dancey's gaze moved to the steps where Davis was squatting now—he's wondering what they're doing to his pa and he wouldn't believe it if somebody told him.

Duane called, "Jimmie!" and one of the men who'd covered Cable from behind came out to the platform. Duane raised his reins, then dropped them and the man came down; but not until he'd picked up the reins did Duane dismount. He stepped down stiffly, straightened his coat, then walked around to the steps and up to the platform, past Davis without even glancing at him though he touched him with his riding quirt, in a gesture of brushing the boy aside.

His full attention was on Cable now. Duane stepped squarely in front of him, close to him, and stood for some moments in silence, his legs apart and his hands fisted on his hips. But before he spoke his hands dropped to his sides.

"I should let Austin kill you," Duane said. "But I can't do it. God knows everyone here would be better off for it, but I can't pass final judgment on a mortal man, not even after he's done what you did."

"What did I do?" Cable asked, not with surprise or

indignation, but calmly, wondering what had suddenly brought Duane here.

"Offended innocence," Duane said. "You'd better keep your mouth shut. I've taken all of you I can stomach."

"I asked a civil question."

Duane's quirt came up and lashed across Cable's face. "And I said shut up!" He stepped back as Cable twisted to free himself. Wynn Dodd stumbled to one knee and Cable almost broke away, but Austin forced Cable's right arm behind his back and jerked up on it.

"I'll break it!"

Cable stopped struggling. He let his breath out slowly and his body seemed to sag. His eyes went to Davis still watching him from the steps, then away from the boy quickly, back to Duane.

"Do you have to do this in front of my children?"

Duane stepped close to him again. "How much respect did you show my daughter?"

"What did Lorraine say I did?"

"She didn't have to say anything. She was all night at your place."

Janroe, near the edge of the platform, looked at Martha, but her eyes were on her husband. He noticed Duane's gaze move to her then.

"You hear that Mrs. Cable? Your husband and my daughter."

"He told me about it," Martha said quietly.

"He told you, did he." Duane's mouth barely moved. "Did he tell you how he dragged Lorraine into that hut?" He turned on Cable and in the motion slashed the quirt across his face. "Did he tell you how he kept her there all night?" The quirt came back across Cable's face. "How he threatened her and forced his will on her?" He swung on Cable again and again, hacking at Cable's cheeks and forehead with the rawhide. Cable's eyes were squeezed closed and he would turn his head with each stinging blow. But he was off balance, leaning forward awkwardly, and he was unable to turn his body with Austin holding his arm twisted behind him. Duane struck him eight times before his arm dropped heavily to his side.

"Did he tell you all that, Mrs. Cable?"

"He told me everything that happened."

"His version."

"If you've finished, Mr. Kidston, may I take my husband inside?"

Duane stared at Martha, his face tight as he held back the temper ready to flare out at her calm, quiet manner.

He said then, "If you want him, take him. Take him anywhere you like, but not back to your house. You're finished here, and I believe you're intelligent enough to realize it. If you think this is unjust, that's too bad; your husband is lucky to be alive. I'll tell you frankly, if it wasn't for your children he would be dead now."

Bill Dancey watched Martha, waiting for her to speak again; but Martha said nothing, her hand on the little girl close to her side. Dancey walked across the platform. Going down the steps he patted Davis's shoulder, but the boy pulled away from him. Dancey mounted, then looked up at Duane.

"You've said it. What're you waiting for?"

Duane still faced Martha. He ignored Dancey, and said, "This evening my men leave for the horse pastures. They'll be gone one week. If you haven't cleared out by the time they return, we will take your husband out and hang him. That's my last warning, Mrs. Cable."

Duane turned and marched stiffly down the steps to his horse. The Dodd brothers followed, almost reluctantly, both of them looking back at Cable as they mounted and rode out after Duane.

Janroe came away from the edge of the platform and studied Cable's face closely. "Duane laid it on you, didn't he?"

Cable said nothing. He felt Martha standing next to him now, but he continued to watch the riders. When they had finally crossed the river and started up the slope, he looked at Janroe.

"That one Duane called Jimmie—what did he do with my gun? Did you see?"

Janroe stepped to the edge of the platform again and looked down. "He dropped it right there."

"Get it for me."

Janroe seemed to smile. "I'd be glad to."

Cable felt Martha's hand on his arm. He looked at her, at her soft, clear expression, at her eyes that seemed moist, though he wasn't sure if she was crying.

She said, "Cabe, come inside now."

He followed her through the store, through the main room to the kitchen, then sat down while Martha went to the sink. She dipped water from a bucket into a kettle, and put the kettle on the stove to heat.

Clare and Davis appeared in the doorway, staring at their father until Martha noticed them and told them to go outside and play.

Cable looked up. "No, let them stay," he said. He motioned to the children. They came in hesitantly, as if this man with the red welts across his face was someone neither of them had ever seen before. But when he smiled and held out his arms, both of them ran to him and pressed against his chest. He kissed Clare on the cheek, then Davis. The boy's arms went around his neck and clung to him and Cable felt the knot in his stomach slowly begin to relax.

Martha poured the warm water into a basin. She carried it to the table, then leaned close to her husband and began bathing the swollen red marks that crossed both of his cheeks, his nose and his forehead. A bruise colored his cheekbone where Austin Dodd had hit him.

Cable's eyes raised. "Where's Sandy?"

"Still taking his nap."

"I'm glad he didn't see it."

Martha said nothing. She moved the two children aside to give herself more room, then pressed the wet cloth gently to Cable's forehead.

The second time they've seen me beaten," Cable said. "Beaten up twice in front of my children—standing there turning the other cheek while a man rawhides my face."

Martha raised his chin with her hand. "Cabe, you don't have to prove yourself to them. You're their father."

"Something they don't have anything to say about."

"They'd love you under any circumstance, you know that."

"Then it's a question of proving myself to me."

Martha shook her head. "It isn't a matter of principle, a question of whether or not you're a man. This is something that affects the whole family. We want to go home and live in peace.

Clare and Davis and even Sandy, we want what is rightfully ours, but we don't want it without you."

"Then you want to leave here," Cable said.

"I didn't say that. If we run away, we lose. But if we have to bury you, we lose even more."

"Martha, I don't have a choice."

She leaned close to him with her hands on the arms of the chair. "Cabe, don't go after them just because of what Duane did."

"You know it's more than that."

"You were beaten up in front of the children. Right now that's all you can think about."

"Sooner or later this will be settled with guns," Cable said. "It might as well be now."

"It doesn't have to be that way," Martha said urgently. "If we wait, if we can put it off—Cabe, something could happen that would solve everything!"

"Like what?"

She hesitated. "I'm not sure."

"Martha, I'm awful tired of waiting."

She looked at him intently. "You could go to Fort Buchanan. Put it up to the authorities."

"You know who they'd side with."

"But we're not sure. Cabe, at least it's worth trying."

From the doorway Janroe said, "I've got the only way to solve your problem." He extended Cable's Walker Colt, holding it in the open palm of his hand. "Right here."

Martha turned, looking at him coldly. "That would solve nothing."

"All right," Janroe said. "Go up to Buchanan. Tell the Yankees you're a Rebel soldier come home to find a gang of Yankee horse-breakers using your land and threatening to hang you." Janroe moved into the kitchen. "You know what they'd do? Supply the rope."

Martha motioned the two children to the back door. She held it open for them, then, closing it behind them, looked at Janroe again.

"Mr. Janroe, I don't think this concerns you."

"Ask your husband whether it concerns me or not." He

stopped in front of Cable and handed him the revolver. "Right?"

Cable said nothing. He took the Walker and looked at it idly, holding it in both hands.

Janroe watched him. "You're going back to your place?"

Cable nodded.

"That's the right direction," Janroe said mildly. His eyes remained on Cable's lowered head. "Did you hear what Duane said about his men going off this evening? They'll go over to some pastures Vern's got way north and west of here and start working the herds home. Duane said they'd be gone a week." Janroe shook his head. "They'll be gone longer than that. And just Duane and maybe Vern will be home, just the two of them."

Cable looked up. "You told me that once before."

Janroe nodded. "And Duane confirmed it." His voice lowered. "It would be easy for a man like you. Ride in there and take both of them."

Martha came away from the door. "You're asking my husband to commit murder!"

Janroe glared at her. "Like any soldier murders."

"This isn't war—he isn't a soldier now!"

"We've been all through that," Janroe said. "Whether it bothers his conscience or not, your husband doesn't have a choice. He's got to kill them before they kill him."

That evening, as soon as it was dark, Janroe slipped under the platform and let himself into the locked storeroom. He measured three strides to the crates of Enfield rifles stacked against the back wall, then stood in the darkness, wondering if there would be room for the wagon-load of rifles due to arrive later that night. The rifles that were here should have been picked up days ago.

You can worry about it, Janroe thought, or you can forget it and ask Luz when she comes. She should be here within two hours. Perhaps they told her in Hidalgo why the rifles had not been picked up. Perhaps not. Either way, there was something more immediate to think about. Something raw and galling, because it was fresh in his mind and seemed to have happened only moments before though it had been this afternoon, hours ago.

He had almost convinced Cable. No, not almost or maybe. He had convinced him. He had handed the man his gun and told him to kill the Kidstons or be killed himself, and Cable had seen the pure reality of this. If he had left at that moment, he would have gone straight to the Kidston place. Janroe was sure of it.

But Martha had interfered. She talked to her husband, soothing the welts on his face with a damp cloth while she soothed his anger with the calm, controlled tone of her voice. And finally Cable had nodded and agreed not to do anything that day. He would go home and watch the house—that much he had to do—but he would not carry the fight to the Kidstons; at least not while he felt the way he did. He agreed to this grudgingly, wearily, part by part, while Martha reasoned in that quiet, firm, insisting, never-varying tone.

Perhaps if he went out to see Cable now? No, the guns were coming and he would have to be here. In the morning then; though by that time the sting would be gone from the welts on Cable's face and that solid patience would have settled in him again.

He had *convinced* Cable—that was the absolute truth of it—until the woman had started in with her moral, monotonous reasoning—

Janroe straightened. He stood listening, hearing the faint sound of a horse approaching. The hoof beats grew louder, but not closer, and when the sound stopped, he knew the horse had reached the back of the store.

Luz? No, it was too early for her. He left the storeroom, carefully, quietly padlocking the door, came out into the open and took his time mounting to the platform and passing through the darkened store. He saw Martha first, standing in the kitchen, then Luz, and saw the girl's eyes raise to his as he moved toward them.

"You're early."

"They're not coming," Luz said.

"What do you mean they're not coming?"

"Not any more."

"All right," Janroe said. "Tell me what you know."

"The war's over."

She said it simply, in the same tone, and for a moment Janroe only stared at her.

"What are you talking about?"

"It's true," Martha said. "They told her as soon as she reached Hidalgo."

He looked at Martha then, seeing her face no longer composed but for the first time flushed and alive and with a smile that was warm and genuine and seemed to include even him, simply because he was here to share the news with them.

He turned to Luz again. "Who told you?"

"Everyone knows it. They told me to come back and tell you."

"But how do they know? How can they be sure?"

"They know, that's all."

"Listen, wars don't just end like that."

"How do they end?" Martha asked, not smiling now.

"There's some warning—days, weeks before, that it's going to end."

"You know how news travels out here," Martha said.

"No"—Janroe shook his head—"we would have heard something. It's a false alarm, or a Yankee trick. It's something else because a war just doesn't end like that."

"We're telling you that the war is over," Martha said. "Whether you believe it or not it ended five days ago, the day we came home."

"And they're just finding out now?" Janroe shook his head again. "Uh-unh, you don't sell me any of that."

"Would they have lied to Luz?"

"I don't even know what they told her! How do I know she even went there?"

Martha was staring at him. "You don't want to believe it."

"What am I supposed to believe—everything this girl comes in and tells me?"

"Luz"—Martha glanced at the girl—"can I take your horse?"

Janroe saw Luz nodding and he said anxiously, "What for?"

"To tell my husband," Martha answered, looking at him again.

"You think you should?" Janroe asked. It was moving too

fast again, rushing at him again, not giving him time to think, and already it was the next step, telling her husband. They would not just stand and talk about it and see how ridiculous the news was; they would bring Cable into it, and if he argued about the sense of her going she would go all the quicker.

"I mean riding out alone at night," Janroe said. He shook his head. "I couldn't see you doing that."

"I think my husband should know," Martha began.

"I believe that," Janroe said. The words were coming easier now. "But I think I better be the one to go tell him."

Martha hesitated. Before she could say anything, Janroe had turned and was gone. She looked at Luz, but neither of them spoke, hearing Janroe just in the next room.

When he came into the kitchen again he was wearing a hat and a coat, the armless sleeve flat and ending abruptly in the pocket, but bulging somewhat with the shape of a shoulder holster beneath the coat.

"You *will* see him?" Martha said. "I mean make sure he finds out?"

"Don't worry about it."

"And you promise to tell him everything?"

"I won't be long." Janroe went out the back door and mounted Luz Acaso's dun mare.

He crossed the river and hurried the dun up the slope to the horse trail, following it north, almost blindly in the night darkness of the trees, brushing branches in his haste and kicking the dun. He moved along the ridge, though with no intention of visiting Cable.

He knew only that there was no time for Cable now. He could admit that to himself without admitting the other, that the war was over. Certainly it could be at the very edge of the end. This could be the last day. It might very well be the last day. All right, it *was* the last day and now there was no time for Cable. The war was not over yet, he told himself, but there was time to do only one thing now.

Four, raging, uninterrupted years of war did not end with two women standing in a kitchen and saying that it was over. You would expect that of women. It was typical. A woman would tell you anything. Lies became truth to them because they felt justified in using any means at hand to hold life to a sweet-smelling, creeping pace; to make this a woman's existence with no room for war or fighting or so many of the things that men did and liked to do and only really proved themselves as men when they were doing them.

If he had not entered the kitchen he wouldn't have heard anything. A man couldn't wait and plan for eight months and know what he had to do, and then see it all canceled by walking into a kitchen. That couldn't be.

So the two women had lied and it was stupid to think about it. And even if it was not a matter of their lying, then it was something else, something equally untrue; and whether the something was a lie from the women or a trick or an untruth from another source was beside the point.

He was hurrying, as if to keep up with time, so that not another moment of it would go by before he reached the Kidston place. But even after half admitting this was impossible he told himself that right now was part of a whole time, not a time before or a time after something. It was a time which started the day he came to live at the store and would end the day he saw the Kidstons dead. So this was part of the time of war. But almost as he thought this, it became more than that. Now, right now, was the whole of the war, the everything of a war that would not end until the Kidstons were dead.

It took him less than an hour altogether. By the time he left the horse trail he had cleared his mind of everything but the Kidstons. Winding, moving more slowly through the sandstone country, he was able to calm himself and think about what he would do after, what he would do about Cable, what he would tell Martha and Luz. Martha . . .

By the time he reached the edge of the timber stand bordering the Kidston place, looking across the open area to the house and outbuildings, he was composed and ready. He was Edward Janroe who happened to be riding by, say, on his way to Fort Buchanan. He was a man they had seen at least once a week for the past eight months. He was the one-armed man who owned the store now and didn't say much. He was nothing to be afraid of or even wonder about. Which was exactly the way Janroe wanted it.

6

JANROE CAME out of the trees, letting the dun mare move
at its own pace toward the house. He was aware of someone
on the veranda, certain that it was Duane when he saw the
pinpoint glow of a cigar.

There was no hurry now. Janroe's eyes rose from the veranda
to the lighted second-story window, then beyond the corner of
the house, past the corral where a dull square of light showed
the open door of the bunkhouse. There were no sounds from
that end of the yard, none from the big adobe that was pale
gray and solid looking in the darkness. The cigar glowed again
and now Janroe was close.

"Good evening, Major."

Duane leaned forward, the wicker chair squeaking. "Who
is it?"

"Edward Janroe." Now, almost at the veranda, Janroe
brought the dun to a halt. He saw Duane rise and come close
to the railing, touching it with his stomach.

"I didn't mean to startle you," Janroe said.

"You didn't startle me." There was indignation in Duane's
tone.

"I meant you sitting here by yourself. . . . Is Vern about?"

"No, he's up at his pastures. You wanted to see him?"

"I'd like to have. But I guess you can't have everything."

"What?"

"Where's Vern, out on the horse drive?"

"Getting it started. He's been gone all day."

"You alone?"

"My daughter's in the house."

"And somebody's out in the bunkhouse."

Duane seemed annoyed, but he said, "A couple of the men."

"I thought everybody went out on the drives," Janroe said.

"We always keep one man here."

"You said a couple of men were there."

As if remembering something, Duane's frown of annoy-
ance vanished. "The second man rode in a while ago to tell
us the news. I've been sitting here ever since thinking about

it." Duane paused solemnly. "Mr. Janroe, the war is over. Lee surrendered the Army of Northern Virginia to General Grant on April ninth."

"Is that a fact?" Janroe said.

"I have been thinking of a place called Chancellorsville," Duane said gravely. "I have been thinking of the men I knew who died there: men I campaigned with who gave their lives that this final victory might be accomplished."

"A touching moment," Janroe said.

Duane's eyes rose. "If you had served, you would know the feeling."

"I served."

"Oh? I didn't know that. In the Union army?"

"With Kirby Smith."

"Oh. . . . You lost your arm . . . were wounded in battle?"

"During the fight at Richmond, Kentucky."

"Is that right? I was in Cincinnati at the time. If I hadn't been on my way to Washington, I would have answered General Nelson's call for volunteers."

"That would have been something," Janroe said, sitting easily and looking down at Duane, "if we'd fought against each other."

Duane nodded gravely. "More terrible things than that have actually happened. Brother fighting brother, friend against friend. The wounds of our minds as well as those of our bodies will have to be healed now if we are to live together in peace." Duane added, for effect, "The war is over."

"You're not just telling me that?" Janroe said.

"What?"

"That the war's over."

"Of course it is. The word came direct from Fort Buchanan. They learned about it this afternoon. Their rider ran into Vern, and Vern sent a man here to tell us. Vern realized I would want to know immediately."

"I haven't been told," Janroe said. "Not officially, and your telling me doesn't count."

Duane was frowning, squinting up at Janroe in the darkness with his cigar poised a few inches from his face. "How could you learn more officially than this? The message came from Fort Buchanan, a military establishment."

"You learned it from your side," Janroe said. "I haven't been told officially from mine."

"Man, you've been out of the war for at least a year! Do you expect them to tell personally every veteran who served?"

"I haven't been out of it." Janroe paused, studying Duane's reaction. "I'm still fighting, just like you've been with your saddle-tramp cavalry, like your brother's been doing supplying Yankee remounts."

Duane was squinting again. "You've been at your store every day. I'm almost sure of it."

"Look under the store," Janroe said. "That's where we keep the Enfields."

"British rifles?"

"Brought in through Mexico, then shipped east."

"I don't believe it." Duane shook his head. "All this time you've been moving contraband arms through the store?"

"About two thousand rifles since I started."

"Well," Duane said, officially now, "if you have any there now, I advise you to turn them over to the people at Fort Buchanan. I presume Confederate officers will be allowed to keep their horses and sidearms, but rifles are another matter."

Janroe shook his head slowly. "I'm not turning anything over."

"You'd rather face arrest?"

"They can't take me if they don't know about the guns."

"Mr. Janroe, if you don't turn them in, don't you think I would be obligated to tell them?"

"I suppose you would."

"Then why did you tell me about them?"

"So you would know how we stand. You see, you can be obligated all you want, but you won't be able to do anything about it."

Duane clamped the cigar in the corner of his mouth. "You've got the nerve to ride in here and threaten me?"

"I guess I do." Janroe was relaxed; he sat with his shoulders hunched loosely and his hand in his lap.

"You're telling me that I won't go to Buchanan?" Duane's voice rose. "Listen, I'll take my saddle-tramp cavalry, as you call it, and drag those guns out myself, and I'll march you right up to the fort with them if I feel like it. So don't go threatening me, mister; I don't take any of it."

Janroe watched him calmly. "It's too bad you didn't volunteer that time you said. That would have made this better. No, it would have made it perfect—if you had been in command of that Yankee artillery company. They were up on a ridge and we had to cross a cornfield that was trampled down and wide open to get at them. They began firing as soon as we started across. Almost right away I was hit and my arm was torn clean from my body."

"I think we've discussed this enough for one evening," Duane said stiffly.

"What if you had given that order to fire?" Janroe said. "Do you see how much better it would make this?" He shook his head then. "But that would be too much to ask; like having Vern here too. Both of you here, and no one else around."

"I would advise you to go home," Duane said, "and seriously consider what I told you. I don't make idle threats."

"I don't either, Major." Janroe's hand rose to the open front of his coat. He drew the Colt from his shoulder holster and cocked it as he trained it on Duane. "Though I don't suppose you'd call this a threat. This is past the threatening stage, isn't it?"

"You don't frighten me," Duane said. He remembered something Vern had told Cable that day at Cable's house, rephrasing it now because he was not sure of the exact words.

"There is a big difference between holding a gun and using it. If you're bluffing, Mr. Janroe, trying to frighten me, I advise you to give it up and go home."

"I'm not bluffing."

"Then you're out of your mind."

"Major, I don't think you realize what's happening."

"I realize I'm talking to a man who hasn't complete control of his faculties."

"That's meant to be an insult, nothing else," Janroe said. "If you believed it, you'd be scared out of your wits."

Duane hesitated. He watched Janroe closely, in silence; the hand holding the cigar had dropped to his side. "You wouldn't dare use that gun," he said finally.

"It's the reason I came."

"But you have no reason to kill me!"

"Call it duty, Major. Call it anything you like." Janroe put the front sight squarely on Duane's chest. "Do you want to run or stand there? Make up your mind."

"But the war's over—don't you realize that!"

Janroe pulled the trigger. In the heavy report he watched Duane clutch the railing, holding himself up, and Janroe fired again, seeing Duane's body jerk with the impact of the bullet before sliding, falling to the porch.

"It's over now," Janroe said.

He reined and kicked the dun to a gallop as he crossed the yard. Behind him he heard a window rise and a woman's voice, but the sounds seemed to end abruptly as the darkness of the trees closed in on him.

Now back to the store. There was no reason to run. He would tell the women that Cable was not at home, that he'd looked for him, but with no luck. Tomorrow he would ride out again, telling the women he would try again to locate Cable.

But he would take his time, giving Vern time to learn about his brother's death; giving him time to convince himself that it was Cable who'd killed Duane; giving him time, then, to go after Cable. No, there was no need to run.

It had been a satisfying time. The best since the days near Opelousas when he'd killed the Yankee prisoners.

Bill Dancey had spent the night in a line shack seven miles north of the Kidston place. The day before, after the incident at Denaman's, after watching Duane demonstrate his authority with a rawhide quirt, after riding back to the Kidston place with Duane and the Dodd brothers and not speaking a word to them all the way, Dancey had decided it was time for a talk with Vern.

But Vern was still away. Since that morning he'd been visiting the grazes, instructing his riders to begin driving the horses to the home range. Vern could be gone all night, Dancey knew, and that was why he went out after him. What he had to say wouldn't wait.

By late evening, after he had roamed the west and north pastures, but always an hour or more behind Vern, Dancey decided to bed down in the line shack. It was deserted now, which suited him fine. It was good to get away from the others once in a while, to sit peacefully or lie in your blanket with quiet all around and be able to hear yourself think. It gave him a chance to review the things he wanted to tell Vern.

With the first trace of morning light he was in the saddle again; and it was at the next pasture that he learned about Duane. There were five men here, still at the breakfast fire. They told him that Vern had been here; but a rider came during the night with news about Duane—one before that with word about the war being over; it had sure as hell been an eventful night—and Vern had left at once, taking only the two Dodd brothers with him.

By six o'clock Dancey was back at the Kidston place. He crossed the yard to the corral, unsaddled and turned his horse into the enclosure before going on to the house.

Austin and Wynn Dodd were sitting on the steps: Wynn sitting low, leaning forward and looking down between his legs; Austin sitting back with his elbows resting on the top step, Austin with his head up, his stained, curled-brim hat straight over his eyes. Both men wore holstered revolvers, the butt of Wynn's jutting out sharply from his hip because of the way he was sitting. Austin, Dancey noticed then, was wearing two revolvers, two Colts that looked like the pair Joe Bob had owned.

Dancey stopped in front of them. "Vern's inside?"

Wynn looked up. Austin nodded.

"He told you to wait for him?"

"Right here." Wynn leaned back saying it, propping his elbows on the step behind him.

"If that's all right with you, Bill," Austin said dryly.

Dancey moved through them to the porch. He opened the screen then stood there, seeing Vern and Lorraine at the stove fireplace across the room. Dancey waited until Vern saw him before moving toward them.

"I've been looking for you." Vern said it bluntly, and the tone stirred the anger Dancey had held under control since yesterday afternoon.

He wanted to snap back at Vern and if it led to his quitting, that was all right. But now Duane was dead and before he argued with Vern he would have to say he was sorry about Duane. And Lorraine was here. Her presence bothered him too. She didn't appear to have been crying, but stood staring at the dead fire; probably not even thinking about her father, more likely wondering what was going to happen to her. She seemed less sure of herself now; though Dancey realized he could be imagining this.

He looked at Vern. "Your brother's dead?" And when Vern nodded Dancey said, "I'm sorry about it. Where is he now?"

"Upstairs. We'll bury him this afternoon."

"All right." Dancey's eyes moved to Lorraine. "What about his girl?"

"I think she'll be going back home," Vern said. "This brought her up pretty short. She might have even grown up in one day."

"It could do that," Dancey said. "When was it, last night?"

Vern nodded. "He rode in while Duane was on the porch. Lorraine was upstairs. She heard the two shots and looked out her window in time to see him riding off."

"Who's he?"

"Who do you think?"

"Did she see him clearly?"

"She didn't have to."

"It's best to be sure."

"All right, Bill, if it's not Cable, who would it be?"

"I know. It's probably him; but you have to be sure."

"I'm sure as I'll ever be."

Vern moved past him and Dancey followed out to the porch. The two Dodd brothers were standing now, watching Vern.

"There'll be just the four of us," Vern told them. He waited until they moved off, then seemed to relax somewhat, leaning against a support post and staring out across the yard. He said to Dancey behind him, "They'll bring you a fresh horse."

"I can get my own," Dancey said.

"I guess you can, but they'll bring it anyway."

"Now we go visit Cable—is that it?"

"You don't have to come."

"Then I sure as hell don't think I will."

Vern turned suddenly from the post, but hesitated then.

"Bill, do you realize the man's killed three people now, one of them my brother?"

"Are you telling me you're going after Cable because you and Duane were so close?"

"Be careful, Bill."

"What would you have done if two men came to your house at night—two men like Royce and Joe Bob? What would you have done if somebody busted your house—"

"I had no part of that; you know it."

"Duane said yesterday he didn't either." Dancey paused. "Maybe Lorraine just made it up." The tone of his voice probed for an answer.

But Vern said only, "Who did it isn't my concern."

"All right," Dancey said. "How would you see it if somebody had taken a rawhide quirt to your face while two others held your arms?"

"I don't have to see it! The man killed my brother, do you understand that?"

"You've got something to say for your stand." Dancey saw the anger etched deeply in Vern's eyes, hardening the solemn, narrow-boned look of his face. "But what are you going to do about it?"

"Take him up to Fort Buchanan."

"You better go in shooting."

"If that's the way it has to be."

"It's the only way you'll beat him," Dancey said. "And even then he'll fight harder than you will. He's got his family and his land at stake."

Vern shook his head. "This has gone beyond arguing over land."

"You've got three hundred horses up in the high pastures," Dancey said. "When you bring them down they're going to have water. That's the point of all the talk. Nothing else. You've got horses relying on you. He's got people. Now who do you think's going to swing the hardest?"

Vern watched the Dodd brothers coming, leading the horses, then looked at Dancey again. "I'll give him a chance to go up to Fort Buchanan peacefully. If he refuses, that's up to him."

Dancey shook his head. "You'll have to kill him."

"I said it's up to him."

"Maybe you'd hold back." Dancey watched the Dodd brothers approaching. "But they wouldn't. They'd give up a month's pay to draw on him." Dancey hesitated, and when Vern said nothing he added, "You've got yourself talked into something you don't even believe in."

"Listen," Vern said tightly, "I've said it, if he won't come peacefully, we'll shoot him out."

"But you're hoping he'll listen to you."

"I don't care now."

"He won't," Dancey said. "And not one person in his family would. I saw that yesterday. I saw it in his wife and kids, his little boy standing there watching his daddy get rawhided and the kid not even flinching or crying or looking the other way. The man's family is with him, Vern. They're part of him. That's why when you fight him you'll think you're fighting five men, not just one."

"There'll be four of us, Bill," Vern said. "So that almost evens it." He started down the steps.

"Three," Dancey said. "I'll drive your horses. I will this time. But I won't take part in what you're doing."

Vern was looking up at Dancey again, studying him, but he said only, "All right, Bill," as if he had started to say something else but changed his mind. He moved to his horse and mounted, not looking at Dancey now, and led the two Dodd brothers out of the yard.

They'll kill Cable, Dancey thought, watching them go. But they'll pay for it, and not all three of them will come back.

Cable was in the barn when Luz Acaso came.

Earlier, while he was fixing something to eat and had gone to the river for a bucket of water, he saw Kidston's mares and foals out on the meadow. He had planned to run them two days ago, but Manuel had come and he had forgotten about the horses until now. So after breakfast he mounted the sorrel and again chased the herd up the curving sweep of the valley to Kidston land.

He was back, less than an hour later, and leading the sorrel into the barn, when he heard the horse coming down through the pines from the ridge trail. He waited. Then, seeing Luz

Acaso appear out of the trees and round the adobe to the front yard, Cable came out of the barn. But in the same moment he stepped back inside again.

Two riders were coming along the bank of the river on the meadow side. Then, as they jumped their horses down the bank, starting across the river, Cable turned quickly to the sorrel. He drew the Spencer from the saddle, skirted the rectangle of light on the barn floor and edged close to the open doorway.

From this angle, looking past the corner of the house, he saw Luz Acaso first, Luz standing close to her dun horse now, staring out across the yard. Then beyond her, he saw the two riders come out of the willows. One was Vern Kidston. Cable recognized him right away. The other was one of the Dodd brothers, and Cable was almost sure it was the one named Austin.

But why didn't they sneak up?

No, they couldn't have seen him. He had stayed close to the trees coming back from running the horses and he had been in the yard, after that, only a moment. Watching them now, he was thinking: If they wanted to kill you they would have sneaked up.

Unless—he thought—there were more than just the two of them. Vern could be drawing him out. Wanting him to show his position, if he was here.

So wait a minute. Just watch them.

But there was Luz to think of.

His gaze returned to the girl. She was facing Vern, still standing by her horse; but now, as Cable watched, she dropped the reins and moved toward the two riders, walking unhurriedly and with barely a trace of movement beneath the white length of her skirt. Vern Kidston came off his saddle as she approached them.

Cable heard him ask, "Where is he?" the words faint and barely carrying to him. Luz spoke. There was no sound but he saw her shrug and gesture with her hands. Then Kidston spoke again, a sound reaching Cable but without meaning, and he saw Luz shake her head.

For several minutes they stood close to each other, Luz looking up at Kidston and now and again making small gestures with her hands, until, abruptly, Vern took her by the arm. Luz resisted, trying to pull away, but his grip held firmly. Vern walked her to the dun, helped her onto the saddle and the moment she was seated, slapped the horse sharply across the rump. He watched her until she passed into the aspen stand a dozen yards beyond the adobe, then motioned to Austin Dodd.

Austin caught up the reins of Vern's horse and came on. Cable watched him, wondering where the other Dodd brother was. Wynn. He had seen them only twice, but still he could not picture one without the other. Perhaps Wynn was close by. Perhaps that was part of these two standing out in the open.

Austin reached Vern and handed him the reins. Cable waited. Would Vern mount and ride out? If he did, it would be over. Over for this time, Cable thought. Then he would wait for the next time—then the next, and the time after that. Unless you do something now, Cable thought.

Tell him, and make it plain—

No, Cable knew that to make his stand clear and unmistakably plain, without the hint of a doubt, he would have to start shooting right now, right this second. And that was something he couldn't do.

He did not see this in his mind during the moments of waiting. He didn't argue it with himself; but the doubt, the conscience, the whatever it was that made him hesitate and be unsure of himself, was part of him and it held him from killing Vern Kidston now just as it had prevented him from pulling the trigger once before.

Briefly, he did think: You can be too honest with yourself and lose everything. He hesitated because this was a simple principle, a matter of almost black or white, and whatever shades of gray appeared, whatever doubts he might have, were still not strong enough to allow him to shoot a man in cold blood.

Though there was more to it than that. A simple principle, but not a simpler matter. Not something as brutally, honestly simple as war. He couldn't shoot Vern in cold blood. But if he *could* . . . If the urge to end this was stronger than anything else, would his shooting Vern end it? Would he be sure of getting Austin, too? Then Wynn and Dancey and Duane . . . and how many more were there?

It wasn't good to think. That was the trouble, thinking about it and seeing it as black and white and good and bad and war or not war. Wouldn't it be good if they could go back six days and start over and not have the Kidstons here or Janroe, not have anything that has happened happen, not even in a dream?

No, it was not merely a question of not being able to shoot Vern in cold blood. It never was just that. It was being afraid, too, of what would happen to his family. To him, and then to his family.

If they would fight, he thought. If they would hurry the hell up and fight, you could fight back and there would be nothing else but that to think about and there wouldn't even be time to think about that.

He saw Vern Kidston draw his revolver. He saw Austin Dodd dismounting, pulling a Sharps rifle from his saddle boot. Both men walked toward the adobe and within a few strides, from this angle, watching them from the barn and looking past the front corner of the house, they passed from Cable's view.

They'll wreck it for good this time, Cable thought.

If you let them.

He felt the tenseness inside of him, but he was not squeezing the Spencer and his legs felt all right. Stepping out from the barn, he glanced toward the back of the adobe. The clearing between the pine slope and the house was empty. Then he was running across the yard, watching the front now, until he reached the windowless side wall of the house. He edged along to the front, cocked the Spencer and stepped around.

Vern and Austin Dodd were coming out of the front door, under the ramada now, Vern with his hands empty, his Colt holstered again, Austin Dodd holding the Sharps in one hand, the barrel angled down but his finger through the trigger guard. Both men saw Cable at the same time, and both were held motionless by the same moment of indecision.

Cable saw it. He stopped, ready to fire if either man moved a finger, waiting now, leaving the decision with them and almost hoping to see the barrel of the Sharps come up.

"Make up your mind," Cable said, even though he felt the moment was past. He moved toward them, along the log section of the house, until less than a dozen strides separated him from the two men.

"You came to wreck it a second time?"

"I came to talk," Vern said flatly. "That first."

"With your gun in your hand."

"So there wouldn't be an argument."

"Well, you've got one now."

Vern's gaze dropped to the carbine. "You better put that down."

"When you get off my land."

"If you want a fight," Vern said, with the same sullen tone, "one of us will kill you. If you want to come along peacefully, I give you my word we won't shoot."

"Come where?"

"To Fort Buchanan."

Cable shook his head. "I've got no reason to go there."

Vern stared at him, his full mustache accentuating the firm line of his mouth. "I'm not leaving before you do," he said. "Either shoot your gun off or let go of it."

Almost at once Cable had sensed the change in Vern Kidston. Four days ago he had stood covering Vern with a gun and Vern had calmly told him that he would outwait him. But now something had changed Vern. Cable could hear it in the flat, grim tone of the man's voice. He could see it on Vern's face: an inflexible determination to have his way now. There would be no reasoning with Vern, no putting it off. Cable was sure of that. Just as he knew he himself would not be budged from this place by anything less persuasive than a bullet.

Still, momentarily, he couldn't help wondering what had brought about the change in Vern, and he said, "So you've lost your patience."

"You visited Duane last night," Vern said. "We're returning the call."

"I never left this house last night."

"Like you don't know anything about it."

"Well, you tell me what I did. So I'll know."

"In case you didn't wait to make sure," Vern said, "I'll tell you this. Duane's dead. Either one of the bullets would have killed him."

Cable stared at Vern, almost letting the barrel of the Spencer drop and then holding it more firmly. He could not picture Duane dead and he wondered if this was a trick. But if Vern was making it up, what would it accomplish? No, Duane was dead. That was a fact. That was the reason Vern was here. And somebody had killed him.

Janroe.

Janroe, tired of waiting. Janroe, carrying the war, his own private version of the war, to Duane. It could be Janroe. It could very well be and probably was without any doubt Janroe.

But he couldn't tell Vern that. Because to convince Vern it was Janroe he'd have to explain about the man, about the guns, and that would involve Luz and Manuel. And then Vern would go to the store and Martha and the children were there now, and they'd seen enough . . . too much. Besides, this thing between him and Vern still had to be settled, no matter what Janroe had done.

Cable said, "I didn't kill your brother. If I had sneaked up to kill anybody, if I'd carried it that far, it would have been to put a sight on you."

"You're the only man who had reason to do it," Vern said.

"That might seem to be true," Cable answered. "But I didn't. Like you're the only one who had reason to wreck my house. Did you do it?"

"I never touched your place."

"So there you are," Cable said. "Maybe we're both lying. Then again, maybe neither of us is."

"You're not talking your way out of it," Vern said flatly.

"I don't have to." Cable raised the carbine slightly. "I'm holding the gun."

"And once you pull the trigger, Austin will put a hole through you."

"If he's alive," Cable said, centering his attention on Austin Dodd who was still holding the Sharps in one hand, the tip of the barrel almost touching the ground. The man seemed even more sure of himself than Kidston. He studied Cable calmly, with an intent, thoughtful expression half closing his eyes.

Like you don't have a gun in your hand, Cable thought, watching him. He's not worried by it because he knows what he's doing. So you go for Austin first if you go at all.

In his mind he practice-swung the Spencer on Austin, aiming to hit him just above his crossed gun belts. When a man is stomach-shot he relaxes and there is no reflex action jerking his trigger, no wild dead-man-firing. Then he pictured swinging the carbine lower and farther to the left. Austin might drop and roll away and it would be a wing shot, firing and letting the man dive into it. No, it wouldn't be like that, but that's the way it would seem. He thought then: That's enough of that. If you have to think when it's happening, you'll be too late.

The silence lengthened before Austin Dodd spoke.

"He talks, but he's scared to do anything."

Kidston said nothing.

Austin Dodd's eyes still held calmly, curiously on Cable. "I've got him thought out but for one thing. Where'd he buy the nerve to kill Joe Bob?"

"Ask him," Kidston said.

"He'll say he killed him fair." Carefully, Austin raised his left hand and pulled on the curled brim of his hat, loosening it on his head and replacing it squarely.

"Maybe," he said then, "we ought to just walk up and take the gun away from him."

Cable watched him. A moment before, as Austin adjusted his hat, he was sure the man's eyes had raised to look past him. And just before that Austin had started talking. Not a word from him until now.

To make sure you keep looking at him, Cable thought. He felt his stomach tighten as he pictured a man behind him, a man at the corner of the house or coming carefully from the direction of the barn with his gun drawn. Austin was staring at him again. Then—there it was—Vern Kidston's gaze flicked out past him. Vern looked at Cable then, quickly, saw his intent stare, and let his gaze wander aimlessly toward the willows.

Now you're sure, Cable thought, wanting to turn and fire and run and not stop running until he was alone and there was quiet all about him with the only sounds in the distance.

But he made himself stand and not move, his mind coldly eliminating the things that could not happen: like whoever it was being able to sneak up close to him without being heard; or suddenly shooting Vern and Austin Dodd standing directly in front of him, in the line of fire.

So, it would be timed. The moment they moved, the second they were out of the way, the man behind him would fire. It came to that in Cable's mind because there was no other way it could be.

And it would come soon.

Watch Austin and go the way he goes.

It would be coming now.

But don't think and listen to yourself.

You'll hear it. God, you'll hear it all right.

You'll even see it. You'll see Austin—

And Cable was moving—spinning to the outside, pushing himself out of the line of fire and throwing the carbine to his shoulder even before Austin Dodd and Kidston hit the ground. With the sound of the single shot still in the air, he was putting the carbine on Wynn Dodd, thirty feet away and in the open, standing, holding his Colt at arm's length.

Cable fired. *Too soon!* He saw Wynn swing the Colt on him as he levered the Spencer, brought it almost to his shoulder and fired again. Wynn was turned, thrown off balance by the impact of the bullet and his Colt was pointing at the willows when it went off. Still, he held it, trying to bring it in line again; but now Cable was running toward him, levering the trigger guard, half raising the carbine and firing again. Wynn's free hand went to his side and he stumbled, almost going down. From ten feet, with Wynn's Colt swinging on him and seeming almost in his face, Cable shot him again, being sure of this one, knowing Wynn would go down; and now levering, turning, snapping a shot at Austin Dodd and missing as the man came to one knee with the Sharps almost to his shoulder.

Austin and Vern had held their fire because of Wynn, but now both of them opened up. Cable's snap shot threw Austin off and he fired quickly, too wide. From the ramada, Kidston fired twice. Before he could squeeze the trigger again Cable was past the corner of the adobe, beyond their view, and within ten strides safely through the open doorway of the barn.

He brought the sorrel out of its stall, thonging the Spencer to the saddle horn, then mounted and drew the Walker.

Now time it, Cable thought.

He knew what Kidston and Austin would do, which was the obvious thing, the first thought to occur to them; and they would respond to it because they would have to act fast to keep up with him or ahead of him and not let him slip away.

Only one man could watch the barn from the corner of the house. The second man would have to expose himself, or else drop back to the willows, to the protection of the cutbank and move along it until he was opposite the barn, directly out from it and little more than a hundred feet away. If that happened he would be pinned down in the barn until he was picked off, burned out or eventually drawn out by a need as starkly simple as a cup of water. If he waited, time would be on their side to be used against him.

So he would move out and he would do it now while they were still realizing what had to be done, while they were still scrambling to seal off his escape. He knew this almost instinctively after two and a half years with Bedford Forrest. You weren't fooled by false security. You didn't wait, giving the other man time to think. You carried the fight, on your own terms and on your own ground.

Now it was a matter of timing. Move fast, but move at the right time.

The sorrel was lined up with the doorway now, though still well back in the barn. From here Cable could see the corner of the adobe. As he watched he saw a man's shoulder, then part of his head and the dull glint of a Colt barrel in the sunlight. Almost at the same time he heard the horse somewhere off beyond the adobe—the other man running for the cutbank.

Cable's eyes clung to the corner of the house.

Now move him back, he thought, raising the Walker and putting the front sight on the edge of the house. He fired once. The man—Cable was sure it was Kidston—drew back out of sight. At that moment Cable moved, abruptly spurring the sorrel. He was suddenly in the sunlight and reining hard to the right, the Walker still covering the corner; and as Kidston appeared, coming suddenly into the open, Cable fired. He had to twist his body then, his arm extended straight back over the sorrel's rump. He fired again, almost at the same time as Kidston did, but both of their shots were hurried. Then he was reining again, swerving the sorrel to the left, passing behind the adobe just as Kidston fired his second shot.

Even as he entered the horse trail up into the pines, Cable saw the way to throw the fight back at them, to swing on them again while they were off guard in the true hell-raising, hit-and-run style of Forrest; and he left the trail, coming back down through the trees. Then he was in the open again behind the adobe, but now cutting to the right and circling the side of the adobe away from the barn. A moment later he broke past the front of the house.

Twenty feet away Kidston was mounting, looking directly at Cable over the pommel of his saddle. He saw Vern trying to bring up his Colt. He saw Vern's face clearly beyond the barrel of his own revolver; he was pulling the trigger when Vern's horse threw its head into the line of fire. Cable reined the sorrel hard to the right then, seeing Vern's horse stumble and go down with Vern falling and rolling clear.

He caught a glimpse of Austin Dodd already mounted and coming up over the cutbank, but that was all. There was one shot left in the Walker and now Cable was spurring, running the sorrel through the light- and dark-streaked aspen stand, then cutting to the left, reaching the willows, brushing through them and feeling the thick, heavy branches behind him, covering him as he splashed across the river and climbed out onto the meadow.

Get distance on Austin, that was the thing to do now. Get time to reload, and at the same time look like you're running. Now he would lead Austin, let Austin think he was chasing him, and perhaps he would become careless.

Austin fired the Sharps as he came out of the willows to the edge of the river, but he hurried the shot and now Cable was almost two hundred yards ahead of him, holding the sorrel to a steady run.

Cable was calm now. Even though he was sure only in a general way what he would do. Somehow, he would stop Austin Dodd just as he had stopped Vern.

But was Vern stopped? For how long? He could be coming too. He would find Wynn's horse, which might or might not take time; but he would come.

So it wasn't over, or even halfway over. It was just starting.

He would have to be careful and keep his eyes open and stop Austin—Austin first. Now it was a matter of leading him on until he found the place he wanted to fight him. He was applying what he had learned well with Bedford Forrest. How to kill and keep from being killed. Though not killing with an urge to kill, not killing Austin Dodd because he was Austin Dodd. Though you could probably even justify that, Cable thought.

He would start up the far side of the meadow and be in the trees while Austin was still in the open. Then Austin would slow up and that would give him time to reload. That would be the way to do it, he thought, lifting his gaze to the piñon trees and the open slope that rose above them.

Yet it was in the same momentary space of time, with the heavy, solid report, with the unmistakable smacking sound of the bullet, that Cable's plan dissolved. The sorrel went down, shot through a hind leg, and Cable was suddenly on the ground. He rolled over, looking back in time to see Austin Dodd mounting again.

The man had reloaded on the run, got down for one last-chance long-shot with the Sharps at two hundred stretching to three hundred yards. And you weren't watching!

Cable started for the sorrel—on the ground with its hind legs kicking in spasms. The Spencer was still thonged to the saddle. The cartridge tubes and loads for the Walker were in the saddle bags. But he knew at once that it was too late to get them. If he delayed, he'd be pinned down behind the sorrel. In Cable's mind it was not a matter of choice. Not with a slope of thick piñon less than forty yards away.

He ran for it, crouched, sprinting, not looking back but hearing the hoof beats gaining on him; then the high, whining report of a Colt.

Before Austin could fire again, Cable was through the fringe of yellow-blossomed mesquite and into the piñons. From here he watched Austin rein in at the sorrel and dismount. Cable was moving at once, higher up on the slope, a dozen yards or more, before he looked back at Austin again.

The gunman was squatting by the sorrel going through the one accessible saddle bag. But now he rose, holding the Spencer down-pointed in one hand, stepped back and shot the sorrel through the head. He threw the carbine aside, looking up at the piñon slope.

"Cable!" Austin shouted the name. He paused while his eyes scanned the dark foliage. "Cable, I'm coming for you!"

Cable watched him, a small figure forty or fifty yards below him and out in the open, now coming toward the trees.

He's sure of himself, Cable thought. Because he's been counting shots and he knows it as well as you do. Cable pulled the Walker and checked it to be sure.

One bullet remained in the revolver. Extra loads, powder and percussion caps were all out in the saddle bag.

Luz kept the dun mare at a steady run, her bare knees pressed tightly to the saddle, holding it and aching with the strain of jabbing her heels into the dun's flanks.

She realized she should have taken the horse trail. It was shorter. But Vern Kidston had sent her off abruptly, and in the moment her only thought had been to keep going, to run for help as fast as the dun would move. And now she was following the curving five-mile sweep of the meadow, already beyond the paths that led up to the horse trail from Cable's land.

They would find Cable in the barn. . . . She had seen him go in as she approached. And if he showed himself, they would kill him. Even if he didn't, he was trapped. She pictured Vern and the other man firing in at him, not showing themselves and taking their time. But if they waited, having trapped him, she might have time also—time to bring help.

If her brother was home. She had thought of no one else, picturing him mounting and rushing back to Cable's aid. He would *have* to be home. God, make him be home, she thought, closing her eyes and thinking hard so God would hear her; he said he would come today, so all You have to do is make sure of it. Not a miracle. Just make him be home.

And if he's not? Then Mr. Janroe.

No! She rejected the thought, shaking her head violently. God is just. He couldn't offer something that's evil to do something that's good.

Yet in the good act, saving Cable, Vern Kidston could be wounded or killed. And there would be nothing good in that.

She closed her eyes as tightly as she could to see this clearly, but it remained confused, the good and the evil overlapping and not clearly defined or facing one another as it should be. Because the wrong ones are fighting, she thought.

But why couldn't they see this? Vern Kidston and Paul Cable should be together, she thought, because they are the same kind of man; though perhaps Paul is more gentle. He has a woman and has learned to be gentle.

But Vern could have a woman. And he could also learn to be gentle. She knew this, feeling it and knowing it from the first time she saw him; feeling it like a warm robe around her body the time he kissed her, which had been almost a year ago and just before Janroe came. Then feeling it again, standing close to him and seeing it in his eyes as they faced each other in front of Cable's house.

She had told him Cable was not at home and he said, then they would wait for him. I will wait with you, Luz said. But Vern shook his head saying, go on home to Janroe. She told him then, without having to stop to think of words, what she thought of Edward Janroe, what kind of a half-man half-animal, what kind of a *nagual* he was. And she could see that Vern believed her when she said she despised Janroe.

She had pleaded with him then to put his guns aside and talk to Cable, to end it between them honestly as two men should. She had thought of the war being over, saying: see, they ended after seeing how senseless it was that so many men should die. End your war, too, she had said.

But he had taken her arm and half dragged her to the dun mare and told her to go. Because now it was this business with Cable and not a time for gentleness. He did not say this, but Luz could feel it. Just as she knew now why he had stopped seeing her after Janroe's coming.

Because Vern Kidston was proud and would rather stay away and clench his fists than risk discovering her living with or in love with Edward Janroe. That meant only one thing. Vern Kidston loved her. He did before and he did now.

But don't think of it now, she thought. Don't think of anything. Just do what you have to do. She told herself that this was beyond her understanding. For how could there be room for love and hate in the same moment? How could good be opposed to good? And how can you be happier than you have ever been and more afraid than you have ever been, both at the same time?

Within a few minutes she was in sight of the store with the dark sweep of willows bunched close beyond. She kept her eyes on the adobe now and soon she was able to make out a figure on the platform. She prayed that it was Manuel.

But it was Janroe, standing rigidly and staring at her, waiting for her as she crossed the yard and reined in the dun.

"Where've you been?"

She saw the anger in his face and in the tense way he held his body. But there was no time to be frightened; she wanted to tell him, she wanted to say all of it at once and make sure he understood.

"I went to the Cable place," she began, out of breath and almost gasping the words.

"I told you I was going there!" Janroe's voice whipped at her savagely, then lowered to the hoarse tone of talking through clenched teeth. "I told you to stay home, that I was going later—but you went anyway! I told you he wasn't there last night and I would see him this morning—but you went anyway!"

"Listen to me!" Luz screamed it, feeling a heat come over her face. "Vern Kidston is there—"

Janroe stared at her and slowly the tightness eased from his face. "Alone?"

"One man with him. Perhaps more."

"What happened?"

"Not anything yet. But something has happened to Vern and he wants to kill Cable. I know it!"

Janroe's chest rose and fell with his breathing, but he said calmly, "He probably just wants to talk to Cable."

"No—he was armed. Vern, and the one called Austin with two guns and a rifle on his saddle. . . . Listen, is my brother here?"

"Not yet."

"He said he was coming today."

"Probably later on."

She was looking at him intently now, trying to see something in him that she could trust, that she could believe. But there was no time even for this and she said, "Come with me. Now, before they kill him."

"Luz, Vern just wants to talk with him." Janroe was completely at ease now. "Vern's a patient man. Why would he change?"

"Then you won't come," Luz said.

"There's no need to. Come in the house and stop worrying about it."

She shook her head. "Then I'm going back."

"Luz, I said come in the house. It's none of your business what's going on between them."

She saw the anger in his face again and she raised the reins. Janroe came off the platform, reaching for the bridle, but the dun was already side-stepping, wheeling abruptly, and Janroe was knocked flat. Luz broke away and was across the yard before Janroe could push himself to his feet.

She held herself low in the saddle and kept the dun running with her heels and with her voice, making the horse strain forward and stretch its legs over the grass that seemed to sweep endlessly toward the curve of the valley.

She would do something, she told herself, because she had to do something. There was no one else. She wouldn't think of it being over. She would arrive before they found Cable and plead with Vern, not leaving this time even if he tried to force her. He would listen. Then Paul would come out and they would talk, and after a while the thing between them would be gone.

But only moments later she knew she was too late. Luz slowed the mare, rising in the saddle and pulling the reins with all her strength to bring the dun finally to a halt. She sat listening.

Now, in the distance, she heard it again: the flat, faraway sound of gunfire, and she knew they had found him and were trying to kill him.

7

SOON THERE would be two of them.

Cable could see the rider now—it would have to be Vern on Wynn's horse—already on this side of the river and coming across the meadow.

Below, closer to him, was Austin Dodd.

Cable waited until Austin came through the yellow mesquite patches at the edge of the piñon pines. As the man reached the trees, Cable began to fall back. He moved carefully up the slope, glancing behind him, not wanting to stumble and lose time, and not wanting to lose sight of Austin. He caught glimpses of the man moving cautiously up through the trees.

The slope was not steep here and the piñon seemed almost uniformly spaced, resembling an abandoned, wild-growing orchard. It was not a place to stand with one shot in his revolver and fight a man who had two Colt guns and all the time in the world.

Cable moved back until he reached the end of the trees. And now he stopped to study the open slope behind him. It was spotted with patches of brittlebush and cliffrose, but nothing to use for cover; not the entire, gravelly, nearly one hundred feet of it that slanted steeply to the sky.

Perhaps he could make it; but not straight up. It was too steep. He would have to angle across the slope and Austin would have time to shoot at him. But it was worth trying and it would be better than staying here. He would have to forget about Austin—and about Vern, almost across the meadow now—and concentrate on reaching the crest, not letting anything stop him.

He was in the open then, running diagonally across the rise, his boots digging hard into the crusted, crumbling sand. Almost at once he felt the knotted pain in his thighs, but he kept going, not looking back and trying not to picture Austin Dodd closing in on him; or Vern, at the foot of the slope now and taking out his rifle.

Cable cut through a patch of brittlebush, getting a better foothold then and running hard, but he came suddenly onto a spine of smooth rock—it humped no more than two feet above the ground—and here he slipped to his hands and knees. He tried to get up and stumbled again, then rolled over the side of the smooth rock surface before lunging to his feet. He was climbing again, less than twenty feet from the top when Austin's voice reached him.

"Cable!"

He stopped, catching his breath and letting it out slowly before coming around. He knew he would never make the crest. He was sure of it then, seeing Austin already well out of the piñon, to his left below him and less than sixty feet away. Austin's Colts were holstered, but his hands hung close to them. He came on slowly, his face calm and his eyes not straying from Cable.

"Pull anytime now," Austin said. He advanced up the slope, not looking at the ground but feeling his way along with each careful step.

"You want to. But you got only one shot." He was reaching the brittlebush now. "Count the other man's shots. That's something I learned a long time ago. Then when I saw your extra loads still out there with the horse I said to myself, 'I wouldn't want to be that boy. He don't have one chance between hell and breakfast.'"

Cable said nothing. He stood facing Austin Dodd, watching him move into the small field of orange-colored brittlebush. There Austin stopped.

"So when you pull," Austin said, "you have to make it good the one time." He seemed almost to be smiling. "That could tighten a man's nerves some."

Austin was ready, standing on his own ground. And to beat him with one shot, Cable knew, he would have to be more than fast. He would have to be dead-center accurate.

But he wouldn't have time to aim, time to be sure.

Unless Austin hesitated. Or was thrown off guard.

Cable's gaze dropped from the brittlebush to the smooth spine of rock where he had slipped. If he could draw Austin to that point. If he could jiggle him, startle him. If he could throw Austin off balance only for a moment, time enough to draw and aim and make one shot count. If he could do all that—

And Vern was into the piñon now.

No—one thing at a time.

Slowly then, Cable began to back away.

Austin shook his head, "You wouldn't come near making it."

Cable was still edging back, covering six, eight, almost ten feet before Austin started toward him again. Cable stopped. He watched Austin come out of the brittlebush, watched him reach the spine of rock and grope with one foot before stepping onto the smooth, rounded surface.

As Austin's foot inched forward again, Cable went to the side, dropping to one knee and bringing up the Walker in one abrupt motion.

Austin was with him, his right-hand Colt out and swinging on Cable; but the movement shifted his weight. His boots slipped on the smooth rock and even as he fired and fired again he was falling back, his free hand outstretched and clawing for balance.

Beyond the barrel of the Walker, Austin seemed momentarily suspended, his back arched and his gun hand high in the air. Cable's front sight held on his chest and in that moment, when he was sure and there was no doubt about it, Cable squeezed the trigger.

He was sliding down the gravel as Austin fell back into the brittlebush, reaching him then, knowing he was dead and concentrating on prying the revolver from the man's fingers. Cable took both of Austin's revolvers, both Colt Army .44s. He waited a moment, but there was no sign of Vern. He rose half crouched, expecting to hear Vern's shot, expecting to feel it, then ran for the piñon pines.

He went down beneath a tree, feeling the sand and grass patches warm and the thick branches close above him, and now he listened.

Vern would be close. In the time, he could have come all the way up through the trees. Perhaps not; but at any rate Vern would have seen him running across the open. Probably he was just not in position for a shot. But now Vern knew where he was; that much was certain.

So move, Cable thought.

He pushed up to one knee and waited, listening, then was running again, keeping low and dodging through the brushlike trees. Almost immediately a rifle report whined through the grove. Cable dropped, clawing then, changing his direction and moving down the slope. The firing began again, this time with the sound of a revolver somewhere between fifty and a hundred feet away from him. Cable kept going and the .44 sound hammered after him, five times, until he dropped into a shallow gully.

Cable rolled to his stomach, holstered one of the Colts, and at once began crawling up the narrow wash, up toward the open slope. He moved quickly, using his knees and forearms, until he was almost to the edge of the trees, roughly thirty feet above the spot where he had entered the gully. He stopped then to listen.

There was no sound. Beyond the brush and rock shadows close in front of him, the slope glared with sunlight. He turned, looking back the way he had come, then removed his hat and rolled on his side, resting the Colt on his thigh so that it pointed down the length of the gully.

Minutes passed in dead silence. Then there was a sound; but not close or in the pines. It was the sound of horse's hoofs, distant, still far out on the meadow.

More of them, Cable thought.

He would have to take Vern quickly, before they came. He would have to keep it even if he expected to come through this.

And if you knew where Vern was maybe you could.

But he didn't. Vern could be close. Vern could even know he was lying here, and if he ran for the slope, Vern could very possibly drop him. Or even if he moved or stood up.

And if times if equals if, and there's no getting out of this. No running. Only waiting and letting it happen. Even Forrest waited sometimes. He waited for them to make mistakes. But he would be waiting this time—God, yes, he would be waiting—whether they made mistakes or not.

The horse sound seemed nearer. He concentrated, listening, until he was sure that it was only one horse coming. One rider. One helper for Vern.

Cable pushed up with one hand, trying to see the meadow over the trees below him, but he could see only the far side of the meadow and the willows marking the river and the dark, quiet, cool-looking slope beyond. The rider would be close to this side by now.

Cable's gaze fell, and held.

Vern Kidston was facing him. Vern not thirty feet away, one leg in the gully, half sitting, half kneeling at the edge of it and partly hidden by the brush. Vern with his revolver extended and watching him.

Neither of them moved. They stared in silence with cocked revolvers pointed at each other. Cable sitting with one hand behind him, the other holding the Colt on his thigh, his face calm and showing clearly in the sunlight that filtered through the trees. Vern's expression, though partly shadowed and solemn with his mustache covering the corners of his mouth, was as relaxed as Cable's. The tension was somewhere between them, waiting for one or the other to move. And as the silence lengthened, it seemed that even a spoken word would pull a trigger.

It was in Vern's tone when finally he said, "Cable," and waited, as if expecting a reaction.

"I could have killed you," he said then. "I had my gun on you and you were looking away. . . . Why didn't I?"

Cable said nothing.

"I could have ended it right then. But I didn't. Do you know why?" He waited again. "I'm asking you."

Cable shook his head, though he saw Vern as he had seen him two days ago—a small figure against the front sight of his Spencer—and remembered how he had not been able to pull the trigger. He had thought about it enough and knew the reason why he had held back; but it was not a clear reason; only a feeling and it might be a different feeling with each man. What did Vern feel? At the same time, what difference did it make? Vern had not been able to pull the trigger when he had the chance, and knowing that was enough. But it would be different with him now, Cable thought, just as it's different with you. The feeling wouldn't apply or hold either of them back at this point.

Tell him anyway, Cable thought; and he said, "I had my sights on you once. The same thing happened. Though I'm not sure I'd let it happen again."

"When was that?"

"Two days ago. You were with Lorraine."

"Why didn't you shoot?"

"It takes some explaining," Cable said. "And I'm not sure it makes sense when you say it out loud."

Vern nodded faintly. "Maybe it's called leaving it up to the other man."

"I didn't start this," Cable said flatly. "I don't feel obliged to keep it going either."

"But you'll finish what you can," Vern said. "What about Austin—he's dead?"

Cable nodded.

"I didn't think you'd have a chance with him."

"Neither did he," Cable said. "That's why he's dead."

"So you killed all three of the Dodd brothers, and Royce—"

"What would you have done?"

"You mean because each time it was them or you?"

"Or my family," Cable said. "I'm asking what you would have done? Two choices. Run or stand?"

"All right." Vern paused. "But Duane. That's something else."

"I didn't shoot your brother."

"There's no one else would have reason to."

"Stay with one thing," Cable said. "I didn't shoot him."

"Even after he rawhided you?"

"If I'd wanted to get back at him for that, I'd have used fists. I never felt a beating was a killing thing."

"That could be true," Vern said. "But how do I know it is?"

"Whether you believe it or not," Cable answered, "your gun's no bigger than mine is." But he said then, "I told you before, I didn't leave the house last night."

"And if you didn't do it—" Vern began.

"Why couldn't it have been one of your own men?"

Vern shook his head. "Everybody was accounted for."

Then it was Janroe, Cable thought, without any doubt of it. He said to Vern, "I can ask you the same kind of question."

"You mean about your house? I never touched it."

"Then it was Duane."

"I know for a fact," Vern said, "it wasn't anyone from my place."

"But you put Royce and Joe Bob on me."

Again Vern shook his head. "They came on their own."

"What about Lorraine?"

"I knew about that," Vern admitted. "I should have stopped her."

"What was the point of it?"

"Lorraine said wedge something between you and your wife. Split you up and you wouldn't have a good reason to stay here."

"Does that make sense to you?"

"I said I should have stopped her."

"Vern, I've lived here ten years. We've been married for eight."

Kidston nodded then, solemnly. "Bill Dancey said you had more reason to fight than I did."

"What did you say?"

"I don't remember."

"Do you believe him?"

"I'll tell you this," Vern said. "I'd like to have known you at a different time."

Cable nodded. "Maybe we would have gotten on. Even worked out this land thing."

"Even that," Vern said.

"I would have been willing to let you put some of your horses on my graze," Cable said, "if it hadn't started the way it did."

"Well, it doesn't matter now," Vern said.

But it could matter, Cable thought. "We were going to wait each other out," Cable said. "But Royce and Joe Bob got into it. Then your brother. I wonder how this would have turned out if he were still alive."

Vern was watching Cable closely. "I wish I could understand you. Either you had nothing to do with killing Duane, or else you're some actor."

"Like trying to understand why you brought Wynn and Austin with you," Cable said. "You're big enough to make your own fight."

"When a man's killed," Vern said, "it's no longer a game or a personal contest. It was time to get you, with the best, surest way I had."

"When the man's your brother," Cable said. "When Royce and Joe Bob were killed you went right on waiting."

"I've been wrong," Vern said, "maybe right from the beginning. I let it get out of hand too. I admit that. But there's nothing I can do about the ways it's developed."

"Then in time you would have backed off," Cable said, "if nothing had happened to Duane."

"Well, with the war on I could look on you as an enemy. Kick you off your land and tell myself it was all right. But now that it's over, I'm not sure about anything, not even my horse business. Though I might probably get a contract from the stage-line people when they start up—"

Cable stopped him. "What did you say?" He was staring at Vern intently. "About the war?"

"It's over. You knew that, didn't you?"

"When was it over?"

"A few days ago."

"You knew it then?"

"We learned yesterday." Vern seemed to frown, studying Cable's expression. "Luz knew about it. She mentioned it when I talked to her a while ago."

"Yesterday," Cable said.

"She would have learned it yesterday." Vern nodded.

And if she knew it, Cable thought, so did Janroe. Yesterday. Before Duane was killed. Janroe would have known. He must have known. But still he killed Duane. Could that be?

You could think about it, Cable thought, and it wouldn't make sense, but still it could be. With anyone else there would be a doubt. But with Janroe there was little room for doubt. This was strange because he hardly knew the man.

But at the same time it wasn't strange, not when he pictured this man who had lost his arm in the war and who had killed over a hundred Union prisoners. Not when he heard him talking again, insisting over and over that Vern and Duane should be killed. Not when he remembered the feeling of trying to answer Janroe. No, it wasn't strange, not when he put everything together that he could remember about Janroe.

It could have been Janroe who tore up his house. It occurred to Cable that moment, but at once he was sure of it: Janroe trying to incite him, trying to make him angry enough to go after the Kidstons. Janroe wanting to see them—the enemy, or whatever they were to him—dead, but without drawing blame on himself.

Janroe could even be insane. Something could have happened to him in the war.

No, don't start that, Cable thought. Just take it at its face value. Janroe killed a man you are being accused of killing. He did it, whether he had reason or not; though the war wasn't the reason, because the war was over and you are almost as sure as you can be sure of something that he knew it was over. So just take that, Cable thought, and do something with it.

He sat up, raising the Colt, then turned the cylinder, letting the hammer down gently on the empty chamber. Vern did not move; though when Cable looked up again he knew Vern had been taken by surprise and was puzzled.

"We're wasting our time," Cable said. "There's a man we ought to see."

He began to tell Vern about Janroe.

Luz reached Cable's dead sorrel before she saw the two horses grazing along the mesquite at the foot of the slope. These would belong to Vern and the one called Austin. She slowed the dun to a walk now, her eyes raised and moving searchingly over the piñon-covered slope. The firing had come from up there, she was sure of it.

But there had been no shots for some time now. They could be hunting for him among the trees. Or it could already be over.

When she saw the two figures coming down through the trees, in view for brief moments as they passed through clearings, she was sure that it was over, that these two were Vern and Austin coming back to their horses. They left the piñon and were down beyond the mesquite for some time. Finally they appeared again and it was not until now that she saw the second man was not Austin but Cable.

She watched them approach with the strange feeling that this could not be happening, that it was a dream. They had been firing at one another; but now they were walking together, both armed, not one bringing the other as a prisoner.

Questions ran through her mind and she wanted to ask all

of them at once; but now they were close and it was Cable who spoke first.

"Luz, did Janroe leave the store last night?"

The question took her by surprize. Without a greeting, without an explanation of the two of them together, without wondering why she was here, Cable asked about Janroe. The question must be so important to him that he skipped all of those other things.

She said, hesitantly, "He went to see you last night. But he said you weren't home."

"Where is he now, at the store?"

"He was a little while ago." She remembered him jumping down from the platform, trying to stop her from leaving. "But he's acting strangely," she said. "I don't think I've ever seen him the way he was."

Vern was looking at Cable. "Your wife and kids are there?" When Cable nodded, glancing at Luz again, Vern said, "I think we'd better go see Mr. Janroe."

Janroe watched Luz until she was almost out of sight. He turned, pausing to brush the dust from his knees, and was aware of Martha in the doorway. He looked up at her; from her expression he knew she had heard Luz.

"Well?" Janroe said.

"I would like to borrow a horse," Martha said tensely.

"You can't do anything."

"Just let me have a horse," Martha said. "I don't need anything else from you, least of all advice."

"And you'll take your kids with you?"

"I'd like to leave them here."

Janroe shook his head. "I don't have time to watch your kids."

Martha came out on the platform. "You would stop me from going to my husband? At a time like this you would stop me from being with him?"

"You couldn't help him," Janroe said. "Neither could I. Luz is wasting her time whether she thinks she's doing something or not. I tried to stop her, tried to talk some sense into her, but she wouldn't listen. That's the trouble with you women. You get all het up and run off without thinking." He had moved to the platform and was now mounting the steps. "If Vern's there to talk to your husband, there's no sense in stopping him. If he's there for any other reason, none of us could stop him if we tried."

"You won't let me have a horse?"

"Sit down on your hands, you won't be so nervous."

"Mr. Janroe, I'm begging you—"

"No, you're not." He moved her into the store in front of him. "You want to do something, get out in the kitchen and do the dishes."

Martha didn't want to back down—he could see that—but there was little she could say as she turned abruptly and walked away, down the length of the store counter.

Janroe said after her, "Don't leave the house. You hear me? Don't even open the door less I say it's all right."

He waited until she was in the next room before he moved around behind the counter that extended along the front of the store. From under the counter he took a short-barreled shotgun with *Hatch & Hodges* carved into the stock—it dated from the time the store had been a stage-line station—checked to see that it was loaded, then laid it on the counter.

From a peg behind him he took his shoulder holster with the Colt fitting snugly in it, and looped it over his armless shoulder. He wound the extra-long leather thong, which held the Colt securely, around his chest and tied the end of it deftly with his one hand.

Just in case, he told himself; though you won't need them. You can be almost absolutely sure of that.

Everything will go all right. Luz would be back within an hour. She would ride in slowly this time, putting off telling Martha what had happened. Then behind her would come Vern and Austin, probably both of the Dodd brothers, with Cable face-down over his horse. Vern would tell it simply, in few words; and if Martha cried or screamed at him, he would say, "He killed my brother." Or, "He should have thought about his family before he killed Duane." Or words that said the same thing. Then they would dump his body. Or let it down easy now that it was over and the anger was drained out of them, and ride away.

Then what? Then he would listen to the woman cry, the

woman and the kids. There was no way of avoiding that. Afterward, he might even offer his services to the new widow. . . .

Then what? Kill Vern? No, forget about that for now.

Then think about it when the time comes. There was no hurry. He could go back to St. Augustine. Or he could stay here. That would be something, to stay here and be a neighbor of Vern's. Talk to him about Duane every once in a while, and Cable, and all the trouble Cable caused. That would be something; but the staying here, the living here and letting the time pass, might not be worth it. He would have to weigh that against the once-in-a-while satisfaction of Vern talking to him and not knowing he had killed Duane.

No, there was no hurry. There would be time later on to think of what he would do. With two arms he would have stayed in the army; even though the war was over.

Janroe caught himself. Is it over?

All right, it's over. You've had no word, he thought. But if they want to say it's over, then it is. It was a good war, part of it was; but now, as of right now, you can say it's over. You can't fight people who won't fight back.

First Luz would come, then Vern. Everything had happened just about the way it was supposed to and there was no reason for it to change now.

Finding Luz gone this morning had affected his nerves. He knew she had gone to see Cable, and he had pictured her telling him that the war was over. Then asking him if he was at home last night. Then why, she would ask, would Janroe lie and say you weren't home? Then he had pictured Cable coming to the store.

But it had worked out all right. Vern was there before her. Vern seeking vengeance.

So now there was no chance of Cable finding out or eluding Vern or beating him or coming here. No, he would come here, all right, but not alive.

But this damn waiting . . .

Janroe paced the length of the space behind the counter, but it was too confining. He went out to the loading platform and for some time stood gazing out at the sunlit sweep of the valley; then at the willows and the slope beyond. He went inside again, through the store to the sitting room. From here he saw Martha still in the kitchen. Davis, the older boy, was with her, standing on a chair to put the breakfast dishes away.

He heard a noise from upstairs, then remembered that the other two children were up there. Martha had sent Clare up to make her bed and the younger one had gone with his sister. They'd probably forgotten all about the bed and were playing.

He was out on the platform again in time to see the rider come down the slope and drop from sight behind the willows. Waiting, Janroe was aware of the tight feeling in his stomach and the ache, the dull, muscle ache, in the arm that wasn't there. But the next moment the tension and the pain were gone. He could feel only relief now, watching Luz appear out of the willows and come toward him across the yard.

He saw her watching him as she came, all the way, until she had reached the platform.

"What happened?"

"It's over."

"He's dead?"

Luz glanced at the doorway behind them, then back to Janroe and nodded quickly.

"Where is he?"

"At home."

"I thought Vern would be coming."

Luz shrugged. "I don't know." She dismounted and came up on the platform. "I'd better go tell her."

Janroe stepped aside. "Go ahead." He said then, "You don't seem broken up any."

Luz said nothing.

"Didn't Vern say he was coming?"

Luz shook her head. "I don't remember." She moved past him into the store.

Janroe followed. "Wait a minute. Tell me what happened."

"After," Luz said. She hurried now to the next room.

Janroe still stood at the edge of the counter after she was gone.

But why wasn't she crying? She could be nervous about telling Martha, but she would have cried, if not now sometime before, and she would show signs of it.

From this the suspicion began to build in his mind. Why wouldn't she tell what happened? She seemed to want to get away from him, to see Martha too quickly; not holding back, putting it off, reluctant to face Martha; but wanting to see her, to tell her . . . to tell her what?

He moved through the store in long, hurried strides, across the sitting room and saw them in the kitchen, Martha and Luz and the little boy: Martha looking at him, her eyes alive and her hand going to Luz suddenly to stop her. "What're you telling her?"

Luz turned, stepping back as he came in. "Nothing. I was just beginning—"

"What did she tell you?" He turned to Martha abruptly.

"This doesn't concern you, Mr. Janroe."

"Answer me!" His hand clamped on Martha's arm and he saw her wince, trying to pull away. "She said your husband was still alive, didn't she? She said not to worry that he was all right, that he was coming." Janroe shook her violently. "Answer me!"

He heard Luz moving. He wheeled, reaching for her, but she was already past him. "Luz—"

She ran through the store ahead of him, out to the loading platform and jumped. Janroe reached the doorway. He pulled the Colt, cocking it, and screamed her name again, a last warning. But beyond Luz he saw Cable step out of the willows with the Spencer in his hand. Then Vern, closer, running past the corner of the building. Janroe pushed back inside. He thought of Martha and ran into the sitting room in time to see her starting for the stairs. She reached the first step before she heard Janroe and turned to face him.

"You couldn't leave the two upstairs, could you?" Janroe said.

Now they were in the willows watching the front of the store. Vern had been down farther, in view of the rear door, but he had come back as Luz ran out of the store and Janroe shouted at her.

"That nails it down," Vern said. "He killed Duane. I wonder what he's thinking, seeing us together."

Cable, at the edge of the trees, said nothing.

Luz was staring vacantly at the adobe. "I shouldn't have run," she said. "I should be there with your wife and children."

"You did the best thing," Cable said.

"But I ran, leaving them alone with him."

"We shouldn't have let you do it," Cable said.

"No," Vern said. "It was the only way and it had to be tried. It was worth that much." The plan had been for Luz to tell Janroe that Cable was dead. Then to tell Martha, somehow without Janroe hearing, to take the children and slip out. That would leave Janroe alone in the adobe and in time they would take him. But now they would have to think of something else.

"Where was Martha?" Cable asked Luz.

"In the kitchen."

"The children with her?"

"Just Davis." She looked at him then. "Could Clare and Sandy be outside?"

"They'd be close. But I haven't seen them." He glanced at Vern. "In back?" When Vern shook his head, Cable said, "Then they're all inside."

"He wouldn't harm them," Luz said. "He would be too afraid to do that."

"Now he'll be thinking of a way out," Vern said.

"Unless he's already thought of it." Cable was still watching the adobe. "I think I'd better talk to him."

Vern looked at him. "Just walk out there?"

"I don't know of any other way," Cable said. He parted the willow branches and started across the yard. Almost at once Janroe's voice stopped him.

"Stay where you are!"

Luz's horse, by the loading platform, raised its head at the sound.

Cable's eyes moved from the screen door to the first window on the right. One of the wooden shutters was open. If Janroe was there he would be in the store, behind the counter that ran along the front wall. Cable started toward the adobe again.

"Stand or I'll kill you!"

That's where he was, by the window. Cable was sure of it now.

"Janroe, you're in enough trouble. Let my family come out."

There was no answer from the store.

"You hear me? Send them out and nobody will harm you." He saw Janroe at the window then, part of his head and shoulder momentarily.

"How do I know that?" Janroe's voice again.

"You've got my word."

"I've got something better than your word."

"Janroe, if you harm my wife and children—"

"I'm through talking to you, Cable!"

"All right"—Cable's tone lowered, became more calm—"what do you want?"

"I'll tell you when I'm ready. Go back where you were. Try sneaking up and you'll hear a shotgun go off."

Cable stared at the window, not moving.

"Go on!"

"Janroe," Cable said finally, "if you harm my family you're a dead man." He turned then and moved back into the willows to stand with Luz and Vern.

Soon after, Luz's horse moved away from the platform, the reins dragging. It wandered aimlessly at first, nosing the ground; but finally the horse's head rose and it came toward them, drawn by the scent of water.

Taking the reins, Luz looked at Cable. "He could threaten us to bring it back. Why doesn't he?"

"He knows he can do it any time he wants," Cable answered.

They waited, watching the store and seldom speaking. The afternoon dragged by and there was no word from Janroe; not a sound reaching them from the adobe.

In the late afternoon, with the first red traces of sunset, a rider came down the slope from the horse trail south. It was Manuel, back from Hidalgo. Back for good, he said.

He looked at Vern, then at Cable inquiringly and Cable told it, beginning with Duane and bridging to the present time. They had been here nearly six hours now, waiting for Janroe to make his move. There was nothing they could do. There wasn't much doubt that Janroe would take a hostage when he decided to make his run. Probably one of the children. Probably, too, he was waiting for dark. But you couldn't count on anything—it was Luz who added this—because something was wrong with the man's mind. But Cable was sure Janroe would know they would hold back for fear of harming the child, and Janroe would lose them long before daylight.

The question then, what would he do with his hostage?

Cable said it bluntly, calmly, though his stomach was tight

and he felt the unceasing urge through his body to move about and to do something with his hands. To do *something*.

It was Vern who brought up the question of the back door. "He can't watch front and back both. Unless he locked the door."

Manuel shook his head. "There's no lock on it. But what if he heard you?"

"That's something else," Vern said.

The evening came gradually with dusk filtering into the willow grove before seeping in long shadows out toward the adobe store. There were faint sounds of birds up in the ridge pines, but close about them the willows were silent. Later on, perhaps, there would be a breeze and the crickets would begin. But now there was a silence that seemed never to end. They waited.

Luz and Vern sat close to each other and occasionally Cable would hear the murmur of their voices. Janroe had split them apart and now he had brought them back together. Maybe they would get married. Maybe some good would come out of this. Later on—days or weeks, sometime later—he and Vern would talk this out that was between them. Cable remained apart from the others, sitting near the edge of the river and watching the dark water.

After a while he began to think of something Vern had said, about the back door. And Manuel had answered that there was no lock on the door. "But what if he heard you?" Manuel had asked.

But, Cable thought, what if he didn't hear you?

He pictured himself keeping to the trees until he had reached the barn, then creeping along its shadows, then across the yard and carefully, quietly, into the kitchen. It would already be dark inside the house. But if you bumped something—

No, he thought then, you know the place well enough. You could blind your eyes and walk through the house without touching or bumping anything.

Janroe wouldn't expect anyone and there would be no sound. Janroe would be by the window watching Martha and the children, but glancing outside often. He would creep to the doorway that led into the store, see Janroe and be very sure of killing him with the first shot.

An hour passed. It was dark in the willows now and the last red traces of sun were gone from the sky. Cable kneeled at the sandy edge of the river to drink, cupping the water in his hands.

In the other time, Martha would be getting the children ready for bed now. They would come in and kiss him good night before Martha sat with them on the bed, their eyes wide and watching her, while she told them a story.

There had been a story the children liked and asked for often, about the little girl and her brother who were lost in the forest. When night came, the little girl began to cry and her brother put his arm around her. They sat huddled together, shivering with cold and listening to the night sounds. And when it seemed they could bear no more, neither the cold nor the frightening sounds, the little girl's guardian angel appeared and led them through the forest to their home.

The children liked the story because it was easily imagined and because of the good feeling of being safely at home while they pictured themselves in the frightening dark.

Soon part of this story would come to life for one of his children. Janroe would take one of them as a hostage, because a child would be easier to handle than Martha. He would need only one horse and hold the child in front of him on the saddle, moving south toward the border and keeping to the wild terrain that offered good cover. But somewhere along the way, when he was sure he had lost the ones trailing him, when he no longer needed his hostage, Janroe would drop the child.

He would have no concern for the child's life. There was no reason even to hope that he might. It could be Sandy. Three years old and alone somewhere in the vast, trackless rock country to the south. If they didn't find him—and it would be almost as miraculous as the story if they did—the boy would survive perhaps two days.

So you have no choice, Cable thought. He would have to stop Janroe before he left the store.

Or while he was leaving it—

Cable pushed himself erect. Perhaps that was it. With the back door idea to make it work.

Perhaps as Janroe came out with the child in front of him. But it would be a long shot, too far, and even now there wasn't enough light. But say Vern worked his way around to the side of the adobe and waited there. That could be done.

Janroe would come out, would call for one of them to come unarmed with a horse, threatening to shoot the child if he wasn't obeyed. He would mount first and pull his hostage up in front of him. Or he would put the child up first. Either way, there would be a moment when Janroe would be seen apart from the child.

That was the time. You'll be there, Cable thought. Through the store as he walks out, right behind him, and fire from the doorway, from close range.

But if the child was in the way then it would be Vern's shot. Vern shooting from about fifty feet, in the dark.

There was no other way.

When he presented his plan to the others there were objections; but finally, after talking it out and seeing no alternatives, they agreed to it. After that each of them thought about what he would do.

Martha sat on an empty packing case with her arm around Davis next to her. It was dark in the store with the night showing in the doorway and in the window behind Janroe. The counter separated them. On it, pointed at Martha and the boy, was the shotgun. It was within easy reach of Janroe sitting on a high stool with the Colt revolver in his hand.

Davis stirred, squirming on the wooden case, making it creak and causing Janroe to look at them. Martha's hand, with her arm around him, patted Davis gently. There was no sound from the other children now.

They were still locked in the upstairs bedroom and through the long afternoon Martha had listened to the faint sounds of their crying. Perhaps they were asleep now, even though they were frightened and had had nothing to eat since breakfast.

That seemed such a long time ago.

First Luz coming, riding in with the excitement on her face and talking to Janroe. Then returning, coming into the kitchen and telling her that it was over and that Cable was alive.

Then Janroe. She remembered the fear, the desperation in his eyes as he herded them upstairs, pushing them to make them hurry. He made Davis go into the bedroom where Clare and Sandy were playing; but as if something occurred to him, he brought Davis out and locked the door. He herded them downstairs again; closed the kitchen door and kicked at it angrily when he saw it had no lock. From the kitchen he moved them into the store, where they now sat.

When Cable came out of the trees and Janroe called to him to halt, Martha stood up. She caught only a glimpse of her husband in the yard before Janroe ordered her to sit down. Once Cable's voice rose threateningly and Martha tensed, seeing the strained look of desperation come over Janroe's face again.

But as the morning stretched into afternoon, Janroe seemed to gain confidence. Gradually his expression became calm and he sat quietly on the stool, his movements, as he looked from the yard to Martha, less nervous and abrupt.

Martha noticed it. She watched him closely, noting each change in his manner as he became more sure of himself. Occasionally, as he looked outside, her eyes would drop to the shotgun on the counter. It was five feet away, no more than that; but it was pointed at her. It would have to be picked up and turned on Janroe; while all he had to do was raise his revolver a few inches and pull the trigger.

Twice she asked him what had happened, why he was holding them; but both times he refused to talk about it.

Janroe came off the stool when Luz's horse wandered from the platform to the trees. He stood at the window, his attention turned from Martha longer than at any time before. But finally he sat down again.

"My horse left me," Janroe said, looking at Martha. "But all I have to do is call and they'll bring it back." He seemed to be reassuring himself.

Martha watched him. "Then you're leaving?"

"In time."

"Alone?"

"Now wouldn't that be something."

"I didn't think so."

"Your boy's going with me."

Martha hesitated. "Will you take me instead?"

Janroe shook his head. "Him. He's big enough to hold on, little enough to be managed."

Martha felt Davis close to her. She glanced down at his hand in her lap, then at Janroe again. "What will you do to him?"

"That's up to him. Tell him if he cries or tries to run, I'll hurt him something awful." Janroe's eyes moved from the boy to Martha. "He's no good to me dead; least not while I'm getting away from here."

"And after that?"

Janroe shrugged. "I suppose I'll let him go."

"Knowing he'd be lost, and possibly never found?"

"Honey, I've got to look out for myself."

"If you leave him or harm him in any way," Martha said quietly, "my husband will kill you."

"If he finds me he'll try."

"He gave you his word," Martha said. "If you release us, he'll let you go."

"But will Vern?"

"At least talk to him again," Martha urged. "Tell him where you'll leave our boy."

"That would be like giving myself up."

They spoke only occasionally after that. Now the room was silent but for Davis's restless movement. Martha watched Janroe, seeing his heavy-boned profile against the dull gray light behind him.

She thought of Clare and Sandy upstairs and of Davis, not looking at him, but feeling his small body pressed close to her side. If Janroe left with him she might never see her son again. Janroe would sacrifice Davis, admitting it with an offhand shrug, to save his own life. Could that happen? Would God let something like that happen?

No, she thought, don't blame God.

Cabe had an idea about that. People, he said, blamed God for bad luck because they had to blame somebody. Some things you can do something about, and with God's help you can do it even better. But others you can't do anything about, so you wait and try not to worry or feel sorry for yourself.

Which was this?

You can do something, Martha thought. Because you have to do something.

Her eyes went to the shotgun. A dull, thin line of light

extended from the breech to the blunt end of the barrel. Two steps to the counter, Martha thought. Her right hand would go to the trigger, raising the gun, swinging it on Janroe at the same time. Three seconds to do that. Four at the most. But it would take him only one.

Janroe turned from the window. "All right. Tell him he's going with me."

"You won't talk to my husband again? To Vern?"

"Tell him!"

She saw Janroe turn to the window again and call out, "Cable—send Luz over here with the horse!" He waited. "You hear me? Just Luz. If anybody else comes I'll kill your boy." His voice rose to a shout. "I mean it!"

Then it's now, Martha thought. She could feel her heart beating as she bent close to Davis and whispered to him. The boy started to speak, but she touched his mouth with the tips of her fingers, her own lips still close to his ear, telling him calmly, carefully, what he would have to do. The boy nodded and Martha kissed his cheek.

Janroe was looking at her again. "Is he ready?"

Martha nodded.

"As soon as she starts over with the horse, we go out to the platform."

Janroe's elbow rested on the window sill, his right shoulder against the side frame. The Colt in his hand was close to his body and pointed to just below the top of the counter.

When he moves it, Martha thought. The moment he turns.

Janroe looked out, but the Colt remained in the same position. Martha's gaze held on it. She heard him call out again, "Luz, bring the horse! You hear me? Luz—"

Janroe wheeled, seeing Martha already at the counter. She was less than four feet from him, raising the shotgun, turning it on him. He slashed out with the Colt, knocking the barrel aside as Martha's finger closed on one trigger. The blast was almost in his face and he struck the barrel again, lunging against the counter and turning Martha with the force of the blow.

"Janroe!"

Martha heard it—Cable's voice—and in the same moment saw Janroe's Colt swing toward the sound of it. Cable was in the doorway to the sitting room. He fired and Janroe stumbled against the wall. Cable fired again, but this shot smashed into the window frame. Janroe was already moving. He had been hit in the body, but he reached the doorway and lunged out to the platform.

Vern stepped away from the corner of the building. He fired three times, deliberately, taking his time, each shot finding Janroe, the last one toppling him from the edge of the platform.

Martha felt Cable move past her, past Davis, moving quickly but making almost no sound in his stockinged feet. She thought of the children upstairs.

"Davis, get Clare and Sandy."

She heard the boy run into the darkness of the next room before she turned and walked out to the platform to where Cable stood at the edge. Martha looked down, not seeing Janroe on the ground, but thinking of her children and her husband and wanting to be held.

The shotgun barrel slipped through her fingers until the stock touched the boards. She let it fall, feeling Cable's arm come around her.

HOMBRE

A T FIRST I wasn't sure at all where to begin. When I asked advice, this man from the *Florence Enterprise* said begin at the beginning, the day the coach departed from Sweetmary with everybody aboard. Which sounded fine until I got to doing it. Then I saw it wasn't the beginning at all. There was too much to explain at one time. Who the people were, where they were going and all. Also, starting there didn't tell enough about John Russell.

He is the person this story is mainly about. If it had not been for him, we would all be dead and there wouldn't be anybody telling this. So I will begin with the first time I ever saw John Russell. I think you will see why after you learn a few things about him. Three weeks went by before I saw him again and that was the day the coach left Sweetmary. It was in the afternoon, right after they had brought the McLaren girl over from Fort Thomas.

Some things, especially concerning the McLaren girl and also some of my ideas about John Russell at the time, are embarrassing to put on paper. But I was advised to imagine I was telling it to a good friend and not worry about what other people might think. Which is what I have done. If there's anything anybody wants to skip, like innermost thoughts in places, just go ahead.

As for the title, it could be called any one of John Russell's names; he had more than one as you will see. But I think *Hombre*, which Henry Mendez and others called him sometimes and just means *man*, is maybe the best.

For the record, the day the coach left Sweetmary was Tuesday, August 12, 1884. Figure back three weeks if you want to know what day I first met John Russell. It was not at Sweetmary, but at Delgado's Station.

Carl Everett Allen
Contention, Arizona

169

1

HERE IS where I think it begins—with Mr. Henry Mendez, the Hatch & Hodges Division Manager at Sweetmary and still my boss at the time, asking me to ride the sixteen miles down to Delgado's with him in the mud wagon. I suspected the trip had to do with the company shutting down this section of the stage line; Mr. Mendez would see Delgado about closing his station and take an inventory of company property. But that was only part of the reason.

It turned out I was the one had to take the inventory. Mr. Mendez had something else on his mind. As soon as we got to the station, he sent one of Delgado's boys out to John Russell's place to get him.

Until that day John Russell was just a name I had written in the Division account book a few times during the past year. So many dollars paid to John Russell for so many stage horses. He was a mustanger. He would chase down green horses and harness-break them; then Mr. Mendez would buy what he wanted, and Russell and two White Mountain Apaches who rode for him would deliver the horses to Delgado's or one of the other relay stations on the way south to Benson.

Mr. Mendez had bought maybe twenty-five or thirty from him during the past year. Now, I suspected, he wanted to tell Russell not to bring in any more since we were shutting down. I asked Mr. Mendez if that was so. He said no, he had already done that. This was about something else.

Like it was a secret. That was the trouble with Mr. Mendez when I worked for him. From a distance you could never tell he was Mexican. He never dressed like one, everything white like their clothes were made out of bedsheets. He didn't usually act like one. Except that his face, with those tobacco-stained looking eyes and drooping mustache, was always the same and you never knew what he was thinking. When he looked at you, it was like he knew something he wasn't telling, or was laughing at you, no matter what it was he said. That's when you could tell Henry Mendez was Mexican. He wasn't old. Not fifty anyway.

Delgado's boy got back while we were having some coffee and said Russell would be here. A little while later we heard horses, so we went outside.

As we stood there seeing these three riders coming toward the adobe with the dust rising behind them, Mr. Mendez said to me, "Take a good look at Russell. You will never see another one like him as long as you live."

I will swear to the truth of that right now. Though it was not just his appearance.

The three riders came on, but giving the feeling that they were holding back some, not anxious to ride right up until they made sure everything was keno. When Russell pulled up, the two White Mountain Apaches with him slowed to a walk and came up on either side of him. Not close, out a ways, as if giving themselves room to move around in. All three of them were armed; I mean *armed*, with revolvers, with cartridge belts over their shoulder and carbines, which looked like Springfields at first.

As he sat there, that's when I got my first real look at John Russell.

Picture the belt down across his chest with the sun glinting on the bullets that filled most of the loops. Picture a stained, dirty looking straight-brim hat worn almost Indian-fashion, that is, uncreased and not cocked to either side, except his brim was curled some and there was a little dent down the crown.

Picture his face half shadowed by the hat. First you just saw how dark it was. Dark as his arms with the sleeves rolled above his elbows. Dark—I swear—as the faces of the two White Mountain boys. Then you saw how long his hair was, almost covering his ears, and how clean-shaved looking his face was. Right then you suspected he was more to those Apaches than a friend or a boss. I mean he could be a blood relation, no matter what his name was, and nobody in the world would bet he wasn't.

When Mr. Mendez spoke to him you believed it all the more. He stepped closer to John Russell's roan horse, and I remember the first thing he said.

He said, "*Hombre.*"

Russell didn't say anything. He just looked at Mr. Mendez, though you couldn't see his eyes in the shadow of his hat brim.

"Which name today?" Mr. Mendez said. "Which do you want?"

Russell answered Mr. Mendez in Spanish then, just a few words, and Mr. Mendez said, in English, "We use John Russell. No symbol names. No Apache names. All right?" When Russell just nodded, Mr. Mendez said, "I was wondering what you decided. You said you would come to Sweetmary in two days."

Russell used Spanish again, more this time, evidently explaining something.

"Maybe it would look different to you if you thought about it in English," Mr. Mendez said and watched him closely. "Or if you spoke about it now in English."

"It's the same," Russell said, all of a sudden in English. In good English that had only a speck of accent, just a faint edge that you would wonder every time you heard him if it really was some kind of accent.

"But it's a big something to think about," Mr. Mendez said. "Going to Contention. Going there to live among white men. To live as a white man on land a white man has given you. To have to speak English to people no matter what language you think in."

"There it is," Russell said. "I'm still thinking all the different ways."

"Sure," Mr. Mendez said. "You could sell the land. Buy a horse and a new gun with some of the money. Give the rest to the hungry ones at the San Carlos Indian agency. Then you got nothing."

Russell shrugged. "Maybe so."

"Or you sell only the herd and grow corn on the land and make *tizwin*, enough to keep you drunk for seven years."

"Even that," Russell said.

"Or you can work the herd and watch it grow," Mr. Mendez said. "You can marry and raise a family. You can live there the rest of your life." He waited a little. "You want some more ways to picture it?"

"I have too many ways now," Russell said. But he didn't sound worried about it.

That didn't satisfy Mr. Mendez. He was trying to convince him of something and kept at it. He said then, "I hear it's a good house."

Russell nodded. "If living there is worth it to you."

"Man," Mendez said, like something good was staring at Russell and he didn't know enough to take it. "What do you want?"

Russell looked down at him. In that unhurried easy way he said, "Maybe a *mescal* if there's some inside, uh?"

Delgado laughed and said something in Spanish. Mr. Mendez shrugged and both of them turned to the adobe.

I was watching Russell though. He dismounted, still holding his carbine, which I now saw was an old .56-56 Spencer, and came right toward me looking at the ground, then looking up quick as he must have sensed me. For a second we were close and I saw his eyes. They had that same tell-nothing-but-know-everything expression as Henry Mendez's eyes. That same Mexican, Indian look. Only John Russell's eyes were blue, light-blue looking in his Indian-dark face. Maybe that doesn't sound like anything, but I'll tell you it gave me the strangest feeling.

The two Apaches carried Springfields, as I had guessed. They held them cradled across one arm and even with the bullet belts and all, they looked kind of funny. Mainly because of their vests and straw hats that were very narrow and turned up all around. They went inside too and I followed.

Only I didn't stay long. Mr. Mendez sent me out to the equipment shed to start the inventory. Then over to see about the feed stores. So it was maybe a half hour before I got back to the main adobe. Five saddle horses along with the mud wagon were standing in front now instead of three.

Inside, I saw Mr. Mendez and John Russell at one end of the long table the stage passengers sat at. Russell's carbine lay on the table, like he never went far without it; another thing that was just like an Apache.

At the bar along the right wall stood his two Apache riders. Down from them were two more men. I didn't look at them good till I sat down next to Mr. Mendez. Right away then I got the feeling something was going on. It was too quiet. Mendez was looking over at the bar; Russell down at his drink, as if thinking or listening.

So I looked at the two men again. I recognized them as hands who rode for a Mr. Wolgast who supplied beef to the reservation up at San Carlos. I would see them in Sweetmary every once in a while and they would most always be drunk. But it was a minute or two before I remembered their names. One was Lamarr Dean, who was about my age, maybe a year older. The other one's name was Early; he was said to have served time at Yuma Prison.

Delgado poured them a whisky like he'd rather be doing something else. Early, who wore his hat funneled down over his eyes and ordinarily didn't talk much, said, "I guess anybody can come in here."

"If they allow Indians," this Lamarr Dean said. He was looking at the two Apaches. They heard him, you could tell, but didn't pay any attention. Of course not, I realized; they didn't know any English.

The one named Early asked Delgado, "When did they start letting Indians drink?" I didn't hear what Delgado answered.

Lamarr Dean stood with his side against the bar so that he was facing the first Apache. "Maybe they have been drinking *tizwin*," he said. "Maybe that's where they bought the nerve to come in here."

Early said, "It would take a week with *tizwin*."

"They got time," Dean said. "What else do they do?"

"That's *mescal*," Early said then.

Lamarr Dean went on staring. "I guess," he said. He moved toward the first Apache, holding his drink, his elbow sliding along the edge of the bar until he was right next to the Apache. Early stayed where he was.

"*Mescal*," Lamarr Dean said. "But it's still not allowed. Not even sticky-sweet Mex drinks."

The first Apache, not even knowing what was going on, raised his glass. It was right up to his mouth when Lamarr Dean nudged him, reaching out and pushing him a little, and the *mescal* spilled over the Apache's chin and down the front of his vest. He looked at Lamarr Dean then, not understanding, I guess not sure if it was an accident or what.

"They just can't hold it," Lamarr Dean said. "Nobody knows why, but it's a fact of nature." He raised his whisky right in front of the Apache, as if daring the Apache to try the same thing on him.

That was when Russell stood up. His eyes never left Lamarr

Dean, but his right hand closed on the Spencer and it was down at his side as he walked over the few steps to the bar.

Lamarr Dean was facing the Apache, starting to drink, sipping at the whisky to give the Apache all the chance he needed. Like saying come on, nudge my arm and see what happens. Then his chin raised as he started to down the whisky.

Russell was right there. But he didn't nudge him. He didn't ask or tell him to leave the Apache alone. Or say anything like, "If you want to pick on somebody, try me." He didn't give Lamarr a chance to know he was there.

He just swung the barrel of the Spencer up clean and quick and before you had a chance to believe it was happening the barrel shattered the glass right against Lamarr Dean's mouth. Lamarr jumped back, dropping the broken pieces and with blood all over his hand and face.

I think he would have tore into Russell the next second, with his fists or his revolver, but now the Spencer was leveled at his belly, almost touching it. Early had his hand on his gun, but it had happened so fast even he couldn't do anything.

Russell said, "No more, uh?"

Lamarr Dean didn't say anything. I don't think he could talk.

Russell said, "Before you leave, put money down for a *mescal*."

That was John Russell, no older than I was at twenty-one and no more Apache than I was. Except he had lived with them—the wild free ones in the mountains and the wild caught ones up at San Carlos—about half his life and that made the difference. He was perhaps one-part Mexican, according to Mr. Mendez, and three-parts white. But I will go into more of that a little later. Right here I just wanted to tell about the first time I ever saw him.

Now, three weeks later, here is where I was advised to begin— with them bringing the McLaren girl over from Fort Thomas in an ambulance wagon and the lieutenant taking her right into the Alamosa Hotel.

I was out in front of the Hatch & Hodges office at the time, directly across the street, and I got a clear look at the girl even with all the people around. She was seventeen or eighteen and certainly pretty. Though maybe pretty wasn't the word, the way her hair was cut almost as short as a boy's and her face dark from the sun. But she looked good anyway. Even after living with Apaches over a month and after all the things they must have done to her.

Somebody said the girl had been taken by Chiricahuas on a raid and held four or five weeks before a patrol out of Fort Thomas surprised their *ranchería* and found her. She had stayed at Thomas a while and now this officer was to put her on a stage for home. Some place around St. David.

Only by now there weren't any more southbound stages, and there hadn't been for over a week. There were notices all over, but that was like the Army to bring her all the way over to Sweetmary not knowing Hatch & Hodges had shut down its stage service. They told the lieutenant over at the hotel, but he wanted to hear it directly from the company. So he sent one of the escort soldiers for Henry Mendez who went right over.

I stayed out front hoping to get another look at the girl if she came out. That's why I was still there when John Russell appeared, which was some fifteen minutes later.

Somebody might laugh, but just for something to do I was picturing the McLaren girl and I sitting alone in the hotel café. We were talking and I heard myself say, "It must have been a very terrible experience, being with those Apaches." Her eyes stayed on her coffee, and she didn't say anything to that.

So we talked about other things. I heard myself speaking calmly in a low tone, telling her how I would be looking into some other business now that this office was closing. Go some place else. With no family here there was nothing to keep me. Then I pictured us traveling together. (Do you see how one thing led to another?) But what would we travel in?

That's when I thought of the mud wagon, the light spring coach Mr. Mendez and I had taken to Delgado's that day. It was still here.

I said to the McLaren girl, "Since you're anxious to leave and there's no regular stage, I wonder if you would like to ride along with me?" (Which proves that using the mud wagon was my idea; whether Mr. Mendez agrees or not.)

Then I skipped the part where she says yes and goes and gets her things and all and pictured the two of us in the coach again. It was night and we were traveling south. Above the wind and the rattle sounds I'd hear her start to cry and put my arm around her and lift her chin and say something that would calm her. She'd sniffle and nestle closer, and even with the peculiar haircut I'd know she wasn't any boy.

We might have rode along in that coach the whole night while I just stood there in front of the office. But both the McLaren girl and the coach disappeared the second I saw John Russell. The new John Russell.

He was sitting his roan horse on this side of the street but down a ways. He was watching the hotel, sitting there like he'd always been there. Smoking a cigarette, I remember that too. But the only thing I recognized about him right away was his hat, worn straight and the brim just curled a little.

Now he had on a suit. It was a pretty worn dark gray one, but it fit him all right. You could see that his hair had been cut. Without the hair covering the ears and that shell belt and all he wasn't someone you would stare at. At least not till you saw him close.

That was not till a few minutes later. Until Mr. Mendez came out of the hotel and Russell nudged his roan up to in front of the office. As he dismounted he looked at me over the saddle and there was that tell-nothing expression, looking at me no different than the way he had looked at Lamarr Dean the moment before he broke a whisky glass against his mouth.

Mr. Mendez was standing there now. He said, "You're going to do it?"

"I'm going there to sell the place," Russell said.

Mr. Mendez seemed to stare at him for awhile, thinking or just looking, I don't know which. Finally he said, "It's up to you. You can be white or Mexican or Indian. But now it pays you to be a white man. To look like a white man for awhile. When you go to Contention, you say, How are you? I'm John Russell. I own the Russell place. Some people will remember you from before; some won't. But they will all know you as John Russell who owns the Russell place. You look at it. If you don't like it, sell it. If you like it, keep it, and see what happens and then decide." Mr. Mendez almost seemed to smile. "Did you know life was that simple?"

"I've learned some things," John Russell said. "That's why I sell it."

He left his roan horse in front and went with Mr. Mendez back across the street to the Alamosa Hotel. Mr. Mendez hadn't bothered to introduce us. In fact he had not bothered to look at me at all. Which was all right.

A little later this Mexican boy who worked for us took Russell's horse around to the stable. I was in the office then, having given up on seeing the McLaren girl again. The boy came in through the back carrying Russell's blanket roll and carbine and put them down on the passenger bench. I remember thinking, What will he do without the Spencer if Lamarr Dean or Early are over there at the Alamosa?

I also remember thinking at the time that dressing like a white man and taking a white man's name wasn't ever going to hide the Apache in him. I don't mean Apache blood. I just mean after the way he had lived, how was he even going to convince anybody he was a white man? He didn't even prefer to speak English. It was things like that gave you the feeling he had no use for white men or our ways.

According to Mr. Mendez he was most likely three-parts white, as I have said, and the rest Mexican on his mother's side. John Russell himself had no memory of his father and only some memory of living in a Mexican village. Probably in Sonora. At that time they say the Apaches were forever raiding the little pueblos and carrying off whatever they needed, clothes, weapons, some women, and sometimes boys young enough to be brought up Apache-style. Which is what must have happened to John Russell. Piecing things together, he must have lived with them about from the time he was six to about age twelve.

Here is where a James Russell, late of Contention, comes in. At that time he owned supply wagons contracted to the army, and he was at Fort Thomas when this boy who was called *Ish-kay-nay* was brought in with some prisoners. The boy was assigned to a work detail under James Russell and that was how the two became friends. Just a month later, when James Russell sold his business and went to settle in Contention, he took the boy with him and gave him his American name,

John Russell. Five years or so passed and the boy even went to school there. Then all of a sudden he left and went up to San Carlos and joined the reservation police as if to become Apache again. (Here they called him *Tres Hombres*, which I will try to tell you about later.)

Now we are almost up to the present. He was with the police about three years, mostly up at Turkey Creek and Whiteriver. Then he moved again. Off on his own now as a mustanger. (I guess to break horses you don't have to be halter-broke yourself, because he was pretty good at it Mr. Mendez said.)

A month ago, then, when Mr. James Russell died, the word was passed to John Russell through Mr. Mendez that he had been left Russell's place outside Contention. Mr. Mendez wanted to put him on a coach and send him down there in style, but Russell kept backing off. Finally, when he did show up willing, there were no more stagecoaches. As I have explained.

Hatch & Hodges was leaving Sweetmary partly because there wasn't enough business from here south; partly because the railroad was taking too much business other places. But that day, all of a sudden, you'd never know we were hard up for business.

First the McLaren girl had come. Then John Russell. Then, right after he and Mr. Mendez left, a mustered-out soldier from Thomas came in looking for passage to Bisbee. He was going to get married in a week and anxious to get there. I told him how it was and he left, walking over to the hotel.

It wasn't long after that Dr. Favor came.

I had never seen him before, but I had heard of him. So when he came in and introduced himself, I knew this was Dr. Alexander Favor, the Indian Agent at San Carlos.

His name was heard because San Carlos was so close, but not too much. You heard of Indian Agents if they were very good, like John Clum, or if they were bad and got caught dealing poorly with the Indians for their own personal gain. You heard when they weren't at the reservation anymore and you heard of the new man arriving. So I didn't know much about Dr. Favor. Only that he had been up at San Carlos about two years and had a wife that was supposed to be very pretty and about fifteen years younger than he was.

He came in so unexpectedly I probably acted dumb at first. He stood with his hands and his hat on the counter which separated the waiting room from the office part, looking straight at me and never away. He was a big man, not so tall but heavy, with kind of reddish-brown hair—what there was of it—and a finely-kept half-moon beard on his chin. But no mustache. You have probably seen the style I am talking about.

He knew the stage line had stopped running. But what about hiring a rig and driver? I told him we were out of business, even for hiring. He said, but what was the possibility? We talked about that for a while and that was when I got the idea of using the mud wagon. Not just for him but for the McLaren girl too, and just like before I could see myself sitting in it with her.

That's when I started to get excited about the idea. I wanted to get away from here. Why not in the mud wagon? I could talk to Dr. Favor on the way to Bisbee, which was where he wanted to go, and ask his advice about what business to get into. A man like Dr. Favor would know, and maybe he would even have some good connections. Between that and the idea of seeing the McLaren girl, it sounded better and better and finally I got the Mexican boy, who was out front again, and sent him after Mr. Mendez.

About fifteen minutes passed. Dr. Favor came through the gate at the end of the counter and sat at Mr. Mendez's desk. We didn't talk much and I felt dumb again. Finally Mr. Mendez came in.

He came right through the gate. I introduced them and Mr. Mendez nodded. Dr. Favor didn't rise or even reach out his hand.

He said, "We're talking about hiring a coach."

Mr. Mendez looked at me. "Didn't Carl tell you? This office is closed."

"But you still have a coach here," Dr. Favor said. "He called it a mud wagon."

"That." Mr. Mendez leaned back against the counter. "We move our office records in it when we leave."

"Come back to get them," Dr. Favor said.

I said, "They have to be in Bisbee Friday." That was in three days. I even added, "If they don't get there, it'll be too late."

Mr. Mendez just shrugged. "If I could do something—"

I said, "Why not use the mud wagon and come back? We could do that without any trouble."

Mr. Mendez was probably already mad because I was talking up, but he still looked patient. He said, "And who would drive it?"

"I could do it," I said. Which just came to me that moment.

"Do you think the company would put an inexperienced driver on a run like that?"

"Well," I said, "How do you get experience?"

"All of a sudden you want to be a driver."

"I'm trying to help Dr. Favor. If he has to be in Bisbee, I think the company should see he gets there."

"Within the company's power," Mr. Mendez said, still patient. "I think you and I can discuss this another time, uh?"

"That doesn't help Dr. Favor any."

Dr. Favor said, "What if I'm willing to let him drive?"

"You might also be willing to bring suit if something happens," Mr. Mendez said.

"If I bought the rig?" Dr. Favor said.

But Mr. Mendez shook his head. "It's not mine to sell."

"Then if I paid more than just our fares."

"You're anxious to get there," Mr. Mendez said.

"I thought you understood that."

Mr. Mendez nodded his head to the side. "Isn't that your buggy by the hotel? Use that."

"It's government property," Dr. Favor said. "There's a regulation about using it for private matters."

"We have regulations too."

"How much do you want?" Dr. Favor seemed just as patient as Mr. Mendez.

"Well, if there was a driver here."

"Then it comes down to a driver."

"And horses. We would have to get four, six horses."

"All right, get them."

"But I couldn't take responsibility for them," Mr. Mendez said. "Now there are no change stations working. The same horses would have to go all the way." Mr. Mendez shrugged. "If they don't make it, who pays for them?"

"I buy the horses," Dr. Favor said. Mr. Mendez started to

nod, very slowly, as if he was just understanding something. "You want to get there pretty bad, uh?"

"I have a feeling," Dr. Favor said, "you're going to find a driver." He pushed up out of the chair, his eyes on Mr. Mendez. "If I went over to the hotel now and had supper, that would give you about an hour to find a man and get ready. Say six-thirty."

"Tonight?"

"Why not?"

"I'll see," Mr. Mendez said.

"Do that," Dr. Favor said. He moved through the gate, taking his hat from the counter.

"But I won't promise you," Mr. Mendez said after him. The Indian agent just walked out, like it was settled.

I said, soon as he was gone, "Mr. Mendez, I know I can drive it."

"Driving a stage isn't something you know you can do," Mr. Mendez said.

"I've pulled the teams around from the yard plenty of times. And that mud wagon's lighter than a Concord."

"The horses pull it," he said. "Not you."

We argued some more, and finally I said, "Well, who else do you have?"

"Don't worry about it," he said.

"Well, I am worrying, because I want to go too."

He looked at me closely with those brown-stained eyes not telling anything, and I hoped my face was just as calm and natural.

"To talk to this Favor, uh? Get to know him?"

"Why not?"

"It's all right, Carl."

"I was thinking of some others too," I said. "An ex-soldier who was in here. And there's the McLaren girl."

Mr. Mendez nodded again as if he was thinking. "The McLaren girl. Sure," he said. "And maybe John Russell."

It was all right with me. "That would be five inside," I said.

"Six," Mr. Mendez said.

"Not if I'm driving."

Mr. Mendez shook his head. "You're inside like a passenger. How does that sound?"

"Well," I said, "could I ask who's going to drive it then?"

"I am," Mr. Mendez said. "Who else?"

The way Mr. Mendez decided to go all of a sudden didn't make any sense at all until I thought about it a while. And then I realized it might not have been so all of a sudden at that. He could have seen money in this right off and been leading Dr. Favor on, seeing to make about a month's wages in three days if he kept all the fares; and why wouldn't he? That was one thing.

The other was John Russell being here. I think Mr. Mendez wanted to get him on his way before he had time to change his mind; before he spent another night staring at the ceiling and counting all the reasons why he shouldn't go to Contention. Put him in a coach now and by morning Russell might be used to being close to white people again. But why Mr. Mendez bothered or cared was something else. Maybe because he was Mexican and John Russell was part Mexican. Does that make sense?

There was a lot to do before six-thirty. I had the Mexican boy get his father; they'd take care of the coach and horses. Mr. Mendez said he would go to the hotel for John Russell and the McLaren girl and also try and find the ex-soldier. So he would see me later.

Before he went though I reminded him I was going too, and he paid me my last wages. From then on I was no longer with Hatch & Hodges. It was a pretty good feeling, even not knowing what I was going to do in life now.

First thing, I went to the boarding house where I lived and put on my suit. It was pretty old and too small now, making me look skinnier than I was, but it would be all right for the trip. I didn't want to buy a new one in Sweetmary. I thought about buying a gun, but decided against that too; I'd be out of money before I left. I wrote to my mother who lived up at Manzanita with her sister, Mrs. R. V. Hungerford, telling her how I was leaving my position and would write again when I had found some place I liked. Then I rolled up my things in a blanket and went out and had something to eat. By the time I got back to the office it was almost six-thirty.

John Russell was waiting. He was sitting on the bench along the wall on the left. His blanket roll, with the cartridge belt wrapped around it and the Spencer inside with part of the barrel and stock showing, was next to him.

I'll admit he gave me a start, because it was dim in the office and I didn't expect to see anybody. I left my blanket roll by the door and went around behind the counter and started making out a passenger list and tickets. Might as well do it right, I thought. Then it started to feel funny, just the two of us there and nobody talking.

So I said, "You ready for your stagecoach ride?"

His eyes raised and he nodded. That was all.

"What about your horse?"

"Henry Mendez bought it."

"How much he give you?"

"Ask him," Russell said.

"I just wondered, that's all."

"Ask him," Russell said again.

Why bother? I thought, and went on making out the list. I put all the names down but the ex-soldier's because I didn't know his. I just put down Ex-Soldier and never did change it, even when he came in a couple of minutes later with this canvas bag on his shoulder. He swung it down, bouncing it off the counter, and reached into his coat pocket.

"What's the fare?"

"I guess you saw Mendez," I said, and told him how much.

"I don't know the whyfor," he said. "But I'm for it."

He waited while I tore off one of the orange-colored tickets, then another one. "If any stops are open on the way, show this for meals. Drinks are extra. You hand it in when you reach your destination. The other one's for him." I nodded to Russell. "You want to hand it to him?"

The ex-soldier looked at the ticket as he walked over to the bench. He was a heavy man and his coat was tight-smooth across the back. I would judge him to have been about thirty-seven or eight. "I see you're going to Contention," he said, handing the ticket to Russell. "I change there for Bisbee. Yesterday I was in the Army. Next week I'm a mining man and the week after I'll have a wife, one already arranged for and waiting. What do you think of that?"

John Russell pulled the blanket roll toward him as the man

sat down, propping his feet on his canvas bag. "You saving your lamp oil?" the ex-soldier said to me.

"I guess we can spare some." I came around and put a match to the Rochester lamp that hung from the ceiling. Just then I heard the coach and I said, "Here it comes, boys."

You could hear the jingling, rattling sound coming from the equipment yard next door. Then through the window you could see it—smaller than a Concord and almost completely open with its canvas side-curtains rolled up and fastened—just turning out of the yard, and the next moment the jingling, rattling sound was right out front. Four horses were pulling the mud wagon; two spares were on twenty-foot lines tied to the back end.

The ex-soldier said, "I wouldn't complain if it was an ore wagon all loaded."

"It's mainly just for rainy spells," I explained. "Sometimes a heavy Concord gets mired down; but three teams can pull a mud wagon through about anything."

The Mexican boy and his father were both up on the boot. Then Mendez, who must have just crossed the street, was standing there. "Everybody's going," he said. Then looked at John Russell. "Your saddle is on the coach. Now I go up and get myself ready."

I waited till we heard him on the stairs, then told them how I had offered to drive this run, but now that I was a passenger it would be against the rules. "There's rules about who can ride up with the driver," I said, looking at John Russell and wondering if he had any ideas. But that was all the farther I got.

The man who came in was wearing range clothes and carrying a saddle which he let go of just inside the door and came on, looking straight at me, but not smiling like he was ready to say something friendly.

He was tall by the time he reached the counter, with that thin, stringy look of a rider and the *ching-ching* sound of spurs. Even the dust and horse-smell seemed to be still with him, and he reminded you of Lamarr Dean and Early and almost every one of them you ever saw: all made of the same leather and hardly ever smiling unless they were with their own look-alike brothers. Then they were always loud, loud talking and loud laughing. This one had a .44 Colt on his hip and his hat tipped forward with the brim curled almost to a point, the hat loose on his head but seeming to be part of him.

"Frank Braden," he said. His hands spread out along the edge of the counter.

I said, "Yessir?" as if I still worked for Hatch & Hodges.

"Write it down for that coach out front."

"That's a special run."

"I heard. That's why I'm going on it."

I looked down at the four orange cards on the counter, lining them up evenly. "I'm afraid that one's full-up. Four here and those two. That is all the coach holds."

"You can get another on," he said. Telling me, not asking.

"Well, I don't see how."

"On top."

"No one's allowed to ride with the driver. That's a company rule. I was just telling these boys here, certain people can ride inside, certain people outside."

"You say they're going?" He nodded toward the bench.

"Yessir. Both of them."

He turned without another word and walked over to John Russell with that soft *ching*-ing spur sound.

He said, "That boy at the counter said you got a stage ticket."

John Russell opened his hand on his lap. "This?"

"That's it. You give it to me and you can take the next stage."

"I have to take this one," Russell said.

"No, you want to is all. But it would be better if you waited. You can get drunk tonight. How does that sound?"

"I have to take this one," John Russell said. "I have to take it and I want to take it."

"Leave him alone," the ex-soldier said then. "You come late, you find your own way."

Frank Braden looked at him. "What did you say?"

"I said why don't you leave him alone." His tone changed. All of a sudden it sounded friendlier, more reasonable. "He wants to take this stage, let him take it," the ex-soldier said.

You heard that *ching* sound again as Frank Braden shifted around to face the ex-soldier. He stared at him and said, "I guess I'll use your ticket instead."

The ex-soldier hadn't moved, his big hands resting on his knees, his feet still propped on the canvas bag. "You just walk in," he said, "and take somebody else's seat?"

Braden's pointed hat brim moved up and down. "That's the way it is."

The ex-soldier glanced at John Russell, then over at me. "Somebody's pulling a joke on somebody," he said.

Russell didn't say anything. He had made a cigarette and now he lit it, looking at Braden as he blew the smoke up in the air.

"You think I come in here to kid?" Braden asked the ex-soldier.

"Look here, this boy is going to Contention," the ex-soldier explained, "and I'm going to Bisbee to get married after twelve years of Army. We got places to go and no reason to give up our seats."

"All this *we*," Braden said. "I'm talking to you."

The ex-soldier didn't know what to say. And, even with his size, he didn't know what to do with Braden standing over him and not giving an inch. He glanced at John Russell again, then over to me like he'd thought of something. "What kind of a business you run?" he said. "You let a man walk in here and say he's taking your seat—after paying your fare and all—and the company doesn't do a thing about it?"

"Maybe I better get Mr. Mendez," I said. "He's upstairs."

"I think he ought to know about this," the ex-soldier said and started to rise. Braden stepped in closer and the ex-soldier looked up, almost straight up, and you could see then that he was afraid but trying hard not to show it.

"This is our business," Braden said. "You don't want somebody else's nose stuck in."

The ex-soldier seemed to get his nerve back—I guess because he realized he had to do something—and he said, "We better settle this right now."

Braden didn't budge. He said, "Are you wearing a gun?"

"Now wait a minute."

"If you aren't," Braden said, "you better get one."

"You can't just threaten a man like that," the ex-soldier said. "There are witnesses here seeing you threaten me."

Braden shook his head. "No, they heard you call me a dirty name."

"I never called you anything."

"Even if they didn't hear it," Braden said. "I did."

"I never said a word!"

"I'm going to walk out on the street," Braden said. "If you don't come out inside a minute, I'll have to come back in."

That's all there was to it. The ex-soldier stared up at Braden, the cords in his neck standing out, his hands spread and clamped on his knees. And even as he gave up, as he let himself lean back against the wall, he was holding on, knowing he had backed down and it was over, but doing it gradually so we wouldn't see the change come over him. Braden held out his hand. The ex-soldier gave him his ticket. Then he picked up his bag and walked out.

Braden didn't even offer to pay him for the ticket. He watched the ex-soldier till he was gone, then walked over to his saddle and carried it out to the coach. I could feel him right outside, but it bothered me that I hadn't done anything. Or Russell hadn't. I motioned him over to the counter and he came, taking his time and stepping out his cigarette.

"Listen," I said, "shouldn't we have done something?"

"It wasn't my business," Russell said.

"But what if he had taken your ticket?" I stared at him and this close you could see that he was young. His face was thin and you saw those strange blue-colored eyes set in the darkness of his skin.

Russell said, "You would have to be sure he was making it something to kill over."

"He made it plain enough," I said.

"If you were sure," Russell said, "and if the ticket was worth it to you, then you'd do something to keep it."

"But I don't think that soldier even had a gun."

Russell said, "That's up to him if he doesn't carry one." Even the way he said it made me mad; so calm about it.

"He would have helped you and you know it," I said.

"I don't know it," Russell said. "If he did, it would be up to him. But it wouldn't be any of his business."

Just like that. He walked back to the bench and just then

Mendez came in. Now he was wearing a coat and hat and carrying a maleta bag and a sawed-off shotgun.

"Time," Mendez said, sounding almost happy about it. He came through the gate to get something from his desk. That gave me the chance to tell what Braden had done, sounding disgusted as I told it so Mendez would have no doubt what I thought about Braden's trick.

"Then we still have six," Mendez said. That was all.

And that was the six—seven counting Mendez—who left Sweetmary that Tuesday, August 12.

Nothing much happened just before we left. Russell asked to ride up with Mendez, saying they could talk about things.

"Talk," Mendez said. "You can't hear yourself." He pushed Russell toward the coach. "Go on. See what it's like."

Then there was a talk between Mendez and Dr. Favor. Probably about all the other people in what was supposed to be a hired coach. I heard Mendez say, "I haven't seen any money yet." They talked a while and finally must have settled it.

The seating inside was as follows: Russell, the McLaren girl, and I riding backwards, across from Braden, Mrs. Favor, and Dr. Favor. Which was perfect. We sat there a while, almost dark inside after Mendez dropped the side curtains, not saying anything, feeling the coach move up and down on its leather thorough braces as the boy who worked for us put the traveling bags in the rear end boot and covered them with a canvas.

I tried to think of something to say to the McLaren girl, hardly believing she was next to me. But I decided to wait a while before speaking. Let her get comfortable and used to everybody.

So I just started picturing her. She was too close to look right at. But I could feel her there. You had the feeling, when you pictured her, that she looked like a boy more than a woman. Not her face. It was a girl's face with a girl's eyes. It was her body and the way she moved; the thinness of her body and the way she had walked up the hotel steps. You had the feeling she would run and swim. I could almost see her come out of the water with her short hair glistening wet and pressed to her forehead. I could see her smiling too, for some reason.

Mrs. Favor was watching the McLaren girl, staring right at her, so I had a chance to look at Mrs. Favor. Audra was her name, and she was nice looking all right: thin, but still very womanly looking, if you understand me. That was the thing about her. If anybody ever says *woman* to me, like "You should have seen that woman," or, "Now there was a woman for you," I would think of Audra Favor, thinking of her as Audra, too, not as Mrs. Favor, the Indian Agent's wife.

That was because one got the feeling she was not with her husband. Dr. Favor was older than she was, at least fifteen years older, which put her about thirty, and he could have been just another man sitting there. That would be something to watch, I decided. To see if she paid any attention to him.

Frank Braden, I noticed, looked right at Mrs. Favor. With his head turned his face was close to hers and he stared right at her, maybe thinking nobody could see him in the dimness, or maybe not caring if they did.

Just before we left, I raised up to straighten my coat and sneaked a look at the McLaren girl. Her eyes were lowered, not closed, but looking down at her hands. Russell, his hat tilted forward a little, was looking at his hands too. They were folded on his lap.

What would these people think, I wondered, if they knew he'd been living like an Apache most of his life, right up until a little while ago? Would it make a difference to them? I had a feeling it would. I didn't think of myself as one of them, then; now I don't see why I should have left myself out. To tell the truth, I wasn't at all pleased about Russell sitting in the same coach with us.

When the coach started to roll I said, "Well, I guess we'll be together for a while."

2

THERE WASN'T much talking at all until Mrs. Favor started after the McLaren girl. I saw her watching the girl for the longest time and finally she said, "Are those Indian beads?"

The McLaren girl looked up. "It's a rosary."

"I don't know why I thought they were Indian beads," Mrs. Favor said. Her voice soft and sort of lazy sounding, the kind of voice that most of the time you aren't sure if the person is kidding or being serious.

"You might say they are Indian beads," the girl said. "I made them."

"During your experience?"

Dr. Favor said, "Audra," very low, meaning for her to keep quiet.

"I hope I didn't remind you of something unpleasant," Mrs. Favor said.

Braden, I noticed, was looking at the McLaren girl too. "What happened?" he said.

The McLaren girl did not answer right away, and Mrs. Favor leaned toward the girl. "If you don't want to talk about it, I can understand."

"I don't mind," the McLaren girl said.

Braden was still looking at her. He said again, "What happened?"

"I thought everybody knew," the McLaren girl said.

"Well," Braden said. "I guess I've been away."

"She was taken by Apaches," Mrs. Favor said. "With them, how long, a month?"

The McLaren girl nodded. "It seemed longer."

"I can imagine," Mrs. Favor said. "Did they treat you all right?"

"As well as you could expect, I guess."

"I suppose they kept you with the women."

"Well, we were on the move most of the time."

"I mean when you camped."

"No, not all the time."

"Did they—bother you?"

"Well," the McLaren girl said, "I guess the whole thing was kind of a bother, but I hadn't thought of it that way. One of the women cut my hair off. I don't know why. It's just now starting to grow back."

"I meant did they *bother* you?" Mrs. Favor said.

Braden was looking right at her. "You can talk plainer than that," he said.

Mrs. Favor pretended she didn't hear him. She kept her eyes on the McLaren girl and you could see what she was trying to get at. Finally she said, "You hear so many stories about what Indians do to white women."

"They do the same thing to them they do to Indian women," Braden said, and after that no one spoke for a minute. All the sounds, the rattling and the wind hissing by, were outside. Inside it was quiet.

I kept thinking that somebody ought to say something to change the subject. In the first place I felt uneasy with the talk about Apaches and John Russell sitting there. Second, I thought Braden certainly shouldn't have said what he did with ladies present, even if Mrs. Favor had started it. I thought Dr. Favor would say something to her again, but he didn't. He could have been seven hundred miles away, his hand holding the side curtain open a little and staring out at the darkness.

I would like to have said that I thought Mr. Braden should be reminded that there were ladies present, but instead I said, "I don't know if the ladies enjoy this kind of talk very much." That was a mistake.

Braden said, "What kind of talk?"

"I mean about Apache Indians and all."

"That's not what you meant," Braden said.

"Mr. Braden." The McLaren girl, her hands folded in her lap, was looking directly at him. "Why don't you just be quiet for a while?"

Braden was surprised, as all of us were, I suppose. He said, "You speak right up, don't you?"

"I don't see any other way," she said.

"I was talking to that boy next to you."

"But it concerned me," the McLaren girl said. "So if you'd be so kind as to shut up, I'd appreciate it."

That was something for her to say. The only trouble was,

it egged Braden on. "A nice girl talking like that," he said, watching her. "Maybe you lived with them too long. Maybe that's it. You live with them a while and you forget how a white person talks."

I couldn't see Russell's face or his reaction to all this. But a minute later I could see what was going to happen, and I began thinking every which way of how to change the subject.

"A white woman," Mrs. Favor said, "couldn't live the way they do. The Apache women rubbing skins and grinding corn, their hair greasy and full of vermin. The men no better. All of them standing around or squatting, picking at themselves and the dogs sniffing them. They even eat the dogs sometimes."

She was watching the McLaren girl again, leading up to something, but I wasn't sure what. "I wonder," she said, "if a woman could fall into their ways and after a while it wouldn't bother her. Like eating with your fingers. Or do you suppose you could eat a dog and not think anything of it?"

Here's where you could see it coming.

John Russell said, "What if you didn't have anything else to eat?" This was the first time he'd spoken since we left Sweetmary. His voice was calm, but still there was an edge to it.

Mrs. Favor looked from the McLaren girl to Russell.

"I don't care how hungry I got. I know I wouldn't eat one of those camp dogs."

"I think," John Russell said, "you have to know the hunger they feel before you can be sure."

"The government supplies them with meat," Mrs. Favor said. "Every week or so I'd see them come in for their beef ration. And they're allowed to hunt. They can hunt whenever their rations are low."

"But they are always low," Russell said. "Or used up, and there's not game enough to take care of everybody."

"You hear all kinds of stories of how the Indian is oppressed by the white man," Dr. Favor said. I was surprised that he had been listening and seemed interested now.

He said, "I suppose you will always hear those stories as long as there is sympathy for the Indian's plight, and that's a good thing. But you have to live on a reservation for a time, like San Carlos, to see that caring for Indians is not a simple matter of giving them food and clothing."

He was watching John Russell all the while and seemed to be picking his words carefully. "You see all the problems then that the Interior Department is faced with," he said. "The natural resentment on the part of the Indians, their distrust, their reluctance to cultivate the soil."

"Having to live where they don't want to live," John Russell said.

"That too," Dr. Favor agreed. "Which can't be helped for the time being." His eyes were still on Russell. "Do you happen to know someone at San Carlos?"

"Many of them," Russell said.

"You've visited the agency?"

"I lived there. For three years."

"I didn't think I recognized you," Dr. Favor said. "Did you work for one of the suppliers?"

"On the police," Russell said.

Dr. Favor didn't say anything. I couldn't see his expression in the dimness, only that he was still looking at Russell.

Then his wife said, "But the police are all Apaches."

She stopped there, and all you heard was the rattling and creaking and wind rushing past and the muffled pounding of the horses.

I thought, Now he'll explain it. Whether he thinks they'll believe him or not, at least he'll say something.

But John Russell didn't say a word. Not one single word. Maybe he's thinking how to explain it, I thought. There was no way of knowing that. But he must have been thinking something and I would have given anything to know what it was. How he could just sit there in that silence was the hardest thing I have ever tried to figure out.

Finally Mrs. Favor said, "Well, I guess you never know."

You never know what? I thought. You never know a lot of things. Still, it was pretty plain what she meant.

Braden was looking at me. He said, "You let anybody on your stage?"

"I don't work for the company anymore," I answered. I'll admit, it was a weak-sister thing to say, but why should I stick up for Russell?

This wasn't any of my business. He couldn't help the ex-soldier, saying it was none of his business. All right, this was none of my business. If he wanted to act like an uncivilized person—which is what he must be and you could see it clearer all the time—then let him alone. Let him act any way he wanted.

I wasn't his father. He was full grown. So let him talk for himself if he had anything to say.

But maybe he even thought he really was Apache. That had never occurred to me before. It would have been something to look into his mind. Not for long. Not for more than a few minutes; just time enough to look around with his eyes, around and back at things that had happened to him. That would tell you a few things.

I started to think of the stories Henry Mendez had told about Russell, piecing little bits of it together now.

How he had been Juan something living in a Mexican pueblo before the Apaches came raiding and took some of the women and children. How he had been named *Ish-kay-nay* and brought up by these Chiricahuas and made the son of Sonsichay, one of the sub-chiefs of the band. Five years with them and he must have learned an awful lot.

Then, after that, living in Contention with Mr. James Russell until he was about sixteen. He had gone to school there. And he had almost killed a boy in a fight. Maybe there was a good reason he did it. But he had left soon after, so maybe there wasn't a good reason; maybe he just couldn't be taught anything.

Then the most interesting part. How John Russell got his next name, *Tres Hombres.*

He had been with the mule packers on that campaign of the Third Cavalry's, chasing down into Mexico after the bands of Chato and Chihuahua, and he got his new name in a meadow high in the Sierra Madre, two days west of the village of Tesorababi.

He had gone out looking for these mule packers who had wandered off the trail, hunting them all day and finding them, three *mozos* and eighteen mules, an hour before dark and a moment before the sudden gunfire came out of the canyon walls and caught them and ended four of the mules.

John Russell, who was sometimes Juan or Juanito, but more often *Ish-kay-nay* to the older ones of the Apache Police, shot six more of the mules in the moments that followed and he and the *mozos* laid behind the dead mules all night and all the next day. The Apaches, nine or ten of them, came twice. Running and screaming the first time they left two dead before they could creep back out of range of John Russell's Spencer. That was the evening of the first day. They came again at dawn, silently through the rocks with their bodies mud-streaked and branches of mesquite in their headbands. They said that John Russell, with the Spencer steadied on the neck of a dead mule, waited until he was sure. He fired seven times with the Spencer, taking his time as they came at him, and emptied his Colt revolver at them as they ran. Maybe two more were hit.

The packers, their eyes closed and their bodies tight against the mules while the firing was going on, smiled at John Russell and laughed with relief at their fear when it was over. And, when they returned to the main column, they told how this one had fought like three men against ten times as many of the barbarians. From then on, among the Apache Police at San Carlos, the trackers at Fort Apache and Cibucu, John Russell was known as *Tres Hombres*.

But knowing all this wasn't the same as seeing things through his eyes. Maybe his past relations with white people explained why he acted the way he did, why he didn't speak up now, but I'm not sure. Maybe you can see it.

It was colder later on, so I got the two robes from the floor and handed one of them to Dr. Favor. He took it and his wife spread it out so it would cover Frank Braden too. I unfolded the other robe for our seat. There was the soft clicking sound of the McLaren girl's beads as she raised her hands. She gathered the end of the robe close to her, wedging it against her leg and not offering any of it to John Russell. I even had the feeling she had moved closer to me, but I wasn't sure.

I heard Dr. Favor say something to his wife; the sound not the words. She told him not to be silly. I asked the McLaren girl if she was comfortable. She said, yes, thank you. Mostly though, no one spoke. It was a lot colder and the canvas curtains, that were all the way down now, would be flat one minute, then snap and billow out with the wind and through the opening you could see the darkness and shapes now and then going by alongside the road.

Frank Braden had eased lower in the seat and his head was very close to Mrs. Favor's. He said something to her, a low murmur. She laughed, not out loud, almost to herself, but you could hear it. Her head moved to his and she said one word or maybe a couple. Their faces were close together for a long time, maybe even touching, and yet her husband was right there. Figure that one out.

We came in to Delgado's Station with the slowing, braking sound of the coach coming off the slope that stretched out toward a wall of trees and the adobes that showed faintly against the trees. The coach kept rolling slower and slower and slower, with the sound of the horses getting clear and heavy, and finally we stopped. We sat there in silence and when Mrs. Favor said, "Where are we?" in just a whisper, it sounded loud inside that coach in the darkness. No one answered until we heard Henry Mendez outside.

"Delgado!" he yelled.

Then close on it came the sound of his steps and the door opened. "Delgado's Station," Mendez said. He stood there holding his leather bag. Beyond him, a man was coming out of the adobe carrying a lantern.

"Mendez?" The man raised the lantern.

"Who else?" Mendez said. "You still got horses?"

"For a few more days," Delgado, the stationmaster, answered.

"Change them for these."

"You got a stage?"

"A long story," Mendez said. "Get your woman to make coffee."

Delgado was frowning. He wore pants with striped suspenders over his underwear. "How do I know you're coming?"

"Just move your people," Mendez said. He turned to the coach again. "You wash at the bench by the door. You follow the path around back for other things." He offered his hand and Mrs. Favor got out. Then the McLaren girl.

"Twice in one night," Delgado said. "An hour ago we are in bed and three men come by."

"You should have stayed up," Mendez said.

Mr. Favor was just getting out of the coach. "Did you know them?" he asked.

"Some riders."

"But did you know them?"

Delgado looked thoughtful. "I don't know. I think they work for Mr. Wolgast."

"Is that usual," Dr. Favor said, "them coming by this time of night?"

"Man, it happens," Delgado said. "People go by here."

By the time I went around back and came out again, just Mendez and Russell were standing there. Mendez took a bottle that looked like brandy out of his leather bag and both of them had a long drink.

Two boys, in shirts and pants but barefooted, came out of the adobe. Both of them smiled at Mendez and one of them called, "Hey, Tio, what have you got?"

"Something for your grease pails," Mendez said, "and the need of clean horses." The boys ran off again, around the adobe, and Mendez turned to John Russell again.

"How do you like a mud wagon?"

Russell said something in Spanish.

"How do you like it in English?" Mendez said.

"That again," Russell said.

"Practice, uh? Then you get good."

"Maybe if I don't speak it's better."

"And what does that mean?" Mendez asked.

Russell didn't say anything. One of the boys came running out again with a bucket and Mendez said, "Paint them good, *chico*."

"This costs more at night," the boy said, still smiling, as if still smiling from before.

"I'll pay you with something," Mendez said. He took a swipe at the boy with the leather bag, but the boy got past him. Then he offered the brandy to Russell again. "For the dust," he said. "Or whatever reason you want."

While Russell was taking a drink, Mendez saw me and offered me one, so I joined them and had a swallow. It was all right, except it was so hot. I don't know how they took the big swigs they did. Mendez took his turn then handed the bottle to Russell and went into the adobe.

The Mexican boy with the grease pail was working on the front wheels now. The other boy had unhitched the lead team and was taking the horses off. We watched them a while. Then I said, "How come you didn't tell them?"

He looked at me, holding the bottle. "Tell them what?"

"That you're not what they think."

His eyes looked at me another second. Then he took a drink of the brandy.

"You want to go in?" I said. He just shrugged.

We went in then—into a low-ceilinged room that was lighted by one lantern hanging from a beam; the lantern had smoked and there was still the oil smell of it in the room.

The Favors and the McLaren girl and Braden were sitting at the main table, a long plank one in the middle of the room. Mendez stood there like he had been talking to them. But he moved away as we came in and motioned us over to a table by the kitchen door. Delgado's wife came out with a pot of coffee, but went over to the main table before pouring us some. Mendez waited, looking at Russell all the while, until she went out to the kitchen again.

"They think you're Apache," he said.

Russell didn't say anything. He was looking at the brandy bottle as if reading the small print. Mendez picked up the brandy and poured some of it in his coffee.

"You hear what I said?"

"Does it make a difference?" Russell said then.

"Dr. Favor says you shouldn't ride in the coach," Mendez said. "That's the difference."

Russell's eyes raised to Mendez. "They all say that?"

"Listen, you wanted to ride with me before."

"Do they all say I shouldn't be in the coach?"

Mendez nodded. "Dr. Favor said they agreed to it. I said this boy isn't Apache, did you ask if he was? Did you ask him anything? But this Favor says he isn't going to argue about it."

Russell kept looking at Mendez. "What did you say?"

"Well—I don't know," Mendez said. "Why have people unhappy? Why not just"—he shrugged—"let them have their way? It isn't a big thing. I mean I don't know if it's something worth making trouble about. He's got this in his mind now and we don't have time to convince him of the truth. So why should we let it worry us, uh?"

"What if I want to ride in the coach?" Russell said.

"Listen, you wanted to ride with me before. Why all of a sudden you like it inside now?"

It was the first time I ever saw Mendez look worried, like something was happening that he couldn't handle or have an answer for. He drank some of his coffee, but looked up quickly, holding the cup, as Braden and Dr. Favor rose from the table. Braden went outside. Dr. Favor went over to the bar where Delgado was, and Mendez seemed to relax a little and sip his coffee.

"Is it worth arguing about?" Mendez said. "Getting people upset and angry? Sure, they're wrong. But is it easier to convince them of it or just forget about it? You understand that?"

"I'm learning," Russell said.

Right there, again, I'd like to have seen what was going on in his mind, because you certainly couldn't tell from his tone. He had such a quiet way of speaking you got the feeling nothing in the world would ever bother him.

While we were still sitting there, Dr. Favor motioned Mendez over to the bar where he and Delgado were. Mendez stood there talking to them for a long time, while we finished our coffee and had another. Finally Mendez came back. He didn't sit down but took a drink of the brandy.

"Dr. Favor wants to go another way," Mendez said. "The road down past the old San Pete Mine."

It was a road Hatch & Hodges had used years before when the mine was still in operation. It ran fifteen or so miles east of the main road, through foothills and on up into high country past the mine, then it joined the present main road again on the way to Benson. But I had never heard of anyone taking it these days. The country through there was wild and climbing, harder to travel over. That's why the new road had been put through after the mine shut down. The only thing you could say about the old road was it was shorter.

But was that reason to take it?

Mendez said why not? Delgado was sure the rest of the stations along the main road had already shut down. At least all their change horses had been moved south by now. Delgado was the only one left with any and his would be gone in a few days. If we have only six horses and there are no more stations, Mendez said. Why not go the short way?

That made sense. We'd have to bring extra food and water, though. Mendez agreed to that. He said as long as Dr. Favor was paying for most of this, why not keep him happy? (Henry Mendez seemed very anxious to keep people happy.)

"Maybe he's a little worried too," Mendez said. "He was talking to Delgado again about those people who came by here. What did they look like? Did they say where they were going? Things like that."

"If he thinks they plan to hold us up," I said, "they couldn't. They wouldn't know a stage was coming by here tonight."

"I told him that," Mendez said. "He said, 'If there is a possibility of being stopped, we should take precautions.' I said, 'Maybe, but, if this was the regular stage, we wouldn't even be talking about it.'"

"Maybe he is really worried," I said.

Mendez nodded. "Like something's after him. And he knows it."

A little later, after Mendez had seen about the provisions and water bags, we got moving again. Frank Braden was already in the coach asleep with his feet on the seat across from him. We just let him be. There was room enough with John Russell up on the boot now.

Soon we were alone in the night with the rumbling and creaking sounds. We turned off the road about two miles south of Delgado's and went through a mesquite thicket with the branches scraping both sides of the coach. Then this trail opened up and you could feel it beginning to climb. We would move through trees, in and out of close darkness, all the time following the winding, climbing road that led on and on, two rutted tracks that were overgrown but I guess still visible to Mendez.

About three hours out of Delgado's, Mendez and Russell changed the teams, giving the two spares a turn in the harness, and watering them. I was the only one who got out of the coach, though I'm sure Dr. Favor was awake too. I had a drink of water from Mendez's canteen (this was kept in the driver's boot; three hide bags of water on the back end were for the passengers and the horses) and then we were off again.

I went to sleep after that, wondering for the longest time if the McLaren girl would say anything if I was to put my arm around her. I never did find out.

With the first signs of daylight and down out of a winding, steep-sided canyon, we came to the abandoned San Pete mine. Mendez and Russell were standing there as we got out, everybody stretching, feeling the stiffness from being cramped up so long, and looking around at the company buildings.

The ones near us were built against the slope so that the front verandas were on stilts and high as a second floor. Out across the canyon the mine works were about two hundred yards off: the crushing mill part way up the slope, the ore tailings that humped in hogbacks down from the mine shaft way up higher. Braden was looking at Mendez. "This isn't the stage road," he said.

"We took a different way," Mendez answered. He was at the back untying one of the water skins.

"What do you mean a different way?"

I noticed John Russell step away from the horses. He watched Braden move toward Mendez who was lifting the water skin to his shoulder.

"You take any road you feel like?"

"Talk to Dr. Favor," Mendez said.

"I'm talking to you."

Mendez had started for the building, but he stopped. "The others agreed on it," he said. "You were asleep. But I thought, if he wants to come with us so bad then this is all right with him."

Braden kept watching him. "Where does it lead?"

"Same places," Mendez answered. He took the water skin under the veranda and came out again stretching, looking up at the sky that was still dull though streaked with traces of sunlight above the far end of the canyon. "We eat now," Mendez said. "Then rest for two hours."

Dr. Favor said, "If you're thinking of us—"

"More of the horses," Mendez said. "And me."

We ate breakfast under the veranda of the main company building, some of the bread and cold meat and coffee Mendez had brought. And after Mendez took his blanket roll to the next house, the only one besides the main one that still had a roof. John Russell went with him and they slept for a couple of hours.

So there was nothing to do but wait during that time. The mud wagon stood alone with the horses grazing farther down the canyon where there was grass and some owl clover. After a while Frank Braden walked out past the coach, gazing at the slope above the mine works, then looking up-canyon, the way he had come. He went on getting smaller and smaller as he crossed the canyon and got up by the crushing mill. He kept going, finally reaching what looked like an assay shack high up by the mine shaft and you couldn't see him any more. I wondered if he was waiting for Mrs. Favor to come up. That or he was just restless.

Whichever, Braden was back in plenty of time. He had calmed down and he asked Mendez how long it would take to reach Benson. Mendez told him this way was shorter than the stage road, but we had the horses to consider. So maybe it would take just as long, arriving in Benson sometime tomorrow morning if the road was all right and if nothing happened.

Well, we left the San Pete mine before eight o'clock and by midnight the first *if* came true.

The trouble was not in following the road, a matter of whether or not the road was "all right." There was just no road to follow. We crossed a shallow arroyo that came down out of the high rocks, and on the other side, where the road should have continued, there was no trace of it.

Wind and rock slides and flash floods had worn the road away or covered it or wiped it clean from the slope. Mendez had no choice. He took the coach down the arroyo, bucking, fighting down through the yellow *palo verdes* that grew along the banks waiting for water, then south again, out into the flat brush country to circle the dry washes and rock formations that extended out from the slopes.

The land lay dead in the heat of the sun, bone dry and thick with greasewood and prickly pear and tall saguaro that looked like fence posts growing wild. Henry Mendez did a good job driving through this, but it took forever. You would look ahead and see an outcropping of rock or a scattering of Joshua trees that looked only a few hundred yards off, but it would take even an hour to reach them and after passing them there would be other marks on the land, like a strangely shaped giant saguaro or more Joshuas or yucca, that would take forever to reach and finally pass. There was nothing to look at, nothing to look forward to.

We stopped to alternate the horses once during the morning, discovering only two waterskins on the back end. We had left one, more than half full, at the San Pete mine.

We stopped again at noon, all of us standing by the coach waiting for the coffee water to boil, Mendez unhitching the teams and feeding them from morrals, Mendez probably waiting for one of the passengers to say this was crazy and why didn't we go back to the stage road? Lose a day, but at least not have to put up with this. But no one said it.

It was strange. There was Mrs. Favor saying it was hot, saying it different ways, but not seeming to mind it. She would glance now and then at the McLaren girl, probably still wondering what the Indians did to her, then look at Braden who had turned quiet today and seemed a different person, as if the effects of whisky had worn off him (though I am not saying he showed any signs of drunkenness the day before). There was the McLaren girl, seeming to be the most patient, aside from Russell (how could it bother him to be out here), and Dr. Favor who watched Mendez, trying to hurry him with his eyes. Nobody asked Mendez if we might get lost or break down. Nobody seemed worried at all. Not even about having left some of our water behind at the San Pete.

We went on, and it was afternoon before we got out of that flat country. Mendez saw the road again up on the slope, a trace of it cutting through the brush, and headed for it. You could see the hills getting bigger and clearer as we approached, shadowed and dark with brush and washes, but up above the peaks looked bare and silent in the sunlight.

We got up to the road and followed it easily for a while, but then it started to climb again, getting higher up into the hills, and finally Mendez pulled in the team.

He leaned down and said, "Everybody takes a nice walk. To the top of the grade."

We got out, all of us looking up, seeing a pretty steep section ahead. Russell was already walking up it, I guess making sure there weren't any washouts we couldn't see from here. The slope wasn't too steep, but Mendez, you could tell, was thinking of the horses.

So we waited until the coach and trailing horses were past us a ways and then started up. Dr. Favor took hold of his wife's arm as if to help her walking, but I think it was so she wouldn't wander off. Frank Braden stood there to make a cigarette, so I fell in with the McLaren girl, thinking hard of something to say. But I didn't have to think for more than a few steps.

She said, "He doesn't look Apache, does he?" as if she'd started right in the middle of her thoughts.

But even that abruptly I knew she was talking about Russell. No question about it. She was squinting a little in the sunlight, looking at him way up on the road.

"You should have seen him a few weeks ago," I said.

She looked at me, waiting for me to explain, and I was a little sorry I'd said it. Still, it was a fact.

"He looked like any other Indian on Army pay."

"Then he *is* Apache?"

"Well, maybe you can't answer that yes or no."

She was frowning a little. "Mr. Mendez said he isn't. That's what I don't understand."

"Well, he wasn't born one. But he's lived with them so long, I mean by his own choice, that maybe he is one by now."

"But why," she said, "would anybody *want* to be one?"

"That's it," I said. "Wanting to be one is just as bad as being one. Maybe worse."

"But wanting to live the way they do," she said.

"You'd have to see things with his eyes to understand that."

"I think I'd be afraid to," she said.

I wanted to say that I didn't think she'd be afraid of anything after what she'd been through, but then thought it best to stay wide of that subject. It could be embarrassing for her. She had talked a little about it in the coach and hadn't seemed embarrassed, but still there could be touchy things. It was like being with a person who has a great big nose or something. You don't want to get caught looking at the nose or even saying the word.

(I hope no one reading this who might have a big nose will take offense. I wasn't making fun of noses.)

The trailing horses were still on the grade, but the coach had passed over the crest and stopped. You could only see the top part of it at first. The road leveled into pinyon and a lot of brush, and on the right side, slanting down at the coach, was a steep cutbank about seven or eight feet high.

"I guess we can get in again," the girl said.

I heard her, but I was watching Mendez. He was looking up at the top of the bank.

We walked around the trailing horses and I looked up there too. My first thought was, what is Russell doing sitting up there? And where did he get the rifle?

Then I saw Russell, not on the cutbank but beyond the Favors and up by the teams. Near him, at the banked side of the road, was another man, holding a revolver. I guess the McLaren girl saw them the same time I did, but she didn't let out a peep.

What is there to say, for that matter? You walk up a road out in the middle of nowhere and there are two armed men waiting for you. Even though you know something is wrong, you act as if this happens every day and twice on Sunday. I mean you don't get excited or act surprised. You just hold yourself in and maybe they will go away if you don't admit they are there. You don't think at the time: I am afraid. You are too busy acting natural.

The man on the bank came down to the edge and squatted there holding the rifle (it was a Henry) on us until we were up even with the coach. Then he jumped down to the road, almost falling, and as he stood up I recognized him at once.

It was the one named Lamarr Dean who rode for Mr. Wolgast. And the other one up by Russell, sure enough, was Early. The same two who had been at Delgado's the first time I ever saw John Russell.

What if they recognize him, I thought. Not—what's going on? Or what are they doing here? But—what if they recognize him? I couldn't help thinking that first because I remembered so well how Russell had broken that whisky glass against Lamarr Dean's mouth. Lamarr Dean must have remembered it even better. But he hadn't recognized him. Early hadn't either, else he wouldn't have just been standing there holding that long-barreled revolver.

Mendez, looking down at Lamarr Dean, said, "You better think before you do something."

"Step down off there and don't worry about it," Lamarr Dean said. Mendez climbed down and Lamarr Dean looked over toward us. He waited; I didn't know why until Braden came up past us and Lamarr Dean's eyes followed him. He said, "We like to not made it."

"I kept thinking," Braden said, "they got some catching up to do once they find the way."

"When you didn't come by the main road," Lamarr Dean said, "we went back to Delgado's early this morning. I said to him, 'Are we hearing things or was that a coach passed us last night?' He said, 'You must have been hearing things; there was a coach but it wasn't on the main road. 'Which way did it go?' I said and that was when he told me you'd taken this other way and I'll tell you we done some riding."

I kept looking at Braden all the time Lamarr Dean was talking. Maybe you aren't surprised now why Braden took the stage in the first place and was so anxious to be on it when we left Sweetmary. It is easy to think back and say I knew it all the time. But I'll tell you I couldn't believe it at first. Braden was not a person you liked, but he was one of us, a passenger like everybody else, and, when he showed himself to be part of this holdup, it must have surprised the others as much as it did me. Though at the time I didn't look to see their reaction. Too much was going on.

Early came over, not saying anything, his face dark with beard growth. He was prodding Russell ahead of him.

Then another man appeared. He looked like a Mexican and wore a straw hat. He was mounted and walked his horse out of the trees, leading two other saddled horses, and stood there in front of the teams. I noticed he wore two .44 revolvers.

Lamarr Dean stood with his hand through the lever of the Henry, his finger on the trigger, but the barrel pointed down and almost touching the ground.

"Old Dr. Favor's pretending he don't see us," Lamarr Dean said.

He moved me aside and motioned the McLaren girl over against the cutbank. "You all spread out so I can see my old friend." Dean was looking directly at Dr. Favor then. "Things start to close in on you?" he asked.

"I'm afraid you're beyond me," Dr. Favor said, though not sounding surprised.

"Ahead of you," Lamarr Dean said. "I've seen this coming for two, three months."

"You've seen what coming?"

"Frank, he's still pretending."

Braden came up beside Lamarr Dean. "He's used to it."

"We're going to Bisbee," Dr. Favor said. "On business. We'll be there two days at most."

"No," Lamarr Dean said. "You'll be there just long enough to get a ride south. You'll hole up in Mexico or else get a boat in Vera Cruz and head out."

"You're sure of that," Dr. Favor said.

"That's how it's done."

"And if I deny it, tell you we're going back in two days?"

"What's the sense?"

"He should be over here with a gun," Braden said.

"No," Lamarr Dean said. "He uses his ink pen. All you do is write down a higher beef tally than what comes in. Pay the trail driver U.S. government scrip for what's delivered and keep the overpayment. Isn't that right, Doctor?"

"Like he never saw you before," Braden said.

Lamarr Dean looked at Mrs. Favor. "You pretending too?"

"I know you," she said, pretty calmly, considering everything. "But I don't remember him," nodding to Braden.

"No, Frank wasn't anywhere near. He was still in Yuma then."

"I guess that's enough," Braden said. "We got things to do."

"I was just trying to understand it," Mrs. Favor said easily. Her eyes shifted to Lamarr Dean who she knew by now was the talker among them. "You were working for the man who had the contract to supply beef."

"Mr. Wolgast."

"And you found out about my husband."

"Audra," Dr. Favor said, sounding unconcerned but hardly taking his eyes from Lamarr Dean or Braden, while the rest of us couldn't help but watch him. (My gosh, the things we were learning all of a sudden!) "Audra," he said, "you know we don't have to talk about our personal business to these people."

Braden moved away. "Let's get to it," he said and nodded to Early who started unhitching the team horses. As he stripped off the harness and brought them out, slapping them and keeping them moving, the Mexican, who was still mounted, bunched the horses and started them along.

The road formed two tracks out across a grassy meadow that was wide, pretty wide across and stetched on at least a mile with slopes rising up on both sides. As soon as the Mexican was off a ways, Early mounted up again and started after him.

Braden was behind the coach now and we saw just part of him as he yanked down the canvas and started pulling the bags off.

Lamarr Dean started looking us over then, I mean to see if we were armed. He took a revolver from inside Dr. Favor's coat, a small caliber gun that he studied for a minute then threw off into the brush on the other side of the road. He went on to Mendez, passing Mrs. Favor and the McLaren girl, and Mendez opened his coat to show he was unarmed.

"What about up in the boot?" Lamarr Dean asked.

"A shotgun," Mendez said.

"See it stays there and you here," Lamarr Dean said. He came on to me and I opened my coat as Mendez had done.

As Lamarr Dean looked me over Mendez said, "You think it's worth it? You won't be able to show your face again."

"I appreciate it," Lamarr said, "but don't give me no advice please."

"I would bet you're dead or arrested in two weeks," Mendez said.

Lamarr glanced at him now. "You won't have nothing to bet with."

"All right, then remember it," Mendez said. "You already have witnesses."

"I don't see any," Lamarr Dean said. Braden came from behind the coach with a leather satchel. "Frank, you see any witnesses?"

"Not here," Braden said. He knelt down to open the satchel.

Lamarr Dean moved on to Russell. "This one doesn't look

like any witness to me. Mister," Lamarr said, "are you a witness?" He pulled Russell's Colt as he said it and flung it back-
handed, high up so that it glinted with the sun catching it, and
down the road, bouncing and skidding way down it.

But Lamarr Dean wasn't watching the gun. He was staring
at Russell, up close to him and squinting, looking right in his
face.

"I've seen you somewhere," Lamarr said. The way he said it
you knew it bothered him. He waited for Russell to help him,
but Russell didn't say a word. They stared at each other and
every second you expected Lamarr to remember that day at
Delgado's, and you could just imagine him suddenly swinging
that Henry rifle up and giving Russell the same thing Russell
gave him, or worse.

Or Braden might say something about "the Indian" and
then Lamarr Dean would remember. You waited for that to
happen too. But, when Braden looked up, the bag open on the
ground in front of him, he said, "I'd say it was a good day's
pay."

Lamarr Dean looked from Braden over to Dr. Favor. "How
much you steal so we won't have to count it?"

Dr. Favor didn't say anything. He was a man in a dark suit
and hat standing there watching, with one thumb hooked in a
vest pocket and the other hand at his side. The McLaren girl,
Mrs. Favor, Mendez, John Russell—all of them in fact just
stood there patiently, as if they had stopped by to watch but
didn't have anything to do with what was going on.

"He figures he's helped out enough without giving us a
tally," Braden said. He rose, handing the satchel to Dean who
took it and transferred the currency to his saddlebags.

"About twelve thousand I figured," Lamarr Dean said.

"Somewhere around it," Braden said.

"He did all right," Lamarr Dean said. "But I guess we did
better." He saw Braden looking at the two horses that still
trailed the coach on a line. "What do you think?" he said then.

"I guess they'll do." Braden looked up at the coach. "And
the two saddles."

Lamarr Dean looked at him. "What do you need two for?"

"You'll see," Braden said. He motioned to me. "You get
them down."

That's how I come to be up on the coach when they rode out. I threw down Braden's saddle, then Russell's, looking at him as I did.

Russell watched, not saying a word as Braden freed the line and pulled in the horses and slipped the hackamores off them. He put his own saddle on one horse and told Russell to put his on the other.

Right then I thought, they're taking Russell along as a hostage. It made sense; they hadn't bothered us up to now, but they certainly weren't going to be so kind as to just ride off. Which turned out to be right. Only it wasn't Russell they took.

It was Mrs. Favor. Braden brought the horse over to her and said, "I thought you'd come along with us a ways," sounding nice about it.

And just as nice she said, "I'd better not," as if they were discussing it and she had a choice.

Braden held out his hand. "You'll be all right."

"I'll be all right here," Mrs. Favor said.

Braden stared at her. "You're coming, one way or the other." And that was the end of the discussion.

He helped her up, Mrs. Favor holding the skirt to cover her legs as she sat the saddle, and they moved off down the road. Braden stayed close to her and neither of them looked back. We all kept watching, nobody saying anything. Dr. Favor in fact didn't say anything even before, when Braden was forcing his wife to go with him.

Lamarr Dean mounted up then. He sat there cradling the Henry across his arms, looking down at the people there and finally up to me, thinking about something, maybe wanting to be sure he hadn't made any mistakes.

He thought of one thing. "The shotgun," he said. "Open it up and throw it away."

I climbed down to the driver's seat and did as I was told, emptying both shells before heaving the gun off into the brush. Lamarr Dean nodded. He wheeled around and took off after Braden and Mrs. Favor, not hurrying though.

By now Braden and Mrs. Favor were about a hundred yards off, out in the wide-open part of the meadow. Way off beyond them there was just dust to show that Early and the Mexican were up there somewhere driving the horse teams.

I felt the coach shake; I remember that. But I didn't look around till a moment later. When I did, there was John Russell kneeling on the roof right behind me unbuckling the cartridge belt from his blanket roll. He glanced up, keeping an eye on Dean who was taking his time moving away from us. Russell slipped the Spencer out, looking at Lamarr Dean again, and that was when he spoke.

He said, "How do they get that sure of themselves?"

I didn't know what he meant, and certainly couldn't believe he intended to shoot Lamarr Dean. I said, "What?"

"How do they get that sure with the mistakes they make?" Already he was slipping a cartridge into the breech, loading it quick for single fire. I guess I didn't say anything then.

He was busy and it was like he was telling it to himself. "Luck then," he said. "They think they know how to do it, but it's luck." I saw him slip three cartridges from the belt and hold them in his left hand. All of a sudden he held still.

I looked around and saw Dean riding back toward us. Braden and Mrs. Favor, two hundred yards off, had come around and reined in as if to wait for him.

Lamarr Dean had put his rifle in the saddle boot, but now, as he approached us, he drew his Colt.

3

L AMARR DEAN was close now.

"I pretty near forgot something," he said. Then he noticed Russell up on the roof behind me. "What're you at up there?"

"Getting my things," John Russell said. The Spencer was down between his legs as he knelt there, sitting back on his feet, his hands flat on his thighs.

"Expect you're going somewhere?"

"Well," Russell shrugged, "why sit here, uh?"

"How far you think you'll get?"

"That's something to find out."

Lamarr Dean heeled his horse, moving to the back of the coach. He stood up in the stirrups to reach one of the two waterskins hanging there, unhooked it, and looped the end thong over his saddle horn. Then he came back with the skin hanging round and tight in front of his left leg. He pulled the horse around so he was facing us again.

"You didn't say how far you'd get," Lamarr Dean said.

Russell's shoulders went up and down. "We find that out after a while."

Lamarr Dean raised the revolver, hesitating, making sure we saw what he was going to do. Mendez yelled something. I'm not sure what, maybe just a sound. But as he yelled it, Lamarr Dean pulled the trigger and the waterskin still hanging from the back of the coach burst open. It gushed and then trickled as the bag sagged, all the water wasting itself on that sandy road, and Lamarr Dean just sat there looking at us. He didn't smile or laugh, but you could see he enjoyed it.

He said to Russell, "Now how far?"

There wasn't supposed to be an answer to that. Lamarr Dean took up his reins and started around. Russell waited till that moment.

"Maybe," he said, "as far as Delgado's."

Lamarr Dean held up, taken off stride and now he was sideways to us, his gun hand on the offside and he had to turn his head around over his shoulder to look up at Russell.

"You said something?"

"Maybe if we get thirsty," Russell said, "we'll go to Delgado's and have *mescal*."

Lamarr Dean didn't move, even with his head turned in that awkward position. He stared up at Russell, and I'm certain that right then something was dawning on him.

He said, "You do that." For a few more seconds he looked up at Russell, then nudged his horse and started off again with his back to us and holding to a walking pace to show that he wasn't afraid of anything.

I kept watching him—thirty, forty, fifty feet away then, about that far when Russell's voice said, "Get down," not suddenly, but calmly and in a quiet tone.

I dropped down on the seat, ducking my head, and Russell said, "All the way *down*—"

And that last word wasn't quiet, still it wasn't yelled or excited. I saw the Spencer suddenly up to his face and I dropped, looking around to see where I was going and catching a glimpse of Lamarr Dean sixty feet out and wheeling his mount and bringing the Colt gun straight out in front of him, thinking he had time to be sure and *bam* the Spencer went off in my ear and Lamarr Dean went out of that saddle like he'd been clubbed in the face, his horse swerving, then running.

Russell must have been sure of his shot, for he was already reloaded and tracking the horse, and, when he fired, the horse stumbled and rolled and tried to get up. And out past the horse you could see Braden coming in. Coming, then swerving as that Spencer went off again, banging hard close to me and cracking thin out in the open. There was the sound of Braden's revolver twice and I hugged the floor of the boot, looking up to see just the barrel of the Spencer. Russell was full length behind it now, resting the barrel on the front rail, tracking Braden with the sights and not hurrying his fire. Braden swerved again and this time kept going all the way around full circle and back the way he had come toward the small figure way out there that was Mrs. Favor, so you knew Russell had come close. At least Braden didn't want any part of him right then.

I raised up. Russell was loading again, now that there was time taking a loading tube from his blanket and putting seven of the .56-56 slugs in it and shoving the tube up through the stock of the Spencer.

"They'll all come back now," I said. "Won't they?"

"As sure as we have what they want," Russell said.

There was a space there where nothing happened. I saw Dr. Favor and Mendez and the McLaren girl, all three of them in a row, crouched against the cutbank where they'd gone when the shooting started. It was quiet now, but still nobody moved.

Russell was buckling on his cartridge belt, over his left shoulder and down across his chest, working it around so that the full cartridge loops were all in front. While he did this, his eyes never left the two specks way out on the meadow.

We had some time, but I did not think of it then. Braden had to get Early and the Mexican before he came back and they could be a mile off running the stage horses. I kept thinking of how Russell had brought up his Spencer and put it on Lamarr Dean, the way a man might aim at a tin can on a fence, and killed him with one shot. Then he had dropped the horse that was running away with the water bag. He had killed a man, sure of it, and in the same second he had known he must get the horse and he did that too.

The space where nothing happened lasted maybe a minute altogether. Then it was over for good.

Russell moved past me, frontwards, stepping on the wheel and then jumping. He was carrying his Spencer of course, and in the other hand his blanket roll and the canteen he and Mendez had used. (Little things you remember: there was no strap on the canteen, only two metal rings a strap had once been fastened to, and Russell hooked a finger through one of the rings to carry it.)

I don't think he even looked at the others, but started off down the road we had come up, only stopping to pick up his Colt gun and shove it in his holster. Down just past there he left the road and started up the slope, moving pretty quickly through the greasewood and other brush.

Dr. Favor woke up first. He yelled at Russell. Then Mendez was out on the road looking up at Russell, and Dr. Favor had run off into the brush on the other side of the coach.

I started down then, taking the grainsack our provisions

were in and my blanket roll. By the time I was on the road, Dr. Favor was coming out of the brush with his little revolver and Mendez's sawed-off shotgun. Mendez and the McLaren girl were still watching Russell.

"He's running," Dr. Favor said. He was not at all calm and at that moment I thought if the shotgun was loaded he would have fired it at Russell.

"We need him," Dr. Favor said then. He knew it right then. He knew it as sure as he thought John Russell was an Apache Indian and we were afoot out in the middle of nowhere.

That's when the rest of us came wide awake. The McLaren girl said, "I wouldn't have any idea where to go. I don't think I even know where we are."

"We're maybe half way," I said. "Maybe more. If we were over on the main road I could tell."

"Then how far's the main road?"

Favor shot a look at her like he was trying to think and she had interrupted him. "Just keep quiet," he said.

It stung her, you could see. "Standing out here in the open," she said, "what good does keeping quiet do?"

Dr. Favor never answered her. He looked at Mendez and said, "Come on," handing him his shotgun, and they hurried out to where Lamarr Dean's horse was, Dr. Favor skirting around Lamarr Dean's body which lay spread-armed like it had been staked out, but Mendez stopped there to take Lamarr Dean's Colt. Then they were both at the dead horse, kneeling there a minute, Favor pulling loose the saddlebags while Mendez got the waterskin. They didn't bother with the Henry rifle, or else it was under the horse and held fast.

While they were at the dead horse, the McLaren girl said, still watching them, "He's not even thinking of his wife. Do you know that?"

"Well, sure he is," I said, not meaning he was actually thinking about her, but at least concerned about her. What did the girl expect him to do? He couldn't just chase after Braden. That wouldn't get his wife back.

"He's forgotten her," the McLaren girl said. "All he's thinking about is the money he stole."

"You can't just say something like that," I said. I meant you couldn't know what somebody was thinking, especially in the jackpot we were in right then. A person *acted*, and thought about it later.

It was getting the things from Lamarr's horse that took time, the reason we were not right behind Russell or had him in sight anymore by the time we got down the road past the cutbank and started up the slope.

Dr. Favor, with the saddlebags over one shoulder, kept ahead of us, following the same direction Russell had taken. The slope was not very difficult at first, a big open sweep that humped up to a bunch of pines along the top; but, as we were hurrying, it wasn't long before our legs started aching and getting so tight you thought something would knot inside and you'd never get it loosened.

We were hurrying because of what was behind us, you can bet all your wages on that. But we were also hurrying to catch Russell, feeling like little kids running home in the dark and scared the house was going to be locked and nobody home. Do you see how we felt? We were worried he had left us to go on his own. In other words knowing we needed Russell if we were going to find our way out of here alive.

When Dr. Favor reached the trees he hesitated, or seemed to, then he was gone. That's when we hurried faster, all worn out by then. You could hear Mendez breathing ten feet away.

But there was no need to hurry. As we reached the top there was Dr. Favor standing just inside the shade of the trees. Russell was just past him. He was sitting down with his blanket open on the ground and his boots off. He was pulling on a pair of curl-toed Apache moccasins, not paying any attention to Dr. Favor who stood there like he had caught Russell and was holding him from getting away, actually pointing his revolver at him. Dr. Favor's chest was moving up and down with his breathing.

Mendez moved in a little closer, watching Russell. "Why didn't you wait for us?" he said. Russell didn't bother to answer. You weren't even sure he heard Mendez.

"He doesn't care what we do," Dr. Favor said. "Long as he gets away."

"Man," Mendez said. "What's the matter with you? We have to think about this and talk it over. What if one of us just ran off? You think that would be a good thing?"

Russell raised his leg to pull a moccasin on. They were the high Apache kind, like leggings which come up past your knees. He began rolling it down, stuffing the pants leg into it and fastening it about calf-high with a strap of something. He didn't look up until he had finished this.

Then he said, "What do you want?"

"What do we want?" Mendez said, surprised. "We want to get out of here."

"What's stopping you?" Russell said.

Mendez kept frowning. "What's the matter with you?"

Russell had both moccasins on now. He took his boots and rolled them inside the blanket. Doing this, not looking at us, he said, "You want to go with me, uh?"

"With you? We all go together. This isn't happening to just one person," Mendez said. "This is happening to all of us."

"But you want me to show you the way," Russell said.

"Sure you show the way. We follow. But we're all together."

"I don't know," Russell said, very slowly, like he was thinking it over. He looked up at Dr. Favor, directly at him. "I can't ride with you. Maybe you can't walk with me . . . uh?"

For a minute, maybe even longer, nobody said a word. Russell finished rolling his blanket and tied it up with a piece of line he'd had inside.

When he stood up, Mendez said—not surprised or excited or frowning now, but so serious his voice wasn't even very loud—he said, "What does that mean?"

Russell looked at him. "It means I can't ride with them and maybe they can't walk with me. Maybe they don't walk the way I walk. You *sabe* that, Mexican?"

"I helped you like you're my own son!" Mendez's voice rose and his eyes opened so that you could see all the whites. But Russell wasn't looking. He was walking off. Mendez kept shouting, "What's the matter with you!"

"Let him go," Dr. Favor said.

We stood there watching Russell move off through the trees.

"What do you expect?" Dr. Favor said. "Do you expect somebody like that to act the way a decent person would?"

"I helped him," Mendez said, as if he couldn't believe what had happened.

"All right, now he'll help us," Dr. Favor said. "He won't

have anything to do with us, but we can follow him, can't we?"

Nobody thought to try to answer that question at the time, because it wasn't really a question. I thought about it later, though. I thought about it for the next two or three hours as we tried to keep up with Russell.

It was about 3:30 or 4 o'clock when the holdup took place, with already a lot of shade on this side of the hills. From then on the light kept getting dimmer. I mean right from the time we started following Russell it was hard to keep him in sight, even when he was out in the open.

In daylight the land was spotted with brush and rock, dead and dusty looking, but with some color, light green and dark green and brown and whitish yellow. In the evening it all turned brown and hazy looking, with high peaks all around us once we'd gone on down through the other side of the pines out into open country again.

I say open, but by that I mean only there weren't any trees. I don't mean to say it was easy to travel over.

We moved along with Dr. Favor usually ahead of us. Way up ahead you would see Russell. Then you wouldn't see him. Not because he had hidden, but because of the time of day and just the way that country was, with little dips and rises and wild with all kinds of scrub brush and cactus. The saguaros that were all over didn't look like fence posts now. They were like grave markers in an Indian burial ground, if there is such a place as that. This wasn't what scared you though, it was what was coming behind us and trying to keep up with Russell that did.

He must have known we were following. But he never once ran or tried to hide on us. The McLaren girl wondered out loud why he didn't. I guess he knew he didn't have to.

There was a pass that led through these hills which Russell followed a little ways, then crossed the half mile or so of openness to the other side and headed up through a barranca that rose as a big trough between two ridges. Following him across the openness we kept looking back, but Braden and his men were not close to us yet.

Russell left the barranca, climbing again up to the cover of trees. I think that climb was the hardest part and wore us out the most, all of us hurrying, wasting our strength as we tried to keep him in sight. Once up on this ridge, though, there was no sign of him.

We kept to the trees, moving north because we figured he would. Then after a mile or so there was the end of the trees. This hump of a ridge trailed off into a bare spine and then we were working our way down again into another pass, a darker, more shadowed one, because now it was later. It was here that we sighted Russell again, and here that we almost gave up and said what was the use. He was climbing again, almost up the other side of this pass, way up past the brush to where the slope was steep and rocky, and we knew then that we would never keep up with him.

Dr. Favor claimed he was deliberately trying to lose us. But the McLaren girl said no, he didn't care if we followed or sprouted wings and flew; he was thinking of Braden and his men on horseback and he was making it as hard for them as he could, making them get off their horses and walk if they wanted to follow him.

When she said this and we thought of Braden again, we went on, tired or not, and climbed right up that grade Russell had, skinning ourselves pretty bad because now it was hard to see your footing in the dim light.

It was up on that slope, in trees again, that we rested and ate some of the dried beef and biscuits from the grainsack. Before we were through it was dark, almost as dark as it would get. This rest, which was our longest one, made it hard to get up and we started arguing about going on.

Mendez was for staying. He said going on wasn't worth it. Let Braden catch up for all he cared.

Dr. Favor said we *had* to go on, practically ordering us to. Braden would have to stop because he couldn't follow our trail in the dark. So we should take advantage of this and keep going.

Keep going, the McLaren girl said. That sounded fine. But which way? How did we know we wouldn't get turned around and walk right back into Braden's hands?

We would head north, Dr. Favor said. And keep heading north. The McLaren girl said she agreed, but which way was it? He pointed off somewhere, but you could tell he wasn't sure.

Or he could go on alone, Dr. Favor suggested, watching us to see our reaction. Go on alone and bring back help. He didn't insist on it and let it die when nobody said anything.

Why didn't he mention his wife then? That's when I started thinking about what the McLaren girl had said earlier: that he had forgotten about his wife and only the money was important to him.

Could that be? I tried thinking what I would do if it was my wife. Hole up and ambush them? Try and get her away from them? My gosh, no, I thought then. Just trade them the money for her! Certainly Dr. Favor must have thought of that.

Then why didn't he do it? Or at least talk about it. When you got down to it, though, it was his business. I mean we had no right to remind him of what he should do. That was his business. I don't mean to sound hard or callous; that's just the way it was. We had enough on our minds without worrying about his wife.

We just sat there until Dr. Favor said he was going. When he started off, the McLaren girl started after him, so Mendez and I did too. I guess we had to follow somebody.

From then on I don't know where we were or even what direction we went.

By then there wasn't much talk among us. Once in a while Dr. Favor said something, usually about what way to go. One time though he brought up the subject again of us hiding somewhere and him going on alone.

Mendez said it was all right with him, not caring one way or the other. But neither the McLaren girl nor I would agree to it. I kept picturing Braden somewhere behind us waiting for morning so he could get on our sign and run us down. Who would want to just sit there waiting for him?

The McLaren girl looked at it another way. She said right to Dr. Favor's face, "That money's been stolen enough. Don't worry about one of us trying to take it."

"As if I'd distrust you people," Dr. Favor said. "The things you think about."

"I'd like to know what you think about," the McLaren girl said. "Since it sure isn't your wife."

Dr. Favor didn't say anything and we went on.

If you were to ask me who was the best one, who took it the

best and never once complained, who even walked with hardly any trouble, I would say the McLaren girl. If you are surprised, remember she had been held by wild Apaches over a month. She had traveled with them as they kept on the move, keeping up with them else they would have killed her. You looked at her and wondered how something like that could have happened to a young girl and still not see it on her face.

Once she offered to take the grainsack or blanket roll I was carrying, but I wouldn't hear of it.

She even said we should still keep going when finally Dr. Favor led us off into a gully and announced we would camp there. He said if we stopped now we would have a better chance of finding Russell when daylight came. I'm not sure what he meant by that and think it was just an excuse, the real reason for his wanting to stop being his tiredness. The McLaren girl argued we should use the darkness while we had it—it was still a few hours before sunup—but gave in when she saw how tired Mendez was. So tired he could hardly stand up.

We had already eaten some of the biscuits and dried meat from the grainsack. Now there was nothing to do but sleep. I was the only one with a blanket, so I offered it to the McLaren girl. She said no, for me to use it. I did, finally, but all rolled up as a pillow. (Somebody might think this was dumb, but I couldn't cover myself with it being the only one. It would have felt good too, I can tell you that.)

It was only a few hours before sunup when we stopped here; so there wasn't much time to sleep, and it was hard getting to sleep, even as tired as I felt. But finally I did.

In the morning there weren't two words said by anyone. You know how it can be in the morning anyway: on top of having slept no more than two and a half hours on the ground and in the cold after walking almost all night. (Yes, it was cold. Even though during the day it was blistering hot.) And on top of that not knowing where you were and Braden coming after us on horseback.

The only thing we were sure of in the morning was the direction north and that was the way we went, having eaten a little more of the dried beef and biscuits and taken a few swallows of water each.

Going toward the north does not mean we went in a straight

line. Unless you wanted to climb steep slopes all the time, and maybe get up there and find no way down, you had to follow the washes and draws that cut through this high country, so that maybe you would walk two, even three miles to get one mile north. You can see nobody talked much. That's the way it was all morning, or until the next part happened which I would judge was an hour or so before noon.

We came out of some trees onto an open meadow, a little graze like that was cupped there in the hills, then crossing the meadow and taking the only way out, we went up a pretty long draw that was deep and lined with thick brush and rocks along both sides, the draw being about sixty feet wide and upwards to three hundred or more feet long, that being a calculation from memory.

We made our way up this draw, looking back across the meadow as we went, finally reached the top and almost dropped everything we carried. Not out of tiredness, out of surprise!

For sitting there with his Spencer across his lap and smoking a cigarette was John Russell.

Mendez yelled his name and ran over to him, Mendez assuming just as I did, I guess, that Russell had changed his mind and gotten the mean feeling out of his system, and now wanted to show us the way out of here.

Mendez scolded him a little, but in a kidding way, that he shouldn't have done what he did. Mendez was too glad to see Russell to be serious or angry at him, telling him how we couldn't keep up with him and how worn out we got trying to.

Russell moved him aside with his arm and motioned all of us back from the crest so we wouldn't be seen from below.

From the way Mendez acted, our troubles were over.

Not so according to Dr. Favor. He said, staring at Russell, "You going to sit there for a while, are you?"

Russell didn't move. "You want to go bad, uh?"

He saw that Russell had no intention of getting up. "Now it comes," Dr. Favor said. "I want to hear how you'll say this."

"You want to go," Russell said, "go on."

Dr. Favor kept looking at him. "What else?"

"Leave the saddlebag and the gun here."

Dr. Favor's big red face almost seemed to relax and smile.

"There," he said. "Right out in the open. It took you all night to realize you'd run off and left something behind."

Mendez, not understanding, had that worried look again. "What is it?" he said to Russell.

"It's my money," Dr. Favor said. "He's thinking it looks pretty good. Out here and no law to stop him. But four people against one. Maybe he hasn't thought about that."

Russell drew on the cigarette. "Maybe one is enough," he said.

That was when the McLaren girl stepped in. "Your money," she yelled at Dr. Favor. I mean *yelled* it. "After you stole it! We're supposed to side with you to protect money you stole!" Then her eyes took in Russell too. "You sit here arguing about money and giving Frank Braden all the time he'd ever need."

"Be careful what you say," Dr. Favor said to her. "I think you are talking without thinking. This is my money, in my possession, and it will take more than the word of a dead outlaw to prove it isn't."

"All this talk," Mendez said, like he had just thought of it. "We have to *move*."

Russell looked up at him. "Where do you want to go?"

Mendez said, "Are you crazy? They're coming!"

"Tell me where," Russell said.

"Where? I don't know. Out of here."

"I'll tell you something," Russell said. "There's open country. Maybe it takes you two, three hours to cross it. And while you're there they come with their horses."

"Then hide somewhere," Mendez said, "and wait for dark to cross it."

Russell nodded. "Or do better than that. Wait for them here. Shoot their horses to make it even, uh? Maybe finish it."

"Finish it," I said, understanding him, but I guess not believing what he was asking us to do. "You mean try and kill them?"

"If they get close enough," Russell said, "they're going to kill you."

"But they didn't harm anybody before. Why would they want to now?"

"Do you want to give them your water?"

"They got water."

"Two canteens which they were drinking out of all day yesterday. Do you want to give them yours?"

"No but—"

"Then they'll kill you for it."

Until then it seemed just a matter of running and getting away or running and being caught and they getting the money after all. But kill them or they would kill us? It was a terrible thing to think about and you couldn't help looking for other ways. Run or hide. Run or hide. Those ways kept popping into your head while Russell just sat there looking down the draw and waiting.

"And if we don't *finish it*," Dr. Favor said, making those last words sound dumb to have ever been thought of. "What then?"

"You don't have a say in this," Russell said, looking up at him. "You can stay or go, but either way you leave the saddlebag."

"You must have kept awake all night," Dr. Favor said.

"It came to me," Russell said back.

"How much you figure I have?"

Russell shrugged. "It doesn't matter."

"Wouldn't take much, would it, to keep you in whisky?"

"You leave the belly gun too," Russell said. And held out his hand for it, turning just a little so that the Spencer in his lap turned with him.

Dr. Favor just stared, not moving. "You're forgetting something," he said. "What if the others decide against you?"

"Then they have you to lead them," Russell answered.

He sat there with his hand still held toward Dr. Favor and you knew he could sit there the rest of his life and never budge. It was his way if we stayed with him. It was either do what he wanted or else go on with Dr. Favor. It was not like choosing between a good thing or a bad thing. Still, one felt to be better than the other and it wasn't much of a hard choice to make.

The McLaren girl was the one who said it out loud, though not very loud. "I would like to go home," she said, hardly glancing at Dr. Favor. "I sure would like to go home. And I know he can't find the way."

Neither Mendez or I had to say anything. If we'd sided with Dr. Favor, we would have.

With us watching him, I believe, Dr. Favor didn't want to

get caught looking awkward or nervous. You had to give him credit for that. He took it calmly, not offering any argument, but I will bet thinking fast all the time. He just shrugged and handed his revolver to Russell.

"Chief make plenty war now," he said. You see how he was passing it off? Like Russell was a bully you had to give in to if you wanted some peace.

Russell didn't pay any attention. He took the gun, then looked at Mendez, noticing Mendez had Lamarr Dean's revolver besides his shotgun.

"You shoot all right?" he asked.

Mendez frowned. "I'm not sure."

"You'll find out," Russell said. "First the shotgun. When they're close. So close you can touch them. Then the other one if you need it."

"I don't know," Mendez said, worried. "Just sit and wait for them like that."

"If there was a better way," Russell said, "we would do it." Just that moment talking to Mendez, Russell's voice was gentle and you remembered they had known each other before and maybe had been friends.

He looked off down the draw, studying the trees over the other side of the meadow. If they were on our sign, he knew, they would come through there and up the draw.

Then he was looking right at me and handing me Dr. Favor's revolver. At first I didn't make any move to take it.

He pushed it out again like telling me, "Come on, take it," and that time I did.

"You have one thing to do," he said and shifted his eyes over to Dr. Favor and back again. "Watch him."

Then it was the McLaren girl's turn. She stood there, her dark nice-looking face very calm, seeing Russell looking at her then.

"You stay with this one," Russell said, meaning me.

"Carl Allen," the McLaren girl said.

It stopped Russell just for a second as if she'd interrupted his thoughts. "You'll have the saddlebag and the water."

"Squaw work," Dr. Favor said. "You ought to like that." He was also saying, "See what you're getting yourself in for?"

It didn't bother her, or else she was so intent on Russell she didn't hear him. She said, "The money and the waterskin, but you carry your own water I see." She meant the canteen that was on the ground next to him. The one he and Mendez had used.

He watched her, getting all the meaning out of her words that she didn't say. "You want it too?"

"Why burden yourself?" she said, and you weren't sure if she was serious or not.

For just a moment there John Russell hesitated, as if handing over the canteen would be giving up his independence. But he did and the McLaren girl took it.

"You and you and you," Russell said, meaning the McLaren girl and Dr. Favor and I, "will be here. You don't stand up. You don't move back away from the edge here and stand up. You sit and don't move." (Like a teacher talking to little children in school!) "Him—"

"Reverend Dr. Favor," the McLaren girl said with that little knife edge in her voice again.

"He can leave up to the time they come," Russell went on. "After that, no." Russell was looking right at me again, but still talking about Dr. Favor.

"If he tries to leave with nothing, shoot him once," Russell said. "If he takes the saddlebag, shoot him twice. If he picks up the water, empty your gun. You understand that?"

(I have thought about those words since then and I am sure Russell was having a little fun with us when he said that. Part serious, part in fun. But can you imagine joking at a time like that? That of course was the reason no one even smiled. He must have thought we were dumb.)

I just nodded, not wanting to say anything with Dr. Favor standing right there.

"I don't know," Mendez said. You could see what had been going on in his mind. "Maybe we should just keep going, try and outrun them."

"You run now," Russell said to him, "they'll catch you and kill you. Believe that more than you believe anything."

Russell told us again to stay where we were, down low. He talked to Mendez, going over it again with him, telling him to wait till they got close and to be sure of hitting something, to shoot first at the men, then at the horses; but watch for the woman. Mendez listened, nodding sometimes, but kept looking over toward us.

After that Russell didn't waste any more talk. He and Mendez crawled out through the brush, working their way about forty feet down the draw, then separating, Mendez staying on the right, Russell crawling way over to the left side so that anybody coming up the draw would pass between them. If one did not have a good shot when the time came, the other probably would.

Both had good cover, for there were sizable rocks that had been washed down the draw, mostly along the sides where they were, and pretty thick brush where there weren't any rocks. Only the middle ground, where water would run off in the spring, was fairly open.

Russell had this timed pretty well, knowing how long it would take them to get on our sign and follow us. He had figured a few other things too. That they wouldn't be as careful by now as they had been yesterday evening and during the first hour or so this morning. There had been good ambush places before this, but nothing had jumped out at them. Why should it now? They would be awake, of course, wide awake coming up something like this draw; but they would tend to keep their eyes on the top and expect it to come from there if it was coming at all.

(It is easy to talk about something like this. It is also interesting to plan and imagine what you would do, but only as long as you aren't there. I wouldn't sit where we were, just waiting there again, no matter what anybody gave me.)

We kept our eyes on the trees that were some kind of pine, big ones, probably ponderosa, across the meadow at the bottom of the draw. Still, when they came, it wasn't sudden at all.

Right at the edge of the trees, in shadow, was a horse and rider and you wondered how long he had been there with you looking right at him. He was awake all right.

He came out of the trees holding to a slow walk and was out in the meadow a ways before the next rider appeared. Then another one came who you knew right away was the Favor woman. (I did not look over at Dr. Favor to see what his face showed. I would have if I had known I was going to write this.) The fourth one was right behind her. That would be Frank

Braden, the big sugar of this outfit. He would be the one telling the others what to do, while he stayed with their hostage
or whatever Mrs. Favor was.

It was the Mexican rider who dismounted and came first
when they reached the bottom of the draw. He seemed to be
making sure of our tracks, walking along a little ways with his
head down. Then he swung back up and he and Early came on,
the Mexican staying a little bit in the lead. They kept looking
up at the sides of the draw, being very watchful now. They
knew we had come this way and I think they smelled it as a
fresh trail. Not so much Early as the Mexican.

You got the feeling he knew by the sign that Russell had
passed through here on his own or ahead of us, or maybe Russell had left no tracks at all and the Mexican saw only that the
four of us had come up this way. There is nothing to prove
this, but I believe he did know. The Mexican seemed so sure of
himself, riding right up the middle of the draw first, seeming
relaxed but his eyes taking everything in.

Braden, with the Favor woman, kept a good ten lengths back
of Early and the Mexican. That was the way they came up,
walking right into it.

It was like watching a play. No, it was realer than that. (My
gosh, it couldn't get more real!) It gave you a strange feeling
to watch it, thinking that in a minute or two you were going
to see somebody get killed.

Russell never moved. We could see just part of him. He lay
full length as if asleep. His hat was off and his head was down,
as if he was listening to them coming up the draw instead of
watching them.

Mendez kept looking over to where Russell was, but I doubt
he could see him, being on about the same level. Then he
would look back up in our direction. You could see he wanted
no part of this. Why couldn't he be up where we were? Or the
rest of us down there helping him, he was probably thinking.
Mendez was nervous. You couldn't blame him for it. Still, it
was strange to see him in that state. (In the last two days I
had certainly learned a lot about show-nothing, tell-nothing
Henry Mendez.)

As Early and the Mexican got up a ways, they started looking up at the top of the draw and studying it. Especially the

Mexican. He was closer to Mendez's side of the draw now and about five horse-lengths ahead of Early. Halfway up, the Mexican drew his right-hand gun and held it ready.

You saw Mendez pressing himself tight against the rock he was behind and not looking around now. He would inch up to sneak a look at the Mexican and then duck down again. You almost knew what he was thinking. You also knew this wasn't something he had done before.

Looking at Russell you couldn't even tell if he was alive, laying there sighting down his carbine now and waiting as if he could wait like that all day, waiting for Early to ride right up to him.

I don't remember what the McLaren girl and Dr. Favor were doing then. I could feel them there. The thing is, the one I really wanted to watch was Russell; then you would see how this was done. But Mendez, the way he was fidgeting, looking up at the Mexican coming and then pressing against the rock, made you nervous and you kept watching him, holding your breath for fear he was going to jump up and start running.

The Mexican was now about a hundred feet away from him, sitting round-shouldered and relaxed, the Colt gun held about chest high and pointed straight up, the sun glinting and moving a little with the motion of the horse and rider.

That was what Mendez saw coming toward him, a man holding a gun that seemed part of his hand, and another gun still holstered; a man you knew was ready, but could still be relaxed about it and not sit stiff in the saddle or with his shoulders hunched.

Maybe if I was Mendez I would have done the same as he did. Which was all of a sudden rise up and fire both barrels of that scatter gun like he couldn't let go fast enough.

At a hundred feet or less, some of the buckshot could have found the Mexican, but Mendez hurried and didn't aim at all. The Mexican straightened and fired three times, faster than I've ever seen a man thumb and fire a Colt revolver, with all three shots zinging off the rocks Mendez had flattened himself behind. Then you saw the Mexican twist in the saddle, like something had pushed him, and grab his side right above the belt.

Russell had fired.

He fired again as the Mexican rolled out of the saddle and into cover. He fired again and the Mexican's horse threw up its head, shaking it, and sunk on its forelegs and fell over.

Early was already off and in cover. You saw him reach up to grab his horse's reins as it reared around and started off down the draw. Early missed. Russell didn't though. He fired twice again, quick, and I swear you heard both shots smack into that horse. The horse went down, rolled on its side and got up again and kept going, following Braden and the Favor woman—Braden holding her horse's reins close at the bit ring and leading it as they rode back down the draw, all the way down to the bottom and around the outcrop of rocks into a little patch of scrubby woods. Even after they were out of sight you heard the horses in the thicket. Then everything was quiet.

It was quiet for the longest time. Mendez kept looking over to about where Russell was, not knowing at all what to do and maybe expecting some signal from him.

Russell didn't move. You could see he had learned a lot from the Apaches, a kind of patience few white men could ever command. He lay there sighting, I think, on the place where Early had gone into the brush, waiting for a movement. He lay like that, I swear, for about two hours, all the while this standoff lasted.

Not much happened during that time. The Mexican started calling out either to Russell or Mendez in Spanish. I didn't know what he was saying, but they were questions, and there was a sound to his voice like the questions were meant to be funny. Not funny, exactly, but like insults or inviting Mendez to step out and show himself, things you wouldn't expect to hear coming out of that draw. You had to give that Mexican something. There was no doubt he had been shot. Still he could yell at Russell and Mendez, trying to draw them out.

Once there was a quick glimpse of Early. He was there and then gone, off behind a scatter of rocks a little farther down the draw. Russell must have been waiting for the Mexican because he didn't fire. We never did see the Mexican squirm out of there and Early only that one time.

Both of them worked their way down though. They stood out in the open for a second, way down at the bottom of the draw. The Mexican, holding his side with one hand, waved to us. Then they were gone into the thicket.

Just for a few minutes we had time to rest, not wondering where they were or worrying about them coming. They would have to think things over and maybe wait until dark to come up that draw again. Though we couldn't count on it. We couldn't sit here for long either. One of them could circle around, even though it would take time, and we wouldn't ever be able to move.

So we had to get out of there. When Russell and Mendez came up, I opened the canteen. Nobody had had any water since this morning. But Russell shook his head. "Tonight," he said. "Not while the sun is out." Meaning, I guess, you would sweat it out right away and be thirsty again before you knew it.

That was all he said, with not one word to Mendez about shooting too soon and spoiling the ambush. That was over as far as he was concerned; he was not the kind of man who would stew over something finished and past fixing. He just picked up his blanket roll and that meant it was time to go.

Maybe we had showed them it wasn't going to be easy, as Russell had said we might. But look at it another way. We might have finished it in the draw, but we didn't and maybe never would. The only good to come out of the ambush was now they had one less horse—maybe two.

But now they were close. Now they knew where we were. And now there was no doubt they would come with guns out and shoot on sight.

4

WE SAT there only a few minutes. That's all the longer our rest time lasted, and it was starting again. Only not the way we expected it to. We didn't go right then. We were about to when the McLaren girl said, "Look—" pointing down the draw.

We looked, but we all crouched down at the same time. There, way down at the bottom, was the Mexican again, his straw hat bright in the sunlight so that you knew it was the Mexican and not one of the others. But we could not tell at first what he was carrying. He had to get up a ways—taking his time, his face raised, his one hand holding his side—before we saw it was a stick with something white tied to the end of it.

He seemed careful, but not scared, keeping his eyes on the ridge, not sure we would honor his white truce flag, I guess, and ready to dive for cover if we let go at him. He was armed with both his revolvers.

Nobody said anything. We just watched. He kept coming, almost reaching the place where Mendez had been during the ambush.

Russell stood up holding his carbine in one hand, pointed down, and the Mexican stopped.

Russell said, "You come to give up?"

The Mexican stood at ease, letting his truce flag dip down to the ground. I think he smiled when Russell said that, but I'm not sure.

I know he shook his head. He said, "When you learn to shoot better." He raised his hand from his side and there was blood on it.

"You didn't do so good."

"I tried to do better," Russell said. "I think you moved."

"Moved," the Mexican said. "How do you like them, tied to a tree?"

"On a horse," Russell said. "Like your friend."

The Mexican grinned. "You like to pull the trigger."

"I can do it again for you," Russell said.

"You could," the Mexican agreed, staring up at Russell, studying him and judging the distance between them. "I have to talk to this other one first. This Favor."

He pronounced it Fa-*vor*, like it was a Spanish word.

"He can hear you," Russell said.

"If he can't you tell him," the Mexican said. "This. He gives us the money . . . and some of the water. We give him his wife and everyone goes home. Ask him how he likes that."

"You're out of water?"

"Almost." The Mexican grinned. "That Early. He put whisky in his canteen. He thought it would be easy."

Russell shook his head. "It will get even harder."

"Not if this Fa*vor* gives us the money."

"He doesn't have it," Russell said.

The Mexican grinned again. "Tell me he hid it."

Russell shook his head. "He gave it to me."

The Mexican nodded, looking up at Russell like he was admiring him. "So now you steal the money." He shrugged his shoulders. "All right, we trade with you then."

"She's not my woman," Russell said.

"We give her to you."

"What else?"

"Your life. How's that?"

"Tell Braden how things are now," Russell said.

"What's the difference who has the money?" the Mexican said. "You give it to us or we shoot that woman."

"All right," Russell said. "You shoot her."

The Mexican kept staring at him. "What about the rest of them? What do they say?"

"They say what they want," Russell said. "I say what I want. Do you see that now?"

He didn't see it. He didn't know what to think, so he just stood there, one hand on his side, the other holding that truce flag.

"Tell Braden how it is," Russell said. "Tell him to think some more."

"He'll say the same thing."

"Tell him anyway."

The Mexican hadn't taken his eyes off Russell for a second,

sizing him up all the while they talked. "Maybe you and I finish something first," he said. "Maybe you come down here a little."

"I'm thinking," Russell said, "whether to kill you right now or wait till you turn around."

Do you know what the Mexican did? He smiled. Not that unbelieving kind of smile, but like he appreciated Russell or enjoyed him. It was about the strangest thing I ever saw. He smiled and said, "If I didn't believe you, I think you would do it. All right, I talk to Braden."

He turned and walked away dragging the truce flag, not with his shoulders hunched like he expected something, but as calmly as he had walked up.

Russell waited until the Mexican was almost down to the bottom. He got his blanket roll and the saddlebags, just glanced at us, and moved off. He didn't tell us what he had planned. If we wanted to follow him that was up to us.

We didn't expect this. We thought he would talk to them again. But who could be sure what Russell was thinking? We knew we couldn't sit in that draw forever. Sooner or later Braden would try to get at us. But was going on right then the best way? Russell must have thought so, though he wasn't telling us why.

We followed him. What choice had we?

That was a funny thing. I felt closer to Dr. Favor than I did to Russell. Dr. Favor might have stolen government money and left his wife to her own fate; but it was something you had to think about before you realized it. He never admitted either right out.

Russell was something else. He had said to the Mexican, not caring who heard him, "All right, shoot her." Like she was nothing to him, so what did he care? Do you see the difference? Russell was so cold and calm about it, it scared you to death. Also, if he didn't care about her, what did he care about us?

Now it was almost like the whole thing was between Braden and Russell and we were in it only because there wasn't any place else to go. Like it was all Russell's fault and he had dragged us into it.

I would say we walked three miles from the time we left that draw until we stopped again, though we did not gain more than one mile in actual distance. We kept pretty much to ridges, high up as possible in the cover of pinyon pine and scrub, and when we stopped it was because flat country opened up at the end of the canyon not far ahead of us. It was a good two or three miles across the openness before the hills took up again.

Russell didn't say it and nobody asked, but we knew he planned to wait for dark to cross that open part. It was no place to be seen in daylight by three men riding horses. (We did not know then whether Russell had killed one or two of their horses.)

We had climbed a pretty steep grade to reach this place we camped at (high up the way Apaches always camp, whether there is water or not) with thick pinyon on three sides of us and the slope, with some cliffrose and scrub, on the open side.

Russell had made it hard for them to follow. If they came directly on our sign, they would have to come up the open slope. If they came any other way, it would take them hours to work around, and then they would be taking a chance of not finding us. So, we figured, they would come directly when they came. All right, but to come up that open slope they would have to wait till dark. Which was what we would be waiting for to slip off through the trees.

Do you see how Russell figured to stay one jump ahead of them? I estimated we would reach the old San Pete mine some time during the night; Delgado's if we were lucky, some time during the next afternoon or evening. Then home. It didn't seem far when you looked ahead. The trouble was you had to keep looking back.

After the little sleep we had had it was good to lie down again. Everybody picked out a spot. We couldn't make a fire so ate some more of the biscuits, which were pretty hard by now, and the dried strip meat which never was very good.

We did not drink any water though. John Russell had said we would have to wait until night. It was mid-afternoon now. Imagine not having had a drink since that morning. The salty beef didn't help your thirst any either. But what could we do?

I kept picturing myself sitting on a shady porch with a big pitcher of ice water, sitting there in a clean shirt having just shaved and taken a bath. Boy!

Mendez looked ten years older, his eyes sunken in and his face covered with beard stubble. Dr. Favor's big, broad face, framed by that half-moon-shaped beard, was sweaty looking. The McLaren girl and John Russell were the only ones who didn't look so bad, I mean not as dirty or sweaty as the rest of us. With her hair too short to muss and her dark skin, she looked like she was taking it all right. John Russell was dusty, of course, but had no beard to make his face look dirty. You could tell he had pulled out the stubbles Indian-fashion when he first started to get a beard, years ago, and now he'd never have one.

Russell stayed mostly by the open side, lying down but propped on his elbows and looking down the way we had come up. I guess he was resting and doing his thinking now, taking time to see things clearly. Whatever he saw in his mind, it got him up on his feet after a while.

He brought the saddlebags over to me and dropped them. He didn't say guard them, but that's what his look meant. All he said was he would go have a look at things and he left, taking only the Spencer carbine; no water or anything else. He didn't go straight down the slope but headed off through the pinyon, I guess to keep high up as he scouted the ground we had covered from the draw.

A little while after he was gone, Dr. Favor went over to where the waterskin and canteen and provisions were. He picked up the canteen and was drinking from it before anyone had time to yell stop. It was the McLaren girl who yelled it.

She jumped up, and Dr. Favor held the canteen out to her. "Your turn," he said.

"We're not to drink till tonight. You know that."

"I forget," Dr. Favor said. She could believe him or not; he didn't care.

Mendez, still sitting down, said, "Maybe we should all take one, to keep it even."

"To keep it even!" the McLaren girl said. "What about later when we don't have any. What good does keeping it even do?"

"I'm thinking of now," Mendez said, rising. "You can think of any time you want."

"All right," the girl said. "And what about Russell?"

"Look"—Mendez had this surprised sound to his voice—"if

he wants to wait till dark, all right. That's up to him. We drink when we want."

"He doesn't even have to know," Dr. Favor said. He saw Mendez liked this idea so he put it out there again. "If you're worried about Russell, why would he even have to know?"

"And you think that would be fair," the McLaren girl said.

"It's his rule," Dr. Favor said. "If it's unfair, he brought it on himself."

"Look," Mendez said, making it sound simple, "If you want to wait, you wait. If you want a drink now, then you take it."

That was when he grabbed the canteen from Dr. Favor and took a good drink, more even than Favor had, so that Dr. Favor reached for it and pulled it out of Mendez's mouth.

"You said keep it even."

Then he handed the canteen to the McLaren girl.

She took it, her eyes right on Dr. Favor and hesitating just a little before she put it to her mouth. If this surprises you, look at it this way: they could drink it all while you sat there obeying Russell's rule. All right, if they were going to have some, a person would be dumb not to take his share. That's why I took a drink right after she did. I'm sure she was thinking the same way.

Dr. Favor was still looking at her, more sure of himself than ever now. He said, "If you want to tell him when he gets back, you just go right ahead." He was even smiling then.

What could she say? On the other hand, knowing her, she might have said something at that. But she didn't.

Everybody settled down again. For a little while there was peace. Then Dr. Favor came over to me.

Right away he said, "That's some Indian chief we got," meaning Russell of course.

"Well," I said, "I guess he knows what he's doing."

"He knows what he wants. That much is sure."

If he thought Russell wanted the money, that was his business. But why talk about something you couldn't prove? I just said, "Maybe he's the best chief we got," kind of joking about it.

"Only we're not his braves," Dr. Favor said, and he was serious, his face close to mine and staring right at me.

"If somebody has another idea," I said, "I'll listen."

"I've got one," he said. "We leave right now."

He'd force you right up against a wall like that; then you'd have to try and wiggle out.

"Well, I don't know about that," I said.

"Let me have my gun then."

He said it all of a sudden and I didn't have any idea in the world what to say back. What I finally said was something like, "Well, I don't think I can do that."

"Because he said so?"

"No, not just because of him."

"Because of the others?"

"We're all in this together."

"But not going by his rules anymore."

"Just the water."

"What's more important than that?"

"I'm holding it," I said. "He's the one took it."

"Now that doesn't make much sense, does it?" Dr. Favor said. "What you're doing, you're keeping something that doesn't belong to you."

I couldn't tell the man to his face I thought he was a thief. That's why I had so much trouble thinking of something to say. Even with the gun in my belt, or maybe because it was there, I felt awkward and dumb. He just kept staring at me.

"Maybe I should take it away from you," he said.

When I hesitated, not knowing what to say or do, the McLaren girl got into it. She said, looking at me, "Are you going to let him?"

She pushed up to a sitting position, about ten or twelve feet away from us. "You know what he wants," she said.

"What's mine," Dr. Favor said. "If you think anything else, you're imagining things."

"I know one thing," the McLaren girl said. "I wouldn't give you the gun if I had it. And if you tried to take it, I'd shoot you."

"For hardly more than a little girl," Dr. Favor said, "you certainly have strong opinions."

"When I know I'm right," the McLaren girl said.

Dr. Favor stood up. He lit a cigar and for a while stood there looking out over the slope and smoking. Time crept along. I laid down with one arm on the saddlebags and my head on my arm. I don't think I have ever been so tired, and it was easy to close my eyes and fall asleep. I fought it for a while, dozing, opening my eyes. Once when I opened them, I saw Dr. Favor sitting by Mendez and Mendez was smoking a cigar too.

I heard Dr. Favor say, "You did fine. It took more nerve than most have to lie there waiting for them."

"He shouldn't have made me do it," Mendez said.

"You didn't have to, you know."

"Listen, he makes sense," Mendez said. "Whether you agree with him or not."

"He makes sense even if it kills you," Dr. Favor said. "That's what you're saying."

"It's just I had never shot at a man before," Mendez said. "It isn't an easy thing."

"It seems easy to him," Dr. Favor said. "And if you can kill one person, you can kill four."

"For what reason?"

"My money," Dr. Favor said.

Mendez shook his head. "I know him better than that."

"Where money is concerned," Dr. Favor said, "you don't know anybody."

Within the next quarter of an hour Dr. Favor proved those words.

I should have taken them as a warning, but I had not for a minute thought he would ever use force. By the time I woke up (I mean actually woke up, for I had dozed off again) it was too late. Dr. Favor was standing over me with Mendez's shotgun pointed right at my head.

Mendez sat there with his legs crossed and his shoulders bunched as if he didn't care what was happening—as if Dr. Favor had just taken the gun and Mendez hadn't lifted an eyebrow to stop him.

The McLaren girl was watching too. She had been lying on her side, but now pushed herself up on one arm as Dr. Favor took the revolver from me first and then the saddlebags. He went over to the waterskin next and filled up the two-quart canteen from it, leaving hardly anything in the skin.

That's when the McLaren girl finally spoke. She said, "Maybe you'll leave us your blessing since you're taking everything else."

Dr. Favor was past arguing with anybody. He didn't say a word. He opened the canvas grainsack, looked at the meat and biscuits inside like he was going to take some out, but he pulled the neck closed and swung it over his shoulder with the saddlebags.

He was standing like that, ready to move off, when John Russell appeared out of the pinyon.

They stood facing each other about twenty feet apart, Russell holding the Spencer against his leg and pointed down; Favor holding the sawed-off shotgun the same way.

"You got everything?" Russell said.

"What's mine," Favor answered.

"You better put it down," Russell said. It sounded like he meant the shotgun.

Mendez must have felt funny about Dr. Favor holding it. He said, "He just took it. I closed my eyes and he had it."

Dr. Favor shook his head slowly. "Like I'm against everybody. Like I was running off on my own."

"You sure had us fooled then," the McLaren girl said, her voice dry and sharp enough to pierce right through him.

"Believe what you like," Dr. Favor said. "I was going to get help. One man can travel faster than five. With food and water he could make it out of here in no time and have help back in less than a day."

"So you elected yourself," the McLaren girl said.

"I've tried to reason with you people before," Dr. Favor said. "I decided it was time to do something besides waste my breath."

Russell's eyes never left Dr. Favor. "Put it down or else use it," he said. "You have two ways to go." His tone seemed to say he didn't care which Favor did. One way would be as easy as the other.

"There's no talking to a man who relies only on force," Dr. Favor said. He shrugged, hesitating, holding on by his fingernails for a moment, waiting for Russell to drop his guard for one second. Maybe he could beat Russell, he was probably thinking. But if he didn't beat him, he would be dead. If he tied Russell, he could also be dead.

Maybe that was the way he thought and he didn't like the

odds. Maybe if he gave in now he would get a better chance later on. I guess he knew nobody believed his story about getting help, but he didn't care what we thought. Whatever he was thinking, it told him today wasn't the day. He let the shotgun and revolver fall, then lifted off the grainsack and saddlebags.

No, it didn't bother him at all what we thought. He turned his back on us and strolled over by the cliffrose bushes to look down the grade. As if telling us he knew we wouldn't do anything to him, so what did he care what we thought?

But that's where he was wrong. John Russell did not just think things.

As Dr. Favor stood there, Russell said, "Keep going."

All we saw was his back for a minute. Dr. Favor seemed to be waiting for the rest of it: "—if you ever try that again." Or "—if you don't behave yourself." You know.

But there wasn't any rest of it. Russell had said it all.

When Dr. Favor realized this, he turned around to look at Russell. His face had lost a little of its calm cocksureness. Not all, just some. But maybe at that point he half believed Russell might be bluffing.

Maybe, he thought, if he could just pass a little time it would blow over.

He said, "You're betting my money I won't survive all alone."

"You could do it," Russell said. "With some luck."

"If I don't, it's the same as murder."

"Like the way you killed those people at San Carlos."

"This is a new one," Dr. Favor said. "First I'm accused of stealing my own money. Now murder."

"Without enough to eat," Russell said, "people sicken and die. I saw that at Whiteriver and also I heard things, how the agent had money to buy more beef, but he had a way of keeping the money for himself."

"A way," Dr. Favor said. "You figure the way and then prove it."

"That one called Dean said enough."

Dr. Favor seemed to smile. "But you went and killed your witness."

"You think I need one?" Russell said.

We weren't in any court. We were fifty miles out in high

desert country, and John Russell was standing there with a .56-56 Spencer in his hand. All he had to do was raise it and Dr. Favor was gone forever.

There wasn't any question, Dr. Favor knew it.

It is hard to try and imagine what was going on in his mind then, because I never did learn much about this Dr. Alexander Favor.

Look at him for a minute. A heavyset man, both in his body and in his opinion of himself. He did what he wanted and did not take much pushing from others. He had been Indian Agent at San Carlos about two years, having come from somewhere in Ohio. The "Doctor" part of his name was not medicine. I have learned that he was a Doctor of the Faith Reform Church. But I had never heard him preaching anything, so you cannot accuse him of not practicing it.

Evidently he got into that profession to make money and for that reason only, thinking it would be an easy way: the same reason he applied to the government to become an Indian Agent and got sent to San Carlos. Though he could have just made up the divinity title and got the appointment through some friend in the Interior Department. I would not like to think that he had ever honestly been a preacher.

He must have started withholding government funds soon after he got to San Carlos to build up the amount in the saddlebags. About twelve thousand dollars. He probably made some of it off supply contractors who paid him in order to get the government business. So you know one thing for sure; he was dishonest. A thief no matter what he hid behind.

You can also say he was a man who cared more about his money than his wife. But maybe he always did. I mean maybe she was just a woman to him. Someone to have around, but not feeling about her the way most men felt about their wives. I mean liking them along with having them there.

Maybe he did like her, but she never liked him and didn't care if he knew it. I think that is the way it was, judging from the way she didn't pay any attention to him on the stagecoach and fooled with Frank Braden right in front of him. I think even then Dr. Favor had finally had enough of her. Leaving her was a good way to pay her back.

You knew good and well he wasn't thinking about her now. I doubt he was even thinking about the money. Right now he just had his life to worry about. Russell wasn't letting him take anything else.

There was that little space of silence where he must have been digging in his mind to say something more to Russell, to scare him or put him in his place or something. But he must have thought what was the use? Why waste breath?

He looked at Mendez though, then at the McLaren girl and said, "You take care of yourselves now. Do everything he tells you." He was turning then to go. "And remember, don't drink any water till tonight."

We watched him step through the cliffrose bushes and he was gone. Russell went over to the edge, but the McLaren girl and Mendez and I didn't move. Not for a moment anyway. Maybe we were afraid Favor would look back up and see us watching him and laugh or say something else about the water.

When I walked over finally and looked down the grade, he was past the steepest part but having an awful time, skidding and raising dust all the way. We watched him down at the bottom, standing there for a minute, looking up canyon to the flat country that opened up there. He crossed the canyon to the other side and started up a little wash (he had learned something from Russell) and after a minute you couldn't see him for the brush and the steepness of the cutbank.

Nobody said a word.

Without Russell I know we could never have sat there in that place until dark. It was too easy to imagine them sneaking up on you, knowing they were out there somewhere and drawing closer all the time. Russell sat watching the slope. Then he'd move off into the trees for a time. He never said anything. He smoked a little, maybe twice. Most of the time though he sat watching; watching and I think listening. But all that time there was no sign of them.

As it started to get dark in the trees, we ate again and Russell held up the canteen and handed it to the McLaren girl.

"Finally, uh?" he said.

She didn't look at him. She took a drink and passed the canteen to me. Mendez was next. Then Russell took his turn.

The McLaren girl watched him drink, holding the water in his mouth before swallowing it, and I kept thinking: She's going to tell him.

Russell lowered the canteen.

Now, I thought, waiting for her to speak.

Russell pushed the cork in tight. She watched him. I think right then she almost told, so near to doing it the words were formed in her mouth. But she didn't say it.

She said instead, "Maybe we should have let him take some." Meaning Dr. Favor.

Russell looked at her.

"I mean just some," the McLaren girl said.

I thought of something then. All of a sudden. "We left a waterskin at the San Pete! Remember that?"

The McLaren girl looked at me. "Will he remember it?"

"I don't know," I said, "I just started thinking, Braden knows about it too."

We did not go down the slope we had come up but went off through the trees, following Russell and not asking any questions.

I remember we crept down through a gully that was very thick with brush and near the bottom of it Russell held up. The open part was next and it was not dark enough to cross it.

When I think of all the waiting we did. It made being out there all the worse because it gave you time to imagine things. We kept quiet because Russell did. I have never seen a man so patient. He would sit with his legs crossed and fool with a stick or something, drawing with it in the sand, making circles and different signs and then smoothing out the sand and doing it all over again. What did a man like that think about? That's what I wondered about every time I looked at him.

From this gully you could not see anything but sky and the dark hump of the slope above us. I kept thinking that if I was back in Sweetmary I would have finished my supper and would be reading or going to visit somebody; seeing the main street then and the lanterns shining through the windows of the saloons; seeing lights way off in the adobes that were situated out from town.

There were some sounds around us, night sounds, which I took as a good sign; nothing was moving nearby. I heard the clicking sound of the McLaren girl's rosary beads, which I had not heard since the first evening in the stagecoach. It was funny, I had forgotten all about making conversation in order to get to know her. If I did not know her after this, I never would. It was something the way she never complained. But maybe she spoke out a little too quickly; even when she was right. That was something I never could do.

When the time came it was like always, coming after you had got tired of waiting for it and wondering when it ever would. There was Russell standing up again, like he knew or felt the exact moment we should leave, and within a few minutes we were down out of the gully with dark, wide-open country stretching out on three sides of us.

We did what Russell did. He didn't tell us. He kept in the lead and we followed with our eyes pretty much of the time. When he stopped, we stopped, which was often, though you could never guess when it was going to be. Or you could listen till your head ached and never know what made him stop.

All of us together made some noise moving through the brush clumps and kicking stones and things, which couldn't be helped. Just grit your teeth and hope nobody else heard it. Yet when Russell moved off from us to scout a little, which he did a few times, he never made a sound going or coming. His Apache-type mocassins had something to do with it, but it was also the way he walked, a way I never learned.

You know how it is outside at night as far as seeing things, shapes and the sky and all. It is never as dark as indoors, in a cellar or in a closed room without a window. We would see a dark patch and it would turn out to be a brush thicket or some Joshua trees. There were those saguaros, but not as many as had been in the higher country. There was greasewood and prickly pear and other bushes I never knew the names of, most of them low to the ground so that you still felt yourself out in the open and unprotected.

I mentioned that Russell would stop and then we would, listening hard to make out some sound. We never heard anything except twice.

The first time, we were maybe halfway across, though it is hard to judge. I remember I was looking down at the ground, then up and I stopped all of a sudden seeing Russell standing still. He had turned and was facing us with his head raised a little.

Then we all heard it, thin and faraway but unmistakable, the sound of a gunshot.

We waited. A few minutes later it came again and seemed a little closer, though I could have imagined that. About ten seconds passed. A third gunshot sounded faintly, off in another direction, way off in the darkness.

Russell moved on, faster now, knowing they were still behind and not somewhere up ahead waiting. I was sure then that the gunshots were signals. Say they had split up to poke through that area where we had hid. Say one group found a sign of us (probably the Mexican) and signaled the others with a shot, then with another one when they did not answer at first. The third shot was when they did answer.

The McLaren girl thought differently. Right after the shots, as we went on, she said to me, "They've killed him."

I had forgotten about Dr. Favor until she said that. I explained what I thought about the signals.

"Maybe," she said. "But if they haven't killed him he'll die of thirst or starvation. He doesn't have any chance at all."

I said, "He sure didn't worry about us."

"Because he would do such a thing," the McLaren girl said, "should we?"

How do you answer a question like that? Anyway it wasn't us that did it, it was Russell. She certainly worried a lot without showing it on her face. I will say that for the McLaren girl.

The second time we heard a sound was a little later. This time it was a horse, sounding close, but far enough out so we couldn't see it. We went down flat and stayed that way for some time. We heard the horse again, never running or galloping, but walking, his shoes clinking against stones. It never came so close you could see it, but there was no doubting what it meant. They were out in the open now looking for us.

When Russell moved off finally it was at his careful, stopping, listening pace again. Nothing could hurry him, not even feeling them out here. He moved along with the Spencer down-pointed in one hand and the saddlebags over the other shoulder, like there wasn't anything in the world could make him hurry. Add that to what you know about his patience.

We saw the shape of the high ground ahead of us by the time we were halfway across. That's what made going slow so hard. There was cover staring right at you, but Russell chose to walk to it.

Finally he led us into some trees that was like going into a house and locking the door, and right away (which surprised nobody) we were climbing again. All the way up to the top of a ridge and along it instead of taking the pass that led into these hills. This part wasn't hard; it was even ground, grassy and with a lot of trees. But when we came to a higher ridge and Russell started climbing again, Mendez complained.

I don't think Russell even looked at him. He went on climbing and the rest of us followed: up through rocks and places you had to grab hold of roots and branches to pull yourself up. Then along a path that was probably a game trail, and finally on up to the top.

A couple of hundred yards along this ridge Russell stopped. There, down below us, was the San Pete mine works.

We had approached it the back way, from up above the shafts and crushing mill and all, which were on this side of the canyon. Way over on the other side you could make out the company buildings, even the one we had eaten breakfast in two days ago.

I think I would have bought John Russell a drink of liquor right then had there been any to buy. The McLaren girl and Mendez just stared; you could see the relief on their faces. That's what seeing something familiar did, letting you forget Braden for a minute and look ahead and start to see a little daylight.

At that point there was the sure feeling with all of us that we would make it to Delgado's without Braden ever getting close again. Except that just a little later on there was another familiar sight. One we had not counted on.

I am referring to Dr. Favor.

But I will get to that in a minute.

It was still dark as we came down the ridge toward the mine works. We didn't go down all the way, only about fifty or sixty feet to a level place where the open mine shafts and a shack were.

Farther along this shelf there was a shute built on scaffolding that went down to the big crushing mill located about forty or fifty yards down the grade. Ore tailings, which were slides of rock and sand and stuff that had been taken out of the shafts and dumped, formed long humps down on the other side of the crushing mill. Everything was quiet and there wasn't even a breeze moving.

As I have said, it was still dark, but you could make out the shapes of things down below: the crushing mill and ore tailings to the left of where we were; the company buildings about two hundred yards away, directly across the canyon from us.

We stood there for a few minutes, Russell looking over the works and I guess, thinking. Finally, when he spoke he said, "This is a good place." Meaning the shack up here on the shelf.

"There's more water for us down there," Mendez said, meaning the waterskin we'd left in that company building the day before yesterday.

Russell shook his head. "If we stay here all day, you want tracks leading up and down?"

"Stay!" Mendez said. The waiting was worrying his nerves. "Man, we're so close now!"

"If you go," Russell said, without any feeling at all, "you go back the way we came."

Mendez looked at him with those solemn eyes of his. He didn't say any more. We went inside the shack which was empty except for a couple of bats which we shooed out. On the two side walls were shelves that held bags of concentrate. (Evidently they had used this shack to test ore samples in.) We just stretched out on the dusty floor and used some of these bags as pillows.

Russell left the door part way open and laid down his head near the opening. I laid down over by one of the windows. There were two of them in front, with board shutters you couldn't close.

Just one small thing: Russell did not offer his blanket to the McLaren girl, but used it himself. I offered mine to her again, as I had done the night before, and this time she took it. Figure that one out.

It was a few hours later, say between six and seven in the morning, after we had slept some and eaten and had our day's water, that we saw Dr. Favor again. The McLaren girl, by the right-hand window at the time, saw him first.

He was already down out of the south pass that approached the mine from the direction of that open country we had crossed. He was moving slow; dead tired you could see, his clothes messier and dirtier looking than before. He walked straight down the middle of the canyon in the sunlight and in the dead silence of those rickety buildings, looking up at the crushing mill for the longest time, then over at the line of company buildings.

Watching him, nobody said a word, waiting to see if he remembered the waterskin.

Alongside one of the buildings was a trough with a hand pump at one end of it. When Dr. Favor saw it, he ran over and started pumping. He fell on his knees and kept on pumping, his shoulders and arms moving up and down, up and down, keeping at it even when he must have known he wasn't going to get any water. After a few minutes he was pumping slower and slower. Finally he fell over the pump and held on there, not moving.

Inside the shack it was quiet as could be.

I remember when the McLaren girl spoke it was hardly above a whisper. I was by the other window with Mendez; Russell was by the door; but we all heard her. "He doesn't remember it," she said.

None of the others spoke.

"We have to tell him," she said then, calm and quiet about it, stating a fact, not just giving in to pity at the sight of him.

"We don't do anything," Russell said from the door. He kept his gaze on Dr. Favor who had sat down now, one arm still on the pump handle.

"You can look at that man," the McLaren girl said, "and not want to help him?" She was staring at Russell now.

"He'll move off," Russell said. "Then you won't have to look at him."

"But he's dying of thirst. You can *see* he is!"

"What did you think would happen?" Russell said. He looked at her then. "You didn't think you'd see him again. So yesterday was all right, uh?"

"If I didn't speak up yesterday," the McLaren girl said, "I was wrong."

"You'd feel better if he had run off with the water?"

"That has nothing to do with him down there now."

"But if you were down there," Russell said, "and he was up here."

"You just don't understand, do you?" the McLaren girl said.

Russell kept staring at her. "What do you want to do?"

"I want to help him!" She raised her voice a little, like she was running out of patience.

It didn't seem to bother Russell any. He said, "You want to go down to him? Make tracks on that slope that hasn't been touched in five years? You want to make signs pointing up where we are?"

"The man's dying of thirst!" She screamed it at Russell. She had run clean out of patience and threw the words right at him.

I don't mean she screamed so loud Dr. Favor heard her. He had now got up from the pump and was moving along the front of the company buildings, reaching the one we had stopped at the day before yesterday and looking up at it.

I held my breath again. Maybe he'd remembered the waterskin. But no, he went on by.

The next thing I knew the McLaren girl was out the window and running down the slope. Russell was out the door but too late to stop her. He stood there in front of the shack, Mendez and I by the window, and watched her raising little dust trails down the grade, seeing her getting smaller and smaller.

Near the bottom the McLaren girl called out. We saw Dr. Favor stop and look around. (He must have been surprised out of his shoes.) He started toward her, but she was yelling something at him now, motioning to the company building.

He stood there a second, then was almost running in his hurry to get to the building, the McLaren girl waiting now to see if he'd find the waterskin.

We were watching all this. We saw him reach the front of the place, just out from the shade formed by the veranda, and that's where he stopped. Right away he started backing off, like edging away. Next thing he had turned and was running toward the McLaren girl who didn't know what was going on any more than we did and stood there watching him.

As he got close he must have said something. The McLaren girl started up the grade, looking back at the company building as she did.

About then was when he appeared. It was Early. He came out of the veranda shade, to the edge of it, and stood there with a Colt gun in one hand and a canteen in the other—evidently the canteen with whisky in it which the Mexican had mentioned to John Russell, for I think Early was drunk or close to it. The way he stood, his boots wide apart, looked like he was steadying himself. I won't swear to it because there wasn't time to get a good look at him.

He started firing his Colt, waving it toward us or at the McLaren girl and Dr. Favor as they came up the grade, causing Mendez and me to duck down, and firing until his gun was empty. He started yelling then, but we couldn't make out any of it.

I kept waiting for Braden and the others to appear, but they didn't. Not right then. Evidently Early had been sent on ahead, Braden figuring we would come this way.

I was still there at the window when the McLaren girl and Dr. Favor reached the shack. She came inside and went out again with the canteen and gave it to Dr. Favor who drank until she yanked it away from his mouth. He yanked back, held onto it and handed it to Russell. I think he could tell from looking at Russell that saving him had been just the McLaren girl's idea. He seemed to be smiling some, like the joke was on Russell.

"You will learn something about white people," he said to Russell. "They stick together."

"They better," Mendez said. "We all better."

Just for a second there was the old tell-nothing Henry Mendez talking. It sounded good after seeing the other side of him for two days. He wasn't looking at Dr. Favor. I noticed then Russell was looking off down the slope too.

Like they had been following Dr. Favor (and no doubt they had), there came the Mexican on foot, Frank Braden and the Favor woman each on a horse, this little procession coming down out of the south pass, keeping close to the other side and in no hurry at all. The Mexican raised his arm up and waved.

We were all back together again. Right back where we had started. Except now we were up on that shelf of rock, looking down and seeing them moving up canyon and dismounting in front of the company building that was straight across from us and drawing their rifles.

You think about an awful lot of things at once. That we should be doing something; getting out of there or doing *something*. That this never should have happened. That if it wasn't for the McLaren girl and her act of kindness to a man who didn't deserve it, they never would have found us; they would have looked up at that bare unmarked slope and gone right on. Maybe you would like to have said something to the McLaren girl. It was a temptation. But only Mendez did.

He said, "You see?" looking at Dr. Favor and then at the McLaren girl in the doorway. "You see?" he said again, wanting to say more, but just shaking his head as he thought of everything at once.

The McLaren girl had been quiet, but I think Mendez made her mad. She said, "I'd do it again. Knowing they were there I'd do it again. What do you think of that!"

"He's not worth it!" Mendez said, keeping his teeth together so he wouldn't scream it at her. Still it was loud.

"Who are you to say who's worth it!" When she got mad, she spoke out, as you have seen.

Dr. Favor didn't get into it. He was running his tongue over his swollen lips, I think still tasting the water.

And Russell. Russell, still outside squatted down, sitting back on his heels. He was smoking a cigarette, gazing over across the canyon. Russell didn't look at the McLaren girl (not then) or say anything to anybody. Russell was Russell.

He just smoked the cigarette as he watched Braden and the others over in front of the company building, watching them take the two horses into the shade of the built-up, second-storey veranda, watching the Mexican come out again in the sunlight and walk up and down in a show-offy way, his hands on his hips and looking up toward where we were.

That's when Russell came inside the shack. Next thing I knew he was at the other window with the Spencer at his shoulder. I doubt the Mexican saw him. I'm sure he didn't else he would have done something before Russell fired.

With the sound of the shot and dust kicking up in front of him, the Mexican stopped dead. Russell fired again and this time the Mexican jumped back into the veranda shade. Russell was not taking anything off that Mexican.

"What do you start that for?" Mendez said, sounding pained.

Russell must have thought there was an awful lot of dumb questions asked. He said to Mendez, "So they'd see us."

Nobody down there returned the fire, but we kept expecting it. Everybody was inside by then. Russell was already piling those bags of concentrate on his window sill. I started building up the other one then, the McLaren girl helping. Mendez brought a few over to Russell, but Dr. Favor didn't lift a hand. He was doing his thinking now, I guess, and eying the saddlebags. Since Russell didn't say anything to him, I didn't either. Hell.

Next Russell pulled the loading tube out of his Spencer and stuck two more cartridges in it from his belt. I kept by the other window wondering if this little revolver I had would do any good.

The minutes went by but the awful nervous feeling I had and tried not to show didn't ease up any. I remember wondering if Russell was scared. He had taken his hat off and I could see the side of his face good. As I have said before, he looked so much younger with his hat off and his hair pressed down on his forehead. He would swallow or scratch his nose, things everybody did, and he didn't seem any different than the rest of us.

Only he was different. As Braden was about to learn first hand.

Frank Braden's idea was to let us worry some, I suppose. About a half hour passed before we heard from him. Then it came all of a sudden.

He yelled out from across the way, "You hear me!" He waited. "I'm coming up to talk! You hold your fire!" He waited and yelled again. Maybe a minute passed.

Then Braden appeared at the edge of the veranda shade. Early and the Mexican were behind him. They waited there as Braden moved out from them carrying a Winchester rifle and a white cloth or something tied to the end of it. Frank Braden's idea of a truce flag.

Russell watched him. As Braden came across the open, out in the sunlight and without any cover close by, Russell raised the Spencer and eared back the hammer.

"He wants to talk," Mendez said. "You heard him. It's no trick. He's got something to say to us!"

Russell didn't bother with Mendez or even look up. He steadied the Spencer on the ore-sample bags and put the front sight on Braden.

5

FRANK BRADEN had nerve. You can put that under his name big. A man does not hold up stagecoaches without nerve, or walk up an open grade in plain sight of people he knows are armed.

If he was afraid at all, he never showed it. The way his hat was funneled and tipped forward over his eyes he had to raise his head to look up. He kept watching, but it did not make him hesitate. He came across the open from the company building like nothing in the world bothered him, the Winchester raised a little and the white truce flag tied to the end of it.

He was putting his faith in that truce flag and the fact that the Mexican had done the same thing yesterday without drawing fire. It showed he still didn't know John Russell very well.

Russell was letting him come. He never took the Spencer away from his shoulder, but the barrel kept lowering a hair at a time as Braden came closer. Anyone else might have been covering Braden; but somehow you knew Russell meant to fire on him, else he never would have raised the gun. The question was how close Braden would get.

"Listen—he just wants to talk," Mendez said, moving toward Russell as you would approach a bronc with your hand out to gentle it. "You can see it's no trick. The man is coming to *talk*. Can't you see that? You want to start something when there's no need to?"

"Look at me!"

Russell's head raised up a little, interrupted from what he was concentrating on. But he kept his eyes on Braden who had now reached some ore-cart tracks that came across from the crushing mill and past a little shack on out into the open a ways. On this side of the tracks Braden was less than a hundred yards off. He kept coming.

"Just see what he wants," Mendez said. "You don't have to talk to him. You don't want to, one of us will." Mendez looked outside, seeing Braden on the grade now and starting up.

"You don't know what he wants. Man, you got to find out what he wants," Mendez kept saying. "Listen to him. He trusts us . . . we have to trust him and see what he wants. Doesn't that make sense to you?" Mendez said it all fast. If it didn't convince Russell, it bothered him enough so he couldn't concentrate on Braden.

By that time Braden was part way up the grade. He stopped there and yelled out, "Anybody home?"

Mendez saw the opportunity looking at him and he grabbed hold of it. "We hear you!" he yelled back.

"Come on out of that boar's nest," Braden called. "We'll talk some."

"Say what you want," Mendez answered.

"I thought maybe you'd like to go home."

"Say something," Mendez said.

"It's looking at you," Braden said back. "We can sit here long as we want. I can send a man for more water and chuck, but you people can't move. You only move if we let you. You see that?"

"What else?"

"There doesn't have to be much else."

"All right, what do you want?"

"You leave the money, we leave the woman."

"And everybody goes home?"

"Everybody goes home."

"We'll have to talk about it."

"You do that." Braden held the Winchester cradled over one arm, the truce flag hanging limp. He stood with his feet spread some, posing, it looked like, confident he knew what he was doing.

"We'll let you look at the woman while you talk," Braden said. "Then when you're ready you bring the money down and take the woman."

"We'll talk about it," Mendez said again. He glanced over at Dr. Favor who was at the other window, then down at Braden again.

"What if," he said "—well, what if nobody wants this woman?"

"Wait a while," Braden answered, "before you think anything like that."

"I just want to make sure what you mean, that's all."

"You just have to be sure of one thing," Braden said. "You don't leave here with the money. You see that?"

Mendez didn't answer. Frank Braden waited a minute then started to go.

"Hey," Russell called out to him and Braden stopped, half way around so that he was looking back over his shoulder.

"I got a question," Russell said.

Braden was squinting to make out Russell in the window. "Ask it," he said.

"How you going to get down that hill?"

Braden knew what he meant. He stood there a moment, then came around slowly to face the shack again, showing us he wasn't afraid.

"Look, I come up here to tell you how things are. I'm making it easy on you."

"We didn't ask you," Russell said. "You walk up here yourself. You come and say we're not leaving with the money . . . uh?"

"You heard what I said." Braden was tenser, you could tell.

"We give up the money or you kill us."

"I said you wouldn't leave here."

"But it's the same thing, uh? . . . Maybe we give up the money and you still kill us."

"You better talk to your friends."

"I think," Russell kept on, "you want to leave dead people who can't tell things."

"If that was so, we'd have killed you at the stagecoach."

"You tried to," Russell said, "taking the water. But it came back to us."

"You think what you want," Braden said, meaning to end it.

Russell nodded. He nodded up and down very slowly two or three times. "I've already thought," he said in that mild way, so calm you did not suspect what he meant until he raised the Spencer. Then there was no doubt what he meant.

"You hold on, boy!" Braden said. "I'm walking down the same way I come up." But he was backing off, keeping his gaze fixed on the window.

Russell had the Spencer at his shoulder, but his head up as he watched Braden.

"You hear me!" Braden yelled. "You hold on!"

It was like Russell was letting out rope, giving Braden a little slack before he yanked it tight. It was coming. We knew it and Braden, still backing away, knew it. But only Russell knew when. That's what finally spooked Braden. He might have had seven miles of nerve inside of him, but all of a sudden he found it all let out and there was only one thing left to do.

He started running, starting so fast across the slope toward the crushing mill that he fell within four or five steps, falling just as Russell pressed his face to that Spencer and fired. Maybe that fall saved Braden's life; for certain it hurried Russell's second shot, trying to get Braden while he was down, but that one kicked sand right in front of Braden who was lunging to his feet, running again, getting some distance as Russell took his time and aimed and when he fired again Braden twisted and rolled a ways down the slope. That's when the gunfire opened up from the company building as the Mexican and Early woke up and started giving Braden some cover. Braden was crawling, then up on his feet and running again, limping-running, favoring one leg—and *bam*, the Spencer went off and Braden was knocked down again, down on his hands and knees, but somehow kept going, clawing the ground and half running half crawling, the Winchester truce flag behind him now and forgotten. Russell fired again, hurrying it because Braden was close to the crushing mill by then and that was Russell's last one; Braden made it, reaching the corner of the building, about forty yards over from us, as the sound of Russell's shot sang off down canyon.

It was the Mexican who got Braden out of there. He came up over on the other side of the crushing mill and brought Braden down the same way, keeping the crushing mill between us and them so they wouldn't get shot at.

Early came out of the veranda shade to help the Mexican take Braden inside: Early looking back like he was afraid Russell would open up again, and Braden walking but dragging his legs and leaning on the two men. He had been shot up good.

Mr. Braden, I thought to myself. Meet John Russell.

But was our situation any better?

Maybe. Depending on Braden. If he was hurt bad enough, they would have to get him to a bed or a doctor. So for a while we watched with that hope. But the hope kept getting smaller and smaller as time passed and nobody rode out from the company building.

When there was no doubt but they were staying, Henry Mendez started on Russell again. Why did you have to do that? Why didn't you let things just happen? he kept saying. It would be worse for us now, Mendez was sure. And it was Russell's fault.

"Nothing is different," Russell said. In other words, they could be mad or shot up or hungry or drunk, they'd still try to kill us. When you thought about it, you knew it was true.

While Mendez and Russell were together I brought up the idea of getting out the way we'd come in.

They'd shoot us off the wall as we climbed up, was Mendez's answer. "Not when it's dark," Russell said; you saw he was thinking of ways.

So far, you will notice, no one had said Russell should give them the money in exchange for Mrs. Favor: do what Braden wanted and *see* what would happen, not just guess. Maybe because it would be wasting breath to mention it to Russell. Or maybe because no one was thinking of Mrs. Favor at that time.

Well, that changed as soon as the Mexican brought her out. Maybe an hour had passed from the time Braden was shot. (It's hard to remember now the different spaces of time.) It had been so quiet over there. Then the Mexican was coming out across the open with Mrs. Favor in front of him. Her hands were tied and there was a length of rope, like a dog leash, tied around her neck with the Mexican holding the other end.

He brought her all the way out to the ore-cart tracks that came down from the crushing mill and made her sit down there. Kneeling, he tied the leash to one of the rails, keeping Mrs. Favor in front of him as he did. He drew his left-hand Colt then, holding his right elbow tight against his side, and ran to a little shed that was just above and over a few yards.

He surprised us then. Instead of going back, keeping the shed in line with us as a cover, he made a run all the way across a pretty open stretch to the crushing mill.

Picture him about forty yards down and over to our left; Mrs. Favor straight down, looking small sitting there and staring up at the shack, about eighty yards away.

It was while the Mexican was making his run that Early came out carrying a rifle and moved off toward the south pass on foot. I did not have to think about it long. Early was circling around to get behind us, closing the back door whether we wanted to use it or not.

That's what Russell said too. He was still at the window watching the corner of the crushing mill where the Mexican was. The McLaren girl asked him where Early was going and Russell said, "Behind us," not taking his eyes off the crushing mill; the Mexican had not shown himself yet.

Dr. Favor, at this time, was at the other window looking down at his wife. It was a strange thing, while he was there no one else went out to the window, as if letting him be alone with her. But he did not stay too long; he walked away and lit up a cigar and sat down, I guess to think some more.

The McLaren girl and Mendez and I finally found ourselves at that window, where we stayed just about all the rest of the time we were there. Of course we kept looking at Mrs. Favor.

Remember Braden saying, "We'll let you look at the woman while you talk?" He knew what he was doing.

She sat there between the ore-cart tracks looking up this way most of the time. We soon learned that she could not stand up straight; the rope tied to her neck was not long enough. She could get in a bent-over position, but that was all. For a time she tried to undo the rope end tied to the track, but evidently the Mexican had tied it too tight.

So she just sat there out in the open with the sun getting higher all the time, sometimes brushing her hair out of her face or picking things off her skirt. The way she would look up—my gosh—you knew what she was thinking. But she certainly was calm about it, not even crying once. It was not till a little later we found out they had not given her any water.

It was after the Mexican started on Russell.

He yelled out from the corner of the crushing mill, just showing part of his head for a second, "Hey, *hombre*! How do you like that woman? . . . You want her? . . . We give her to you!" Things like that.

John Russell did not answer. Except he put his face against the stock of the Spencer and the front sight on the corner of the crushing mill.

The Mexican waited a while. Then he yelled, "If you want that, *hombre*, you better hurry! Maybe there won't be nothing left in the sun!"

It was about 10 o'clock by then, maybe a little earlier.

Then the Mexican yelled, "Man, why don't you come out and give her a drink of water? She hasn't had none . . . not since yesterday morning!"

There he was, just a little part of him at the corner, and *bam* the Spencer went off and you saw the wood splinter right where the Mexican's face had been.

It was quiet right after, long enough for us to wonder if Russell had got him. Long enough for the McLaren girl to say, "That woman hasn't had any water." Then to Russell: "Did you hear what he said? She hasn't had water since yesterday."

Russell was watching the corner still. The McLaren girl kept staring at him. "Is that why you want to kill him?" she said then. "To shut him up? So you won't have to hear about her?"

I touched her arm to calm her, but she jerked away. "It won't help to get fighting among ourselves," I said.

"Are we all on the same side?" she said. "Do you really think that?"

"Well, we're all sitting here."

She was looking at Russell again. "He's sitting here with twelve thousand dollars of somebody else's money and that woman is tied like an animal out there in the sun." She looked at me like somebody should do something.

"Well, what do you want him to do?"

The McLaren girl never answered. The Mexican yelled out again, letting us know he was still alive. "Hey, *hombre*!" he called out. "You got wood in my eyes! . . . Come down here and help me get it out!" Honest to gosh, like he thought it was funny to be shot at.

He kept it up, yelling at Russell from time to time, trying to get him outside. We heard from Early a few times too. Rocks coming down on the roof from above: Early still feeling his whisky and being playful, or else just letting us know he was up there and not to try anything.

The McLaren girl was quiet for a while. I guess she had calmed down. The sole of one of her shoes was loose and she kept fooling with it, trying to twist it off, even when she was looking at Mrs. Favor who sat with her shoulders hunched over now and her head down. The McLaren girl could not look at her too long, or fool with that shoe forever.

She started looking at Russell and finally went over and kneeled down next to him. Russell was smoking, sitting back on his feet, the Spencer resting on the ore bags lining the window sill.

"We have to give them the money," she said, very quietly, "I think you know that."

He looked at her, not just glancing but taking his time to look at her dark sun-browned face good.

"Like you had to give that one water," Russell said. Meaning Dr. Favor.

"That's over with." She bristled up a little.

"You think he would have done it for you?"

"Somebody would have."

"How do you know that?"

"I just know. People help other people."

"People kill other people too."

"I've seen that."

"You're going to see some more."

"If you want to say it's my fault we're stuck here, go ahead," the McLaren girl said. "It might make you feel better, but it won't change anything."

Russell shook his head. "The thing I want to know is why you helped."

"Because he *needed* help! I didn't ask if he deserved it!"

She let her temper calm down and said, half as loud, "Like that woman needs to live. It's not up to us to decide if she deserves it."

"We only help her, uh?"

"Do we have another choice?"

Russell nodded. "Not help her."

"Just let her die." The McLaren girl kept staring at him.

"That's up to Braden," Russell said. "We have another thing to look at. If we don't give him the money, he has to come get it."

The McLaren girl almost let go of her temper then. "You'd sacrifice a human life for that money. That's what you're saying."

Russell started making a cigarette, looking out the window at the crushing mill as he shaped it, then at the McLaren girl again. "Go ask that woman what she thinks of human life. Ask her what a human life is worth at San Carlos when they run out of meat."

"That isn't any fault of hers."

"She said those dirty Indians eat dogs. You remember that? She couldn't eat a dog no matter how hungry she was." Everybody was watching him. He lit his cigarette and blew out smoke. "Go ask her if she'd eat a dog now."

"That's why!" the McLaren girl said, like it was all clear to her now. "She insulted the poor hungry miserable Indians and you'd let her die for that!"

Russell shook his head. "We were talking about human life."

"Even if there was no money, nothing to be gained, you'd let her die!" All the McLaren girl's temper was showing now, and she was just letting it come. "Because she thinks Indians are dirty and no better than animals you'd sit there and let her die!"

Russell held the cigarette close to his mouth, watching her. "It makes you angry, why talk about it?"

"I want to talk about it," she shot back. "I would like you to ask me what I think a human life is worth . . . a dirty human Apache life. Go on, ask me. Ask me about the ones that took me from my home and kept me past a month. Ask me about the dirty things they did, what the women did when the men weren't around and what the men did when we weren't running but were hiding somewhere and there was time to waste. I dare you to ask me!"

She knelt there tensed, like she was to spring on him if he moved, though it was just she was so intent on telling him what she'd just said.

It was all out of her system then. I think everybody wasn't so tense anymore. She sank back to a sitting position, taking her eyes off Russell, looking down at that loose sole on her shoe and fooling with it as she thought something over.

Next thing, she was saying, "I haven't seen my folks in almost two months . . . or my little brother. Just he and I were home and he ran and I don't know what happened to him, whether they caught him or what."

She looked up at Russell again, all the softness gone out of her that quick, like it was starting all over again. "What do they think of an eight-year-old human life?" she said. "Do they just kill little boys who can't defend themselves?"

Russell had not taken his eyes off her, still holding the cigarette up near his face. "If they don't want them," he said, and kept looking right at her.

That ended it. For a thin little seventeen-year-old girl she was tougher than most men and I think you know that by now. But she had to give some time. I thought she was going to cut at Russell again, but the words didn't come. Her eyes filled up first. She sat there trying to keep her chin from quivering or crying so we'd hear her, still looking right at Russell even with her eyes wet, daring him to say something else.

Right at that time (and it was almost welcome) the Mexican started again. He yelled out, "Hey man, you hear me!" Russell turned and looked down the barrel of the Spencer. The Mexican wasn't showing himself now and his voice sounded a little farther away. You knew he was there though.

"Come on down here," the Mexican yelled out, "I got something for you!"

Russell had something for him too if he showed even part of his face.

"Man!" the Mexican yelled then. "We both come out—talk to each other!"

He waited.

"You bring that piece of iron you got. I bring one, uh?"

Every word he yelled echoed up canyon and came back again.

"Hey, *hombre*, whatever your name is—you hear me!"

After that he said some things I had better not put down here, terrible words that were embarrassing to hear with the McLaren girl in the same room. He was trying to get Russell out by insulting him, but he could have been yelling at a tree stump for all the good it did. Russell sat there waiting for the Mexican to show himself; which he never did.

Something Russell had said to the McLaren girl bothered me, so I asked him about it: about them having to come up here if they wanted the money. Why couldn't they just outwait us? Our water would run out (there was about a quart and a half left) then what would we do?

Theirs would run out too, Russell said. But, I said, they can go get more.

All the way to Delgado's? Russell said. Who would go, the one up behind us? The Mexican? Then who would watch us? No, Russell said. Some time they have to come up here. They know it.

I said that may be, but the Favor woman would be dead by then. Russell didn't answer.

About two o'clock in the afternoon the Favor woman started screaming.

It could not get any hotter than it was then. There was no breeze, no clouds; the sun was bright, boiling hot and you would not even dare look up to see where it was.

The Favor woman sat down there near the bottom of the grade, no hat or anything to cover her head, no shade to crawl into. As I have said, there was a little shack near where she was, but the rope tied to her neck would not even let her stand up straight much less get over to the shack. She had given up trying to undo the rope.

For the longest time she sat hunched over, her face buried in her arm resting on her raised knees. Now she was looking up toward us, as she had done when the Mexican first put her there, and now every once in a while she would scream out to her husband, calling his name at first.

"Alex!" she would call, but drawn out and faint sounding, not sharp and loud as you would imagine a real scream.

"Alex . . . help me!" Sounding far away almost, like hearing only an echo of the words. She had not had water since yesterday. It was something that she could call out at all.

Dr. Favor raised up when she started and looked down at her for a while. I don't know what he was thinking. I don't even know if he felt sorry for her, because his expression never changed; he was just looking at something. He didn't call back to her or say a word.

Some people can hide their feelings very well, so I had better not pass judgment on Dr. Favor. I remember picturing him and his wife alone and wondering what they ever talked about and if they had ever got along well together. (I couldn't help having that feeling she had been just a woman to him. You know what I mean, just a woman to have around.) I tried to imagine her calling him Alex when they were alone. But it didn't sound right. He was not the kind of man you thought of as having a first name. Especially not a name like Alex or Alexander.

There it was though, faintly, coming from out of that big open canyon, "Alex . . ." And he just sat there looking down at her, not moving much other than to feel his beard, to rub it gently under his chin with the back of his fingers.

Once she stood up, as far as she could, and yelled his name louder than she ever did before. "Alex!" And this time it was sharp and clear enough and with an echo coming back to give you goose pimples at the sound of it.

And then again, which I will hear every day of my life.

"Alex . . . please help me!" The words all alone outside, echoing and fading to nothing.

It was strange to be in a room with four people and not hear one sound. Everybody sat there holding still, waiting for the Favor woman to cry out again. Maybe a couple of minutes passed; maybe more than that, it seemed longer. It was so quiet that when the sound came—the sound of a match scraping and popping aflame—everybody looked up and right at John Russell.

He lit his cigarette, shook the match out and threw it up past his shoulder, out the window.

The McLaren girl, closer to the window where Mendez and I still were, kept staring at Russell. Do you see how his calm rubbed her? I think any of the rest of us could have lit a cigarette at that time and it would have been all right. But not Russell. Lighting that match touched it off again. Just the way she was looking at him you could see it coming, so I tried to head it off.

I said, "I've been thinking"—though I hadn't, it just came to me then—"when it gets dark, why can't a couple of us sneak down and get her? Maybe we could get her up here without them even seeing us."

"But if they heard you—" Mendez said.

"By dark she'll be dead," the McLaren girl said.

"You don't *know* that," I said.

"Do you want to wait and find out?"

"I was thinking something else," I said. "Braden's watching her too. What if he sees it's not working or he feels sorry for her or something and has that Mexican bring her back in?"

"You just think nice things, don't you?" the McLaren girl said.

"It could happen."

"The day he changes into a human being." She looked at Russell smoking his cigarette. "Or the day *he* does. That's the only thing will save her."

Russell was watching her, but just then the Mexican yelled out from the crushing mill, and Russell's head turned to look down the barrel of the Spencer.

"Hey, *hombre*!" the Mexican yelled, followed by a string of words some of which were in Spanish and were probably as obscene as the English ones mixed in. "Come on down and see me!"

Russell kept looking down the Spencer for at least a minute. When he turned to us again, he drew on his cigarette and dropped it out the window. The hand came down on the saddlebags next to him. He lifted them up, feeling the weight of them, then let them swing a little and threw them so they fell out in the middle of the floor.

"You want to save her?" Russell said. He looked at Mendez and me and then over to Dr. Favor sitting with his back to the wall a few feet from me. "Somebody want to walk down there and save her?"

Nobody answered.

"Somebody wants to, go ahead," Russell said. "But I'll tell you one thing first. You walk down there you won't walk back. Leave that bag and start to take the woman and they'll kill both of you."

The McLaren girl was watching him, leaning forward a little. "You're saying that so nobody will take the money and try it."

"They'll kill both of you," Russell said. "That's why I'm saying it." He looked over at Dr. Favor before the McLaren girl could say anything else.

"That woman's your wife," Russell said to him. "You want to go untie her?"

Dr. Favor, his head down a little, had his eyes on Russell, but he didn't say one word.

Russell took his time, making it awful embarrassing, so you wouldn't dare look over at Dr. Favor. Finally Russell turned to us again.

"Mr. Mendez," he said, "you want to save her? . . . Or Mr. Carl Allen, I think your name is, you want to walk down there? This man won't. It's his wife, but he won't do it. He doesn't care about his own woman, but maybe someone else does, uh? That's what I want to know."

He was looking right at the McLaren girl then and said, "I don't think I know your name. We live together some, uh? But I don't know your name."

"Kathleen McLaren," she said. He must have surprised her, caught her without anything else ready to say.

"All right, Kathleen McLaren," Russell said. "How would you like to walk down there and untie her and start up again and get shot in the back? Or in the front if that one by the mill does it. In the back or in the front, but one way or the other."

She kept looking at him but didn't say a word.

"There it is," Russell said, nodding to the saddlebags. "Take it. You worry more about his wife than he does. You say I'm not sure or I'm not telling the truth—all right, you go find out what happens."

Russell did a strange thing then. He took off his Apache moccasins and threw them over to the McLaren girl.

"Wear those," he said. "You run faster when they start shooting."

He opened up his blanket and took out his boots and pulled them on. While he did, the McLaren girl kept staring at him; but she never spoke. And when he looked up at her again, her eyes held only for a second before looking away.

It was one thing to know a woman would die if she didn't get help. It was another thing to say you'd die helping her.

I kept thinking of what Russell had said right to me ". . . do you want to walk down there?"

No, I didn't, and I will admit that right here. I believed Braden would shoot anybody who went down there with the money. I think everybody believed it by then. Yes, even the McLaren girl.

The best thing to do, I decided, was just sit there and wait and see what happened. That sounds like a terrible thing to say when a woman's life is at stake, Mrs. Favor's; but I will tell you now it's easier to think of your own life than someone else's. I don't care how brave a person is.

I will admit, too, that Dr. Favor being there made it easier on your conscience. If anybody should go down there it was him. He wasn't going though; that was certain.

Some more time passed. The Mexican, who was patient and had as much time as we did, yelled out at Russell once in a while. Russell stayed with his face pressed to that Spencer longer every time the Mexican insulted him or tried to draw him out. You could see Russell was anxious to get the Mexican. After quite a while passed and the Mexican did not yell at him again, Russell turned around to lean against the wall and make a cigarette. I noticed he threw the tobacco sack away after. It was his last one. He did not light it though; not yet.

Time passed as we sat there and nobody said a word. Russell was thinking, working something out and picturing how it would be; I was sure of that.

About four o'clock the Favor woman started screaming for her husband again; the sounds coming not so loud as before, but it was an awful thing to hear. She would call his name, then say something else which was never clear but like she was pleading with him to help her.

Sitting there in the shack you heard it faintly out in the canyon, "Alex"—the name drawn out, then again maybe and the rest of the words coming like a long moan.

It was quiet when Russell stood up. He looked out the window, not long, just a minute or so, then went over and picked up the grainsack, emptying out what meat and bread and coffee were left, and brought it back to the window. He took one of the ore bags from the sill and put it in the sack. Nobody else moved, all of us watching him. That was when he lit his last cigarette. He drew on it very slowly, very carefully. We kept watching him, maybe not trusting him either, knowing he was about to do something.

"I need somebody," Russell said, looking right at me. Not knowing what he meant I just sat there. "Right here," he said, nodding to the window.

I went over, not in any hurry, staring at him to show I didn't understand. But he didn't explain until he'd motioned again and I was kneeling there with the stock of his Spencer between us. Russell put his hand on it.

"You know how to shoot this?"

"I'm not sure." Frowning at him.

"Push the trigger guard down with your thumb. That ejects and loads . . . uh? Right now it's ready and maybe you only need the one." He added, almost under his breath, "Man, I hope you only need one."

I said, "I'm going to shoot at them?"

"The one by the mill." Russell looked out the window. "He'll come across and walk past that shack by the woman and stand with his back to you, up this way from the shack a little. Then, be sure then, you keep the front sight on him."

"I don't understand what you mean," I said.

"What's there to understand?" There was just a little surprise in his voice, mostly it was quiet and patient. "If he touches his gun, you shoot him."

"But," I said, "in the *back*?"

"I'll ask him if he'll turn around," Russell said.

"Look," I said, "I just don't understand what's going to happen. That's what I'm talking about."

"You'll see it," Russell said. He thought a minute. "Maybe you have to see something else. The money—that it gets up to San Carlos."

"Look, if you'd just explain—"

He touched my arm. "Maybe it's you who has to take it up to San Carlos after. That's easy, uh?"

I kept staring at him. "You never were keeping it for yourself, were you?"

He just looked at me—like he was tired—or like what was the use explaining now?

He put his hat on, straight and pulled down a little over his eyes. He picked up the grainsack, swinging it up over his left shoulder. All of us were watching him, the McLaren girl never moving.

She kept staring and said, "You're going." Just those two words.

Russell made a little shrugging motion. "Maybe try something."

"What if they don't think you've got the money in there?"

"They come out and see," Russell answered.

"They might," the McLaren girl nodded. "They just might."

"They have to," Russell said.

The McLaren girl kept staring at him, wanting to ask why he was doing it, I think. But Russell was looking at Mendez then. "You'll watch this Dr. Favor. Good this time?" he said.

Mendez said something in Spanish and Russell answered also in Spanish, shrugging his shoulders. Mendez appeared like he was afraid to breathe. Russell turned to Dr. Favor. He had something for everybody.

"All that trouble you went to, uh?"

Dr. Favor didn't answer, not caring what anybody said or thought about him now. He sat there staring up at Russell, his big face pale-looking with that reddish hair around it and with hardly any expression. He probably thought this John Russell was the biggest fool God ever made.

We were watching him, every one of us; perhaps still not certain he was going down there and having to see it to believe it.

He was at the door when the McLaren girl picked up his moccasins and threw them over to him. "Wear those," she said. "You run faster when they start shooting."

Do you see what she was doing? Giving it right back to him. Using the same words even that he had used before. Saying it calmly and watching to see his reaction.

And seeing his smile then; a smile you were sure he meant. Even with his hat on, at that moment he looked young and like anybody else.

Russell stood with his hand on the door, looking over his shoulder at the McLaren girl, at her only.

"Maybe we should talk more sometime," he said.

"Maybe," the McLaren girl answered. She was looking at him the same way, intently, like seeing something in him that was not there before. "When things calm down," she said.

I had the feeling she wanted to say more than that, but she didn't.

Russell nodded, his strange light-blue-colored eyes not moving from the girl's. "When things calm down," he said back.

He pulled the door open and stepped outside with the grain-sack over his shoulder. The next time I was close enough to John Russell to see his face, he was dead.

Not long ago I was talking to a man from Benson who said they were playing a song now about Frank Braden and the woman he stole for reasons of love, and that I would appreciate it. I said are they playing a song about John Russell? He said who is John Russell?

What took place that afternoon at the San Pete mine has been written many times and different ways. (Including the song now.) Maybe you have read some of them. All I want to say is the account that appeared in the *Florence Enterprise* is a true one, even to the number of shots that were fired. Except even that account does not tell enough. (Which is what caused me to write this.) It describes a man named John Russell; but you still do not know John Russell after you have read it.

I am not saying anything against the *Florence Enterprise*. Their account was written in one hour or so, just telling what happened. I have been writing this for three months trying to tell you about John Russell as he was, so you will understand him. Yet, after three months of writing and thinking and all, I can't truthfully say I understand him myself. I only feel I know why he walked down that slope.

I watched him from the window. I was also keeping an eye out for the Mexican. The Mexican must have seen Russell as he started down, but he did not come out from the crushing mill until Russell was about half way.

That was when Russell held up the grainsack. "Hey!" He yelled out, the same way the Mexican had been yelling at him, "I got something for you!"

The Mexican was being careful as he moved across the grade, keeping his eyes on Russell all the time. By then the Favor woman had seen him; sitting stooped over, her hair hanging and straggly, she was watching him come.

Russell did not look at the Mexican, though he must have known the Mexican was moving down and across the grade as if to head him off. By then you could see part of the Mexican's back. I got down lower and, as Russell had instructed, put the front sight of the Spencer square on him, getting an awful feeling as I did.

At that moment, Early, up above us on the ridge, was probably putting his sights on Russell.

I kept expecting the Mexican to do something; but as he got over more by that little shack he slowed up so that he was hardly moving; not taking his eyes from Russell for a second, his right elbow bent and the elbow pressed against where he had been shot, his left hand hanging free. That was the hand I watched, feeling the trigger of the Spencer and ready to pull it if the hand went to the Colt gun along side it.

The Mexican stopped.

He was almost in line but a little to the left; so that from here you would look down past his right side to Russell who was nearing the Favor woman. She did not call out or appear to have said a word; she just kept staring at him, maybe not believing what she saw.

It was as Russell reached her that Frank Braden showed himself.

Braden came out of the veranda shade. He was limping some, I think trying not to show it, though he kept his left hand on his thigh, gripping it with his fingers spread.

The Mexican had not moved. I kept sighting on him, trying to watch Braden and Russell at the same time. Russell was kneeling by the woman, not paying any attention to Braden who kept coming. Braden called something, but Russell did not look up.

Braden called out again, slowing up and ready, you could tell.

Russell rose to his feet, helping the Favor woman as he did and you saw she was untied now. You also saw the grainsack lying over on the other side of the ore-cart tracks.

Russell and the Favor woman had taken only a few steps when Braden called out again. This time Russell stopped, though he motioned the Favor woman to keep going. She did, but looking back as Russell stood there watching Braden. She got up as high as the Mexican. He paid no attention to her. She was walking kind of sideways, coming up but looking back all the time.

The next thing I knew the front of the Spencer was on her. She had wandered just enough, looking back and not watching where she was going, to get behind the Mexican. I looked up, about to yell at her, but didn't. The Mexican would hear it too.

All I could do was keep telling her to get out of the way in my mind. Please hurry up and get out of the way.

Braden had reached the grainsack. He stood by it saying something to Russell who was about ten feet from him. Russell answered him. (What this was about, no one knows. Braden could have said to open the sack, show him the money. Russell would have told him to look in it himself if he doubted it was there.)

The Favor woman looked up at where we were. I stood up and waved my arm, but as I did she was looking back the other way again.

Even standing and sighting down with the Spencer against the side frame, the Favor woman was still in the way. I could only see part of the Mexican.

In my mind I kept telling her over and over again to get out of the way, to please, for the Lord's sake move one way or the other and to *hurry*! Now, right now, just move or look up here again or sit down or do *something*!

She stood there. She turned around to watch what was happening below and did not move from the spot.

Braden, his left hand still holding his thigh, straightened the grainsack with his boot toe so that the open end was toward him. Russell watched.

Braden went down to one knee, his right one, and now the hand came away from his thigh and unloosened the opening of the grainsack. Russell watched.

Braden straightened up, still kneeling. He said something to Russell. What? Warning him? Telling him not to try anything because the Mexican was behind him?

I saw Braden's hand reach inside the grainsack.

Move! I thought. Get somewhere else!

If there was time—

Just move! I actually heard it in my mind, and I was to the door and out the door, running along the shelf, seven, eight, ten yards to be sure of the angle, to be sure of not hitting the woman.

But I had not even brought up the gun to aim when Braden's hand came out of the grainsack. He was rising, trying to get out his revolver, but was already too late. Russell drew and fired twice with his Colt extended and aimed . . . his other arm coming up as he fired the second round and he was stumbling forward as if kicked in the back. The Mexican had pulled his long-barreled .44 and fired three shots in the time Russell had hit Braden twice and Braden and Russell both went down, Russell to his hands and knees, but turning with his revolver already raised and he fired as the Mexican fired again, fired as the Mexican stumbled forward, fired as the Mexican staggered and dropped to his knees and fell face down with his arms spread. There were three more shots at that time, exactly three, because I can hear them every time I picture what took place; the shots coming from the ridge above us, from Early who was up there. I turned, aiming the Spencer almost straight up, but there was no sign of him. (There was no sign of him ever again that I know of.) When I turned back again, I saw Russell lying face-down between the ore-cart tracks. In the quiet that followed, all of us went down there.

Frank Braden had been shot twice in the chest; there was also the wound in his left thigh and a bullet crease across the shin of his left boot which had not touched him. Frank Braden was dead.

The Mexican had been hit in the chest twice and once in the stomach; plus the wound in his side that looked awful enough to have killed him. He lived another hour or so, but never told us his name, though he asked what Russell's was.

John Russell had been shot three times low in the back. We turned him over and saw he had been hit twice again, through the neck and chest. He was dead.

I was the one rode to Delgado's, running the horse most of the way, and ruining it, not intending to but not caring either. Delgado sent one of his boys to Sweetmary for the deputy. Delgado and I rode back to the San Pete in a wagon and got there in the dark of early morning. You could hear the crickets in the old buildings. Down in the open the McLaren girl and Henry

Mendez and Dr. Favor and his wife were by a fire they'd kept going. Only Mrs. Favor had slept. Mendez had dug two graves.

Delgado and I sat with them and by the time it started to get light the Sweetmary deputy, J. R. Lyons, arrived.

He looked at the bodies, Braden's and the Mexican's by the graves, Russell's in the wagon. Dig a hole for him too, J. R. Lyons said. What's the difference? He's dead. The McLaren girl said look all you want, but keep your opinions; we were taking Russell to Sweetmary for proper burial with a Mass and all and if Mr. J. R. Lyons didn't like it he didn't have to attend.

J. R. Lyons said of course he would. Once Dr. Favor and the stolen government money were handed over to a United States marshal.

(Which was done. Dr. Favor was tried in the District Court at Florence about a month later and sentenced to seven years in Yuma prison. Mrs. Favor was not at the trial.)

John Russell was buried at Sweetmary. It was strange that neither the McLaren girl nor Henry Mendez nor I said much about him until after the funeral, and when we did talk found there wasn't much to be said.

You can look at something for a long time and not see it until it has moved or run off. That was how we had looked at Russell. Now, nobody questioned why he had walked down that slope. What we asked ourselves was why we ever thought he wouldn't.

Maybe he was showing off a little bit when he asked each of us if we wanted to walk down to the Favor woman, knowing nobody would but himself.

Maybe he let us think a lot of things about him that weren't true. But as Russell would say, that was up to us. He let people do or think what they wanted while he smoked a cigarette and thought it out calmly, without his feelings getting mixed up in it. Russell never changed the whole time, though I think everyone else did in some way. He did what he felt had to be done. Even if it meant dying. So maybe you don't have to understand him. You just know him.

"Take a good look at Russell. You will never see another one like him as long as you live." That first day, at Delgado's, Henry Mendez said it all.

VALDEZ
IS
COMING

1

Picture the ground rising on the east side of the pasture with scrub trees thick on the slope and pines higher up. This is where everybody was. Not all in one place but scattered in small groups, about a dozen men in the scrub, the front line, the shooters who couldn't just stand around. They'd fire at the shack when they felt like it, or when Mr. Tanner passed the word, they would all fire at once.

Others were up in the pines and on the road that ran along the crest of the hill, some three hundred yards from the shack across the pasture. Those watching made bets whether the man in the shack would give himself up or get shot first.

It was Saturday and that's why everybody had the time. They would arrive in Lanoria, hear about what happened, and shortly after, head out to the cattle company pasture. Most of the men went out alone, leaving their families in town, though there were a few women who came. The other women waited. And the people who had business in town and couldn't leave waited. Now and then a few would come back from the pasture to have a drink or their dinner and would tell what was going on. No, they hadn't got him yet. Still inside the line shack and not showing his face. But they'd get him. A few more would go out from town when they heard this. Also a wagon from De Spain's went out with whiskey. That's how the saloon was set up in the pines overlooking the pasture. Somebody said it was like the goddam Fourth of July.

Barely a mile from town those going out would hear the gunfire—like a skirmish way over the other side of the woods, thin specks of sound—and this would hurry them. They were careful though, topping the slope, looking across the pasture, getting their bearings, then peering around to see who was there. They would see a friend and ask about this Mr. Tanner, and the friend would point him out.

The man there in the dark suit: thin and bony, not big especially, but looking like he was made of gristle and hard to kill, with a moustache and a thin nose and a dark dusty hat worn over his eyes. That was him. They had heard about Frank Tanner, but not many had ever seen him. He had a place south in the foothills of the Santa Ritas and almost to the border. They said he had an army riding for him, Americans and Mexicans, and that his place was like a barracks except for the women. They said he traded horses and cattle and guns across into Mexico to the revolutionary forces and he had all the riders in case the Federales came down on him; also in case his customers ever decided not to pay. Sure he had at least twenty-five men and he didn't graze a head of beef himself. Where were they? somebody wanted to know. Driving a herd south. That's what he had come here for, cattle; bought them from Maricopa.

Somebody else said he had brought his wife along—"God*dam*, a good-looking young woman, I'll tell you, some years younger than he is"—and she was waiting for him at the Republic Hotel right now, staying up in his room, and not many people had seen her.

They would look at Mr. Tanner, then across the cattle pasture to the line shack three hundred yards away. It was a little bake-oven of a hut, wood framed and made of sod and built against a rise where there were pines so the hut would be in shade part of the day. There were no windows in the hut, no gear lying around to show anybody lived there. The hut stood in the sun now with its door closed, the door chipped and splintered by all the bullets that had poured into it and through it.

Off to the right where the pine shapes against the sky rounded and became willows, there in the trees by the creek bed, was the man's wagon and team. In the wagon were the supplies he'd bought that morning in Lanoria before Mr. Tanner spotted him.

Out in front of the hut about ten or fifteen feet there was something on the ground. From the slope three hundred yards away nobody could tell what it was until a man came who had field glasses. He looked up and said, frowning, it was a doll: one made of cloth scraps, a stuffed doll with buttons for eyes.

"The woman must have dropped it," somebody said.

"The *woman*?" the man with the field glasses said.

A Lipan Apache woman who was his wife or his woman or

just with him. Mr. Tanner hadn't been clear about that. All they knew was that there was a woman in the hut with him and if the man wanted her to stay and get shot that was his business.

A Mr. Beaudry, the government land agent for the county, was there. Also Mr. Malson, manager of the Maricopa Cattle Company, and a horsebreaker by the name of Diego Luz, who was big for a Mexican but never offensive and who drank pretty well.

Mr. Beaudry, nodding and also squinting so he could picture the man inside the line shack, said, "There was something peculiar about him. I mean having a name like Orlando Rincón."

"He worked for me," Mr. Malson said. He was looking at Mr. Tanner. "I mistrusted him and I believe that was part of it, his name being Orlando Rincón."

"Johnson," Mr. Tanner said.

"I hired him two, three times," Mr. Malson said. "For heavy work. When I had work you couldn't pay a white man to do."

"His name is Johnson," Mr. Tanner said. "There is no fuzzhead by the name of Orlando Rincón. I'm telling you this fuzzhead is from the Fort Huachuca Tenth fuzzhead Cavalry and his name was Johnson when he killed James C. Erin six months ago and nothing else."

He spoke as you might speak to young children to press something into their minds. This man seemed to have no feeling and he never smiled, but there was no reason to doubt him.

Bob Valdez arrived at the Maricopa pasture about noon. He was riding shotgun on the Hatch and Hodges run from St. David. He swung down from the boot, holding his sawed-off shotgun in the air, as the stage edged past the whiskey wagon.

Somebody standing at the tailgate with a glass in his hand said, "Hey, here's the town constable," and those nearby looked toward Bob Valdez in his dark suit and buttoned-up shirt, wearing a collar button but no tie or bandana; Valdez with his hat straight and slightly forward, the brim flat and the low crown undented.

"We'll get that nigger out of there now," somebody said, and a couple of others gave a little laugh to show they knew the person who said it was kidding.

Bob Valdez smiled, going along with it, though not knowing what they meant. "Out of where?" he said.

They explained it to him and he nodded, listening, his gaze moving over the shooters in the scrub, out to the line shack across the pasture and back to the slope, to the group of men a little way down from him. He saw Mr. Beaudry and Mr. Malson and Diego Luz, and the one they said was Mr. Tanner, there, talking to an R. L. Davis, who rode for Maricopa when he was working.

Bob Valdez watched the two men, both of them cut from the same stringy hide and looking like father and son: Mr. Tanner talking, never smiling, barely moving his mouth; R. L. Davis standing hip-cocked, posing with his revolver and rifle and a cartridge belt hanging over one shoulder, and the funneled, pointed brim of his sweaty hat nodding up and down as he listened to Mr. Tanner, grinning at what Mr. Tanner said, laughing out loud while Mr. Tanner did not show the twitch of a lip. Bob Valdez did not like R. L. Davis or any of the R. L. Davises in the world. He was civil, he listened to them, but God, there were a lot of them to listen to.

Well, all right, Bob Valdez thought. He walked down the slope to the group of men, nodding to Mr. Beaudry and Mr. Malson as they looked up. He waited a moment, not looking directly at Tanner, waiting for one of them to introduce him. Finally he held out his hand. "I'm Bob Valdez," he said, smiling a little.

Mr. Tanner looked at him, but did not shake hands. His gaze shifted as Mr. Malson said, "Bob's a town constable. He works a few nights a week in the Mexican part of town."

"The nights I'm here," Bob Valdez said. "Not on a stage run. See, I work for Hatch and Hodges too."

This time Mr. Tanner turned to say something to R. L. Davis, a couple of words that could have been about anything, and R. L. Davis laughed. Bob Valdez was a grown man; he was forty years old and as big as Mr. Tanner, but he stood there and didn't know what to do. He gripped the shotgun and was glad he had something to hold on to. He would have to stay near Mr. Tanner because he was the center of what was going on here. Soon they would discuss the situation and decide what to do. As the law-enforcement man he, Bob Valdez, should be in on the discussion and the decision. Of course. If someone was going to arrest Orlando Rincón or Johnson or whatever his name was, then he should be the one to do it; he was a town constable. They were out of town maybe, but where did the town end? The town had moved out here now; it was the same thing.

He could wait for Rincón to give up. Then arrest him.

If he wasn't dead already.

"Mr. Malson." Bob Valdez stepped toward the cattle company manager, who glanced over but looked out across the pasture again, indifferent.

"I wondered if maybe he's already dead," Valdez said.

Mr. Malson said, "Why don't you find out?"

"I was thinking," Valdez said, "if he was dead we could stand here a long time."

R. L. Davis adjusted his hat, which he did often, grabbing the funneled brim, loosening it on his head and pulling it down close to his eyes again and shifting from one cocked hip to the other. "Valdez here's got better things to do," R. L. Davis said. "He's busy."

"No," Bob Valdez said. "I was thinking of the one inside there, Rincón. He's dead or he's alive. He's alive, maybe he wants to give himself up. In there he has time to think, uh? Maybe——" He stopped. Not one of them was listening. Not even R. L. Davis.

Mr. Malson was looking at the whiskey wagon; it was on the road above them and over a little ways, with men standing by it being served off the tailgate. "I think we could use something," Mr. Malson said. His gaze went to Diego Luz the horsebreaker and Diego straightened up; not much, but a little. He was heavy and very dark and his shirt was tight across the thickness of his body. They said that Diego Luz hit green horses on the muzzle with his fist and they minded him. He had the hands for it; they hung at his sides, not touching or fooling with anything. They turned open, gestured when Mr. Malson told him to get the whiskey, and as he moved off climbing the slope, one hand held his holstered revolver to his leg.

Mr. Malson looked up at the sky, squinting and taking his hat off and putting it on again. He took off his coat and held it hooked over his shoulder by one finger, said something, gestured, and he and Mr. Beaudry and Mr. Tanner moved a few yards down the slope to a hollow where there was good shade. It was about two or two thirty then, hot, fairly still and quiet considering the number of people there. Only some of them in the pines and down in the scrub could be seen from where Bob Valdez stood wondering whether he should follow the three men down to the hollow or wait for Diego Luz, who was at the whiskey wagon now where most of the sounds that carried came from: a voice, a word or two that was suddenly clear, or laughter, and people would look up to see what was going on. Some of them by the whiskey wagon had lost interest in the line shack. Others were still watching though: those farther along the road sitting in wagons and buggies. This was a day people would remember and talk about. "Sure, I was there," the man in the buggy would be saying a year from now in a saloon over in Benson or St. David or somewhere. "The day they got that Army deserter, he had a Big-Fifty Sharps and an old dragoon pistol, and I'll tell you it was ticklish business."

Down in that worn-out pasture, dusty and spotted with desert growth, prickly pear and brittlebush, there was just the sun. It showed the ground clearly all the way to just in front of the line shack where now, toward midafternoon, there was shadow coming out from the trees and from the mound the hut was set against.

Somebody in the scrub must have seen the door open. The shout came from there, and Bob Valdez and everybody on the slope were looking by the time the Lipan Apache woman had reached the edge of the shade. She walked out from the hut toward the willow trees carrying a bucket, not hurrying or even looking toward the slope.

Nobody fired at her, though this was not so strange. Putting the front sight on a sod hut and on a person are two different things. The men in the scrub and in the pines didn't know this woman. They weren't after her. She had just appeared. There she was; and no one was sure what to do about her.

She was in the trees by the creek awhile, then she was in the open again, walking back toward the hut with the bucket and not hurrying at all, a small figure way across the pasture almost without shape or color, with only the long skirt reaching to the ground to tell it was the woman.

So he's alive, Bob Valdez thought. And he wants to stay alive and he's not giving himself up.

He thought about the woman's nerve and whether Orlando Rincón had sent her out or she had decided this herself. You couldn't tell about an Indian woman. Maybe this was expected of her. The woman didn't count; the man did. You could lose the woman and get another one.

Mr. Tanner didn't look at R. L. Davis. His gaze held on the Lipan Apache woman, inched along with her toward the hut; but he must have known R. L. Davis was right next to him.

"She's saying she don't give a goddam about you and your rifle," Mr. Tanner said.

R. L. Davis looked at him funny. Then he said, "Shoot her?" like he hoped that's what Mr. Tanner meant.

"You could make her jump some," Mr. Tanner said.

Now R. L. Davis was on stage and he knew it, and Bob Valdez could tell he knew it by the way he levered the Winchester, raised it, and fired all in one motion, and as the dust kicked behind the Indian woman, who kept walking and didn't look up, R. L. Davis fired and fired and fired as fast as he could lever and half aim and with everybody watching him, hurrying him, he put four good ones right behind the woman. His last bullet socked into the door just as she reached it, and now she did pause and look up at the slope, staring up like she was waiting for him to fire again and giving him a good target if he wanted it.

Mr. Beaudry laughed out loud. "She don't give a goddam about your rifle."

It stung R. L. Davis, which it was intended to do.

"I wasn't aiming at her."

"But she doesn't know that." Mr. Beaudry was grinning, twisting his moustache, turning then and reaching out a hand as Diego Luz approached them with the whiskey.

"Hell, I wanted to hit her she'd be laying there, you know it."

"Well now, you tell her that," Mr. Beaudry said, working the cork loose, "and she'll know it." He took a drink from the bottle and passed it to Mr. Malson, who offered the bottle to Mr. Tanner, who shook his head. Mr. Malson took a drink and saw R. L. Davis staring at him, so he handed the bottle to him.

R. L. Davis jerked the bottle up, took a long swallow and that part was over.

Mr. Malson said to Mr. Tanner, "You don't want any?"

"Not right now," Mr. Tanner answered. He continued to stare out across the pasture.

Mr. Malson watched him. "You feel strongly about this Army deserter."

"I told you," Mr. Tanner said, "he killed a man was a friend of mine."

"No, I don't believe you did."

"James C. Erin, sutler at Fort Huachuca," Mr. Tanner said. "He came across a tulapai still this nigger soldier was working with some Indians. The nigger thought Erin would tell the Army people, so he shot him and ran off with a woman."

"And you saw him this morning."

"I had come in last night to see this gentleman," Mr. Tanner said, nodding toward Malson. "This morning I was getting ready to leave when I saw him, him and the woman."

"I was right there," R. L. Davis said. "Right, Mr. Tanner? Him and I was on the porch by the Republic Hotel and Rincón goes by in the wagon. Mr. Tanner said, 'You know that man?' I said, 'Only that he's lived up north of town a few months. Him and his woman.' 'Well, I know him,' Mr. Tanner said. 'That man's an Army deserter wanted for murder.' I said, 'Well let's go get him.' He had a start on us and that's how he got to the hut before we could grab on to him. He's been holed up ever since."

Mr. Malson said, "Then you didn't talk to him."

"Listen," Mr. Tanner said, "I've kept that man's face before my eyes this past year."

Bob Valdez, somewhat behind Mr. Tanner and to the side, moved in a little closer. "You know this is the same man?"

Mr. Tanner looked around. He stared at Valdez. That's all he did, just stared.

"I mean, we have to be sure," Bob Valdez said. "It's a serious thing."

Now Mr. Malson and Mr. Beaudry were looking up at him. "We," Mr. Beaudry said. "I'll tell you what, Roberto. We need help we'll call you. All right?"

"You hired me," Bob Valdez said, standing alone above

them. He was serious, but he shrugged and smiled a little to take the edge off the words. "What did you hire me for?"

"Well," Mr. Beaudry said, acting it out, looking up past Bob Valdez and along the road both ways. "I was to see some drunk Mexicans, I'd point them out."

After that, for a while, the men with the whiskey bottle forgot Bob Valdez. They stayed in the shade of the hollow watching the line shack, waiting for the Army deserter to realize it was all over for him. He would realize it and open the door and be cut down as he came outside. It was a matter of time only.

Bob Valdez stayed on the open part of the slope that was turning to shade, sitting now like an Apache with a suit on and every once in a while making a cigarette and smoking it slowly and thinking about himself and Mr. Tanner and the others, then thinking about the Army deserter, then thinking about himself again.

He didn't have to stay here. He didn't have to be a town constable. He didn't have to work for the stage company. He didn't have to listen to Mr. Beaudry and Mr. Malson and smile when they said those things. He didn't have a wife or any kids. He didn't have land that he owned. He could go anywhere he wanted.

Diego Luz was coming over. Diego Luz had a wife and a daughter almost grown and some little kids and he had to stay, sure.

Diego Luz squatted next to him, his arms on his knees and his big hands that he used for breaking horses hanging in front of him.

"Stay near if they want you for something," Bob Valdez said. He was watching Beaudry tilt the bottle up. Diego Luz said nothing.

"One of them bends over," Bob Valdez said then, "you kiss it, uh?"

Diego Luz looked at him, patient about it. Not angry or stirred. "Why don't you go home?"

"He says get me a bottle, you run."

"I get it. I don't run."

"Smile and hold your hat, uh?"

"And don't talk so much."

"Not unless they talk to you first."

"You better go home," Diego said.

Bob Valdez said, "That's why you hit the horses."

"Listen," Diego Luz said. "They pay me to break horses. They pay you to talk to drunks and keep them from killing somebody. They don't pay you for what you think or how you feel. So if you take their money keep your mouth shut. All right?"

Bob Valdez smiled. "I'm kidding you."

Diego Luz got up and walked away, down toward the hollow. The hell with him, he was thinking. Maybe he was kidding, but the hell with him. He was also thinking that maybe he could get a drink from that bottle. Maybe there would be a half inch left nobody wanted and Mr. Malson would tell him to kill it.

But it was already finished. R. L. Davis was playing with the bottle, holding it by the neck and flipping it up and catching it as it came down. Beaudry was saying, "What about after dark?" And looking at Mr. Tanner, who was thinking about something else and didn't notice.

R. L. Davis stopped flipping the bottle. He said, "Put some men on the rise right above the hut; he comes out, bust him."

"Well, they should get the men over there," Mr. Beaudry said, looking at the sky. "It won't be long till dark."

"Where's he going?" Mr. Malson said.

The others looked up, stopped in whatever they were doing or thinking by the suddenness of Mr. Malson's voice.

"Hey, Valdez!" R. L. Davis yelled out. "Where you think you're going?"

Bob Valdez had circled them and was already below them on the slope, leaving the pines now and entering the scrub brush. He didn't stop or look back.

"Valdez!"

Mr. Tanner raised one hand to silence R. L. Davis, all the time watching Bob Valdez getting smaller, going straight through the scrub, not just walking or passing the time but going right out to the pasture.

"Look at him," Mr. Malson said. There was some admiration in his voice.

"He's dumber than he looks," R. L. Davis said, then jumped a little as Mr. Tanner touched his arm.

"Come on," Mr. Tanner said. "With the rifle." And he started down the slope, hurrying and not seeming to care if he might stumble on the loose gravel.

Bob Valdez was now halfway across the pasture, the shotgun pointed down at his side, his eyes not leaving the door of the line shack. The door was probably already open enough for a rifle barrel to poke through. He guessed the Army deserter was covering him, letting him get as close as he wanted; the closer he came the easier to hit him.

Now he could see all the bullet marks in the door and the clean inner wood where the door was splintered. Two people in that little bake-oven of a place. He saw the door move.

He saw the rag doll on the ground. It was a strange thing, the woman having a doll. Valdez hardly glanced at it but was aware of the button eyes looking up and the discomforted twist of the red wool mouth. Then, just past the doll, when he was wondering if he would go right up to the door and knock on it and wouldn't that be a crazy thing, like visiting somebody, the door opened and the Negro was in the doorway filling it, standing there in pants and boots but without a shirt in that hot place, and holding a long-barreled dragoon that was already cocked.

They stood twelve feet apart looking at each other, close enough so that no one could fire from the slope.

"I can kill you first," the Negro said, "if you raise it."

With his free hand, the left one, Bob Valdez motioned back over his shoulder. "There's a man there said you killed some-body a year ago."

"What man?"

"Said his name is Tanner."

The Negro shook his head, once each way.

"Said your name is Johnson."

"You know my name."

"I'm telling you what he said."

"Where'd I kill this man?"

"Huachuca."

The Negro hesitated. "That was some time ago I was in the Tenth. More than a year."

"You a deserter?"

"I served it out."

"Then you got something that says so."

"In the wagon, there's a bag there my things are in."

"Will you talk to this man Tanner?"

"If I can hold from busting him."

"Listen, why did you run this morning?"

"They come chasing. I don't know what they want." He lowered the gun a little, his brown-stained tired-looking eyes staring intently at Bob Valdez. "What would you do? They come on the run. Next thing I know they firing at us."

"Will you go with me and talk to him?"

The Negro hesitated again. Then shook his head. "I don't know him."

"Then he won't know you."

"He didn't know me this morning."

"All right," Bob Valdez said. "I'll get your paper says you were discharged. Then we'll show it to this man, uh?"

The Negro thought it over before he nodded, very slowly, as if still thinking. "All right. Bring him here, I'll say a few words to him."

Bob Valdez smiled a little. "You can point that gun some other way."

"Well . . ." the Negro said, "if everybody's friends." He lowered the revolver to his side.

The wagon was in the willow trees by the creek. Off to the right. But Bob Valdez did not turn right away in that direction. He backed away, watching Orlando Rincón for no reason that he knew of. Maybe because the man was holding a gun and that was reason enough.

He had backed off six or seven feet when Orlando Rincón shoved the revolver down into his belt. Bob Valdez turned and started for the trees.

It was at this moment that he looked across the pasture. He saw Mr. Tanner and R. L. Davis at the edge of the scrub trees but wasn't sure it was them. Something tried to tell him it was them, but he did not accept it until he was off to the right, out of the line of fire, and by then the time to yell at them or run toward them was past. R. L. Davis had the Winchester up and was firing.

They say R. L. Davis was drunk or he would have pinned

him square. As it was, the bullet shaved Rincón and plowed past him into the hut.

Bob Valdez saw Rincón half turn and he saw Rincón's accusing eyes as Rincón pulled the long-barreled dragoon from his belt.

"They weren't supposed to," Bob Valdez said, holding one hand out as if to stop Rincón. "Listen, they weren't supposed to do that!"

The revolver was free, and Rincón was cocking it. "Don't!" Bob Valdez said. "Don't do it!" Looking right into the Negro's eyes and seeing it was no use, that Rincón was going to shoot him, and suddenly hurrying, he jerked the shotgun up and pulled both triggers so that the explosions came out in one blast and Orlando Rincón was spun and thrown back inside.

They came out across the pasture to have a look, some going inside where they found the woman and brought her out, everybody noticing she would have a child in about a month. Those by the doorway made room as Mr. Tanner and R. L. Davis approached.

Diego Luz came over by Bob Valdez, who had not moved. Valdez stood watching them and he saw Mr. Tanner look down at Rincón and after a moment shake his head.

"It looked like him," Mr. Tanner said. "It sure looked like him."

He saw R. L. Davis squint at Mr. Tanner. "It ain't the one you said?"

Mr. Tanner shook his head again. "I've seen him before though. I know I've seen him somewheres."

Bob Valdez saw R. L. Davis shrug. "You ask me, they all look alike," He was yawning then, fooling with his hat, and then his eyes swiveled over to Bob Valdez standing with the empty shotgun.

"Constable," R. L. Davis said. "You went and killed the wrong coon."

Bob Valdez started for him, raising the shotgun to swing it like a club, but Diego Luz caught him from behind and locked a big arm around his neck, under his chin, until he was still and Mr. Tanner and the others had moved off.

2

A MAN CAN be in two different places and he will be two different men. Maybe if you think of more places he will be more men, but two is enough for now. This is Bob Valdez washing his hands in the creek and resting in the willows after digging the hole and lowering Orlando Rincón into it and covering him with dirt and stones, resting and watching the Lipan Apache woman who sat in silence by the grave of the man whose child she would have in a month.

This is one Bob Valdez. The forty-year-old town constable and stage-line shotgun rider. A good, hard-working man. And hard looking, with a dark hard face that was creased and leathery; but don't go by looks, they said, Bob Valdez was kindly and respectful. One of the good ones. The whores in Inez's place on Commercial Street would call to him from their windows; even the white-skinned girls who had come from St. Louis, they liked him too. Bob Valdez would wave at them and sometimes he would go in and after being with the girl would have a cup of coffee with Inez. They had known each other when they were children in Tucson. That was all right, going to Inez's place. Mr. Beaudry and Mr. Malson and the others could try to think of a time when Bob Valdez might have drunk too much or swaggered or had a certain smart-aleck look on his face, but they would never recall such a time. Yes, this Bob Valdez was all right.

Another Bob Valdez inside the Bob Valdez in the willows that evening had worked for the Army at one time and had been a contract guide when General Crook chased Geronimo down into the Madres. He was a tracker out of Whipple Barracks first, then out of Fort Thomas, then in charge of the Apache police at Whiteriver. He would sit at night eating with them and talking with them as he learned the Chiricahua dialect. He would keep up with them all day and shoot his Springfield carbine one hell of a lot better than any of them could shoot. He had taken scalps but never showed them to anyone and had thrown them away by the time Geronimo was in Oklahoma and he had gone to work for the stage company,

Hatch and Hodges, to live as a civilized man. Shortly after that he was named town constable in Lanoria at twenty-five dollars a month, getting the job because he got along with people, including the Mexicans in town who drank too much on Saturday night, and this was the Bob Valdez that Mr. Beaudry and Mr. Malson and the others knew. They had never met the first Bob Valdez.

And they had forgotten about the second Bob Valdez; they had gone, everyone cleared out of the Maricopa pasture. He was alone with the Lipan Apache woman as evening settled and the grove in the willow trees became dark.

He had not spoken to the woman. He had touched her shoulder before digging the grave—when she had tried to take the shovel from him to do it herself—he had touched her, easing her to the ground, and she had sat unmoving while he formed the hole and dug deep into the soil. He would look at her and smile, but her expression gave him nothing in return. She wasn't an attractive woman. She was a round shape in a dirty gray dress with yellow strands of beads. He did not know how old she was. She was something sitting there watching him but not watching him. She would build a fire and sit here all night and in the morning she would probably be gone.

He had never seen the woman before. He had seen Orlando Rincón in Lanoria. He had recognized him, but had never spoken to him before today. Rincón had a one-loop spread a half day's ride south of Lanoria that he and the woman tended alone. That much was all Bob Valdez knew about them. They had come into town for something and now the man was dead and the woman was alone with her unborn child. Like that, her life, whatever it had been before, good or bad, was gone.

He watched the woman rise from the grave to water the wagon horses in the creek. She returned and made a fire, lighting it with a match. Valdez went over to her then, fashioning a cigarette and leaning in to light it in the fire, taking his time because he wasn't sure of the words he wanted to use.

In Spanish he said, "Where will you go?" and repeated it in the Chiricahua dialect when she continued to stare at him, and now she pointed off beyond the creek.

"This should not have happened," he said. "Your husband had done nothing. It was a mistake." He leaned closer to see her clearly in the firelight. "I did it to him, but I didn't want to. He didn't understand and he was going to kill me."

Christ, if you can't say anything, Valdez thought, quit talking.

He said, "It isn't your fault this has happened. I mean, you are made to suffer and yet you did nothing to cause it. You understand?"

The woman nodded slightly, looking into the fire now. "All right, we can't give him back to you, but we should give you something. You take something from a person, then you have to pay for it. We have to pay. We have to pay you for taking your husband. You see that?"

The woman did not move or speak.

"I don't know how much you pay a woman for killing her husband, but we'll think of something, all right? There were many men there; I don't know them all. But the ones I know I go to and ask them to give me something for you. A hundred dollars. No, *five* hundred dollars we get and give it to you so you can do what you want with it. Have your baby and go home, wherever your home is, or stay here. Buy some, I don't know, something to grow, and a cow and maybe some goats, uh? You know goats?"

Christ, let her buy what she wants. Get it done.

"Look," Valdez said then. "We get in the wagon and go back to town. I see the men and talk to them—you stay in town also. I find a place for you, all right?"

The woman's gaze rose from the fire, her dark face glistening in the light, the shapeless, flat-faced Lipan Apache woman looking at him. A person, but Christ, barely a person.

Why did Rincón choose this one? Valdez thought. He smiled then. "How does that sound? You stay in town, sleep in a bed. You don't have to worry or think about it. We pay for everything."

A Maricopa rider came into De Spain's, where Mr. Beaudry and Mr. Malson were playing poker with another gentleman and the house man, and told them it was the goddamedest thing he'd seen in a while: Bob Valdez walking into the Republic Hotel with that blown-up Indian woman.

R. L. Davis came over from the bar and said, "What about

the Indian woman? Hell, I could have knocked her flat if I'd wanted. Nobody believes that then they never seen me shoot."

Mr. Malson told him to shut up and said to the Maricopa rider, "What's this about Bob Valdez?"

"He's in the Republic registering that nigger's squaw," the rider said. "I saw them come up in the team and go inside, so I stuck my head in."

Mr. Beaudry was squinting in his cigar smoke. "What'd the clerk do?"

"I guess he didn't know what to do," the rider said. "He went and got the manager, and him and Bob Valdez were talking over the counter, but I couldn't hear them."

Mr. Malson, the manager of Maricopa, looked at Mr. Beaudry, the government land agent, and Mr. Beaudry said, "I never heard of anything like that before."

Mr. Malson shook his head. "They won't give her a room. Christ Almighty."

Mr. Beaudry shook his head too. "I don't know," he said. "Bob Valdez. You sure it was Bob?"

"Yes sir," the Maricopa rider said. He waited a minute while the men at the poker table thought about it, then went over to the bar and got himself a glass of whiskey.

Next to him, R. L. Davis said, "Were you out there today?" The rider shook his head, but said he'd heard all about it. R. L. Davis told him how he had taken the Winchester and put four good ones right behind the woman when she came out for water and one smack in the door as she went back inside. "Hell," R. L. Davis said, "I'd wanted to hit her I'd have hit her square."

The Maricopa rider said, "God*dam*, I guess she's a big enough something to shoot at for anybody."

"I was two hundred yards off!" R. L. Davis stiffened up and his face was tight. "I put them shots right where I aimed!"

The Maricopa rider said, "All right, I believe you." He was tired and didn't feel like arguing with some stringy drunk who was liable to make something out of nothing.

For a Saturday night there was only a fair crowd in De Spain's, the riders and a few town merchants lined up and lounged at the bar and some others played poker and faro, with tobacco smoke hanging above them around the brass lamps. They were drinking and talking, but it didn't seem loud enough for a Saturday. There had been more men in here earlier, right after supper, a number of them coming in for a quick glass or a jug to take with them, heading back to their spreads with their families, but, now it was only a fair-sized crowd. The moment of excitement had been Mr. Tanner coming in. He had stood at the bar and lit a cigar and sipped two glasses of whiskey while Mr. Malson stood with him. Those who were out at the Maricopa pasture pointed out Mr. Tanner to those who hadn't been there. The reactions to seeing him were mostly the same. So that was Frank Tanner. He didn't look so big. They expected a man with his name and reputation to look different—a man who traded goods to Mexican rebels and had a price on his head across the border and two dozen guns riding for him. Imagine paying all those men. He must do pretty well. He was a little above average height and was straight as a post, thin, with a thin, sunken-in face and a heavy moustache and eyes in the shadow of his hatbrim. He made a person look at him when he walked in, but once the person had looked, Tanner wasn't that different from anybody else. That was the reaction to Frank Tanner. That he was not so much after all. Still, while he was in De Spain's, it seemed quieter, like everybody was holding back, though most of the men were trying to act natural and somebody would laugh every once in a while. Frank Tanner stayed fifteen minutes and left. He'd gone over to the Republic and shortly after, he and his wife were seen riding out of Lanoria in their buggy with a mounted Mexican trailing them, everyone coming to doors and windows to get a look at them. The men said boy, his wife was something— a nice young thing and not too frail either, and the women admitted yes, she was pretty, but she ought to knot or braid her hair instead of letting it hang down like that; it made her look awful bold.

Frank Tanner had left De Spain's over two hours ago. Now, the next one to come in, just a little while after the Maricopa rider, was Bob Valdez.

The house man saw him and nudged Mr. Malson under the table. Mr. Malson looked at him funny, frowning—What was the little bald-headed son of a bitch up to?—then saw the house man looking toward the door. Bob Valdez was coming directly toward their table, his gaze already picking out Mr. Malson, who looked at him and away from him and back again, and Bob Valdez was still looking right at him.

"I buried him," Valdez said.

Mr. Malson nodded. "Good. There were enough witnesses, I didn't see any need for an inquest." He looked up at Bob Valdez. "Everybody knows how he died."

"Unless his wife wants him buried at home," Valdez said.

Mr. Beaudry said, "Let her move him if she wants. Phew, driving that team in the sun with him on the back. How'd you like to do that?"

R. L. Davis, who had moved over from the bar, said, "I guess that boy stunk enough when he was alive." He looked around and got a couple of the riders to laugh at it.

"I haven't asked her if she wants to," Valdez said. "It's something she'll think about later when she's home. But I told her one thing," he said then. "I told her we'd pay her for killing her husband."

There was a silence at the table. Mr. Beaudry fooled with the end of his moustache, twisting it, and Mr. Malson cleared his throat before he said, "We? Who's we?"

"I thought everybody who was there," Bob Valdez said. "Or everybody who wants to give something."

Mr. Malson said, "You mean take up a collection? Pass the hat around?"

Valdez nodded. "Yes sir."

"Well, I suppose we could do that." He looked at Beaudry. "What do you think, Earl?"

Mr. Beaudry shrugged. "I don't care. I guess it would be all right. Give her a few dollars for a stake."

Mr. Malson nodded. "Enough to get home. Where does she live?"

"Their place is north of here," Valdez said.

"No, I mean where is she from?"

"I don't know."

"Probably across the border," Mr. Beaudry said. "She could collect about ten dollars and it'd be more than any of her kin had ever seen before."

Mr. Malson said, "I suppose we could do it."

"I was thinking of more than ten dollars," Valdez said.

Mr. Malson looked up at him. "How much more?"

Bob Valdez cleared his throat. He said, "I was thinking five hundred dollars."

The silence followed again. This time R. L. Davis broke it. He moved, shifting his weight, and there was a chinging sound of his spurs. He said, "I would like to know something. I would like to know why we're listening to this greaser. It was him killed the nigger. What's he coming to us for?"

"R. L.," Mr. Malson said, "keep your mouth closed, all right?"

"Why can't I say what I want?" R. L. Davis said, drunk enough to tell the manager of Maricopa to his face, "He killed him. Not us."

Mr. Malson said, "Shut up or go to bed." He took his time shifting his gaze to Bob Valdez, then holding it there, staring at him. "That's a lot of money, five hundred dollars."

"Yes sir," Bob Valdez nodded, speaking quietly. "I guess it is, but she needs it. What does she have now? I mean, we take her husband from her and now she doesn't have anything. So I thought five hundred dollars." He smiled a little. "It just came to me. That much."

Mr. Beaudry said, "That's as much as most men make in a year."

"Yes sir," Bob Valdez said. "But her husband won't earn anything anymore. Not this year or any year. So maybe five hundred is not so much."

Mr. Beaudry said, "Giving that much is different than giving her a few dollars. I don't mean the difference in the amount. I mean you give her a sum like five hundred dollars it's like admitting we owe it to her. Like we're to blame."

"Well?" Bob Valdez said. "Who else is to blame?"

Mr. Beaudry said, "Now wait a minute. If you're anxious to fix blame then I'll have to go along with what this man said." He nodded toward R. L. Davis. "You killed him. We didn't. We were there to help flush him out, a suspected murderer. We weren't there to kill anybody unless we had to. But you took it on yourself to go down and talk to him and it was you that killed him. Am I right or wrong?"

Bob Valdez said, "Everybody was shooting——"

Mr. Beaudry held up his hand. "Wait just a minute. Shooting isn't killing. Nobody's shot killed him but yours and there are ninety, a hundred witnesses will testify to it."

"I said it before," R. L. Davis said. "He killed the coon. Nobody else. The wrong coon at that."

A few of them laughed and Bob Valdez looked over at R. L. Davis standing with his funneled hat over his eyes and his thumbs hooked in his belt trying to stand straight but swaying a little. He was good and drunk, his eyes watery looking and the corners of his mouth sticky. But it would be good to hit him anyway, Bob Valdez was thinking. Come in from the side and get his cheek and rip into his nose without hitting those ugly teeth and maybe cut your hand. With gloves on hit the mouth, but not without gloves. He could see R. L. Davis sitting on the floor of De Spain's saloon with his nose bleeding and blood down the front of him. That would be all right.

And who else? No, he should be able to talk to Mr. Malson and Mr. Beaudry, the manager of a cattle company and a government land agent, but he was having one son of a bitch of a hard time because they didn't see it, what he meant, or they didn't want to see it.

He said, "I mean this way. What if she went to court——"

"Jesus Christ," R. L. Davis said, shaking his head.

"What if she went there"—Valdez kept his eyes on Mr. Beaudry now—"with a lawyer and said she wanted to sue everybody that was out there, or this city?"

"Bob," Mr. Beaudry said, "that woman doesn't know what a lawyer is."

"But if she did and they went to court, wouldn't she get some money?"

The house man said, "I thought we were playing cards."

"Since she's never heard of a lawyer or a county seat," Mr. Beaudry said, "you're talking straight into the wind, aren't you?"

"I mean if she did. Like if you drive cattle over a man's property and damage something," Bob Valdez went on, holding on, "and the man goes to court, then the cattle company has to pay him for the damage. Isn't that right?"

Mr. Malson smiled. He said, "That doesn't sound like much

of a cattle company to me," and the others laughed. "I was to get involved in court suits, a man would be out from Chicago and I'd be out of a job."

"But it's happened," Valdez said, staying with it. "The person or persons responsible have had to pay."

Mr. Beaudry said, "I wouldn't worry about it, Bob."

"The person has to stand up and prove damage," Mr. Malson said. "You don't go to court, even if you know where it is, without a case. And by that I mean evidence."

"All right," Valdez said. "That's what I mean. The woman doesn't know anything about court, but we know about the evidence, uh? Because we were there. If we weren't there her husband would be alive."

"Or if he hadn't opened the door," Mr. Beaudry said. "Or if you hadn't pulled the trigger."

"Or," Mr. Malson said, "if he hadn't come to town this morning and if Frank Tanner hadn't seen him."

"Goddam, I was there," R. L. Davis said. "We was on the steps of the Republic."

"There you are," Mr. Beaudry said. "If Frank Tanner hadn't been here this morning it never would have happened. So maybe it's his fault. Tanner's."

Somebody in the group behind Mr. Beaudry said, "Go tell him that," and some of the men laughed, picturing it.

"Now that's not so funny," Mr. Beaudry said. "If this happened because of Frank Tanner, then maybe he's to blame. What do you think, Bob?" he asked him seriously, patiently, as he would ask a stupid, thick-headed person.

"I guess so," Bob Valdez said.

"Well, if you think he's to blame," Mr. Beaudry said, "why don't you ask him for the money? And I'll tell you what. If he agrees to the five hundred dollars, we will too. How's that?"

Valdez kept his eyes on Mr. Beaudry. "I don't know where he is."

"He's south of town," Mr. Beaudry said. "Probably at the relay station for the night if his cattle got that far. Or he might have gone on."

"He mentioned stopping there," Mr. Malson said.

"All right," Valdez said because there was nothing else he could say. "I'll go talk to him."

"Do that," Mr. Beaudry said.

Mr. Malson waited until Bob Valdez was turning and the men who had crowded in were stepping aside. "Bob," he said, "that Apache woman—somebody said she was over to the hotel trying to get a room."

"No." Valdez shook his head. "The manager said they were full up."

"Uh-huh," Mr. Malson said. "Well, where is she now?"

"I took her to Inez's place," Valdez said. "She's staying there tonight."

Nobody said anything until he was gone. Then R. L. Davis, as drunk as he was, said, "Je-sus H. Christ. Now he's turned that Indin creature into a whore."

He went unarmed, riding south through the darkness, feeling the chill of night settling on the land. He didn't want to go; he was tired. He had come up this road this morning from St. David on the bouncing, bucking, creaking boot of the Hatch and Hodges stage, throwing gravel at the wheelers and yelling, urging the horses on as the driver held the heavy reins and snapped them over the teams. Sun and dust this morning, and sweat soaking his body under the dark suit; now cold darkness over the same ruts that stretched across the mesquite flats and climbed through barrancas to crest a hill and drop curving into the endless flats again, forever, it seemed, on the boot or now in the saddle of a stage company horse.

He said in his mind, Mr. Tanner, I'm Bob Valdez. You remember, I was out at the pasture today when the man was killed.

When the man was killed. When *you* killed him, he said to himself.

We were talking about doing something for his wife and Mr. Beaudry, the land agent, said——

He said go out and try to get it from Frank Tanner, you dumb Mexican son of a bitch. That's what he said. Do you know it?

He knew it. Sure. But what was he supposed to do? Forget about the woman? He had told her they would give her money. God, it would be easy to forget about her. No, it would be good, but it wouldn't be easy. But with all of them watching him he had had to walk out and get a horse and he would have

to ride the ten goddam miles or more to the goddam swing station and, getting it over with, smile and be respectful and ask
Mr. Tanner if he would please like to give something for this
fat squaw who had lived with Rincón and was having his child.

And Frank Tanner, like the rest of them, would say——

No, they said this Tanner had a lot of money. Maybe he
would say, "Sure, I'll give you something for her. How much
do you want?" Maybe it would be easy to talk to him. Maybe
now, at night, after it was over and the man had had time to
think about it, maybe he would talk a little and say yes.

A mile or a little more from the stage station he saw low
shapes out among the brush patches, cattle grazing, bedded
for the night, and among them, the taller shape of a rider. But
they were well off from the stage road and none of the cattle he
saw or the mounted man came near him. During the last mile
he was certain a rider was behind him, but he didn't stop or
slow down to let the horse sound catch up with him. It could
be somebody on the road, anybody, or one of Tanner's men
watching him; but he had nothing to say to whoever it was.
His words were for Tanner, even if he didn't know how to put
the words to convince the man. It would be easier to say it in
Spanish. Or in Chiricahua.

Now, coming over a low rise, he could see the glow of their
fires, three of them, where the swing station would be in the
darkness. Gradually then, as he approached, he could make
out the adobe building, the fires reflecting on pale walls in the
night. The front of the building, beneath the mesquite-pole
ramada, was in deep shadow. Closer now and he could see the
low adobe outer wall across the front yard, shielding the well
and the horse corral from open country.

Valdez listened as he approached. He could hear the men by
the fire, the thin sound of voices coming across the yard. He
could hear horses moving in the corral and a shrill whinnying
sound. He was aware of horses closer to him, off in the darkness, but moving in with the heavy muffled sound of hooves on
the packed sand. He did not look toward the sound but continued on, coming to the wall and walking his horse through the
open gate, feeling the riders out of the darkness close behind
him as he entered the yard.

A figure by the wall with a rifle said, "Hold it there," and a voice behind him, in English also but with an accent said, "We have him." The man with the rifle came toward him, raising the barrel of a Henry or a Winchester—Valdez wasn't sure in the dimness.

He said in Spanish, "I have no gun."

And the voice behind him said, also in Spanish, "Get down and show us."

Valdez swung down. He dropped the reins and opened his coat as the man with the rifle, a Winchester, came up to him.

"The saddle," the voice behind him said in English.

Not looking around Valdez said, "You make sure, don't you?" The man behind him didn't answer. He walked his horse forward and dismounted close to Valdez, looking into his face.

"You go where?"

"Here," Valdez said. "To speak to Señor Tanner."

"About what?"

"Money," Valdez said.

The man who had dismounted continued to study him for a moment. He handed his reins to the one with the rifle and walked off toward the adobe. Valdez watched him and saw the men by the fires, on the side of the adobe, looking out toward him. It was quiet now except for the stirring of the horses in the corral. He saw the light in the doorway as the man went inside. The door remained open, but he could see nothing within.

There was a bar inside the room and two long tables. The station man, Gregorio Sanza, would be behind the bar maybe, serving Tanner. He remembered Tanner did not take anything to drink at the pasture.

He said to the one with the rifle, "The company I work for owns that building. The Hatch and Hodges."

The man said nothing. Beyond him now two figures appeared in the doorway, in the light for a moment and out of it into darkness. Not Tanner, neither of them. The one who had gone inside called out, "Bring him over." The two men in shadow came out a few steps and the second one, also with an accent, said, "Against the wall," motioning with a nod of his head to the side.

Some of the men by the fires had stood up or were rising as Valdez walked toward them. Others sat and lounged on their sides—dark faces, dark leather, firelight reflecting on cartridge belts and mess tins—and Valdez had to walk around them to reach the wall. As he turned, the man who had come out of the house walked over to stand across the fire from him, the men standing or sitting there quickly making room for him.

The *segundo*, Valdez thought. They move.

He was a big man, almost as big as Diego Luz, with a straw Sonora hat and a heavy moustache that gave him a solemn expression and a strip of beard beneath his mouth. The segundo, with one cartridge bandolier and two long-barreled .44s on his legs.

Valdez nodded to him and said in Spanish, "Good evening," almost smiling.

"I don't know you," the segundo said.

"Because we have never met."

"I know everyone who does business with Señor Tanner."

"I have no business with him. A private matter."

"You told them business."

"I told them money."

The segundo was silent, watching him. "He doesn't know you," he said then.

"Señor Tanner? Sure, I met him today. I killed a man for him."

The segundo hesitated again, undecided or taking his own time, watching him. He motioned with his hand then, and the Mexican who had gone into the house before moved away, turning the corner. The segundo continued to stare. Valdez shifted his gaze to the left and to the right and saw all of them watching him in the light of the fires. There were Americans and Mexicans, some of them bearded, most of them with their hats on, all of them armed. He counted, looking about idly, and decided there were at least twelve of them here. More of them out in the darkness.

He said in his mind, Mr. Tanner, do you remember me? Bob——

Tanner came around the corner. He took a stub of cigar out of his mouth and stood looking at Valdez.

Now. "Mr. Tanner, do you remember me? Bob Valdez, from the pasture today."

Tanner held the cigar in front of him. He was in his shirtsleeves and vest and without the dark hat that had hidden his eyes, his hair slanting down across his forehead, the skin pale-looking in the firelight. He seemed thinner now and smaller, but his expression was the same, the tell-nothing expression and the mouth that looked as if it had never smiled.

"What do you want?"

"I just wanted to talk to you for a minute."

"Say it."

"Well, it's about the man today."

"What man?"

"The one that was killed. You know he had a wife with him." Valdez waited.

"Say what you want and get out of here."

"Well, we were talking—Mr. Beaudry and Mr. Malson. You know who I mean?"

"You don't have much time left," Mr. Tanner said.

"We were saying maybe we should give something to the woman now that she doesn't have a husband."

"They sent you out here?"

"No, I thought of it. I thought if we all put in to give her some money"—he hesitated—"about five hundred dollars."

Mr. Tanner had not moved his gaze from Valdez. "You come out here to tell me that?"

"Well, we were talking about it and Mr. Beaudry said why don't I see you about it."

"You want me to pay money," Mr. Tanner said, "to that red nigger he was holed up with?"

"You said it wasn't the right man——"

"What's that got to do with it?"

"It was an accident, not the woman's fault, and she doesn't have anything now. And she's got that child she's going to have. Did you see that?"

Mr. Tanner looked at his segundo. He said, "Get rid of him," and started to turn away.

"Wait a minute!"

Valdez watched him half turn to look at him again.

"What did you say?"

"I mean if you could take time to listen a minute so I can explain it." The hard-working, respectful Bob Valdez speaking again, smiling a little.

"Your minute's up, boy." He glanced at his segundo again. "Teach him something." He turned and was gone.

Valdez called out, "Mr. Tanner——"

"He don't hear you so good," the segundo said. "It's too loud out here." He drew the .44 on his right leg, cocked it and fired as he brought it up, and with the explosion the adobe chipped next to Bob Valdez's face.

"All this shooting," the segundo said. "Man, he can't hear anything." He fired again and the adobe chipped close to the other side of Valdez's face. "You see how easy it would be?" the segundo said.

The Mexican rider who had brought him in said, "Let me have one," his revolver already drawn. "Where do you want it?"

"By the right hand," the segundo said.

Valdez was looking at the Mexican rider. He saw the revolver lift as the man pulled the trigger and saw the muzzle flash with the heavy solid noise and heard the bullet strike close to his side.

"Too high," the segundo said.

Now those who were sitting and lounging by the fires rose and drew their revolvers, looking at the segundo and waiting their turn. One of them, an American, said, "I know where I'm going to shoot the son of a bitch." One of them laughed and another one said, "See if you can shoot his meat off." And another one said, "It would fix this squaw-lover good."

Bob Valdez did not want to move. He wanted to run and he could feel the sweat on his face, but he couldn't move a hand or an elbow or turn his head. He had to stay rigid without appearing to be rigid. He edged his left foot back and the heel of his boot touched the wall close behind him. He did that much, touching something solid and holding on, as the men faced him across the fires, five or six strides away from him, close enough to put the bullets where they wanted to put them—if all of the men knew how to shoot and if they hadn't had too much mescal or tequila since coming to the station. Valdez held on and now kept his eyes on the segundo for a place to keep them, a point to fix on while they played their game with him.

The first few men fired in turn, calling their shots; but now the rest of them were anxious and couldn't wait and they began firing as they decided where to shoot, raising the revolvers in front of them but not seeming to aim, pulling the triggers in the noise and smoke and leaning in to see where their bullets struck. Valdez felt his hat move and felt powder dust from the adobe brick in his eyes and in his nose and felt chips of adobe sting his face and hands and felt a bullet plow into the wall between his knees and a voice say, "A little higher you get him good." Another voice, "Move up a inch at a time and watch him poop his drawers."

He kept his eyes on the segundo in the Sonora straw, not telling the segundo anything with his gaze, looking at him as he would look at any man, if he wanted to look at the man, or as he would look at a horse or a dog or a steer or an object that was something to look at. But as he saw the segundo staring back at him he realized that he was telling the segundo something after all. Good. He had nothing to lose and now was aware of himself staring at the segundo.

What can you do? he was saying to the segundo. You can kill me. Or one of them can kill me not meaning to. But what else can you do to me? You want me to get down on my knees? You don't have enough bullets, man, and you know it. So what can you do to me? Tell me.

The segundo raised his hand and called out, "Enough!" in English and in Spanish and in English again. He walked between the fires to Bob Valdez and said, "You ride out now."

Bob Valdez took his hat off, adjusting it, loosening it on his head. He didn't touch his face to wipe away the brick dust and sweat or look at his hands, though he felt blood on his knuckles and running down between his fingers.

He said, "If you're through," and walked away from the segundo. He mounted the company horse and rode out the gate, the segundo watching him until he was into the darkness and only a faint sound of him remained.

The men were talking and reloading, spinning the cylinders of their revolvers, sitting by the fires to rest and to tell where they had put their bullets. The segundo walked away from them out into the yard, listening to the silence. After a few minutes he went under the ramada to enter the adobe.

The station man, Gregorio Sanza, behind the plank bar and beneath the smoking oil lamp, raised a mescal bottle to the segundo, pale yellow in the light; but the segundo shook his head; he walked over to the long table where Tanner was sitting with the woman. She was sipping a tin cup of coffee.

The woman had gone into a sleeping room shortly after they had arrived in the buggy and had remained there until now. The segundo saw she was still dressed and he wondered what she had been doing in the room. In the months she had been with them—since Tanner had brought her over from Fort Huachuca—the segundo could count the times he had spoken to her on his hands. She seldom asked for anything; she never gave the servants orders as the woman of the house was supposed to do. Still, she had the look of a woman who would be obeyed. She did not seem afraid or uneasy; she looked into your eyes when she spoke to you; she spoke loud enough yet quietly. But something was going on in her head beneath the long gold-brown hair that hung past her shoulders. She was a difficult woman to understand because she did not give herself away. Except that she smiled only a little, and he had never seen her laugh. Maybe she laughed when she was alone with Señor Tanner.

If she was my woman, the segundo was thinking, I could make her laugh and scream and bite.

He said to Tanner, "The man's gone."

"How did he behave?"

"He stood up."

Tanner drew on the fresh cigar he was smoking. "He did, uh?"

"As well as a man can do it."

"He didn't beg?"

The segundo shook his head. "He said nothing."

"He shot the nigger square," Tanner said. "He did that well. But outside, I thought he would crawl."

The segundo shook his head again. "No crawling or begging."

"All right, tell that man to close his bar and go to bed."

The segundo nodded and moved off.

Tanner waited until the segundo had stopped at the bar and had gone outside. "Why don't you go to bed, too," he said to the woman.

"I will in a minute." She kept her finger in the handle of the coffee cup.

"Go in and pretty yourself up," he said then. "I'll take a turn around the yard and be in directly."

"What did the man do?"

"He wasted my time."

"So they put him against the wall?"

"It was the way he spoke to me," Tanner said. "I can't have that in front of them." He sat close to her, staring into her face, at the gray-green eyes and the soft hair close to her cheek. His hand came up to finger the end strands of her hair. Quietly, he said, "Gay, go on in the room."

"I'll finish my coffee."

"No, right now would be better. I'll be there in a minute."

She waited until he was out of the door before rising and going into the sleeping room. In the dim lamplight she began to undress, stepping out of her dress and dropping it on the bed next to her nightgown. The light blue one. Thin and limp and patched beneath one arm. There had been a light blue one and a light green one and a pink one and a yellow one, all with the white-scrolled monogram GBE she had embroidered on the bodice when she was nineteen years old and living in Prescott, a girl about to be married. The girl, Gay Byrnes, had brought the nightgowns and her dresses and linens to Fort Huachuca to become the bride of James C. Erin. During five and a half years as his wife she discarded the nightgowns one by one and used them as dust rags. When her husband was killed six months ago, and she left Huachuca with Frank Tanner, she had only the light blue one left.

Gay Erin slipped the nightgown over her head, brushed her hair and got into the narrow double bed, pulling the blanket up over her shoulder as she rolled to her side, her back to the low-burning lamp.

When Tanner came in and began to undress, she remained with her back to him. She could see him from times before: removing his boots, his shirt and trousers, standing in his long cotton underwear as he unfastened the buttons. He would stand naked scratching his stomach and chest, then go to the wall hook and take his revolver from the holster, making sure the hammer was on an empty chamber as he moved toward the bed.

She felt the mattress yield beneath his weight. The gun would be at his side, under the blanket and next to his hip. He would lie still for a few moments, then roll toward her and put his hand on her shoulder.

"What have you got the nightgown on for?"

"I'm cold."

"Well now, what do you think I'm for?"

"Tell me," Gay Erin said.

"I'll show you."

"As a lover or a husband?"

Tanner groaned. "Jesus Christ, are you going to start that?"

"Six months ago you said we'd be married in a few weeks."

"Most people probably think we already are. What's the difference?"

She started to get up, to throw back the blanket, and his hand tightened on her arm.

"I said we'd be married, we will."

"When?"

"Well not right now, all right?" His hand stroked her arm beneath the flannel. "Come on, take this thing off."

She lay without moving, her eyes open in the darkness, letting her hesitation stretch into silence, a long moment, before she sat up slowly and worked the nightgown out from beneath her. She pulled it over her head, turning to him.

3

I NEZ WAS fat and took her time coming over from the stove with the coffeepot. Filling the china cup in front of Bob Valdez and then her own, Inez said, "She left early. It must have been before daybreak."

"You hear her?"

"No, maybe one of the girls did. I can ask."

"It doesn't matter."

"I heard what you're doing," Inez said.

"Well, I'm not doing very good. I wanted to tell the woman maybe it would take me a little longer."

"You're crazy."

"Listen, I'm tired," Valdez said. "I'm not going to argue with you, all right?"

"Go upstairs."

"I said I'm tired."

"So are the girls. I mean take a room and go to sleep."

"I have a run to St. David this afternoon and don't come back till the morning."

"Tell them you're sick."

"No, they don't have anybody."

"That Davis was in here last night. I threw him out."

"You can do it," Valdez said.

"He was in no condition. Only talk. I don't need talk," Inez said. She made a noise sipping her coffee and watched Valdez shape a cigarette. He handed it to her and made another one and lit them with a kitchen match.

"Now what do you do, forget the whole thing?"

"I don't know." He rubbed a gnarled brown hand over his hair, pulling it down on his forehead. "I think maybe talk to this Mr. Tanner again."

"You're crazy."

"I didn't explain it to him right. The part that it's like a court where you get money for something done to you. Not like a court, but, you know."

"You're still crazy. He won't listen to you. Nobody will."

"But if he does, the others will, uh?" Valdez sipped his coffee.

"Put a gun in his back if you can get close to him," Inez said. "That's the only way."

"No guns."

"The little shotgun."

Valdez nodded, thinking about it. "That would be good, wouldn't it?"

"Boom!" Inez laughed out and the sound of her voice filled the kitchen.

Valdez smiled. "Has he ever been in here?"

"They say he's got a woman. Maybe he beats her or does strange things to her."

"He's never been here, but you don't like him," Valdez said. "Why?"

"My book."

"Ah, your book. I forgot about it."

"You're in it."

"Sure, I remember now."

Inez called out, "Polly!" and waited a moment and called again.

A dark-haired girl in a robe came through the door from the front room. She smiled at Bob Valdez, holding the robe together in front of her. "Early bird," she said.

"No early bird. Get me the book," Inez said.

"Which, the black one?"

"No, the one before," Inez said. "The green one."

Valdez shook his head. "Black ones and green ones. How many do you have?"

"They go back about twelve years. To your time."

"Like I'm an old man now."

"Sometime you act it."

The girl came into the kitchen again with the scrapbook under her arm. "The green one," she said, winking at Bob Valdez and handing it to Inez, who pushed her coffee cup out of the way to open the book on the table. Inez sat at the end of the kitchen table with Polly standing behind her now, looking over her shoulder. Sitting to the side, Valdez lowered and cocked his head to look at the newspaper clippings and photographs mounted in the book.

"He seems familiar," Valdez said.

Inez looked at him. "I hope so. It's Rutherford Hayes."

"Well, that was twelve, fourteen years ago," Valdez said. He looked up as Polly laughed. She was leaning over Inez and the top of her robe hung partly open.

There were photographs of local businessmen, territorial officials and national figures, including two presidents, Rutherford Hayes and Chester A. Arthur, Porfirio Díaz and Carmelita at Niagara Falls, and the Prince of Wales on his visit to Washington.

"Have they been to your place?" Valdez asked.

"No, but if they come I want to recognize them." Inez turned a page. "Earl Beaudry, on his appointment as land agent." Inez moved to the next page, her finger tracing down the column of newspaper clippings.

"Here it is," she said. "The first mention of him. August 13, 1881—Frank Tanner and a Carlisle Baylor were convicted of cattle theft and sent to Yuma Penitentiary."

Valdez seemed as pleased as he was surprised. "He's been to prison."

"For a few years, I think," Inez said. "It doesn't say how long. He was stealing cattle and driving them across the border. There's more about him." Her hand moved down the column and went to the next page. "Here, October, 1886, Frank J. Tanner, cattle broker, arraigned on a charge of murder in Contention, Arizona."

"Cattle broker now," Valdez said.

"The case was dismissed."

"It's getting better."

Inez turned the page. "Ah, here's the picture. You see him there?" Inez turned the book halfway toward Valdez and he leaned in, recognizing Tanner standing with a group of Army officers in front of an adobe building.

Inez read the caption. "It says he has a contract with the government to supply remounts to the Tenth United States Cavalry at Fort Huachuca." She turned a few more pages. "I think that's all."

"Nothing about him now, uh?"

"There's something else sticks in my mind about Huachuca," Inez said, "but I don't see it. Unless—sure, it would be in the other book. She sat back in her chair looking up over her shoulder. "Polly?"

Valdez watched the girl straighten and draw the robe together.

"Should I take this one?" the girl asked.

Inez was turning pages again. "No, I want to show Bob something."

"What have you got now?" he asked her.

Coming to a page, she pressed it flat and turned the book to him. "You remember?"

Valdez smiled a little. "That one."

It was a photograph of Bob Valdez taken at Fort Apache, Arizona, September 7, 1884: Bob Valdez standing among small trees and cactus plants the photographer had placed in his studio shed as a background: Bob Valdez with a Sharps .50 cradled in one arm and a long-barreled Walker Colt on his leg. He was wearing a hat, with a bandana beneath it that covered half of his forehead, a belt of cartridges for the Sharps, and knee-length Apache moccasins. The caption beneath the picture described Roberto Valdez as chief of scouts with Major General George Crook, Department of Arizona, during his expedition into Sonora against hostile Apaches.

"That's the way I still picture you," Inez said. "When someone says Bob Valdez, this is the one I see. Not the one that wears a suit and a collar."

Valdez was concentrating on the book, looking now at a photograph of a young Apache scout in buckskins and holding a rifle, standing against the same background used in the photo of himself. He remembered the photographer, a man named Fly. And the day the pictures were taken at Fort Apache. He remembered the scout washing himself and brushing his hair and putting on the buckskin shirt he had bought and had never worn before.

"Peaches," Valdez said. "General Crook's guide. His real name was Tso-ay, but the soldiers and the general called him Peaches. His skin." Valdez continued to study the photograph. He said, "They'd put a suit and a collar on him too, if they ever took his picture again."

Inez looked up as Polly came in with the other scrapbook. She took it from her and held it over the table.

"I don't know where he is now," Valdez was saying. "Maybe Fort Sill, Oklahoma, with the rest of them. Planting corn."

He shook his head. "Man, I would like to see that sometime. Those people growing things in a garden."

Inez opened the book and laid it over the page Valdez was studying. He sat back as she turned a few pages and raised his gaze to Polly, who was looking over Inez's shoulder again, letting her robe come open. She was built very well and had very white skin.

"Here it is," Inez said. "Sutler murdered at Fort Huachuca. James C. Erin was found shot to death a few miles from the fort today——"

Valdez stopped her. "When was this?"

Inez looked at the date on the clipping. "March. Six months ago."

"That's the one Orlando Rincón was supposed to have killed."

"It says he was found by some soldiers and"—her finger moved down the column—"here's the part. 'Held for questioning was Frank J. Tanner of Mimbreño, said to be the last person to have seen Erin alive. Mr. Tanner stated he had spent the previous evening with Mr. and Mrs. Erin at the fort, but had left for a business appointment in Nogales and had not seen Erin on the day he was reported to have been killed.'"

"He was sure it was Rincón," Valdez said. "And that his name was Johnson."

Inez nodded, looking at the book. "They mention a Johnson, listed as a deserter and also a suspect. A trooper with the Tenth Cavalry."

"Maybe they know this Johnson did it now," Valdez said.

Inez looked over the pages facing her. "I don't see anything more about it."

Valdez raised his eyes from the open robe to the nice-looking face of the dark-haired girl. "It's too bad he doesn't come here," he said.

Inez closed the book. "He never has and I would guess he knows where it is."

"If he did," Valdez said, his gaze still on Polly. "I could wait for him."

Diego Luz had a dream in which he saw himself sitting on a corral fence watching his men working green horses in the enclosure. In the dream, which he would look at during the day as well as at night, Diego Luz was manager of the Maricopa Cattle Company. He lived with his family in the whitewashed adobe off beyond the corral, where the cedars stood against the sky: a house with trees and a stone well in the yard and a porch to sit on in the evening. Sometimes he would picture himself on the porch with his family about him, his three sons and two daughters, his wife and his wife's mother and whatever relatives might be visiting them. But his favorite dream was to see himself on the corral fence with his eldest son, who was almost a man, sitting next to him.

The hands were very nervous when he watched them with the horses because they knew he was the greatest mustanger and horsebreaker who ever lived. They knew he could subdue the meanest animals and they were afraid to make mistakes in his presence. He had told them how to do it, what they must do and not do, and he liked to watch them at work.

In the dream Diego and his son would watch R. L. Davis hanging on to the crow-hopping bronc until finally they saw him thrown and land hard on his shoulder. His son would shake his head and say, "Should I do it, Papa?" But he would say no, it was good for the man. He made R. L. Davis ride only the rough string, the outlaws and spoiled horses, when they were on roundup or a drive, and made R. L. Davis call him Señor Luz.

R. L. Davis mounted the bronc and was thrown again and this time he went after the horse with a loaded quirt and began beating the animal over the head. At this point in the dream Diego Luz walked over to R. L. Davis and said to him, "Hey," and when R. L. Davis looked around Diego Luz hit him in the face with one of his big fists. R. L. Davis went down and the eldest son poured a bucket of water on him and when the man shook his head and opened his eyes, he said "What did I do?" Diego Luz said, "You hit the horse." R. L. Davis frowned, holding his jaw. "But you hit them when you broke horses," he said. And Diego Luz smiled and said, "Maybe, but now I hit whoever I want to."

R. L. Davis was a good one to hit. Once in a while though, he would leave R. L. Davis alone and hit Mr. Malson, not hitting him too hard, but letting him know he was hit. And sometimes he would fire Mr. Malson, call him over and say, "It's too bad, but you're too goddam weak and stupid to do this work anymore so we got to get rid of you. And don't come back."

Diego Luz would think of these things as he worked his land and broke the mustangs he and his eldest son drove down out of the high country. His place was southeast of Lanoria, well off the road to St. David and only a few miles from the village of Mimbreño, though there was no wagon road in that direction, only a few trails if a man knew where to find them.

His place was adobe with straw blinds that rolled down to cover the doorway and windows and an open lean-to built against the house for cooking. There were a few chickens and two goats in the yard with the three youngest children and a brown mongrel dog that slept in the shade of the house most of the day. There was a vegetable garden for growing beans and peppers, and the peppers that were drying hung from the roof of the ramada that shaded the front of the house, which faced north, on high ground. Down the slope from the house was the well, and beyond it, on flat, cleared ground, the mesquite-pole corral where Diego Luz broke and trained the mustangs he flushed out of the hills. He worked here most of the time. Several times a year he drove a horse string down to the Maricopa spread near Lanoria, and he would go down there at roundup time and when they drove the cattle to Willcox.

When Bob Valdez appeared, circling the corral—two days following the incident at the pasture—Diego Luz and his eldest son were at the well, pulling up buckets of water and filling the wooden trough that ran to the corral. They stood watching Bob Valdez walking his horse toward them and waited, after greeting him, as he stepped down from the saddle and took the dipper of water Diego's son offered him.

There was no hurry. If a man rode all the way here he must have something to say, and it was good to wonder about it first and not ask him questions. Though Diego Luz had already decided Bob Valdez had not come to see them but was passing through on his way to Mimbreño. And who lived in Mimbreño? Frank Tanner. There it was. Simple.

They left the boy and climbed the slope to the house, Bob Valdez seeing the children in the yard, Diego's wife and her mother watching them from the lean-to where they were both holding corn dough, shaping tortillas. The small children ran up to them and the eldest daughter appeared now in the doorway of the house. Hey, a good looking girl now, almost a woman. Anita. She would be maybe sixteen years old. Valdez had not been up here in almost a year.

When they were in the shade and had lighted cigarettes, Diego Luz said, "There's something different about you. What is it?"

Valdez shrugged. "I'm the same. What are you talking about?"

"Your face is the same." Diego Luz squinted, studying him. Slowly then his face relaxed. "I know what it is. You don't have your collar on."

Valdez's hand went to his neck where he had tied a bandana.

"Or your suit. What is this, you're not dressed up?"

"It's too hot," Valdez said.

"It's always hot," Diego Luz said. His gaze dropped to Valdez's waist. "No gun though."

Valdez frowned. "What's the matter with you? I don't have a coat on, that's all."

"And you're going to see Mr. Tanner."

"Just to say a few things to him."

"My son rode to Lanoria yesterday. He heard about the few things you said the other night."

Valdez shook his head. "People don't have anything to talk about."

"Listen, the woman doesn't need any money. She doesn't know what it is."

"But we know," Valdez said. "I just want to ask you something about Tanner."

Diego Luz drew on his cigarette and squinted out into the sunlight, down the slope to the horse corral. "I know what others know. That's all."

"He lives in Mimbreño?"

"For about two years maybe."

"How do the people like him?"

"There are no people. Most of them left at the time of the Apache. The rest of them left when Frank Tanner come.

He's there with his men," Diego Luz said, "and some of their women."

"How many men?"

"At least thirty. Sometimes more."

"Do they ever come here?"

"Sometimes they pass by."

"What do they do, anything?"

"They have a drink of water and go on."

"They never make any trouble?"

"No, they don't bother me. Never."

"Maybe because you work for Maricopa."

Diego Luz shrugged. "What do I have they would want?"

"Horses," Valdez said.

"Once they asked to buy a string. I told them to see Mr. Malson."

"Did Tanner himself come?"

"No, his segundo and some others."

"Do you know any of them?"

"No, I don't think any of them are from around here."

"Do you think that's strange?"

"No, these are guns he hires, not hands. I think they hear of Tanner and what he pays and they come from all over to get a job with him."

"He pays good, uh?"

"You see them sometimes in St. David," Diego Luz said. "They spend the money. But you see different ones each time, so maybe he lose some in Mexico or they get a stomach full of it and quit."

"What, driving cattle?"

"Cattle and guns. He gets the guns somewhere and sneaks them over the border to people who are against Díaz and want to start a revolution. So over there the *rurales* and federal soldiers look for him and try to stop him. Everybody knows that."

"I've been learning the stageline business," Valdez said.

"Keep doing it," Diego Luz said, "and live to be an old man."

"Sometimes I feel old now." He watched the chickens pecking the hard ground and heard Diego Luz's children calling out something and laughing as they played somewhere on the other side of the house. What do you need besides this? he was thinking. To have a place, a family. Very quiet except for the children sometimes, and no trouble. No Apaches. No bandits raiding from across the border. Trees and water and a good house. The house could be fixed up better. A little work, that's all. He said, "I'll trade you. I become the horsebreaker, you work for the stage company."

Diego Luz was looking out at the yard. "You want this?"

"Why not? It's a good place."

"If I had something to do I wouldn't be here."

"You do all right," Valdez said.

"Do it forever," Diego Luz said. "See how you like it."

"Maybe sometime. After I see this Tanner."

Diego Luz was studying Valdez's horse. "You don't have a rifle either."

"What do I need it for?"

"Maybe you meet a couple of them on a trail, they don't like your face."

"I'll talk to them," Valdez said.

"Maybe they don't let you talk."

"Come on, they know who I am. I'm going there to talk, that's all."

"You talk better with a rifle," Diego Luz said. "I give you mine."

From habit, approaching the top of the rise—before he would be outlined for a moment against the sky—Bob Valdez looked back the way he had come, his eyes, half-closed in the sun's glare, holding on the rock shapes and darker patches of brush at the bottom of the draw. He sat motionless until he was sure of the movement, then dismounted and led his claybank mare off the trail to one side, up into young piñon pines.

For a few moments he did not think of the rider coming up behind him; he thought of his own reaction, the caution that had stopped him from topping the rise. There were no more Chiricahuas or White Mountain bands around here. There was nothing to worry about to keep him alert and listening and looking back as well as to the sides and ahead. But he had stopped. Sure, habit, he thought. Something hanging on of no use to him now.

What difference did it make who the man was? The man wasn't following him. The man was riding southeast from the St. David road and must have left the road not far back to cut cross-country toward Mimbreño maybe, or to a village across the border. Sure, it could be one of Tanner's men. You can ride in with him, Valdez thought, and smiled at the idea of it. He would see who it was and maybe he would come out of the pines, giving the man some warning first, or maybe he wouldn't.

Now, as the man drew nearer, for some reason he was sure it was one of the Maricopa riders: the slouched, round-shouldered way the man sat his saddle, the funneled brim of his hat bobbing up and down with the walking movement of the horse.

Maybe he had known all time who it was going to be. That was a funny thing. Because when he saw it was R. L. Davis, looking at the ground or deep in thought, the stringy, mouthy one who thought he was good with the Winchester, Valdez was not surprised, though he said to himself, Goddam. How do you like that?

He let him go by, up over the rise and out of sight, while he stayed in the pines to shape a cigarette and light it, wondering where the man was going, curious because it was this one and not someone else, and glad now of the habit that had made him look around when he did. He was sure the man had not been following him. The man would have been anxious and looking around and would have stopped before he topped the rise. But the question remained, Where was he going?

When Valdez moved out, keeping to the trees over the crest of the rise, he hung back and let the distance between them stretch to a hundred yards. He followed R. L. Davis this way for several miles until the trail came to open grazing land, and as R. L. Davis crossed toward the scrub trees and hills beyond the flats, a column of dust came down the slope toward him.

You look around, Bob Valdez thought. That habit stays with you. But you don't bring the field glasses.

He remained in the cover of trees and, in the distance, watched three riders meet R. L. Davis and stand close to him for some time, forming a single shape until the group came apart and the riders, strung out now, one in front of Davis and two behind, rode with him into the deep shadow at the base of the far hills. He saw them briefly again up on the slope and at the crest of the hill.

They wonder about him too, Valdez thought. What do you want? Who do you want to see? They ask questions and take their jobs very seriously because they feel they're important. They should relax more, Valdez thought. He mounted the claybank again and rode out into the sunlight, holding the horse to a walk, keeping his eyes on the slope the riders came down and wondering if they had left someone there to watch.

No, they did it another way. One of them who had been with R. L. Davis came back. When Valdez was little more than halfway up the trail, following the switchbacks that climbed through the brush, he saw the mounted rider waiting for him, his horse standing across the trail.

As Valdez came on, narrowing the distance between them, he recognized the rider, the Mexican who had brought him into the yard of the stage station.

"Far enough," the Mexican said. He held a Winchester across his lap, but did not raise it. He studied Valdez, who reined in a few feet from him. "You come back again."

"I didn't finish talking to him," Valdez said.

"I think he finish with you, though."

"Let's go ask him."

"Maybe he don't want to see you," the Mexican said.

"It's about money again."

"You said that before. For the woman. He don't care anything about the woman."

"Maybe this time when I tell him."

"What do you have on you?"

"Nothing." Valdez raised his hands and dropped one of them to the stock of Diego Luz's rifle in its leather boot. "Only this."

"That could be enough," the Mexican said.

"You want it?" Valdez smiled. "You don't trust me?"

"Sure, I trust you." The Mexican raised the Winchester and motioned Valdez up the grade. "But I ride behind you."

Valdez edged past him up the trail and kept moving until he reached the top of the slope. Now he could see the village of Mimbreño across the valley, a mile from them beyond open land where Tanner's cattle grazed. Valdez had been to this village once before, the day after White Mountain Apaches had raided and killed three men and carried off a woman and burned the mission church. He remembered the blackened walls; the roof had collapsed into the church and the beams were still smoking. He remembered the people in the square when they rode in, the people watching the Apache scouts and company of cavalry and saying to themselves, Why weren't you here yesterday, you soldiers? What good are you?

As they crossed the grazing land Valdez recognized the church, the roofless shell that had never been repaired. It stood at the end of the single street of adobes where the street widened into a square and there was a well with a pump and a stone trough for watering the horses. Beyond the cluster of buildings was a stand of cottonwood trees and a stream that came down out of the high country to the east. Valdez saw the women in the trees, some of them walking this way carrying baskets of clothes. Then he was entering the street, the Mexican next to him now, with the dogs barking and the smell of wood fires, seeing the freight wagons along the adobe fronts and more horses than would ever be in a village this size. It was a village preparing to make war. It was a military camp, the base of a revolutionary army. Or the base of a heavily armed scouting force that would stay here until they were driven out. But at the same time it was not a village. Yes, there were people. There were women among the armed men, women in front of the adobes and a group of them at the well with gourds and wooden pails. But there were no children; no sound of children nor a sign of children anywhere.

"He's there waiting for you," the Mexican said.

Valdez was looking at the church. A gate of mesquite poles had been built across the arched opening of the doorway, and there were horses penned inside the enclosure. He felt the Mexican close to him, moving him to the east side of the square, to the two-story adobe with the loading platform across the front, the building that had been the village's general store and mill and grain warehouse.

Frank Tanner stood at the edge of the loading platform looking down at a group of riders, standing over them with his hands on his hips. A woman was behind him near the open doorway, not a Mexican woman, a blond-haired woman, golden hair in the sunlight hanging below her shoulders to the front of her white dress. Valdez looked at the woman until they were close to the platform and the riders sidestepped their horses to let the Mexican in, Valdez holding back now; and as they moved in among the riders he saw that one of them was the segundo. He saw R. L. Davis, then, mounted on a sorrel next to the segundo. He didn't look at Davis, who was watching him, but up at Tanner now, the man so close above him that he had to bend his head back, feeling awkward and unprotected and foolish with the woman watching him, to look at Tanner.

Tanner stared down at Valdez as if this would be enough, no words necessary. Valdez did not want to smile because he knew he would feel foolish, but he eased his expression to show he was sincere and had come here as an honest man with nothing to hide.

He said, "I'd like to talk to you once more."

"You've talked," Tanner said. "You get one time and you've had yours."

Maybe he was joking, so Valdez smiled a little bit now, though he didn't want to smile with the woman watching him. "I know you're a busy man," he said, "but you must be a fair man also, uh? I mean you have all these people working for you. You recognize the worth of things and pay a just wage. A man like that would also see when someone is owed something."

Goddam, it didn't sound right, hearing himself speaking with his goddam neck bent back and Tanner looking down at him like God in black boots and a black hat over his eyes.

"I mean if the woman was to go to the courthouse and say some men have killed my husband, by mistake, as an accident. So I think somebody should pay me for that—don't you think the court would say sure and order that we pay her something?"

"Jesus Christ," R. L. Davis said. Valdez did not look at him, but he knew it was Davis. He saw Tanner's eyes shift to the side, slide over and back to him again.

"I'm talking about what's fair," Valdez said. "I'm not trying to cheat anybody—if you think I want to take the money and run off. No, you can give it to the woman yourself. I mean have one of your men do it. I don't care who gives it to her."

Tanner continued to stare at him until finally he said, "You don't learn. I guess I have to keep teaching you."

"Tell me why you don't think she should have something," Valdez said. "You explain it to me, I understand it."

"No, I think there's only one thing you'll understand." Tanner's gaze went to his segundo. "You remember that one tried to run off with the horses?"

Valdez lowered his head to look at the segundo, who was nodding, picturing something. "The one who liked to walk," the segundo said.

Valdez heard Tanner say, "That one," and the segundo continued to nod his head, then raised it and gazed about the square.

"We can use the poles from the gate," the segundo said, looking toward the church, "and have some more cut."

Tanner was saying, "All right," and the segundo was looking at Valdez now. He nodded once.

Valdez felt the hand at his shoulder, fingers clawing into his neck as the hand clutched his bandana, and his own hands went to the horn of his saddle. He felt the Mexican's horse tight against his left leg, then moving away and the Mexican pulling him, choking him, until his hands slipped from the saddle horn and he was dragged from his horse, stumbling but not able to fall, held up by the Mexican's fist twisted in the tight fold of his neckerchief. They were around him and someone hit him in the face with a fist. It didn't hurt him, but it startled him; he was struck again on the back of the neck, then in the stomach, seeing the man close to him swing his fist and not being able to turn away from it. He went down and was kicked in the back, pushed over and pressed flat to the hard-packed ground. His hat was off now. A foot came down on his neck, pinning him, face turned to the side against the ground. Now they pulled his arms straight out to the sides and he felt a sharp pain through his shoulder blades as he was held in this position. Several minutes passed and he rested, breathing slowly to relax and not be tensed if they hit him again. Boots were close to his face. The boots moved and dust rose into his nostrils, but no one kicked him.

They placed a mesquite pole across his shoulders that extended almost a foot on either side beyond his outstretched hands, and tied it with leather thongs to his wrists and neck. They placed another pole down the length of his back, from above his head to his heels, and lashed this one to the crosspole and also around his neck and body. When this was done the segundo told him all right, stand up.

Valdez could not press his hands to the ground. He raised his head, turning it, and pushed his forehead against the hard-pack, arching against the pole down his spine, straining the muscles of his neck, and gradually, kicking and scraping the ground, worked his knees up under him.

"The other one didn't get up so quick," the segundo said.

Valdez was on his knees raising his body, and he was kicked hard from behind and slammed onto his face again.

"This one don't get up either," the Mexican said.

Valdez heard Tanner's voice say, "Get him out of here," and this time they let him work his way to his knees and stand up. But as he straightened, the bottom of the vertical pole struck the ground and held him in a hunched position, a man with a weight on his back, his eyes on the ground, unable to raise his head. Someone put his hat on his head, too low and tight on his forehead.

"That way," the segundo said, nodding across the square. "The way you came."

"My horse," Valdez said.

"Don't worry about the horse," the segundo said. "We take care of."

There was nothing more to say. Valdez turned and started off, hunched over, raising his eyes and able to see perhaps twenty feet in front of him, but not able to hold his gaze in this strained position.

The segundo called after him. "Hey, don't fall on your back. You'll be like a turtle." He laughed, and some of the others laughed with him.

Frank Tanner watched the stooped figure circle the water pump and move down the street past the women who had come out of the adobes to look at him.

"You fixed him," R. L. Davis said.

Tanner's eyes shifted to Davis, sliding on him and away from him, as he had looked at him before. "I don't remember asking you here," Tanner said.

"Listen," R. L. Davis began to say.

Tanner stopped him. "Watch your mouth, boy. I don't listen to you. I don't listen to anybody I don't want to listen to."

R. L. Davis squinted up at him. "I didn't mean it that way. I come here to work for you."

Tanner's gaze dropped slowly from the bent figure down the street to Davis. "Why do you think I'd hire you?"

"You need a gun, I'm your man."

"I didn't see you hit anything the other day."

"Jesus Christ, I wasn't aiming at her. You said yourself just make her jump some."

"Are you telling me what I said?"

"I thought that's what it was."

"Don't think," Tanner said. "Ride out."

"Hell, you can always use another man, can't you?"

"Maybe a man," Tanner said. "Ride out."

"Try me out. Put me on for a month."

"We'll put some poles on your back," Tanner said, "if you want to stay here."

"I was just asking." R. L. Davis lifted his reins and flicked them against the neck of his sorrel, bringing the animal around and guiding it through the group of riders, trying to take his time.

Tanner watched Davis until he was beyond the pump and heading down the street. The small stooped figure was now at the far end of the adobes.

The woman, Gay Erin, who had been married to the sutler at Fort Huachuca and had been living with Frank Tanner since her husband's death, waited for Tanner to turn and notice her in the doorway behind him. But he didn't turn; he stood on the edge of the platform over his men.

She said, "Frank?" and waited again.

Now he looked around and came over to her, taking his time. "I didn't know you were there," he said.

She kept her eyes on him, waiting for him to come close. "I don't understand you," she said.

"I don't need that boy. Why should I hire him?"

"The other one. He asks you a simple thing, to help someone."

"We won't talk about it out here," Tanner said. They went

into the dimness of the warehouse, past sacks of grain and stacked wooden cases, Tanner holding her arm and guiding her to the stairway. "I let you talk to me the way you want," Tanner said, "but not in front of my men."

Upstairs, in the office that had been made into a sitting room, Gay Erin looked out the window. She could see R. L. Davis at the end of the street; the hunched figure of Bob Valdez was no longer in sight.

"You better keep up here from now on," Tanner said, "unless I call you down."

She turned from the window. "And how long is that?"

"I guess as long as I want." Tanner went into the bedroom. He came out wearing his coat, strapping on a gunbelt. "I'm going to Nogales; I'll be back in the morning." He looked down at his belt, buckling it. "You can come if you want a twenty-mile ride."

"Or sit here," the girl said.

He looked up at her. "What else?"

"If you say sit I'm supposed to sit." Her expression and the sound of her voice were mild, but her eyes held his and hung on. "No one can be that sure," she said. "Not even you."

"Well, you're not going to leave," Tanner said. He moved toward her, settling the gunbelt on his hips. "You don't have anything at Huachuca. You don't have anything left at Prescott. Whatever you have is here."

"Whatever I have," the girl said, "as your woman."

"Aren't I nice enough to you?"

"Sometimes."

"Take what you get."

"Sometimes you act like a human being."

"When I'm in my drawers," Tanner said. "When I'm in my boots that's a different time."

"You had them on outside."

"You bet I did, lady."

"He was trying to help a woman who'd lost her husband; that's all he was doing."

"And I'm helping one already," Tanner said. "One poor widow woman's enough." He was close to her, looking into her face, and he touched her cheek gently with his hand. He said, "I guess I could stay a few more minutes if you like."

"Frank, send someone to cut him loose."

Tanner shook his head, tired of it. "Lady, you sure can break the spell . . ." He moved away from her toward the door, then looked back as he opened it. "Nobody cuts him loose. I don't want to see that man again."

You've looked at the ground all your life, Valdez thought at one point. But never this close for so long.

The pain reached from the back of his head down into his shoulders. He would try to arch his back, and the pole, with a knot in it, would press against his head and push his hat forward. The hat was low and stuck to his forehead and sweat stung his eyes. He told himself, The hell with it; don't think about it. Go home. You've walked home before.

God, but he had never walked home like this. The ground across the grazing land was humped and spotted with brush, but he had little trouble with his footing. No, God, he could see where he was going all right. He could hear Tanner's cattle and he thought once, What if some bull with swords on his head sees you and doesn't like you? God, he said to himself, give that bull good grass to eat or a nice cow to do something with.

A mile across the grazing land and then up into the foothills, following a gully and angling out of it, climbing the side of a brush slope, not finding the trail and taking a longer way to the top, trying to look up to see where he was going with the pole pressed against his head. He couldn't go straight up. He couldn't lose his footing and fall backward on the crossed poles. He remembered what the segundo had said about the turtle, and at that time he had pictured himself lying on his back in the sun of midday and through the afternoon. No, he would take longer and he wouldn't fall. It was the pain in his legs that bothered him now; it turned his thighs into cords and pulled so, as he neared the top, that his legs began to tremble.

They're old legs, he said to himself. Be good to them. They have to walk twenty miles. Or over to Diego Luz, he thought then. Ten miles. Twenty miles, ten miles, what was the difference?

He wished he could wipe the sweat and dust from his face. He wished he could loosen his hat and rub his nose and bring his arms down and straighten up just for a minute.

Before he reached the crest of the slope he crouched forward and gradually lowered himself to his knees, bending over and twisting his body as he fell forward so that a tip of the crosspole touched the slope first; but this did little to break his fall, and with his head turned his cheekbone struck the ground with the force of a heavy, solid blow. It stunned him and he lay breathing with his mouth open. His hat, tight to his forehead, had remained on; good. Now he rested for perhaps a quarter of an hour, until the pain through his shoulder blades became unbearable. Valdez got to his feet and continued on.

R. L. Davis waited for him in the trees, across the meadow on the far side of the slope. He had watched Valdez work up through the ravine and down the switchback trail on this side. He had waited because maybe Tanner's men were also watching—the lookouts up on the slope—and he had waited because he wasn't sure what they'd do. He thought they might come out and push Valdez down the trail, have some fun with him; but no one appeared, and Valdez had come all the way down to the meadow now and was coming across, hurrying some as he saw the shade of the trees waiting for him.

R. L. Davis moved his sorrel into heavy foliage. There wasn't any hurry: watch him a while and then play with him.

Goddam, now what was he doing, kicking at the leaves? Clearing a spot, R. L. Davis decided. He could hear Valdez in the silence, the sound of the leaves scuffing, and could see him through the pale birch trunks, the bent-over hunched-back figure in the thin shafts of sunlight. He watched Valdez go to his knees; he winced and then smiled as Valdez fell forward on the side of his face. That was pretty good. But as Valdez lay there not moving, R. L. Davis became restless and started to fidget and tried to think of something. You could trample him some, he thought. Ride over him a few times. He decided maybe that was the thing to do and raised his reins to flick the sorrel.

But now the man was stirring, arching onto his head and getting his knees under him.

Valdez rose and stood there, trying to turn his head to look about him. He moved forward slowly, shuffling in the leaves. He turned sideways to edge between trees that grew close together. Farther on he stopped and placed one end of the crosspole against a birch trunk and waved the other end of the pole toward a tree several feet from him, but the pole was too short. R. L. Davis watched him move on, touching a trunk and trying to reach another with the crosspole until finally there it was, and R. L. Davis saw what he was trying to do.

Valdez stood between two trees that were a little less than six feet apart. Now, with the ends of the crosspole planted against the trunks, holding him there, he tried to move forward, straining, digging in with his boots and slipping in the leaves. He bent his wrists so that his hands hung down and were out of the way. Now he moved back several steps and ran between the two trees. The ends of the crosspole struck the trunks and stopped him dead. He strained against the pole, stepping back and slamming the pole ends against the trunks again and again. Finally he moved back eight or ten feet and again ran at the space between the trees and this time as the ends struck, R. L. Davis heard a gasp of breath in the silence.

He moved the sorrel out of the foliage. Valdez must hear him, but the man didn't move; he hung there on the crosspole leaning against the trunks, his arms seeming lower than they were before.

R. L. Davis saw why as he got closer. Sure enough, the pole had splintered. And it looked like a sharp end had pierced his back. R. L. Davis sat in his saddle looking down at the blood spreading over Valdez's back. He reined the sorrel around the near birch tree and came up in front of him.

"I swear," R. L. Davis said, "you are sure one dumb son of a bitch, aren't you? When that pole broke, where did you suppose it was going to go?" He saw Valdez try to raise his head. "It's your old amigo you tried to swing a scatter gun at the other day. You remember that? You went and shot the wrong coon and you was going to come at me for it."

Davis sidestepped the sorrel closer to Valdez, pulling his coiled *reata* loose from the saddle thong and playing out several feet of it. He reached over, looping the vertical pole above Valdez's head and snugged the knot tight. "You're lucky a white man come along," Davis said.

Valdez tried to raise his eyes to him. "Look at my back," he said.

"I saw it. You cut yourself."

"God, I think so," Valdez said. "Cut my wrists loose first, all right?"

"Well, not right yet," Davis said. He moved away, letting out rope, and when he was ten feet away dallied the line to his saddle horn. "Come on," he said.

Valdez had to move to the side to free an end of the crosspole and was almost jerked from his feet, stumbling to get between the trees and keep up with the short length of rope. He was pulled this way, through the birch trees and through the brush that grew along the edge of the grove, and out into the glare of the meadow again.

"You must ache some from stooping over," R. L. Davis said.

"Cut my hands and I'll tell you about it."

"You know I didn't like you trying to hit me with that scatter gun."

"I won't do it anymore," Valdez said. "How's that?"

"It made me sore, I'll tell you."

"Cut me loose and tell me, all right?"

R. L. Davis moved in close in front and lifted the loop from the upright pole. He kept the sorrel close against Valdez as he coiled the rope and thonged it to his saddle again.

"Your animal doesn't smell so good," Valdez said.

"Well, I'll give you some air," R. L. Davis said. "How'll that be?" He moved the sorrel tight against Valdez, kicking the horse's left flank to sidestep it and keep it moving.

Valdez said, "You crazy, you put me over. Hey!" He could feel the bottom of the upright pole pushing into the ground, wedged tight, and his body lifting against R. L. Davis' leg. The sorrel jumped forward, sidestepping, swinging its rump hard against Valdez, and he went over, seeing Davis above him and seeing the sky and tensing and holding the scream inside him and gasping as his spine slammed the ground and the splintered pole gouged into his back.

After a moment he opened his eyes. His hat was off. It was good, the tight band gone from his forehead. But he had to close his eyes again because of the glare and the pain in his body, the sharp thing sticking into his back that made him strain to arch his shoulders. A shadow fell over him and he opened his eyes to see R. L. Davis far above him on the sorrel, the funneled hat brim and narrow face staring down at him.

"A man ought to wear his hat in the sun," R. L. Davis said.

Valdez closed his eyes and in a moment the sun's glare pressed down on his eyelids again. He heard the horse break into a gallop that soon faded to nothing.

4

S t. francis of Assisi was the kindest man who ever lived.
Maybe not kinder than Our Lord; that was different. But
kinder than any real living man. Sure, St. Francis had been a
soldier once and got wounded and after that he wouldn't step
on bugs or kill animals. Hell, he talked to the animals; like the
time he talked to the wolf—probably a big gray lobo—who was
scaring everybody and he told the wolf to stop it. Stop it or I'll
skin you, you son of a bitch, and wear you for a coat. You would
talk to a wolf different than you would talk to other animals.
But he talked to all of them, birds, everything; they were all
his friends he said. He even talked to the stars and the sun and
the moon. He called the sun Brother Sun.

But not today you couldn't call it Brother Sun, Bob Valdez
thought.

It was strange the things he thought about, lying in the
meadow on a pole like a man crucified, remembering his older
sister reading to him a long time ago about St. Francis of Assisi
and his prayer, or whatever it was, The Canticle of the Sun. Yes,
because he had pictured the sun moving, spinning and doing
things, the sun smiling, as his sister read it to him. Today the
sun filled the sky and had no edges. It wasn't smiling; this day
the sun was everything over him, white hot pressing down on
him and dancing orange, red, and black dots on his closed
eyelids.

He remembered a man who had no eyelids, who had been
staked out in the sun and his eyelids cut off. And his ears cut
off also and his right hand. He remembered finding the man's
hand and finding the man's son in the burned-out farmhouse
on the Gila River south of San Carlos, after Geronimo had
jumped the reservation and raided down into old Mexico. They
didn't find the man's wife. No, he didn't remember a woman
there. Maybe she had been away visiting relatives. Or they had
taken her. No, they had been moving fast and she wouldn't
have been able to keep up with them. It was funny, he wondered what the woman looked like.

She could look like the Lipan Apache woman and have a

child inside her. She could look like the woman with Tanner standing on the loading platform—he remembered her blond hair and her eyes watching him, a blond-haired woman in that village of guns and horses and freight wagons. Her face was brown and she looked good with the sun on her hair, but she should be inside in a room with furniture and gold statue lamps on the tables.

He remembered the girl Polly at Inez's place and her robe coming open as she leaned over to look at the green book and then the black one. He should have stayed. It would be good to be there. It didn't matter about the girl—later—but to be in a bed with the shades down, lying on one side and then the other and moving his arms, bending them all he wanted while he slept. He would only wake up at night when the sun was down and Brother Moon or Sister Moon or whatever the hell St. Francis called it was in the sky with its soft light, and he would drink cool water from the pitcher next to the bed. When the girl came in he would turn his head and see her face, her eyes in the darkness, close to him. She had dark hair, but he thought of her with light hair, and this didn't make sense to him.

He remembered turning his head against the thong holding him to the upright post, the thong cutting his neck as he strained to twist his face away from the white heat pressing him and the colors dancing in his eyes. He remembered thinking that if the thong was wet with his sweat it would shrink when it dried and perhaps strangle him to death if he was still alive. Then he wouldn't be thirsty anymore and it wouldn't matter if his eyes were burned out. It wouldn't matter if Brother Wolf came to see him; he wouldn't have to talk to any Brother Wolf and ask him to go away.

He remembered the knife pain in his shoulders and back. He remembered feeling sick and trying to calm himself and breathe slowly so he wouldn't vomit and drown in his own bile in a mountain meadow. He remembered the worst, the heat and the pain and the thirst, and he remembered opening his eyes to a blue sky turning gray and streaked with red. He remembered a numbness in his body, looking at his hands and unable to move them.

He remembered darkness, opening his eyes and seeing darkness and hearing night sounds coming from the birch trees. He remembered the breeze moving the grass close to his face. He remembered pieces of the whole, sleeping and opening his eyes: the girl from Inez's place over him, lifting his head and holding a canteen to his lips. Why would she use a canteen when the pitcher was on the table? He remembered getting up, standing and falling and the girl holding his arms, bending them carefully, working the joints and feeling a sweet pain that would have made his eyes water if he had water left in him to come out. He remembered stretching and walking and falling and walking and crawling on his hands and knees. He remembered voices, the voices of children and a voice that he knew well and an arm that he knew helping him.

Diego Luz said, "Are you awake?"

Valdez lay with his eyes open, his eyes moving slowly from the ceiling of the room to Diego Luz, a white figure in the dimness. "I think so," he said. "I woke up before, I think; but I didn't know where I was."

"You were saying some crazy things."

"How did you find me?"

"Find you? You crawled into the yard last night. I heard the dogs; I almost shot you."

"I came here myself?"

Diego Luz moved closer to the bed. "What happened to you?"

"Maybe I'm dead," Valdez said. "Am I dead?" He could see the children of Diego Luz behind their father, in the doorway.

"You looked near to it. Somebody stabbed you in the back."

"No, a tree did that."

Diego Luz nodded. "A tree. What kind of a tree is it does that?"

His daughter came into the room with a gourd and a tin cup, and the small children followed her, crowding up to the bed. Valdez smiled at them and at the girl and got up on his elbow to sip the water. He could see the wife of Diego Luz and his wife's mother in the doorway, staying in the other room but raising their faces to look at him on the bed.

"I don't see your boy," Valdez said.

"He's watching."

"For what?"

"To see if they follow you. Or whoever it was."

"Don't worry," Valdez said. "I'm leaving when I find my pants."

"I don't worry," the horsebreaker said. "I'm careful. I wonder when I see a man crawl in half dead."

Valdez handed the cup to the girl. "Have you got some whiskey?"

"Mescal."

"Mescal then."

"You haven't eaten yet."

"I want to sleep, not eat," Valdez said. "In the back of your wagon when you take me to Lanoria."

"Stay here, you be better."

"No," Valdez said. "You said they come by here. Maybe they come by again."

"Maybe they know where you live too."

"I'm not going where I live." He motioned Diego Luz closer and whispered to him as his children and his wife and his wife's mother watched.

Diego Luz straightened, shaking his head. "Half dead and you want to go to that place."

"Half alive," Valdez said. "There is a difference."

Diego Luz brought him in through the kitchen at almost four in the morning. Valdez had passed out in the wagon, his wound beginning to bleed again. But as they dragged him up the stairs and along the dark hallway, Diego Luz and the large woman, Inez, supporting him between them, he hissed at them, "God*dam*, put my arms down!"

"We carry you and you swear at us," Inez hissed back.

"God and St. Francis, put me down!"

"Now he prays," Inez said. She opened a door, and inside they lowered him gently to the bed, settling him on his stomach and hearing him let out his breath. Inez bent over him, lifting his shirt to look at the bloodstained bandage.

"In the back," she said. "The only way you could kill this one." She looked at Diego Luz. "Who shot him? I didn't hear anything."

"A tree," Diego Luz said. "Listen, get something to clean him and talk after."

Valdez heard the woman close the door. He was comfortable

and he knew he would be asleep again in a moment. He said, "Hey," bringing Diego Luz close to the side of the bed. "I'm going to leave you everything I have when I die."

"You're not going to die. You got a little cut."

"I know I'm not going to die now. I mean when I die."

"Don't talk about it," Diego Luz said.

"I leave you everything I have if you do one more thing for me, all right?"

"Go to sleep," Diego Luz said, "and shut up for a while."

"If you get me something from my room at the boarding house."

"You want me to go now?"

"No, this time of night that old lady'll shoot you. During the day. Tomorrow."

"What is it you want?"

"In the bottom drawer of the dresser," Valdez said. "Everything that's there."

Goddam, he wished he could tell somebody about it.

R. L. Davis stood at the bar in the Republic Hotel drinking whiskey. He didn't have anything to do. He'd been fired for not being where he was supposed to be, riding fence and not riding all over the goddam country, Mr. Malson had said. He'd told Mr. Malson he'd gone to see Diego Luz about a new horse, but Mr. Malson didn't believe him, the tight-butt son of a bitch. Sure he had gone off to Tanner's place to see about working for him, figuring the chance of getting caught and fired was worth it. What surprised him was Tanner not hiring him. Christ, he could shoot. Probably good or better than any man Tanner had. He saw himself riding along with Tanner's bunch, riding into Lanoria, stampeding in and swinging down in front of the Republic or De Spain's.

He could go over to De Spain's. At least he'd been paid off. Maybe there was somebody over there he could tell. God, it was hard to keep something that good inside you. But he wasn't sure how everybody would take it, telling how he'd pushed Valdez over like a goddam turtle in the sun. The segundo had mentioned the turtle and it had given him the idea, though he thought one of Tanner's men would do it first.

Maybe if he told Tanner what he did——

No, Tanner would look at him and say, "You come all the way out here to tell me that?"

He was a hard man to talk to. He looked right through you without any expression. But it would be something to ride for him, down into old Mexico with guns and beef and shoot up the federals.

R. L. Davis finished his whiskey and had another and said to himself all right, he'd go over to De Spain's. Maybe there was a way of telling it that it wouldn't sound like he'd done it to him deliberately. Hell, he hadn't killed him, he'd pushed him over, and there were seven hundred miles between pushing and killing. If the son of a bitch was still out there it was his own fault.

Outside, he mounted the sorrel and moved up the street. He came to the corner and looked around, seeing who was about, not for any reason, just looking. He saw Diego Luz coming out of the boardinghouse two doors from the corner: Diego Luz coming toward him, carrying something wrapped up in newspaper, a big bundle that could be his wash. Except a Mexican horsebreaker wasn't going to have any wash done in there. He had his own woman for that.

He waited for him to reach the corner. "Hey, Diego, what you got there, your laundry?"

The Mexican looked funny, surprised, like he'd been caught stealing chickens. Then he gave a big smile and waved, like R. L. Davis was his best friend and he was really glad to see him.

Dumb Mexican. He was all right; just a dumb chili-picker. Christ, R. L. Davis thought, it'd be good to tell him what he'd done to Bob Valdez. And then he thought, Hey, that's the boardinghouse Bob Valdez lives in, isn't it?

Each of the seven doors in the upstairs hall bore the name of a girl in a flowery pink and blue scroll—Anastacia, Rosaria, Evita, Elisaida, Maria, Tranquiliña, and Edith. The names were a nice touch and Inez liked them, though only one of the original seven girls was still here. Because of the turn-over during the past two years, and because the Mexican sign painter had moved away, Inez had not bothered to have the doors relettered. Maybe she would sometime, though none of her customers seemed to mind that the name on the door didn't match the girl. They didn't care what the girls' names were, long as they were there.

Inez tiptoed down the hall, but the floor still creaked beneath her weight. It was semidark, with one lamp lit at the end of the hall and a faint light coming from the stairway landing. Polly followed her, carrying a tray of ham and greens and fried potatoes and coffee: Bob Valdez's supper if he was awake and felt like eating. He had been here since yesterday morning: two days and going on the second night, sleeping most of the time and sitting up drinking water out of the pitcher when he wasn't sleeping. She had never seen a man drink so much water. Diego Luz had come yesterday afternoon with a bundle of clothes—at least what looked to be clothing—and hadn't been back since then. Diego Luz never came here ordinarily, unless he was looking for someone for Mr. Malson, so it would seem strange if he were seen coming in and out. This was why Bob Valdez told him to stay away. No one was to know he was here. "As far as anybody thinks, I have disappeared," Bob Valdez had said. He had told Inez what happened to him, but she had the feeling he didn't tell her everything. That was all right; it was his business. He told what he wanted, but he always told the truth.

At Rosaria's door Inez paused, listening, taking a key from the folds of her skirt. She turned it in the lock and opened the door quietly, in case he was asleep.

She was surprised to see light from the overhead lamp; she was even more surprised to see Bob Valdez standing by the dresser. She got Polly into the room and locked the door and saw the look on Polly's face as she stared at Bob Valdez.

"Put it down," Inez said. "Before you drop it."

"Over here," Valdez said. "If you will."

Crossing the room, Polly kept her eyes on him as he moved aside the newspaper and oil can and revolver so she could place the tray on the dresser. He was holding his sawed-off ten-bore Remington shotgun, wiping it with a cloth that two days before had been his shirt.

Inez smiled a little watching him, noticing the shotgun shells now on the dresser, the shells standing upright with their crimped ends peeled open. "Roberto Valdez returned," she said.

He smiled back at her. "Bob is easier."

"Bob wears a starched collar," Inez said. "Roberto makes war."

"Just a little war, if he wants it," Valdez said.

"You get crazier every day."

"I ask him once more; that's all."

"You've asked him twice."

"But this time will be different."

"You expect to fight him?"

"If he wants a little. We'll see."

"*We*. There's one of you."

"The ham smells good. Potatoes, fresh vegetables." He smiled at Polly, then moved his gaze back to Inez. "You got any beef tallow?"

"I'll look," Inez said. "Or maybe you can use ham fat."

"I cut lean slices specially," Polly said. She was frowning, trying to understand why a man would want beef tallow when he had a plate of baked ham in front of him.

"He doesn't want it to eat," Inez said, watching Valdez. "He puts the tallow in the shotgun shell; it holds the charge together so it doesn't fly all over the place. How far would you say, Roberto?"

Bob Valdez shrugged. "Maybe a hundred and fifty feet."

"Boom, like a cannon," Inez said. "His own army. Listen, we'll give you food to take, whatever you want."

"I'm grateful."

"When are you going?"

"When Diego brings the horse."

"You're not taking him, are you?"

"No. One is as good as two."

"But not as good as two dozen."

"Maybe a little whiskey with the coffee, if you got some."

"And some to take for your nerve," Inez said. "When do you plan to be back?"

"Two days, three. I don't know."

"So if you're not back in three days—" Inez said.

Valdez smiled. "Pray for me."

A little while later they watched him leave to begin his war: the Valdez from another time, the Valdez in leather *chivarra* pants and the long-barreled Walker Colt on his right thigh, carrying his shotgun and a Sharps carbine and field glasses and a big canteen and a warbag for the ham and biscuits, the Valdez no one had seen in ten years.

He reached the birch forest before dawn, dismounting and leading his buckskin gelding through the gray shapes of the trees to the far side, to the edge of the meadow that reached to the slope where Tanner's lookouts were stationed. The night was clear and there was no sign of life on the hill. But they would be there, he was sure; how many, he would have to wait and see.

In the first light he moved along the edge of the thicket to the place where R. L. Davis had crowded his horse against him and pushed him over. Valdez did not leave the cover of the trees; he could see the cruciformed poles lying in the open; he could see, at the ends of the crosspole and in the middle, the leather thongs that had been cut by someone in the darkness, a shape close to him, an arm raising his head to give him water, hands helping him to his feet. He must have been out of his head not to remember; he must have been worse off than he imagined. Three days ago he had been lying here in the sun. Already it seemed as if it had happened in another time, years before. He moved back to a place where he would have a good view of the slopes across the meadow, and here he dropped his gear and settled down to wait, propping his field glasses on his warbag and canteen and lying behind them to hold his gaze on the slope.

About six o'clock, not quite an hour after first light, three riders appeared against the sky at the top of the slope. They came down into the deep shadows, and shortly after, a single rider passed over the crest going the other way. One at night, Valdez marked down in his mind, and three during the day. Though maybe not all day.

But it did turn out to be all day. Valdez remained in the thicket watching the slope, seeing very little movement; no one came down the trail or crossed the meadow toward the slope; the lookouts remained in dense brush most of the time, and if he did not know where to look for them through the glasses, he probably wouldn't have noticed them. At about five o'clock in the evening a rider came over the crest of the ridge, and soon after the three lookouts climbed the switchbacks and disappeared.

There you are, Valdez said to himself. How do you like it now? It doesn't get any better.

He had not eaten all day and had taken only a few sips of water. Now he ate some of the ham and biscuits and a handful of red peppers; he took a sip of the whiskey Inez had given him and a good drink from the canteen. Valdez was ready.

Crossing the meadow, he let his hand fall to the Walker Colt and eased the barrel in its holster. The stock of the Sharps carbine rested against the inside of his left knee, in the saddle boot; the sawed-off Remington hung on the right side, looped to the saddle horn by a short length of suspender strap. By now the lookout would have seen him and studied him and would be ready. Three of them yesterday came down to meet R. L. Davis, but one up there now would stay put and plan to take him by surprise. Valdez let the buckskin walk, but nudged his heels into its flanks as they reached the rocks and brush and started up the trail.

Now it comes, Valdez thought. When he's ready. Any time. He let himself slouch in the saddle, his shoulders moving with the gait of the horse, a rider climbing a trail, a man relaxed and off guard, in no hurry. Surprise me, he said in his mind to the lookout. I'm nothing to be afraid of. Come out in the open and stop me. I could be one of your friends.

He was a little more than halfway up the slope when the rider appeared, fifty yards and three switchback levels above him. Valdez pretended not to see him and came on, rounding a switchback and reaching an almost level stretch of the trail before the man called out in Spanish, "Enough!"

The Mexican. Valdez recognized the voice and, as he looked up now, the shape of the man on his horse—brown man and brown horse against the evening shadows of the brush slope. The Mexican came down the trail toward him, stopping and coming on again, the sound of his horse's hooves clear in the stillness, reaching the level above Valdez, then tight-reining, his horse moving loose shale as he came down to the stretch of trail where Bob Valdez waited. The Mexican stopped about fifty feet away, facing him on the narrow ledge of the path.

"I thought it was you, but I said no, that man carries a cross on his back."

"I got tired of it," Valdez said.

"Somebody found you, uh?"

"Somebody."

"You had luck with you that time."

"If people help you," Valdez said, "you don't need luck."

"That's it, uh? I didn't know that."

"Sure, like you and me," Valdez said. "We can be friends if we want. We talk awhile. I give you a drink of whiskey. What do you think about something like that?"

"I think I see a lot of guns," the Mexican said. "You come up here to talk and you bring all those guns?" He was at ease, smiling now.

"This little thing?" Valdez raised the cutoff Remington in his right hand, his fingers around the neck of the stock, the stubby barrels pointing straight up. "You think this could hurt somebody? It's for rabbits."

"For rabbits," the Mexican said, nodding. "Sure, there are plenty of rabbits around here. That's what you come for, uh, to hunt rabbits?"

"If I see any maybe. No, I come to ask you to do something for me."

"Because we're good friends," the Mexican said.

"That's right. As a friend I want you to go see Mr. Tanner and tell him Valdez is coming."

The Mexican was silent for a moment, his head nodding slightly as he studied Valdez and thought about him. "You come to see me," the Mexican said then. "How do you know I'm here?"

"You or somebody else," Valdez said. "It doesn't matter."

"You mean me *and* somebody else. Somebody over in the rocks behind you."

"I'll tell you something," Valdez said. "I've been here all day. I saw three of you come and one of you leave. I saw one of you come and three of you leave. There's no somebody else in the rocks—there's just you in front of me. That's all."

The Mexican watched him, unmoving. "You're certain of that? You'd bet your life on it?"

"It's on the table," Valdez said.

The Mexican grinned. "What is this kind of talk with two friends? You want me to go tell him something? All right, I tell him. Put the rabbit gun down." He lifted his reins and began sidestepping his horse to turn around on the narrow trail. Looking at Valdez again, he said, "You wait here, all right? I go tell him what you say and then I come back and tell you what he say. How is that?"

Valdez nodded. "I'll be here." He lowered the shotgun, resting it across his lap.

"Sure, stay right there. It don't take me any time."

The Mexican turned in his saddle and started away, his back to Valdez until he reached the end of the ledge and kicked his horse up over the shale at the switchback, and now, on the level above Valdez and seventy or eighty feet away, came back toward him.

Valdez's right thumb eased back both hammers, his finger curled inside the guard and felt the tension of the first trigger. The Mexican was spurring his horse now, kicking it to a gallop up the low angle of the trail, holding the reins in his left hand. Valdez saw nothing but the Mexican coming and it was in his mind that the man would go past him and suddenly turn and fire from behind. But thirty feet away closing to twenty, he saw the Mexican's right hand come up with the revolver and there it was, right now, the Mexican hunched low in the saddle, screaming *Aiiiii* for the horse or for himself, the revolver across the horse's mane, the man offering only his left leg and side and shoulder, but it was enough. Valdez brought up the barrels of the Remington from his lap, and with the ten-bore explosion close in front of him, the Mexican came out of his saddle, flung back over the horse's rump, his revolver discharging as he struck the ground, and the buckskin beneath Valdez throwing its head and trying to dance away from the man, and loose shale coming down the slope at them. The Mexican rolled to his back almost beneath the buckskin, his clothes filmed with fine dust, a dark, wet stain spreading from his side down over his thigh. His eyes were open and he had his left arm tight to his side.

"How do you feel?" Valdez asked.

The Mexican said nothing, staring up at him with a dazed expression.

Valdez dismounted and went to his knees over the man, raising his arm gently to look at the wound. The shotgun charge had torn through his side at the waist, ripping away his belt and part of his shirt and leather chaps.

"You should have this taken care of," Valdez said. "You know somebody can sew you up?"

The Mexican's eyes were glazed, wet looking. "What do you put in that thing?"

"I told you, something for rabbits. Listen, I'm going to get your horse and put you on it."

"I can't ride anywhere."

"Sure you can." Valdez lowered the Mexican's arm and gave his shoulder a pat. The Mexican winced and Valdez smiled. "You ride to Mr. Tanner, all right? Tell him Valdez is coming. You hear what I said? Valdez is coming. But listen, friend, I think you better go there quick."

5

"HE's DYING," the Segundo said. "Maybe before tonight."
The Mexican was on his back at the edge of the loading
platform where they had taken him off his horse and laid him
on his back. His eyes looked up at the segundo and at Frank
Tanner standing over him. He could hear the people in the
street, but he did not have the strength or the desire to turn
his head to look at them. He heard the segundo say he was
dying and he knew he was dying, now, as the sun went down.
He was thinking, I should have gone past him and turned and
shot him. Or I should have shot him as he came up, before he
saw me. Or I could have gone higher and used the rifle. He
wished he could begin it again, do it over from the time Valdez
started up the trail, but it was too late. He could see Valdez
raising the gun, the blunt double barrels looking at him; he
could see Mr. Tanner looking at him, the mouth beneath the
moustache barely moving.

"What else did he say?"

The Mexican who was dying stared up at Mr. Tanner, and
the segundo said, "Valdez is coming. That's all."

"How do we know it's the same one?"

"It's his name."

"There are a hundred Valdezes."

"Maybe, but it must be the same one," the segundo said.
"You said he killed the Negro with a shotgun."

"A farmer gun," Tanner said.

"I don't know," the segundo said. "The way he used it."

Tanner looked up from the Mexican, his gaze lifting beyond
the square, beyond the adobes to the ridge of hills in the distance, to the cold red slash of sky above the shadowed slopes.
This Valdez killed one of his men up there and said he was
coming. For what? It couldn't be to help any dead nigger's
Indian woman. He couldn't come in and pull a gun to get
money. He'd never get in or out. Then what was he doing?
Who was he?

The segundo followed Tanner's gaze to the hills. "He's
gone. He wouldn't be there waiting."

"Send somebody and make sure."

"He could be anywhere."

"Well, goddam it, you've got people who read signs?"

"We've got some, sure."

"Then send them," Tanner said. "I want people all over those hills, and if he's there I want him brought in, straight up or face down. I don't care. I want some men sent to Lanoria to look every place he might be and talk to anybody knows him. I want a sign put up on the main street that says Bob Valdez is a dead man and anybody known to be helping him is also dead. You understand me?"

"We start the drive tomorrow," the segundo said.

Tanner looked at him. "We start the drive when I tell you we start it."

The man lying on his back dying, with the wet stain of his blood on the platform now—thinking that this shouldn't have happened to him because of the life in him an hour ago and because of the way he saw himself, aware of himself alive and never thinking of himself dying—looked up at the sky and didn't have to close the light from his eyes. He saw the beard on the segundo's face and the under-brim of his straw hat, and then he didn't see the segundo. He saw Mr. Tanner's face and then he didn't see Mr. Tanner anymore. He saw the open sky above him and that was all there was to see. But the sky wasn't something to look at. If he wasn't on the hill tonight he would be in the adobe that was the cantina, with the oil smoke and the women coming in, lighting a cigar as he looked at them and feeling his belly beneath his gunbelts full of beef and tortillas, bringing a woman close to him and drinking mescal with his hand on the curve of her shoulder, touching her neck and feeling strands of her hair between his fingers. But he had done it the wrong way. He should have looked at the three guns on the man and known something. But he had thought of the man as he had remembered him from before, against the wall and with the cross on his back, and he had listened to the man talk even while he planned to kill the man, being careful but not being careful enough, not giving the man enough. He should have thought more about the way the man stood at the wall and watched them shoot at him. He should have remembered the way the man got up with the cross on his back and was kicked down and got up again and walked away. Look—someone should have said to him, or he should have told himself—the man wears three guns and hangs a Remington from his saddle. What kind of man is that? And then he thought, You should know when you're going to die. It should be something in your life you plan. It shouldn't happen but it's happening. He tried to raise his left arm but could not. He had no feeling in his left side, from his chest into his legs. His side was hanging open and draining his life as he looked at the sky. He said to himself, What is the sky to me? He said to himself, What are you doing here alone?

"Ask him if he's sure it's the same one," Tanner said.

The segundo stepped close to the Mexican again. He knew he was dead as he looked at him, though the man's eyes were open, staring at the sky.

The Mexican had reached the village, his head hanging, letting the horse take him, but he seemed to be still alive as he entered the street between the adobes.

You can die any time after you tell them, Valdez had thought, watching through the field glasses at the top of the trail. He had nothing against the man except a kick in the back and the certainty the man had wanted to kill him. He knew the man would die, and it would be better if he did; but he didn't wish the man dead. It would happen, that was all.

Soon they would come out. They would come out in all directions or they would come strung out across the graze toward the trail into the hills. As the Mexican had reached the adobes, Valdez had climbed higher, off the trail now, leading the buckskin up into the rocks. From here he watched the three riders coming first, letting their horses out across the open land. They came up through the ravines and went down the switchbacks on the other side, not stopping. Three more came behind them, but not running their horses, taking their time. They climbed over the trail looking at the ground; coming to the place where Valdez had shot the Mexican they dismounted.

There were others coming out from the village, fanning out, not knowing where they were going. They were nothing. The three looking for his sign were little better than nothing; they had less than an hour of light and no chance of catching up with him. He counted seventeen men who had come out of the village. There would be others with the herd and perhaps others somewhere else. There was no way of knowing how many were still in the village. There was no way of knowing if Tanner had come out or was still in the village. He would have to go there to find out. And if Tanner was not in the village he would have to think of another way to do it and come back another time. There was no hurry. It wasn't something that had to be done today or tomorrow or this week. It could be done any time. But you'd better do it tonight, Valdez said to himself, before you think about it too much. Do it or don't do it.

Do it, he thought. He took a sip of the whiskey and put the bottle back in the warbag that hung from his saddle.

Do it before you get too old.

He took the reins of the buckskin and began working down through the rocks toward the village. He would circle and approach from the trees on the far side, coming up behind the burned-out church.

The clerk from the Republic Hotel, as soon as he was off duty, went over to De Spain's and asked if the three Tanner riders had been there.

Hell, yes, they had. They'd been here and to Bob Valdez's boardinghouse and the Hatch and Hodges office and had stuck their heads into almost every store along the street. They moved fast and didn't waste any questions and you could tell they wanted him bad. Bad? Did you see the sign out in front? Nailed to the post?

It was a square of board, and one of them had lettered on it with charcoal: BOB VALDEZ IS A DEAD MAN. ANYONE HELPING HIM IS ALSO DEAD.

That was how bad they wanted him. They were going to kill him.

If they ever found him. Where the hell was Valdez? Nobody knew. Nobody remembered seeing him in days. The last time was Saturday when he rode out to see Tanner. No, somebody said, he had made the run to St. David the next day. How about since then? Nobody could recall. Maybe he'd been around; maybe he hadn't. Bob Valdez wasn't somebody who stuck in your mind and you remembered.

Mr. Malson said to Mr. Beaudry, "If he's got Tanner on him and knows it, he'll be seven hundred miles away by now." "Or farther," Mr. Beaudry said. "If he don't know it," somebody said, "then he's a dead man, like the sign says." "There must be something wrong with his head," Mr. Malson said. "Christ, we should have known it the minute he started talking about the Lipan woman something was wrong with him."

R. L. Davis didn't say anything. He wanted to, but he still wasn't sure what people would say. They might say he was crazy. If he'd pushed Valdez over in the sun, then what had he gone back for?

They'd listen to him tell it. "Sure, I pushed him over. I was teaching him a lesson for coming at me with the scatter gun the other day—after he shot the nigger." They'd look at him and say, "You killed a man like that? Like a Indin would do it?"

And he'd say "No, I was teaching him a lesson is all. Hell, I went back and cut him loose and left him a canteen of water." And they'd say "Well, if you cut him loose, where is he?" Somebody else'd say, "If you wanted to kill him, what did you cut him loose for?"

And he'd say "Hell, if there's something between me and Bob Valdez, we'll settle it with guns. I'm no goddam Apache."

But he had a feeling they wouldn't believe a word of it.

All right, three days ago he'd left Valdez in the meadow. And this evening Tanner's men come in looking for him and write his death sentence. So Valdez must have gone back and done something to them.

Valdez hadn't been here; at least nobody remembered seeing him. So where would he have been the past three days? Not at his boardinghouse.

But, goddam, Diego Luz had been to his boardinghouse! He could see Diego again coming out of it and the funny look on the man's face when he realized he'd been spotted.

What would Frank Tanner say about that? R. L. Davis said

to himself. If you could hand him Bob Valdez he'd hire you the same minute, wouldn't he?

Go up to Tanner and cock the Walker in his face and say, All right, give me the money, Valdez was thinking. Not asking him, telling him this time. A hundred dollars or five hundred or whatever he had. Take it and get out and don't think about later until later. He would have to leave Lanoria and go someplace else and maybe worry about Tanner the rest of his life—because he had wanted to help the woman; because he had started it and gotten into it and now was so far in he couldn't turn around and walk out. You must be crazy, Valdez thought. Like Inez had said. Or an idiot. But he was here and was going through with it and he wasn't going to think about why he was here.

He was behind the church, bringing the buckskin along close to the wall, then into the alley that led to the yard of the church. At the far end of the yard was the building with the loading platform. Past the low wall of the churchyard he could see the square and the water pump and stone trough. There was no one in the square now. Farther down the street, in the dusk, he could make out people in front of the adobes, a few of the women sitting outside to talk; he could hear voices and laughter, the sound clear in the silence.

Valdez left the buckskin in the yard. He went over the wall and through the narrow space between the platform and two freight wagons that stood ready for loading. He mounted the steps at the far end. On the platform he looked out at the square again and at the church doorway and the fence across the opening. There were a few horses inside; he wondered if one of them was his claybank. Maybe after, he would have time to look. He crossed the platform and went into the building, into the room crowded with wooden cases and sacks of grain. Maybe this wasn't Tanner's place. Maybe he would have to work his way down the street, hurrying before it was full dark and they gave up looking for him. It was already dark in the room. He had to feel his way at first, moving between the cases to the stairway. The boards creaked and his boots on the stairs made a hard, sharp sound that Tanner would hear if he was upstairs; he would be ready or he would think it was one of his men. Valdez reached the hall and opened the door in front of him.

The room was still and seemed empty, until the woman moved and he saw her profile and the soft curve of her hair against the window. She watched him cross the room and open the door to the bedroom, waiting for him to look toward her again.

"He's not here."

Valdez walked toward her. He stopped to look out the window at the square below. "He went with them?"

"I guess he did," the woman said. "He didn't say."

"Are you his wife?"

She didn't answer for a moment, and Valdez looked at her.

"I will be his wife, soon."

"Do you know him?"

"That's a strange question. I guess I know him if I'm going to marry him."

"Well, it's up to you."

There was a silence between them until she said, "Are you going to wait for him?"

"I don't know yet—wait or come back another time."

"He won't give you another time. You killed one of his men."

"He died. I thought he would die," Valdez said. "Unless you had a doctor."

She watched him look out the window again. "Did you come here to kill Frank?"

"It would be up to him," Valdez said.

"Then what do you want?"

"The same thing as before. Something for the woman."

"Why? I mean why do you bother?"

"Listen," Valdez said. He hesitated. "If I tell you what I think, it doesn't sound right. It's something I know. You understand that?"

"Maybe you'll kill him," the woman said, "but you won't get anything out of him."

Valdez nodded slowly. "I've been thinking of that. If he doesn't want to give me anything, how do I make him? I push a gun into him and tell him, but if I have to shoot him, then I don't get anything."

"If he doesn't kill you first," the woman said.

"I've been thinking," Valdez said. "If I have something he wants, then maybe we make a trade. If he wants it bad enough."

She watched him and said nothing. He was looking at her now.

"Like I say to him, 'You give me the money and I give you your woman.'"

She continued to look at him, studying him. "And if he doesn't give you the money?" she said finally.

"Then he doesn't get his woman," Valdez said.

"You'd kill me?"

"No, the question would be how much does he like you?"

"He'll outwait you. He'll put his men around the building and sooner or later you'll have to go out."

"Not if I'm already out," Valdez said. His face went to the window before he looked at her again. "Listen, if you want to take something with you, get it now."

A woman who belonged to one of Tanner's men saw them leave. She had gone to the water pump in the square and stood looking at them as they came out to the loading platform: the woman of Mr. Tanner with a blanket roll and the man carrying a grain pack with something in it and an empty water skin. She looked at them and they looked at her, but she didn't call out. She told Mr. Tanner she was afraid the man would do something to her or to the woman of Mr. Tanner.

"Go on," Tanner said. "Then what?" He was still mounted, standing with his segundo and several of his men in the lantern glow of the square—the lantern on the seat of a freight wagon so Tanner could see the woman while she told what had happened.

"They went to the yard of the church," the woman said to Tanner. Then the man came over the wall toward her and told her to get a horse from the church, asking for a particular claybank horse if it was there. The woman brought out a horse but was not sure of its color in the darkness of the church and it wasn't the claybank but a brown horse. Then he told her to bring a saddle and bridle and a half sack of dried corn.

While this was taking place, the woman of Mr. Tanner was astride a horse in the churchyard, sitting in the saddle as a man does, though she was wearing a dress. "I think a white or a gray dress," the woman said. When Valdez was ready and had mounted the brown horse, he rode into the churchyard and told the woman of Mr. Tanner to follow him.

"Did she say anything to him?" Tanner asked.

"Not that I heard," the woman said.

They left through the alley next to the church. The woman waited until they were in the alley and followed, but by the time she reached the back of the church they were gone.

"Could you hear them?" Tanner asked.

"I think going toward the river," the woman said.

"To reach cover," the segundo said. He was sitting his horse close to Frank Tanner. "Then maybe south into the mountains."

"How long ago?" asked Tanner.

The woman thought about it and said, "Not long. They would be maybe two or three miles away only. Or a little more if they ran their horses."

"You know what to do," Tanner said to the segundo. "Whoever's here, send them out again."

"In the dark," the segundo said, "how do we see them?"

"You listen," Tanner said. "Somebody could run into them."

The segundo waited, about to speak, but looked at Tanner and then only nodded. It was Tanner's business. No, his business was in the morning with the arms and grain and cattle, taking it all across the border and coming back without being killed. That was his business.

But in the morning the freight wagons stood empty, and Frank Tanner waited on the loading platform for his men to come in. Some of the women stood in the square, watching him, waiting to see what he was going to do. The men came in singly and in small groups and would talk to the segundo while they watered their horses and while the women watched. It was almost midmorning when the three trackers came in. One of them was dead, the other two were wounded.

These three who came along the street single file, one of them facedown over his saddle, were the segundo's best hunters and trackers. They had been in the Army and had lived through the campaigns against the Apache. But now one was dead and another would soon be dead.

Tanner sat in a rocking chair in the morning sunlight and watched them brought in: another dead man on the loading platform and a man coughing blood and a third one, luckier than the first two, shot through the left forearm, the bone shattered, and there was no doubt about that. This one could talk and he told what had happened, his the only voice in the stillness. Tanner listened to the man and did not interrupt. He heard how the three had put themselves in Valdez's place and decided he would follow the river south into the hills of the Santa Ritas, then maybe work his way west around toward Lanoria or maybe not, but they'd take a look.

With the first light this morning they had found tracks, fresh prints of two horses that showed the horses were walking. They weren't sure of this man they were following; he didn't try to keep to rocky ground or cover his tracks, and he walked the horses, maybe thinking he had enough time. Still, when they came to the flat open stretch with the trees in the distance, they were careful, knowing he could be waiting for them in the trees. So they made a plan as they crossed the flat stretch: they would spread out before they got to the cover and come up from three sides and if he was in there they'd have him. But they never got to the trees.

"Listen, it was flat open," the man with the shattered arm said, "out to the sides as far as you could see and a mile in front of us. There was no cover near, hardly any brush to speak of. So it was like he rose up out of the ground behind us. He says, 'Throw down your guns and come around.' This voice out there in the middle of nothing. We stop and come around, keeping our iron though, and there he is standing there. I swear to God there was nothing for him to hide behind, yet we'd come over the ground he was standing on just a moment before.

"He says, 'Go back and tell Mr. Tanner we're waiting for him.' That's what he said, waiting for *him*. Meaning he wasn't talking to anybody else. Then he says, 'Tell Mr. Tanner I got something to trade him.' We looked, but she wasn't anywheres around. Just him, and three of us. I guess we all had it in mind to bust him and he must have saw it. He says again, 'Throw down the guns.' We don't move. He says it again and this time when we don't move he brings up the Colt gun in his right hand and puts one through my arm."

He looked toward the dead man and the man who was lying

on the ground shot through the lungs. "They went for theirs with the sound of his piece, and he brings up this little scatter gun in his left hand and lets go both barrels and them two boys take it square. This here boy partly in front of the other, a little closer, and it killed him in his boots.

"Then he says to me, 'You tell him, he wants his woman, come out here with five hundred dollars.'

"I say to him, 'Well, where's Mr. Tanner supposed to come? You going to have signs put up?' And then he points."

The man with the shattered arm, standing by the loading platform, turned half around and raised his right arm, his finger extended; he moved it gradually southwest.

"There, you can see it," the man said, "though it was closer where we were at and you could see it better—twin peaks, the one a little higher than the other. He says for you to point to them and he'll get in touch with you.

"I say to him, 'Well, what if Mr. Tanner don't feel like coming?'

"And he says, standing there with the shotgun and the Colt gun, 'Then I kill his woman.'"

Frank Tanner stared at the twin peaks ten miles in the distance. After a few minutes, when he became aware that he was sitting in a rocking chair on the loading platform and his people were below him in the square, waiting for him to say something, he waved his hand and they cleared out, taking the dead man and the lung-shot man and the man with the shattered left arm, who thought Mr. Tanner might say something to him personally. But he didn't—just the wave of the hand.

The segundo stayed; he was the only one. He waited awhile, getting the words straight in his mind. When he was ready he said, "You go after him, we don't make the trip."

He waited, giving Mr. Tanner a chance to say something, but the only sound was someone working the pump handle, a rattly metal sound in the heat settling over the village.

"We go out there and look for him," the segundo said. "Sure, we find him, but maybe it take us a few days, a week, if he knows what he's doing. We're out there, we're not in Sonora giving the man the things he's paying for. How much is he paying?" The segundo waited again. He said then, "He pay plenty, but nobody pay you to go up in those mountains."

The segundo stood in the sun waiting for Mr. Tanner to say something. He could stand here all day and this son of a bitch Mr. Tanner might never say anything. The segundo was hot and thirsty. He'd like a nice glass of mescal and some meat and peppers, but he was standing here waiting for this son of a bitch Americano to make up his mind.

So he said, smiling a little, "Hey, what if you don't go out? You let him kill her." His smile broadened and he gestured as if to say, Do you see how simple it is? He said, "Then what? You get another woman."

Frank Tanner, sitting in the rocker, looked at his segundo. He said, "If you were up here I'd bust your face open. And if you wanted any more I'd give you that too. Do you see the way it is?"

The segundo had killed five men in his life that he knew of and had probably killed more if some of them died later or if he wanted to count Apaches. He had hanged a man he caught stealing his horses. He had killed a man with a knife in a cantina. He had shot a man who once worked for him and insulted him and drew his revolver. He had killed two Federales when the soldiers set an ambush to take the goods they were delivering in Sonora. And with others he had wiped out an Apache *ranchería*, shooting or knifing every living person they found, including the old people and the children. But the segundo was also a practical man. He had a wife in this village and two or three more wives in villages south of here, in Sonoita and Naco and Nogales. He had nine children that he knew of. Maybe he had eleven or twelve. Maybe he had fifteen. He had not wanted to kill the Apache children, but they were Apache. He also liked mescal and good horses and accurate rifles and revolving pistols. He was number two and Mr. Tanner was number one. He was thinking, *Shit.* But he smiled at Mr. Tanner and said, "Why didn't you say so? You want to get this man, we go get him for you."

Frank Tanner nodded, thinking about the woman.

The time he was in Yuma he thought about women every day. He'd thought about women before that, but not the same way he did in that stone prison overlooking the river. He remembered how the men smelled at Yuma, breaking rocks for twelve hours in the sun, working on the road, and coming back in to eat the slop. That's when they'd start talking about women. Frank Tanner would think, They don't know a real woman if they see one, except for some whore who'd smile and laugh and give them everything and rot their insides. No, when he was at Yuma he pictured a blond-haired girl, real long hair and a pretty face and big round breasts, though she wouldn't be too big in the gut or the hips. The hips could be more than a handful, but she'd have to have a nice sucked-in white gut. That's the one he pictured at Yuma, after he and Carlisle Baylor got caught with the goddam branded cows they were running into old Mexico without any bill of sale. Three years picturing the blond golden-haired woman. Two years more raising money and buying stock to sell across the border, buying and selling horses and cattle and dynamite and about anything he could lay his hands on they didn't have down there. He'd bought twenty-five-year-old Confederate muskets and sold them. He bought a few old Whitworth field pieces and sold them too. He'd made money and met people who knew people and pretty soon he was even selling remounts to the United States Cavalry at Fort Huachuca. And that was where he saw the woman, the girl or woman or however you wanted to think of her, there at Huachuca, married to the drunk-ass sutler, who never went a day without a quart of whiskey or a bottle of mescal or even corn beer if he couldn't get any mescal. There she was, the one he'd seen every day at Yuma and about every day since, the blond golden-haired girl who was built for the kind of man he was, sitting in their place talking to the drunk-ass sutler and looking at the woman every chance he got. A year of that; a little more than a year. Talking to her when he wasn't around and trying to find out things about her, about them. Trying to find out if she felt anything for the drunk or not. She felt something when he beat her—sometimes you could see the bruises on her face she couldn't hide with powder—but maybe she liked it. You could never tell about women.

He would have taken her away from the drunk alive, and once he was dead there wasn't anything else to think over. He took her and she came with him. He would marry her, too, but he had things to do and she'd have to wait on that; but in the meantime there wasn't any reason they couldn't live as husband and wife. She saw that and agreed, and she was better than he ever imagined in Yuma she would be. She was real now and she was his, and there wasn't any goddam broken-down Mexican nigger-loving town constable going to run off with her into the hills and threaten to kill her. Valdez, or whatever his name, was a dead man and he could roll over right now and save everybody a lot of time.

Tanner was looking off at the hills that climbed into the Santa Ritas and the twin peaks, far away against the hot sky.

"What's up there?" he said to the segundo.

"Nothing," the segundo answered.

"Why would he want us to track up there?"

"I don't know," the segundo said. "Maybe he's got a place somewhere."

"What kind of place?"

"An Apache camp he's been to," the segundo said. "He knows the Apache—the thing he did to the three of them in the open country, hiding where there's no place to hide."

"He didn't seem like much," Frank Tanner said.

"Maybe," the segundo said. "But he knows the Apache."

R. L. Davis got drunk trying to work up nerve to tell what he did to Bob Valdez and never did tell it. He went over to Inez's, but they wouldn't let him in. Then he didn't remember anything after that. He woke up in the Maricopa bunkhouse when a hand came in and poured water all over him. God, he felt awful. So it was afternoon by the time he got out to Mimbreño.

There seemed to be more activity than the time he was here before, more men in the village sitting around waiting for something, and more horses and more noise. He rode up the street not looking around too much, but not missing anything either. He hoped Mr. Tanner would be outside, and he was, the same place he was the last time, up on the loading platform. The problem was to tell him before Mr. Tanner gave any orders to have him run off or tied to a cross or whatever he might do; so he kept his eyes on Mr. Tanner and the second he saw Mr. Tanner's gaze land on him, R. L. Davis yelled out, "I know where he is!"

They looked at him, all the people standing around there, and let him ride over toward the platform where Mr. Tanner was waiting.

"I think I know where he is," R. L. Davis said to Mr. Tanner.

"You think so or you know so," Tanner said.

"I'd bet a year's wage on it."

"Where?"

"A place up in the mountains."

"I asked you where."

"I was thinking," R. L. Davis said. "Let me ride along and I can show you. Take you right to it."

Tanner kept looking at him deciding something, but showing nothing in his face. Finally he said, "Step down and water your horse."

6

MOST OF the day the woman, Gay Erin, rode behind Valdez as they climbed out of the flatland and across sloping meadows that stretched toward pine timber, in the open sunlight all morning and into the afternoon, until they reached the deep shade of the forest. She noticed that Valdez seldom looked back now. When they had stopped to rest and he stood waiting as the horses grazed, he would look north sometimes, the way they had come, but he stood relaxed and could be looking at nothing more than the view.

Earlier this morning, once it was light, he had looked back. He stopped and looked back for some time as they were crossing flat, open country. When they reached the trees he made her dismount and tied their horses to a dead trunk that had fallen. She watched him walk out of the trees, out across the flats until he was a small figure in the distance. She watched him squat or kneel by a low brush clump and then she didn't see him again, not for more than an hour, not until the three riders appeared and she heard the gunfire. He came back carrying his shotgun; they mounted again and continued on. She asked him, "Did you kill them?" And he answered, "One. Maybe another." She asked, "Why didn't you tie me? I could have run away." He said to her, "Where would you go?"

They spoke little after that. They stopped to rest in a high meadow and she asked him where they were going. "Up there," he answered, nodding toward the rock slopes above them.

Another time she said to him, "Maybe you don't have a natural call to do certain things, but I do." He smiled a little and told her to go ahead, he wouldn't look. She stayed on the off side of her horse and didn't know if he looked or not.

At first she wondered about him, and there were questions she wanted to ask; but she followed him in silence, watching the slope of his shoulders, the easy way he sat his saddle. In time the pain began to creep down her back and into her thighs; she held on to the saddle horn, following the movement of the horse and not thinking or wondering about him after a while, wanting this to be over but knowing he wasn't going to stop until he was ready.

When they reached the edge of the pine timber he dismounted. Gay Erin went to the ground and stretched out on her back in the shade. She could feel her lips cracked and hard and dirt in the corners of her eyes. She wanted water, to drink and to bathe in, but more than water she wanted to stretch the stiffness from her body and sleep.

She heard Valdez say, "We're going to move. Not far, over a little bit." Looking up at the pine branches she closed her eyes and thought, He'll have to drag me or carry me. She could hear him moving in the pine needles and could hear the horses. She waited for him to come over and tell her to get up or kick her or pull her to her feet, but after a while there was no sound, and in the silence she fell asleep.

When she opened her eyes she wasn't sure where she was and wondered if he had moved her. The trees above were a different color now, darker, and she could barely see the sky through the branches. She stretched, feeling the stiffness, and rolled to her side. Valdez was sitting on the ground a few feet away smoking a cigarette, watching her. She pushed herself to a sitting position. "I thought we were moving."

"It's waiting for you," Valdez said.

He led her on foot along the dark-shadowed edge of the timber. Off from them, in the open, dusk was settling over the hills. They walked for several minutes, until she smelled wood burning and saw the horses picketed close below them in the meadow. The camp was just inside the timber, in a cutbank that came down through the pines like a narrow road, widening where it reached the meadow and dropping into the valley below.

At times she looked at him across the low fire, at this man who had taken her up a mountain and let her sleep for a few hours and then served her pan bread and ham and peppers and strong coffee. When they had finished he took a bottle of whiskey from a canvas bag. She watched him now. She could see Jim Erin with his bottle every evening, saying he was going to have a couple to relax and pouring a glass and then another glass, smoking a cigar and taking another drink, his voice becoming louder as he talked. Sometimes she would go out, visit one of the officers' wives, and if she could stay long enough he would be asleep when she got home. But sometimes he wouldn't allow her to go out and she would have to listen to him as he pretended he was a man, hearing his complaints and his obscenities and his words of abuse; the goddam Army and the goddam fort and the goddam heat and the goddam woman sitting there with her goddam nose up in the air. The first time he hit her she doubled her fist and hit him back, solidly in the mouth, and he beat her until she was unconscious. For months he didn't take a drink and was kind to her. But he started again, gradually, and by the time he had worked up to his bottle an evening he was slapping her and several times hit her with his fist. She never fought back after the first time. She was married to him, a man old enough to be her father, who perhaps might grow up one day. Sometimes she thought she loved him; most of the time she wasn't sure, and there were moments when she hated him. But he didn't change; he beat her for the last time and no man would ever beat her again.

It surprised her when Valdez offered the bottle. "For the cold," he said. "Or to make you sleep." She hesitated, then took a sip and handed it back to him. Valdez raised the bottle. When he lowered it he popped in the cork and got up to put the bottle away.

"I've never seen a man take one drink," she said.

Valdez sat down again by the fire. "Maybe it has to last."

"I was married to a man who drank." He made no comment and she said, "He was killed."

Valdez nodded. "I see."

"What do you see?"

"I mean you were married and now you're not. What's your name?"

"Gay Erin."

He was looking at her but said nothing for a moment. "That's your marriage name?"

"Mrs. James C. Erin."

"Of Fort Huachuca," Valdez said. "Your husband was killed six months ago."

"You knew him?"

He shook his head.

She waited. "Then you heard about it."

Valdez said, "You were in Lanoria Saturday when the man was killed?"

"Frank said an Army deserter was shot."

"No, he wasn't a deserter. Frank Tanner said it was the man that killed your husband, but when he looked at him dead he said no, it was somebody else."

Gay Erin said, "And the Indian woman, the widow——"

"Was the wife of the man we killed by mistake."

She nodded slowly. "I see." She said then, "Frank didn't tell me that."

Valdez watched her. "But you're going to marry him."

"What difference does it make to you?"

"I like to know how much he wants you—if you're worth coming after."

"He'll come," she said.

"I think so too. I think he wants you pretty bad." Valdez placed a stick on the fire and pushed the ends of the sticks that had not burned into the center of the flame. "You know what else I think. I think maybe he wanted you pretty bad when you were still married."

The flame rose to the fresh wood. He could see her face in the light, her eyes holding on his.

"He knew my husband," she said. "Sometimes he'd come to visit. Anyone who was at the hearing knows that."

"And after it you go to live with him."

She was staring at him in the flickering light. "Why don't you say it right out?"

"It's just something I started to wonder."

"You think Frank killed my husband."

"He could do it."

"He could," the woman said, "but he didn't."

"You're sure of that, uh?"

"I know he didn't."

"How do you know?"

"Because I killed him."

She had come from Prescott with her nightgowns and linens to marry James C. Erin, and five years and six months later she fired three bullets into him from a service revolver and left him dead.

Tell this man about it, she thought. The time in the draw at night, a single moment in her life she would see more clearly than anything she had ever experienced. She had told no one about it and now she was telling this man sitting across the low-burning fire, not telling him everything, but not sure what to tell and what to leave out.

She began telling him about Jim Erin and found she had to tell him about her father and the years of living on Army posts and her mother dying of fever when she was a little girl. She remembered Jim Erin when she was younger, in her early teens, and her father was stationed at Whipple Barracks. She remembered Jim Erin and her father drinking together and remembered them stumbling and knocking the dishes from the table. A few years later she remembered her father—after he retired and they were living in Prescott—mentioning Jim Erin and saying he was coming to see them. And when he came she remembered Jim Erin again, the man with the nice smile and the black hair who had a way of holding her arm as he talked to her, his fingers moving, feeling her skin. She remembered her father drinking and cursing the Army and a system that would pass over a man and leave him a lieutenant after sixteen years on frontier station. Now a sutler was something else; he had a government contract to sell stores to the soldiers and could do well. Like his friend Jim Erin. The girl who gets him is getting something, her father had told her, leading up to it, and within a year had arranged the marriage. A year and a half later her father was dead of a stroke.

A lot of men drink, but their wives don't kill them. Of course. It wasn't his drinking. Yes, it was his drinking, but it was more than that. If he wasn't the kind of man he was and he didn't beat her it wouldn't have happened. This was in her mind, though she didn't try to explain it to Valdez. He put wood on the fire, keeping the flame low, while she told him about the night she killed her husband.

It was after Frank Tanner had left. He had come to see Jim Erin on business, with a proposition to supply the sutler's store with leather and straw goods he could bring up from Mexico.

She stared into the fire, remembering that night. "They were drinking when I left to visit for a while," she said. "When I got back Frank was gone and Jim was out of whiskey. He couldn't borrow any. No one would lend it to him, and that night he didn't have enough money to buy any. So he said he was going out to get corn beer . . ."

"He liked tulapai, uh?"

"He liked anything you could drink. He said someone not far away would sell him a bucket of it. I told him he was too drunk to go out alone, and he said then I was coming with him if I was so concerned. Jim got his gun and we took the buggy, not past the main gate, because he didn't want anybody questioning him. There was no stockade and it was easy to slip out if you didn't want to be seen.

"I don't know where we went except it was a few miles from the fort and off the main road. When we finally stopped Jim got out and left me there. He said 'here,' handing me his gun, 'so you won't be scared.' He didn't mean it as kindness; he was saying 'here, woman, I'm going off alone, but I don't need any gun.' Do you see what I mean?"

She looked at Valdez. He nodded and asked her then, "Was he drunk at this time?"

"Fairly. He'd had the bottle with Frank. He stumbled some, weaving, as he walked away from the buggy. There wasn't a house around or a sign of light. He walked off toward a draw you could see because of the brush in it."

"It must have been a half hour before I saw him coming back, hearing him first, because it was so dark that night, then seeing him. He was carrying a gourd in front of him with both hands and when he got to the buggy he raised it and said, 'Here, take it.' He put his foot up on the step plate to rest the gourd on his knee, but as he did it his foot slipped and he dropped the gourd on the rocks. He looked down at the broken pieces and the corn beer soaking into the ground, then up at me and said it was my fault, I should have taken it. He started screaming at me, saying he was going to beat me up good. I said, 'Jim, don't do it. Please,' I remember that. He started to step up into the buggy, reaching for me, and I jumped out the other side. I ran toward the draw, but he got ahead of me, turning me. I said to him, 'Jim, I've got your gun. If you touch me I'll use it.' I remember saying that too. He kept coming, working around me as I faced him, until I was against the side of the draw and couldn't turn. I said to Jim, please.

He came at me and I pulled the trigger. Jim fell to his knees, though I wasn't sure I had hit him. He picked up something, I guess a rock, and came at me again, and this time I shot him twice and knew I had killed him."

Valdez rolled a cigarette and leaned into the fire to light it, and raising his eyes he saw the woman staring into the light. She sat unmoving; she was in another time, remembering, her hands folded in her lap. She seemed younger at this moment and smaller, this woman who had killed her husband.

Valdez said, "You didn't tell anyone?"

She shook her head slowly.

"Why didn't you?"

"I don't know. I was afraid. I went back to the post. The next day, after they found him, they asked me questions. I told them Jim had gone out late, but I didn't know where. They told me he was dead and I didn't say anything, because I couldn't pretend to be sorry. When I didn't tell them then, I couldn't tell them later, at the hearing. They decided it must have been the man who deserted, a soldier named Johnson who everybody knew was buying corn beer from the Indians and selling it at the post."

Valdez drew on his cigarette, letting the smoke out slowly. "You haven't told Frank Tanner?"

"No. I almost did. But I thought better of it."

"Then why did you tell me?"

Her eyes raised now in the firelight. "I don't know," she said softly. "Maybe it's this place. Maybe it's because I've wanted to tell somebody so bad. I just don't know." She paused, and with the soft sound gone from her voice said, "Maybe I told you because you're not going to live long enough to tell anyone else."

"You want to stay alive," Valdez said. "Everybody wants to stay alive."

She was staring at him again. "Do you?"

"Everybody," Valdez said.

"Well, remember that when you close your eyes," she said. "I killed a man to be free of him, to stay alive."

"I'll remember that," Valdez said. "I'll remember something else, too, a man lying on his back tied to a cross and someone cutting him loose and giving him water."

He watched closely but there was no change of expression on her face. He said, "The man believes a woman did this. He thought the woman had dark hair, because he had been thinking of a woman with dark hair. But maybe he thought it was dark hair because it was night. Maybe it was a woman with light hair. A woman who lived near this place and knew where he was and could find him."

She was listening intently now, hunched forward, her long hair hanging close to her face. She said, "It could have been one of the Mexican women."

"No, it wasn't one of them, I know that. They live with those men and they would be afraid."

She waited, thoughtful, but still did not move her eyes from his. She said, almost cautiously, "You believe I'm the woman?"

"There's no one else."

She said then, still thoughtful, watching him, "If you believe I saved you, why are you doing this to me?"

Valdez took a last draw on the cigarette and dropped it in the fire. "I'm not doing it to you. I'm doing it to Frank Tanner."

"But if he doesn't give you the money——"

"Let's see what happens," Valdez said. He got to his knees and spread his blanket so that his feet would be toward the fire.

Gay Erin didn't move. She said, "Why do you think I cut you loose?"

"I don't know. Because you felt sorry for me?"

"Maybe." She watched him. "Or maybe because of Frank. To do something against him."

"You're going to marry him," Valdez said.

"He says I'm going to marry him."

"Well, if you don't want to, why didn't you leave?"

"Because I've no place to go. So I'll marry him whether I want to or not." She looked into the fire, moving her hair from the side of her face gently, with the tips of her fingers. "I have no family to go to. People I used to know are scattered all over the territory. I think even when I was married to Jim I felt alone. I stayed with him, I guess, for the same reason I'm going to marry Frank."

Valdez knelt on his blanket, half turned to look at her. "You want to get married so bad, there are plenty of men."

"Are there?" She got up and smoothed her skirt, standing close to the fire. "Where should I spread my blanket?"

"Where do you want to?"

Looking down at him she said, "Wherever you tell me."

Look at him again as he looked at himself that night. His name was Roberto Eladio Valdez, born July 23, 1854, in an adobe village on the San Pedro, where the valley land climbed into the Galiuros. His father was a farmer until they moved to Tucson and his father went to work for a freight company and sent his children to the mission school. Roberto Eladio Valdez, born of Mexican parents in the United States Territory of Arizona, a boy who lived in the desert and knew of many people who had been killed by the Apaches, boy to man in the desert and in the mountains, finally working for the Army, leading the Apache trackers when the hostiles jumped San Carlos and went raiding, and finally through with that and deciding it was time to work the land or work for a company, as most men did, and do it now if it wasn't already too late. Roberto Eladio Valdez worked for Hatch and Hodges, and they put him on the boot with the shotgun because he was good with it. He asked the municipal committee of Lanoria for a town job and they made him a part-time constable and put a shotgun in his hands because he was good with it and because he was quiet and because everybody liked him or at least abided him, because he was one of the good ones who kept himself clean and neat, even wearing the starched collar and the suit when everybody else was in shirtsleeves, and never drank too much or was abusive. Remember, there is the Bob Valdez who knew his place, and the one looking for a normal life and a home and a family.

Now this one is inside the one at the high camp above the mountain meadow at the edge of the timber. Bob and Roberto both there, both of them looking at the woman across the fire-light, but Roberto doing the thinking now, saying to himself but to the woman, "All right, that's what you want."

He was not smiling now or holding open the coach door or touching his hat and saying yes, ma'am. He was on his own ground and he was unbuckling the Walker Colt from his leg.

He said, "Bring it over here."

He rose to his feet as she came around the fire with the

rolled blanket, now taller and bigger than she was. She spread the blanket next to his, and when she straightened, he took her shoulders in his hands, not feeling her pull back, feeling only the soft firmness of her arms. He said, "You don't want to be alone, uh?"

She said nothing.

"You want somebody to hold you and take care of you. Is that it?"

Her face was close, her eyes looking at him, her lips slightly parted.

"What else do you want? You want me to let you go?"

Slowly her hands came up in front of her and she began unbuttoning her shirt, her hands working down gradually from her throat to her waist. She said, "I told you I killed my husband. I told you I don't want to marry Frank Tanner. I told you I have nothing. You decide what I want."

"I heard something," Diego Luz said.

His wife lay beside him with her eyes closed. He knew she was awake because sunlight filtered through the straw blind covering the window, the way the early morning sunlight looked each day when they rose to work in the yard and the fields and the horse corral until the sun left for the night. Without opening her eyes his wife said, sleep in her voice and on her face, "What did you hear?"

Diego Luz sat up now. "I heard something."

"Your horses," his wife said.

"Horses, but not my horses."

"The chickens," she said.

"Horses." Diego Luz got out of the bed Bob Valdez had slept in a few days before. He looked at the two children on the mat beneath the window; they were asleep. He went into the front room and looked at his daughter and his youngest child and his wife's mother in the bed. His mother-in-law lay on her back staring at the ceiling. Diego Luz said, "What is it?"

"Outside," his wife's mother said.

"What outside? What did you hear?"

"They killed the dogs," the old woman said.

He turned to look at his oldest son, sleeping, and said to himself, Wake him. But he let the boy sleep. Diego Luz pushed aside the straw mat covering the doorway and went outside, out under the mesquite-pole ramada, and saw them in the yard.

An army of them, a half-circle of armed men in their saddles. No sound now, not even from the horses. A dozen of them or more. A dog lying on its side in the yard with a saddle blanket covering its bead. The dog smothered. Twelve riders looking at him, staring at him or at the ramada or at the house, facing him and not moving. He heard hooves on the hardpack and two riders appeared from the side of the house. Diego Luz looked that way and saw more of them at the corral and coming up from the horse pasture. They were all around the place; they had been everywhere; they had closed in from all sides and now they were here.

Diego Luz moved to the edge of the ramada shade looking out. He said nothing because there was nothing for him to say; he didn't ask them here; they came. But he said to himself, He did something to them and they're looking for him.

He saw Mr. Tanner and his segundo and several people that he recognized who had been by here. He saw R. L. Davis and this puzzled him, R. L. Davis being with them; but the way they were here, not passing by and stopping for water, *here*, made him too afraid to wonder about R. L. Davis.

Diego Luz, the horsebreaker, who they said broke horses with his fists, looked out at them and said in his mind to them, Go out to the corral and eat horseshit, goddam you sitting there. But he thought of his wife and his children and his oldest daughter and he said, Jesus, son of God, help me. Jesus, if you listen to anything or have listened to anything. Jesus, from now on——

The segundo said in Spanish, "How are you, friend? How is your family? Are they awake?"

Goddam him, Diego Luz thought and said, "How does it pass with you? Come down and have something with us. I'll wake up the old woman."

"Good," the segundo said, "Bring the woman out. Bring out your daughter."

Over from him several riders, R. L. Davis said, "Mr. Tanner you want me to ask him? I'll get it from him."

The segundo looked at R. L. Davis from under the straw brim of his Sonora hat. R. L. Davis saw the look, not moving his eyes to Mr. Tanner, knowing better, and decided to keep his mouth shut for a while.

"Now they come," the segundo said pleasantly, smiling, touching the brim of his hat.

Diego Luz could hear them behind him. He thought, Jesus, make them stay inside. But they were out and coming out: his wife and his son and his daughter, standing close to him now; he could hear one of the smaller children, the high questioning voice, and heard the witch voice of his wife's mother, the too-loud annoying sound telling them to be silent; God bless the toothless hag this time, now, Jesus, give her power to keep them inside.

Diego Luz tried to be calm and let this happen, what was going to happen. He wet his lips and tried not to wet his lips. He did not see the segundo motion or hear him speak, but now a rider dismounted, letting his reins trail, and came toward them.

He was an American, a bony man who had not shaved for several days and wore boots to his knees and spurs that chinged as he came forward. He moved past Diego Luz and took his son by the arm and brought him out several strides into the yard. He positioned the boy, moving him by his shoulders, to face his family as the boy looked up at him. The man glanced at the segundo. His gaze dropped slowly to the boy and when he was looking at him, standing a stride in front of him, he stepped in swinging his gloved right fist and slammed it into the boy's face.

Diego Luz did not move. He looked at his boy on the ground and at the man who had struck him and at the segundo.

The segundo said, "We ask you one time. Where is Valdez?"

Diego Luz did not hesitate or think about it. He said, "I don't know." He added then, "No one here knows." And then, because he had said this much, he said, "He hasn't been here in four days." He saw the segundo looking at him and he wished he had said only that he didn't know.

The American with the bony face and the high boots walked over to the ramada. Diego Luz glanced aside and then half turned as he saw his small children out of the doorway. The American picked up the littlest girl, his three-year-old, and held her up in front of him. The man grinned with no teeth, with his mouth sunken. He said, "How're you, honey?" The little girl smiled as he carried her out into the yard. The American looked out toward the mounted men and he said, "Mr. Tanner, I could swing this young'n by her feet and bash her head agin the wall."

Diego Luz screamed, "I don't know!"

Now several men dismounted and came toward him. One of them pushed him aside and they brought his daughter out into the yard. She was wearing only a nightdress, and in the sunlight he could see the shape of his daughter's hips and legs beneath the cotton cloth and saw the men by the ramada looking at her. The man who brought her out was behind her now. He took her nightdress at the neck and pulled down on it. The girl twisted, wrenching away from him, screaming. Some of the men laughed, staring at her now as she tried to hold up her shredded nightdress to cover herself.

The segundo said to Diego Luz, "Maybe we take her inside and mount her one at a time. Or maybe we do it out here so your family can see."

"I don't know where he is," Diego Luz said.

The segundo looked at Mr. Tanner, who was mounted on a bay horse. The segundo stepped out of his saddle. He took a plug of tobacco and bit off a corner as he walked up to Diego Luz, who watched him, feeling his hands hanging heavily at his sides.

He said to the segundo in Spanish, "Tell him to put my little girl down."

"He's talking," the segundo said.

"Not that one."

"He's a little crazy maybe."

"Tell him to put her down."

"I won't let him do it," the segundo said. "She's too young. Maybe she grow up to be something, like your daughter."

Diego Luz said, "If you touch her you'd better kill me."

"We can do that," the segundo said.

"I don't know where he is. Man, who do you think I put first, him?"

"We only asking you," the segundo said. "Maybe you give us a lot of shit and we believe it. That's a nice-looking girl," he said, looking at the man's daughter. "I like a little more up there, but first one of the day, maybe it's all right."

"Shoot her first," Diego Luz said. "You'd do it to a corpse, you filthy son of a whore."

The segundo said, "Man, hold on to yourself if you can do it. Just tell us."

"I don't know where he is," Diego Luz said.

"Listen, leave Maricopa, you can ride for me."

"I don't know where he is," Diego Luz said.

"I don't care where he is," the segundo said. "I mean it, ride for me."

Diego Luz said, "Come here alone to ask me, I'd try to kill you."

The segundo nodded, smiling. "You'd try it, wouldn't you? That's why I want you."

R. L. Davis came out of his saddle. He walked part way toward Tanner and stopped. He eased his funneled hat up and pulled it down again.

"Mr. Tanner, I'd like to ask him something."

"Go ahead," Tanner said. He brought a cigar out of a vest pocket and bit off the tip.

"I want to ask Diego about seeing him in town with Bob Valdez's clothes three days ago."

Tanner lit his cigar and blew out the smoke. "You hear that?"

Diego Luz nodded his head up and down. "I was taking his clothes to him."

"Where?" Tanner said.

"He was hiding."

"I said where."

"In the line shack. At the Maricopa pasture."

To the segundo Tanner said, "They look in the shack?"

"I'll find out," the segundo said.

"If he wasn't there," Tanner said to Diego Luz, "you're a dead man."

"He brought him his clothes," R. L. Davis said, "and he must've brought him his guns too."

"We've stayed long enough," Tanner said. "Tend to the horsebreaker."

R. L. Davis was standing in the yard. He wanted to say more, but it was passing him by. "Mr. Tanner, I could talk to him some——"

But Tanner wasn't paying any attention to him.

Two men and then a third one brought Diego Luz out in the yard. They bent his arms behind him, forcing him to his knees and this way got him facedown on the hardpack, spreading his arms, a man sitting on him and a man clamping each of his arms flat to the ground with a boot.

The segundo went to one knee at Diego Luz's head. He worked the tobacco from one side of his mouth to the other with his tongue and spit a brown stream close to Diego Luz. He said, "I believe you; you don't know where he is. But maybe you're lying. Or maybe you lie some other time to us. You understand?"

The American with the bony face and the high boots went down to his knees close to Diego Luz's left hand that was palm-flat on the ground. The man drew his Colt revolver and flipped it, catching it by the barrel, and brought the butt down hard on Diego Luz's hand. The hand clenched to protect itself as Diego Luz screamed and the gun butt came down on the tight white knuckles and Diego Luz screamed again. This way they broke both of the horsebreaker's hands while his family watched from the shade of the ramada.

"I mean it," the segundo said, as Diego Luz lay there after the men holding him had moved away. "You come work for me sometime."

They herded the family into the yard to get them out of the way while they destroyed the house and burned everything that would burn, beginning inside, pouring kerosene on the beds and the furniture, while outside two mounted men were fixing their ropes to the support posts of the ramada. The flames took the straw blinds covering the windows; the men inside poured out with smoke, and as they cleared the doorway, the mounted men spurred away to bring the mesquite-pole awning down over the front of the house. They burned the ramada and the outbuildings and the corn crib. They pulled his corral apart, scattering the horses, and came back across the yard, gathering and riding out southeast, leaving their dust hanging in the air and the sound of them fading in the early morning sunlight.

They were a good mile from the place, moving single file down the bank of an arroyo, the riders milling in the dry stream bed as they moved one at a time up the other side.

R. L. Davis looked back, squinting at the gray smoke rising in the near distance—not a lot of smoke now; the house would be burned out and most of the smoke was probably coming from the corn crib. He turned in his saddle. Tanner was already up the cutbank, but he saw the segundo still in the dry stream bed, waiting for the file of riders to move up. R. L. Davis walked his horse over to him.

"You see that smoke?"

The segundo looked at R. L. Davis, not at the sky.

"I reckon you can see that smoke a good piece," R. L. Davis said. "We're about a mile. I reckon you could still see it eight, ten miles."

The segundo said, "If he's no farther than that and if he's looking this way."

R. L. Davis grinned, "You see what I mean, huh? I was sure you would, though I wasn't putting much stock in Tanner getting it."

"Be careful," the segundo said. "He'll eat you up."

"I don't mean that insulting. I mean he might want to think about it a while, seeing things I don't see——"

"Hey," the segundo said. He took time to squirt a stream of tobacco to the dry-caked earth. "Why do you think he'd come if he sees the smoke?"

"Because they're friends. He brought him clothes and his guns."

"Would you go? If you saw your friend's place burning?"

"Sure I would."

"No, you wouldn't," the segundo said. "But he might. If he sees it he might."

"It's worth staying to find out," R. L. Davis said.

The segundo nodded. "Worth leaving you and maybe a few more." He started off, reining his horse toward the far bank, then came around to look at Davis again. "Hey," the segundo said, maybe smiling in the shadow of his Sonora hat. "What are you going to do if he comes?"

7

"YOU DON'T have to tie me," the Erin woman said. "I'll wait for you; I won't run."

Valdez said nothing. Maybe he had to tie her and maybe he didn't, but a mile from Diego Luz's place now and the smoke gone from the sky an hour, he tied her and left her in the arroyo, marking the place in his mind: willows on the bank and yellow brittlebrush in the dry bed. He left her in deep shade, not speaking or looking at her face.

Though he looked at her over and over as he made his way to Diego Luz's place, picturing her in the darkness of the high meadow, the woman lying with him under the blanket, holding her and feeling her against him and for a long time, after she was asleep, staring up at the cold night sky, at the clouds that moved past the moon.

In the morning the sky was clear, until he saw the smoke in the distance, seven miles northwest, and knew what it was as he saw it. Valdez packed their gear without a word and they moved out, across the meadow and down through the foothills toward the column of smoke. At one point she said to him, "What if they're waiting for you?" And he answered, "We'll see."

They could be waiting or not waiting. Or he could have not seen the smoke. Or he could have continued with the woman southeast and been near the twin peaks by this evening. Or he never could have asked Diego Luz to help him. Or he never could have started this. Or he never could have been born. But he was here and he was pointing northwest instead of southeast because he had no choice. At first he had thought only about Diego Luz and his family. But when there was no sign of Tanner, no dust rising through the field glasses, he began to think of the woman more. When she was still with him when they reached the arroyo, he knew he wanted to keep her and tied her up to make sure of it.

Following the dry stream bed north, Valdez saw the tracks where Tanner's men had crossed; he noticed the prints of several horses leading south. He continued on a short distance before climbing out of the arroyo to move west. This way he circled Diego Luz's place and approached from a thicket beyond the horse pasture, studying the house and yard for some time before he moved into the open.

It might have been a dozen years ago after an Apache raid, the look of the place, the burned-out house and the dog lying in the yard; but there were people here, alive, and a team hitched to a wagon, and that was the difference. They waited for him by the wagon, Diego Luz and his family.

Valdez dismounted, "What did they do to you?"

"What you see," Diego Luz said. He raised his hands in front of him, his hands open, the swollen, discolored fingers apart.

"Did they harm your family?"

"A little. If they did any more I wouldn't be here."

"I'm sorry," Valdez said.

"We're friends. They would have come with or without Mr. R. L. Davis."

"He was with them?"

"He saw me in Lanoria with your clothes. Jesus, my hands hurt."

"Let me look at them."

"No looking today. Get out of here."

"What did they ask you?"

"Where you are. Man, what did you do to them?"

"Enough," Valdez said.

"They want you bad."

"They could have followed me."

"But Mr. Davis brought them here. Listen," Diego Luz said, "if you see him, give him something for me."

"For myself too," Valdez said. "You're going to Lanoria?"

"My son is taking me to get these fixed." He looked at his hands again.

"Will they be all right?"

"How do I know? We'll see. I just need to get one finger working."

"I'll take you," Valdez said.

"Go to hell. No, go where they can't find you," Diego Luz said. "I have my boy and my family."

* * *

R. L. Davis came across the Erin woman because he was hot
and tired of riding in the sun.

He had moved south along the arroyo with the three riders
who would watch with him. "If he comes he'll come from the
southeast," the segundo had said. But after the segundo left,
R. L. Davis thought, Who says he'll come in a straight line? He
could work around and come from any direction. He told this
to the three riders with him and one of them, the bony-faced
one who'd picked up the little girl and who'd broken Diego
Luz's hands, said sure, it was a waste of time; he'd like to get a
shot at this Valdez, but it didn't have to be today; the greaser
was in the hills and they'd find him.

That one, God, when he'd picked up the little girl, R. L.
Davis wasn't sure he could watch what the man wanted to do.
Her being a tiny girl.

After a while he said well, he'd double back and take a swing
to the north. The others said they'd get up on the banks and
look around and head back pretty soon. Good. He was glad to
get away from the bony-faced one, a face like a skeleton face,
only with skin.

So R. L. Davis moved back up the arroyo. He wasn't looking
for anything in particular; there was nothing out here but the
hot sun beating down on him. He saw the willow shade up
ahead and the bright yellow blossoms of the brittlebush growing along the cutbank. The shade looked good. He headed for
it. And when he found the Erin woman in there, sitting in the
brush, tied up, he couldn't believe his eyes.

It was a lot to think about all at once. Valdez was here. Had
been here. He'd put the woman here out of the way and gone
to see Diego Luz. And if he left her like this, tied hand and
foot, with a bandana over her mouth, then he was coming back
for her. The woman was looking at him and he had to make
up his mind fast.

He could pull her up behind him on the sorrel and deliver
her to Tanner and say, "Here you are, Mr. Tanner. What else
you need done?"

Or he could wait for Bob Valdez. Throw down on him and
bring him in as well as the woman. Or gun him if that's the
way Valdez wanted it.

The woman looked good. He'd like to slip the bandana from

her mouth and get a close look at her. But he'd better not. There was a little clearing in here and rocks that had come down the cutbank. There was room in here to face him. There was room deeper in the brittlebush for his horse, if the son of a bitch didn't make any noise.

God Almighty, R. L. Davis thought. How about it? Bring them both in.

Once he'd moved the sorrel into the brush, he got his Winchester off the saddle and settled down behind the woman, behind some good rock cover. He saw her twist around to the side to look at him, her eyes looking but not saying anything. Probably scared to death. He motioned her to turn around and put one finger to his mouth. *Shhhh.* Don't worry; it won't be long.

Crossing the pasture from Diego Luz's place, Valdez saw the willows in the distance marking the arroyo. There had been some luck with him so far, coming in and going out, though he didn't know Tanner and he wasn't sure if it was luck or not. He didn't know yet how the man thought, if he was intelligent and could anticipate what the other man might do, or if he ran in all directions trusting only to luck. Luck was all right when you had it, but it couldn't be counted on. It worked good and bad, but it worked more good than bad if you knew what you were doing, if you were careful and watched and listened. He shouldn't be here, but he was here, and if the luck or whatever it was continued, he would be in high country again late this afternoon, letting Tanner find him and follow him, but not letting him get too close until the time was right for that.

When he talked to Tanner again it had to be on his own ground, not Tanner's.

The sawed-off Remington was across his lap as he approached the willows and entered the cavern of shade formed by the hanging branches. Holding the Remington, he dismounted and stood still to listen. There was no sound in the trees. He moved along the bank of the arroyo, beyond the thick brush below, to a place where the bank slanted down in deep slashes to the dry bed. He worked his way down carefully. At the bottom, as he entered the brittlebush, he cocked the right barrel of the Remington.

The Erin woman sat where he had placed her. She did not hear him or look this way. The bandana covered the side of her face and pulled her long hair behind her shoulders, which sagged with the weariness of sitting here for nearly an hour. You hold her all night and tie her in the morning, he thought. You make love to her, but you've never said her name. Now she turned her head this way.

He saw the startled expression jump into her eyes. He moved toward her, watching her eyes, wide open; her head moved very slightly to the side and then her eyes moved in that direction. Off to the right of her or behind her. Valdez shifted his gaze to the rocks and deep brush.

He moved forward again, a half step, and a voice he recognized said, "That's far enough!"

"Hey!" Valdez said. "Is that Mr. R. L. Davis?"

"Put down the scattergun and unfasten your belt."

Valdez's gaze shifted slightly. There. He could see the glint of the Winchester barrel in the brush and part of Davis's hat. He was behind an outcropping of rock, looking out past the left side, which meant he would have to expose half of his body to fire from that place. If he's right handed, Valdez thought. He remembered Davis firing at the Lipan woman across the Maricopa pasture and he said to himself, Yes, he's right-handed.

"You hear me? I said put it down!"

"Why don't you come out?" Valdez said.

The sawed-off Remington was in his right hand, pointed down, but with his finger curled on the trigger. He looked at the brush and the edge of the rock outcropping, judging the distance. He imagined swinging the shotgun up and firing, deciding how high he would have to swing it. You get one time, Valdez thought. No more.

"I'm going to count to three," R. L. Davis said.

"Listen," Valdez called. "Why don't you cut out this game and use your gun if you want to use it? What're you hiding in the bushes for?"

"I'm warning you to put it down!"

"Come on, boy, use the gun. Hey, pretend I'm an Indian woman, you yellow-ass son of a bitch."

There. His shoulder and the rifle barrel sliding higher on the outcropping, more of him in the brush, and Valdez swung up the Remington, squeezing his hand around the narrow neck and seeing the brush fly apart with the explosion.

"Hey, you still there?" He shifted the gun to his left hand and drew the Walker. There was a silence. He glanced at the woman, seeing her eyes on him, and away from her.

"I'm hit!" Davis called out.

"What do you expect?" Valdez said. "You want to play guns."

"I'm *bleeding*!"

"Wipe it off and try again."

Silence.

"Boy, I'm coming in for you. You ready?"

He saw Davis at the edge of the rock again, seeing him more clearly now with part of the brush torn away. Davis came out a little more, his left hand covering his ear and the side of his face.

"Don't shoot. Listen to me, don't."

"The first one was for Diego," Valdez said. "The next one's from me. I owe you something."

"I didn't leave you, did I? I didn't let you die. I could've, but I didn't."

"Pick up your gun."

"Listen, I cut you loose!"

Valdez paused, letting the silence come over the clearing. He heard another sound, far away, off behind him, but his gaze held on Davis.

"Say it again."

"After I pushed you over. That night I come back and cut you loose, didn't I?"

"I didn't see you that night."

"Well, who do you think did it?"

His gaze dropped to the woman, to her eyes looking at him above the bandana. He heard the sound again and knew it was a horse approaching, coming fast up the arroyo.

"I left you my canteen. I can prove it's mine, it's got my initials scratched in the tin part, inside."

Valdez raised his Walker to shut him up and motion him out of the brush. Davis started out, then stopped. He could hear the horse.

"Come on," Valdez hissed.

But Davis hesitated. The sound was louder down the arroyo,

rumbling toward them. Davis waited another moment then yelled out, "He's in here!" throwing himself behind the outcropping. "Get him! He's in here!"

Valdez reached the woman and pushed her over. He turned, moving crouched through the brittlebush, at the edge of it now, and stepping out of it as the first rider came at him from thirty yards away, drawing his revolver as he saw Valdez and the barrels of the Remington, then seeing nothing as the ten-bore charge rocked him from the saddle. The second rider was down the arroyo coming fast, low in the saddle and spurring his horse, his handgun already drawn, firing it from the off side of his horse. Valdez raised the Walker. He thumbed the hammer and fired and thumbed and fired and saw the horse buckle and roll, the rider stiff, with his arms outstretched in the air for a split moment, and Valdez shot him twice before he hit the ground. The horse was on its side, pawing with its forelegs, trying to rise. Valdez looked down the arroyo, waiting, then stepped to the horse and shot it through the head. He walked over to the man, whose death's head face looked up at him with sunken mouth and open eyes.

"I hope you're one of them Diego wanted," Valdez said. He turned toward the yellow brittlebush, loading the Remington.

"Where was he?" the segundo asked.

"He must have been in them bushes and fired on them as they come by," the rider said. "I was back a piece, up on the west side looking for his sign. When I heard the gunfire I lit up this way and they was coming out of the draw."

The segundo held up his hand. "Wait. You don't want to tell it so many times." He squinted under his straw hat brim toward Tanner, mounted on his bay, looking down at them in the arroyo.

Tanner saw the two bodies sprawled in the dry bed. He saw the dead horse and the yellow-baked ground stained dark at the horse's head. He saw the segundo and a man standing next to him and a half dozen mounted men and a riderless horse nibbling at the brittlebush. Tanner kicked the bay down the bank to the stream bed. He stared at the dead men, then at the segundo, a stub of a cigar clamped in his jaw.

"This man," the segundo said, "is one of the four we left."

"You left," Tanner said.

"I left. He says they went south looking for a sign of him. Then after a while the piss-ant you hired, something Davis, he come back this way."

"Let him tell it," Tanner said, judging the man next to the segundo as he looked at him.

"Well, as he says we worked south a ways," the rider said. "Davis come back first and we spread out some. Then these two here must have started back. I was down there a mile and a half, two miles"—he pointed south, more at ease now, a thumb hooked in his belt—"when I heard the shots and come on back."

"Where were they?" Tanner said.

"When I come back? They were laying there. He must have been in the bushes and fired on them as they come by. As I got close they was coming up out of the draw and going west."

"Who's they?" Tanner asked him.

"Two men and a woman."

"You saw them good?"

"Well, I was off a ways, but I could see her hair, long hair flying in the wind."

"You're saying it was Mrs. Erin?"

"Yes sir, I'd put my hand on the Book it was."

"You see Valdez?"

"Not his face, but it must have been him. One of these boys here was blowed off by a scatter gun."

"That one," the segundo said. "This one, I don't know, forty-four or forty-five, in the chest twice, close together."

"That's five men he's killed," Tanner said. He drew on the cigar stub; it was out, and he threw it to the ground. "What about Davis?"

The rider looked up. "I figured he was the other one with them. Once I saw he wasn't around here."

"That's the strange thing," the segundo said. "Why would the man want to take him? He's worth nothing to him."

"Unless he went with him on his own," Tanner said. "Mark him down as another one, a dead man when we catch up with them."

"We'll get him for you," the rider said.

Tanner looked down at him from the bay horse. "Did you fire at them?"

"Yes sir, I got down and laid against the cutbank for support and let go till they was out of range."

"Did you hit anybody?"

"I don't believe so."

"But you might have."

"Yes sir, I might've."

"That range you couldn't tell."

"They was two hundred yards when I opened up."

"You could have hit one though."

"Yes sir."

"You could have hit the woman," Tanner said to him.

"No sir, I wasn't aiming at her. No, I couldn't have hit her. There wasn't any chance I could've. See, I was aiming just at Valdez and he was a good piece from the woman."

Tanner looked at the segundo. "Put him against the bank and shoot him."

The rider said, "Mr. Tanner, there was no chance I could've hit her! I swear to God that's the truth!"

The segundo felt the tobacco in his cheek, rolling it with his tongue as his eyes moved from the rider to Frank Tanner, looking at Tanner now but aware of the mounted men behind him and those up on the bank watching. The segundo said, "We lost five now. We shoot our own, that's six, but the same as Valdez killed him. How many you want to give for this man?"

"As many as it takes," Tanner said.

"Instead of shoot him," the segundo said, "we make him ride point. The first one Valdez sees if he's up there waiting. What do you think of that?"

The rider was watching Tanner. "I'll ride point. Mister, I'll cut his sign, too, and get him for you."

Tanner stared down from his judgment seat on the bay horse. He let the man hang on the edge for a long moment before he said, "All right, this time," saying no more than that, but holding his eyes on the man to let him know how close he had come.

The segundo said to the rider, "Start now, come on." He was aware of the men on the bank, beyond Tanner, moving in their saddles, a man wiping his hand across his mouth and another loosening his hat and putting it on again. They were glad it was over. They had killed men, most of them had, but they didn't want to put this one against the bank and shoot him. That would be the end of it. In a few days they would all be gone.

So that was done. The segundo walked over to Tanner's bay; he touched the horse's withers, feeling the smooth flesh quiver and patting it gently. "We have him now," the segundo said, in a voice only for Tanner. "Yesterday he could take us where he wants with plenty of time. Today he has maybe an hour. He has to run and now he doesn't have no more time."

"Say it," Tanner said.

The segundo's hand remained on the horse, patting the firm flesh. "I was thinking to myself, we got eighteen men here. We got six at Mimbreño. We could send eight or ten back and they could start south with the drive. Then when we finish with him we catch up, maybe lose only two days."

Tanner waited. "You through?"

"I mean we don't need so many," the segundo said, but he knew by the way the man was looking at him his words had been wasted.

"I'm going up the mountain," Tanner said. "You're going up the mountain, and all my men are going up the mountain. My men, segundo. You savvy that?"

"If you say it."

"I say it," Tanner said.

Through the field glasses he watched them come up the slope: small dots that he could not count yet, spread in a line, all of them moving this way, one dot ahead of the others, far in front, the only one that he could identify through the field glasses as a mounted rider.

It wasn't happening the way it was supposed to happen. There was open country behind him and he needed more time, a bigger space between them, if he expected to reach the twin peaks. But they were driving him now, running him and making sure he wasn't going to move around them.

It was late afternoon, three hours and a little more until sunset. Three hours to hold them here—if he could hold them—before he could take his two people and slip out. He lay on the ground with good rock cover in front of him and all along the ridge. Next to him were his guns and Davis's Winchester. Looking at the dots coming up he thought, The Winchester or the Sharps? And said to himself, The Sharps. You know it better. You know what it can do.

Well, he had better let them know. Pretty soon now.

He rolled slightly to look at the Erin woman and R. L. Davis. Gay Erin, he said in his mind. Aloud he said, "Mr. R. L. Davis, I would like you to come over here, please, and go down there about fifty feet. You see where those rocks are?"

Davis stood up awkwardly, his wrists tied to his belt with pieces of rope. His elbows pointed out and he looked as though he was holding his stomach. There was dried blood on the side of his face and in his hair and down the arm of his jacket, which was torn and shredded.

"What do you want me down there for?"

"I want you in front of me," Valdez said. "So I can see you."

"What if they come?"

"They're already coming."

Davis gazed down the slope, squinting. "I don't see nothing."

"Take my word," Valdez said.

"Well listen now, if they start shooting I'm going to be in the line of fire."

"Behind the rocks, you'll be all right."

Davis stood his ground. "You still don't believe me, do you? I can prove it by my canteen."

"I don't have your canteen."

"You had it. It's somewhere."

"And we're here," Valdez said. "Let's talk some other time."

"If I didn't cut you loose, who did?"

"You can walk down or I can throw you down," Valdez said.

He looked toward the woman. Say it, he thought. He said, "Gay Erin. Gay. That's your name? Come over here." He watched Davis moving hunch-shouldered down the slope to the cover of low rocks. He felt the woman near him. As she sank to the ground, he handed her the field glasses. "Count them for me."

He raised up to take Davis's Colt out of his belt. The barrel was cutting into his hip. He placed it on the ground next to him and took the heavy Sharps, the Big Fifty, and laid it on the flat surface of the rock in front of him. He would load from the cartridge belt across his chest. With the stock against his cheek, aware of the oiled metal smell of the gun, he sighted down the barrel. Nothing. Not without the glasses.

"Seventeen," the Erin woman said.

He took the glasses from her. Putting them to his eyes the lower part of the slope came up to him.

They were still far enough away that he could see all of them without sweeping the glasses. He estimated the distance, the first man, the point rider, at six hundred yards, the rest of them at least two hundred yards behind him. The brave one, Valdez thought. Maybe the segundo. Maybe Tanner. He held the glasses on the man until he knew it was not Tanner. Nor the segundo, because of the man's dark hat.

Valdez lowered the glasses. He said, "Nineteen. You missed two of them, but that's very good." He looked at her, at her hair in the afternoon sunlight, the bandana pulled down from her face, loose around her neck now. He reached over and touched the bandana, feeling the cotton cloth between his fingers. "Put this on your head."

"The sun doesn't bother me," she said. She had not spoken since they left the arroyo.

"I'm not thinking of the sun. I'm thinking how far you can see yellow hair."

As she untied the knot behind her neck she said, "You believed I cut you loose. I didn't tell you I did."

"But you let me believe it."

"How do you know he did?"

"Because he told me. Because if someone else did it, he would think I knew who did it and he wouldn't bother to lie. I think I was dreaming of a woman giving me water," Valdez said. "So when I tried to remember what happened, I thought it was a woman."

"I didn't mean to lie to you," she said. "I was afraid."

"I can see it," Valdez said. "If you saved my life, I'm not going to shoot you. Or if you get under a blanket with me."

"I tried to explain how I felt," she said.

"Sure, you're all alone, you need somebody. Don't worry anymore. I know a place you can work, make a lot of money."

"If you think I'm lying," the woman said, "or if you think I'm a whore, there's nothing I can do about it. Think what you like."

"I've got something else to think about," Valdez said. He studied the slope through the field glasses, past Davis lying behind the rock looking up at him, to the point rider. He raised up then and said to Davis, "If you call out, I give you the first one."

He put the glasses on the point man again, three hundred yards away, and held him in focus until he was less than two hundred yards and he could see the man's face and the way the man was squinting, his gaze inching over the hillside. I don't know you, Valdez said to the man. I have nothing against you. He put down the field glasses and turned the Sharps on the point rider. He could still see the man's face, his eyes looking over the slope, not knowing it was coming. You shouldn't have looked at him, Valdez thought.

Then take another one and show them something. But not Tanner. Anyone else.

Through the field glasses he picked out Tanner almost four hundred yards away and put the glasses down again and placed the front sight of the Sharps on the man next to Tanner, not having seen the man or thinking about him now as a man. He let them come a little more, three hundred and fifty yards, and squeezed the trigger. The sound of the Sharps cracked the stillness, echoing across the slope, and the man, whoever he was, dropped from the saddle. Valdez looked and fired and saw a horse go down with its rider. He fired again and dropped another horse as they wheeled and began to fall back out of range. The Sharps echoed again, but they were moving in confusion and he missed with this shot and the next one. He picked up the Winchester, getting to his knees, and slammed four shots at the point rider, chasing him down the slope, and with the fourth shot the man's horse stumbled, throwing him from the saddle. He fired the Winchester twice again, into the distance, then lowered it, the ringing aftersound of the gunfire in his ears.

"Now think about it," Valdez said to Tanner.

He would think and then he would send a few, well out of

range, around behind them. Or he would have some of them try to work their way up the slope without being seen.

Or they would all come again.

As they did a few minutes later, spread out and running their horses up the slope. Valdez used the Sharps again. He hit the first man he aimed at, dumping him out of the saddle, and dropped two horses. Before they had gotten within two hundred yards they were turning and falling back. He looked for the two riders whose horses he had hit. One of them was running, limping down the hill, and the other was pinned beneath his dead animal.

You'd better move back or work around, Valdez said to Tanner, before you lose all your horses.

Make him believe you.

He raised the angle of the Sharps and fired. He fired again and saw a horse go down at six hundred yards. They pulled back again.

Now, Valdez thought, get out of here.

They could wait until dark, but that would be too late if Tanner was sending people around. He had to be lucky to win and he had to take chances in order to try his luck.

He could leave R. L. Davis.

But he looked at him down there with his wrists tied to his belt, and for some reason he said to himself, Keep him. Maybe you need him sometime.

He called to Davis, "Come up now. Slowly, along the brush there."

The woman sat on the ground watching him. The woman who was alone and needed someone and wanted to be held and got under the blanket. In this moment before they made their run, Valdez looked at her and said, "What do you want? Tell me."

"I want to get out of here," she said.

"Where? Where do you want to be?"

"I don't know."

"Gay Erin," Valdez said, "think about it and let me know."

Tanner and the men with him had gotten to the ridge and were looking at the ground and back down the slope to where they had been, seeing it as Valdez had seen it. Now they heard the gunfire in the distance, to the south.

They stopped and looked that way, all of them, out across the open, low-rolling country to the hills beyond.

"They caught him," one of them said.

Another one said, "How many shots?"

They listened and in the silence a man said, "I counted five, but it could've been more."

"It was more than five," the first man said. "It was all at once, like they were firing together."

"That's it," a man said. "The four of them got him in their sights and all fired at once to finish him."

The segundo was standing at the place where Valdez had positioned himself belly-down behind the rocks to fire at them. He picked up an empty brass cartridge and looked at it—fifty-caliber big bore, from a Sharps or some kind of buffalo gun. He noticed the .44 cartridges that had been fired from the Winchester. A Sharps and a Winchester, a big eight- or ten-bore shotgun and a revolver; this man was armed and he knew how to use his guns. The segundo counted fourteen empty cartridges on the ground and tallied what the bullets had cost them: two dead on the slope, two wounded, five horses shot. Now seven dead in the grand total and, counting the men without horses, who would have to walk to Mimbreño and come back, twelve men he had wiped from the board, leaving twelve to hunt him and kill him.

He said to Mr. Tanner, "This is where he was, if you want to see how he did it."

Tanner walked over, looking at the ground and down the slope. "He had some luck," Tanner said, "but it's run out."

The segundo said nothing. Maybe the man had luck—there was such a thing as luck—but God in heaven, he knew how to shoot his guns. It would be something to face him, the segundo was thinking. It would be good to talk to him sometime, if this had not happened and if he met the man, to have a drink of mescal with him, or if they were together using their guns against someone else.

How would you like to have him? the segundo thought. Start over and talk to him different. He remembered the way

Valdez had stood at the adobe wall as they fired at him, shooting close to his head and between his legs. He remembered the man not moving, not tightening or pleading or saying a word as he watched them fire at him. You should have known then, the segundo said to himself.

Tanner had sent four to circle around behind Valdez on the ridge and close his back door. A half hour after they heard the gunfire in the distance, one of them came back.

The man's horse was lathered with sweat, and he took his hat off to feel the evening breeze on the ridge as he told it.

"We caught them, out in the open. They had miles to go yet before they'd reach cover, and we ran them, hard," the man said. "Then we see one of the horses pull up. We know it must be him and we go right at him, getting into range to start shooting. But he goes flat on the ground, out in the open but right flat, and doesn't give us nothing to shoot at. He opened up at about a hunnert yards, and first one boy went down and then he got the horse of this other boy. The boy run toward him and he cut him clean as he was a-running. So two of us left, we come around. We see Valdez mount up and chase off again for the hills. We decide, one of us will follow them and the other will come back here."

Tanner said, "Did you hit him?"

"No sir, he didn't look to be hit."

"You know where he went?"

"Yes sir, Stewart's out there. He's going to track them and leave a plain enough trail for us to follow."

Tanner looked at the segundo. "Is he any good?"

The segundo shrugged. "Maybe he's finding out."

They moved out, south from the ridge, across the open, rolling country. In the dusk, before the darkness settled over the hills, they came across the man's horse grazing, and a few yards farther on the man lying on his back with his arms flung out. He had been shot through the head.

Ten, the segundo thought, looking down at the man. Nine left.

"Take his guns," Tanner said. "Bring his horse along."

It was over for this day. With the darkness coming they would have to wait until morning. He took out a cigar and bit off the end. Unless they spread out and worked up into the hills tonight. Tanner lighted the cigar, staring up at the dim, shadowed slopes and the dark mass of trees above the rocks.

He said to the segundo, "Come here. I'll tell you what we're going to do."

8

"CHRIST," R. L. Davis said. "I need more than this to eat." Christ, some bread and peppers and a half cup of stale water. "I didn't have nothing all day."

"Be thankful," Valdez told him.

Davis's saddle was on the ground in front of him, his hands tied to the horn. He was on his stomach and had to hunch his head down to take a bite of the pan bread he was holding. The Erin woman, next to him, held his cup for him when he wanted a sip of water. She listened to them, to their low tones in the darkness, and remained silent.

"I don't even have no blanket," R. L. Davis said. "How'm I going to keep warm?"

"You'll be sweating," Valdez said.

"Sweating, man it gets *cold* up here."

"Not when you're moving."

Davis looked over at him in the darkness, the flat, stiff piece of bread close to his face. "You don't even know where you're going, do you?"

"I know where I want to go," Valdez answered. "That much."

Toward the twin peaks, almost a day's ride from where they were camped now for a few hours, in the high foothills of the Santa Ritas: a dry camp with no fire, no flickering light to give them away if Tanner's men were prowling the hills. They would eat and rest and try to cover a few miles before dawn.

Ten years before, he had camped in these hills with his Apache trackers, following the White Mountain band that had struck Mimbreño and burned the church and killed three men and carried off a woman: renegades, fleeing into Mexico after jumping the reservation at San Carlos, taking what they needed along the way.

Ten years ago, but he remembered the ground well, and the way toward the twin peaks.

Valdez had worked ahead with his trackers and let the cavalry troop try to keep up with them, moving deep into the hills and

climbing gradually into rock country, following the trail of the
White Mountain band easily, because the band was running,
not trying to cover their tracks, and because there were many
of them: women and several children in addition to the fifteen
or so men in the raiding party. He knew he would catch them,
because he could move faster with his trackers and it was only
a matter of time. They found cooking pots and jars that had
been stolen and now thrown away. They found a lame horse
and farther on a White Mountain woman who was sick and
had been left behind. They moved on, climbing the slopes and
up through the timber until they came out of the trees into a
canyon: a gama grass meadow high in the mountains, with an
escarpment of rock rising steeply on both sides and narrowing
at the far end to a dark, climbing passage that would allow only
one man at a time to enter.

The first tracker into the passage was shot from his saddle.
They carried him back and dismounted in the meadow to look
over the situation.

This was the reason the White Mountain band had made a
run for it and had not bothered to cover their tracks. Once they
made it through the defile they were safe. One of them could
squat up there in the narrows and hold off every U. S. soldier
on frontier station, as long as he had shells, giving his people
time to run for Mexico. They studied the walls of the canyon
and the possible trails around. Yes, a man could climb it maybe,
if he had some goat blood in him. But getting up there didn't
mean there was a way to get down the other side. On the other
hand, to go all the way back down through the rocks and find
a trail that led around and brought them out at the right place
could take a week if they were lucky. So Valdez and his trackers
sat in that meadow and smoked cigarettes and talked and let
the White Mountain people run for the border. If they didn't
get them this year they'd get them next year.

Valdez could see Tanner's men dismounted in the meadow,
looking up at the canyon walls, studying the shadowed crevices and the cliff rose that grew along the rim, way up there
against the sky. Anyone want to try it? No thank you, not
today. Tanner would send some men to scout a trail that led
around. But before he ever heard from them again, after a day

or two in the meadow, seeing the bats flicking and screeching around the canyon's wall at night, he'd come to the end of his patience and holler up through the narrow defile, "All right, let's talk!"

That was the way Bob Valdez had pictured it taking place: leading Tanner with plenty of time and setting it up to make the deal. "Give me the money for the Lipan woman or you don't get your woman back."

He had almost forgotten the Lipan woman. He couldn't picture her face now. It wasn't a face to remember, but now the woman had no face at all. She was somewhere, sitting in a hut eating corn or *atole*, feeling the child inside her and not knowing this was happening outside in the night. He would say to Tanner, "You see how it is? The woman doesn't have a man, so she needs money. You have money, but you don't have a woman. All right, you pay for the man and you get your woman."

It seemed simple because in the beginning it was simple, with the Lipan woman sitting at her husband's grave. But now there was more to it. The putting him against the wall and tying him to the cross had made it something else. Still, there was no reason to forget the Lipan woman. No matter if she didn't have a face and no matter what she looked like. And no matter if it was not happening the way it was supposed to happen. The trouble now was, Tanner could stop him before he reached the narrow place, before he reached the good position to talk and make a trade.

No, the trouble was more than that. The trouble was also the woman herself, this woman sitting without speaking anymore, the person he would have to trade. He said in his mind, St. Francis, you were a simple man. Make this goddam thing that's going on simple for me.

"You say you know where you're going," R. L. Davis said. "Tell us so we'll all know."

You don't need him, Valdez thought. He said, "If we get there, you see it. If we don't get there, it doesn't matter, does it?"

"Listen, you know how many men he's got?"

"No so much anymore."

"He's still got enough," R. L. Davis said. "They're going to take you and string you up, if you aren't shot dead before. But either way it's the end of old Bob Valdez."

"How's your head?"

"It still hurts."

"Close your mouth or I make it hurt worse, all right?"

"I helped you," R. L. Davis said. "You owe me something. I could have left you out there, but being a white man I went back and cut you loose."

"What do you want?" Valdez asked.

"What do you think? I cut you loose, you cut me loose and let me go."

Valdez nodded slowly. "All right. When we leave."

Davis looked at him hard. "You mean it?"

Valdez felt the Erin woman looking at him also. "As you say, I owe it to you."

"It's not some kind of trick?"

"How could it be a trick?"

"I don't know, I just don't trust you."

Valdez shrugged. "If you're free, what difference does it make?"

"You're cooking something up," R. L. Davis said.

"No." Valdez shook his head. "I only want you to do me a favor."

"What's that?"

"Give Mr. Tanner a message from me. Tell him he has to pay the Lipan, but now I'm not sure I give him back his woman."

He felt her staring at him again, but he looked out into the darkness thinking about what he had said, realizing that it was all much simpler in his mind now.

It was two o'clock in the morning when Valdez and the Erin woman moved out leading Davis's bareback sorrel horse. They left Davis tied to his saddle with his own bandana knotted around his mouth. As Valdez tied it behind his head, Davis twisted his neck, pushing out his jaw.

"You gag me I won't be able to yell for help!"

"Very good," Valdez said.

"They might not find me!"

"What's certain in life?" Valdez asked. He got the bandana

between Davis's teeth and tightened it, making the knot. "There. When it's light stand up and carry your saddle down the hill. They'll find you."

He would have liked to hit Davis once with his fist. Maybe twice. Two good ones in the mouth. But he'd let it go; he'd cut him fairly good with the Remington. Mr. R. L. Davis was lucky.

Now a little luck of your own, Valdez thought.

They walked the horses through the darkness with ridges and shadowed rock formations above them, Valdez leading the way and taking his time, moving with the clear sound of the horses on broken rock and stopping to listen in the night silence. Once, in the hours they traveled before dawn, they heard a single gunshot, a thin sound in the distance, somewhere to the east; then an answering shot far behind them. Tanner's men firing at shadows, or locating one another. But they heard no sounds close to them that could have been Tanner's riders. Maybe you're having some more luck and you'll get through, Valdez thought. Maybe St. Francis listened and he's making it easier. Hey, Valdez said. Keep Sister Moon behind the clouds so they don't see us. They moved through the night until a faint glow began to wash the sky and the ground shadows became diffused and the shapes of the rock formations and trees were more difficult to see. The moment before dawn when the Apache came through the brush with bear grass in his headband and you didn't see him until he was on you. The time when it was no longer night, but not yet morning. A time to rest, Valdez thought.

They moved into a canyon, between walls that rose steeply and were darkly shadowed with brush. Valdez knew the place and the horses snorted and threw their heads when they smelled the water, the pool of it lying still, undercutting one side of the canyon.

The Erin woman moved around the pool while Valdez stripped off the bridles and saddles to let the horses drink and graze freely. He watched her, looking past the horses, watched her kneel down at the edge of the water and drink from her cupped hands. Valdez took off his hat and slipped the heavy Sharps cartridge belt over his head. A time to rest at dawn, before the day brought whatever it would bring. He moved around the pool toward her.

"Are you hungry?"

She looked up at him, shaking her head, then brushing her hair from her face. "No, not really. Are you?"

"I can wait."

"Are you going to sit down?"

"If you're not going to stand up," Valdez said. He went down next to her, touching her hair, feeling his finger brush her cheek and seeing her eyes on him.

He said, "Gay Erin. That's your name, uh? What was it before?"

"Gay Byrnes."

He took her face gently, his palm covering her chin, and kissed her on the mouth. "Gay Erin. That's a good name. You like it?"

"It's my name because I was married to him."

"What do you want to talk about that for?"

"I don't want to talk about it."

"Then don't. Do you know my name?"

"Valdez."

"Roberto Valdez. How do you like Roberto?"

"I think it's fine."

"Or Bob. Which do you like better?"

"Roberto."

"It's Mexican."

"I know it is."

"Listen, I've been thinking about something."

She waited.

"You heard me tell him I don't know if I'm going to give you back or not."

"I told you before," the Erin woman said. "I don't want to go back."

"That's what you told me." Valdez nodded. "All right, I believe you. Do you know why? Because it's easier if I believe you. If I think about you too much, then I don't have time to think about other things."

"What do you think about me?"

"I think I'd like to live with you and be married to you."

She waited. "We've been together two days."

"And two nights," Valdez said. "How long does it take?" He could see her face more clearly now in the dawn light.

Her eyes did not leave his. "You'd marry me?"

"I think I know you well enough."

"I killed my husband."

"I believe you."

"I've been living with Frank Tanner."

"I know that."

"But you want to marry me."

"I think so, yes."

"Tell me why."

"Listen, I don't like this. I don't feel right, but I don't know what else to say. I believe you because I want to believe you. I say to myself, You want her? I say, Yes. Then I say, What if she's lying? And then I say, Goddam, believe her and don't think anymore. Listen, I couldn't do anything to you. I mean if he says, I won't give you the money, shoot her, you think I'd shoot you?"

She shook her head. "No, I didn't think you would."

"So don't worry about that."

"I never have," the Erin woman said. "I may have been feeling sorry for myself, but I didn't lie down with you just because I wanted to be held."

"Why did you then?"

She hesitated again. "I don't know. I wanted to be with you. I still want to be with you. If I'm in love with you then I'm in love with you. I don't know, I've never loved a man before."

"I've never been married," Valdez said.

She took his hand and brought it up to her face. "I haven't either, really."

"Maybe we can talk about it again. When there's time, uh?"

"I hope so," she said.

Believe that, Valdez thought, and don't think about it. He gave her R. L. Davis's Colt revolver and that sealed it. If she was lying to him she could shoot him in the back. She had already killed one man.

Still, it was easier in his mind now. Much easier.

They found R. L. Davis a little after sunup, a hunched-over figure on the brush slope, dragging a saddle and a thin trail of dust. The two men who found him cut him loose. One of them took the saddle and the other pulled R. L. Davis up behind him and they rode double over to where Mr. Tanner had spent the night. He was alone; all the others were still out on scout.

He looked different. Mr. Tanner had not shaved for two or three days, and the collar of his shirt was dirty and curled up. His moustache looked bigger and his face thinner.

R. L. Davis noticed this, though God Almighty, his back ached from dragging the goddam saddle all over the countryside.

"I wouldn't mind a drink of water from somebody."

The rider who'd brought him in was about to hand him a canteen, but Tanner stopped him.

"Wait'll we're through."

"I haven't had no water since last night."

"You won't die," Tanner said. "'Less I see I should kill you."

"Mr. Tanner, look at me. He drew down with that scattergun, like to took my head off."

"Where are they?"

"He let me go about four hours ago and headed south."

"Mrs. Erin was with him?"

"Yes sir."

"How is she?"

"She looks fine to me. I mean I don't think he's mistreated her any."

"God help him," Tanner said. "Did you speak to her?"

"No, he was right there all the time. There wasn't nothing I could say he wouldn't've heard."

"Then she didn't say anything to you."

"No sir. He said something he wanted me to tell you, though."

Tanner waited. "Well, goddam it, go ahead."

"He said, 'Tell him he still has to pay the Indin, but I'm not sure now I'm giving him his woman back.'"

Frank Tanner hit him. He clubbed Davis in the face with his right fist and the man sprawled on his back in the dust.

"I didn't say it—he said it! Them are his words."

"Tell it again."

"I swear it's what he said."

"Tell it!"

"He said you're to pay the Indin, but he wasn't so sure he was going to give you your woman back. Them words exactly."

"Did she say anything?"

"No sir, not a word, the whole time I was there."

"He keep her tied?"

"When she was in the draw, but not when he's around. I mean riding or when he's made camp."

"Why'd he let you go?" Davis hesitated and Tanner said, "I asked you a question."

"Well, I reckon to tell you what he said. There's no other reason I know of."

"God help you if there is," Tanner said.

He was mounting his bay horse, when two riders came in with a string of fresh horses. They had walked all night back to Mimbreño from the place where they had left their dead mounts on the slope.

Tanner looked at R. L. Davis. "Put your saddle on one of them," he said. "I want you present when we run him down."

During the early morning the segundo, whose name was Emilio Avilar but who had been called only segundo for the past six years, found three of his men in the mountain wilderness and signaled them, gathering them in. The men were tired and their horses were worn and needed water. They were ready to head back, and Frank Almighty Tanner could whistle out his ass if he didn't like it. They were paid to drive cattle and freight wagons and shoot *rurales*; they had not signed on to chase a man who'd run off with Tanner's woman. That was his lookout if he couldn't keep her home. After all night in the saddle, it was time to unroll the blankets.

The segundo said, "You think he doesn't want to sleep? Man, he has to stay awake, doesn't he? He got to watch the woman, he got to watch for us. Man, ask him what it's like to be tired."

Two of the riders were American and one Mexican, the Mexican a young man who had been hired only a few months before by the segundo.

One of the Americans said it was none of their business. And the segundo said maybe not, but look, the sooner they caught this crazy man the sooner they could ride to Mexico and have a good time.

"You want some fresh water, uh?" the segundo said. "Don't you think he want some fresh water?"

"If he know where it was," one of the Americans said.

"Listen, when are you going to understand what kind of man he is?" the segundo said. "Sure he's crazy, but he knows what he's doing. You think he come down this way if he don't know there's water? Where it is? He's not that crazy."

"Well, him knowing doesn't help us," the other American said.

The segundo took his hat off and wiped his forehead with his sleeve and set the Sonora hat over his eyes again. He shook his head and said to the man, "Where do I get people like you? You think I work around here six years I don't know where the goddam water is? What kind of segundo doesn't know where the water is?"

"Well, let's go get it," the rider said.

Emilio Avilar, the segundo, smiled. "Sure, I thought that was what you want."

A little later that morning, watering their horses at the pool, the cliffs and sloping canyon walls reflected in the still water, the three riders looked at the segundo and the segundo smiled again. God, there were fresh tracks all over the place close to the bank, two horses and two people: no doubt about it, a man and a woman. They filled their canteens and wiped down their horses and at this moment were willing to follow the segundo anyplace he wanted to go. Hell, let's get him!

"Which way would you go?" the segundo asked.

"Follow their tracks."

"But that take too long," the segundo said. "What if we know where they going?"

"How could you figure that?"

"Two days ago," the segundo said, "he told Señor Tanner to approach the two peaks. You remember?" He lifted his gaze. "We come from a different way now, but there are the two peaks. Why should he change his mind and not go there? The only difference is now he don't have so much time."

The two American riders thought about it and nodded and one of them said, "What's up there?"

The segundo answered, "We find out."

This is all, he thought, watching the three men move out, slouched in their saddles, heads bobbing, sweat staining a column down their spines. No more. He watched them another moment before calling out, "Hey, Tomás!" The riders looked around and the young Mexican he had hired a few months before reined in to wait for him.

In Spanish the segundo said, "You have a ride the other way. Bring Señor Tanner."

The young Mexican picked up his reins, getting ready. "How will I know where to bring him?"

"You'll hear us," the segundo said.

9

THE TWIN peaks reached above them, beyond the slope that was swept with owl clover and cholla brush, beyond the scrub oak and dark mass of timber, stone pinnacles against the sky, close enough to touch in the clean, clear air.

"Up there," Valdez said. "We go through the trees and come out in a canyon. At the end of the canyon is a little trail that goes up through the rocks and passes between the two peaks and down the other side. You stand in there and look straight up and the peaks look like they're moving in the wind."

The Erin woman's eyes were half closed in the glare; she shielded her eyes with her hand.

"Once we go through there, we see if we can make a slide to block the trail," Valdez said. "Then we don't hurry anymore. We take our time because it takes them a few days to find a way around."

Her gaze lowered and she looked at him now. "A few days. Is that all we'll have?"

"It's up to us," Valdez said. "Or it's up to him. We can go to Mexico. We can go to China if there's a way to go there. Or we can go to Lanoria."

"Where do you want to go?" she asked him.

"To Lanoria."

"He'll come for us."

"If he wants to," Valdez said. "I run today, but not forever. Today is enough."

"Whatever you want to do," the Erin woman said, "I want to do."

Valdez looked at her and wanted to reach over to touch her hair and feel the skin of her sun-darkened cheek and move the tips of his fingers gently over her cracked lips. But he kept his hand in his lap, around the slender neck of the Remington.

He said, "If you want to go back now, you can. I let you go, you're free. Go wherever you want. Tell him you got away from me."

Next to him, sitting in their saddles, their legs almost touching, she said again, "Whatever you want to do."

"We'll go," he said, reaching back and flicking the rope that trailed from his saddle to R. L. Davis's sorrel horse.

They left the trail and started up across the slope on an angle, moving through the owl clover and around the cholla bushes that were like dwarf trees, Valdez leading, aware of the woman behind him, wanting to turn to look at her, but only glancing at her as his gaze swept the hillside and back the way they had come.

Roberto Valdez kept watch up the slope and Bob Valdez, inside him, pictured the woman coming out of an adobe into the front yard: a place like Diego Luz's, alone in the high country, but larger than Diego's, with glass in the windows and a plank front porch beneath the ramada. The woman in a white dress open at the throat and her hair hanging below her shoulders, her hair shining in the sunlight. He would be coming up from the horse pasture and see her and she would raise her arm to wave. God, he would like to ride up to her, twisting out of the saddle, and take hold of her with her arm still raised, his hands moving under her arms and around her and hold her as tightly as a man can hold a woman without injuring her. But he would stop at the pump and have a drink of water and wash himself and then go to the yard, walking his horse, because he would have the rest of his life to do this.

As Bob Valdez pictured this, finally reaching the yard and the woman, Roberto Valdez saw the riders far below them starting across the slope in single file. Six of them and three horses in a string.

Valdez took the field glasses from his saddlebag. He picked out Frank Tanner and R. L. Davis. He saw them looking up this way and saw one of the men pointing, saying something.

Come on, Valdez thought, as they spread apart now and spurred their horses up through the brush. When you get here we'll be gone. But still watching them, counting them again, he thought, If Tanner is here, where is his segundo?

Emilio Avilar watched from above, from the shadowed edge of the timber.

They had the man almost in their sights, Valdez coming across the slope through the scrub oak, leading the horse and the woman behind him, coming at a walk and angling directly toward them, walking into their guns, and now Tanner the Almighty, the white barbarian, had ruined the ambush and was running him again.

God, the man would have been dead in a moment, shot out of his saddle, but now with the woman behind him, kicking their mounts straight up the grade, Valdez had reached the top of the slope and was entering the timber. Not here, where the segundo had waited with his two Americans for almost an hour, but more than a hundred yards away: a last glimpse of Valdez and the woman disappearing into the trees.

The segundo had scouted the timber and the canyon beyond, studying the canyon and the narrow defile at the end of it, and known at once Valdez was coming here. Where else? This man knew the ground and the water sinks and fought like an Apache. Sure Valdez was coming here: to escape through the defile or to stand in it and shoot them one at a time as they came for him.

Don't let him get in the canyon, the segundo had thought. Don't take a chance with him. Wait for him at the canyon mouth and shoot him as he enters. But Valdez would be coming through the cover of the trees and maybe his nose or his ears would tell him something, warn him, and he would run off another way. You have to think of him as you would a mountain lion, the segundo thought. Trap him in the open, away from cover.

So the segundo had gone back through the timber to the edge overlooking the slope and had told his two men very carefully what they would do: how they would watch for him, then study his angle of approach from the cover of the trees, and be waiting for him to walk into it, waiting until he was close to the trees but still in the open, and kill him before he saw them.

But now Valdez was already in the timber. The segundo had told his men to be quiet and keep their horses quiet and listen.

One of them said, "You know he's going for the canyon."

"He reached it, that's all," the other one said. "Once he gets in the hole ain't nobody going in after him."

"Not this child," the first man said. "Tanner can go in himself he wants him so bad."

Christ Jesus, the segundo said to himself. "Will you be quiet!"

They listened.

"I don't hear him," one of them said. "I don't hear a sound."

The segundo drew the two men closer to him, listening, and they listened with him. "Do you know why?" he said. "Because he's not moving, he's listening. He knows we're in here with him."

"He didn't see us."

"When are you going to know him?" the segundo said. "He doesn't have to see you."

"He's got to move sometime," one of them said.

The segundo nodded. "Before Tanner and the others come up. All right, we separate, spread out a little. But all of us move toward the canyon." His voice dropped to a hushed tone. "Very quietly."

There were open patches where sunlight streaked through the pine branches a hundred feet above, and there were thickets of scrub oak and dense brush. There was an occasional sound close to them, a small scurrying sound in the brush, and there were the shrill faraway cries of unseen birds in the treetops. The birds would stop and in the shadowed forest, high in the Santa Ritas, a silence would settle.

They moved deep into the trees from the open slope before Valdez brought them up to listen. And as he listened he thought, You should have kept going and taken the chance. You don't have time to wait.

He heard the sound through the trees, a twig snapping, then silence. In a moment he heard it again and the sound of movement in dead leaves.

He was right, some of them were already in the trees. But it did no good to be right this time. They should have kept going and not stopped. They weren't going to sneak through and keep running, and now he wondered if the woman should go first or follow him. Follow him through the trees and in the open, if they reached the canyon, then first into the defile while he held them off. He couldn't remember the distance to the canyon. Perhaps fifty yards, a little more. He was certain of the general direction, the way they would point and keep going.

He said to the woman, "The last time we run. Are you ready?"

She nodded once, up and down. Both of her hands were on her saddle horn, but she didn't seem tense or to be holding on.

"I go first," Valdez said. He nodded in the direction. "That way. You come behind me. Don't go another way around the trees, keep behind me. If you see them in front of us, stay close to me, as close as you can. At the end of the canyon you'll see the opening. You go in first. Don't get off, ride in—it's wide enough—and I'll come in after you."

She nodded again. "All right."

He smiled at her. "Just a little ride, it's over."

She nodded again and tried to smile and now he saw she was afraid.

Valdez dismounted. He untied the sorrel, moving it aside, holding the bridle under the horse's muzzle. As soon as Tanner's men entered the trees he would send the sorrel galloping off and hope they would take off after its sound. He waited, telling Tanner's men to hurry so he would hear them soon; and when it came, moments later, the sound of their horses rushing into the timber, he hissed into the sorrel's ear, yanking the bridle and slapping the Remington hard across the horse's rump as it jumped to a start and ran off through the trees.

"Now," Valdez said.

They were moving, running through the shafts of sunlight and darkness with the beating, breathing sound of the horses and the tree branches cutting at their faces, running through the brush, through the wall of leaves and snapping branches and through a clearing into trees again, now hearing Tanner's men calling out somewhere behind and somewhere off in the timber. Valdez could see the canyon ahead through the foliage, the open mouth of the meadow, the rock escarpment slanting to the sky.

He saw the opening and he saw a rider slash out of the trees in front of him and come around, his horse rearing with the sudden motion. Valdez broke out of the trees straight for the rider, seeing him broadside now and kicking his mount. He bore down on the man, raising the Remington in front of him, and at point-blank range blew the man off the back of his horse.

He was aware of horses behind him and felt the next man before he saw him or heard him coming up on the left. He switched the Remington to that hand, extending it at arm's length, and when he looked, he fired as the rider fired and saw the man go out of his saddle. The man's horse kept running, racing him, and now he felt the wind in the open and saw the sun balanced on the west rim of the escarpment and heard the Erin woman's horse holding close behind him.

A high whine sang through the narrows as a rifle opened up on him. He remembered the sound of gunfire in the canyon from a time before. He remembered the shadowed crevices high on the walls and the thick gama grass. But he remembered the meadow longer than this, a half mile long in his mind. Now it was not half that distance and he was almost to the end.

Another rifle shot sang out as he reached the defile and came around.

The woman would be there, behind him, and ride in and he would follow her.

But the horse that came behind him was riderless.

The horse veered off, seeing the canyon wall. As it moved out of the way, Valdez saw her: she was about thirty yards from him, her horse was down, and she was rising to her feet, holding her head with both hands and looking at the dead horse.

He saw the segundo close beyond her, dismounting and coming up with a rifle in his hands. Valdez wanted to call out to her, "Run! Come on, do it!" But it was too late. The segundo came on, walking through the gama grass with the rifle in his right hand, his finger through the trigger guard. He stopped before reaching the Erin woman.

Valdez loaded the Remington—not thinking about it, but loading it because it was empty and saying to the segundo with his gaze, You want to do something, come on, do it. He was tired, God, at the end of it, but this is what he was saying to the segundo. With the Remington loaded and cocked he walked out to the woman.

She stood with one hand covering the side of her face, dirt and pieces of grass on her dress and in her hair, as she watched Valdez coming. She looked tired and still afraid, her eyes dull and without question or hope.

"Almost, uh?" Valdez said.

"Almost," the Erin woman said.

"Are you all right?" She nodded and he said then, "You don't have to go back with him. Remember that."

A look of awareness came into her eyes, as if she had been suddenly awakened from sleep. "Don't say that."

"It has to be said."

"I go with you. I don't go with him."

"Frank Tanner doesn't know that." Valdez paused. He said then, "Frank," smiling with the weariness etched in his face. "Francisco. Francis. I have a friend named Francis. I don't know what happened to him."

He laughed out loud and saw the startled look come over her and saw the segundo looking at him.

He heard his own laughter again in the canyon and at the far end saw Frank Tanner and men on both sides of him coming out into the meadow. He saw Tanner stop, looking this way.

Gay Erin touched his arm, holding on to it. He said to her, "I don't know why I thought it was funny. This Frank and my friend having the same name. They're not much alike." He smiled, still thinking of it, and watched the segundo approach, the segundo staring at him, trying to understand what would make him laugh.

With his left hand Emilio Avilar raised his hat and wiped his forehead with the same hand and put his hat on again. He said to Valdez, "You have tobacco? For chewing?"

"Cigarette," Valdez said.

The segundo nodded. "All right."

Valdez brought the sack and paper out of his pocket and moved toward the segundo, who stepped forward to meet him. The segundo rolled a cigarette and returned the sack to Valdez, who made one for himself, and the segundo lighted the cigarettes. Valdez stepped back, the cigarette in his mouth, the Remington in his right hand, pointed down.

The segundo said, blowing out smoke and shaking the match, "Tell me something—who you are."

"What difference does it make?" Valdez answered. He looked beyond the segundo to Tanner coming up with his men spread behind him.

"You hit one yesterday," the segundo said. "I think five hundred yards."

"Six hundred," Valdez said.

"What was it you use?"

"Sharps."

"I thought some goddam buffalo gun. You hunt buffalo?"

"Apache," Valdez said.

"Man, I know it. When?"

"When they were here."

"You leave any alive?"

"Some. In Oklahoma now."

"Goddam, you do it," the segundo said. "You know how many of mine you kill?"

"Twelve," Valdez said.

"You count them."

"You better, uh?" Valdez said.

The segundo drew deeply on the cigarette and exhaled slowly. He was looking at Valdez and thinking, How would you like about four of him? All the rest of them could go home. Four of him and no Tanner and they could drive cattle to Mexico and become rich. And then he was thinking, Who would you rather shoot, him or Tanner? It was too bad the two of them couldn't trade places. Tanner liked to put people against the wall. This one knew how to do it. He didn't need a wall. He could kill a man at six hundred yards, and the son of a bitch kept count.

"It's too bad it turns out like this," the segundo said.

"Well," Valdez shrugged. "It will be settled now. It will be finished."

The segundo continued to study him. "Why don't you give him his woman. Tell him you won't do it again."

"It's not his woman now."

The segundo smiled. "Like that."

"Sure, it's up to him. He wants her back, he has to take her."

"You think he can't do it?"

Valdez shrugged again. "If he tries, he's dead. Somebody will get me, there are enough of you. But he still will be dead."

"He don't think that way," the segundo said.

Valdez held his gaze. "What do you think?"

"I believe it." The segundo saw Valdez's gaze lift and he moved to the side, looking over his shoulder to see Frank Tanner coming toward them. The segundo backed away several more steps, but Tanner stopped before reaching him. He was holding a Colt revolver at his side. A man behind Tanner took his horse, and the rest of the men, five of them, spread out, moving to both sides, keeping their eyes on Valdez. R. L. Davis was next to Tanner, a few feet to his right.

Tanner was looking at the Erin woman, who had not moved as he approached. He stared at her and his expression showed nothing, but he was making up his mind.

He said finally, "Come over here next to me."

The woman made no move. "I'm all right where I am."

"You better start thinking straight," Tanner said. "You better have something to tell me when we get home."

"I'm not going home with you."

Tanner took his time. "That's how it is, huh?" His gaze shifted to Valdez. "She better than a Mexican bitch?"

Valdez said nothing.

"If that's how it is, you better tell that whore next to you go get out of the way."

Quietly, Valdez said to her, "Move over a little. Just a little."

Tanner waited. "Have you got something you want to say to me?"

"I've said it," Valdez answered.

Tanner's eyes held on Valdez. He said, "Put this man against the wall over there and shoot him."

He waited and said then, "Emilio!"

"I hear you," the segundo said.

"Take him."

The segundo did not make a move or seem about to speak.

"Number two"—Tanner's voice rose—"I'm telling you something!"

The segundo looked at Tanner now, directly at him. He said, "It's not my woman."

Valdez's eyes shifted to the man, hung there, and returned to Tanner. His hand gripped the Remington lightly, feeling the weight of the gun, the sawed-off barrel hanging at his knee.

Tanner turned his head slowly to the left, to the three men standing off from him, then to the right, to R. L. Davis and the two men beyond him.

"I'm going to give the word," Tanner said.

"Wait a minute!" R. L. Davis said. "I'm no part of this." He saw Tanner looking at him as he edged back a few steps, bumping against his horse and pushing it. "I don't even have a gun."

"I give you mine," the segundo said.

"I don't want one!" Davis was edging back, taking himself out of the group, his eyes holding on the Remington at Valdez's side. "I don't have any fight with him."

In Spanish, the segundo said to the young Mexican on Tanner's left, "Tomás, go home. This isn't yours."

The young man wasn't sure. "I work for him," he said.

"Not anymore. I let you go."

Tanner's head jerked toward the segundo. "What're you telling him?"

"That she's your woman," the segundo said easily. "A man holds his woman or he doesn't. It's up to him, a personal thing between him and the man who took the woman. All these men are thinking, What have we got to do with it?"

"You do what I tell you. That's what you've got to do with it." Tanner glanced both ways and said, "I'm talking to everybody present. Everybody hears me and I'm telling you now to shoot him. Now!"

He looked at his men again, not believing it, seeing them standing watching him, none of them ready to make a move.

"You hear me—I said shoot him!"

Valdez waited in the silence that followed. He waited as Tanner looked at his men, from one to the next. He drew on the cigarette, finishing it, and dropped it and said, "Hey."

As Tanner turned to him, Valdez said, "I got an idea, Frank," and waited another moment. "You have a gun in your hand. Why don't you shoot me?"

Tanner faced him, the Colt revolver at his side. He stared at Valdez and said nothing, eyes sunken in the shadow of his hat brim, dusty and beard stubbled, still looking like he was made of gristle and hard to kill.

But he's not looking at himself, Valdez was thinking, and it isn't an easy thing to raise and fire a Colt at someone. So he jabbed at Tanner saying, "See if your gun is as good as mine. What do you think of something like that? You and I, that's all, uh? What do you need anybody else for?"

Tanner stood stiffly, no part of him moving.

"Let me say it to you this way," Valdez said. "You give me money for the Lipan woman whose husband was killed or you use the gun. One or the other, right now. Make up your mind."

Tanner's hand tightened on the Colt and his thumb lifted to the hammer. He could feel the move he would make and he was looking squarely at Valdez twenty feet away from him, looking at him dead center where the cartridge belt crossed his chest. The moment was there, *now*, but his gaze flickered to the stubby barrel of the Remington and lingered there and the moment was past. His thumb came off the hammer.

"Not today," Tanner said. "Another time."

Valdez shook his head slowly. "No, that was your time. You get one time, mister, to prove who you are."

"I should have killed you three days ago," Tanner said. "I should have killed you, but I let you go."

"No"—the segundo started past him toward the horses, pausing to take the Colt from Tanner's hand—"three days ago you should have started for Mexico."

"Or paid the Lipan woman," Valdez said. "It wouldn't have cost you so much."

FORTY LASHES
LESS ONE

1

THE TRAIN was late and didn't get into Yuma until after dark. Then the ticket agent at the depot had to telephone the prison and tell them they had better get some transportation down here. He had three people waiting on a ride up the hill: a man he had never seen before who said he was the new prison superintendent, and another man he knew was a deputy sheriff from Pima County and he had a prisoner with him, handcuffed, a big colored boy.

Whoever it was on the phone up at the prison said they had sent a man two hours ago and if the train had been on time he would have met them. The ticket agent said well, they were here now and somebody better hurry with the transportation, because the Southern Pacific didn't care for convicts hanging around the depot, even if the boy was handcuffed.

The Pima deputy said hell, it wasn't anything new; every time he delivered a man he had to sit and wait on the prison people to get off their ass. He asked the big colored boy if he minded waiting, sitting in a nice warm train depot, or would he rather be up there in one of them carved-out cells with the wind whistling in across the river? The Pima deputy said something about sweating all day and freezing at night; but the colored boy, whose name was Harold Jackson, didn't seem to be listening.

The new prison superintendent—the new, temporary superintendent—Mr. Everett Manly, heard him. He nodded, and adjusted his gold-frame glasses. He said yes, he was certainly familiar with Arizona winters, having spent seven years at the Chiricahua Apache Mission School. Mr. Manly heard himself speak and it sounded all right. It sounded natural.

On the train Mr. Manly had exchanged a few words with the deputy, but had not spoken to the colored boy. He could have asked him his name and where he was from; he could have asked him about his sentence and told him that if he behaved himself he would be treated fairly. He could have asked him if he wanted to pray. But with the Pima deputy sitting next to the colored boy—all afternoon and evening on the wicker

seats, bumping and swaying, looking out at the sun haze on
the desert and the distant, dark brown mountains—Mr. Manly
had not been able to get the first words out, to start a conversation. He was not afraid of the colored boy, who could have
been a cold-blooded killer for all he knew. It was the idea of
the deputy sitting there listening that bothered him.

He thought about starting a friendly conversation with the
ticket agent: ask him if he ever got up to the prison, or if he
knew the superintendent, Mr. Rynning, who was in Florence
at the present time seeing to the construction of the new
penitentiary. He could say, "Well, it won't be long now, there
won't be any more Yuma Territorial Prison," and kidding, add,
"I suppose you'll be sorry to see it closed." Except maybe he
wasn't supposed to talk about it in idle conversation. It had
been mentioned in newspapers—"Hell-Hole on the Bluff to
Open Its Doors Forever by the Spring of 1909"—pretty clever,
saying opening its doors instead of closing them. And no doubt
the station agent knew all about it. Living here he would have
to. But a harmless conversation could start false rumors and
speculation, and before you knew it somebody from the Bureau
would write and ask how come he was going around telling
everybody about official government business.

If the ticket agent brought up the subject that would be different. He could be noncommittal. "You heard the old prison's
closing, huh? Well, after thirty-three years I imagine you won't
be too sorry to see it happen." But the ticket agent didn't bring
up the subject.

A little while later they heard the noise outside. The ticket
agent looked at them through his barred window and said,
"There's a motor conveyance pulling into the yard I reckon is
for you people."

Mr. Manly had never ridden in an automobile before. He asked
the driver what kind it was and the driver told him it was a
twenty-horsepower Ford Touring Car, powerful and speedy,
belonged to the superintendent, Mr. Rynning. It was comfortable, Mr. Manly said, but kind of noisy, wasn't it? He wanted
to ask how much a motor rig like this cost, but there was the
prison above him: the walls and the guard towers against the
night sky, the towers, like little houses with pointed roofs;

dark houses, nobody home. When the gravel road turned and climbed close along the south wall, Mr. Manly had to look almost straight up, and he said to the guard driving the car, "I didn't picture the walls so high." And the guard answered, "Eighteen feet up and eight feet thick. A man can't jump it and he can't bore through neither."

"My last trip up this goddamn rock pile," the Pima deputy said, sitting in the back seat with his prisoner. "I'm going to the railroad hotel and get me a bottle of whiskey and in the morning I'm taking the train home and ain't never coming back here again."

The rest of the way up the hill Mr. Manly said nothing. He would remember this night and the strange feeling of riding in a car up Prison Hill, up close to this great silent mound of adobe and granite. Yuma Territorial Prison, that he had heard stories about for years—that he could almost reach out and touch. But was it like a prison? More like a tomb of an ancient king, Mr. Manly was thinking. A pyramid. A ghostly monument. Or, if it was a prison, then one that was already deserted. Inside the walls there were more than a hundred men. Maybe a hundred and fifty counting the guards. But there was no sound or sign of life, only this motor car putt-putting up the hill, taking forever to reach the top.

What if it did take forever, Mr. Manly thought. What if they kept going and going and never reached the prison gate, but kept moving up into stoney darkness for all eternity—until the four of them realized this was God's judgment upon them. (He could hear the Pima deputy cursing and saying, "Now, wait a minute, I'm just here to deliver a prisoner!") It could happen this way, Mr. Manly thought. Who said you had to die first? Or, how did a person know when he was dead? Maybe he had died on the train. He had dozed off and opened his eyes as they were pulling into the depot—

A man sixty years old could die in his sleep. But—and here was the question—if he was dead and this was happening, why would he be condemned to darkness? What had he done wrong in his life?

Not even thinking about it very hard, he answered at once, though quietly: What have you done right? Sixty years of life, Mr. Manly thought. Thirty years as a preacher of the Holy

Word, seven years as a missionary among pagan Indians. Half his life spent in God's service, and he was not sure he had converted even one soul to the Light of Truth.

They reached the top of the bluff at the west end of the prison and, coming around the corner, Mr. Manly saw the buildings that were set back from the main gate, dim shapes and cold yellow lights that framed windows and reflected on the hard-packed yard. He was aware of the buildings and thought briefly of an army post, single- and two-story structures with peaked roofs and neatly painted verandas. He heard the driver point out the guard's mess and recreation hall, the arsenal, the stable, the storehouses; he heard him say, "If you're staying in the sup'rintendent's cottage, it's over yonder by the trees."

Mr. Manly was familiar with government buildings in clean-swept areas. He had seen them at the San Carlos reservation and at Fort Huachuca and at the Indian School. He was staring at the prison wall where a single light showed the main gate as an oval cavern in the pale stone, a dark tunnel entrance crisscrossed with strips of iron.

The driver looked at Mr. Manly. After a moment he said, "The sally port. It's the only way in and, I guarantee, the only way out."

Bob Fisher, the turnkey, stood waiting back of the inner gate with two of his guards. He seemed either patient or half asleep, a solemn-looking man with a heavy, drooping mustache. He didn't have them open the iron lattice door until Mr. Manly and the Pima deputy and his prisoner were within the dark enclosure of the sally port and the outer gate was bolted and locked behind them. Then he gave a sign to open up and waited for them to step into the yard light.

The Pima deputy was pulling a folded sheaf of papers out of his coat pocket, dragging along his handcuffed prisoner. "I got a boy name of Harold Jackson wants to live with you the next fifteen years." He handed the papers to the turnkey and fished in his pants pocket for the keys to the handcuffs.

Bob Fisher unfolded the papers close to his stomach and glanced at the first sheet. "We'll take care of him," he said, and folded the papers again.

Mr. Manly stood by waiting, holding his suitcase.

"I'll tell you what," the Pima deputy said. "I'll let you buy me a cup of coffee 'fore I head back."

"We'll see if we got any," Fisher said.

The Pima deputy had removed the handcuffs from the prisoner and was slipping them into his coat pocket. "I don't want to put you to any trouble," he said. "Jesus, a nice friendly person like you."

"You won't put us to any trouble," Fisher answered. His voice was low, and he seemed to put no effort or feeling into his words.

Mr. Manly kept waiting for the turnkey to notice him and greet him and have one of the guards take his suitcase; but the man stood at the edge of the yard light and didn't seem to look at any of them directly, though maybe he was looking at the prisoner, telling him with the sound of his voice that he didn't kid with anybody. What does he look like, Mr. Manly was thinking. He lowered his suitcase to the ground.

A street car motorman, that was it. With his gray guard uniform and gray uniform hat, the black shiny peak straight over his eyes. A tough old motorman with a sour stomach and a sour outlook from living within the confinement of a prison too many years. A man who never spoke if he didn't have to and only smiled about twice a year. The way the man's big mustache covered the sides of his mouth it would be hard to tell if he ever smiled at all.

Bob Fisher told one of the guards to take the Pima deputy over to the mess hall, then changed his mind and said no, take him outside to the guard's mess. The Pima deputy shrugged; he didn't care where he got his coffee. He took time to look at Mr. Manly and say, "Good luck, mister." As Mr. Manly said, "Good luck to you too," not looking at the turnkey now but feeling him there, the Pima deputy turned his back on them; he waited to get through the double gates and was gone.

"My name is Everett Manly," Mr. Manly said. "I expect—"

But Fisher wasn't ready for him yet. He motioned to the guards and watched as they led the prisoner off toward a low, one-room adobe. Mr. Manly waited, also watching them. He could see the shapes of buildings in the darkness of the yard, here and there a light fixed above a doorway. Past the corner of a two-story building, out across the yard, was the massive outline of a long, windowless adobe with a light above its crisscrossed iron door. Probably the main cellblock. But in the darkness he couldn't tell about the other buildings, or make any sense of the prison's layout. He had the feeling again that the place was deserted except for the turnkey and the two guards.

"I understand you've come here to take charge."

All the waiting and the man had surprised him. But all was forgiven, because the man was looking at him now, acknowledging his presence.

"I'm Everett Manly. I expect Mr. Rynning wrote you I was coming. You're—"

"Bob Fisher, turnkey."

Mr. Manly smiled. "I guess you would be the man in charge of the keys." Showing him he had a sense of humor.

"I've been in charge of the whole place since Mr. Rynning's been gone."

"Well, I'm anxious to see everything and get to work." Mr. Manly was being sincere now, and humble. "I'm going to admit though, I haven't had much experience."

In his flat tone, Fisher said, "I understand you haven't had any."

Mr. Manly wished they weren't standing here alone. "No *prison* experience, that's true. But I've dealt with people all my life, Mr. Fisher, and nobody's told me yet convicts aren't people." He smiled again, still humble and willing to learn.

"Nobody will have to tell you," Fisher said. "You'll find out yourself."

He turned and walked off toward the one-room adobe. Mr. Manly had no choice but to pick up his suitcase and follow—Lord, with the awful feeling again and wishing he hadn't put so many books in with his clothes; the suitcase weighed a ton and he probably looked like an idiot walking with quick little steps and the thing banging against his leg. And then he was grateful and felt good again, because Bob Fisher was holding the door open for him and let him go inside first, into the lighted room where the colored boy was jackknifed over a table without any clothes on and the two guards were standing on either side of him.

One of the guards pulled him up and turned him around by the arm as Fisher closed the door. "He's clean," the guard said. "Nothing hid away down him or up him."

"He needs a hosing is all," the other guard said.

Fisher came across the plank floor, his eyes on the prisoner. "He ain't worked up a sweat yet."

"Jesus," the first guard said, "don't get close to him. He stinks to high heaven."

Mr. Manly put down his suitcase. "That's a long dusty train ride, my friend." Then, smiling a little, he added, "I wouldn't mind a bath myself."

The two guards looked over at him, then at Fisher, who was still facing the prisoner. "That's your new boss," Fisher said, "come to take Mr. Rynning's place while he's gone. See he gets all the bath water he wants. This boy here washes tomorrow with the others, after he's put in a day's work."

Mr. Manly said, "I didn't intend that to sound like I'm interfering with your customs or regulations—"

Fisher looked over at him now, waiting.

"I only meant it was sooty and dirty aboard the train."

Fisher waited until he was sure Mr. Manly had nothing more to say. Then he turned his attention to the prisoner again. One of the guards was handing the man a folded uniform and a broad-brimmed sweat-stained hat. Fisher watched him as he put the clothes on the table, shook open the pants and stepped into them: faded, striped gray and white convict pants that were short and barely reached to the man's high-top shoes. While he was buttoning up, Fisher opened the sheaf of papers the Pima deputy had given him, his gaze holding on the first sheet. "It says here you're Harold Jackson."

"Yes-suh, captain."

The Negro came to attention as Fisher looked up, a hint of surprise in his solemn expression. He seemed to study the prisoner more closely now and took his time before saying, "You ain't ever been here before, but you been somewhere. Where was it you served time, boy?"

"Fort Leavenworth, captain."

"You were in the army?"

"Yes-suh, captain."

"I never knew a nigger that was in the army. How long were you in it?"

"Over in Cuba eight months, captain. At Leavenworth four years hard labor."

"Well, they learned you some manners," Fisher said, "but they didn't learn you how to stay out of prison, did they? These papers say you killed a man. Is that right?"

"Yes-suh, captain."

"What'd you kill him with?"

"I hit him with a piece of pipe, captain."

"You robbing him?"

"No-suh, captain, we jes' fighting."

Mr. Manly cleared his throat. The pause held, and he said quickly, "Coming here he never gave the deputy any trouble, not once."

Fisher took his time as he looked around. He said, "I generally talk to a new man and find out who he is or who he believes he is, and we get a few things straightened out at the start." He paused. "If it's all right with you."

"Please go ahead," Mr. Manly said. "I just wanted to say he never acted smart on the trip, or was abusive. I doubt he said more than a couple words."

"That's fine." Fisher nodded patiently before looking at Harold Jackson again. "You're our last nigger," he said to him. "You're the only one we got now, and we want you to be a good boy and work hard and do whatever you're told. Show you we mean it, we're going to help you out at first, give you something to keep you out of trouble."

There was a wooden box underneath the table. Mr. Manly didn't notice it until one of the guards stooped down and, with the rattling sound of chains, brought out a pair of leg-irons and a ball-peen hammer.

Mr. Manly couldn't hold back. "But he hasn't done anything yet!"

"No, sir," Bob Fisher said, "and he ain't about to with chains on his legs." He came over to Mr. Manly and, surprising him, picked up his suitcase and moved him through the door, closing it firmly behind them.

Outside, Fisher paused. "I'll get somebody to tote your bag

over to Mr. Rynning's cottage. I expect you'll be most comfortable there."

"I appreciate it."

"Take your bath if you want one, have something to eat and a night's sleep—there's no sense in showing you around now—all right?"

"What are you going to do to the colored boy?"

"We're going to put him in a cell, if that's all right."

"But the leg-irons."

"He'll wear them a week. See what they feel like."

"I guess I'm just not used to your ways," Mr. Manly said. "I mean prison ways." He could feel the silence again among the darkened stone buildings and high walls. The turnkey walked off toward the empty, lighted area by the main gate. Mr. Manly had to step quickly to catch up with him. "I mean I believe a man should have a chance to prove himself first," he said, "before he's judged."

"They're judged before they get here."

"But putting leg-irons on them—"

"Not all of them. Just the ones I think need them, so they'll know what irons feel like."

Mr. Manly knew what he wanted to say, but he didn't have the right words. "I mean, don't they hurt terrible?"

"I sure hope so," Fisher answered.

As they came to the lighted area, a guard leaning against the iron grill of the gate straightened and adjusted his hat. Fisher let the guard know he had seen him, then stopped and put down the suitcase.

"This Harold Jackson," Fisher said. "Maybe you didn't hear him. He killed a man. He didn't miss Sunday school. He beat a man to death with an iron pipe."

"I know—I heard him."

"That's the kind of people we get here. Lot of them. They come in, we don't know what's on their minds. We don't know if they're going to behave or cause trouble or try and run or try and kill somebody else."

"I understand that part all right."

"Some of them we got to show right away who's running this place."

Mr. Manly was frowning. "But this boy Harold Jackson, he seemed all right. He was polite, said yes-sir to you. Why'd you put leg-irons on him?"

Now it was Fisher's turn to look puzzled. "You saw him same as I did."

"I don't know what you mean."

"I mean he's a nigger, ain't he?"

Looking up at the turnkey, Mr. Manly's gold-frame spectacles glistened in the overhead light. "You're saying that's the only reason you put leg-irons on him?"

"If I could tell all the bad ones," Bob Fisher said, "as easy as I can tell a nigger, I believe I'd be sup'rintendent."

Jesus Christ, the man was even dumber than he looked. He could have told him a few more things: sixteen years at Yuma, nine years as turnkey, and he hadn't seen a nigger yet who didn't need to wear irons or spend some time in the snake den. It was the way they were, either lazy or crazy; you had to beat 'em to make 'em work, or chain 'em to keep 'em in line. He would like to see just one good nigger. Or one good, hardworking Indian for that matter. Or a Mexican you could trust. Or a preacher who knew enough to keep his nose in church and out of other people's business.

Bob Fisher had been told two weeks earlier, in a letter from Mr. Rynning, that an acting superintendent would soon be coming to Yuma.

Mr. Rynning's letter had said: "Not an experienced penal administrator, by the way, but, of all things, a preacher, an ordained minister of the Holy Word Church who has been wrestling with devils in Indians schools for several years and evidently feels qualified to match his strength against convicts. This is not my doing. Mr. Manly's name came to me through the Bureau as someone who, if not eminently qualified, is at least conveniently located and willing to take the job on a temporary basis. (The poor fellow must be desperate. Or, perhaps misplaced and the Bureau doesn't know what else to do with him but send him to prison, out of harm's way.) He has had some administrative experience and, having worked on an Apache reservation, must know something about inventory control and logistics. The bureau insists on an active administrator at Yuma while, in the same breath, they strongly suggest I remain in Florence during the new prison's final stage of preparation. Hence, you will be meeting your new superintendent in the very near future. Knowing you will oblige him with your utmost cooperation I remain . . ."

Mr. Rynning remained in Florence while Bob Fisher remained in Yuma with a Holy Word Pentacostal preacher looking over his shoulder.

The clock on the wall of the superintendent's office said ten after nine. Fisher, behind the big mahogany desk, folded Mr. Rynning's letter and put it in his breast pocket. After seeing Mr. Manly through the gate, he had come up here to pick up his personal file. No sense in leaving anything here if the preacher was going to occupy the office. The little four-eyed son of a bitch, maybe a few days here would scare hell out of him and run him back to Sunday school. Turning in the swivel chair, Fisher could see the reflection of the room in the darkened window glass and could see himself sitting at the desk; with a thumb and first finger he smoothed his mustache and continued to fool with it as he looked at the clock again.

Still ten after nine. He was off duty; had been since six. Had waited two hours for the preacher.

It was too early to go home: his old lady would still be up and he'd have to look at her and listen to her talk for an hour or more. Too early to go home, and too late to watch the two women convicts take their bath in the cook shack. They always finished and were gone by eight-thirty, quarter to nine. He had been looking forward to watching them tonight, especially Norma Davis. Jesus, she had big ones, and a nice round white fanny. The Mexican girl was smaller, like all the Mexican girls he had ever seen; she was all right, though; especially with the soapy water on her brown skin. It was a shame; he hadn't watched them in about four nights. If the train had been on time he could have met the preacher and still got over to the cook shack before eight-thirty. It was like the little son of a bitch's train to be late. There was something about him, something that told Fisher the man couldn't do anything right, and would mess up anything he took part in.

Tomorrow he'd show him around and answer all his dumb questions.

Tonight—he could stare at the clock for an hour and go home.

He could stare out at the empty yard and hope for something to happen. He could pull a surprise inspection of the guard posts, maybe catch somebody sleeping.

He could stop at a saloon on the way home. Or go down to Frank Shelby's cell, No. 14, and buy a pint of tequila off him.

What Bob Fisher did, he pulled out the papers on the new prisoner, Harold Jackson, and started reading about him.

One of the guards asked Harold Jackson if he'd ever worn leg-irons before. Sitting tired, hunch-shouldered on the floor, he said yeah. They looked down at him and he looked up at them, coming full awake but not showing it, and said yes-suh, he believed it was two times. That's all, if the captain didn't count the prison farm. He'd wore irons there because they liked everybody working outside the jail to wear irons. It wasn't on account he had done anything.

The guard said all right, that was enough. They give him a blanket and took him shuffling across the dark yard to the main cell block, then through the iron-cage gate where bare overhead lights showed the stone passageway and the cell doors on both sides. The guards didn't say anything to him. They stopped at Cell No. 8, unlocked the door, pushed him inside, and clanged the ironwork shut behind him.

As their steps faded in the passageway, Harold Jackson could make out two tiers of bunks and feel the closeness of the walls and was aware of a man breathing in his sleep. He wasn't sure how many were in this cell. He let his eyes get used to the darkness before he took a step, then another, the leg chains clinking in the silence. The back wall wasn't three steps away. The bunks, three decks high on both sides of him, were close enough to touch. Which would make this a six-man room, he figured, about eight feet by nine feet. Blanket-covered shapes lay close to him in the middle bunks. He couldn't make out the top ones and didn't want to feel around; but he could see the bottom racks were empty. Harold Jackson squatted on the floor and ducked into the right-side bunk.

The three-tiered bunks and the smell of the place reminded him of the troopship, though it had been awful hot down in the hold. Ten days sweating down in that dark hold while the ship was tied up at Tampa and they wouldn't let any of the Negro troops go ashore, not even to walk the dock and stretch their legs. He never did learn the name of that ship, and he didn't care. When they landed at Siboney, Harold Jackson walked off through the jungle and up into the hills. For two weeks he stayed with a Cuban family and ate sugar cane and got a kick out of how they couldn't speak any English, though they were Negro, same as he was. When he had rested and felt good he returned to the base and they threw him in the stockade. They said he was a deserter. He said he came back, didn't he? They said he was still a deserter.

He had never been in a cell that was this cold. Not even at Leavenworth. Up there in the Kansas winter the cold times were in the exercise yard, stamping your feet and moving to keep warm; the cell was all right, maybe a little cold sometimes. That was a funny thing, most of the jails he remembered as being hot: the prison farm wagon that was like a circus cage and the city jails and the army stockade in Cuba. He'd be sitting on a bench sweating or laying in the rack sweating, slapping mosquitoes, scratching, or watching the cockroaches fooling around and running nowhere. Cockroaches never looked like they knew where they were going. No, the heat was all right. The heat, the bugs were like part of being in jail. The cold was something he would have to get used to. Pretend it was hot. Pretend he was in Cuba. If he had to pick a jail to be in, out of all the places—if somebody said, "You got to go to jail for ten years, but we let you pick the place"—he'd pick the stockade at Siboney. Not because it was a good jail, but because it was in Cuba, and Cuba was a nice-looking place, with the ocean and the trees and plenty of shade. That's a long way away, Harold Jackson said to himself. You ain't going to see it again.

There wasn't any wind. The cold just lay over him and didn't go away. His body was all right; it was his feet and his hands. Harold Jackson rolled to his side to reach down below the leg-irons that dug hard into his ankles and work his shoes off, then put his hands, palms together like he was praying, between the warmth of his legs. There was no use worrying about where he was. He would think of Cuba and go to sleep.

In the morning, in the moments before opening his eyes, he

wasn't sure where he was. He was confused because a minute ago he'd have sworn he'd been holding a piece of sugar cane, the purple peeled back in knife strips and he was sucking, chewing the pulp to draw out the sweet juice. But he wasn't holding any cane now, and he wasn't in Cuba.

The bunk jiggled, strained, and moved back in place as somebody got down from above him. There were sounds of movement in the small cell, at least two men.

"You don't believe it, take a look."

"Jesus Christ," another voice said, a younger voice. "What's he doing in here?"

Both of them white voices. Harold Jackson could feel them standing between the bunks. He opened his eyes a little bit at a time until he was looking at prison-striped legs. It wasn't much lighter in the cell than before, when he'd gone to sleep, but he could see the stripes all right and he knew that outside it was morning.

A pair of legs swung down from the opposite bunk and hung there, wool socks and yellow toenails poking out of holes. "What're you looking at?" this one said, his voice low and heavy with sleep.

"We got a coon in here with us," the younger voice said.

The legs came down and the space was filled with faded, dirty convict stripes. Harold Jackson turned his head a little and raised his eyes. His gaze met theirs as they hunched over to look at him, studying him as if he was something they had never seen before. There was a heavy-boned, beard-stubbled face; a blond baby-boy face; and a skinny, slick-haired face with a big cavalry mustache that drooped over the corners of the man's mouth.

"Somebody made a mistake," the big man said. "In the dark."

"Joe Dean seen him right away."

"I smelled him," the one with the cavalry mustache said.

"Jesus," the younger one said now, "wait till Shelby finds out."

Harold Jackson came out of the bunk, rising slowly, uncoiling and bringing up his shoulders to stand eye to eye with the biggest of the three. He stared at the man's dead-looking deep-set eyes and at the hairs sticking out of a nose that was scarred and one time had been broken. "You gentlemen excuse me," Harold Jackson said, moving past the young boy and the one who was called Joe Dean. He stood with his back to them and aimed at the slop bucket against the wall.

They didn't say anything at first; just stared at him. But as Harold Jackson started to go the younger one murmured, "Jesus Christ—" as if awed, or saying a prayer. He stared at Harold as long as he could, then broke for the door and began yelling through the ironwork, "Guard! Guard! Goddamn it, there's a nigger in here pissing in our toilet!"

2

R AYMOND SAN CARLOS heard the sound of Junior's voice
before he made out the words: somebody yelling—for a
guard. Somebody gone crazy, or afraid of something. Something happening in one of the cells close by. He heard quick
footsteps now, going past, and turned his head enough to look
from his bunk to the door.

It was morning. The electric lights were off in the cell block
and it was dark now, the way a barn with its doors open is
dark. He could hear other voices now and footsteps and, getting louder, the metal-ringing sound of the guards banging
crowbars on the cell doors—good morning, get up and go to
the toilet and put your shoes on and fold your blankets—the
iron clanging coming closer, until it was almost to them and
the convict above Raymond San Carlos yelled, "All right, we
hear you! God Almighty—" The other convict in the cell,
across from him in an upper bunk, said, "I'd like to wake
them sons of bitches up some time." The man above Raymond
said, "Break their goddamn eardrums." The other man said,
"No, I'd empty slop pails on 'em." And the crowbar clanged
against the door and was past them, banging, clanging down
the passageway.

Another guard came along in a few minutes and unlocked
each cell. Raymond was ready by the time he got to them,
standing by the door to be first out. One of the convicts in the
cell poked Raymond in the back and, when he turned around,
pointed to the bucket.

"It ain't my turn," Raymond said.

"If I want you to empty it," the convict said, his partner close
behind him, looking over his shoulder, "then it's your turn."

Raymond shrugged and they stood aside to let him edge past
them. He could argue with them and they could pound his
head against the stone wall and say he fell out of his bunk. He
could pick up the slop bucket and say, "Hey," and when they
turned around he could throw it at them. Thinking about it
afterward would be good, but the getting beat up and pounded
against the wall wouldn't be good. Or they might stick his face

in a bucket. God, he'd get sick, and every time he thought of it after he'd get sick.

He had learned to hold onto himself and think ahead, looking at the good results and the bad results, and decide quickly if doing something was worth it. One time he hadn't held onto himself—the time he worked for the Sedona cattle people up on Oak Creek—and it was the reason he was here.

He had held on at first, for about a year while the other riders—some of them—kidded him about having a fancy name like Raymond San Carlos when he was Apache Indian down to the soles of his feet. Chiricahua Apache, they said. Maybe a little taller than most, but look at them black beady eyes and the flat nose. Pure Indin.

The Sedona hands got tired of it after a while; all except two boys who wouldn't leave him alone: a boy named Buzz Moore and another one they called Eljay. They kept at him every day. One of them would say, "What's that in his hair?" and pretend to pick something out, holding it between two fingers and studying it closely. "Why, it's some fuzz off a turkey feather, must have got stuck there from his headdress." Sometimes when it was hot and dry one of these two would look up at the sky and say, "Hey, chief, commence dancing and see if you can get us some rain down here." They asked him if he ever thought about white women, which he would never in his life ever get to have. They'd drink whiskey in front of him and not give him any, saying it was against the law to give an Indian firewater. Things like that.

At first it hadn't been too hard to hold on and go along with the kidding. Riding for Sedona was a good job, and worth it. Raymond would usually grin and say nothing. A couple of times he tried to tell them he was American and only his name was Mexican. He had made up what he thought was a pretty good story.

"See, my father's name was Armando de San Carlos y Zamora. He was born in Mexico, I don't know where, but I know he come up here to find work and that's when he met my mother who's an American, Maria Ramirez, and they got married. So when I'm born here, I'm American too."

He remembered Buzz Moore saying, "Maria Ramirez? What kind of American name is that?"

The other one, Eljay, who never let him alone, said, "So, are Apache Indins American if you want to call everybody who's born in this country American. But anybody knows Indins ain't citizens. And if you ain't a citizen, you ain't American." He said to Raymond, "You ever vote?"

"I ain't never been where there was anything to vote about," Raymond answered.

"You go to school?"

"A couple of years."

"Then you don't know anything about what is a U. S. citizen. Can you read and write?"

Raymond shook his head.

"There you are," Eljay said.

Buzz Moore said then, "His daddy could have been Indin. They got Indins in Mexico like anywhere else. Why old Geronimo himself lived down there and could have sired a whole tribe of little Indins."

And Eljay said, "You want to know the simple truth? He's Chiricahua Apache, born and reared on the San Carlos Indin reservation, and that's how he got his fancy name. Made it up so people wouldn't think he was Indin."

"Well," Buzz Moore said, "he could be some part Mexican."

"If that's so," Eljay said, "what we got here is a red greaser."

They got a kick out of that and called him the red greaser through the winter and into April—until the day up in the high meadows they were gathering spring calves and their mammas and chasing them down to the valley graze. They were using revolvers and shotguns part of the time to scare the stock out of the brush stands and box canyons and keep them moving. Raymond remembered the feel of the 12-gauge Remington, holding it pointed up with the stock tight against his thigh. He would fire it this way when he was chasing stock—aiming straight up—and would feel the Remington kick against his leg. He kept off by himself most of the day, enjoying the good feeling of being alone in high country. He remembered the day vividly: the clean line of the peaks towering against the sky, the shadowed canyons and the slopes spotted yellow with arrowroot blossoms. He liked the silence; he liked being here alone and not having to think about anything or talk to anybody.

It wasn't until the end of the day he realized how sore his

leg was from the shotgun butt punching it. Raymond swung down off the sorrel he'd been riding and limped noticeably as he walked toward the cook fire. Eljay was standing there. Eljay took one look and said, "Hey, greaser, is that some kind of one-legged Indin dance you're doing?" Raymond stopped. He raised the Remington and shot Eljay square in the chest with both loads.

On this morning in February, 1909, as he picked up the slop bucket and followed his two cellmates out into the passageway, Raymond had served almost four years of a life sentence for second-degree murder.

The guard, R. E. Baylis, didn't lay his crowbar against No. 14, the last door at the east end of the cellblock. He opened the door and stepped inside and waited for Frank Shelby to look up from his bunk.

"You need to be on the supply detail today?" R. E. Baylis asked,

"What's today?"

"Tuesday."

"Tomorrow," Shelby said. "What's it like out?"

"Bright and fair, going to be warm."

"Put me on an outside detail."

"We got a party building a wall over by the cemetery."

"Hauling the bricks?"

"Bricks already there."

"That'll be all right," Shelby said. He sat up, swinging his legs over the side of the bunk. He was alone in the cell, in the upper of a double bunk. The triple bunk opposite him was stacked with cardboard boxes and a wooden crate and a few canvas sacks. A shelf and mirror hung from the back wall. There was also a chair by the wall with a hole cut out of the seat and a bucket underneath. A roll of toilet paper rested on one of the arms. The convicts called the chair Shelby's throne. "Get somebody to empty the bucket, will you?" Looking at the guard again, Shelby said, "You need anything?"

R. E. Baylis touched his breast pocket. "Well, I guess I could use some chew."

"Box right by your head," Shelby said. "I got Mail Pouch and Red Man. Or I got some Copenhagen if you want."

R. E. Baylis fished a hand in the box. "I might as well take a couple—case I don't see you again today."

"You know where to find me." Shelby dropped to the floor, pulled on half-boots, hopping a couple of times to keep his balance, then ran a hand through his dark hair as he straightened up, standing now in his boots and long underwear. "I believe I was supposed to get a clean outfit today."

"Washing machine broke down yesterday."

"Tomorrow then for sure, uh?" Shelby had an easy, unhurried way of talking. It was known that he never raised his voice or got excited. They said the way you told if he was mad or irritated, he would fool with his mustache; he would keep smoothing it down with two fingers until he decided what had to be done and either did it himself or had somebody else do it. Frank Shelby was serving forty-five years for armed robbery and second-degree murder and had brought three of his men with him to Yuma, each of them found guilty on the same counts and serving thirty years apiece.

Junior was one of them. He banged through the cell door as Shelby was getting into his prison stripes, buttoning his coat. "You got your mean go-to-hell look on this morning," Shelby said. "Was that you yelling just now?"

"They stuck a nigger in our cell last night while we was asleep." Junior turned to nail the guard with his look, putting the blame on him.

"It wasn't me," R. E. Baylis said. "I just come on duty."

"You don't throw his black ass out, we will," Junior said. By Jesus, this was Worley Lewis, Jr. talking, nineteen-year-old convict going on forty-nine before he would ever see the outside of a penitentiary, but he was one of Frank Shelby's own and that said he could stand up to a guard and mouth him if he had a good enough reason. "I'm telling you, Soonzy'll kill the son of a bitch."

"I'll find out why—" the guard began.

"It was a mistake," Shelby said. "Put him in the wrong cell is all."

"He's in there now, great big buck. Joe Dean seen him first, woke me up, and I swear I couldn't believe my eyes."

Shelby went over to the mirror and picked up a comb from the shelf. "It's nothing to get upset about," he said, making a part and slanting the dark hair carefully across his forehead. "Tonight they'll put him someplace else."

"Well, if we can," the guard said.

Shelby was watching him in the mirror: the gray-looking man in the gray guard uniform, R. E. Baylis, who might have been a town constable or a deputy sheriff twenty years ago. "What's the trouble?" Shelby asked.

"I mean he might have been ordered put there, I don't know."

"Ordered by who?"

"Bob Fisher. I say I don't know for sure."

Shelby turned from the mirror. "Bob don't want any trouble."

"Course not."

"Then why would he want to put Sambo in with my boys?"

"I say, I don't know."

Shelby came toward him now, noticing the activity out in the passageway, the convicts standing around and talking, moving slowly as the guards began to form them into two rows. Shelby put a hand on the guard's shoulder. "Mr. Baylis," he said, "don't worry about it. You don't want to ask Bob Fisher; we'll get Sambo out of there ourselves."

"We don't want nobody hurt or anything."

The guard kept looking at him, but Shelby was finished. As far as he was concerned, it was done. He said to Junior, "Give Soonzy the tobacco. You take the soap and stuff."

"It's my turn to keep the tally."

"Don't give me that look, boy."

Junior dropped his tone. "I lugged a box yesterday."

"All right, you handle the tally, Joe Dean carries the soap and stuff." Shelby paused, as if he was going to say something else, then looked at the guard. "Why don't you have the colored boy empty my throne bucket?"

"It don't matter to me," the guard said.

So he pulled Harold Jackson out of line and told him to get down to No. 14—as Joe Dean, Soonzy, and Junior moved along the double row of convicts in the dim passageway and sold them tobacco and cigarette paper, four kinds of plug and scrap, and little tins of snuff, matches, sugar cubes, stick candy, soap bars, sewing needles and thread, playing cards, red bandana handkerchiefs, shoelaces, and combs. They didn't take money; it would waste too much time and they only had ten minutes to go down the double line of eighty-seven men. Junior put the purchase amount in the tally book and the customer had one week to pay. If he didn't pay in a week, he couldn't buy any more stuff until he did. If he didn't pay in two weeks Junior and Soonzy would get him in a cell alone and hit him a few times or stomp the man's ribs and kidneys. If a customer wanted tequila or mescal, or corn whiskey when they had it, he'd come around to No. 14 after supper, before the doors were shut for the night, and pay a dollar a half-pint, put up in medicine bottles from the sick ward that occupied the second floor of the cell block. Shelby only sold alcohol in the morning to three or four of the convicts who needed it first thing or would never get through the day. What most of them wanted was just a day's worth of tobacco and some paper to roll it in.

When the figure appeared outside the iron lattice Shelby said, "Come on in," and watched the big colored boy's reaction as he entered: his gaze shifting twice to take in the double bunk and the boxes and the throne, knowing right away this was a one-man cell.

"I'm Mr. Shelby."

"I'm Mr. Jackson," Harold said.

Frank Shelby touched his mustache. He smoothed it to the sides once, then let his hand drop to the edge of his bunk. His eyes remained on the impassive dark face that did not move now and was looking directly at him.

"Where you from, Mr. Jackson?"

"From Leavenworth."

That was it. Big time con in a desert prison hole. "This place doesn't look like much after the federal pen, uh?"

"I been to some was worse, some better."

"What'd you get sent here for?"

"I killed a man was bothering me."

"You get life?"

"Fifteen years."

"Then you didn't kill a man. You must've killed another colored boy." Shelby waited.

Harold Jackson said nothing. He could wait too.

"I'm right, ain't I?" Shelby said.

"The man said for me to come in here."

"He told you, but it was me said for you to come in."

Harold Jackson waited again. "You saying you the man here?"

"Ask any of them out there," Shelby said. "The guards, anybody."

"You bring me in to tell me about yourself?"

"No, I brought you in to empty my slop bucket."

"Who did it before I come?"

"Anybody I told."

"If you got people willing, you better call one of them." Harold turned and had a hand on the door when Shelby stopped him.

"Hey, Sambo—"

Harold came around enough to look at him. "How'd you know that was my name?"

"Boy, you are sure starting off wrong," Shelby said. "I believe you need to be by yourself a while and think it over."

Harold didn't have anything to say to that. He turned to the door again and left the man standing there playing with his mustache.

As he fell in at the end of the prisoner line, guard named R. E. Baylis gave him a funny look and came over.

"Where's Shelby's bucket at?"

"I guess it's still in there, captain."

"How come he didn't have you take it?"

Harold Jackson stood at attention, looking past the man's face to the stone wall of the passageway. "You'll have to ask him about that, captain."

"Here they come," Bob Fisher said, "Look over there."

Mr. Manly moved quickly from the side of the desk to the window to watch the double file of convicts coming this way. He was anxious to see everything this morning, especially the convicts.

"Is that all of them?"

"In the main cell block. About ninety."

"I thought there'd be more." Mr. Manly studied the double file closely but wasn't able to single out Harold Jackson. All the convicts looked alike. No, that was wrong; they didn't all look alike.

"Since we're shutting down we haven't been getting as many."

"They're all different, aren't they?"

"How's that?" Bob Fisher said.

Mr. Manly didn't answer, or didn't hear him. He stood at the window of the superintendent's office—the largest of a row of offices over the mess hall—and watched the convicts as they came across the yard, passed beyond the end of a low adobe, and came into view again almost directly below the window. The line reached the door of the mess hall and came to a stop.

Their uniforms looked the same, all of them wearing prison stripes, all faded gray and white. It was the hats that were different, light-colored felt hats and a few straw hats, almost identical hats, but all worn at a different angle: straight, low over the eyes, to the side, cocked like a dandy would wear his hat, the brim funneled, the brim up in front, the brim down all around. The hats were as different as the men must be different. He should make a note of that. See if anything had been written on the subject: determining a man's character by the way he wore his hat. But there wasn't a note pad or any paper on the desk and he didn't want to ask Fisher for it right at the moment.

He was looking down at all the hats. He couldn't see any of their faces clearly, and wouldn't unless a man looked up. Nobody was looking up.

They were all looking back toward the yard. Most of them turning now so they wouldn't have to strain their necks. All those men suddenly interested in something and turning to look.

"The women convicts," Bob Fisher said.

Mr. Manly saw them then. My God—two women.

Fisher pressed closer to him at the window. Mr. Manly could smell tobacco on the man's breath. "They just come out of the latrine, that adobe there," Fisher said. "Now watch them boys eyeing them."

The two women walked down the line of convicts, keeping

about ten feet away, seeming at ease and not in any hurry, but not looking at the men either.

"Taking their time and giving the boys sweet hell, aren't they? Don't hear a sound, they're so busy licking their lips."

Mr. Manly glanced quickly at the convicts. The way they were looking, it was more likely their mouths were hanging open. It gave him a funny feeling, the men dead serious and no one making a sound.

"My," Fisher said, "how they'd like to reach out and grab a handful of what them girls have got."

"Women—" Mr. Manly said almost as a question. Nobody had told him there were women at Yuma.

A light-brown-haired one and a dark-haired one that looked to be Mexican. Lord God, two good-looking women walking past those men like they were strolling in the park. Mr. Manly couldn't believe they were convicts. They were *women*. The little dark-haired one wore a striped dress—smaller stripes than the men's outfits—that could be a dress she'd bought anywhere. The brown-haired one, taller and a little older, though she couldn't be thirty yet, wore a striped blouse with the top buttons undone, a white canvas belt and a gray skirt that clung to the movement of her hips as she walked and flared out as it reached to her ankles.

"Tacha Reyes," Fisher said.

"Pardon me?"

"The little chilipicker. She's been here six months of a ten-year sentence. I doubt she'll serve it all though. She behaves herself pretty good."

"What did she do? I mean to be here."

"Killed a man with a knife, she claimed was trying to make her do dirty things."

"Did the other one—kill somebody?"

"Norma Davis? Hell, no. Norma likes to do dirty things. She was a whore till she took up armed robbery and got caught holding up the Citizens' Bank of Prescott, Arizona. Man with her, her partner, was shot dead."

"A woman," Mr. Manly said. "I can't believe a woman would do that."

"With a Colt forty-four," Fisher said. "She shot a policeman during the hold-up but didn't kill him. Listen, you want to keep a pretty picture of women in your head don't get close to Norma. She's serving ten years for armed robbery and attempted murder."

The women were inside the mess hall now. Mr. Manly wanted to ask more questions about them, but he was afraid of sounding too interested and Fisher might get the wrong idea. "I notice some of the men are carrying buckets," he said.

"The latrine detail." Fisher pointed to the low adobe. "They'll go in there and empty them. That's the toilet and wash house, everything sewered clear out to the river. There—now the men are going into mess. They got fifteen minutes to eat, then ten minutes to go to the toilet before the work details form out in the exercise yard."

"Do you give them exercises to do?"

"We give them enough work they don't need any exercise," Fisher answered.

Mr. Manly raised his eyes to look out at the empty yard and was surprised to see a lone convict coming across from the cellblock.

"Why isn't that one with the others?"

Bob Fisher didn't answer right way. Finally he said, "That's Frank Shelby."

"Is he a trusty?"

"Not exactly. He's got some special jobs he does around here."

Mr. Manly let it go. There were too many other things he wanted to know about. Like all the adobe buildings scattered around, a whole row of them over to the left, at the far end of the mess hall. He wondered where the women lived, but didn't ask that.

Well, there was the cook shack over there and the tailor shop, where they made the uniforms. Bob Fisher pointed out the small one-story adobes. Some equipment sheds, a storehouse, the reception hut they were in last night. The mattress factory and the wagon works had been shut down six months ago. Over the main cellblock was the hospital, but the doctor had gone to Florence to set up a sick ward at the new prison. Anybody broke a leg now or crushed his hand working the rocks, they sent for a town doctor.

And the chaplain, Mr. Manly asked casually. Was he still here?

No, there wasn't any chaplain. The last one retired and they decided to wait till after the move to get another. There wasn't many of the convicts prayed anyway.

How would you know that? Mr. Manly wanted to ask him. But he said, "What are those doors way down there?"

At the far end of the yard he could make out several iron-grill doors, black oval shapes, doorways carved into the solid rock. The doors didn't lead outside, he could tell that, because the top of the east wall and two of the guard towers were still a good piece beyond.

"Starting over back of the main cellblock, you can't see it from here," Bob Fisher said, "a gate leads into the TB cellblock and exercise yard."

"You've got consumptives here?"

"Like any place else. I believe four right now." Fisher hurried on before Mr. Manly could interrupt again. "The doors you can see—one's the crazy hole. Anybody gets mean loco they go in there till they calm down. The next one they call the snake den's a punishment cell."

"Why is it called—"

"I don't know, I guess a snake come in through the air shaft one time. The last door there on the right goes into the women's cell block. You seen them. We just got the two right now."

There, he could ask about them again and it would sound natural. "The one you said, Norma something, has she been here long?"

"Norma Davis. I believe about a year and a half."

"Do the men ever—I mean I guess you have to sort of watch over the women."

"Mister, we have to watch over everybody."

"But being women—don't they have to have their own, you know, facilities and bath?"

Fisher looked right at Mr. Manly now. "They take a bath in the cook shack three, four times a week."

"In the cook shack." Mr. Manly nodded, surprised. "After the cooks are gone, of course."

"At night," Fisher said. He studied Mr. Manly's profile—the

soft pinkish face and gold-frame glasses pressed close to the window pane—little Bible teacher looking out over his prison and still thinking about Norma Davis, asking harmless sounding questions about the women.

Fisher said quietly, "You want to see them?"

Mr. Manly straightened, looking at Fisher now with a startled expression. "What do you mean?"

"I wondered if you wanted to go downstairs and have another look at Norma and Tacha."

"I want to see everything," Mr. Manly said. "Everything you have here to show me."

3

WHEN FRANK SHELBY entered the mess hall he stepped in line ahead of Junior. In front of him, Soonzy and Joe Dean looked around.

"You take care of it?" Junior asked him.

"He needs some time in the snake den," Shelby said.

Soonzy was looking back down the line. "Where's he at?"

"Last one coming in."

"I'll handle him," Junior said.

Shelby shook his head. "I want somebody else to start it. You and Soonzy break it up and get in some licks."

"No problem," Junior said. "The spook's already got leg-irons on."

They picked up tin plates and cups and passed in front of the serving tables for their beans, salt-dried beef, bread, and coffee. Soonzy and Joe Dean waited, letting Shelby go ahead of them. He paused a moment, holding his food, looking out over the long twelve-man tables and benches that were not yet half filled. Joe Dean moved up next to him. "I see plenty people that owe us money."

"No, I see the one I want. The Indin," Shelby said, and started for his table.

Raymond San Carlos was pushing his spoon into the beans that were pretty good but would be a lot better with some ketchup. He looked up as Frank Shelby and Junior put their plates down across from him. He hurried and took the spoonful of beans, then took another one more slowly. He knew they had picked him for something. He was sure of it when Soonzy sat down on one side of him and Joe Dean stepped in on the other. Joe Dean acted surprised at seeing him. "Well, Raymond San Carlos," he said, "how are you today?"

"I'm pretty good, I guess."

Junior said, "What're you pretty good at, Raymond?"

"I don't know—some things, I guess."

"You fight pretty good?"

It's coming, Raymond said to himself, and told himself to be

449

very calm and not look away from this little boy son-of-a-bitch friend of Frank Shelby's. He said, "I fight sometimes. Why, you want to fight me?"

"Jesus," Junior said. "Listen to him."

Raymond smiled. "I thought that's what you meant." He picked up his coffee and took a sip.

"Don't drink it," Shelby said.

Raymond looked directly at him for the first time. "My coffee?"

"You see that colored boy? He's picking up his plate." As Raymond looked over Shelby said, "After he sits down I want you to go over and dump your coffee right on his woolly head."

He was at the serving table now, big shoulders and narrow hips. Some of the others from the latrine had come in behind him. He was not the biggest man in the line, but he was the tallest and seemed to have the longest arms.

"You want me to fight him?"

"I said I want you to pour your coffee on his head," Shelby answered. "That's all I said to do. You understand that, or you want me to tell you in sign language?"

Harold Jackson took a place at the end of a table. There were two men at the other end. Shifting his gaze past them as he took a bite of bread, he could see Frank Shelby and the mouthy kid and, opposite them, the big one you would have to hit with a pipe or a pick handle to knock down, and the skinny one, Joe Dean, with the beard that looked like ass fur off a sick dog. The dark-skinned man with them, who was getting up now, he hadn't seen before.

There were five guards in the room. No windows. One door. A stairway—at the end of the room behind the serving tables—where the turnkey and the little man from the train were coming down the stairs now: little man who said he was going to be in charge, looking all around—my, what a fine big mess hall—looking and following the turnkey, who never changed his face, looking at the grub now, nodding, smiling—yes, that would sure stick to their ribs—taking a cup of coffee the turnkey offered him and tasting it. Two of the guards walked over and now the little man was shaking hands with them.

That was when Harold felt somebody behind him brush him,

and the hot coffee hitting his head was like a shock, coming into his eyes and feeling as if it was all over him.

Behind him, Raymond said, "What'd you hit my arm for?"

Harold wiped a hand down over his face, twisting around and looking up to see the dark-skinned man who had been with Shelby, an Indian-looking man standing, waiting for him. He knew Shelby was watching, Shelby and anybody else who had seen it happen.

"What's the matter with you?" Harold said.

Raymond didn't move. "I want to know why you hit my arm."

"I'll hit your mouth, boy, you want. But I ain't going to do it here."

Raymond let him have the tin plate, back-handing the edge of it across his eyes, and Harold was off the bench, grabbing Raymond's wrist as Raymond hit him in the face with the coffee cup. Harold didn't get to swing. A fist cracked against his cheekbone from the blind side. He was hit again on the other side of the face, kicked in the small of the back, and grabbed by both arms and around his neck and arched backward until he was looking at the ceiling. There were faces looking at him, the dark-skinned boy looking at him calmly, people pressing in close, then a guard's hat and another, and the turnkey's face with the mustache and the expression that didn't change.

"Like he went crazy," Junior said. "Just reared up and hit this boy."

"I was going past," Raymond said.

Junior was nodding. "That's right. Frank seen it first, we look over and this spook has got Raymond by the neck. Frank says help him, and me and Soonzy grabbed the spook quick as we could."

The turnkey reached out, but Harold didn't feel his hand. He was looking past him.

"Let him up," Fisher said.

Somebody kicked him again as they jerked him to his feet and let go of his arms. Harold felt his nose throbbing and felt something wet in his eyes. When he wiped at his eyes he saw the red blood on his fingers and could feel it running down his face now. The turnkey's face was raised; he was looking off somewhere.

Fisher said, "You saw it, Frank?"

Shelby was still sitting at his table. He nodded slowly. "Same as Junior told you. The colored boy started it. Raymond hit him to get free, but he wouldn't let go till Junior and Soonzy got over there and pinned him."

"That's all?"

"That's all," Shelby said.

"Anybody else see it start?" Fisher looked around. The convicts met his gaze as it passed over them. They waited as Fisher took his time, letting the silence in the room lengthen. When he looked at Harold Jackson again there was a moment when he seemed about to say something to him. The moment passed. He turned away and walked back to the food tables where Mr. Manly was waiting, his hands folded in front of him, his eyes wide open behind the gold-frame glasses.

"You want to see the snake den," Bob Fisher said. "Come on, we got somebody else wants to see it too."

After breakfast, as the work details were forming in the yard, the turnkey and the new superintendent and two guards marched Harold Jackson past the groups all the way to the snake den at the back of the yard.

Raymond San Carlos looked at the colored boy as he went by. He had never seen him before this morning. Nobody would see him now for about a week. It didn't matter. Dumb nigger had done something to Shelby and would have to learn, that's all.

While Raymond was still watching them—going one at a time into the cell now—one of the guards, R. E. Baylis, pulled him out the stone quarry gang and took him over to another detail. Raymond couldn't figure it out until he saw Shelby in the group and knew Shelby had arranged it. A reward for pouring coffee on a man. He was out of that man-breaking quarry and on Shelby's detail because he'd done what he was told. Why not?

As a guard with a Winchester marched them out the main gate Raymond was thinking: Why not do it the easy way? Maybe things were going to be better and this was the beginning of it: get in with Shelby, work for him; have all the cigarettes he wanted, some tequila at night to put him to sleep, no hard-labor details. He could be out of here maybe in twenty years if he never did nothing to wear leg-irons or get put in the snake den. Twenty years, he would be almost fifty years old. He couldn't change that. Or he could do whatever he felt like doing and not smile at people like Frank Shelby and Junior and the two convicts in his cell. He could get his head pounded against the stone wall and spend the rest of his life here. It was a lot to think about, but it made the most sense to get in with Shelby. He would be as dumb as the nigger if he didn't.

Outside the walls, the eight-man detail was marched past the water cistern—their gaze going up the mound of earth past the stonework to the guard tower that looked like a bandstand sitting up there, a nice shady pavilion where a rapid-fire weapon was trained on the main gate—then down the grade to a path that took them along the bluff overlooking the river. They followed it until they reached the cemetery.

Beyond the rows of headstones an adobe wall, low and uneven, under construction, stood two to three feet high on the river side of the cemetery.

Junior said, "What do they want a wall for? Them boys don't have to be kept in."

"They want a wall," Shelby said, "because it's a good place for a wall and there ain't nothing else for us to do."

Raymond agreed four years' worth to that. The work was to keep them busy. Everybody knew they would be moving out of here soon, but every day they pounded rocks into gravel for the roads and made adobe bricks and built and repaired walls and levees and cleared brush along the river bank. It was a wide river with a current—down the slope and across the flat stretch of mud beach to the water—maybe a hundred yards across. There was nothing on the other side—no houses, only a low bank and what looked to be heavy brush. The land over there could be a swamp or a desert; nobody had ever said what it was like, only that it was California.

All morning they laid the big adobe bricks in place, gradually raising the level string higher as they worked on a section of wall at a time. It was dirty, muddy work, and hot out in the open. Raymond couldn't figure out why Shelby was on this detail, unless he felt he needed sunshine and exercise. He laid about half as many bricks as anybody else, and didn't talk to anybody except his three friends. It surprised Raymond when Shelby began working on the other side of the wall from him and told him he had done all right in the mess hall this morning. Raymond nodded; he didn't know what to say. A few minutes went by before Shelby spoke again.

"You want to join us?"

Raymond looked at him. "You mean work for you?"

"I mean go with us," Shelby said. He tapped a brick in place with the handle of his trowel and sliced off the mortar oozing out from under the bride. "Don't look around. Say yes or no."

"I don't know where you're going."

"I know you don't. You say yes or no before I tell you."

"All right," Raymond said. "Yes."

"Can you swim?"

"You mean the river?"

"It's the only thing I see around here to swim," Shelby said. "I'm not going to explain it all now."

"I don't know—"

"Yes, you do, Raymond. You're going to run for the river when I tell you. You're going to swim straight across and find a boat hidden in the brush, put there for us, and you're going to row back fast as you can and meet us swimming over."

"If we're all swimming what do you want the boat for?"

"In case anybody can't make it all the way."

"I'm not sure I can, even."

"You're going to find out," Shelby said.

"How wide is it here?"

"Three hundred fifty feet. That's not so far."

The river had locked cool and inviting before; not to swim across, but to sit in and splash around and get clean after sweating all morning in the adobe mud.

"There's a current—"

"Don't think about it. Just swim."

"But the guard—what about him?"

"We'll take care of the guard."

"I don't understand how we going to do it." He was frowning in the sunlight trying to figure it out.

"Raymond, I say run, you run. All right?"

"You don't give me any time to think about it."

"That's right," Shelby said. "When I leave here you come

over the wall and start working on this side." He got up and moved down the wall about ten or twelve feet to where Soonzy and Junior were working.

Raymond stepped over the three-foot section of wall with his mortar bucket and continued working, facing the guard now who was about thirty feet away, sitting on a rise of ground with the Winchester across his lap and smoking a cigarette. Beyond him, a hundred yards or so up the slope, the prison wall and the guard tower at the northwest corner stood against the sky. The guard up there could be looking this way or he could be looking inside, into the yard of the TB cell block. Make a run for the river with two guns within range. Maybe three, counting the main tower. There was some brush, though, a little cover before he got to the mud flat. But once they saw him, the whistle would blow and they'd be out here like they came up out of the ground, some of them shooting and some of them getting the boat, wherever the boat was kept. He didn't have to stay with Shelby, he could go up to the high country this spring and live by himself. Maybe through the summer. Then go some place nobody knew him and get work. Maybe Mexico.

Joe Dean came along with a wheelbarrow and scooped mortar into Raymond's bucket. "If we're not worried," Joe Dean said, leaning on the wall, "what're you nervous about?"

Raymond didn't look up at him. He didn't like to look at the man's mouth and tobacco-stained teeth showing in his beard. He didn't like having anything to do with the man. He didn't like having anything to do with Junior or Soonzy either. Or with Frank Shelby when he thought about it honestly and didn't get it mixed up with cigarettes and tequila. But he would work with them and swim the river with them to get out of this place. He said to Joe Dean, "I'm ready any time you are."

Joe Dean squinted up at the sun, then let his gaze come down to the guard. "It won't be long," he said, and moved off with his wheelbarrow.

The way they worked it, Shelby kept his eye on the guard. He waited until the man started looking for the chow wagon that would be coming around the corner from the main gate any time now. He waited until the guard was finally half-turned, looking up the slope, then gave a nod to Junior.

Junior jabbed his trowel into the foot of the man working next to him.

The man let out a scream and the guard was on his feet at once, coming down from the rise.

Shelby waited until the guard was hunched over the man, trying to get a look at the foot. The other convicts were crowding in for a look too and the man was holding his ankle, rocking back and forth and moaning. The guard told him goddamn-it, sit still and let him see it.

Shelby looked over at Raymond San Carlos, who was standing now, the wall in front of him as high as his hips. Shelby nodded and turned to the group around the injured man. As he pushed Joe Dean aside he glanced around again to see the wall empty where Raymond had been standing. "What time is it?" he said.

Joe Dean took out his pocket watch. "Eleven-fifty about."

"Exactly."

"Eleven-fifty-two."

Shelby took the watch from Joe Dean as he leaned in to see the clean tear in the toe of the man's shoe and the blood starting to come out. He waited a moment before moving over next to the wall. The guard was asking what happened and Junior was trying to explain how he'd tripped over the goddamn mortar bucket and, throwing his hand out as he fell, his trowel had hit the man's shoe. His foot, the guard said—you stabbed him. Well, he hadn't meant to, Junior told the guard. Jesus, if he'd meant to, he wouldn't have stabbed him in the foot, would he?

From the wall Shelby watched Raymond moving quickly through the brush clumps and not looking back—very good—not hesitating until he was at the edge of the mud flats, a tiny figure way down there, something striped, hunched over in the bushes and looking around now. Go on, Shelby said, looking at the watch. What're you waiting for? It was eleven fifty-three.

The guard was telling the man to take his shoes off, he wasn't going to do it for him; and goddamn-it, get back and give him some air.

When Shelby looked down the slope again Raymond was in the water knee-deep, sliding into it; in a moment only his head was showing. Like he knew what he was doing, Shelby thought.

Between moans the injured man said Oh God, he believed his toes were cut off. Junior said maybe one or two; no trowel was going to take off all a man's toes, 'less you come down hard with the edge; maybe that would do it.

Twenty yards out. Raymond wasn't too good a swimmer, about average. Well, that was all right. If he was average then the watch would show an average time. He sure seemed to be moving slow though. Swimming was slow work.

When the chow wagon comes, the guard said, we'll take him up in it. Two of you men go with him.

It's coming now, somebody said.

There it was, poking along close to the wall, a driver and a helper on the seat, one of the trusties. The guard stood up and yelled for them to get down here. Shelby took time to watch the injured man as he ground his teeth together and eased his shoe off. He wasn't wearing any socks. His toes were a mess of blood, but at least they all seemed to be there. He was lucky.

Raymond was more than halfway across now. The guard was motioning to the wagon, trying to hurry it. So Shelby watched Raymond: just a speck out there, you'd have to know where to look to find him. Wouldn't that be something if he made it? God Almighty, dumb Indin probably could if he knew what to do once he got across. Or if he had some help waiting. But he'd look for the boat that wasn't there and run off through the brush and see all that empty land stretching nowhere.

Eleven fifty-six. He'd be splashing around out there another minute easy before he reached the bank.

Shelby walked past the group around the injured man and called out to the guard who had gone part way up the slope, "Hey, mister!" When the guard looked around Shelby said, "I think there's somebody out there in the water."

The guard hesitated, but not more than a moment before he got over to the wall. He must have had a trained eye, because he spotted Raymond right away and fired the Winchester in the air. Three times in rapid succession.

Joe Dean looked up as Shelby handed him his pocket watch. "He make it?" Joe Dean asked.

"Just about."

"How many minutes?"

"Figure five anyway, as a good average."

Junior said to Shelby, "What do you think?"

"Well, it's a slow way out of here," Shelby answered. "But least we know how long it takes now and we can think on it."

Mr. Manly jumped in his chair and swiveled around to the window when the whistle went off, a high, shrieking sound that ripped through the stillness of the office and seemed to be coming from directly overhead. The first thing he thought of, immediately, was, *somebody's trying to escape!* His first day here . . .

Only there wasn't a soul outside. No convicts, no guards running across the yard with guns.

Of course—they were all off on work details.

When he pressed close to the window Mr. Manly saw the woman, Norma Davis, standing in the door of the tailor shop. Way down at the end of the mess hall. He knew it was Norma, and not the other one. Standing with her hands on her hips, as if she was listening—Lord, as the awful piercing whistle kept blowing. After a few moments she turned and went inside again. Not too concerned about it.

Maybe it wasn't an escape. Maybe it was something else. Mr. Manly went down the hall and opened the doors, looking into empty offices, some that hadn't been used in months. He turned back and, as he reached the end of the hall and the door leading to the outside stairway, the whistle stopped. He waited, then cautiously opened the door and went outside. He could see the front gate from here: both barred doors closed and the inside and outside guards at their posts. He could call to the inside guard, ask him what was going on.

And what if the man looked up at him on the stairs and said it was the noon dinner whistle? It was just about twelve.

Or what if it was an exercise he was supposed to know about? Or a fire drill. Or anything for that matter that a prison superintendent should be aware of. The guard would tell him, "That's the whistle to stop work for dinner, sir," and not say anything else, but his look would be enough.

Mr. Manly didn't know where else he might go, or where

he might find the turnkey. So he went back to his office and continued reading the history file on Harold Jackson.

Born Fort Valley, Georgia, September 11, 1879.

Mr. Manly had already read that part. Field hand. No formal education. Arrested in Georgia and Florida several times for disorderly conduct, resisting arrest, striking an officer of the law. Served eighteen months on a Florida prison farm for assault. Inducted into the army April 22, 1898. Assigned to the 24th Infantry Regiment in Tampa, Florida, June 5. Shipped to Cuba.

He was going to read that part over again about Harold Jackson deserting and being court-martialed.

But Bob Fisher, the turnkey, walked in. He didn't knock, he walked in. He looked at Mr. Manly and nodded, then gazed about the room. "If there's something you don't like about this office, we got some others down the hall.

"Caught one of them trying to swim the river, just about the other side when we spotted him." Fisher stopped as Mr. Manly held up his hand and rose from the desk.

"Not right now," Mr. Manly said. "I'm going to go have my dinner. You can give me a written report this afternoon."

Walking past Fisher wasn't as hard as he thought it would be. Out in the hall Mr. Manly paused and looked back in the office. "I assume you've put the man in the snake den."

Fisher nodded.

"Bring me his file along with your report, Bob." Mr. Manly turned and was gone.

4

HAROLD JACKSON recognized the man in the few moments the door was open and the guards were shoving him inside. As the man turned to brace himself Harold saw his face against the outside sunlight, the dark-skinned face, the one in the mess hall. The door slammed closed and they were in darkness. Harold's eyes were used to it after half a day in here. He could see the man feeling his way along the wall until he was on the other side of the ten-by-ten-foot stone cell. It had been almost pitch dark all morning. Now, at midday, a faint light came through the air hole that was about as big around as a stovepipe and tunneled down through the domed ceiling. He could see the man's legs good, then part of his body as he sat down on the bare dirt floor. Harold drew up his legs and stretched them out again so the leg-iron chains would clink and rattle—in case the man didn't know he was here.

Raymond knew. Coming in, he had seen the figure sitting against the wall and had seen his eyes open and close as the sunlight hit his face, black against blackness, a striped animal in his burrow hole. Raymond knew. He had hit the man a good lick across the eyes with his tin plate, and if the man wanted to do something about it, now it was up to him. Raymond would wait, ready for him—while he pictured again Frank Shelby standing by the wall and tried to read Shelby's face.

The guards had brought him back in the skiff, making him row with his arms dead-tired, and dragged him wet and muddy all the way up the hill to the cemetery. Frank Shelby was still there. All of them were, and a man sitting on the ground, his foot bloody. Raymond had wanted to tell Shelby there wasn't any boat over there, and he wanted Shelby to tell him, somehow, what had gone wrong. He remembered Shelby staring at him, but not saying anything with his eyes or his expression. Just staring. Maybe he wasn't picturing Shelby's face clearly now, or maybe he had missed a certain look or gesture from him. He would have time to think about it. Thirty days in here. No mattress, no blanket, no slop bucket, use the corner, or piss on the nigger if he tried something. If the nigger hadn't done something to Shelby he wouldn't be here and you wouldn't be here, Raymond thought. Bread and water for thirty days, but they would take the nigger out before that and he would be alone. There were men they took from here to the crazy hole after being alone in the darkness too long. It can happen if you think about being here and nothing else, Raymond said to himself. So don't think about it. Go over and hit the nigger hard in the face and get it over with. God, if he wasn't so tired.

Kick him in the face to start, Harold was thinking, as he picked at the dried blood crusted on the bridge of his nose. Two and a half steps and aim it for his cheekbone, either side. That would be the way, if he didn't have on the irons and eighteen inches of chain links. He try kicking the man, he'd land flat on his back and the man would be on top of him. He try sneaking up, the man would hear the chain. 'Less the man was asleep and he worked over and got the chain around the man's neck and crossed his legs and stretched and kicked hard. Then they come in and say what happen? And he say I don't know, captain, the man must have choked on his bread. They say yeah, bread can kill a man all right; you stay in here with the bread the rest of your life. So the best thing would be to stand up and let the man stand up and hit him straight away and beat him enough but not too much. Beat him just right.

He said, "Hey, boy, you ready?"

"Any time," Raymond answered.

"Get up then."

Raymond moved stiffly, bringing up his knees to rise.

"What's the matter with you?"

"I'll tell you something," Raymond said. "If you're any good, maybe you won't get beat too bad. But after I sleep and rest my arms and legs I'll break your jaw."

"What's the matters with your arms and legs?"

"From swimming the river."

Harold Jackson stared at him, interested. He hadn't thought of why the man had been put in here. Now he remembered the whistle. "You saying you tried to bust out?"

"I got across."

"How many of you?"

Raymond hesitated. "I went alone."

"And they over there waiting."

"Nobody was waiting. They come in a boat."

"Broad daylight—man, you must be one dumb Indin fella."

Raymond's legs cramped as he started to rise, and he had to ease down again, slowly.

"We got time," Harold Jackson said. "Don't be in a hurry to get yourself injured."

"Tomorrow," Raymond said, "when the sun's over the hole and I can see your black nigger face in here."

Harold saw the chain around the man's neck and his legs straining to pull it tight. "Indin, you're going to need plenty medicine before I'm through with you."

"The only thing I'm worried about is catching you," Raymond said. "I hear a nigger would rather run than fight."

"Any running I do, red brother, is going to be right at your head."

"I got to see that."

"Keep your eyes open, Indin. You won't see nothing once I get to you."

There was a silence before Raymond said, "I'll tell you something. It don't matter, but I want you to know it anyway. I'm no Indian. I'm Mexican born in the United States, in the territory of Arizona."

"Yeah," Harold Jackson said. "Well, I'm Filipina born in Fort Valley, Georgia."

"Field nigger is what you are."

"Digger Indin talking, eats rats and weed roots."

"I got to listen to a goddamn field hand."

"I've worked some fields," Harold said. "I've plowed and picked cotton, I've skinned mules and dug privies and I've busted rock. But I ain't never followed behind another convict and emptied his bucket for him. White or black. *No*body."

Raymond's tone was lower. "You saw me carrying a bucket this morning?"

"Man, I don't have to see you, I know you carry one every morning. Frank Shelby says dive into it, you dive."

"Who says I work for Frank Shelby?"

"He say scratch my ass, you scratch it. He say go pour your coffee on that nigger's head, you jump up and do it. Man, if I'm a field nigger you ain't no better than a house nigger." Harold

Jackson laughed out loud. "Red nigger, that's all you are, boy. A different color but the same thing."

The pain in Raymond's thighs couldn't hold him this time. He lunged for the dark figure across the cell to drive into him and slam his black skull against the wall. But he went in high. Harold got under him and dumped him and rolled to his feet. They met in the middle of the cell, in the dim shaft of light from the air hole, and beat each other with fists until they grappled and kneed and strained against each other and finally went down.

When the guard came in with their bread and water, they were fighting on the hard-packed floor. He yelled to another guard who came fast with a wheelbarrow, pushing it through the door and the short passageway into the cell. They shoveled sand at Harold and Raymond, throwing it stinging hard into their faces until they broke apart and lay gasping on the floor. A little while later another guard came in with irons and chained them to ring bolts on opposite sides of the cell. The door slammed closed and again they were in darkness.

Bob Fisher came through the main gate at eight-fifteen that evening, not letting on he was in a hurry as he crossed the lighted area toward the convicts' mess hall.

He'd wanted to get back by eight—about the time they'd be bringing the two women out of their cellblock and over to the cook shack. But his wife had started in again about staying here and not wanting to move to Florence. She said after sixteen years in this house it was their *home*. She said a rolling stone gathered no moss, and that it wasn't good to be moving all the time. He reminded her they had moved twice in twenty-seven years, counting the move from Missouri. She said then it was about time they settled; a family should stay put, once it planted roots. What family? he asked her. Me and you? His wife said she didn't know anybody in Florence and wasn't sure she wanted to. She didn't even know if there was a Baptist church in Florence. What if there wasn't? What was she supposed to do then? Bob Fisher said that maybe she would keep her fat ass home for a change and do some cooking and baking, instead of sitting with them other fatties all day making patchwork quilts and bad-mouthing everybody in town who wasn't a paid-up member of the church. He didn't honestly care where she spent her time, or whether she baked pies and cakes or not. It was something to throw at her when she started in nagging about staying in Yuma. She said how could anybody cook for a person who came home at all hours with whiskey stinking up his breath? Yes, he had stopped and had a drink at the railroad hotel, because he'd had to talk to the express agent about moving equipment to Florence. Florence, his wife said. She wished she had never heard the name—the same name as her cousin who was still living in Sedalia, but now she didn't even like to think of her cousin any more and they had grown up together as little girls. Bob Fisher couldn't picture his wife as a little girl. No, that tub of fat couldn't have ever been a little girl. He didn't tell her that. He told her he had to get back to the prison, and left without finishing his coffee.

Fisher walked past the outside stairway and turned the corner of the mess hall. There were lights across the way in the main cellblock. He moved out into the yard enough to look up at the second floor of the mess hall and saw a light on in the superintendent's office. The little Sunday school teacher was still there, or had come back after supper. Before going home Fisher had brought in his written report of the escape and the file on Raymond San Carlos. The Sunday school teacher had been putting his books away, taking them out of a suitcase and lining them up evenly on the shelf. He'd said just lay the report on the desk and turned back to his books. What would he be doing now? Probably reading his Bible.

Past the latrine adobe Fisher walked over to the mess hall and tried the door. Locked for the night. Now he moved down the length of the building, keeping close to the shadowed wall though moving at a leisurely pace—just out for a stroll, checking around, if anybody was curious. At the end of the building he stopped and looked both ways before crossing over into the narrow darkness between the cook-shack adobe and the tailor shop.

Now all he had to do was find the right brick to get a free show. About chin-high it was, on the right side of the cook-shack chimney that stuck out from the wall about a foot and would partly hide him as he pressed in close. Fisher worked a finger in on both sides of the brick that had been chipped loose some months before, and pulled it out as slowly as he could. He didn't look inside right away; no, he always put the brick on the ground first and set himself, his feet wide apart and his shoulders hunched a little so the opening would be exactly at eye level. They would be just past the black iron range, this side of the work table where they always placed the washtub, with the bare electric light on right above them.

Fisher looked in. Goddamn Almighty, just in time.

Just as Norma Davis was taking off her striped shirt, already unbuttoned, slipping it off her shoulders to let loose those round white ninnies that were like nothing he had ever seen before. Beauties, and she knew it, too, the way she stuck them out, standing with her hands on her hips and her belly a round little mound curving down into her skirt. What was she waiting for? Come on, Fisher said, take the skirt off and get in the tub. He didn't like it when they only washed from the waist up. With all the rock dust in the air and bugs from the mattresses and sweating under those heavy skirts, a lick-and-a-promise, armpits-and-neck wash wasn't any good. They had to wash theirselves all over to be clean and healthy.

Maybe he could write it into the regulations: Women convicts must take a full bath every other day. Or maybe every day.

The Mexican girl, Tacha Reyes, appeared from the left, coming from the end of the stove with a big pan of steaming water, and poured it into the washtub. Tacha was still dressed. Fisher could tell by her hair she hadn't bathed yet. She had to wait on Norma first, looking at Norma now as she felt the water. Tacha had a nice face; she was just a little skinny. Maybe give her more to eat—

Norma was taking off her skirt. Yes, *sir*, and that was all she had. No underwear on. Bare-ass naked with black stockings that come up over her knees. Norma turned, leaning against the work table to pull the stockings off, and Bob Fisher was looking at the whole show. He watched her lay her stockings on the table. He watched her pull her hair back with both hands and look down at her ninnies as she twisted the hair around so it would stay. He watched her step over to the tub, scratching under one of her arms, and say, "If it's too hot I'll put you in it."

"It should be all right," Tacha said.

Another voice, not in the room but out behind him, a voice he knew, said, "Guard, what's the matter? Are you sick?"

Twisting around, Bob Fisher hit the peak of his hat on the chimney edge and was straightening it, his back to the wall, as Mr. Manly came into the space between the buildings.

"It's me," Fisher said.

"Oh, I didn't know who it was."

"Making the rounds. I generally check all the buildings before I go to bed."

Mr. Manly nodded. "I thought somebody was sick, the way you were leaning against the wall."

"No, I feel fine. Hardly ever been sick."

"It was the way you were standing, like you were throwing up."

"No, I was just taking a look in here. Dark places you got to check good." He couldn't see Mr. Manly's eyes, but he knew the little son of a bitch was looking right at him, staring at him, or past him, where part of the brick opening might be showing and he could see light coming through. "You ready to go," Fisher said, "I'll walk you over to the gate."

He came out from the wall to close in on Mr. Manly and block his view; but he was too late.

What's that hole?" Mr. Manly said.

"A hole?"

"Behind you, I can see something—"

Bob Fisher turned to look at the opening, then at Mr. Manly again. "Keep your voice down."

"Why? What is it?"

"I wasn't going to say anything. I mean it's something I generally check on myself. But," Fisher said, "if you want to take a look, help yourself."

Mr. Manly frowned. He felt funny now standing here in the darkness. He said in a hushed tone, "Who's in there?"

"Go ahead, take a look."

Through the slit of the opening something moved, some-body in the room. Mr. Manly stepped close to the wall and peered in.

The light glinted momentarily on his glasses as his head came around, his eyes wide open.

"She doesn't have any clothes on!"

"Shhhh." Fisher pressed a finger to his heavy mustache. "Look and see what they're doing."

"She's bare-naked, washing herself."

"We want to be sure that's all," Fisher said.

"What?"

"Go on, see what she's doing."

Mr. Manly leaned against the wall, showing he was calm and not in any hurry. He peered in again, as though looking around a corner. Gradually his head turned until his full face was pressed against the opening.

What Norma was doing, she was sliding a bar of yellow soap over her belly and down her thighs, moving her legs apart, and coming back up with the soap almost to her breasts before she slid it down again in a slow circular motion. Mr. Manly couldn't take his eyes off her. He watched the Mexican girl bring a kettle and pour water over Norma's shoulders, and watched the suds run down between her breasts, Lord Jesus, through the valley and over the fertile plain and to the dark forest. He could feel his heart beating and feel Bob Fisher close behind him. He had to quit looking now; Lord, it was long enough. It was too long. He wanted to clear his throat. She was turning around and he got a glimpse of her behind as he pulled his face from the opening and stepped away.

"Washing herself," Mr. Manly said. "That's all I could see she was doing."

Bob Fisher nodded. "I hoped that was all." He stooped to pick up the brick and paused with it at the opening. "You want to look at Tacha?"

"I think I've seen enough to know what they're doing," Mr. Manly answered. He walked out to the open yard and waited there for Fisher to replace the brick and follow him out.

"What I want to know is what you're doing spying on them."

"Spying? I was checking, like I told you, to see they're not doing anything wrong."

"What do you mean, wrong?"

"Anything that ain't natural, then. You know what I mean. Two women together without any clothes on—I want to know there ain't any funny business going on."

"She was washing herself."

"Yes, sir," Fisher said, "that's all I saw too. The thing is, you never know when they might start."

Mr. Manly could still see her, the bar of yellow soap moving over her body. "I've never heard of anything like that. They're both *women*."

"I'll agree with you there," Fisher said, "but in a prison you never know. We got men with no women, and women with no men, and I'll tell you we got to keep our eyes open if we don't want any funny business."

"I've heard tell of men," Mr. Manly said—the sudsy water running down between her breasts—"but *women*. What do you suppose they do?"

"I hope I never find out," Fisher said. He meant it, too.

He got Mr. Manly out of there before the women came out and saw them standing in the yard; he walked Mr. Manly over to the main gate and asked him if he had read the report on the escape attempt.

Mr. Manly said yes, and that he thought it showed the guards to be very alert. He wondered, though, wasn't this Raymond San Carlos the same one the Negro had assaulted in the mess hall? The very same, Fisher said. Then wasn't it dangerous to put them both in the same cell? Dangerous to who? Fisher asked. To *them*, they were liable to start fighting again and try and kill each other. They already tried, Fisher said. They were chained to the floor now out of each other's reach. Mr. Manly asked how long they would leave them like that, and Fisher said until they made up their minds to be good and kind to each other. Mr. Manly said that could be never if there was a grudge between them. Fisher said it didn't matter to him, it was up to the two boys.

Fisher waited in the lighted area as Mr. Manly passed through the double gates of the sally port and walked off toward the superintendent's cottage. He was pretty sure Mr. Manly had believed his story, that he was checking on the women to see they didn't do queer things. He'd also bet a dollar the little Sunday school teacher wouldn't make him chink the hole up either.

That was dumb, taking all his books over to the office. Mr. Manly sat in the living room of the superintendent's cottage, in his robe and slippers, and didn't have a thing to read. His Bible was on the night table in the bedroom. Yes, and he'd made a note to look up what St. Paul said about being in prison, something about all he'd gone through and how one had to have perseverance. He saw Norma Davis rubbing the bar of soap over her body, sliding it up and down. No—what he wished he'd brought were the file records of the two boys in the snake den. He would have to talk to them when they got out. Say to them, look, boys, fighting never solved anything. Now forget your differences and shake hands.

They were different all right, a Negro and an Indian. But they were alike too.

Both here for murder. Both born the same year. Both had served time. Both had sketchy backgrounds and no living relatives anybody knew of. The deserter and the deserted.

A man raised on a share-crop farm in Georgia; joined the army and, four months later, was listed as a deserter. Court-martialed, sentenced to hard labor.

A man raised on the San Carlos Indian reservation; deserted by his Apache renegade father before he was born. Father believed killed in Mexico; mother's whereabouts unknown.

Both of them in the snake den now, a little room carved out of stone, with no light and hardly any air. Waiting to get at each other.

Maybe the sooner he talked to them the better. Bring them both out in ten days—no matter what Bob Fisher thought about it. Ten days was long enough. They needed spiritual guidance as much as they needed corporal punishment. He'd tell Fisher in the morning.

As soon as Mr. Manly got into bed he started thinking of Norma Davis again, seeing her clearly with the bare light right over her and her body gleaming with soap and water. He saw her in the room then, her body still slippery-looking in the moonlight that was coming through the window. Before she could reach the bed, Mr. Manly switched on the night-table lamp, grabbed hold of his Bible and leafed as fast as he could to St. Paul's letters to the Corinthians.

For nine days neither of them spoke. They sat facing each other, their leg-irons chained to ring bolts that were cemented in the floor. Harold would stand and stretch and lean against the wall and Raymond would watch him. Later on Raymond would get up for a while and Harold would watch. They never stood up at the same time or looked at each other directly. There was silence except for the sound of the chains when they moved. Each pretended to be alone in the darkness of the cell, though each was intently aware of the other's presence. Every day about noon a guard brought them hardtack and water. The guard was not allowed to speak to them, and neither of them spoke to him. It was funny their not talking, he told the other guards. It was spooky. He had never known a man in the snake den not to talk a storm when he was brought his bread and water. But these two sat there as if they had been hypnotized.

The morning of the tenth day Raymond said, "They going to let you out today." The sound of his voice was strange, like someone else's voice. He wanted to clear his throat, but wouldn't let himself do it with the other man watching him. He said, "Don't go anywhere, because when I get out of here I'm going to come looking for you."

"I be waiting," was all Harold Jackson said.

At midday the sun appeared in the air shaft and gradually faded. Nobody brought their bread and water. They had been hungry the first few days but were not hungry now. They waited and it was early evening when the guard came in with a hammer and pounded the ring bolts open, both of them, Raymond watching him curiously but not saying anything. Another guard came in with shovels and a bucket of sand and told them to clean up their mess.

Bob Fisher was waiting outside. He watched them come out blinking and squinting in the daylight, both of them filthy stinking dirty, the Negro with a growth of beard and the Indian's bony face hollowed and sick-looking. He watched their gaze creep over the yard toward the main cellblock where the convicts were standing around and sitting by the wall, most of them looking this way.

"You can be good children," Fisher said, "or you can go back in there, I don't care which. I catch you fighting, twenty days. I catch you looking mean, twenty days." He looked directly at Raymond. "I catch you swimming again, thirty days and leg-irons a year. You understand me?"

For supper they had fried mush and syrup, all they wanted. After, they were marched over to the main cellblock. Raymond looked for Frank Shelby in the groups standing around outside, but didn't see him. He saw Junior and nodded. Junior gave him a deadpan look. The guard, R. E. Baylis, told them to get their blankets and any gear they wanted to bring along.

"You putting us in another cell?" Raymond asked him. "How about make it different cells? Ten days, I'll smell him the rest of my life."

"Come on," Baylis said. He marched them down the passageway and through the rear gate of the cellblock.

"Wait a minute," Raymond said. "Where we going?"

The guard looked around at him. "Didn't nobody tell you? You two boys are going to live in the TB yard."

5

A WORK DETAIL was making adobe bricks over by the south wall, inside the yard. They mixed mud and water and straw, stirred it into a heavy wet paste and poured it into wooden forms. There were bricks drying all along the base of the wall and scrap lumber from the forms and stacks of finished bricks, ready to be used here or sold in town.

Harold Jackson and Raymond San Carlos had to come across the yard with their wheelbarrows to pick up bricks and haul them back to the TB cellblock that was like a prison within a prison: a walled-off area with its own exercise yard. There were eight cells here, in a row facing the yard, half of them empty. The four tubercular convicts stayed in their cells most of the time or sat in the shade and watched Harold and Raymond work, giving them advice and telling them when a line of bricks wasn't straight. They were working on the face wall of the empty cells, tearing out the weathered, crumbling adobe and putting in new bricks; repairing cells that would probably never again be occupied. This was their main job. They worked at it side by side without saying a word to each other. They also had to bring the tubercular convicts their meals, and sometimes get cough medicine from the sick ward. A guard gave them white cotton doctor masks they could put on over their nose and mouth for whenever they went into the TB cells; but the masks were hot and hard to breathe through, so they didn't wear them after the first day. They used the masks, and a few rags they found, to pad the leg-irons where the metal dug into their ankles.

The third day out of the snake den Raymond began talking to the convicts on the brick detail. He recognized Joe Dean in the group, but didn't speak to him directly. He said, man alive, it was good to breathe fresh air again and feel the sun. He took off his hat and looked up at the sky. All the convicts except Joe Dean went on working. Raymond said, even being over with the lungers was better than the snake den. He said somebody must have made a mistake, he was supposed to be in thirty days for trying to escape, but they let him out after ten. Raymond smiled; he said he wasn't going to mention it to them, though.

Joe Dean was watching him, leaning on his shovel. "You take care of him yet?"

"Take care of who?" Raymond asked him.

"The nigger boy. I hear he stomped you."

"Nobody stomped me. Where'd you hear that?"

"Had to chain him up."

"They chained us both."

"Looks like you're partners now," Joe Dean said.

"I'm not partners with him. They make us work together, that's all."

"You going to fight him?"

"Sure, when I get a chance."

"He don't look too anxious," another convict said. "That nigger's a big old boy."

"I got to wait for the right time," Raymond said. "That's all."

He came back later for another wheelbarrow load of bricks and stood watching them as they worked the mud and mixed in straw. Finally he asked if anybody had seen Frank around.

"Frank who you talking about?" Joe Dean asked.

"Frank Shelby."

"Listen to him," Joe Dean said. "He wants to know has anybody seen Frank."

"I got to talk to him," Raymond said. "See if he can get me out of there."

"Scared of TB, huh?"

"I mean being with the black boy. I got enough of him."

"I thought you wanted to fight him."

"I don't know," Joe Dean said. "It sounds to me like you're scared to start it."

"I don't want no more of the snake den. That's the only thing stopping me."

"You want to see Frank Shelby," one of the other convicts said, "there he is." The man nodded and Raymond looked around.

Shelby must have just come out of the mess hall. He stood by the end-gate of a freight wagon that Junior and Soonzy and a couple of other convicts were unloading. There was no guard with them, unless he was inside. Raymond looked up at the guard on the south wall.

"I'll tell you something," Joe Dean said. "You can forget about Frank helping you."

Raymond was watching the guard. "You know, uh? You know him so good he's got you working in this adobe slop."

"Sometimes we take bricks to town," Joe Dean said. "You think on it if you don't understand what I mean."

"I got other things to think on."

As the guard on the south wall turned and started for the tower at the far end of the yard, Raymond picked up his wheelbarrow and headed for the mess hall.

Shelby didn't look up right away. He was studying a bill of lading attached to a clipboard, checking things off. He said to Junior, "The case right by your foot, that should be one of ours."

"Says twenty-four jars of Louisiana cane syrup."

"It's corn whiskey." Shelby still didn't look up, but he said then, "What do you want?"

"They let me out of the snake den," Raymond said. "I was suppose to be in thirty days, they let me out."

Shelby looked at him now. "Yeah?"

"I wondered if you fixed it."

"Not me."

"I thought sure." He waited as Shelby looked in the wagon and at the clipboard again. "Say, what happened at the river? I thought you were going to come right behind me."

"It didn't work out that way."

"Man, I thought I had made it. But I couldn't find no boat over there."

"I guess you didn't look in the right place," Shelby said.

"I looked where you told me. Man, it was work. I don't like swimming so much." He watched Shelby studying the clipboard. "I was wondering—you know I'm over in a TB cell now."

Shelby didn't say anything.

"I was wondering if you could fix it, get me out of there."

"Why?"

"I got to be with that nigger all the time."

"He's got to be with you," Shelby said, "so you're even."

Raymond grinned. "I never thought of it that way." He waited again. "What do you think?"

"About what?"

"About getting me back with everybody."

Shelby started fooling with his mustache, smoothing it with his fingers. "Why do you think anybody wants you back?"

Raymond didn't grin this time. "I did what you told me," he said seriously. "Listen, I'll work for you any time you want."

"I'm not hiring today."

"Well, what about getting me out of the TB yard?"

Shelby looked at him. He said, "Boy, why would I do that? I'm the one had you put there. Now you say one more word Soonzy is going to come down off the wagon and break both your arms."

Shelby watched Raymond pick up his wheelbarrow and walk away. "Goddamn Indin is no better than a nigger," he said to Junior. "You treat them nice one time and you got them hanging around the rest of your life."

When Raymond got back to the brick detail Joe Dean said, "Well, what did he say?"

"He's going to see what he can do," Raymond answered. He didn't feel like talking any more, and was busy loading bricks when Harold Jackson came across the yard with his wheelbarrow. Harold wore his hat pointed low over his eyes. He didn't have a shirt on and, holding the wheelbarrow handles, his shoulders and arm muscles were bunched and hard-looking. One of the convicts saw him first and said to Raymond, "Here comes your buddy." The other convicts working the adobe mud looked up and stood leaning on their shovels and hoes as Harold Jackson approached.

Raymond didn't look at him. He stacked another brick in the wheelbarrow and got set to pick up the handles. He heard one of the convicts say, "This here Indian says you won't fight him. Says you're scared. Is that right?"

"I fight him any time he wants."

Raymond had to look up then. Harold was staring at him.

"Well, I don't know," the convict said. "You and him talk about fighting, but nobody's raised a hand yet."

"It must be they're both scared," Joe Dean said. "Or it's

because they're buddies. All alone in that snake den they got to liking each other. Guard comes in thinks they're rassling on the floor—man, they're not fighting, they're buggering each other."

The other convicts grinned and laughed, and one of them said, "Jesus Christ, what they are, they're sweethearts."

Raymond saw Harold Jackson take one step and hit the man in the face as hard as he could. Raymond wanted to say no, don't do it. It was a strange thing and happened quickly as the man spun toward him and Raymond put up his hands. One moment he was going to catch the man, keep him from falling against him. The next moment he balled up a fist and drove it into the man's face, right out in the open yard, the dumbest thing he had ever done, but doing it now and not stopping or thinking, going for Joe Dean now and busting him hard in the mouth as he tried to bring up his shovel. God, it felt good, a wild hot feeling, letting go and stepping into them and swinging hard at all the faces he had been wanting to smash and pound against a wall.

Harold Jackson held back a moment, staring at the crazy Indian, until somebody was coming at him with a shovel and he had to grab the handle and twist and chop it across the man's head. If he could get room and swing the shovel—but there were too many of them too close, seven men in the brick detail and a couple more, Junior and Soonzy, who came running over from the supply detail and grabbed hunks of lumber and started clubbing at the two wild men.

By the time the guard on the south wall fired his Winchester in the air and a guard came running over from the mess hall, Harold lay stunned in the adobe muck; Raymond was sprawled next to him and neither of them moved.

"Lord," Junior said, "we had to take sticks this time to get them apart."

Soonzy shook his head. "I busted mine on that nigger, he went right on fighting."

"They're a scrappy pair," Junior said, "but they sure are dumb, ain't they?"

Bob Fisher told the guard to hose them off and throw them in the snake den. He told Soonzy and Junior and the men on the brick detail to get back to work. Chained? the guard wanted to know. Chained, Fisher said, and walked off toward the stairs at the end of the mess hall, noticing the convicts who had come out of the adobe huts and equipment sheds, brought out by the guard's rifle fire, all of them looking toward the two men lying in the mud. He noticed Frank Shelby and some convicts by the freight wagon. He noticed the cooks in their white aprons, and the two women, Norma and Tacha, over by the tailor shop.

Fisher went up the stairs and down the hall to the superintendent's office. As he walked in, Mr. Manly turned from the window.

"The same two," Fisher said.

"It looked like they were all fighting." Mr. Manly glanced at the window again.

"You want a written report?"

"I'd like to know what happened."

"These two start fighting. The other boys try to pull them apart and the two start swinging at everybody. Got to hit 'em with shovels to put 'em down."

"I didn't see them fighting each other."

"Then you must have missed that part." Past Mr. Manly's thoughtful expression—through the window and down in the yard—he saw a convict walking toward the tailor shop with a bundle under his arm. Frank Shelby. This far away he knew it was Shelby. Norma Davis stood in the door waiting for him.

"Soon as I heard the shots," Mr. Manly said, "I looked out. They were separated, like two groups fighting. They didn't look close enough to have been fighting each other."

Bob Fisher waited. "You want a written report?"

"What're you going to do to them?"

"I told them before, they start fighting they go back in the snake den. Twenty days. They know it, so it won't be any surprise."

"Twenty days in there seems like a long time."

"I hope to tell you it is," Fisher said.

"I was going to talk to them when they got out the other day. I meant to—I don't know, I put it off and then I guess some other things came up."

Fisher could see Shelby at the tailor shop now, close to the woman, talking to her. She turned and they both went inside.

"I'm not saying I could have prevented their fighting, but you never know, do you? Maybe if I *had* spoken to them, got them to shake hands—you understand what I mean, Bob?"

Fisher pulled his gaze away from the tailor shop to the little man by the window. "Well, I don't know about that."

"It could have made a difference."

"I never seen talking work much on anybody."

"But twenty days in there," Mr. Manly said, "and it could be my fault, because I didn't talk to them." He paused. "Don't you think, Bob, in this case, you ought to give them no more than ten days? You said yourself ten days was a long time. Then soon as they come out I'll talk to them."

"That Indian was supposed to be in thirty days," Fisher said, "and you changed it to ten. Now I've already told them twenty and you want to cut it down again. I tell a convict one thing and you say something else and we begin to have problems."

"I'm only asking," Mr. Manly said, "because if I could have done something, if I'm the one to blame, then it wouldn't be fair to those two boys."

"Mister, they're convicts. They do what we tell them. Anything."

Mr. Manly agreed, nodding. "That's true, we give the orders and they have to obey. But we still have to be fair, no matter who we're dealing with."

Bob Fisher wondered what the hell he was doing here arguing with this little four-eyed squirt. He said, "They don't know anything about this. They don't know you meant to talk to them."

"But I know it," Mr. Manly said, "and the more I think about it the more I know I got to talk to them." He paused. "Soon."

Fisher saw it coming, happening right before his eyes, the little squirt's mind working behind his gold-frame glasses.

"Yes, maybe you ought to bring them in tomorrow."

"Just a minute ago you said ten days—"

"Do you have any children, Bob?"

The question stopped Fisher. He shook his head slowly, watching Mr. Manly.

"Well, I'm sure you know anyway you got to have patience

with children. Sure, you got to punish them sometimes, but first you got to teach them right from wrong and be certain they understand it."

"I guess my wife's got something wrong with her. She never had any kids."

"That's God's will, Bob. What I'm getting at, these two boys here, Harold and Raymond, they're just like children." Mr. Manly held up his hand. "I know what you're going to say, these boys wasn't caught stealing candy, they took a life. And I say that's true. But still they're like little children. They're grown in body but not in mind. They got the appetites and temptations of grown men. They fight and carry on and, Lord knows, they have committed murder, for which they are now paying the price. But we don't want no more murders around here, do we, Bob? No, sir. Nor do we want to punish anybody for something that isn't their fault. We got two murderers wanting to kill each other. Two mean-looking boys we chain up in a dungeon. But Bob, tell me something. Has anybody ever spoke kindly to them? I mean has anybody ever helped them overcome the hold the devil's got on them? Has anybody ever showed them the path of righteousness, or explained to them Almighty God's justice and the meaning of everlasting salvation?"

Jesus Christ, Bob Fisher said—not to Mr. Manly, to himself. He had to get out of here; he didn't need any sermons today. He nodded thoughtfully and said to Mr. Manly, "I'll bring them in here whenever you want."

When Junior and Soonzy came back from clubbing the Indian and the colored boy, Frank Shelby told them to get finished with the unloading. He told them to leave a bottle of whiskey in the wagon for the freight driver and take the rest of it to his cell. Soonzy said Jesus, that nigger had a hard head, and showed everybody around how the hunk of wood was splintered. Junior said my, but they were dumb to start a fight out in the yard. This old boy over there called them sweethearts and that had started them swinging. If they wanted to fight, they should have it out in a cell some night. A convict standing there said, boy, he'd like to see that. It would be a good fight.

Shelby was looking at Norma Davis outside the tailor shop. He knew she was waiting for him, but what the convict said caught in his mind and he looked at the man.

"Which one would you bet on?"

"I think I'd have to pick the nigger," the convict said. "The way he's built."

Shelby looked around at Soonzy. "Who'd you pick?"

"I don't think neither of them look like much."

"I said who'd you pick."

"I don't know. I guess the nigger."

"How about in the mess hall," Shelby said. "The Indin showed he's got nerve. Pretty quick, too, the way he laid that plate across the boy's eyes."

"He's quick," Junior said.

"Quick and stronger than he looks," Shelby said. "You saw him swimming against the river current."

"Well, he's big for an Indin," Junior said. "Big and quick and, as Frank says, he's got some nerve. Another thing, you don't see no marks on him from their fighting in the snake den. He might be more'n the nigger can handle."

"I'd say you could bet either way on that fight," Shelby said. He told Junior to hand him the bundle for the tailor shop—a bolt of prison cloth wrapped in brown paper—and walked off with it.

Most of them, Shelby was thinking, would bet on the nigger. Get enough cons to bet on the Indin and it could be a pretty good pot. If he organized the betting, handled the whole thing, he could take about ten per cent for the house. Offer some long-shot side bets and cover those himself. First, though, he'd have to present the idea to Bob Fisher. A prize fight. Fisher would ask what for and he'd say two reasons. Entertain the cons and settle the problem of the two boys fighting. Decide a winner and the matter would be ended. Once he worked out the side bets and the odds.

"Bringing me a present?" Norma asked him.

Shelby reached the shade of the building and looked up at her in the doorway. "I got a present for you, but it ain't in this bundle."

"I bet I know what it is."

"I bet you ought to. Who's inside?"

"Just Tacha and the old man."

"Well, you better invite me in," Shelby said, "before I start stripping you right here."

"Little anxious today?"

"I believe it's been over a week."

"Almost two weeks," Norma said. "Is there somebody else?"

"Two times I was on my way here," Shelby said, "Fisher stopped me and sent me on a work detail."

"I thought you got along with him."

"It's the first time he's pulled anything like that."

"You think he knows about us?"

"I imagine he does."

"He watches me and Tacha take a bath."

"He comes in?"

"No, there's a loose brick in the wall he pulls out. One time, after I was through, I peeked out the door and saw him sneaking off."

Shelby grinned. "Dirty old bastard."

"Maybe he doesn't feel so old."

"I bet he'd like to have some at that." Shelby nodded slowly. "I just bet he would."

Norma was watching him. "Now what are you thinking?"

"But he wouldn't want anybody to know about it. That's why he don't come in when you're taking a bath. Tacha's there."

Norma smiled. "I can see your evil mind working. If Tacha wasn't there—"

"Yes, sir, then he'd come in."

"Ask if I wanted him to soap my back."

"Front and back. I can see him," Shelby said. "One thing leads to another. After the first time, he don't soap you. No, sir, he gets right to it."

"Then one night you come in"—Norma giggled—"and catch the head guard molesting a woman convict."

Shelby shook his head, grinning.

"He's trying to pull his pants on in a hurry and you say, 'Good evening, Mr. Fisher. How are tricks?'"

"God *damn*," Shelby said, "that's good."

"He's trying to button his pants and stick his shirt in and

thinking as hard as he can for something to say." Norma kept giggling and trying not to. "He says, uh—"

"What does he say?"

"He says, 'I just come in for some coffee. Can I get you a cup, Mr. Shelby?' And you say, 'No, thank you. I was just on my way to see the superintendent.' He says, 'About what, Mr. Shelby?' And you say, 'About how some of the guards have been messing with the women convicts.'"

"It's an idea," Shelby said, "but I don't know of anything he can do for me except open the gate and he ain't going to do that, no matter what I get on him. No, I was wondering—if you and him got to be good friends—what he might tell you if you were to ask him."

Norma raised her arm and used the sleeve to wipe the wetness from her eyes. "What might he tell me?"

"Like what day we're supposed to move out of here. If we're going by train. If we're all going at once, or in groups." Shelby spoke quietly and watched her begin to nod her head as she thought about it. "Once we know when we're moving we can begin to make plans. I can talk to my brother Virgil, when he comes to visit, get him working on the outside. But we got to know *when*."

Norma was picturing herself in the cook shack with Fisher. "It would have to be the way I asked him. So he wouldn't suspect anything."

"Honey, you'd know better than I could tell you."

"I suppose once I got him comfortable with me."

"You won't have any trouble at all."

"It'll probably be a few times before he relaxes."

"Get him to think you like him. A man will believe anything when he's got his pants off."

"We might be having a cup of coffee after and I'll make a little face and look around the kitchen and say, 'Gee, honey, I wish there was some place else we could go.'"

"Ask him about the new prison."

"That's what I'm leading to," Norma said. "I'll tell him I hope we'll have a better place than this. Then I'll say, like I just thought of it, 'By the way, honey, when are we going to this new prison?'"

"Ask him if he's ever done it on a train?"

"I'll think of a way. I bet he's a horny old bastard."

"So much the better. He's probably never got it off a good-looking woman before in his life."

"Thank you."

"You're welcome."

"The only thing is what to do about Tacha."

"I'll have to think on that," Shelby said.

"Maybe he'd like both of us."

"Honey, he don't even have dreams like that anymore."

Tacha Reyes looked up from her sewing machine as they came into the shop and Shelby dropped the bundle on the work table. The old man, who had been a tailor here for twenty-six years since murdering his wife, continued working. He sat hunched over with his legs crossed, sewing a button to a striped convict coat.

Norma didn't say anything to them. She followed Shelby into the back room where the supplies and bolts of material were kept. The first few times they went back there together she said they were going to inventory the material or look over the thread supply or count buttons. Now she didn't bother. They went into the room and closed the door.

Tacha sat quietly, not moving. She told herself she shouldn't listen, but she always did. Sometimes she heard Norma, the faint sound of her laughing in there; she never heard Frank Shelby. He was always quiet.

Like the man who owned the café in St. David. He would come up behind her when she was working in the kitchen and almost before she heard him he would be touching her, putting his hands on her hips and bringing them up under her arms, pretending to be counting her ribs and asking how come she was so skinny, how come, huh, didn't she like the cooking here? And when she twisted away from him—what was the matter, didn't she like working here?

"How can he come in," Tacha said, "do whatever he wants?"

The tailor glanced over at the stock-room door. He didn't look at Tacha. "Norma isn't complaining."

"She's as bad as he is."

"I wouldn't know about that."

"She does whatever he wants. But he's a convict, like any of them."

"I'll agree he's a convict," the tailor said.

"You're afraid to even talk about him."

"I'll agree to that too," the tailor said.

"Some people can do whatever they want. Other people have to let them." Tacha was silent again. What good was talking about it?

The owner of the café in St. David thought he could do whatever he wanted because he paid her seven dollars a week and said she didn't have to stay if she didn't want to. He would kiss her and she would have to close her eyes hard and hold her breath and feel his hand coming up over her breast. Her sister had said so what, he touches you a little. Where else are you going to make seven dollars a week? But I don't want him to, Tacha had said. I don't love him. And her sister had told her she was crazy. You don't have to love a man even to marry him. This man was providing for her and she should look at it that way. He gave her something, she should give him something.

She gave him the blade of a butcher knife late one afternoon when no one was in the café and the cook had gone to the outhouse. She jabbed the knife into him because he was hurting her, forcing her back over the kitchen table, smothering her with his weight and not giving her a chance to speak, to tell him she wanted to quit. Her fingers touched this knife on the table and, in that little moment of panic, as his hand went under her skirt and up between her legs, she pushed the knife into his stomach. She would remember his funny, surprised expression and remember him pushing away from her again with his weight, and looking down at the knife handle, touching it gently with both hands then, standing still, as if afraid to move, and looking down at the knife. She remembered saying, "I didn't mean to—" and thinking, Take it out, you can do whatever you want to me, I didn't mean to do this.

"Some people lead," the tailor said, "some follow."

Tacha looked over at him, hunched over his sewing. "Why can Frank Shelby do whatever he wants?"

"Not everything, he can't."

"Why can he go in there with her?"

"Ask him when he's through."

"Do you know something?" Tacha said. "You never answer a question."

"I've been here—" the tailor began, and stopped as the outside door opened.

Bob Fisher stepped inside. He closed the door quietly behind him, his gaze going to the stock room, then to Tacha and past her to the tailor.

"Where's Norma at?"

Tacha waited. When she knew the tailor wasn't going to answer she said, "Don't you know where she is?"

Fisher's dull expression returned to Tacha. "I ask a question, I don't need a question back."

"She's in there," Tacha said.

"I thought I saw a convict come in here."

"He's in there with her."

"Doing what?"

"Doing *it*," Tacha said. "What do you think?"

Bob Fisher took time to give her a look before he walked over to the stock room. Then he didn't hesitate: he pushed the door and let it bang wide open and stood looking at them on the flat bolts of striped prison material they had spread on the floor, at the two of them lying close and pulling apart, at their upturned faces that were momentarily startled.

"You through?" Fisher said.

Shelby started to grin and shake his head. "I guess you caught us, boss."

Tacha could see Norma's skirt pulled up and her bare thighs. She saw Shelby, behind Fisher, getting to his feet. He was buttoning the top of his pants now. Norma was sitting up, slowly buttoning her blouse, then touching her hair, brushing it away from her face.

Tacha and the tailor began working again as Fisher looked around at them. He motioned Norma to get up. "You go on to your cell till I'm ready for you."

Shelby waited, while Norma gave Fisher a look and a shrug and walked out. He said then, "Were me and her doing something wrong? Against regulations?"

"You come with me," Fisher said.

Once outside, they moved off across the yard, toward the far end of the mess hall. Fisher held his set expression as his gaze moved about the yard. Shelby couldn't figure him out.

"Where we going?"

"I want to tell the new superintendent what you were doing."

"I didn't know of any law against it."

Fisher kept walking.

"What's going on?" Shelby said. Christ, the man was actually taking him in. Before they got to the latrine adobe Shelby said, "Well, I wanted to talk to him anyway." He paused. "About this guard that watches the girls take their bath. Pulls loose a brick and peeks in at them."

Fisher took six strides before saying, "She know who this guard is?"

"You bet," Shelby said.

"Then tell the sup'rintendent."

Son of a bitch. He was bluffing. Shelby glanced at him, but couldn't tell a thing from the man's expression.

Just past the latrine Shelby said, "I imagine this guard has got a real eyeful, oh man, but looking ain't near anything like doing, I'll tell you, 'cause I've done both. That Norma has got a natural-born instinct for pleasing a man. You know what she does?"

Fisher didn't answer.

Shelby waited, but not too long. "She knows secret things I bet there ain't ten women in the world can do. I been to Memphis, I been to Tulsa, to Nogales, I know what I'm talking about. You feel her mouth brushing your face and whispering dirty things in your ear—you know something? Once a man's had some of that woman—I mean somebody outside—he'd allow himself to be locked up in this place the rest of his life if he thought he could get some every other night. Get her right after she comes out of the bath."

Shelby paused to let Fisher think about it. As they were nearing the outside stairs he said, "Man, I tell you, anybody seen her bare-ass naked knows that's got to be a woman built for pleasure."

"Upstairs," Fisher said.

Shelby went up two steps and paused, looking around over his shoulder. "The thing is, though. She don't give it out to nobody but me. Less I say it's all right." Shelby looked right at his eyes. "You understand me, boss?"

Mr. Manly heard them coming down the hall. He swiveled around from the window and moved the two file folders to one side of the desk, covering the Bible. He picked up a pencil. On his note pad were written the names *Harold Jackson* and *Raymond San Carlos*, both underlined, and the notations: *Ten days will be Feb. 23, 1909. Talk to both at same time. Ref. to St. Paul to the Corinthians 11: 19–33 and 12: 1–9.*

When the knock came he said, "Come in" at once, but didn't look up until he knew they were in the room, close to the desk, and he had written on the note paper: *See Ephesians 4: 1–6.*

Bob Fisher came right out with it. "He wants to tell you something."

In that moment Shelby had no idea what he would say; because Fisher wasn't bluffing and wasn't afraid of him; because Fisher stood up and was a tough son of a bitch and wasn't going to lie and lose face in front of any con. Maybe Fisher would deny the accusation, say prove it. Shelby didn't know what Fisher would do. He needed time to think. The next moment Mr. Manly was smiling up at him.

"I'm sorry I don't know everybody's name yet."

"This is Frank Shelby," Fisher said. "He wants to tell you something."

Shelby watched the little man rise and offer his hand and say, "I'm Everett Manly, your new superintendent." He watched Mr. Manly sit down again and look off somewhere.

"Frank Shelby . . . Shelby . . . forty-five years for armed robbery. Is that right?"

Shelby nodded.

"Forty-five years," Mr. Manly said. "That's a long time. Are you working to get some time off for good behavior?"

"I sure am," Shelby said. He didn't know if the man was serious or not, but he said it.

"How long have you been here at Yuma?"

"Little over a year."

"Have you got a good record here? Keep out of fights and trouble?"

"Yes, *sir.*"

"Ever been in the snake den?"

"No, sir."

"Got two boys in there now for fighting, you know."

Shelby smiled a little and shook his head. "It's funny you should mention them," he said. "Those two boys are what I wanted to talk to you about."

Bob Fisher turned to look at him but didn't say a word.

"I was wondering," Shelby went on, "what you'd think of us staging a prize fight between those two boys?"

"A prize fight?" Mr. Manly frowned. "Don't you think they've done enough fighting? Lord, it seems all they like to do is fight."

"They keep fighting," Shelby said, "because they never get it settled. But, I figure, once they have it out there'll be peace between them. You see what I mean?"

Mr. Manly began to nod, slowly. "Maybe."

"We could get them some boxing gloves in town. I don't mean the prison pay for them. We could take us up a collection among the convicts."

"I sure never thought of fighting as a way to achieve peace. Bob, have you?"

Fisher said quietly, "No, I haven't."

Shelby shrugged. "Well, peace always seems to follow a war."

"You got a point there, Frank."

"I know the convicts would enjoy it. I mean it would keep their minds occupied a while. They don't get much entertainment here."

"That's another good point," Mr. Manly said.

Shelby waited as Mr. Manly nodded, looking as if he was falling asleep. "Well, that's all I had to say. I sure hope you give it some thought, if just for the sake of those two boys. So they can get it settled."

"I promise you I will," Mr. Manly said. "Bob, what do you think about it? Off-hand."

"I been in prison work a long time," Fisher said. "I never heard of anything like this."

"I'll tell you what, boys. Let me think on it." Mr. Manly got up out of the chair, extending a hand to Shelby. "It's nice meeting you, Frank. You keep up the good work and you'll be out of here before you know it."

"Sir," Shelby said, "I surely hope so."

Bob Fisher didn't say a word until they were down the stairs and Shelby was heading off along the side of the building, in the shade.

"Where you going?"

Shelby turned, a few steps away. "See about some chow."

"You can lose your privileges," Fisher said. "All of them inside one minute."

Go easy, Shelby thought, and said, "It's up to you."

"I can give it all to somebody else. The stuff you sell, the booze, the soft jobs. I pick somebody, the tough boys will side with him and once it's done he's the man inside and you're another con on the rock pile."

"I'm not arguing with you," Shelby said. "I used my head and put together what I got. You allow it because I keep the cons in line and it makes your job easier. You didn't give me a thing when I started."

"Maybe not, but I can sure take it all away from you."

"I know that."

"I will, less you stay clear of Norma Davis."

Shelby started to smile—he couldn't help it—even with Fisher's grim, serious face staring at him.

"Watch yourself," Fisher said. "You say the wrong thing, it's done. I'm telling you to keep away from the women. You don't, you lose everything you got."

That was all Bob Fisher had to say. He turned and went back up the stairs. Shelby watched him, feeling better than he'd felt in days. He sure would keep away from the women. He'd give Norma all the room she needed. The state Bob Fisher was in, Norma would have his pants off him before the week was out.

6

"**B**OYS, I tell you the Lord loves us all as His children; but you cross Him and He can be mean as a roaring lion. Not mean because he hates you boys, no-sir; mean because he hates sin and evil so much. You don't believe me, read your Psalms, fifty, twenty-two, where it says, 'Now consider this, ye that forget God, lest I tear you in pieces'—you hear that?—'tear you in *pieces* and there be none to deliver. . . .' None to deliver means there ain't nothing left of you."

Mr. Manly couldn't tell a thing from their expressions. Sometimes they were looking at him, sometimes they weren't. Their heads didn't move much. Their eyes did. Raymond's eyes would go to the window and stay there a while. Harold would stare at the wall or the bookcase, and look as if he was asleep with his eyes open.

Mr. Manly flipped back a few pages in his Bible. When he looked up again his glasses gleamed in the overhead light. He had brought the two boys out of the snake den after only three days this time. Bob Fisher hadn't said a word. He'd marched them over, got them fed and cleaned up, and here they were. Here, but somewhere else in their minds. Standing across the desk fifteen, twenty minutes now, and Mr. Manly wondered if either of them had listened to a word he'd said.

"Again in the Psalms, boys, chapter eleven, sixth verse, it says, 'Upon the wicked shall rain snares, fire and brimstone and a horrible tempest'—that's like a storm—'and this shall be the portion of their cup.'

"Raymond, look at me. 'He that keepeth the commandments keepeth his own soul'—Proverbs, chapter nineteen, verse sixteen—'but he that despiseth His way shall die.'

"Harold Jackson of Fort Valley, Georgia, 'There shall be no reward for the evil man.' That's Proverbs again, twenty-four, twenty. 'The candle of the wicked shall be put out.' Harold, you understand that?"

"Yes-suh, captain."

"What does it mean?"

"It mean they put out your candle."

"It means God will put *you* out. You're the candle, Harold. If you're evil you get no reward and the Lord God will snuff out your life. You want that to happen?"

"No-suh, captain."

"Raymond, you want to have your life snuffed out?"

"No, sir, I don't want no part of that."

"It will happen as sure as it is written in the Book. Harold, you believe in the Book?"

"What Book is that, captain?"

"The Holy Bible."

"Yes-suh, I believe it."

"Raymond, you believe it?"

"What is that again?"

"Do you believe in the Holy Bible as being the inspired word of Almighty God as told by Him directly into the ears of the boys that wrote it?"

"I guess so," Raymond said.

"Raymond, you don't guess about your salvation. You believe in Holy Scripture and its truths, or you don't."

"I believe it," Raymond said.

"Have you ever been to church?"

"I think so. When I was little."

"Harold, you ever attend services?"

"You mean was I in the arm service, captain?"

"I mean have you ever been to church."

"Yes, I been there, captain."

"When was the last time?"

"Let's see," Harold said. "I think I went in Cuba one time."

"You *think* you went to church?"

"They talk in this language I don't know what they saying, captain."

"That was ten years ago," Mr. Manly said, "and you don't know if it was a church service or not."

"I think it was."

"Raymond, what about you?"

"Yes, sir, when I was little, all the time."

"What do you remember?"

"About Jesus and all. You know, how they nail him to this cross."

"Do you know the Ten Commandments?"

"I think I know some of them," Raymond said. "Thou shall not steal. Thou shall not commit adultery."

"Thou shalt not kill," Mr. Manly prompted.

"Thou shall not kill. That's one of them."

"The one that sent you here. Both of you. And now you're disobeying that commandment again by fighting. Did you know that? When you fight you break the Lord's commandment against killing?"

"What if you only hit him?" Raymond asked. "Beat him up good, but he don't die."

"It's the same thing. Look, when you hit somebody you hurt him a little bit or you hurt him a lot. When you kill somebody you hurt him for good. So hitting is the same as killing without going all the way. You understand that, Harold?"

"What was that, captain?"

Mr. Manly swiveled around slowly to look out the window, toward the convicts standing by the main cellblock. Close to a hundred men here, and only a handful of them, at the most, understood the Divine Word. Mr. Manly was sixty years old and knew he would never have time to teach them all. He only had a few months here before the place was closed. Then what? He had to do what he could, that's all. He had to begin somewhere, even if his work was never finished.

He came around again to face them and said, "Boys, the Lord has put it on the line to us. He says you got to keep His commandments. He says you don't keep them, you die. That doesn't mean you die and they put in a grave—no-sir. It means you die and go straight down to hell to suffer the fires of the damned. Raymond, you ever burn yourself?"

"Yes, sir, my hand one time."

"Boys, imagine getting burned all over for the rest of your life by the hottest fire you ever saw, hotter'n a blast furnace."

"You'd die," Raymond said.

"Only it doesn't kill you," Mr. Manly said quickly. "See, it's a special kind of fire that hurts terrible but never burns you up."

They looked at him, or seemed to be looking at him; he wasn't sure.

He tried again. "Like just your head is sticking out of the fire. You understand? So it don't suffocate you. But, boy, these flames are licking at your body and it's so hot you're a-screaming your lungs out, 'Water, water, somebody give me just a drop of water—please!' But it's too late, because far as you're concerned the Lord is fresh out of mercy."

Raymond was looking at the window again and Harold was studying the wall.

"Hell—" Mr. Manly began. He was silent for a while before he said, "It's a terrible place to be and I'm glad you boys are determined not to go there."

Harold said, "Where's that, captain?"

After they were gone Mr. Manly could still see them standing there. He got up and walked around them, picturing them from the back now, seeing the Negro's heavy, sloping shoulders, the Indian standing with a slight cock to his hip, hands loose at his sides. He'd like to stick a pin in them to see if they jumped. He'd like to holler in their ears. What's the matter with you? Don't you understand plain English? Are you too ignorant, or are you too full of evil? Answer me!

If they didn't understand the Holy Word, how was he ever going to preach it to them? He raised his eyes to the high ceiling and said, "Lord, if You're going to send me sinners, send me some with schooling, will you, please?"

He hadn't meant to say it out loud. In the silence that followed he hurried around the desk to sit down again.

Maybe that was the answer, though, and saying it out loud was the sign. Save somebody else, somebody who'd understand him, instead of two boys who couldn't even read and write. Sixty years old, he didn't have time to start saving illiterates. Somebody like Frank Shelby. Save him.

No, Frank was already trying. It was pretty clear he'd seen the error of his past life and was trying to correct it.

Norma Davis.

Get Norma in here and ask her if she was ready to accept the Lord Jesus Christ as her saviour. If she hadn't already.

No, something told Mr. Manly she hadn't yet. She was in for robbery, had shot a man, and had been arrested for prostitution in Wichita, Kansas. It wasn't likely she'd had time to be saved. She looked smart though.

Sit her down there, Mr. Manly thought.

He wasn't sure how he'd begin, but he'd get around to

picking some whores out of the Bible to tell her about—like that woman at the well. Jesus knew she was a whore, but He was still friendly and talked to her. See, He wasn't uppity about whores, they were just sinners to him like any other sinners. Take the time they're stoning the whore and He stops them, saying, Wait, only whoever of ye is without sin may cast a stone. And they had to quit doing it. See, Norma, we are all of us sinners in one way or another.

He kept looking at the way her top buttons were undone and the blouse was pulled open so he could see part of the valley between her breasts.

Where the soap had run down and over her belly.

She was sitting there trying to tempt him. Sure, she'd try to tempt him, try to show him up as a hypocrite.

She would undo a couple more buttons and he'd watch her calmly. He would say quietly, shaking his head slowly, "Norma, Norma."

She'd pull that blouse wide open and her eyes and her breasts would be staring right smack at him.

Sit back in the swivel chair then; show her he was at ease. Keep the expression very calm. And kindly.

She'd get up and lean over the desk then so they'd hang down. Great big round things with big reddish-brown tips. Then she'd jiggle them a little and he'd say in his quiet voice, "Norma, what are you doing that for? Don't you feel silly?"

Maybe he wouldn't ask her if she felt silly, but he'd say something.

She'd see she wasn't getting him, so then she'd take off her belt and slowly undo her skirt, watching him all the time, and let it fall. She'd back off a little bit and put her hands on her hips so he could see her good.

"Norma, child, cover your nakedness."

No, sir, that wasn't going to stop her. She was coming around the desk now. She'd stepped out of the skirt and was taking off the blouse, all the way off, coming toward him now without a stitch on.

He had better stand up, or it would be hard to talk to her.

Mr. Manly rose from the chair. He reached out to place his hands on Norma's bare shoulders and, smiling gently, said, "Child, 'If ye live after the flesh ye shall die'—Romans, eight, thirteen—'but if ye mortify the deeds of the body, ye shall live.'"

From the doorway Bob Fisher said, "Excuse me."

Mr. Manly came around, seeing the open door that had been left open when the two went out; he dropped his hands awkwardly to the edge of the desk.

Bob Fisher kept staring at him.

"I was just seeing if I could remember a particular verse from Romans," Mr. Manly said.

"How'd you do with Harold and Raymond?"

"It's too early to tell. I want to see them again in the morning."

"They got work to do."

"In the morning," Mr. Manly said.

Bob Fisher thought it over, then nodded and left the office. Walking down the hall, he was thinking that the little preacher may have been trying to remember a verse, but he sure looked like a man about to get laid.

Lord, give me these two, Mr. Manly said to the window and to the yard below. Give me a sign that they understand and are willing to receive the Lord Jesus Christ into their hearts.

He didn't mean a tongue of fire had to appear over the two boys' heads, or they had to get knocked to the ground the way St. Paul did. All they had to do was show some interest, a willingness to accept their salvation.

Lord, I need these two to prove my worthiness and devotion as a preacher of your Holy Writ. I need them to show for thirty years service in your ministry. Lord, I need them for my record, and I expect You know it.

Sit them down this time. Maybe that would help. Mr. Manly turned from the window and told them to take chairs. "Over there," he said. "Bring them up close to the desk."

They hesitated, looking around. It seemed to take them forever to carry the chairs over, their leg chains clinking on the wooden floor. He waited until they were settled, both of them looking past him, seeing what there was to see at this lower angle than yesterday.

"I'm going to tell you something. I know you both had humble beginnings. You were poor, you've been hungry, you've experienced all kinds of hardships and you've spent time in jail. Well, I never been to jail before I got sent here by the Bureau"—Mr. Manly paused as he grinned; neither of them noticing it—"I'll tell you though, I'll bet you I didn't begin any better off than you boys did. I was born in Clayburn County, Tennessee—either of you been there?"

Raymond shook his head. Harold said nothing.

"Well, it's in the mountains. I didn't visit Knoxville till I was fifteen years old, and it wasn't forty miles from home. I could've stayed there and farmed, or I could have run off and got into trouble. But you know what I did? I joined the Holy Word Pentecostal Youth Crusade and pledged myself to the service of the Lord Jesus. I preached over twenty years in Tennessee and Kentucky before coming out here to devote the rest of my life to mission work—the rest of it, five years, ten years. You know when your time is up and the Lord's going to call you?"

Harold Jackson's eyes were closed.

"Harold"—the eyes came open—"you don't know when you're going to die, do you?"

"No-suh, captain."

"Are you ready to die?"

"No-suh, captain. I don't think I ever be ready."

"St. Paul was ready."

"Yes-suh."

"Not at first he wasn't. Not until the Lord knocked him smack off his horse with a bolt of lightning and said, 'Saul, Saul, why do you persecuteth me?' Paul was a Jew-boy at that time and he was persecuting the Christians. Did you know that, Raymond?"

"No, I never knew that."

"Yes, sir, before he became Paul he was a Jew-boy name of Saul, used to put Christians to death, kill them in terrible ways. But once he become a Christian himself he made up for all the bad things he'd done by his own suffering. Raymond, you ever been stoned?"

"Like with rocks?"

"Hit with big rocks."

"I don't think so."

"Harold, you ever been shipwrecked?"

"I don't recall, captain."

Mr. Manly opened his Bible. "You boys think you've experienced hardships, listen, I'm going to read you something. From two Corinthians. 'Brethren, gladly you put up with fools, because you are wise . . .' Let me skip down. 'But whereas any man is bold . . . Are they ministers of Christ?' Here it is. '. . . in many more labors, in lashes above measure, often exposed to death. From the Jews'—listen to this—'five times I received forty lashes less one. Thrice I was scourged, once I was stoned, thrice I suffered shipwreck, a night and a day I was adrift on the sea; on journeyings often, in perils from floods, in perils from robbers, in perils from my own nation . . . in labor and hardships, in many sleepless nights, in hunger and thirst, in fastings often, in cold and nakedness.'"

Mr. Manly looked up. "Here's the thing, boys. St. Paul asked God three times to let him up from all these hardships. And you know what God said to him?" Mr. Manly's gaze dropped to the book. "He said, 'My grace is sufficient for thee, for strength is made perfect in weakness.'"

Now Mr. Manly sat back, just barely smiling, looking expectantly from Raymond to Harold, waiting for one of them to speak. Either one, he didn't care.

He didn't even care what they said, as long as one of them spoke.

Raymond was looking down at his hands, fooling with one of his fingernails. Harold was looking down too, his head bent low, and his eyes could have been open or closed.

"Strength—did you hear that, boys?—is made perfect in weakness."

He waited.

He could ask them what it meant.

He began thinking about the words. If you're weak the Lord helps you. Or strength stands out more in a weak person. Like it's more perfect, more complete, when a weak person gets strong.

No, that wasn't what it meant.

It meant no matter how weak you were you could get strong if you wanted.

Maybe. Or else it was the part just before which was the important part. God saying My grace is sufficient for thee. That's right, no matter what the temptation was.

Norma Davis could come in here and show herself and do all kinds of terrible things—God's grace would be sufficient. That was good to know.

It wasn't helping those two boys any, though. He had to watch that, thinking of himself more than them. They were the ones had to be saved. They had wandered from the truth and it was up to him to bring them back. For . . . 'whoever brings back a sinner from the error of his ways will save his own soul from death'—James, five-something—'and it will cover a multitude of sins.'"

That was the whole thing. If he could save these two boys he'd have nothing to worry about the rest of his life. He could maybe even slip once in a while—give in to temptation—without fear of his soul getting sent to hell. He wouldn't give in on purpose. You couldn't do that. But if somebody dragged you in and you went in scrapping, that was different.

"Boys," Mr. Manly said, "whoever brings back a sinner saves his own soul from death and it will cover a multitude of sins. Now do you want your souls to be saved, or don't you?"

Mr. Manly spent two days reading and studying before he called Raymond and Harold into the office again.

While they were standing by the desk he asked them how they were getting along. Neither of them wanted to answer that. He asked if there had been any trouble between them since the last time they were here. They both said no, sir. He asked if there had been any mean words between them. They said no, sir. Then it looked like they were getting somewhere, Mr. Manly said, and told them to bring the chairs over and sit down.

"'We know,'" he said to Raymond, "'that we have passed from death unto life because we love the brethren. He that loveth not his brethren abideth in death.'" Mr. Manly looked at Harold Jackson. "'Whoever hateth his brother is a murderer, and ye know that no murderer hath eternal life abiding in him.' James, chapter three, the fourteenth and fifteenth verses."

They were looking at him. That was good. They weren't

squinting or frowning, as if they were trying to figure out the words, or nodding agreement; but by golly they were looking at him and not out the window.

"Brethren means brother," he said. "You know that. It doesn't mean just your real brother, if you happen to have any brothers. It means everybody's your brethren. You two are brethren and I'm your brethren, everybody here at Yuma and everybody in the whole world, we are all brethren of Jesus Christ and sons of Almighty God. Even women. What I'm talking about, even women are your brethren, but we don't have to get into that. I'm saying we are all related by blood and I'll tell you why. You listening?"

Raymond's gaze came away from the window, his eyes opening wide with interest.

Harold said, "Yes-suh, captain."

"We are all related," Mr. Manly said, watching them, "because we all come from the first two people in the world, old Adam and Eve, who started the human race. They had children and their children had children and the children's children had some more, and it kept going that way until the whole world become populated."

Harold Jackson said, "Who did the children marry?"

"They married each other."

"I mean children in the same family."

Mr. Manly nodded. "Each other. They married among theirselves."

"You mean a boy did it with his sister?"

"Oh," Mr. Manly said. "Yes, but it was different then. God said it was all right because it was the only way to get the earth populated. See, in just a few generations you got so many people they're marrying cousins now, and second cousins, and a couple hundred years it's not even like they're kin any more."

Mr. Manly decided not to tell them about Adam living to be nine hundred and thirty and Seth and Enoch and Kenan and Methuselah, all of them getting up past nine hundred years old before they died. He had to leave out details or it might confuse them. It was enough to tell them how the population multiplied and the people gradually spread all over the world.

"If we all come from the same people," Raymond said, "where do niggers come from?"

So Mr. Manly had to tell them about Noah and his three sons, Shem, Ham, and Japheth, and how Ham made some dirty remark on seeing his daddy sleeping naked after drinking too much wine. For that Noah banished Ham and made his son a "slave of slaves." Ham and his family had most likely gone on down to Africa and that was where niggers came from, descendents of Ham.

Harold Jackson said, "Where does it say Indins come from?"

Mr. Manly shook his head. "It don't say and it don't matter. People moved all over the world, and those living in a certain place got to look alike on account of the climate. So now you got your white race, your yellow race, and your black race."

"What's an Indin?" Harold said. "What race?"

"They're not sure," Mr. Manly answered. "Probably somewhere in between. Like yellow with a little nigger thrown in. You can call it the Indian race if you want. The colored race is the only one mentioned in the Bible, on account of the story of Noah and Ham."

Harold said, "How do they know everybody was white before that?"

Mr. Manly frowned. What kind of a question was that? "They just know it. I guess because Adam and Eve was white." He said then, "There's nothing wrong with being a nigger. God made you a nigger for a reason. I mean some people have to be niggers and some have to be Indians. Some have to be white. But we are all still brethren."

Harold's eyes remained on Mr. Manly. "It say in the Bible this man went to Africa?"

"It wasn't called Africa then, but they're pretty sure that's where he went. His people multiplied and before you know it they're living all over Africa and that's how you got your different tribes. Your Zulus. Your Pygmies. You got your—oh, all different ones with those African names."

"Zulus," Harold Jackson said. "I heard something about Zulus one time."

Mr. Manly leaned forward on the edge of the desk. "What did you hear about them?"

"I don't know. I remember somebody talking about Zulus. Somebody saying the word."

"Harold, you know something? For all you know you might be a Zulu yourself."

Harold gave him a funny look. "I was born in Fort Valley, Georgia."

"Where was your mama and daddy born?"

"Fort Valley."

"Where was your granddaddy born?"

"I don't know."

"Or your great granddaddy. You know, he might have been born in Africa and brought over here as a slave. Maybe not him, but somebody before him, a kin of yours, was brought over. All your kin before him lived in Africa, and if they lived in a certain part of Africa then, by golly, they were Zulus."

Mr. Manly had a book about Africa in his collection. He remembered a drawing of a Zulu warrior, a tall Negro standing with a spear and a slender black and white cowhide shield.

He said, "Harold, your people are fine hunters and warriors. Oh, they're heathen, they paint theirselves up red and yellow and wear beads made out of lion's claws; but, Harold, they got to kill the lion first, with spears, and you don't go out and kill a lion unless you got plenty of nerve."

"With a spear, huh?" Harold said.

"Long spear they use, and this shield made out of cowhide. Some of them grow little beards and cut holes in the lobes of their ears and stick in these big hunks of dried sugar cane, if I remember correctly."

"They have sugar cane?"

"That's what it said in the book."

"They had a lot of sugar cane in Cuba. I never see anybody put it in their ear."

"Like earrings," Mr. Manly said. "I imagine they use all kinds of things. Gold, silver, if they got it."

"What do they wear?"

"Oh, just a little skimpy outfit. Some kind of cloth or animal skin around their middle. Nothing up here. Wait a second," Mr. Manly said. He went over to his bookcase. He found the book right away, but had to skim through it twice before he found the picture and laid the book open in front of Harold. "There. That's your Zulu warrior."

Harold hunched over the book. As he studied the picture Mr. Manly said, "Something else I remember. It says in there these Zulus can run. I mean *run*. The boys training to be warriors, they'd run twenty miles, take a little rest and run some more. Run thirty-forty miles a day isn't anything for a Zulu. Then go out and kill a lion. Or a elephant."

Mr. Manly noticed Raymond San Carlos glancing over at the book and he said quickly, "Same with your Indians; especially your desert tribes, like the Apaches. They can run all day long, I understand, and not take a drink of water till sundown. They know where to find water, too, way out in the middle of the desert. Man told me once, when Apaches are going where they know there isn't any water they take a horse's intestine and fill it full of water and wrap it around their bodies. He said he'd match an Apache Indian against a camel for traveling across the desert without any water."

"There's plenty of water," Raymond said, "if you know where to look."

"That's what I understand."

"Some of the older men at San Carlos, they'd take us boys and make us go up in the mountains and stay there two, three days without food or water."

"You did that?"

"Plenty of times."

"You'd find water?"

"Sure, and something to eat. Not much, but enough to hold us."

"Say, I just read in the paper," Mr. Manly said. "You know who died the other day? Geronimo."

"Is that right?"

"Fort Sill, Oklahoma. Died of pneumonia."

"That's too bad," Raymond said. "I mean I think he would rather have got killed fighting."

"You ever see him? No, you would have been too young."

"Sure, I seen him. Listen, I'll tell you something I never told anybody. My father was in his band. Geronimo's."

"Is that a fact?"

"He was killed in Mexico when the soldiers went down there."

"My goodness," Mr. Manly said, "we're talking about warriors, you're the son of an Apache warrior."

"I never told anybody that."

"Why not? I'd think you'd be proud to tell it."

"It doesn't do me any good."

"But if it's true—"

"You think I'm lying?"

"I mean since it's a fact, why not tell it?"

"It don't make any difference to me. I could be Apache, I could be Mexican, I'm in Yuma the rest of my life."

"But you're living that life," Mr. Manly said. "If a person's an Indian then he should look at himself as an Indian. Like I told Harold, God made him a nigger for a reason. All right, God made you an Indian. There's nothing wrong with being an Indian. Why, do you know that about half our states have Indian names? Mississippi. The state I come from, Tennessee. Arizona. The Colorado River out yonder. Yuma."

"I don't know," Harold said, "that spear looks like it could break easy."

Mr. Manly looked over at him and at the book. "They know how to make 'em."

"They fight other people?"

"Sure they did. Beat 'em, too. What I understand, your Zulus owned most of the southern part of Africa, took it from other tribes and ruled over them."

"Never got beat, uh?"

"Not that I ever heard of. No, sir, they're the greatest warriors in Africa."

"Nobody ever beat the Apache," Raymond said, "till the U. S. Army come with all their goddamn guns."

"Raymond, don't ever take the Lord's name in vain like that."

"Apaches beat the Pimas, the Papagoes, Maricopas—took anything we wanted from them."

"Well, I don't hold with raiding and killing," Mr. Manly said, "but I'll tell you there is something noble about your uneducated savage that you don't see in a lot of white men. I mean just the way your warrior stands, up straight with his shoulders back and never says too much, doesn't talk just to hear himself, like a lot of white people I know. I'll tell you something else, boys. Savage warriors have never been known to lie or go back on their word, and that's a fact. Man up at the reservation told me that Indians don't even have a word in their language for lie. Same thing with your Zulus. I reckon if a boy can run all day long and kill lions with a spear, he don't ever *have* to lie."

"I never heard of Apaches with spears," Raymond said.

"Oh, yes, they had them. And bows and arrows."

Harold was waiting. "I expect the Zulus got guns now, don't they?"

"I don't know about that," Mr. Manly answered. "Maybe they don't need guns. Figure spears are good enough." A smile touched his mouth as he looked across the desk at Raymond and Harold. "The thing that tickles me," he said, "I'm liable to have a couple of real honest-to-goodness Apache and Zulu warriors sitting right here in my office and I didn't even know it."

That evening, when Bob Fisher got back after supper, the guard at the sally port told him Mr. Manly wanted to see him right away. Fisher asked him what for, and the guard said how was he supposed to know. Fisher told the man to watch his mouth, and headed across the compound to see what the little squirt wanted.

Fisher paused by the stairs and looked over toward the cook shack. The women would be starting their bath about now.

Mr. Manly was writing something, but put it aside as Fisher came in. He said, "Pull up a chair," and seemed anxious to talk.

"There's a couple of things I got to do yet tonight."

"I wanted to talk to you about our Apache and our Zulu."

"How's that?"

"Raymond and Harold. I've been thinking about Frank Shelby's idea—he seems like a pretty sensible young man, doesn't he?"

Jesus Christ, Bob Fisher thought. He said, "I guess he's smart enough."

Mr. Manly smiled. "Though not smart enough to stay out of jail. Well, I've been thinking about this boxing-match idea. I want you to know I've given it a lot of thought."

Fisher waited.

"I want Frank Shelby to understand it too—you might mention it to him if you see him before I do."

"I'll tell him," Fisher said. He started to go.

"Hey, I haven't told you what I decided."

Fisher turned to the desk again.

"I've been thinking—a boxing match wouldn't be too good. We want them to stop fighting and we tell them to go ahead and fight. That doesn't sound right, does it?"

"I'll tell him that."

"You're sure in a hurry this evening, Bob."

"It's time I made the rounds is all."

"Well, I could walk around with you if you want and we could talk."

"That's all right," Fisher said, "go ahead."

"Well, as I said, we won't have the boxing match. You know what we're going to have instead?"

"What?"

"We're going to have a race. I mean Harold and Raymond are going to have a race."

"A race," Fisher said.

"A foot race. The faster man wins and gets some kind of a prize, but I haven't figured that part of it out yet."

"They're going to run a race," Fisher said.

"Out in the exercise yard. Down to the far end and back, maybe a couple of times."

"When do you want this race held?"

"Tomorrow I guess, during free time."

"You figure it'll stop them fighting, uh?"

"We don't have anything to lose," Mr. Manly said. "A good race might just do the trick."

Get out of here, Bob Fisher thought. He said, "Well, I'll tell them."

"I've already done that."

"I'll tell Frank Shelby then." Fisher edged toward the door and got his hand on the knob.

"You know what it is?" Mr. Manly was leaning back in his chair with a peaceful, thoughtful expression. "It's sort of a race of races," he said. "You know what I mean? The Negro against the Indian, black man against red man. I don't mean to prove that one's better than the other. I mean as a way to stir up their pride and get them interested in doing something with theirselves. You know what I mean?"

Bob Fisher stared at him.

"See, the way I figure them—" Mr. Manly motioned to the chair again. "Sit down, Bob, I'll tell you how I see these two boys, and why I believe we can help them."

By the time Fisher got down to the yard, the women had taken their bath. They were back in their cellblock and he had to find R. E. Baylis for the keys.

"I already locked everybody in," the guard said.

"I know you did. That's why I need the keys."

"Is there something wrong somewhere?"

Bob Fisher had never wanted to look at that woman as bad as he did this evening. God, he felt like he *had* to look at her, but everybody was getting in his way, wasting time. His wife at supper nagging at him again about moving to Florence. The little squirt preacher who believed he could save a couple of bad convicts. Now a slow-witted guard asking him questions.

"Just give me the keys," Fisher said.

He didn't go over there directly. He walked past the TB cellblock first and looked in at the empty yard, at the lantern light showing in most of the cells and the dark ovals of the cells that were not occupied. The nigger and the Indian were in separate cells. They were doing a fair job on the wall; but, Jesus, they'd get it done a lot sooner if the little squirt would let them work instead of wasting time preaching to them. Now foot races. God Almighty.

Once you were through the gate of the women's cellblock, the area was more like a room than a yard—a little closed-in courtyard and two cells carved into the granite wall.

There was lantern light in both cells. Fisher looked in at Tacha first and asked her what she was doing. Tacha was sitting on a stool in the smoky dimness of the cell. She said, "I'm reading," and looked down at the book again. Bob Fisher told himself to take it easy now and not to be impatient. He looked in Tacha's cell almost a minute longer before moving on to Norma's.

She was stretched out in her bunk, staring right at him when he looked through the iron strips of the door. A blanket covered her, but one bare arm and shoulder were out of the blanket and, Jesus, it didn't look like she had any clothes on. His gaze moved around the cell to show he wasn't too interested in her.

"Everything all right?"

"That's a funny thing to ask," Norma said. "Like this is a hotel."

"I haven't looked in here in a while."

"I know you haven't."

"You need another blanket or anything?"

"What's anything?"

"I mean like kerosene for the lantern."

"I think there's enough. The light's awful low though."

"Turn it up."

"I can't. I think the wick's stuck. Or else it's burned down."

"You want me to take a look at it?"

"Would you? I'd appreciate it."

Bob Fisher brought the ring of keys out of his coat pocket with the key to Norma's cell in his hand. As he opened the door and came in, Norma raised up on one elbow, holding the blanket in front of her. He didn't look at her; he went right to the lamp and peered in through the smoky glass. As he turned the wick up slowly, the light grew brighter, then dimmed again as he turned it down.

"It seems all right now." Fisher glanced at her twisted bare back. He tried the lantern a few more times, twisting the wick up and down and knowing her bare back—and that meant her bare front too—wasn't four feet away from him. "It must've been stuck," he said.

"I guess it was. Will you turn it down now? Just so there's a nice glow."

"How's that?"

"That's perfect."

"I think you got enough wick in there."

"I think so. Do you want to get in bed with me?"

"Jesus Christ," Bob Fisher said.

"Well, do you?"

"You're a nervy thing, aren't you?"

Norma twisted around a little more and let the blanket fall. "I can't help it."

"You can't help what?"

"If I want you to do it to me."

"Jesus," Bob Fisher said. He looked at the cell door and then at Norma again, cleared his throat and said in a lower tone, "I never heard a girl asking for it before."

"Well," Norma said, throwing the blanket aside as she got up from the bunk and moved toward him, "you're hearing it now, daddy."

"Listen, Tacha's right next door."

"She can't see us."

"She can hear."

"Then we'll whisper." Norma began unbuttoning his coat.

"We can't do nothing here."

"Why not?"

"One of the guards might come by."

"Now you're teasing me. Nobody's allowed in here at night, and you know it."

"Boy, you got big ones."

"There, now slip your coat off."

"I can't stay here more'n a few minutes."

"Then quit talking," Norma said.

7

F RANK SHELBY said, "A race, what do you mean, a race?"
"I mean a foot race," Fisher told him. "The nigger and the Indin are going to run a race from one end of the yard to the other and back again, and you and every convict in this place are going to be out here to watch it."

"A race," Shelby said again. "Nobody cares about any foot race."

"You don't have to care," Fisher said. "I'm not asking you to care. I'm telling you to close your store and get everybody's ass out of the cellblock. They can stand here or over along the south wall. Ten minutes, I want everybody out."

"This is supposed to be our free time."

"I'll tell you when you get free time."

"What if we want to make some bets?"

"I don't care, long as you keep it quiet. I don't want any arguments, or have to hit anybody over the head."

"Ten minutes, it doesn't give us much time to figure out how to bet."

"You don't know who's going to win," Fisher said. "What's the difference?"

About half the convicts were already in the yard. Fisher waited for the rest of them to file out: the card players and the convicts who could afford Frank Shelby's whiskey and the ones who were always in their bunks between working and eating. They came out of the cellblock and stood around waiting for something to happen. The guards up on the wall came out of the towers and looked around too, as if they didn't know what was going on. Bob Fisher hadn't told any of them about the race. It wouldn't take more than a couple of minutes. He told the convicts to keep the middle area of the yard clear. They started asking him what was going on, but he walked away from them toward the mess hall. It was good that he did. When Mr. Manly appeared on the stairway at the end of the building Fisher was able to get to him before he reached the yard.

"You better stay up on the stairs."

Mr. Manly looked surprised. "I was going over there with the convicts."

"It's happened a sup'rintendent's been grabbed and a knife put at his throat till the gate was opened."

"You go among the convicts; all the guards do."

"But if any of us are grabbed the gate stays closed. They know that. They don't know about you."

"I just wanted to mingle a little," Mr. Manly said. He looked out toward the yard. "Are they ready?"

"Soon as they get their leg-irons off."

A few minutes later, Raymond and Harold were brought down the length of the yard. The convicts watched them, and a few called out to them. Mr. Manly didn't hear what they said, but he noticed neither Raymond nor Harold looked over that way. When they reached the stairs he said, "Well, boys, are you ready?"

"You want us to run," Raymond said. "You wasn't kidding, uh?"

"Course I wasn't."

"I don't know. We just got the irons off. My legs feel funny."

"You want to warm up first?"

Harold Jackson said, "I'm ready any time he is."

Raymond shrugged. "Let's run the race."

Mr. Manly made sure they understood—down to the end of the yard, touch the wall between the snake den and the women's cellblock, and come back past the stairs, a distance Mr. Manly figured to be about a hundred and twenty yards or so. He and Mr. Fisher would be up at the top of the stairs in the judge's stand. Mr. Fisher would fire off a revolver as the starting signal. "So," Mr. Manly said, "if you boys are ready—"

There was some noise from the convicts as Raymond and Harold took off as the shot was fired and passed the main cellblock in a dead heat. Raymond hit the far wall and came off in one motion. Harold stumbled and dug hard on the way back but was five or six yards behind Raymond going across the finish.

They stood with their hands on their hips breathing in and out while Mr. Manly leaned over the rail of the stair landing, smiling down at them. He said, "Hey, boys, you sure gave it the old try. Rest a few minutes and we'll run it again."

Raymond looked over at Harold. They got down again and went off with the sound of the revolver, Raymond letting Harold set the pace this time, staying with him and not kicking out ahead until they were almost to the finish line. This time he took it by two strides, with the convicts yelling at them to *run*.

Raymond could feel his chest burning now. He walked around breathing with his mouth open, looking up at the sky that was fading to gray with the sun below the west wall, walking around in little circles and seeing Mr. Manly up there now. As Raymond turned away he heard Harold say, "Let's do it again," and he had to go along.

Harold dug all the way this time; he felt his thighs knotting and pushed it some more, down and back and, with the convicts yelling, came in a good seven strides ahead of the Indian. Right away Harold said, "Let's do it again."

In the fourth race he was again six or seven strides faster than Raymond.

In the fifth race, neither of them looked as if he was going to make it back to the finish. They ran pumping their arms and gasping for air, and Harold might have been ahead by a half-stride past the stairs; but Raymond stumbled and fell forward trying to catch himself, and it was hard to tell who won. There wasn't a sound from the convicts this time. Some of them weren't even looking this way. They were milling around, smoking cigarettes, talking among themselves.

Mr. Manly wasn't watching the convicts. He was leaning over the railing looking down at his two boys: at Raymond lying stretched out on his back and at Harold sitting, leaning back on his hands with his face raised to the sky.

"Hey, boys," Mr. Manly called, "you know what I want you to do now? First I want you to get up. Come on, boys, get up on your feet. Raymond, you hear me?"

"He looks like he's out," Fisher said.

"No, he's all right. See?"

Mr. Manly leaned closer over the rail. "Now I want you two to walk up to each other. Go on, do as I say. It won't hurt you. Now I want you both to reach out and shake hands. . . .

"Don't look up here. Look at each other and shake hands."

Mr. Manly started to grin and, by golly, he really felt good. "Bob, look at that."

"I see it," Fisher said.

Mr. Manly called out now, "Boys, by the time you get done running together you're going to be good friends. You wait and see."

The next day, while they were working on the face wall in the TB cellblock, Raymond was squatting down mixing mortar in a bucket and groaned as he got to his feet. "Goddamn legs," he said.

"I know what you mean," Harold said. He was laying a brick, tapping it into place with the handle of his trowel, and hesitated as he heard his own voice and realized he had spoken to Raymond. He didn't look over at him; he picked up another brick and laid it in place. It was quiet in the yard. The tubercular convicts were in their cells, out of the heat and the sun. Harold could hear a switch-engine working, way down the hill in the Southern Pacific yard; he could hear the freight cars banging together as they were coupled.

After a minute or so Raymond said, "I can't hardly walk today."

"From running," Harold said.

"They don't put the leg-irons back on, uh?"

"I wondered if they forgot to."

"I think so. They wouldn't leave them off unless they forgot."

There was silence again until Harold said, "They can leave them off, it's all right with me."

"Sure," Raymond said, "I don't care they leave them off."

"Place in Florida, this prison farm, you got to wear them all the time."

"Yeah? I hope I never get sent there."

"You ever been to Cuba?"

"No, I never have."

"That's a fine place. I believe I like to go back there sometime."

"Live there?"

"Maybe. I don't know."

"Look like we need some more bricks," Raymond said.

The convicts mixing the adobe mud straightened up with their shovels in front of them as Raymond and Harold came across the yard pushing their wheelbarrows. Joe Dean stepped around to the other side of the mud so he could keep an eye on the south-wall tower guard. He waited until the two boys were close, heading for the brick pile.

"Well, now," Joe Dean said, "I believe it's the two sweethearts."

"If they come back for some more," another convict said, "I'm going to cut somebody this time."

Joe Dean watched them begin loading the wheelbarrows. "See, what they do," he said, "they start a ruckus so they'll get sent to the snake den. Sure, they get in there, just the two of them. Man, they hug and kiss, do all kinds of things to each other."

"That is Mr. Joe Dean talking," Harold said. "I believe he wants to get hit in the mouth with a 'dobe brick."

"I want to see you try that," Joe Dean said.

"Sometime when the guard ain't looking," Harold said. "Maybe when you ain't looking either."

They finished loading their wheelbarrows and left.

In the mess hall at supper they sat across one end of a table. No one else sat with them. Raymond looked around at the convicts hunched over eating. No one seemed aware of them. They were all talking or concentrating on their food. He said to Harold, "Goddamn beans, they always got to burn them."

"I've had worse beans," Harold said. "Worse everything. What I like is some chicken, that's what I miss. Chicken's good."

"I like a beefsteak. With peppers and catsup."

"Beefsteak's good too. You like fried fish?"

"I never had it."

"You never had fish?"

"I don't think so."

"Man, where you been you never had fish?"

"I don't know, I never had it."

"We got a big river right outside."

"I never seen anybody fishing."

"How long it take you to swim across?"

"Maybe five minutes."

"That's a long time to swim."

"Too long. They get a boat out quick."

"Anybody try to dig out of here?"

"I never heard of it," Raymond said. "The ones that go they always run from a work detail, outside."

"Anybody make it?"

"Not since I been here."

"Man start running he got to know where he's going. He got to have a place to go to." Harold looked up from his plate. "How long you here for?"

"Life."

"That's a long time, ain't it?"

They were back at work on the cell wall the next day when a guard came and got them. It was about mid-afternoon. Neither of them asked where they were going; they figured they were going to hear another sermon from the man. They marched in front of the guard down the length of the yard and past the brick detail. When they got near the mess hall they veered a little toward the stairway and the guard said, "Keep going, straight ahead."

Raymond and Harold couldn't believe it. The guard marched them through the gates of the sally port and right up to Mr. Rynning's twenty-horsepower Ford Touring Car.

"Let me try to explain it to you again," Mr. Manly said to Bob Fisher. "I believe these boys have got to develop some pride in theirselves. I don't mean they're supposed to get uppity with us. I mean they got to look at theirselves as man in the sight of men, and children in the eyes of God."

"Well, I don't know anything about that part," Bob Fisher said. "To me they are a couple of bad cons, and if you want my advice based on years of dealing with these people, we put their leg-irons back on."

"They can't run in leg-irons."

"I know they can't. They need to work and they need to get knocked down a few times. A convict stands up to you, you better knock him down quick."

"Have they stood up to you, Bob?"

"One of them served time in Leavenworth, the other one tried to swim the river and they're both trying to kill one another. I call that standing up to me."

"You say they're hard cases, Bob, and I say they're like little children, because they're just now beginning to learn about living with their fellowman, which to them means living with white men and getting along with white men."

"Long as they're here," Fisher said, "they damn well better. We only got one set of rules."

Mr. Manly shook his head. "I don't mean to change the rules for them." It was harder to explain than he thought it would be. He couldn't look right at Fisher; the man's solemn expression, across the desk, distracted him. He would glance at Fisher and then look down at the sheet of paper that was partly covered with oval shapes that were like shields, and long thin lines that curved awkwardly into spear heads. "I don't mean to treat them as privileged characters either. But we're not going to turn them into white men, are we?"

"We sure aren't."

"We're not going to tell them they're just as good as white men, are we?"

"I don't see how we could do that," Fisher said.

"So we tell them what an Indian is good at and what a nigger is good at."

"Niggers lie and Indians steal."

"Bob, we tell them what they're good at as members of their race. We already got it started. We tell them Indians and niggers are the best runners in the world."

"I guess if they're scared enough."

"We train them hard and, by golly, they begin to believe it."

"Yeah?"

"Once they begin to believe in something, they begin to believe in theirselves."

"Yeah?"

"That's all there is to it."

"Well, maybe you ought to get some white boys to run against them."

"Bob, I'm not interested in them running *races*. This has got to do with distance and endurance. Being able to do something no one else in this prison can do. That race out in the yard was all wrong, more I think about it."

"Frank Shelby said he figured the men wouldn't mind seeing different kinds of races instead of just back and forth. He said run them all over and have them jump things—like climb up the wall on ropes, see who can get to the top first. He said he thought the men would get a kick out of that."

"Bob, that is a show. It doesn't prove nothing. I'm talking about these boys running *miles*."

"Miles, uh?"

"Like their granddaddies used to do."

"How's that?"

"Like Harold Jackson's people back in Africa. Bob, they kill lions with *spears*."

"Harold killed a man with a lead pipe."

"There," Mr. Manly said. "That's the difference. That's what he's become because he's forgot what it's like to be a Zulu nigger warrior."

Jesus Christ, Bob Fisher said to himself. The little squirt shouldn't be sitting behind the desk, he should be over in the goddamn crazy hole. He said, "You want them to run miles, uh?"

"Start them out a few miles a day. Work up to ten miles, twenty miles. We'll see how they do."

"Well, it will be something to see, all right, them running back and forth across the yard. I imagine the convicts will make a few remarks to them. The two boys get riled up and lose their temper, they're back in the snake den and I don't see you've made any progress at all."

"I've already thought of that," Mr. Manly said. "They're not going to run in the yard. They're going to run outside."

The convicts putting up the adobe wall out at the cemetery were the first ones to see them. A man raised up to stretch the kinks out of his back and said, "Look-it up there!"

They heard the Ford Touring Car as they looked around and saw it up on the slope, moving along the north wall with the two boys running behind it. Nobody could figure it out. Somebody asked what were they chasing the car for. Another convict said they weren't chasing the car, they were being taken somewhere. See, there was a guard in the back seat with a rifle. They could see him good against the pale wall of the prison. Nobody had ever seen convicts taken somewhere like that. Any time the car went out it went down to Yuma, but no convicts were ever in the car or behind it or anywhere near it. One of the convicts asked the work-detail guard where he supposed they were going. The guard said it beat him. That motor car belonged to Mr. Rynning and was only used for official business.

It was the stone-quarry gang that saw them next. They looked squinting up through the white dust and saw the Ford Touring Car and the two boys running to keep up with it, about twenty feet behind the car and just barely visible in all the dust the car was raising. The stone-quarry gang watched until the car was past the open rim and the only thing left to see was the dust hanging in the sunlight. Somebody said they certainly had it ass-backwards; the car was supposed to be chasing the cons. They tried to figure it out, but nobody had an answer that made much sense.

Two guards and two convicts, including Joe Dean, coming back in the wagon from delivering a load of adobe bricks in town, saw them next—saw them pass right by on the road— and Joe Dean and the other convict and the two guards turned around and watched them until the car crossed the railroad tracks and passed behind some depot sheds. Joe Dean said he could understand why the guards didn't want the spook and the Indin riding with them, but he still had never seen anything like it in all the time he'd been here. The guards said they had never seen anything like it either. There was funny things going on. Those two had raced each other, maybe they were racing the car now. Joe Dean said Goddamn, this was the craziest prison he had ever been in.

That first day, the best they could run in one stretch was a little over a mile. They did that once: down prison hill and along the railroad tracks and out back of town, out into the country. Most of the time, in the three hours they were out, they would run as far as they could, seldom more than a quarter of a mile—then have to quit and walk for a while, breathing hard with their mouths open and their lungs on fire. They would drop thirty to forty feet back of the car and the guard with the Winchester would yell at them to come on, get the lead out of their feet.

Harold said to Raymond, "I had any lead in my feet I'd take and hit that man in the mouth with it."

"We tell him we got to rest," Raymond said.

They did that twice, sat down at the side of the road in the meadow grass and watched the guard coming with the rifle and the car backing up through its own dust. The first time the guard pointed the rifle and yelled for them to get on their feet. Harold told him they couldn't move and asked him if he was going to shoot them for being tired.

"Captain, we *want* to run, but our legs won't mind what we tell them."

So the guard gave them five minutes and they sat back in the grass to let their muscles relax and stared at the distant mountains while the guards sat in the car smoking their cigarettes.

Harold said to Raymond, "What are we doing this for?"

Raymond gave him a funny look. "Because we're tired, what do you think?"

"I mean running. What are we running for?"

"They say to run, we run."

"It's that little preacher."

"Sure it is. What do you think, these guards thought of it?"

"That little man's crazy, ain't he?"

"I don't know," Raymond said. "Most of the time I don't understand him. He's got something in his head about running."

"Running's all right if you in a hurry and you know where you going."

"That road don't go anywhere."

"What's up ahead?"

"The desert," Raymond said. "Maybe after a while you come to a town."

"You know how to drive that thing?"

"A car? I never even been in one."

Harold was chewing on a weed stem, looking at the car. "It would be nice to have a ride home, wouldn't it?"

"It might be worth the running," Raymond said.

The guard got them up and they ran some more. They ran and walked and ran again for almost another mile, and this time when they went down they stretched out full length: Harold on his stomach, head down and his arms propping him up; Raymond on his back with his chest rising and falling.

After ten minutes the guard said all right, they were starting back now. Neither of them moved as the car turned around and rolled past them. The guard asked if they heard him. He said goddamn-it, they better get up quick. Harold said captain, their legs hurt so bad it didn't look like they could make it. The guard levered a cartridge into the chamber of the Winchester and said their legs would hurt one hell of a lot more with a .44 slug shot through them. They got up and fell in behind the car. Once they tried to run and had to stop within a dozen yards. It wasn't any use, Harold said. The legs wouldn't do what they was told. They could walk though. All right, the guard said, then walk. But god*damn*, they were so slow, poking along, he had to keep yelling at them to come on. After a while, still not in sight of the railroad tracks, the guard driving said to the other guard, if they didn't hurry they were going to miss supper call. The guard with the Winchester said well, what was he supposed to do about it? The guard driving said it looked like there was only one thing they *could* do.

Raymond liked it when the car stopped and the guard with the rifle, looking like he wanted to kill them, said all right, goddamn-it, get in.

Harold liked it when they drove past the cemetery work detail filing back to prison. The convicts had moved off the road and were looking back, waiting for the car. As they went by Harold raised one hand and waved. He said to Raymond, "Look at them poor boys. I believe they convicts."

8

"YOU KNOW why they won't try to escape?" Mr. Manly said. Bob Fisher stood at the desk and didn't say anything, because the answer was going to come from the little preacher anyway.

"Because they see the good in this. They realize this is their chance to become something."

"Running across a pasture field."

"You know what I mean."

"Take a man outside enough times," Fisher said, "he'll run for the hills."

"Not these two boys."

"Any two. They been outside every day for a week and they're smelling fresh air."

"Two weeks, and they can run three miles without stopping," Mr. Manly said. "Another couple of weeks I want to see them running five miles, maybe six."

"They'll run as long as it's easier than working."

Mr. Manly smiled a little. "I see you don't know them very well."

"I have known them all my life," Bob Fisher said. "When running becomes harder than working, they'll figure a way to get out of it. They'll break each other's legs if they have to."

"All right, then I'll talk to them again. You can be present, Bob, and I'll prove to you you're wrong."

"I understand you write a weekly report to Mr. Rynning," Fisher said. "Have you told him what you're doing?"

"As a matter of fact, I have."

"You told him you got them running outside?"

"I told him I'm trying something out on two boys considered incorrigible, a program that combines spiritual teaching and physical exercise. He's made no mention to me what he thinks. But if you want to write to him, Bob, go right ahead."

"If it's all the same to you," Fisher said, "I want it on the record I didn't have nothing to do with this in any way at all."

* * *

Three miles wasn't so bad and it was easier to breathe at the end of the stretch. It didn't feel as if their lungs were burning any more. They would walk for a few minutes and run another mile and then walk again. Maybe they could do it again, run another mile before resting. But why do it if they didn't have to, if the guards didn't expect it? They would run a little way and when Raymond or Harold would call out they had to rest the car would stop and wait for them.

"I think we could do it," Raymond said.

"Sure we could."

"Maybe run four, five miles at the start."

"We could do that too," Harold said, "but why would we want to?"

"I mean to see if we could do it."

"Man, we could run five miles right now if we wanted."

"I don't know."

"If we had something to run for. All I see it doing is getting us tired."

"It's better than laying adobes, or working on the rock pile."

"I believe you're right there," Harold said.

"Well," Raymond said, "we can try four miles, five miles at any time we want. What's the hurry?"

"What's the hurry," Harold said. "I wish that son of a bitch would give us a cigarette. Look at him sucking on it and blowing the smoke out. Man."

They were getting along all right with the guards, because the guards were finding out this was pretty good duty, driving around the countryside in a Ford Touring Car. Ride around for a few hours. Smoke any time they wanted. Put the canvas top up if it got too hot in the sun. The guards weren't dumb, though. They stayed away from trees and the river bank, keeping to open range country once they had followed the railroad tracks out beyond town.

The idea of a train going by interested Harold. He pictured them running along the road where it was close to the tracks and the train coming up behind them out of the depot, not moving too fast. As the guards watched the train, Harold saw himself and Raymond break through the weeds to the gravel roadbed, run with the train and swing up on one of those iron-rung ladders they had on boxcars. Then the good part. The guards are watching the train and all of a sudden the guards see them on the boxcar—*waving to them.*

"Waving good-bye," Harold said to Raymond when they were resting one time and he told him about it.

Raymond was grinning. "They see the train going away, they don't know what to do."

"Oh, they take a couple of shots," Harold said. "But they so excited, man, they can't even hit the train."

"We're waving bye-bye."

"Yeah, while they shooting at us."

"It would be something, all right." Raymond had to wipe his eyes.

After a minute Harold said, "Where does the train go to?"

"I don't know. I guess different places."

"That's the trouble," Harold said. "You got to know where you going. You can't stay on the train. Sooner or later you got to get off and start running again."

"You think we could run five miles, uh?"

"If we wanted to," Harold said.

It was about a week later that Mr. Manly woke up in the middle of the night and said out loud in the bedroom, "All right, if you're going to keep worrying about it, why don't you see for yourself what they're doing?"

That's what he did the next day: hopped in the front seat of the Ford Touring Car and went along to watch the two boys do their road work.

It didn't bother the guard driving too much. He had less to say was all. But the guard with the Winchester yelled at Raymond and Harold more than he ever did before to come on, pick 'em up, keep closer to the car. Mr. Manly said the dust was probably bothering them. The guard said it was bothering him too, because he had to see before he could watch them. He said you get a con outside you watch him every second.

Raymond and Harold ran three miles and saw Mr. Manly looking at his watch. Later on, when they were resting, he came over and squatted down in the grass with them.

"Three miles in twenty-five minutes," he said. "That's pretty good. You reckon you could cover five miles in an hour?"

"I don't think so," Raymond said. "It's not us, we want to do it. It's our legs."

"Well, wanting something is half of getting it," Mr. Manly said. "I mean if you want something bad enough."

"Sure, we want to do it."

"Why?"

"Why? Well, I guess because we got to do it."

"You just said you wanted to."

"Yeah, we like to run."

"And I'm asking you why." Mr. Manly waited a moment. "Somebody told me all you fellas want to do is get out of work."

"Who tole you that?"

"It doesn't matter who it was. You know what I told him? I told him he didn't know you boys very well. I told him you were working harder now, running, than you ever worked in your life."

"That's right," Raymond said.

"Because you see a chance of doing something nobody else in the prison can do. Run twenty miles in a day."

Raymond said, "You want us to run twenty miles?"

"*You* want to run twenty miles. You're an Apache Indian, aren't you? And Harold's a Zulu. Well, by golly, an Apache Indian and a Zulu can run twenty miles, thirty miles a day, and there ain't a white man in this territory can say that."

"You want us to run twenty miles?" Raymond said again.

"I want you to start thinking of who you are, that's what I want. I want you to start thinking like warriors for a change instead of like convicts."

Raymond was watching him, nodding as he listened. He said, "Do these waryers think different than other people?"

"They think of who they are." An angry little edge came into Mr. Manly's tone. "They got pride in their tribe and their job, and everything they do is to make them better warriors— the way they live, the way they dress, the way they train to harden theirselves, the way they go without food or water to show their bodies their will power is in charge here and, by golly, their bodies better do what they're told. Raymond, you say you're Apache Indian?"

"Yes, sir, that's right."

"Harold, you believe you're a Zulu?"

"Yes-suh, captain, a Zulu."

"Then prove it to me, both of you. Let me see how good you are."

As Mr. Manly got to his feet he glanced over at the guards, feeling a little funny now in the silence and wondering if they had been listening. Well, so what if they had? He was superintendent, wasn't he? And he answered right back, You're darn right.

"You boys get ready for some real training," he said now. "I'm taking you at your word."

Raymond waited until he walked away and had reached the car. "Who do you think tole him we're doing this to get out of work?"

"I don't know," Harold said. "Who do you think?"

"I think that son of a bitch Frank Shelby."

"Yeah," Harold said, "he'd do it, wouldn't he?"

On Visiting Day the mess-hall tables were placed in a single line, dividing the room down the middle. The visitors remained on one side and the convicts on the other. Friends and relatives could sit down facing each other if they found a place at the tables; but they couldn't touch, not even hands, and a visitor was not allowed to pass anything to a convict.

Frank Shelby always got a place at the tables and his visitor was always his brother, a slightly older and heavier brother, but used to taking orders from Frank.

Virgil Shelby said, "By May for sure."

"I don't want a month," Frank said. "I want a day."

"I'm telling you what I know. They're done building the place, they're doing something inside the walls now and they won't let anybody in."

"You can talk to a workman."

"I talked to plenty of workmen. They don't know anything."

"What about the railroad?"

"Same thing. Old boys in the saloon talk about moving the convicts, but they don't know when."

"Somebody knows."

"Maybe they don't. Frank, what are you worried about?

Whatever the day is we're going to be ready. I've been over and across that rail line eight times—nine times now—and I know just where I'm going to take you off that train."

"You're talking too loud."

Virgil took time to look down the table both ways, at the convicts hunched over the tables shoulder to shoulder and their visitors crowded in on this side, everyone trying to talk naturally without being overheard. When Virgil looked at his brother again, he said, "What I want to know is how many?"

"Me. Junior, Soonzy, Joe Dean. Norma." Frank Shelby paused. "No, we don't need to take Norma."

"It's up to you."

"No, we don't need her."

"That's four. I want to know you're together, all in the same place, because once we hit that train there's going to be striped suits running all over the countryside."

"That might be all right."

"It could be. Give them some people to chase after. But it could mess things up too."

"Well, right now all I hear is you wondering what's going to happen. You come with more than that, or I live the next forty years in Florence, Arizona."

"I'm going to stay in Yuma a while, see what I can find out about the train. You need any money?" Virgil asked.

"If I have to buy some guards. I don't know, get me three, four hundred."

"I'll send it in with the stores. Anything else?"

"A good idea, buddy."

"Don't worry, Frank, we're going to get you out. I'll swear to it."

"Yeah, well, I'll see you."

"Next month," Virgil said. He turned to swing a leg over the bench, then looked at his brother again. "Something funny I seen coming here—these two convicts running behind a Ford automobile. What do you suppose they was doing, Frank?"

Shelby had to tear his pants nearly off to see Norma again. He ripped them down the in-seam from crotch to ankle and told the warehouse guard he'd caught them on some bailing wire and, man, it had almost fixed him good. The guard said to get another pair out of stores. Shelby said all right, and he'd leave his ripped pants at the tailor's on the way back. The guard knew what Shelby was up to; he accepted the sack of Bull Durham Shelby offered and played the game with him. It wasn't hurting anybody.

So he got his new pants and headed for the tailor shop. As soon as he was inside, Norma Davis came off the work table, where she was sitting smoking a cigarette, and went into the stock room. Shelby threw the ripped pants at the tailor, told Tacha to watch out the window for Bob Fisher, and followed Norma into the back room, closing the door behind him.

"He's not as sure of himself as he used to be," Tacha said. "He's worried."

The tailor was studying the ripped seam closely.

Tacha was looking out the window, at the colorless tone of the yard in sunlight: adobe and granite and black shadow lines in the glare. The brick detail was at work across the yard, but she couldn't hear them. She listened for sounds, out in the yard and in the room behind her, but there were none.

"They're quiet in there, uh?"

The tailor said nothing.

"You expect them to make sounds like animals, those two. That old turnkey makes sounds. God, like he's dying. Like somebody stuck a knife—" Tacha stopped.

"I don't know what you're talking about," the tailor said.

"I'm talking about Mr. Fisher, the turnkey, the sounds he makes when he's in her cell."

"And I don't want to know." The tailor kept his head low over his sewing machine.

"He sneaks in at night—"

"I said I don't want to hear about it."

"He hasn't been coming very long. Just the past few weeks. Not every night either. He makes some excuse to go in there, like to fix the lantern or search the place for I don't know what. One time she say, 'Oh, I think there is a tarantula in here,' and the turnkey hurries in there to kill it. I want to say to him, knowing he's taking off his pants then, 'Hey, mister, that's a funny thing to kill a tarantula with.'"

"I'm not listening to you," the tailor said. "Not a word."

*   *   *

In the closeness of the stock room Shelby stepped back to rest his arm on one of the shelves. Watching Norma, he loosened his hat, setting it lightly on his forehead. "Goodness," he said, "I didn't even take off my hat, did I?"

Norma let her skirt fall. She smoothed it over her hips and began buttoning her blouse. "I feel like a mare, standing like that."

"Honey, you don't look like a mare. I believe you are about the trickiest thing I ever met."

"I know a few more ways."

"I bet you do, for a fact."

"That old man, he breathes through his nose right in your ear. Real loud, like he's having heart failure."

Shelby grinned. "That would be something. He has a stroke while he's in there with you."

"I'll tell you, he isn't any fun at all."

"You ain't loving him for the pleasure, sweetheart. You're supposed to be finding out things."

"He doesn't know yet when we're going."

"You asked him?"

"I said to him, 'I will sure be glad to get out of this place.' He said it wouldn't be much longer and I said, 'Oh, when are we leaving here?' He said he didn't know for sure, probably in a couple of months."

"We got to know the day," Shelby said.

"Well, if he don't know it he can't hardly tell me, can he?"

"Maybe he can find it out."

"From who?"

"I don't know. The superintendent, somebody."

"That little fella, he walks around, he looks like he's lost, can't find his mama."

"Well, mama, maybe you should talk to him."

"Get him to come to my cell."

"Jesus, you'd eat him up."

Norma giggled. "You say terrible things."

"I mean by the time you're through there wouldn't be nothing left of him."

"If *you're* through, you better get out of here."

"I talked to Virgil. He doesn't know anything either."

"Don't worry," Norma said. "One of us'll find out. I just want to be sure you take me along when the time comes."

Shelby gave her a nice little sad smile and shook his head slowly. "Sweetheart," he said, "how could I go anywhere without you?"

Good timing, Norma Davis believed, was one of the most important things in life. You had to think of the other person. You had to know his moods and reactions and know the right moment to spring little surprises. You didn't want the person getting too excited and ruining everything before it was time.

That's why she brought Bob Fisher along for almost two months before she told him her secret.

It was strange; like instinct. One night, as she heard the key turning in the iron door of the cellblock, she knew it was Bob and, for some reason, she also knew she was going to tell him tonight. Though not right away.

First he had to go through his act. He had to look in at Tacha and ask her what was she doing, reading? Then he had to come over and see Norma in the bunk and look around the cell for a minute and ask if everything was all right. Norma was ready. She told him she had a terrible sore ankle and would he look at it and see if it was sprained or anything. She got him in there and then had to slow down and be patient while he actually, honest to God, looked at her ankle and said in a loud voice it looked all right to him. He whispered after that, getting out of his coat and into the bunk with her, but raising up every once in a while to look at the cell door.

Norma said, "What's the matter?"

"Tacha, she can hear everything."

"If she bothers you, why don't you put her some place else?"

"This is the woman's block. There isn't any place else."

Norma got her hand inside his shirt and started fooling with the hair on his chest. "How does Tacha look to you?"

"Cut it out, it tickles," Fisher said. "What do you mean, how does she look?"

"I don't know, I don't think she looks so good. I hear her coughing at night."

"Listen, I only got a few minutes."

Norma handled the next part of it, making him believe he was driving her wild, and as he lay on the edge of the bunk breathing out of his nose, she told him her secret.

She said, "Guess what? I know somebody who's planning to escape."

That got him up and leaning over her again.

"Who?"

"I heard once," Norma said, "if you help the authorities here they'll help you."

"Who is it?"

"I heard of convicts who helped stop men trying to escape and got pardoned. Is that right?"

"It's happened."

"They were freed?"

"That's right."

"You think it might happen again?"

"It could. Who's going out?"

"Not out of here. From the train. You think if I found out all about it and told you I'd get a pardon?"

"I think you might," Fisher said. "I can't promise, but you'd have a good chance."

"It's Frank Shelby."

"That's what I thought."

"His brother Virgil's going to help him."

"Where do they jump the train?"

"Frank doesn't know yet, but soon as I find out I'll tell you."

"You promise?"

"Cross my heart."

"You're a sweet girl, Norma. You know that?"

She smiled at him in the dim glow of the lantern and said, "I try to be."

Another week passed before Bob Fisher thought of something else Norma had said.

He was in the tailor shop that day, just checking, not for any special reason. Tacha looked up at him and said, "Norma's not here."

"I can see that."

"She's at the toilet—if you're looking for her."

"I'm not looking for her," Fisher said.

He wasn't sure if Tacha was smiling then or not—like telling him she knew all about him. Little Mexican bitch, she had better not try to get smart with him.

It was then he thought of what Norma had said. About Tacha not looking so good. Coughing at night.

Hell, yes, Bob Fisher said to himself and wondered why he hadn't thought of it before. There was only one place around here to put anybody who was coughing sick. Over in the TB cellblock.

9

THE GUARD, R. E. Baylis, was instructed to move the Mexican girl to the TB area after work, right before supper. It sounded easy enough.

But when he told Tacha she held back and didn't want to go. What for? Look at her. Did she look like she had TB? She wasn't even sick. R. E. Baylis told her to get her things, she was going over there and that's all there was to it. She asked him if Mr. Fisher had given the order, and when he said sure, Tacha said she thought so; she should have known he would do something like this. Goddamn-it, R. E. Baylis thought, he didn't have to explain anything to her. He did though. He said it must be they were sending her over there to help out—bring the lungers their food, get them their medicine. He said there were two boys in there supposed to be looking after the lungers, but nobody had seen much of them the past couple of months or so, what with all the running they were doing. They would go out early in the morning, just about the time it was getting light, and generally not get back until the afternoon. He said some of the guards were talking about them, how they had changed; but he hadn't seen them in a while. Tacha only half listened to him. She wasn't interested in the two convicts, she was thinking about the TB cellblock and wondering what it would be like to live there. She remembered the two he was talking about; she knew them by sight. Though when she walked into the TB yard and saw them again, she did not recognize them immediately as the same two men.

R. E. Baylis got a close look at them and went to find Bob Fisher.

"She give you any trouble?" Fisher asked.

He sat at a table in the empty mess hall with a cup of coffee in front of him. The cooks were bringing in the serving pans and setting up for supper.

"No trouble once I got her there," R. E. Baylis said. "What I want to know is what the Indin and the nigger are doing."

"I don't know anything about them and don't want to know. They're Mr. Manly's private convicts." Fisher held his cup close to his face and would lean in to sip at it.

"Haven't you seen them lately?"

"I see them go by once in a while, going out the gate."

"But you haven't been over there? You haven't seen them close?"

"Whatever he's got them doing isn't any of my business. I told him I don't want no part of it."

"You don't care what they're doing?"

"I got an inventory of equipment and stores have to be tallied before we ship out of here and that ain't very long away."

"You don't care if they made spears," R. E. Baylis said, "and they're throwing them at a board stuck in the ground?"

Bob Fisher started coughing and spilled some of his coffee down the front of his uniform.

Mr. Manly said, "Yes, I know they got spears. Made of bamboo fishing poles and brick-laying trowels stuck into one end for the point. If a man can use a trowel to work with all day, why can't he use one for exercise?"

"Because a spear is a weapon," Fisher said. "You can kill a man with it."

"Bob, you got some kind of stain there on your uniform."

"What I mean is you don't let convicts make *spears*."

"Why not, if they're for a good purpose?"

No, Bob Fisher said to himself—with R. E. Baylis standing next to him, listening to it all—this time, goddamn-it, don't let him mix you up. He said, "Mr. Manly, for some reason I seem to have trouble understanding you."

"What is it you don't understand, Bob?"

"Every time I come up here, it's like you and me are talking about two different things. I come in, I know what the rules are here and I know what I want to say. Then you begin talking and it's like we get onto something else."

"We look at a question from different points of view," Mr. Manly said. "That's all it is."

"All right, R. E. Baylis here says they got spears. I haven't been over to see for myself. We was downstairs—I don't know, something told me I should see you about it first."

"I'm glad you did."

"How long have they had 'em?"

"About two weeks. Bob, they run fourteen miles yesterday. Only stopped three times to rest."

"I don't see what that's got to do with the spears."

"Well, you said you wanted it to show in the record you're not having anything to do with this business. Isn't that right?"

"I want it to show I'm against their being taken outside."

"I haven't told you anything what's going on, have I?"

"I haven't asked neither."

"That's right. This is the first time you've mentioned those boys in over two months. You don't know what I'm teaching them, but you come in here and tell me they can't have spears."

"It's in the rules."

"It says in the rules they can't have spears for any purpose whatsoever?"

"It say a man found with a weapon is to be put under maximum security for no less than ten days."

"You mean put in the snake den."

"I sure do."

"You believe those two boys have been found with weapons?"

"When you make a spear out of a trowel, it becomes a weapon."

"But what if I was the one told them to make the spears?"

"I was afraid you might say that."

"As a matter of fact, I got them the fishing poles myself. Bought them in town."

"Bought them in town," Bob Fisher said. His head seemed to nod a little as he stared at Mr. Manly. "This here is what I meant before about not understanding some things. I would sure like to know why you want them to have spears?"

"Bob," Mr. Manly said, "that's the only way to learn, isn't it? Ask questions." He looked up past Fisher then, at the wall clock. "Say, it's about supper time already."

"Mr. Manly, I'll wait on supper if you'll explain them spears to me."

"I'll do better than that," Mr. Manly said, "I'll show you. First though we got to get us a pitcher of ice water."

"I'll even pass on that," Fisher said. "I'm not thirsty *or* hungry."

Mr. Manly gave him a patient, understanding grin. "The ice water isn't for us, Bob."

"No sir," Fisher said. He was nodding again, very slowly, solemnly. "I should've known better, shouldn't I?"

Tacha remembered them from months before wearing leg-irons and pushing the wheelbarrows. She remembered the Negro working without a shirt on and remembered thinking the other one tall for an Indian. She had never spoken to them or watched them for a definite reason. She had probably not been closer than fifty feet to either of them. But she was aware now of the striking change in their appearance and at first it gave her a strange, tense feeling. She was afraid of them.

The guard had looked as if he was afraid of them too, and maybe that was part of the strange feeling. He didn't tell her which cell was to be hers. He stared at the Indian and the Negro, who were across the sixty-foot yard by the wall, and then hurried away, leaving her here.

As soon as he was gone the tubercular convicts began talking to her. One of them asked if she had come to live with them. When she nodded he said she could bunk with him if she wanted. They laughed and another one said no, come on in his cell, he would show her a fine old time. She didn't like the way they stared at her. They sat in front of their cells on stools and a wooden bunk frame and looked as if they had been there a long time and seldom shaved or washed themselves.

She wasn't sure if the Indian and the Negro were watching her. The Indian was holding something that looked like a fishing pole. The Negro was standing by an upright board that was as tall as he was and seemed to be nailed to a post. Another of the poles was sticking out of the board. Neither of them was wearing a shirt; that was the first thing she noticed about them from across the yard.

They came over when she turned to look at the cells and one of the tubercular convicts told her again to come on, put her blanket and stuff in with his. Now, when she looked around, not knowing what to do, she saw them approaching.

She saw the Indian's hair, how long it was, covering his ears, and the striped red and black cloth he wore as a headband. She saw the Negro's mustache that curved around his mouth into a short beard and the cuts on his face, like knife scars, that slanted down from both of his cheekbones. This was when she was afraid of them, as they walked to her.

"The cell on the end," Raymond said. "Why don't you take that one?"

She made herself hold his gaze. "Who else is in there, you?"

"Nobody else."

Harold said, "You got the TB?"

"I don't have it yet."

"You do something to Frank Shelby?"

"Maybe I did," she said, "I don't know."

"If you don't have the TB," Harold said, "you did something to somebody."

She began to feel less afraid already, talking to them, and yet she knew there was something different about their faces and the way they looked at her. "I think the turnkey, Mr. Fisher, did it," Tacha said, "so I wouldn't see him going in with Norma."

"I guess there are all kinds of things going on," Harold said. "They put you in here, it's not so bad. It was cold at night when we first come, colder than the big cellblock, but now it's all right." He glanced toward the tubercular convicts. "Don't worry about the scarecrows. They won't hurt you."

"They lock everybody in at night," Raymond said. "During the day one of them tries something, you can run."

That was a strange thing too: being afraid of them at first because of the way they looked, then hearing them say not to worry and feeling at ease with them, believing them.

Raymond said, "We fixed up that cell for you. It's like a new one."

She was inside unrolling her bedding when the guard returned with the superintendent and the turnkey, Mr. Fisher. She heard one of them say, "Harold, come out here," and she looked up to see them through the open doorway: the little man in the dark suit and two in guard uniforms, one of them, R. E. Baylis, holding a dented tin pitcher. The Indian was still in the yard, not far from them, but she didn't see the Negro. The superintendent was looking toward her cell now, squinting into the dim interior.

Mr. Manly wanted to keep an eye on Bob Fisher and watch his reactions, but seeing the woman distracted him.

"Who's that in there, Norma Davis?"

"The other one," Fisher said, "the Mexican."

"I didn't see any report on her being sick."

"She's working here. Your two boys run off, there's nobody to fetch things for the lungers."

Mr. Manly didn't like to look at the tubercular convicts; they gave him a creepy feeling, the way they sat there all day like lizards and never seemed to move. He gave them a glance and called again, "Harold, come on out here."

The Negro was buttoning a prison shirt as he appeared in the doorway. "You want me, captain?"

"Come over here, will you?"

Mr. Manly was watching Fisher now. The man's flat open-eyed expression tickled him: old Bob Fisher staring at Harold, then looking over at Raymond, then back at Harold again, trying to figure out the change that had come over them. The change was something more than just their appearance. It was something Mr. Manly felt, and he was pretty sure now Bob Fisher was feeling it too.

"What's the matter, Bob, ain't you ever seen an Apache or a Zulu before?"

"I seen Apaches."

"Then what're you staring at?"

Fisher looked over at Harold again. "What're them cuts on his face?"

"Tell him, Harold."

"They tribal marks, captain."

Fisher said, "What the hell tribe's a field nigger belong to?"

Harold touched his face, feeling the welts of scar tissue that were not yet completely healed. He said, "My tribe, captain."

"He cut his own face like that?"

Fisher kept staring at the Negro as Mr. Manly said, "He saw it in a Africa book I got—picture of a native with these marks like tattoos on his face. I didn't tell him to do it, you understand. He just figured it would be all right, I guess. Isn't that so, Harold?"

"Yes-suh, captain."

"Same with Raymond. He figured if he's a full-blooded Apache Indian then he should let his hair grow and wear one of them bands."

"We come over here to look at spears," Fisher said.

Mr. Manly frowned, shaking his head. "Don't you see the connection yet? A spear is part of a warrior's get-up, like a tool is to a working man. Listen, I told you, didn't I, these boys can run fifteen miles in a day now and only stop a couple of times to rest."

"I thought it was fourteen miles," Fisher said.

"Fourteen, fifteen—here's the thing. They can run that far *and* go from morning to supper time without a drink of water, any time they want."

"A man will do that in the snake den if I make him." Bob Fisher wasn't backing off this time.

Mr. Manly wasn't letting go. "Inside," he said, "is different than running out in the hot sun. Listen, they each pour theirselves a cup of water in the morning and you know what they do? They see who can go all day without taking a drink or more than a couple of sips." He held his hand out to R. E. Baylis and said, "Let me have the pitcher." Then he looked at Raymond and Harold again. "Which of you won today?"

"I did," Raymond said.

"Let's see your cups."

Raymond went into his cell and was back in a moment with a tin cup in each hand. "He drank his. See, I got some left."

"Then you get the pitcher of ice water," Mr. Manly said. "And, Harold, you get to watch him drink it."

Raymond raised the pitcher and drank out of the side of it, not taking very much before lowering it again and holding it in front of him.

"See that?" Mr. Manly said. "He knows better than to gulp it down. One day Raymond wins, the next day Harold gets the ice water. I mean they can both do it any time they want."

"I would sure like to see them spears," Fisher said.

Mr. Manly asked Harold where they were and he said, "Over yonder by the wall, captain."

Tacha watched them cross the yard. The Negro waited for the Indian to put the pitcher on the ground and she noticed they gave each other a look as they fell in behind the little man in the dark suit and the two guards. They were over by the wall a few minutes talking while Mr. Fisher hefted one of the bamboo spears and felt the point of it with his finger.

Then the superintendent took the spear from him and gave it to the Indian. The Negro picked up the other spear from against the wall and they came back this way, toward the cells, at least a dozen paces before turning around. Beyond them, the group moved away from the upright board. The Indian and the Negro faced the target for a moment, then stepped back several more feet, noticing Tacha now in the doorway of her cell.

She said, "You're going to hit that, way down there?"

"Not today," Raymond answered.

Everyone in the yard was watching them now. They raised the spears shoulder high, took aim with their outstretched left arms pointing, and threw them hard in a low arc, almost at the same moment. Both spears fell short and skidded along the ground past the board to stop at the base of the wall.

Raymond and Harold waited. In the group across the yard Mr. Manly seemed to be doing the talking, gesturing with his hands. He was facing Bob Fisher and did not look over this way. After a few minutes they left the yard, and now Mr. Manly, as he went through the gate last, looked over and waved.

"Well," Raymond said—he stooped to pick up the tin pitcher—"who wants some ice water?"

Within a few days Tacha realized that, since moving to the TB cellblock, she felt better—whether it made sense or not. Maybe part of the feeling was being outside most of the day and not bent over a sewing machine listening to Norma or trying to talk to the old man. Already that seemed like a long time ago. She was happier now. She even enjoyed being with the tubercular convicts and didn't mind the way they talked to her sometimes, saying she was a pretty good nurse though they would sure rather have her be something else. They needed to talk like men so she smiled and didn't take anything they said as an offense.

In the afternoon the Apache and the Zulu would come in through the gate, walking slowly, carrying their shirts. One of the tubercular convicts would yell over, asking how far they had run and one or the other would tell them twelve, fifteen, sixteen miles. They would drink the water in their cups. One of the convicts would fill the cups again from the bucket they kept in the shade. After drinking the second cup they would decide who the winner would be that day and pour just a little more water into his cup, leaving the other one empty. The TB convicts got a kick out of this and always laughed. Every day it was the same. They drank the water and then went into the cell to lie on their bunks. In less than an hour the TB convicts would be yelling for them to come out and start throwing their spears. They would get out their money or rolled cigarettes when the Apache and the Zulu appeared and, after letting them warm up a few minutes, at least two of the convicts would bet on every throw. Later on, after the work crews were in for the day, there would be convicts over from the main yard watching through the gate. None of them ever came into the TB yard. They were betting too and would yell at the Apache and the Zulu—calling them by those names—to hit the board, cut the son of a bitch dead center. Frank Shelby appeared at the gate only once. After that the convicts had to pay to watch and make bets. Soonzy, Junior, and Joe Dean were at the grillwork every day during free time.

Harold Jackson, the Zulu, walked over to the gate one time. He said, "How come we do all the work, you make all the money?"

Junior told him to get back over there and start throwing his goddamn spear or whatever it was.

Harold let the convicts get a good look at his face scars before he walked away. After the next throw, when he and Raymond were pulling their spears out of the board, Harold said, "Somebody always telling you what to do, huh?"

"Every place you go," Raymond said.

They were good with the spears. Though when the convicts from the outside yard were at the gate watching they never threw from farther than thirty-five feet away, or tried to place the spears in a particular part of the board. If they wanted to, they could hit the board high or low at the same time.

It was Tacha who noticed their work shoes coming apart from the running and made moccasins for them, sewed them by hand—calf-high Apache moccasins she fashioned out of old leather water bags and feed sacks.

And it was Tacha who told Raymond he should put war paint on his face. He wasn't scarey enough looking.

"Where do you get war paint?" Raymond asked her, "At the store?"

"I think from berries."

"Well, I don't see no berries around here."

The next day she got iodine and a can of white enamel from the sick ward and, after supper, sat Raymond on a stool and painted a white streak across the bridge of his nose from cheekbone to cheekbone, and orange-red iodine stripes along the jawline to his chin.

Harold Jackson liked it, so Tacha painted a white stripe across his forehead and another one down between his eyes to the tip of his nose.

"Hey, we waryers now," Raymond said.

They looked at themselves in Tacha's hand mirror and both of them grinned. They were pretty mean-looking boys. Harold said, "Lady, what else do these waryers put on?"

Tacha said she guessed anything they wanted. She opened a little sack and gave Raymond two strands of turquoise beads, a string for around his neck and another string, doubled, for around his right arm, up high.

She asked Harold if he wanted a ring for his nose. He said no, thank you, lady, but remembered Mr. Manly talking about the Zulus putting chunks of sugar cane in their ear lobes and he let Tacha pierce one of his ears and attach a single gold earring. It looked good with the tribal scars and the mustache that curved into a short beard. "All I need me is a lion to spear," Harold said. He was Harold Jackson the Zulu, and he could feel it without looking in the mirror.

He didn't talk to Raymond about the feeling because he knew Raymond, in a way of his own, Raymond the Apache, had the same feeling. In front of the convicts who watched them throw spears or in front of the two guards who took them out to run, Harold could look at Raymond, their eyes would meet for a moment and each knew what the other was thinking. They didn't talk very much, even to each other. They walked slowly and seemed to expend no extra effort in their movements. They knew they could do something no other men in the prison could do—they could run all day and go without water—and it was part of the good feeling.

They began to put fresh paint on their faces almost every day, in the afternoon before they threw the spears.

10

THE EVENING Junior and Joe Dean came for them they were sitting out in front of the cells with Tacha. It was after supper, just beginning to get dark. For a little while Tacha had been pretending to tell them their fortunes, using an old deck of cards and turning them up one at a time in the fading light. She told Harold she saw him sleeping under a banana tree with a big smile on his face. Sure, Cuba, Harold said. With the next card she saw him killing a lion with his spear and Harold was saying they didn't have no lions in Cuba, when Junior came up to them. Joe Dean stood over a little way with his hands in his pockets, watching.

"Frank wants to see you," Junior said. "Both of you." He took time to look at Tacha while he waited for them to get up. When neither of them moved he said, "You hear me? Frank wants you."

"What's he want?" Harold said.

"He's going to want me to kick your ass you don't get moving."

Raymond looked at Harold, and Harold looked at Raymond. Finally they got up and followed them across the yard, though they moved so goddamn slow Worley Lewis, Jr. had to keep waiting for them with his hands on his hips, telling them to come on, *move*. They looked back once and saw Joe Dean still over by the cells. He seemed to be waiting for them to leave.

Soonzy was in the passageway of the main cellblock, standing in the light that was coming from No. 14. He motioned them inside.

They went into the cell, then stopped short. Frank Shelby was sitting on his throne reading a newspaper, hunched over before his own shadow on the back wall. He didn't look up; he made them wait several minutes before he finally rose, pulled up his pants and buckled his belt. Junior and Soonzy crowded the doorway behind them.

"Come closer to the light," Shelby said. He waited for them to move into the space between the bunks, to where the

541

electric overhead light, with its tin shield, was almost directly above them.

"I want to ask you two something. I want to know how come you got your faces painted up like that."

They kept looking at him, but neither of them spoke.

"You going to tell me?"

"I don't know," Raymond said. "I guess it's hard to explain."

"Did anybody tell you to put it on?"

"No, we done it ourselves."

"Has this Mr. Manly seen it?"

"Yeah, but he didn't say nothing."

"You just figured it would be a good idea, uh?"

"I don't know," Raymond said. "We just done it, I guess."

"You want to look like a couple of circus clowns, is that it?"

"No, we didn't think of that."

"Maybe you want to look like a wild Indin," Shelby said, "and him, he wants to look like some kind of boogey-man native. Maybe that's it."

Raymond shrugged. "Maybe something like that. It's hard to explain."

"What does Mr. Jackson say about it?"

"If you know why we put it on," Harold said, "what are you asking us for?"

"Because it bothers me," Shelby answered. "I can't believe anybody would want to look like a nigger native. Even a nigger. Same as I can't believe anybody would want to look like a Wild West Show Indin 'less he was paid to do it. Somebody paying you, Raymond?"

"Nobody's paying us."

"See, Raymond, what bothers me—how can we learn people like you to act like white men if you're going to play you're savages? You see what I mean? You want to move back in this cell block, but who do you think would want to live with you?"

"We're not white men," Raymond said.

"Jesus Christ, I know that. I'm saying if you want to live with white men then you got to try to act like white men. You start playing you're an Apache and a goddamn Zulu or something, that's the same as saying you don't want to be a white man, and that's what bothers me something awful, when I see that going on."

There was a little space of silence before Harold said, "What do you want us to do?"

"We'll do it," Shelby said. "We're going to remind you how you're supposed to act."

Soonzy took Harold from behind with a fist in his hair and a forearm around his neck. He dragged Harold backward and as Raymond turned, Junior stepped in and hit Raymond with a belt wrapped around his fist. He had to hit Raymond again before he could get a good hold on him and pull him out of the cell. Joe Dean and a half-dozen convicts were waiting in the passageway. They got Raymond and Harold down on their backs on the cement. They sat on their legs and a convict stood on each of their outstretched hands and arms while another man got down and pulled their hair tight to keep them from moving their heads. Then Joe Dean took a brush and the can of enamel Tacha had got from the sick ward and painted both of their faces pure white.

When R. E. Baylis came through to lock up, Shelby told him to look at the goddamn mess out there, white paint all over the cement and dirty words painted on the wall. He said that nigger and his red nigger friend sneaked over and started messing up the place, but they caught the two and painted them as a lesson. Shelby said to R. E. Baylis goddamn-it, why didn't he throw them in the snake den so they would quit bothering people. R. E. Baylis said he would tell Bob Fisher.

The next morning after breakfast, Shelby came out of the mess hall frowning in the sunlight and looking over the work details forming in the yard. He was walking toward the supply group when somebody called his name from behind. Bob Fisher was standing by the mess hall door: grim-looking tough old son of a bitch in his gray sack guard uniform. Shelby sure didn't want to, but he walked back to where the turnkey was standing.

"They don't know how to write even their names," Fisher said.

"Well"—Shelby took a moment to think—"maybe they got the paint for somebody else to do it."

"Joe Dean got the paint."

"Joe did that?"

"Him and Soonzy and Junior are going to clean it up before they go to work."

"Well, if they did it—"

"You're going to help them."

"Me? I'm on the supply detail. You know that."

"Or you can go with the quarry gang," Fisher said. "It don't make any difference to me."

"Quarry gang?" Shelby grinned to show Fisher he thought he was kidding. "I don't believe I ever done that kind of work."

"You'll do it if I say so."

"Listen, just because we painted those two boys up. We were teaching them a lesson, that's all. Christ, they go around here thinking they're something the way they fixed theirselves up— somebody had to teach them."

"I do the teaching here," Fisher said. "I'm teaching that to you right now."

Dumb, stone-face guard son of a bitch. Shelby said, "Well," half-turning to look off thoughtfully toward the work groups waiting in the yard. "I hope those people don't get sore about this. You know how it is, how they listen to me and trust me. If they figure I'm getting treated unfair, they're liable to sit right down and not move from the yard, every one of them."

"If you believe that," Fisher said, "you better tell them I'll shoot the first man that sits down, and if they all sit down at once I'll shoot you."

Shelby waited. He didn't look at Bob Fisher; he kept his gaze on the convicts. After a moment he said, "You're kneeling on me for a reason, aren't you? You're waiting to see me make a terrible mistake."

"I believe you've already made it," Fisher said. He turned and went into the mess hall.

Scraping paint off cement was better than working in the quarry. It was hot in the passageway, but there was no sun beating down on them and they weren't breathing chalk dust. Shelby sat in his cell and let Junior, Soonzy, and Joe Dean do the work, until Bob Fisher came by. Fisher didn't say anything; he looked in at him and Shelby came out and picked up a trowel and started scraping. When Fisher was gone, Shelby sat back on his heels and said, "I'm going to bust me a guard, I'll tell you, if that man's anywhere near us when we leave."

The scraping stopped as he spoke, as Junior and Soonzy and Joe Dean waited to hear whatever he had to say.

"There is something bothering him," Shelby said. "He wants to nail me down. He could do it any time he feels like it, couldn't he? He could put me in the quarry or the snake den—that man could chain me to the wall. But he's waiting on something."

Joe Dean said, "Waiting on what?"

"I don't know. Unless he's telling me he knows what's going on. He could be saying, 'I got my eye on you, buddy. I'm waiting for you to make the wrong move.'"

"What could he know?" Joe Dean said, "We don't know anything ourselves."

"He could know we're thinking about it."

"He could be guessing."

"I mean," Shelby said, "he could *know*. Norma could have told him. She's the only other person who could."

Junior was frowning. "What would Norma want to tell him for?"

"Jesus Christ," Shelby said, "because she's Norma. She don't need a reason, she does what she feels like doing. Listen, she needs money she gets herself a forty-four and pours liquor into some crazy boy and they try and rob a goddamn *bank*. She's seeing Bob Fisher, and she's the only one could have told him anything."

"I say he's guessing," Joe Dean said. "The time's coming to move all these convicts, he's nervous at the thought of it, and starts guessing we're up to something."

"That could be right," Shelby said. "But the only way I can find out for sure is to talk to Norma." He was silent a moment. "I don't know. With old Bob watching every move I got to stay clear of the tailor shop."

"Why don't we bring her over here?" Junior said. "Right after supper everybody's in the yard. Shoot, we can get her in here, anywhere you want, no trouble."

"Hey, boy," Shelby grinned, "now you're talking."

Jesus, yes, what was he worrying about that old man turnkey

for? He had to watch that and never worry out loud or raise his voice or lose his temper. He had to watch when little pissy-ant started to bother him. The Indin and the nigger had bothered him. It wasn't even important; but goddamn-it, it had bothered him and he had done something about it. See—but because of it Bob Fisher had come down on him and this was not any time to get Bob Fisher nervous and watchful. Never trust a nervous person unless you've got a gun on him. That was a rule. And when you've got the gun on him shoot him or hit him with it, quick, but don't let him start crying and begging for his life and spilling the goddamn payroll all over the floor—the way it had happened in the paymaster's office at the Cornelia Mine near Ajo. They would have been out of there before the security guards arrived if he hadn't spilled the money. The paymaster would be alive if he hadn't spilled the money, and they wouldn't be in Yuma. There was such a thing as bad luck. Anything could happen during a holdup. But there had been five payroll and bank robberies before the Cornelia Mine job where no one had spilled the money or reached for a gun or walked in unexpectedly. They had been successful because they had kept calm and in control, and that was the way they had to do it again, to get out of here.

It had surely bothered him though—the way the Indin and the nigger had painted their faces.

Junior pushed through the mess-hall door behind Norma as she went out, and told her to go visit Tacha. That's how easy it was. When Norma got to the TB yard Joe Dean, standing by the gate, nodded toward the first cell. She saw Tacha sitting over a ways with the Indian and the Negro, and noticed there was something strange about them: they looked sick, with a gray pallor to their skin, even the Negro. Norma looked at Joe Dean and again he nodded toward the first cell.

Soonzy stepped out and walked past her as she approached the doorway. Shelby was waiting inside, standing with an arm on the upper bunk. He didn't grin or reach for her, he said, "How're you getting along with your boy friend?"

"He still hasn't told me anything, if that's what you mean."

"I'm more interested in what you might have told him."

Norma smiled and seemed to relax. "You know, as I walked in here I thought you were a little tense about something."

"You haven't answered my question."

"What is it I might have told him?"

"Come on, Norma."

"I mean what's there to tell him? You don't have any plan you've told me about."

"I don't know," Shelby said, "it looks to me like you got your own plan."

"I ask him. Every time he comes in I bring it up. 'Honey, when are we going to get out of this awful place?' But he won't tell me anything."

"You were pretty sure one time you could squeeze it out of him."

"I don't believe he knows any more than we do."

"I'll tell you what," Shelby said. "I'll give you three more days to find out. You don't know anything by then, I don't see any reason to take you with us."

Norma took her time. She kept her eyes on Shelby, holding him and waiting a little, then stepped in close so that she was almost touching him with her body. She waited again before saying, quietly, "What're you being so mean for?"

Shelby said, "Man." He said, "Come on, Norma, if I want to put you on the bunk I'll put you on the bunk. Don't give me no sweetheart talk, all right? I want you to tell me if you're working something with that old man. Now hold on—I want you to keep looking right at me and tell me to my face yes or no—yes, 'I have told him,' or no, 'I have not told him.'"

Norma put on a frown now that brought her eyebrows together and gave her a nice hurt look.

"Frank, what do you want me to tell you?" She spaced the words to show how honest and truthful she was being, knowing that her upturned, frowning face was pretty nice and that her breasts were about an inch away from the up-curve of his belly.

She looked good all right, and if he put her down on the bunk she'd be something. But Frank Shelby was looking at a train and keeping calm, keeping his voice down, and he said, "Norma, if you don't find out anything in three days you don't leave this place."

It was Sunday, Visiting Day, that Mr. Manly decided he would make an announcement. He called Bob Fisher into his office to tell him, then thought better of it—Fisher would only object and argue—so he began talking about Raymond and Harold instead of his announcement.

"I'll tell you," Mr. Manly said, "I'm not so much interested in who did it as I am in *why* they did it. They got paint in their eyes, in their nose. They had to wash theirselves in gasoline and then they didn't get it all off."

"Well, there's no way of finding out now," Fisher said. "You ask them, there isn't anybody knows a thing."

"The men who did it know."

"Well, sure, the ones that did it."

"I'd like to know what a man thinks like would paint another person."

"They were painting theirselves before."

"I believe you see the difference, Bob."

"These are convicts," Fisher said. "They get mean they don't need a reason. It's the way they are."

"I'm thinking I better talk to them."

"But we don't know who done it."

"I mean talk to all of them. I want to talk to them about something else any way."

"About what?"

"Maybe I can make the person who did it come forward and admit it."

"Mister, if you believe that you don't know anything a-tall about convicts. You talked to Raymond and Harold, didn't you?"

"Yes, I did."

"And they won't even tell you who done it, will they?"

"I can't understand that."

"Because they're convicts. They know if they ever told you they'd get their heads beat against a cell wall. This is between them and the other convicts. If the convicts don't want them to paint up like savages then I believe we should stay out of it and let them settle it theirselves."

"But they've got rights—the two boys. What about them?"

"I don't know. I'm not talking about justice," Fisher said. "I'm talking about running a prison. If the convicts want these two to act a certain way or not act a certain way, we should keep out of it. It keeps them quiet and it don't cost us a cent. When you push against the whole convict body it had better be important and you had better be ready to shoot and kill people if they push back."

"I told them they could put on their paint if they wanted."

"Well, that's up to you," Fisher said. "Or it's up to them. I notice they been keeping their faces clean."

When Mr. Manly didn't speak right away, Fisher said, "If it's all right with you I want to get downstairs and keep an eye on things. It's Visiting Day."

Mr. Manly looked up. "That's right, it is. You know, I didn't tell you I been wanting to make an announcement. I believe I'll do it right now—sure, while some of them have their relatives here visiting." Mr. Manly's expression was bright and cheerful, as if he thought this was sure a swell idea.

"I don't know what you're doing," Shelby said, "but so far it isn't worth a rat's ass, is it?" He sat facing his brother, Virgil, who was leaning in against the table and looking directly at Frank to show he was sincere and doing everything he could to find out when the goddamn train was leaving. There were convicts and their visitors all the way down the line of tables that divided the mess hall: hunched over talking, filling the room with a low hum of voices.

"It ain't like looking up a schedule," Virgil said. "I believe this would be a special train, two or three cars probably. All right, I ask a lot of questions over at the railroad yard they begin wondering who I am, and somebody says hey, that's Virgil Shelby. His brother's up on the hill."

"That's Virgil Shelby," Frank said. "Jesus, do you believe people know who you are? You could be a mine engineer. You could be interested in hauling in equipment and you ask how they handle special trains. 'You ever put on a special run? You do? Like what kind?' Jesus, I mean you got to use your head and think for a change."

"Frank, I'm ready. I don't need to know more than a day ahead when you leave. I got me some good boys and, I'm telling you, we're going to *do* it."

"You're going to do what?"

"Get you off that train."

"How?"

"Stop it if we have to."

"How, Virgil?"

"Dynamite the track."

"Then what?"

"Then climb aboard."

"With the guards shooting at you?"

"You got to be doing something too," Virgil said. "Inside the train."

"I'm doing something right now. I'm seeing you don't know what you're talking about. And unless we know when the train leaves and where it stops, we're not going to be able to work out a plan. Do you see that, Virgil?"

"The train goes to Florence. We know that."

"Do we know if it stops anywhere? If it stops, Virgil, wouldn't that be the place to get on?"

"If it stops."

"That's right. That's what you got to find out. Because how are you going to know where to wait and when to wait if you don't know when the train's leaving here? Virgil, are you listening to me?"

His brother was looking past him at something. Shelby glanced over his shoulder. He turned then and kept looking as Mr. Manly, with Bob Fisher on the stairs at the far end of the mess hall, said, "May I have your attention a moment, please?"

Mr. Manly waited until the hum of voices trailed off and he saw the faces down the line of tables looking toward him: upturned, solemn faces, like people in church waiting for the sermon. Mr. Manly grinned. He always liked to open with a light touch.

He said, "I'm not going to make a speech, if any of you are worried about that. I just want to make a brief announcement while your relatives and loved ones are here. It will save the boys writing to tell you and I know some of them don't write as often as they should. By the way, I'm Everett Manly, the acting superintendent here in Mr. Rynning's absence." He paused to clear his throat.

"Now then—I am very pleased to announce that this will be the last Visiting Day at Yuma Territorial Prison. A week from tomorrow the first group of men will leave on the Southern Pacific for the new penitentiary at Florence, a fine new place I think you all are going to be very pleased with. Now you won't be able to tell your relatives or loved ones what day exactly you'll be leaving, but I promise you in three weeks everybody will be out of here and this place will open its doors forever and become a page in history. That's about all I can tell you right now for the present. However, if any of you have questions I will be glad to try and answer them."

Frank Shelby kept looking at the little man on the stairway. He said to himself, It's a trick. But the longer he stared at him—the little fellow standing up there waiting for questions—he knew Mr. Manly was telling the truth.

Virgil said, "Well, I guess that answers the question, doesn't it?"

Shelby didn't look at his brother. He was afraid he might lose his temper and hit Virgil in the mouth.

11

For three sacks of Mail Pouch, R. E. Baylis told Shelby the convicts would be sent out in groups of about forty at a time, going over every other day, it looked like, on the regular morning run.

R. E. Baylis even got Shelby a Southern Pacific schedule. Leave Yuma at 6:15 A.M. Pass through Sentinel at 8:56; no stop unless they needed coal or water. They'd stop at Gila at 9:51, where they'd be fed on the train; no one allowed off. They'd arrive in Phoenix at 2:40 P.M., switch the cars over to a Phoenix & Eastern train and arrive at Florence about 5:30 P.M. Bob Fisher planned to make the first run and the last one, the first one to see what the trip was like and the last one so he could lock up and officially hand over the keys.

Shelby asked R. E. Baylis if he would put him and his friends down for the first run, because they were sure anxious to get out of here. R. E. Baylis said he didn't know if it could be done, but maybe he could try to arrange it. Shelby gave him fifty dollars to try as hard as he could.

The guard told Bob Fisher about Shelby's request, since Fisher would see the list anyway. Why the first train? Fisher wanted to know. What was the difference? R. E. Baylis asked. All the trains were going to the penitentiary. Fisher put himself in Shelby's place and thought about it a while. Maybe Shelby was anxious to leave, that could be a fact. But it wasn't the reason he wanted to be on the first train. It was so he would know exactly which train he'd be on, so he could tell somebody outside.

Fisher said all right, tell him he could go on the first train. But then, when the time came, they'd pull Shelby out of line and hold him for the last train. "I want him riding with me," Fisher said, "But not before I look over the route."

It bothered R. E. Baylis because Shelby had always treated him square and given him tobacco and things. He stopped by Shelby's cell that evening and said Lord, he could sure use that fifty dollars, but he would give it back. Bob Fisher was making them go on the last train. Shelby looked pretty disappointed. By God, he was big about it though. He let R. E. Baylis keep the fifty dollars anyway.

The next morning when he saw Junior and Soonzy and Joe Dean, Shelby grinned and said, "Boys, always trust a son of a bitch to be a son of a bitch. We're taking the last train."

All he had to do now was to get a letter of instructions to Virgil at the railroad hotel in Yuma. For a couple more sacks of Mail Pouch R. E. Baylis would probably deliver it personally.

Virgil Shelby and his three men arrived at Stout's Hotel in Gila on a Wednesday afternoon. Mr. Stout and a couple of Southern Pacific division men in the lobby got a kick out of these dudes who said they were heading south into the Saucedas to do some prospecting. All they had were bedrolls and rifles and a pack mule loaded with suitcases. The dudes were as serious about it though as they were ignorant. They bought four remount horses at the livery and two 50-pound cases of No. 1 dynamite at Tom Child's trading store, and on Thursday morning they rode out of Gila. They rode south two miles before turning west and doubling back to follow the train tracks.

They arrived in sight of the Southern Pacific water stop at Sentinel that evening and from a grove of trees studied the wooden buildings and frame structure that stood silently against a dark line of palo verdes. A water tank, a coaling shed, a section house and a little one-room station with a light showing in the window, that's all there was here.

As soon as Virgil saw the place he knew Frank was right again. Sometimes it made him mad when he sounded dumb in front of his brother. He had finished the sixth grade and Frank had gone on to the seventh or eighth. Maybe when Frank was looking at him, waiting, he would say the wrong thing or sound dumb; but Jesus, he had gone into places with a gun and put the gun in a man's face and got what he wanted. Frank didn't have to worry about him going in with a gun. He had not found out the important facts of the matter talking to the railroad people. He had not thought up the plan in all the time he'd had to do it. But he could sure do what Frank said in his letter. He had three good boys who would go with him for two hundred and fifty dollars each and bring the guns and know how to use them. These boys drank too much and got in fights, but they were the captains for this kind of work. Try and pick them. Try and get three fellows who had the nerve to stop a prison train and take off the people you wanted and do it right, without a lot of shooting and getting nervous and running off into the desert and hiding in a cave. He wished he had more like them, but these three said they could do the job and would put their guns on anybody for two hundred and fifty dollars.

He had a man named Howard Crowder who had worked for railroad lines in both the United States and Mexico, before he turned to holding up trains and spent ten years in Yuma.

He had an old hand named Dancey who had ridden with him and Frank before, and had been with them at the Cornelia Mine payroll robbery and had got away.

He had a third one named Billy Santos who had smuggled across the border whatever could be carried and was worth anything and knew all the trails and water holes south of here.

Five o'clock the next morning it still looked good and still looked easy as they walked into the little station at Sentinel with their suitcases and asked the S.P. man when the next eastbound train was coming through.

The S.P. man said 8:56 this morning, but that train was not due to stop on account of it was carrying convicts some place.

Virgil asked him if there was anybody over in the section house. The S.P. man said no, he was alone. A crew had gone out on the 8:45 to Gila the night before and another crew was coming from Yuma sometime today.

Virgil looked over at Billy Santos. Billy went outside. Howard Crowder and Dancey remained sitting on the bench. The suitcases and bedrolls and rifles and two cases of dynamite were on the floor by them. No, the S.P. man behind the counter said, they couldn't take the 8:56, though they could get on the 8:48 this evening if they wanted to hang around all day. But what will you do with your horses? he said then. You rode in here, didn't you?

Virgil was at the counter now. He nodded to the telegrapher's key on the desk behind the S.P. man and said, "I hope you can work that thing, mister."

The S.P. man said, "Sure, I can work it. Else I wouldn't be here."

"That's good," Virgil said. "It's better if they hear a touch they are used to hearing."

The S.P. man gave Virgil a funny look, then let his gaze shift over to the two men on the bench with all the gear in front of them. They looked back at him; they didn't move or say anything. The S.P. man was wondering if he should send a message to the division office at Gila; tell them there were three dudes hanging around here with rifles and dynamite and ask if they had been seen in Gila the day before. He could probably get away with it. How would these people know what he was saying? Just then the Mexican-looking one came back in, his eyes on the one standing by the counter, and shook his head.

Virgil said, "You all might as well get dressed."

The S.P. man watched them open the suitcases and take out gray and white convict suits. He watched them pull the pants and coats on over the clothes they were wearing and shove revolvers down into the pants and button the coats. One of them brought a double-barrel shotgun out of a suitcase in two pieces and sat down to fit the stock to the barrels. Watching them, the S.P. man said to Virgil Shelby, "Hey, what's going on? What is this?"

"This is how you stop a train," Virgil told him. "These are prisoners that escaped off the train that come through the day before yesterday."

"Nobody escaped," the S.P. man said.

Virgil nodded up and down. "Yes, they did, mister, and I'm the deputy sheriff of Maricopa County who's going to put them back on the train for Florence."

"If you're a deputy of this county," the S.P. man said, "then you're a new one."

"All right," Virgil said, "I'm a new one."

"If you're one at all."

Virgil pulled a .44 revolver from inside his coat and pointed it in the S.P. man's face. He said, "All you got to do is telegraph the Yuma depot at exactly six A.M. with a message for the prison superintendent, Mr. Everett Manly. You're going to say three escaped convicts are being held here at Sentinel and you request the train to stop and take them aboard. You also request an immediate answer and, mister," Virgil said, "I don't want you to send it one word different than I tell it to you. You understand?"

The S.P. man nodded. "I understand, but it ain't going to work. If three were missing at the head-count when they got to Florence, they would have already told Yuma about it."

"That's a fact," Virgil said. "That's why we had somebody wire the prison from Phoenix Wednesday night and report three missing." Virgil looked around then and said, "Howard?"

The one named Howard Crowder had a silver dollar in his hand. He began tapping the coin rapidly on the wooden bench next to him in sharp longs and shorts that were loud in the closed room. Virgil watched the expression on the S.P. man's face, the mouth come open a little.

"You understand that too?" Virgil asked him.

The S.P. man nodded.

"What did he say?"

"He said, 'Send correct message or you are a dead man.'"

"I'm happy you understand it," Virgil said.

The S.P. man watched the one named Dancey pry open a wooden case that was marked *High Explosives—Dangerous* and take out a paraffin-coated packet of dynamite sticks. He watched Dancey get out a coil of copper wire and detonator caps and work the wire gently into the open end of the cap and then crimp the end closed with his teeth. The Mexican-looking one was taking a box plunger out of a canvas bag. The S.P. man said to himself, My God, somebody is going to get killed and I am going to see it.

At six A.M. he sent the message to the depot at Yuma, where they would then be loading the convicts onto the train.

The Southern Pacific equipment that left Yuma that Friday morning was made up of a 4-4-0 locomotive, a baggage car, two day coaches for regular passengers (though only eleven people were aboard), another baggage car, and an old wooden coach from the Cannanea-Rio Yaqui-El Pacifico line. The last twenty-seven convicts to leave the prison were locked inside this coach along with Bob Fisher and three armed guards. Behind, bringing up the rear, was a caboose that carried Mr. Manly and three more guards.

Bob Fisher had personally made up the list of prisoners for this last run to Florence: only twenty-seven, including Frank Shelby and his bunch. Most of the others were short-term prisoners and trusties who wouldn't be expected to make trouble. A small, semi-harmless group which, Bob Fisher believed, would make it easy for him to keep an eye on Shelby. Also aboard were the TB convicts, the two women and Harold Jackson and Raymond San Carlos.

Harold and Raymond were near the rear of the coach. The only ones behind them were Bob Fisher and the guards. Ahead of them were the TB convicts, then two rows of empty seats, then the rest of the prisoners scattered along both sides of the aisle in the back-to-back straw seats. The two women were in the front of the coach. The doors at both ends were padlocked. The windows were glass, but they were not made to open.

Before the train was five minutes out of Yuma every convict in the coach knew they were going to stop in Sentinel to pick up three men who had escaped on Wednesday and had been recaptured the next day. There was a lot of talk about who the three were.

Bob Fisher didn't say a word. He sat patiently waiting for the train to reach Sentinel, thinking about the message they had received Wednesday evening: *Three convicts missing on arrival Phoenix. Local and county authorities alerted.* Signed, *Sheriff, Maricopa County.* What bothered Fisher, there had been no information sent from Florence, nothing from Mr. Rynning, no further word from anybody until the wire was received at the depot this morning. Mr. Manly had wired back they would stop for the prisoners and Bob Fisher had not said a word to anybody since. Something wasn't right and he had to think it through.

About 7:30 A.M., halfway to Sentinel, Fisher said to the guard sitting next to him, "Put your gun on Frank Shelby and don't move it till we get to Florence."

Harold Jackson, next to the window, looked out at the flat desert country that stretched to distant dark mounds, mountains that would take a day to reach on foot, maybe half a day if a man was to run. But a mountain was nothing to run to. There was nothing out there but sky and rocks and desert growth that looked as if it would never die, but offered a man no hope of life. It was the same land he had looked at a few months before, going in the other direction, sitting in the same upright straw seat handcuffed to a sheriff's man. The Indian sitting next to him now nudged his arm and Harold looked up.

The Davis woman was coming down the aisle from the front of the coach. She passed them and a moment later Harold heard the door to the toilet open and close. Looking out the window again, Harold said, "What's out there, that way?"

"Mexico," Raymond answered. "Across the desert and the mountain, and if you can find water, Mexico."

"You know where the water is?"

"First twenty-five, thirty miles there isn't any."

"What about after that?"

"I know some places."

"You could find them?"

"I'm not going through the window if that's what you're thinking about."

"The train's going to stop in Sentinel."

"They open the door to put people on," Raymond said. "They ain't letting anybody off."

"We don't know what they going to do," Harold said, "till we get there." He heard the woman come out of the toilet compartment and waited for her to walk past.

She didn't appear. Harold turned to look out the window across the aisle. Over his shoulder he could see the Davis woman standing by Bob Fisher's seat. She was saying something but keeping her voice down and he couldn't make out the words. He heard Fisher though.

Fisher said, "Is that right?" The woman said something else and Fisher said, "If you don't know where what's the good of telling me? How are you helping? Anybody could say what you're saying and if it turns out right try to get credit. But you haven't told me nothing yet."

"All right," Norma Davis said. "It's going to be at Sentinel."

"You could be guessing, for all I know."

"Take my word," the woman said.

Bob Fisher didn't say anything for a while. The train swayed and clicked along the tracks and there was no sound behind Harold Jackson. He glanced over his shoulder. Fisher was getting up, handing his revolver to the guard sitting across the aisle. Then he was past Harold, walking up the aisle and hold-ing the woman by the arm to move her along ahead of him.

Frank Shelby looked up as they stopped at his seat. He was sitting with Junior; Soonzy and Joe Dean were facing them.

"This lady says you're going to try to escape," Fisher said to Shelby. "What do you think about that?"

Shelby's shoulders and head swayed slightly with the motion of the train. He looked up at Fisher and Norma, looking from one to the other before he said, "If I haven't told her any such thing, how would she know?"

"She says you're getting off at Sentinel."

"Well, if she tells me how I'm going to do it and it sounds good, I might try it." Shelby grinned a little. "Do you believe her?"

"I believe she might be telling a story," Fisher said, "but I also believe it might be true. That's why I've got a gun pointed at your head till we get to Florence. Do you understand me?"

"I sure do." Shelby nodded, looking straight up at Bob Fisher. He said then, "Do you mind if I have a talk with Norma? I'd like to know why she's making up stories."

"She's all yours," Fisher said.

Harold nudged Raymond. They watched Fisher coming back down the aisle. Beyond him they saw Junior get up to give the Davis woman his seat. Tacha was turned around watching. She moved over close to the window as Junior approached her and sat down.

Behind Harold and Raymond one of the guards said, "You letting the woman sit with the men?"

"They're all the same as far as I can see," Fisher answered. "All convicts."

Virgil Shelby, holding a shotgun across his arm, was out on the platform when the train came into sight. He heard it and saw its smoke first, then spotted the locomotive way down the tracks. This was the worst part, right now, seeing the train getting bigger and bigger and seeing the steam blowing out with the screeching sound of the brakes. The locomotive was rolling slowly as it came past the coaling shed and the water tower, easing into the station, rolling past the platform now hissing steam, the engine and the baggage cars and the two coaches with the half-dozen faces in the windows looking out at him. He could feel those people staring at him, wondering who he was. Virgil didn't look back at them. He kept his eyes on the last coach and caboose and saw them jerk to a stop before reaching the platform—out on open ground just this side of the water tower.

"Come on out," Virgil said to the station house.

Howard Crowder and Dancey and Billy Santos came out into the sunlight through the open door. Their hands were behind their backs, as though they might have been tied. Virgil moved them out of the doorway, down to the end of the platform and stood them against the wall of the building: three convicts waiting to be put aboard a prison train, tired-looking, beaten, their hat brims pulled down against the bright morning glare.

Virgil watched Bob Fisher, followed by another guard with a rifle come down the step-rungs at the far end of the prison coach. Two more guards with rifles were coming along the side of the caboose and somebody else was in the caboose window: a man wearing glasses who was sticking his head out and saying something to the two guards who had come out of the prison coach.

Bob Fisher didn't look around at Mr. Manly in the caboose window. He kept his gaze on the three convicts and the man with the shotgun. He called out, "What're the names of those men you got?"

"I'm just delivering these people," Virgil called back. "I wasn't introduced to them."

Bob Fisher and the guard with him and the two guards from the caboose came on past the prison coach but stopped before they reached the platform.

"You the only one guarding them?" Fisher asked.

"Yes, sir, I'm the one found them, I'm the one brought them in."

"I've seen you some place," Fisher said.

"Sure, delivering a prisoner. About a year ago."

"Where's the station man at?"

"He's inside."

"Call him out."

"I reckon he heard you." Virgil looked over his shoulder as the S.P. man appeared in the doorway. "There he is. Hey, listen, you want these three boys or don't you? I been watching them all night, I'm tired."

"I want to know who they are," Fisher said. "If you're not going to tell me, I want them to call out their names."

There was silence. Virgil knew the time had come and he had to put the shotgun on Fisher and fill up the silence and get this thing done right now, or else drop the gun and forget the whole thing. No more than eight seconds passed in the silence, though it seemed like eight minutes to Virgil. Bob Fisher's hand went inside his coat and Virgil didn't have to think about it any more. He heard glass shatter as somebody kicked through a window in the prison coach. Bob Fisher drew a revolver, half turning toward the prison coach at the same time, but not turning quickly enough as Virgil put the shotgun on him and gave him a load point-blank in the side of the chest. And as the guards saw Fisher go down and were raising their rifles the three men in convict clothes brought their revolvers from behind their backs and fired as fast as they could swing their guns from one gray suit to another. All three guards were dropped where they stood, though one of them, on his knees, shot Billy Santos through the head before Virgil could get his shotgun on the man and finish him with the second load.

A rifle came out the caboose window and a barrel smashed the glass of a window in the prison coach, but it was too late. Virgil was pressed close to the side of the baggage car, out of the line of fire, and the two men in prison clothes had the S.P. man and were using him for a shield as they backed into the station house.

Virgil could look directly across the platform to the open doorway. He took time to reload the shotgun. He looked up and down the length of the train, then over at the doorway again.

"Hey, Dancey," Virgil called over, "send that train man out with the dynamite."

He had to wait a little bit before the S.P. man appeared in the doorway, straining to hold the fifty-pound case in his arms, having trouble with the dead weight, or else terrified of what he was holding.

"Walk down to the end of the platform with it," Virgil told him, "so they can see what you got. When you come back, walk up by that first passenger coach. Where everybody's looking out the window."

Jesus, the man could hardly take a step he was so scared of dropping the case. When he was down at the end of the platform, the copper wire trailing behind him and leading into the station, Virgil stepped away from the baggage car and called out, "Hey, you guards! You hear me? Throw out your guns and come out with your hands in the air, or we're going to put dynamite under a passenger coach and blow everybody clear to hell. You hear me?"

They heard him.

Mr. Manly and the three guards who were left came out to stand by the caboose. The prisoners began to yell and break the windows on both sides of the coach, but they quieted down when Frank Shelby and his three boys walked off the train and wouldn't let anybody else follow.

They are going to shoot us, Mr. Manly said to himself. He saw Frank Shelby looking toward them. Then Frank was looking at the dead guards and at Bob Fisher in particular. "I wish you hadn't of killed him," he heard Shelby say.

"I had to," the man with the shotgun said.

And then Shelby said, "I wanted to do it."

Junior said that if he hadn't kicked out the window they might still be in there. That was all they said for a while that Mr. Manly heard. Shelby and his three convict friends went into the station house. They came out a few minutes later wearing work clothes and might have been ranch hands for all anybody would know to look at them.

Mr. Manly didn't see who it was that placed the case of dynamite at the front end of the train, under the cowcatcher, but saw one of them playing out the wire back along the platform and around the off side of the station house. Standing on the platform, Frank Shelby and the one with the shotgun seemed to be in a serious conversation. Then Frank said something to Junior, who boarded the train again and brought out Norma Davis. Mr. Manly could see she was frightened, as if afraid they were going to shoot her or do something to her. Junior and Joe Dean took her into the station house. Frank Shelby came over then. Mr. Manly expected him to draw a gun.

"Four of us are leaving," Shelby said. "You can have the rest."

"What about the woman?"

"I mean five of us. Norma's going along."

"You're not going to harm her, are you?" Shelby kept staring at him, and Mr. Manly couldn't think straight. All he could say was, "I hope you know that what you're doing is wrong, an offence against Almighty God as well as your fellowman."

"Jesus Christ," Shelby said, and walked away.

Lord, help me, Mr. Manly said, and called out, "Frank, listen to me."

But Shelby didn't look back. The platform was deserted now except for the Mexican-looking man who lay dead with his arm hanging over the edge. They were mounting horses on the other side of the station. Mr. Manly could hear the horses. Then, from where he stood, he could see several of the horses past the corner of the building. He saw Junior stand in his stirrups to reach the telegraph wire at the edge of the roof and cut it with a knife. Another man was on the ground, stooped over a wooden box. Shelby nodded to him and kicked his horse, heading out into the open desert, away from the station. As the rest of them followed, raising a thin dust cloud, the man on the ground pushed down on the box.

The dynamite charge raised the front end of the locomotive off the track, derailed the first baggage car and sent the coaches slamming back against each other, twisting the couplings and tearing loose the end car, rolling it a hundred feet down the track. Mr. Manly dropped flat with the awful, ear-splitting sound of the explosion. He wasn't sure if he threw himself down or was knocked down by the concussion. When he opened his eyes there was dirt in his mouth, his head throbbed as if he had been hit with a hammer, and for a minute or so he could see nothing but smoke or dust or steam from the engine, a cloud that enveloped the station and lay heavily over the platform.

He heard men's voices. He was aware of one of the guards lying close to him and looked to see if the man was hurt. The guard was pushing himself up, shaking his head. Mr. Manly got quickly to his feet and looked around. The caboose was no longer behind him; it was down the track and the prison coach was only a few feet away where the convicts were coming out, coughing and waving at the smoke with their hands. Mr. Manly called out, "Is anybody hurt?"

No one answered him directly. The convicts were standing around; they seemed dazed. No one was attempting to run away. He saw one of the guards with a rifle now on the platform, holding the gun on the prisoners, who were paying no attention to him. At the other end of the platform there were a few people from the passenger coach. They stood looking at the locomotive that was shooting white steam and stood leaning awkwardly toward the platform, as if it might fall over any minute.

He wanted to be doing something. He had to be doing something. Five prisoners gone, four guards dead, a train blown up, telegraph line cut, no idea when help would come or where to go from here. He could hear Mr. Rynning saying, "You let them do all that? Man, this is your responsibility and you'll answer for it."

"Captain, you want us to follow them?"

Mr. Manly turned, not recognizing the voice at first. Harold Jackson, the Zulu, was standing next to him.

"What? I'm sorry, I didn't hear you."

"I said, you want us to follow them? Me and Raymond."

Mr. Manly perked up. "There are horses here?"

"No-suh, man say the nearest horses are at Gila. That's most of a day's ride."

"Then how would you expect to follow them?"

"We run, captain."

"There are eight of them—on horses."

"We don't mean to fight them, captain. We mean maybe we can follow them and see which way they go. Then when you get some help, you know, maybe we can tell this help where they went."

"They'll be thirty miles away before dark."

"So will we, captain."

"Follow them on foot—"

"Yes-suh, only we would have to go right now. Captain, they going to run those horses at first to get some distance and we would have to run the first five, six miles, no stopping, to keep their dust in sight. Raymond say it's all flat and open, no water.

Just some little bushes. We don't have to follow them all day. We see where they going and get back here at dark."

Mr. Manly was frowning, looking around because, Lord, there was too much to think about at one time. He said, "I can't send convicts to chase after convicts. My God."

"They do it in Florida, captain. Trusties handle the dogs. I seen it."

"I have to get the telegraph wire fixed, that's the main thing."

"I hear the train man say they busted his key, he don't know if he can fix it," Harold Jackson said. "You going to sit here till tonight before anybody come—while Frank Shelby and them are making distance. But if me and the Apache follow them we can leave signs."

Mr. Manly noticed Raymond San Carlos now behind Harold. Raymond was nodding. "Sure," he said, "we can leave pieces of our clothes for them to follow if you give us something else to wear. Maybe you should give us some guns too, in case we get close to them, or for firing signals."

"I can't do that," Mr. Manly said. "No, I can't give you guns."

"How about our spears then?" Raymond said. "We get hungry we could use the spears maybe to stick something."

"The spears might be all right." Mr. Manly nodded.

"Spears and two canteens of water," Raymond said. "And the other clothes. Some people see us they won't think we're convicts running away."

"Pair of pants and a shirt," Mr. Manly said.

"And a couple of blankets. In case we don't get back before dark and we got to sleep outside. We can get our bedrolls and the spears," Raymond said. "They're with all the baggage in that car we loaded."

"You'd try to be back before dark?"

"Yes, sir, we don't like to sleep outside if we don't have to."

"Well," Mr. Manly said. He paused. He was trying to think of an alternative. He didn't believe that sending these two out would do any good. He pictured them coming back at dusk and sinking to the ground exhausted. But at least it would be doing something—now. Mr. Rynning or somebody would ask him, What did you do? And he'd say, I sent trackers out after them. I got these two boys that are runners. He said, "Well, find your stuff and get started. I'll tell the guards."

They left the water stop at Sentinel running almost due south. They ran several hundred yards before looking back to see the smoke still hanging in a dull cloud over the buildings and the palo verde trees. They ran for another half-mile or so, loping easily and not speaking, carrying their spears and their new guard-gray pants and shirts wrapped in their blanket rolls. They ran until they reached a gradual rise and ran down the other side to find themselves in a shallow wash, out of sight of the water stop.

They looked at each other now. Harold grinned and Raymond grinned. They sat down on the bank of the wash and began laughing, until soon both of them had tears in their eyes.

12

Harold said, "What way do we go?"

Raymond got up on the bank of the dry wash and stood looking out at the desert that was a flat burned-out waste as far as they could see. There were patches of dusty scrub growth, but no cactus or trees from here to the dark rise of the mountains to the south.

"That way," Raymond said. "To the Crater Mountains and down to the Little Ajos. Two days we come to Ajo, the town, steal some horses, go on south to Bates Well. The next day we come to Quitobaquito, a little water-hole village, and cross the border. After that, I don't know."

"Three days, uh?"

"Without horses."

"Frank Shelby, he going the same way?"

"He could go to Clarkstown instead of Ajo. They near each other. One the white man's town, the other the Mexican town."

"But he's going the same way we are."

"There isn't no other way south from here."

"I'd like to get him in front of me one minute," Harold said.

"Man," Raymond said, "you would have to move fast to get him first."

"Maybe we run into him sometime."

"Only if we run," Raymond said.

Harold was silent a moment. "If we did, we'd get out of here quicker, wouldn't we? If we run."

"Sure, maybe save a day. If we're any good."

"You think we couldn't run to those mountains?"

"Sure we could, we wanted to."

"Is there water?"

"There used to be."

"Then that's probably where he's heading to camp tonight, uh? What do you think?"

"He's got to go that way. He might as well."

"We was to get there tonight," Harold said, "we might run into him."

"We might run into all of them."

567

"Not if we saw them first. Waited for him to get alone."

Raymond grinned. "Play with him a little."

"Man, that would be good, wouldn't it?" Harold said. "Scare him some."

"Scare hell out of him."

"Paint his face," Harold said. He began to smile thinking about it.

"Take his clothes. Paint him all over."

"Now you talking. You got any?"

"I brought some iodine and a little bottle of white. Listen," Raymond said, "we're going that way. Why don't we take a little run and see how Frank's doing?"

Harold stood up. When they had tied their blanket rolls across one shoulder and picked up their spears, the Apache and the Zulu began their run across the southern Arizona desert.

They ran ten miles in the furnace heat of sand and rock and dry, white-crusted playas and didn't break their stride until the sun was directly over head. They walked a mile and ran another mile before they stopped to rest and allowed themselves a drink of water from the canteens, a short drink and then a mouthful they held in their mouths while they screwed closed the canteens and hung them over their shoulders again. They rested fifteen minutes and before the tiredness could creep in to stiffen their legs they stood up without a word and started off again toward the mountains.

For a mile or so they would be aware of their running. Then, in time, they would become lost in the monotonous stride of their pace, running, but each somewhere else in his mind, seeing cool mountain pastures or palm trees or thinking of nothing at all, running and hearing themselves sucking the heated air in and letting it out, but not feeling the agony of running. They had learned to do this in the past months, to detach themselves and be inside or outside the running man but not part of him for long minutes at a time. When they broke stride they would always walk and sometimes run again before resting. At times they felt they were getting no closer to the mountains, though finally the slopes began to take shape, changing from a dark mass to dun-colored slopes and shadowed contours. At mid-afternoon they saw the first trace of dust rising in the distance. Both of them saw it and they kept their eyes on the wispy, moving cloud that would rise and vanish against the sky. The dust was something good to watch and seeing it was better than stretching out in the grass and going to sleep. It meant Frank Shelby was only a few miles ahead of them.

They came to the arroyo in the shadowed foothills of the Crater Mountains a little after five o'clock. There was good brush cover here and a natural road that would take them up into high country. They would camp above Shelby if they could and watch him, Raymond said, but first he had to go out and find the son of a bitch. You rest, he told Harold, and the Zulu gave him a dead-pan look and stared at him until he was gone. Harold sat back against the cool, shaded wall of the gulley. He wouldn't let himself go to sleep though. He kept his eyes open and waited for the Apache, listening and not moving, letting the tight weariness ease out of his body. By the time Raymond returned the arroyo was dark. The only light they could see were sun reflections on the high peaks above them.

"They're in some trees," Raymond said, "about a half-mile from here. Taking it easy, they even got a fire."

"All of them there?"

"I count eight, eight horses."

"Can we get close?"

"Right above them. Frank's put two men up in the rocks— they can see all around the camp."

"What do you think?" Harold said.

"I think we should take the two in the rocks. See what Frank does in the morning when nobody's there."

The grin spread over Harold's face. That sounded pretty good.

They slept for a few hours and when they woke up it was night. Harold touched Raymond. The Indian sat up without making a sound. He opened a canvas bag and took out the small bottles of iodine and white paint and they began to get ready.

There was no sun yet on this side of the mountain, still cold dark in the early morning when Virgil Shelby came down out of the rocks and crossed the open slope to the trees. He could make out his brother and the woman by the fire. He could hear the horses and knew Frank's men were saddling them and gathering up their gear.

Frank and the woman looked up as Virgil approached, and Frank said, "They coming?"

"I don't know. I didn't see them."

"What do you mean you didn't see them?"

"They weren't up there."

Frank Shelby got up off the ground. He dumped his coffee as he walked to the edge of the trees to look up at the tumbled rocks and the escarpment that rose steeply against the sky.

"They're asleep somewhere," he said. "You must've looked the wrong places."

"I looked all over up there."

"They're asleep," Shelby said. "Go on up there and look again."

When Virgil came back the second time Frank said, Jesus Christ, what good are you? And sent Junior and Joe Dean up into the rocks. When they came down he went up himself to have a look and was still up there as the sunlight began to spread over the slope and they could feel the heat of day coming down on them.

"There's no sign of anything," Virgil said. "There's no sign they were even here."

"I put them here," Frank Shelby said. "One right where you're standing, Dancey over about a hundred feet. I put them here myself."

"Well, they're not here now," Virgil said.

"Jesus Christ, I know that." Frank looked over at Junior and Soonzy. "You counted the horses?"

"We'd a-heard them taking horses."

"I asked if you counted them!"

"Christ, we got them saddled. I don't have to count them."

"Then they walked away," Frank Shelby said, his tone quieter now.

Virgil shook his head. "I hadn't paid them yet."

"They walked away," Shelby said again. "I don't know why, but they did."

"Can you see Dancey walking off into the mountains?" Virgil said. "I'm telling you I hadn't *paid* them."

"There's nothing up there could have carried them off. No animal, no man. There is no sign they did anything but walk away," Shelby said, "and that's the way we're going to leave it."

He said no more until they were down in the trees again, ready to ride out. Nobody said anything.

Then Frank told Joe Dean he was to ride ahead of them like a point man. Virgil, he said, was to stay closer in the hills and ride swing, though he would also be ahead of them looking for natural trails.

"Looking for trails," Virgil said. "If you believe those two men walked off, then what is it that's tightening up your hind end?"

"You're older than me," Frank said, "but no bigger, and I will sure close your mouth if you want it done."

"Jesus, can't you take some kidding?"

"Not from you," his brother said.

They were in a high meadow that had taken more than an hour to reach, at least a thousand feet above Shelby's camp. Dancey and Howard Crowder sat on the ground close to each other. The Apache and the Zulu stood off from them leaning on their spears, their blankets laid over their shoulders as they waited for the sun to spread across the field. They would be leaving in a few minutes. They planned to get out ahead of Shelby and be waiting for him. These two, Dancey and Crowder, they would leave here. They had taken their revolvers and gun belts, the only things they wanted from them.

"They're going to kill us," Dancey whispered.

Howard Crowder told him for God sake to keep quiet, they'd hear him.

They had been in the meadow most of the night, brought here after each had been sitting in the rocks, drowsing, and had felt the spear point at the back of his neck. They hadn't got a good look at the two yet. They believed both were Indians—even though there were no Indians around here, and no Indians had carried spears in fifty years. Then they would have to be loco Indians escaped from an asylum or kicked out of their village. That's what they were. That's why Dancey believed they were going to kill him and Howard.

Finally, in the morning light, when the Zulu walked over to them and Dancey got a close look at his face—God Almighty, with the paint and the scars and the short pointed beard and the earring—he closed his eyes and expected to feel the spear in his chest any second.

Harold said, "You two wait here till after we're gone."

Dancey opened his eyes and Howard Crowder said "What?"

"We're going to leave, then you can find your way out of here."

Howard Crowder said, "But we don't know where we are."

"You up on a mountain."

"How do we get down?"

"You look around for a while you find a trail. By that time your friends will be gone without you, so you might as well go home." Howard started to turn away.

"Wait a minute," Howard Crowder said. "We don't have horses, we don't have any food or water. How are we supposed to get across the desert?"

"It's up to you," Harold said. "Walk if you want or stay here and die, it's up to you."

"We didn't do nothing to you," Dancey said.

Harold looked at him. "That's why we haven't killed you."

"Then what do you want us for?"

"We don't want you," Harold said. "We want Frank Shelby."

Virgil rejoined the group at noon to report he hadn't seen a thing, not any natural trail either that would save them time. They were into the foothills of the Little Ajos and he sure wished Billy Santos had not got shot in the head in the train station, because Billy would have had them to Clarkstown by now. They would be sitting at a table with cold beer and fried meat instead of squatting on the ground eating hash out of a can. He asked if he should stay with the group now. Norma Davis looked pretty good even if she was kind of sweaty and dirty; she was built and had nice long hair. He wouldn't mind riding with her a while and maybe arranging something for that night.

Frank, it looked like, was still not talking. Virgil asked him again if he should stay with the group and this time Frank said no and told him to finish his grub and ride out. He said, "Find the road to Clarkstown or don't bother coming back, because there would be no use of having you around."

So Virgil and Joe Dean rode out about fifteen minutes ahead of the others. When they split up Virgil worked his way deeper into the foothills to look for some kind of a road. He crossed brush slopes and arroyos, holding to a south-southeast course, but he didn't see anything that resembled even a foot path. It was a few hours after leaving the group, about three o'clock in the afternoon, that Virgil came across the Indian and it was the damnedest thing he'd ever seen in his life.

There he was out in the middle of nowhere sitting at the shady edge of a mesquite thicket wrapped in an army blanket. A real Apache Indian, red headband and all and even with some paint on his face and a staff or something that was sticking out of the bushes. It looked like a fishing pole. That was the first thing Virgil thought of: an Apache Indian out in the desert fishing in a mesquite patch—the damnedest thing he'd ever seen.

Virgil said, "Hey, Indin, you sabe English any?"

Raymond San Carlos remained squatted on the ground. He nodded once.

"I'm looking for the road to Clarkstown."

Raymond shook his head now. "I don't know."

"You speak pretty good. Tell me something, what're you doing out here?"

"I'm not doing nothing."

"You live around here?"

Raymond pointed off to the side. "Not far."

"How come you got that paint on your face?"

"I just put it there."

"How come if you live around here you don't know where Clarkstown is?"

"I don't know."

"Jesus, you must be a dumb Indin. Have you seen anybody else come through here today?"

"Nobody."

"You haven't seen me, have you?"

"What?"

"You haven't seen nobody and you haven't seen me either."

Raymond said nothing.

"I don't know," Virgil said now. "Some sheriff's people ask you you're liable to tell them, aren't you? You got family around here?"

"Nobody else."

"Just you all alone. Nobody would miss you then, would they? Listen, buddy, I don't mean anything personal, but I'm afraid you seeing me isn't a good idea. I'm going to have to shoot you."

Raymond stood up now, slowly.

"You can run if you want," Virgil said, "or you can stand there and take it, I don't care; but don't start hollering and carrying on. All right?"

Virgil was wearing a shoulder rig under his coat. He looked down as he unbuttoned the one button, drew a .44 Colt and looked up to see something coming at him and gasped as if the wind was knocked out of him as he grabbed hold of the fishing pole sticking out of his chest and saw the Indian standing there watching him and saw the sky and the sun, and that was all.

Raymond dragged Virgil's body into the mesquite. He left his spear in there too. He had two revolvers, a Winchester rifle and a horse. He didn't need a spear any more.

Joe Dean's horse smelled water. He was sure of it, so he let the animal have its head and Joe Dean went along for the ride—down into a wide canyon that was green and yellow with spring growth. When he saw the cottonwoods and then the round soft shape of the willows against the canyon slope, Joe Dean patted the horse's neck and guided him with the reins again.

It was a still pool, but not stagnant, undercutting a shelf of rock and mirroring the cliffs and canyon walls. Joe Dean dismounted. He led his horse down a bank of shale to the pool, then went belly-down at the edge and drank with his face in the water. He drank all he wanted before emptying the little bit left in his canteen and filling it to the top. Then he stretched out and drank again. He wished he had time to strip off his clothes and dive in. But he had better get the others first or Frank would see he'd bathed and start kicking and screaming again. Once he got them here they would probably all want to take a bath. That would be something, Norma in there with them, grabbing some of her under the water when Frank wasn't looking. Then she'd get out and lie up there on the bank to dry off in the sun. Nice soft white body—

Joe Dean was pushing himself up, looking at the pool and aware now of the reflections in the still water: the slope of the canyon wall high above, the shelf of rock behind him, sandy brown, and something else, something dark that resembled a man's shape, and he felt that cold prickly feeling up between his shoulder blades to his neck.

It was probably a crevice, shadowed inside. It couldn't be a man. Joe Dean got to his feet, then turned around and looked up.

Harold Jackson—bare to the waist, and a blanket over one shoulder, with his beard and tribal scars and streak of white paint—stood looking down at him from the rock shelf.

"How you doing?" Harold said. "You get enough water?"

Joe Dean stared at him. He didn't answer right away. God, no. He was thinking and trying to decide quickly if it was a good thing or a bad thing to be looking up at Harold Jackson at a water hole in the Little Ajo Mountains.

He said finally, "How'd you get here?"

"Same way you did."

"You got away after we left?"

"Looks like it, don't it?"

"Well, that must've been something. Just you?"

"No, Raymond come with me."

"I don't see him. Where is he?"

"He's around some place."

"If there wasn't any horses left, how'd you get here?"

"How you think?"

"I'm asking you, Sambo."

"We run, Joe."

"You're saying you run here all the way from Sentinel?"

"Well, we stop last night," Harold said, and kept watching him. "Up in the Crater Mountains."

"Is that right? We camped up there too."

"I know you did," Harold said.

Joe Dean was silent for a long moment before he said, "You killed Howard and Dancey, didn't you?"

"No, we never killed them. We let them go."

"What do you want?"

"Not you, Joe. Unless you want to take part."

Joe Dean's revolver was in his belt. He didn't see a gun or a knife or anything on Harold, just the blanket over his shoulder and covering his arm. It looked like it would be pretty easy. So he drew the revolver.

As he did, though, Harold pulled the blanket across his body with his left hand. His right hand came up holding Howard Crowder's .44 and he shot Joe Dean with it three times in the chest. And now Harold had two revolvers, a rifle, and a horse. He left Joe Dean lying next to the pool for Shelby to find.

They had passed Clarkstown, Shelby decided. Missed it. Which meant they were still in the Little Ajo Mountains, past the chance of having a sit-down hot meal today, but that much closer to the border. That part was all right. What bothered him, they had not seen Virgil or Joe Dean since noon.

It was almost four o'clock now. Junior and Soonzy were riding ahead about thirty yards. Norma was keeping up with Shelby, staying close, afraid of him but more afraid of falling behind and finding herself alone. If Shelby didn't know where they were, Norma knew that she, by herself, would never find her way out. She had no idea why Shelby had brought her, other than at Virgil's request to have a woman along. No one had approached her in the camp last night. She knew, though, once they were across the border and the men relaxed and quit looking behind them, one of them, probably Virgil, would come to her with that fixed expression on his face and she would take him on and be nice to him as long as she had no other choice.

"We were through here one time," Shelby said. "We went up through Copper Canyon to Clarkstown the morning we went after the Cornelia Mine payroll. I don't see any familiar sights, though. It all looks the same."

She knew he wasn't speaking to her directly. He was thinking out loud, or stoking his confidence with the sound of his own voice.

"From here what we want to hit is Growler Pass," Shelby said. "Top the pass and we're at Bates Well. Then we got two ways to go. Southeast to Dripping Springs and on down to Sonoyta. Or a shorter trail to the border through Quitobaquito. I haven't decided yet which way we'll go. When Virgil comes in I'll ask him if Billy Santos said anything about which trail's best this time of the year."

"What happened to the two men last night?" Norma asked him.

Shelby didn't answer. She wasn't sure if she should ask him again. Before she could decide, Junior was riding back toward them and Shelby had reined in to wait for him.

Junior was grinning. "I believe Joe Dean's found us some water. His tracks lead into that canyon yonder and it's chock full of green brush and willow trees."

"There's a tank somewhere in these hills," Shelby said.

"Well, I believe we've found it," Junior said.

They found the natural tank at the end of the canyon. They found Joe Dean lying with his head and outstretched arms in the still water. And they found planted in the sand next to him, sticking straight up, a spear made of a bamboo fishing pole and a mortar trowel.

13

THEY CAMPED on high ground south of Bates Well and in the morning came down through giant saguaro country, down through a hollow in the hills to within sight of Quitobaquito.

There it was, a row of weathered adobes and stock pens beyond a water hole that resembled a shallow, stagnant lake—a worn-out village on the bank of a dying pool that was rimmed with rushes and weeds and a few stunted trees.

Shelby didn't like it.

He had pictured a green oasis and found a dusty, desert water hole. He had imagined a village where they could trade for food and fresh horses, a gateway to Mexico with the border lying not far beyond the village, across the Rio Sonoyta.

He didn't like the look of the place. He didn't like not seeing any people over there. He didn't like the open fifty yards between here and the water hole.

He waited in a cover of rocks and brush with Norma and Junior and Soonzy behind him, and Mexico waiting less than a mile away. They could go around Quitobaquito. But if they did, where was the next water? The Sonoyta could be dried up, for all he knew. They could head for Santo Domingo, a fair-sized town that shouldn't be too far away. But what if they missed it? There was water right in front of them and, goddamn-it, they were going to have some, all they wanted. But he hesitated, studying the village, waiting for some sign of life other than a dog barking, and remembering Joe Dean with the three bullets in his chest.

Junior said, "Jesus, are we going to sit here in the sun all day?"

"I'll let you know," Shelby said.

"You want me to get the water?"

"I did, I would have told you."

"Well, then tell me, goddamn-it. You think I'm scared to?"

Soonzy settled it. He said, "I think maybe everybody's off some place to a wedding or something. That's probably what it is. These people, somebody dies or gets married, they come from all over."

"Maybe," Shelby said.

"I don't see no other way but for me to go in there and find out. What do you say, Frank?"

After a moment Shelby nodded. "All right, go take a look."

"If it's the nigger and the Indin," Soonzy said, "if they're in there, I'll bring 'em out."

Raymond held the wooden shutter open an inch, enough so he could watch Soonzy coming in from the east end of the village, mounted, a rifle across his lap. Riding right in, Raymond thought. Dumb, or sure of himself, or maybe both. He could stick a .44 out the window and shoot him as he went by. Except that it would be a risk. He couldn't afford to miss and have Soonzy shooting in here. Raymond let the shutter close.

He pressed a finger to his lips and turned to the fourteen people, the men and women and children who were huddled in the dim room, sitting on the floor and looking up at him now, watching silently, even the two smallest children. The people were Mexican and Papago. They wore white cotton and cast-off clothes. They had lived here all their lives and they were used to armed men riding through Quitobaquito. Raymond had told them these were bad men coming who might steal from them and harm them. They believed him and they waited in silence. Now they could hear the horse's hoofs on the hard-packed street. Raymond stood by the door with a revolver in his hand. The sound of the horse passed. Raymond waited, then opened the door a crack and looked out. Soonzy was nowhere in sight.

If anybody was going to shoot at anybody going for water, Soonzy decided, it would have to be from one of the adobes facing the water hole. There was a tree in the backyard of the first one that would block a clear shot across the hole. So that left him only two places to search—two low-roofed, crumbling adobes that stood bare in the sunlight, showing their worn bricks and looking like part of the land.

Soonzy stayed close to the walls on the front side of the street. When he came to the first adobe facing the water hole, he reached down to push the door open, ducked his head, and walked his horse inside.

He came out into the backyard on foot, holding a revolver now, and seeing just one end of the water hole because the tree was in the way. From the next adobe, though, a person would have a clear shot. There weren't any side windows, which was good. It let Soonzy walk right up to the place. He edged around the corner, following his revolver to the back door and got right up against the boards so he could listen. He gave himself time; there was no hurry. Then he was glad he did when the sound came from inside, a little creaking sound, like a door or a window being opened.

Harold eased open the front door a little more. He still couldn't see anything. The man had been down at the end of the street, coming this way on his horse big as anything, and now he was gone. He looked down half a block and across the street, at the adobe, where Raymond was waiting with the people, keeping them quiet and out of the way. He saw Raymond coming out; Harold wanted to wave to him to get inside. What was he doing?

The back door banged open and Soonzy was standing in the room covering him with a Colt revolver.

"Got you," Soonzy said. "Throw the gun outside and turn this way. Where's that red nigger at?"

"You mean Raymond?" Harold said. "He left. I don't know where he went."

"Which one of you shot Joe Dean, you or him?"

"I did. I haven't seen Raymond since before that."

"What'd you do with Virgil?"

"I don't think I know any Virgil."

"Frank's brother. He took us off the train."

"I haven't seen him."

"You want me to pull the trigger?"

"I guess you'll pull it whether I tell or not." Harold felt the door behind him touch the heel of his right foot. He had not moved the foot, but now he felt the door push gently against it.

"I'll tell Frank Shelby," Harold said then. "How'll that be? You take me to Frank I'll tell him where his brother is and them other two boys. But if you shoot me he won't ever know where his brother's at, will he? He's liable to get mad at somebody."

Soonzy had to think about that. He wasn't going to be talked into anything he didn't want to do. He said, "Whether I shoot you now or later you're still going to be dead."

"It's up to you," Harold said.

"All right, turn around and open the door."

"Yes-suh, captain," Harold said.

He opened the door and stepped aside and Raymond, in the doorway, fired twice and hit Soonzy dead center both times.

Shelby and Junior and Norma Davis heard the shots. They sounded far off, but the reports were thin and clear and unmistakable. Soonzy had gone into the village. Two shots were fired and Soonzy had not come out. They crouched fifty yards from water with empty canteens and the border less than a mile away.

Norma said they should go back to Bates Well. They could be there by evening, get water, and take the other trail south.

And run into a posse coming down from Gila, Shelby said. They didn't have time enough even to wait here till dark. They had to go with water or go without it, but they had to go, now.

So Junior said Jesus, give me the goddamn canteens or we will be here all day. He said maybe those two could paint theirselves up and bushwack a man, but he would bet ten dollars gold they couldn't shoot worth a damn for any distance. He'd get the water and be back in a minute. Shelby told Junior he would return fire and cover him if they started shooting, and Junior said that was mighty big of him.

"There," Raymond said. "You see him?"

Harold looked out past the door frame to the water hole. "Whereabouts?"

Raymond was at the window of the adobe. "He worked his way over to the right, coming in on the other side of the tree. You'll see him in a minute."

"Which one?"

"It looked like Junior."

"He can't sit still, can he?"

"I guess he's thirsty," Raymond said. "There he is. He thinks that tree's hiding him."

Harold could see him now, over to the right a little, approaching the bank of the water hole, running across the open in a hunch-shouldered crouch, keeping his head down behind nothing.

"How far do you think?" Raymond said.

Harold raised his Winchester and put the front sight on Junior. "Hundred yards, a little more."

"Can you hit him?"

Harold watched Junior slide down the sandy bank and begin filling the canteens, four of them, kneeling in the water and filling them one at a time. "Yeah, I can hit him," Harold said, and he was thinking, He's taking too long. He should fill them all at once, push them under and hold them down.

"What do you think?" Raymond said.

"I don't know."

"He ever do anything to you?"

"He done enough."

"I don't know either," Raymond said.

"He'd kill you. He wouldn't have to think about it."

"I guess he would."

"He'd enjoy it."

"I don't know," Raymond said. "It's different, seeing him when he don't see us."

"Well," Harold said, "if he gets the water we might not see him again. We might not see Frank Shelby again either. You want Frank?"

"I guess so."

"I do too," Harold said.

They let Junior come up the bank with the canteens, up to the rim before they shot him. Both fired at once and Junior slid back down to the edge of the still pool.

Norma looked at it this way: they would either give up, or they would be killed. Giving up would be taking a chance. But it would be less chancey if she gave up on her own, without Shelby. After all, Shelby had forced her to come along and that was a fact, whether the Indian and the Negro realized it or not. She had never been really unkind to them in prison; she had had nothing to do with them. So there was no reason for them to harm her now—once she explained she was more on their side than on Frank's. If they were feeling mean and had rape on their mind, well, she could handle that easily enough.

There was one canteen left, Joe Dean's. Norma picked it up and waited for Shelby's reaction.

"They'll shoot you too," he said.

"I don't think so."

"Why, because you're a woman?"

"That might help."

"God Almighty, you don't know them, do you?"

"I know they've got nothing against me. They're mad at you, Frank, not me."

"They've killed six people we know of. You just watched them gun Junior—and you're going to walk out there in the open?"

"Do you believe I might have a chance?"

Shelby paused. "A skinny one."

"Skinny or not, it's the only one we have, isn't it?"

"You'd put your life up to help me?"

"I'm just as thirsty as you are."

"Norma, I don't know—two days ago you were trying to turn me in."

"That's a long story, and if we get out of here we can talk about it sometime, Frank."

"You really believe you can do it."

"I want to so bad."

Boy, she was something. She was a tough, good-looking woman, and by God, maybe she could pull it. Frank said, "It might work. You know it?"

"I'm going way around to the side," Norma said, "where those bushes are. Honey, if they start shooting—"

"You're going to make it, Norma, I know you are. I got a feeling about this and I *know* it's going to work." He gave her a hug and rubbed his hand gently up and down her back, which was damp with perspiration. He said, "You hurry back now."

Norma said, "I will, sweetheart."

Watching her cross the open ground, Shelby got his rifle up between a notch in the rocks and put it on the middle adobe across the water hole. Norma was approaching from the

left, the same way Junior had gone in, but circling wider than
Junior had, going way around and now approaching the pool
where tall rushes grew along the bank. Duck down in there,
Shelby said. But Norma kept going, circling the water hole, following the bank as it curved around toward the far side. Jesus,
she had nerve; she was heading for the bushes almost to the
other side. But then she was past the bushes. She was running.
She was into the yard where the big tree stood before Shelby
said, "Goddamn you!" out loud, and swung his Winchester
on the moving figure in the striped skirt. He fired and levered
and fired two more before they opened up from the house and
he had to go down behind the rocks. By the time he looked
again she was inside.

Frank Shelby gave up an hour later. He waved a flour sack at
them for a while, then brought the three horses down out of
the brush and led them around the water hole toward the row
of adobes. He had figured out most of what he was going to
say. The tone was the important thing. Take them by surprise.
Bluff them. Push them off balance. They'd expect him to run
and hide, but instead he was walking up to them. He could
talk to them. Christ, a dumb nigger and an Indin who'd been
taking orders and saying yes-sir all their lives. They had run
scared from the train and had been scared into killing. That's
what happened. They were scared to death of being caught and
taken back to prison. So he would have to be gentle with them
at first and calm them down, the way you'd calm a green horse
that was nervous and skittish. There, there, boys, what's all this
commotion about? Show them he wasn't afraid, and gradually
take charge. Take care of Norma also. God, he was dying to
get his hands on Norma.

Harold and Raymond came out of the adobe first, with rifles,
though not pointing them at him. Norma came out behind
them and moved over to the side, grinning at him, goddamn
her. It made Shelby mad, though it didn't hold his attention.
Harold and Raymond did that with their painted faces staring
at him; no expression, just staring, waiting for him.

As he reached the yard Shelby grinned and said, "Boys, I
believe it's about time we cut out this foolishness. What do
you say?"

Harold and Raymond waited.

Shelby said, "I mean what are we doing shooting at each other for? We're on the same side. We spent months together in that hell hole on the bluff and, by Jesus, we jumped the train together, didn't we?"

Harold and Raymond waited.

Shelby said, "If there was some misunderstanding you had with my men we can talk about it later because, boys, right now I believe we should get over that border before we do any more standing around talking."

And Harold and Raymond waited.

Shelby did too, a moment. He said then, "Have I ever done anything to you? Outside of a little pissy-ass difference we had, haven't I always treated you boys fair? What do you want from me? You want me to pay you something? I'll tell you what, I'll pay you both to hire on and ride with me. What do you say?"

Harold Jackson said, "You're going to ride with us, man. Free."

"To where?"

"Back to Sentinel."

Norma started laughing as Shelby said, "Jesus, are you crazy? What are you talking about, back to Sentinel? You mean back to *prison*?"

"That's right," Harold said. "Me and Raymond decide that's the thing you'd like the worst."

She stopped laughing altogether as Raymond said, "You're going too, lady."

"Why?" Norma looked dazed, taken completely by surprise. "I'm not with him. What have I ever done to you?"

"Nobody has ever done anything to us," Raymond said to Harold. "Did you know that?"

The section gang that arrived from Gila told Mr. Manly no, they had not heard any news yet. There were posses out from the Sand Tank Mountains to the Little Ajos, but nobody had reported seeing anything. At least it had not been reported to the railroad.

They asked Mr. Manly how long he had been here at Sentinel and he told them five days, since the escape. He didn't tell them Mr. Rynning had wired and instructed him to stay. "You have five days," Mr. Rynning said. "If convict pair you released do not return, report same to sheriff, Maricopa. Report in person to me."

Mr. Manly took that to mean he was to wait here five full days and leave the morning of the sixth. The first two days there had been a mob here. Railroad people with equipment, a half-dozen guards that had been sent over from Florence, and the Maricopa sheriff, who had been here getting statements and the descriptions of the escaped convicts. He had told the Maricopa sheriff about sending out the two trackers and the man had said, trackers? Where did you get trackers? He told him and the man had stared at him with a funny look. It was the sheriff who must have told Mr. Rynning about Harold and Raymond.

The railroad had sent an engine with a crane to lift the locomotive and the baggage car onto the track. Then the train had to be pulled all the way to the yard at Gila, where a new locomotive was hooked up and the prisoners were taken on to Florence. There had certainly been a lot of excitement those two days. Since then the place had been deserted except for the telegrapher and the section gang. They were usually busy and it gave Mr. Manly time to think of what he would tell Mr. Rynning.

It wasn't an easy thing to explain: trusting two convicts enough to let them go off alone. Two murderers, Mr. Rynning would say. Yes, that was true; but he had still trusted them. And until this morning he had expected to see them again. That was the sad part. He sincerely believed he had made progress with Harold and Raymond. He believed he had taught them something worthwhile about life, about living with their fellowman. But evidently he had been wrong. Or, to look at it honestly, he had failed. Another failure after forty years of failures.

He was in the station house late in the afternoon of the fifth day, talking to the telegrapher, passing time. Neither had spoken for a while when the telegrapher said, "You hear something?" He went to the window and said, "Riders coming in." After a pause he said, "Lord in heaven!" And Mr. Manly knew.

He was off the bench and outside, standing there waiting for them, grinning, beaming, as they rode up: his Apache and his

Zulu—thank you, God, just look at them!—bringing in Frank Shelby and the woman with ropes around their necks, bringing them in tied fast and making Mr. Manly, at this moment, the happiest man on earth.

Mr. Manly said, "I don't believe it. Boys, I am looking at it and I don't believe it. Do you know there are posses all over the country looking for these people?"

"We passed some of them," Raymond said.

"They still after the others?"

"I guess they are," Raymond said.

"Boys, I'll tell you, I've been waiting here for days, worried sick about you. I even began to wonder—I hate to say it but it's true—I even began to wonder if you were coming back. Now listen, I want to hear all about it, but first I want to say this. For what you've done here, for your loyalty and courage, risking your lives to bring these people back—which you didn't even have to do—I am going to personally see that you're treated like white men at Florence and are given decent work to do."

The Apache and the Zulu sat easily in their saddles watching Mr. Manly, their painted faces staring at him without expression.

"I'll tell you something else," Mr. Manly said. "You keep your record clean at Florence, I'll go before the prison board myself and make a formal request that your sentences be commuted, which means cut way down." Mr. Manly was beaming. He said, "Fellas, what do you think of that?"

They continued to watch him until Harold Jackson the Zulu, leaning on his saddle horn, said to Mr. Manly, "Fuck you, captain."

They let go of the ropes that led to Frank Shelby and the woman. They turned their horses in tight circles and rode out, leaving a mist of fine dust hanging in the air.

STORIES

Trail of the Apache

U NDER THE thatched roof ramada that ran the length of the agency office, Travisin slouched in a canvas-backed chair, his boots propped against one of the support posts. His gaze took in the sun-beaten, gray adobe buildings, all one-story structures, that rimmed the vacant quadrangle. It was a glaring, depressing scene of sun on rock, without a single shade tree or graceful feature to redeem the squat ugliness. There was not a living soul in sight. Earlier that morning, his White Mountain Apache charges had received their two-weeks' supply of beef and flour. By now they were milling about the cook fires in front of their wickiups, eating up a two-weeks' ration in two days. Most of the Indians had built their wickiups three miles farther up the Gila, where the flat, dry land began to buckle into rock-strewn hills. There the thin, sparse Gila cottonwoods grew taller and closer together and the mesquite and prickly pear thicker. And there was the small game that sustained them when their government rations were consumed.

At the agency, Travisin lived alone. By actual count there were forty-two Coyotero Apache scouts along with the interpreter, Barney Fry, and his wife, a Tonto woman, but as the officers at Fort Thomas looked at it, he was living alone. There is no question that to most young Eastern gentlemen on frontier station, such an alien means of existence would have meant nothing more than a very slow way to die, with boredom reading the services. But, of course, they were not Travisin.

From Whipple Barracks, through San Carlos and on down to Fort Huachuca, it went without argument that Eric Travisin was the best Apache campaigner in Arizona Territory. There was a time, of course, when this belief was not shared by all and the question would pop up often, along the trail, in the barracks at Fort Thomas, or in a Globe barroom. Barney Fry's name would always come up then—though most discounted him for his one-quarter Apache blood. But that was a time in the past when Eric Travisin was still new; before the sweltering

591

sand-rock Apache country had burned and gouged his features, leaving his gaunt face deep-chiseled and expressionless. That was while he was learning that it took an Apache to catch an Apache. So, for all practical purposes, he became one. Barney Fry taught him everything he knew about the Apache; then he began teaching Fry. He relied on no one entirely, not even Fry. He followed his own judgment, a judgment that his fellow officers looked upon as pure animal instinct. And perhaps they were right. But Travisin understood the steps necessary to survival in an enemy element. They weren't included in Cooke's "Cavalry Tactics": you learned them the hard way, and your being alive testified that you had learned well. They said Travisin was more of an Apache than the Apaches themselves. They said he was cold-blooded, sometimes cruel. And they were uneasy in his presence; he had discarded his cotillion demeanor the first year at Fort Thomas, and in its place was the quiet, pulsing fury of an Apache war dance.

This was easy enough for the inquisitive to understand. But there was another side to Eric Travisin.

For three years he had been acting as agent at the Camp Gila subagency, charged with the health and welfare of over two hundred White Mountain Apaches. And in three years he had transformed nomadic hostiles into peaceful agriculturalists. He was a dismounted cavalry officer who sometimes laid it on with the flat of his saber, but he was completely honest. He understood them and took their side, and they respected him for it. It was better than San Carlos.

That's why the conversation at the officers' mess at Fort Thomas, thirty miles southwest, so often dwelled on him: he was a good Samaritan with a Spencer in his hand. They just didn't understand him. They didn't realize that actually he was following the line of least resistance. He was accepting the situation as it was and doing the best job with the means at hand. To Travisin it was that simple; and fortunately he enjoyed it, both the fighting and the pacifying. The fact that it made him a better cavalryman never entered his mind. He had forgotten about promotions. By this time he was too much a part of the savage everyday existence of Apache country. He looked at the harsh, rugged surroundings and liked what he saw.

He shuffled his feet up and down the porch pole and sank deeper into his camp chair. Suddenly in his breast he felt the tenseness. His ears seemed to tingle and strain against an unnatural stillness, and immediately every muscle tightened. But as quickly as the strange feeling came over him, he relaxed. He moved his head no more than two inches, and from the corner of his eye saw the Apache crouched on hands and knees at the corner of the ramada. The Indian crept like an animal across the porch, slowly and with his back arched. A pistol and a knife were at his waist, but he carried no weapon in his hands. Travisin moved his right hand across his stomach and eased open the holster flap. Now his arms were folded across his chest, with his right hand gripping the holstered pistol. He waited until the Apache was less than six feet away before he wheeled from his chair and pushed the long-barreled revolving pistol into the astonished Apache's face.

Travisin grinned at the Apache and holstered the handgun. "Maybe someday you'll do it."

The Indian grunted angrily. With victory almost in his grasp he had failed again. Gatito, sergeant of Travisin's Apache scouts, was an old man, the best tracker in the Army, and it cut his pride deeply that he was never able to win their wager. Between the two men was an unusual bet of almost two years' standing. If at any time, while not officially occupied, the scout was able to steal up to the officer and place his knife at Travisin's back, a bottle of whiskey was his. For such a prize the Indian would gladly crawl through anything. He tried constantly, using every trick he knew, but the officer was always ready. The result was a grumbling, thirsty Indian, but an officer whose senses were razor-sharp. Travisin even practiced staying alive.

Gatito gave the report of the morning patrol and then added, almost as an afterthought, "Chiricahua come. Two miles away."

Travisin wheeled from the office doorway. "Where?"

Gatito spoke impassively. "Chiricahua come. He come with troop from Fort."

Travisin considered the Apache's words in silence, squinting through the afternoon glare toward the wooden bridge across the Gila that was the end of the trail from Thomas. They would come from that direction. "Go get Fry immediately. And turn out your boys."

2

Second Lieutenant William de Both, West Point's newest contribution to the "Dandy 5th," had the distinct feeling that he was entering a hostile camp as he led H troop across the wooden bridge and approached Camp Gila. As he drew nearer to the agency office, the figures in front of it appeared no friendlier. Good God, were they all Indians? After guarding the sixteen hostiles the thirty miles from Fort Thomas, Lieutenant de Both had had enough of Indians for a long time. Even with the H troopers riding four sides, he couldn't help glancing nervously back to the sixteen hostiles and expecting trouble to break out at any moment. After thirty miles of this, he was hardly prepared to face the gaunt, raw-boned Travisin and his sinister-looking band of Apache scouts.

His fellow officers back at Fort Thomas had eagerly informed de Both of the character of the formidable Captain Travisin. In fact, they painted a picture of him with bold, harsh strokes, watching the young lieutenant's face intently to enjoy the mixed emotions that showed so obviously. But even with the exaggerated tales of the officers' mess, de Both could not help learning that this unusual Indian agent was still the best army officer on the frontier. Three months out of the Point, he was only too eager to serve under the best.

Leading his troop across the square, he scanned the ragged line of men in front of the office and on the ramada. All were armed, and all stared at the approaching column as if it were bringing cholera instead of sixteen unarmed Indians. He halted the column and dismounted in front of the tall, thin man in the center. The lieutenant inspected the man's faded blue chambray shirt and gray trousers, and unconsciously adjusted his own blue jacket.

"My man, would you kindly inform the captain that Lieutenant de Both is reporting? I shall present my orders to him." The lieutenant was brushing trail dust from his sleeve as he spoke.

Travisin stood with hands on hips looking at de Both. He shook his head faintly, without speaking, and began to twist one end of his dragoon mustache. Then he nodded to the foremost of the Chiricahuas and turned to Barney Fry.

"Barney, that's Pillo, isn't it?"

"Ain't nobody else," the scout said matter-of-factly. "And the skinny buck on the paint is Asesino, his son-in-law."

Travisin turned his attention to the bewildered lieutenant. "Well, mister, ordinarily I'd play games with you for a while, but under the circumstances, when you bring along company like that, we'd better get down to the business at hand without the monkeyshines. Fry, take care of our guests. Lieutenant, you come with me." He turned abruptly and entered the office.

Inside, de Both pulled out a folded sheet of paper and handed it to Travisin. The captain sat back, propped his boots on the desk and read the orders slowly. When he was through, he shook his head and silently cursed the stupidity of men trying to control a powder-keg situation two thousand miles from the likely explosion. He read the orders again to be certain that the content was as illogical as it seemed.

HEADQUARTERS, DEPARTMENT OF ARIZONA
IN THE FIELD, FORT THOMAS, ARIZONA
August 30, 1880
E. M. Travisin. Capt. 5th Cav. Reg.
Camp Gila Subagency
Camp Gila, Arizona

You are hereby directed, by order of the Department of the Interior, Bureau of Indian Affairs, to place Pillo and the remnants of his band (numbering fifteen) on the Camp Gila White Mountain reservation. The Bureau compliments you on the remarkable job you are doing and has confidence that the sixteen hostile Chiricahuas, placed in your charge, will profit by the example of their White Mountain brothers and become peaceful farmers.

The bearer, Second Lieutenant William de Both, is, as of this writing, assigned to Camp Gila as second in command. Take him under your wing, Eric; he's young, but I think he will make a good officer.

EMON COLLIER
BRIGADIER GENERAL COMMANDING

He looked up at the lieutenant, who was gazing about the bare room, taking in the table, the rolltop desk along the back wall, the rifle rack and three straight chairs. De Both looked no more than twenty-one or -two, pink-cheeked, neat, every inch a West Point gentleman. But already, after only three months on the frontier, his face was beginning to lose that expression of anticipated adventure, the young officer's dream of winning fame and promotion in the field. The thirty miles from Fort Thomas alone presented the field as something he had not bargained for. To Travisin, it wasn't a new story. He'd had younger officers serve under him before, and it always started the same way, ". . . take him under your wing . . . teach him about the Apache." It was always the old campaigner teaching the recruit what it was all about.

To Eric Travisin, at twenty-eight, only seven years out of the Point, it was bound to be amusing. The cavalry mustache made him look older, but that wasn't it. Travisin had been a veteran his first year. It was something that he'd had even before he came West. It was that something that made him stand out in any group of men. It was the strange instinct that made him wheel and draw his handgun when Gatito stole up behind him. It was a combination of many things, but not one of them did Travisin himself understand, even though they made him the youngest captain in Arizona because of it.

And now another one to watch him and not understand. He wondered how long de Both would last.

He said, "Lieutenant, do you know why you've been sent here?"

"No, sir." De Both brought himself to attention. "I do not question my orders."

Travisin was faintly amused. "I'm sure you don't, Lieutenant. I was referring to any rumors you might have heard. . . . And relax."

De Both remained at attention. "I don't make it a practice to repeat idle rumors that have no basis in fact."

Travisin felt his temper rise, but suppressed it from long practice. It wasn't the way to get things done. He circled the desk and drew a chair up behind de Both. "Here, rest your legs." He placed a firm hand on the lieutenant's shoulder and half forced him into the chair. "Mister, you and I are going to spend a lot of time together. We'll be either in this room or out on the desert with nothing to think about except what's in front of us. Conversation gets pretty thin after a while, and you might even make up things just to hear yourself talk. You're the only other Regular Army man here, so you can see it isn't going to be a parade-grounds routine. I've been here for three years now, counting White Mountain Indians and making patrols. Sometimes things get a bit hot; otherwise you just sit around and watch the desert. I probably don't look like much of an officer to you. That doesn't matter. You can keep up the spit and polish if you want, but I'd advise you to relax and play the game without keeping the rule book open all the time. . . . Now, would you mind telling me what in hell the rumors are at Thomas?"

De Both was surprised, and disturbed. He fidgeted in his chair, trying to feel official. "Well, sir, under the circumstances . . . Of course, as I said, there is no basis for its authenticity, but the word is that Crook is being transferred back to the Department to lead an expedition to the border. They say that he will probably ask for you. So I am being assigned here to replace you when the time comes. This is, of course, only gossip that is circulating about."

"Do you believe it?"

"Sir, I don't even think about it."

Travisin said, "You mean you don't want to think about it. Sitting by yourself at a Godforsaken Indian agency with almost two hundred and fifty White Mountains living across the street. Not to mention the scouts." He paused and smiled at de Both. "I don't know, Lieutenant, you might even like it after a while."

"I accept my orders, Captain. My desires have nothing to do with my orders."

But Travisin was not listening. Long strides took him to the doorway and he leaned out with a hand against the door frame on each side.

"*Fryyyyyyyyyyyy! Hey, Fryyyy!*"

The men of H troop looked over to the office as they prepared to mount. Barney Fry left the sergeant and strode toward the agency office. "Come in here, Barney."

The clatter of trotting horses beat across the quadrangle as Fry stepped up on the porch and entered the office. His short strides were slightly pigeon-toed and he held his head tilted down as if he were self-conscious of his appearance. He looked to be in his early twenties, but, like Travisin, his face was a hard, bronzed mask, matured beyond his age. When he took off his gray wide-brimmed hat, thick, black hair clung close to his scalp, smeared with oily perspiration.

"What do you think, Barney?"

Fry leaned against the edge of the desk. "I think probably the same thing you do. Those 'Paches aren't goin' to stay long at Gila even if we'd give them all the beef critters in Arizona. You notice there wasn't any women in the band?"

"Yes, I noticed," Travisin answered. "They'll never learn, will they?" He looked at de Both. "You see, Lieutenant, the Bureau thinks that if they separate them from their families for a while, the hostiles will become good little Indians and make plows out of their Spencers and grow corn to eat instead of drink. What would you do if some benevolent race snatched your women and children from you and sent you to a barren rock pile over a hundred miles away? And do you know why? For something you'd been doing for the past three hundred years. For that simple but enigmatic something that makes you an Apache and not a Navajo. For that quirk of fate that makes you a tiger instead of a Persian cat. Mister, I've got over two hundred White Mountains here raising crops and eating government beef. I can assure you that they're not doing it by nature! And now they sent sixteen Chiricahuas! Sixteen men with the smell of gunpowder still strong in their nostrils and blood lust in their eyes." Travisin shook his head wearily. "And they send them here without their women."

De Both cleared his throat before speaking. "Well, frankly, Captain, I don't see what the problem is. Obviously, these hostiles have done wrong. The natural consequence would be a punishment of some sort. Why pamper them? They're not little children."

"No, they're not little children. They're Apaches," Travisin reflected. "You know, I used to know an Indian up near Fort Apache by the name of Skimitozin. He was an Arivaipa. One day he was sitting in the hut of a white friend of his, a miner, and they were eating supper together. Then, for no reason at all, Skimitozin drew his handgun and shot his friend through the head. Before they hung him he said he did it to show his Arivaipa people that they should never get too friendly with the *blancos.* The Apache has never gotten a real break from the whites. So Skimitozin wanted to make sure that his people never got to the point of expecting one, and relaxing. Mister, I'm here to kill Indians and keep Indians alive. It's a paradox—no question about that—but I gave up rationalizing a long time ago. Most Apaches have always lived a life of violence. I'm not here primarily to convert them; but by the same token I have to be fair—when they are fair to me."

De Both raised an objection. "I see nothing wrong with our treatment of the Indians. As a matter of fact, I think we've gone out of our way to treat them decently." He recited the words as if he were reading from an official text.

Fry broke in. "Go up to San Carlos and spend a week or two," he said. "Especially when the government beef contractors come around with their adjusted scales and each cow with a couple of barrels of Gila water in her. Watch how the 'Pache women try to cut each other up for a bloated cow belly." Fry spoke slowly, without excitement.

Travisin said to the lieutenant, "Fry's not talking about one or two incidents. He's talking about history. You were with Pillo all the way up from Thomas. Did you see his eyes? If you did, you saw the whole story."

3

The early afternoon sun blazed heavily against the adobe houses and vacant quadrangle. The air was still, still and oppressive, and seemed to be thickened by the fierce, withering rays of the Arizona sun. To the east, the purplish blur of the Pinals showed hazily through the glare.

Travisin leaned loosely against a support post under the brush ramada. His gray cotton shirt was black with sweat in places, but he seemed unmindful of the heat. His sun-darkened face was impassive, as if asleep, but his eyes were only half closed in the shadow of his hat brim, squinting against the glare in the direction from which Fry would return.

Earlier that morning, the scout and six of his Coyoteros had traveled upriver to inspect the tracts selected by Pillo and his band. The hostiles had erected their wickiups without a murmur of complaint and seemed to have fallen into the alien routines of reservation life without any trouble; but it was their silence, their impassive acceptance of this new life that bothered Travisin. For the two weeks the hostiles had been at Camp Gila, Travisin's scouts had been on the alert every minute of the day. But nothing had happened. When Fry returned, he would know more.

De Both appeared in the office door behind him. "Not back yet?"

"No. He might have stopped to chin with some of the White Mountain people. He's got a few friends there," Travisin said. "Barney's got a little Apache blood in him, you know."

De Both was openly surprised. "He has? I didn't know that!" He thought of the countless times he had voiced his contempt for the Apaches in front of Fry. He felt uncomfortable and a little embarrassed now, though Fry had never once seemed to take it as a personal affront. Travisin read the discomfort on his face. There was no sense in making it more difficult.

"His mother was a half-breed," Travisin explained. "She married a miner and followed him all over the Territory while he dug holes in the ground. Barney was born somewhere up in the Tonto country on one of his dad's claims. When he was about eight or nine his ma and dad were killed by some Tontos and he was carried off and brought up in the tribe. That's where he got his nose for scouting. It's not just in his blood like some people think; he learned it, and he learned it from the best in the business. Then, when he was about fifteen, he came back to the world of the whites. About that time there was a campaign operating out of Fort Apache against the Tontos. One day a patrol came across the rancheria where Barney lived and took him back to Fort Apache. All the warriors were out and only the women and children were around. He remembered enough about the white man's life to want to go back to the Indians, but he knew too much about the Apache's life for the Army to let him go; so he's been a guide since that day. He was at Fort

Thomas when I arrived there seven years ago, and he's been with me ever since I've been here at Gila."

De Both was deep in thought. "But can you trust him?" he asked. "After living with the Apaches for so long."

"Can you trust the rest of the scouts? Can you trust those rocks and mesquite clumps out yonder?" Travisin looked hard into the lieutenant's eyes. "Mister, you watch the rocks, the trees, the men around you. You watch until your eyes ache, and then you keep on watching. Because you'll always have that feeling that the minute you let down, you're done for. And if you don't have that feeling, you're in the wrong business."

A little past four, Fry and his scouts rode in. He threw off and ran toward the agency office. Travisin met him in the doorway. "They scoot, Barney?"

Fry paused to catch his breath and wiped the sweat from his face with a grimy, brown hand.

"It might be worse than that. When we got there this morning only a few of Pillo's band were around. I questioned them, but they kept trying to change the subject and get us out of there. I thought they were actin' strange, talkin' more than usual, and then it dawned on me. Gatito had spotted it right away. They'd been drinkin' tizwin. You know you got to drink a whoppin' lot of that stuff to really get drunk. I figure these boys ain't had much yet, cuz they were still too quiet. But the others were probably off at the source of supply so we rode out and tried to cut their sign. We tried every likely spot in the neighborhood until afternoon, and we still couldn't find a trace of them."

Travisin considered the situation silently for a moment. "They've probably been at it since they got here. Taking their time to pick a spot we wouldn't find right away. No wonder they've been so quiet." Travisin had much to think about, for a drunken Apache will do strange things. Bloody things. He asked the scout, "What does Gatito think?"

Fry hesitated, and then said, "I don't like the way he was lickin' his lips while we were on the hunt."

Fry did not have to say more. Travisin knew him well enough to know that the scout felt Gatito could bear some extra attention. To de Both, watching the scene, it was a new experience. The captain and the quarter-breed scout talking like brothers. Saying more with eyes and gestures than with words. He looked from one to the other intently, then for the first time noticed the young Apache standing next to Travisin. A moment ago he had not been there. But there had not been a sound or a footstep!

The young brave spoke swiftly in the Apache tongue for almost a minute and then disappeared around the corner of the office. De Both could still see vividly the red calico cloth around thick, black hair, and his almost feminine features.

Fry and Travisin began to talk again, but de Both interrupted.

"What in the name of heaven was that?"

Travisin grinned at the young officer's astonishment. "I thought you knew Peaches. Forgot he hadn't been around for a while."

"Peaches!"

Travisin said, "Let's go inside."

They gathered around his table, lighted cigarettes, and Travisin went on. "I'd just as soon you didn't speak his name aloud around here. You see, that young, gentle-looking Apache has one of the toughest jobs on the reservation. He's an agency spy. Only Fry and I, and now you, know what he is. Not even any of the scouts know. The Indians suspect that someone on their side is reporting to me, but they have no idea who it is. He's got a dangerous job, but it's necessary. If trouble ever breaks out, we have to be able to nip it in the bud. Peaches is the only way for us to determine where the bud is."

"May I ask what he told you just now?"

Travisin drew hard on his cigarette before replying. "He said that he knew much, but he would be back sometime before sunup tomorrow to tell what he knew. He made one last point very emphatic. He said, 'Watch Gatito!'"

A rear room of the agency office adobe served as sleeping quarters for both of the officers. Their cots were against opposite walls, lockers at the feet, and two large pine-board wardrobes, holding uniforms and personal gear, were flush with the wall running along the heads of their bunks.

A full moon pointed its light through the window frame over de Both's bed, carpeted the plank flooring with a delicate sheen, and reached as far as the gleaming upper portion of Travisin's body, motionless on the cot. One arm was beneath the gray blanket that reached just above his waist, the other was folded across his bare chest.

A floorboard creaked somewhere near. His eyes opened at once and closed just as suddenly. Beneath the blanket his hand groped near his thigh and quietly covered the grip of his pistol. He opened his eyes slightly and glanced across the room. De Both was dead asleep. The latch on the door leading to the front office rattled faintly, and then hinges creaked as the door began to open. Travisin quietly drew his arm from beneath the blanket and leveled the pistol at the doorway. His thumb closed on the hammer and drew it back, and the click of the cocking action was a sharp, metallic sound. The opening-door motion stopped.

"Nantan, do not shoot." The words were just above a whisper.

Travisin threw the blanket from his legs, swung them to the floor and moved to the doorway without a sound. Peaches backed into the office as he approached.

"Chiricahua leave."

"How long?"

"They go maybe five mile now. Gatito go with them."

Travisin stepped back to the doorway and slammed the butt of his pistol against the wooden door. "Hey, mister, roll out!" De Both sat bolt upright. "Be ready to ride in a few minutes," Travisin said, and ran out of the office toward Barney Fry's adobe across the quadrangle.

In less than twenty minutes, thirteen riders streaked out of the quadrangle westward. Behind them, orange light was just beginning to show above the irregular outline of the Pinals. The morning was cool, but still, and the stillness held the promise of the blistering heat of the day to come.

The sun was only a little higher when Travisin and his scouts rode up to four wickiups along the bank of the Gila. Travisin halted the detail, but did not dismount. He sat motionless in the saddle, his senses alert to the quiet. He said something in

Apache and one of the scouts threw off and cautiously entered the first wickiup. He reappeared in an instant, shaking his head from side to side. In the third hut, the scout remained longer than usual. When he reappeared he was dragging an unconscious Indian by the legs.

Travisin said, "That one of them, Barney?"

Fry swung down from his pony and leaned over the prostrate Indian, saying a few words in Apache to the scout still holding the Indian's legs. "He's a Chiricahua, Captain. Dead drunk. Must have been drinking for at least two days." He nodded his head toward the Apache scout. "Ningun says there's a jug inside with a little tizwin in it."

Travisin pointed to two of the scouts and then swept his arm in the direction of the fourth wickiup. They kicked their ponies to a leaping start, dashed to the hut and gave it a quick inspection. In a minute they were back.

The scouts watched Travisin intently as he studied the situation. They knew what the signs meant. They sat their ponies now with restless anticipation, fingering their carbines, checking ammunition belts, holding in the small, wiry horses that also seemed to be charged with the excitement of the moment—for there is no love lost between the Coyotero and the Chiricahua. Eric Travisin knew as well as any of them what the sign meant: sixteen drunken Apaches screaming through the countryside with blood in their eyes and a bad taste in their mouths. It was something that had to be stopped before the Indians regained their senses. Now they were loco Apaches, bloodthirsty, but a bit careless. By the next day, unless stopped, they would again be cold, patient guerrilla fighters led by the master strategist, Pillo.

From the direction of the agency a scout rode into sight beating his pony to a whirlwind pace. He reined in abruptly and shouted something to Fry through the dust cloud.

"We been sleepin', Captain. He says Gatito made off with a dozen carbines and two hundred rounds of forty-fours. Must have sneaked them out sometime last night."

In Travisin, the excitement of what lay ahead was building up continually. Now it was beginning to break through his calm surface. "We're awake now, Barney. I figure they'll either streak south for the Madres right away, or contact their people up near Apache by dodging through the Basin and then heading east for the reservation. I know if I was going to hide out for a while, I'd sure want my wife along. Let's find out which it is."

4

By midmorning Travisin's scouts had followed the tracks of the hostiles to an elevated stretch of pines wedged tightly among bare, rolling hills. They halted a few hundred yards from the wooded area, in the open. Before them the land, dotted with mesquite and catclaw, climbed gradually to the pine plateau; and the sun-glare made shimmering waves, hazy and filmy white, as they looked ahead to the contrasting black of the pines. A shallow arroyo cut its way down from the ridge past where the detail stood, finally ending at the banks of the Gila, twelve miles behind them. On both sides of the crusted edges of the arroyo, the unshod tracks they had been following all morning moved straight ahead.

Ningun, the Apache scout, rode up the arroyo a hundred yards, circled and returned. He mumbled only a few words to Fry, who glanced at the pine ridge again before speaking.

"He says the tracks go all the way up. Ain't no other place they could go."

"Does he think they're still up there?" Travisin asked the question without taking his eyes from the ridge.

"He didn't say, but I know he don't think so." Barney Fry pulled out a tobacco plug and bit off a generous chew, mumbling, "And I don't either." He moved the front of his open vest aside with a thumb and dropped the plug into the pocket of his shirt. "I figure it this way, Captain," he said. "They know who's followin' 'em, and they know we ain't about to get caught in a simple jackpot like that one up yonder without flushin' it out first. So they ain't goin' to waste their time settin' a trap that we won't fall right into."

"Sounds good, Barney, only there's one thing that's been troubling me," Travisin said. "Notice how clean the sign's been all the way? Not once have they tried to throw us off the track— and they've had more than one opportunity to at least make it pretty tough. No Apache, no matter if he's drunker than seven hundred dollars, is going to leave a trail that plain—that is, unless he wants to." He looked at the scout, suggesting a reply with his expression, and added, "Now why do you suppose old Pillo would want us to follow him?"

Fry pushed his hat from his forehead and passed the back of his hand across his mouth. It was plain that the captain's words gave him something to think about, but he had been riding with Travisin too long to show surprise with the officer's uncanny familiarity with what an Apache would do at a given time. He was never absolutely sure himself, but for some unexplainable reason Travisin's judgment was almost always right. And when dealing with an unknown quantity, the Apache, this judgment sometimes seemed to reach a superhuman level.

Fry was quiet, busy putting himself in Pillo's place, but de Both spoke up at once. "I take it you're suggesting that the Indians are not really drunk. But what about that unconscious Indian back at the reservation?" He asked the question as if he were purposely trying to shoot holes in the captain's theory.

"No, Lieutenant. I'm only saying what if," Travisin agreed, with a faint smile. "Could be one way or the other. I just want to impress you that we're not chasing Harvard sophomores across the Boston Common. If you ever come up against a better general than Pillo, you can be sure of one thing—he'll be another Apache."

Though he was sure of Fry's and Ningun's judgment, Travisin sent scouts ahead to flank the pine woods before taking his command through.

In another hour they were over the ridge, in the open, descending noisily over the loose gravel that was strewn down the gradual slope that led to the valley below. On level ground again, they followed the tracks to the north, up the raw, rolling valley, flat and straight from a distance; but as they traveled, the sandrock ground buckled and heaved into shallow crevices and ditches every few hundred feet. The monotony of the bleak scene was interrupted only by the grotesque outlines of giant saguaro and low, thick mesquite clumps.

Even in this comparatively open ground, de Both noticed that Travisin and all of the scouts rode half-tensed in their saddles, their eyes sweeping the area to the front and to both sides, studying every rock or shrub clump large enough to conceal a man. It was a vigilance that he himself was slowly acquiring just from noticing the others. Still he was more than willing to let the scouts do the watching. The damned stifling heat and the dazzling glare were enough for a white man to worry about. He mopped his face continually, and every once in a while pulled the white bandanna around his throat up over his nose and mouth. But that caused the heat to be even more smothering. He could feel the Apache scouts laughing at him. How could they remain so damned cool-looking in this heat! With every step of the horses, the dust rose around him and seemed to cling to his lungs until he would cough and cover his nose again with the kerchief. Ahead, but slightly to the east, he studied the jagged, blue outline of a mountain range. The Sierra Apaches. The purplish blue of the mountains and the soft blue of the cloudless sky were the only pleasant tones to redeem the ragged, wild look of the valley.

He pressed his heels into his horse's flanks and rode up abreast of Travisin. The climate and the unyielding country were grinding de Both's nerves raw; he wanted to scream at somebody, anybody.

"I sincerely hope you know where you're going, Captain."

Travisin ignored the sarcasm. "You'll feel better after we camp this evening. First day's always the toughest." He was silent for a few minutes, his head swinging in an arc studying the signs that did not even exist to de Both, and then he added, "Those mountains up ahead are the Sierra Apaches. Lot farther than they look. Before we pass them we're going to camp at a rancher's place. His name's Solomon, a really fine old gentleman. I think you'll like him, Bill." It was the first time Travisin had used de Both's first name. The lieutenant looked at him strangely.

It was close to six o'clock when they reached the road leading to Solomon's place. The road cut an arc through the brush flat and then passed through a grove of cottonwoods. From where they stood, they could see the roof of the ranch house through the clearing in the trees made by the road. The house stood a few hundred yards the other side of the cottonwoods, and just to the right of it a few acres of pines edged toward the house from the foothills of the Sierra Apaches towering to the east. Fry pointed to the wide path of trampled brush a hundred feet to the left of the road they were following.

"There's one I wouldn't care to try to figure out. Why didn't they take the road?"

Travisin was watching Ningun circle the cottonwoods and head back. "They're making it a bit *too* easy now," he replied idly.

Ningun made his report to Fry and pointed above the cottonwoods in the direction of the pines. A faint wisp of dark smoke curled skyward in a thin line. Against the glare it was hardly noticeable.

"Know what that means?" Travisin asked. He looked at no one in particular.

Fry answered, "I got an idea."

They dismounted in the cottonwoods and approached the clearing on foot. The ranch house, barn and corral behind it seemed deserted.

Travisin said, "Go take a look, Barney." Fry beckoned to four of the Apache scouts and they followed him into the clearing. They walked across the open space toward the house slowly, all abreast. They made no attempt to conceal themselves by crouching or hunching their shoulders—a natural instinct, but futile precaution with no cover in sight. They walked perfectly erect with their carbines out in front. Suddenly they all stopped and one of the scouts dropped to his hands and knees and put his ear to the earth. He arose slowly, and the others back at the cottonwoods saw them watching the pines more closely as they approached the house. Fry walked up to the log wall next to the front door and placed his ear to it. He made a motion with his right hand and three of the scouts disappeared around the corner of the house. Without hesitating, Fry approached the front door, kicked it open and darted into the dimness of the interior, the fourth Apache scout behind him. In a few moments, Fry reappeared in the doorway and waved to the rest in the cottonwoods.

He was still in the doorway when Travisin brought the others up. "Just the missus is inside" was all he said.

Travisin, with de Both behind him, walked past the scout

into the dimly lit ranch house. The room was a shambles, every piece of furniture and china broken. But what checked their gaze was Mrs. Solomon lying in the middle of the floor. Her clothes had been almost entirely ripped from her body and the flesh showing was gouged and slashed with knife wounds. Her scalp had been torn from her head.

De Both stared at the dead woman with a frozen gaze. Then the revulsion of it overcame him and he half turned to escape into the fresh air outside. He checked himself, thinking then of Travisin, and turned back to the room. The captain and the scout studied the scene stoically; but beneath their impassive eyes, almost any kind of emotion could be present. He tried to show the same calm. A cavalry officer should be used to the sight of death. But this was a form of death de Both had not counted on. He wheeled abruptly and left the room.

The next step was the pines. Travisin ordered the horses put in the corral. In case of a fight, they would be better off afoot; though he was sure that Pillo was hours away by now. They threaded through the nearer, sparsely growing pines that gradually grew taller and heavier as they advanced up the almost unnoticeable grade. Soon the pines entwined with junipers and thick clumps of brush so that they could see no more than fifty feet ahead into the dimness. They were far enough into the thicket so that they could no longer see the wisp of smoke, but now a strange odor took its place. The Coyotero scouts sniffed the air and looked at Travisin.

Fry said, "I'll send some of 'em ahead," and without waiting for a reply called an order to Ningun in the Apache tongue. As five of the scouts went on ahead, he said, "Let 'em do a little work for their pay," and propped his carbine against a pine. He eased his back against the same tree and looked at Travisin.

"You know, that's a funny thing back there at the cabin," Fry said, pointing his thumb over his shoulder. "That's only the second time in my life that I ever knew of a 'Pache scalpin' anybody."

"I was thinking about that myself," Travisin answered. "Then I remembered hearing once that Pillo was one of the few Apaches with Quana Parker at Adobe Walls six years ago. Don't know how Apaches got tied up with Comanches, but some Comanche dog soldier might have taught him the trick."

"Well," Fry reflected, picking up his carbine, "that's about the only trick a 'Pache might be taught."

Ningun appeared briefly through the trees ahead and waved his arm. They walked out to where he stood. Fry and Travisin listened to Ningun speak and then looked past his drooping shoulders to where he pointed. The nauseating odor was almost unbearable here. De Both tried to hold his breath as he followed the others into a small clearing. In front of him, Travisin and the scout moved apart as they reached the open ground and de Both was struck with a scene he was to remember to his dying day. He stared wide-eyed, swallowing repeatedly, until he could no longer control the saliva rising in his throat, and he turned off the path to be sick.

Fry scraped a boot along the crumbly earth and kicked sand onto the smoldering fire. The smoke rose heavy and thick for a few seconds, obscuring the grotesque form that hung motionless over the center of the small fire; and then it died out completely, revealing the half-burned body of Solomon suspended head-down from the arc of three thin juniper poles that had been stuck into the ground a few feet apart and lashed together at the tops. The old man's head hung only three feet above the smothered ashes of the fire. His head and upper portion of his body were burned beyond recognition, the black rawness creeping from this portion of his body upward to where his hands were tied tightly to his thighs; there the blackness changed to livid red blisters. All of his clothing had been burned away, but his boots still clung to his legs, squeezed to his ankles where the rawhide thongs wound about them and reached above to the arch of junipers. He was dead. But death had come slowly.

"The poor old man." The words were simple, but Travisin's voice cracked just faintly to tell more. "The poor, poor old man."

Fry looked around the clearing slowly, thinking, and then he said, "Bet he screamed for a bullet. Bet he screamed until his throat burst, and all the time they'd just be dancin' around jabbin' him with their knives and laughin'." Fry stopped and looked at the captain.

Travisin stared at old Solomon without blinking, his jaw muscles tightening and relaxing, his teeth grinding against one another. Only once in a while did Fry see him as the young man with feelings. It was a strange sight, the man fighting the boy; but always the man would win and he would go on as relentlessly as before, but with an added ruthlessness that had been sharpened by the emotional surge. Travisin never dealt in half measures. He felt sorrow for the old man cut to the bottom of his stomach, and he swore to himself a revenge, silently, though the fury of it pounded in his head.

5

They camped at Solomon's cabin that night, after burying the man and woman, and were up before dawn, in the saddle again on the trail of Pillo. They rode more anxiously now. Caution was still there, for that was instinct with Travisin and the scouts, but every man in the small company could feel an added eagerness, a gnawing urge to hound Pillo's spoor to the end and bring about a violent revenge.

De Both sensed it in himself and saw it easily in the way the Apache scouts clutched their carbines and fingered the triggers almost nervously. He felt the tightness rise in him and felt as if he must shriek to be relieved of the tension. Then he knew that it was the quickness of action mounting within him, that charge placed in a man's breast when he has to go on to kill or be killed. He watched Travisin for a sign to follow, a way in which to react; but as before he saw only the impassive, sun-scarred mask, the almost indolent look of half-closed eyes searching the surroundings for an unfamiliar sign.

By early afternoon, the thrill of the chase was draining from Second Lieutenant William de Both. His legs ached from the long hours in the saddle, and he gazed ahead, welcoming the green valley stretching as far as the eye could see, twisting among rocky hills, looking thick and cool. Over the next rise, they forded the Salt River, shallow and motionless, just west of Cherry Creek, and continued toward the wild, rugged rock and greenery in the distance. De Both heard Fry mention that it was the southern edges of the Tonto Basin, but the name meant little to him.

Toward sundown they were well into the wildness of the Basin. For de Both, the promise of a shady relief had turned into an even more tortuous ride. Through thick, stabbing chapparal and over steep, craggy mounds of rock they made their way. The trees were there, but they offered no solace; they only urged a stronger caution. The sun was falling fast when Travisin stopped the group on the shoulder of a grassy ridge. Below them the ground fell gradually to the west, green and smooth, extending for a mile to a tangle of trees and brush that began to climb another low hill. Behind it, three or four miles in the distance, the facing sun painted a last, brilliant yellow streak across the jagged top of a mountain.

Ningun jumped down from his pony as the others dismounted, and stared across the grass valley for a full minute or more. Then he spoke in English, pointing to the light-streaked mountain of rock. "There you find Pillo."

Fry conversed with him in Apache for a while, shooting an occasional question at one of the other scouts, and then said to Travisin, "They all agree that's most likely where Pillo is. One of 'em says Pillo used to have a rancheria up there. Pro'bly a favorite spot of his." The scout sat down in the grass and reached for his tobacco chew.

Travisin squatted next to him, Indian fashion, and poked the ground idly with a short stick. "It's still following, Barney," he said. "He must have known that at least one of our boys would have heard of this place and remember it. He purposely picked a place we'd be sure to come to, and on top of that he made it double easy to find."

"Well, you got to admit he'll be fair hard to root out, sittin' on top of that hill. Maybe he just wanted a good advantage."

"He had advantages all along the way. Here's the key, Barney. Did he ever once try to get away?" Travisin sat back and watched the outline of the mountain in the fading light. "Now why the devil did he want to bring us here?" He spoke to himself more than to anyone else.

Fry bit off a chew, packing it into his cheek with his tongue. He mumbled, "You've had more luck figurin' the 'Paches than anyone else. You tell me."

"I can't tell you anything, Barney, but I guess one thing's sure. We're going to play Pillo's game just a little longer." He looked up over Fry's shoulder toward the group of scouts. They sat in a semicircle. All wore breechcloths, long moccasins rolled just below the knees, and red calico bands around jet-black hair. Only their different-colored shirts distinguished them. Ningun wore a blue, cast-off army shirt. A leather belt studded with cartridges crossed it over one shoulder. Travisin beckoned to him. "Hey, Ningun. *Aquí!*"

The Apache squatted next to them silently as Travisin began to draw a map in a bare portion of ground with his stick. "Here's where we are and here's that mountain yonder." He indicated, drawing a circle in the earth. "Now you two get together and tell me what's up there and what's in between." He handed the stick to Fry. "And talk fast; it's getting dark."

Not more than an hour later the sun was well behind the western rim of the Basin. The plan had been laid. Travisin and Ningun gave their revolving pistols a last inspection and strode off casually into the darkness of the valley. It struck de Both that they might have been going for an after-dinner stroll.

They kept to the shadows of the trees and rocks as much as possible, Travisin a few steps behind the Apache, who would never walk more than twenty paces without stopping for what seemed like minutes. And then they would go on after the silence settled and began to sing in their ears. Travisin muttered under his breath at the full moon that splashed its soft light on open areas they had to cross. Ningun would walk slowly to the thinnest reaches of the shadows and then dart across the strips of moonlight. For a few seconds he would be only a dark blur in the moonlight and then would disappear into the next shadow. Travisin was never more than ten paces behind him. Soon they were out of the valley ascending the pine-dotted hill. The sand was soft and loose underfoot, muffling their footsteps, but they went on slowly, making sure of each step. In the silence, a dislodged stone would be like a trumpet blast.

On the crest of the hill, Travisin looked back across the valley. The shadowy bulk of the ridge they had left earlier showed in the moonlight, but there was no sign of life on the shoulder. He had not expected to see any, but there was always the young officer. It took more than one patrol to learn about survival in Apache country.

They made their way down the side of the slope into a rugged country of twisting rock formations and wild clumps of desert growth. The mountain loomed much closer now, a gigantic patch of soft gray streaking down from its peak where the moonlight pressed against it. At first, they progressed much slower than before, for the irregular ground rose and fell away without warning; grotesque desert trees and scattered boulders limited their vision to never more than fifty feet ahead. Though at a slower pace, Ningun went ahead with an assurance that he knew where he was going.

Soon they reached a level, bare stretch that seemed to extend into the darkness without end. Ningun changed his direction to the right for a good five hundred yards, and then turned back toward the mountain and the bare expanse of desert leading toward it. He beckoned to Travisin and slid down the crumbly bank of an arroyo that led out into the desert. In five months it would be a rushing stream, carrying the rain that washed down from the mountain. Now it was a dark path offering a stingy protection up to the door of Pillo's stronghold.

They followed the erratic, weaving course of the arroyo until it turned sharply, as the ground began to rise, and passed out of sight around the southern base of the mountain. The top of the mountain still lay almost a mile above them—up a gradual slope at first, dotted with small trees, then to rougher ground. The last few hundred yards climbed tortuously over steep jagged rock to the mesa above.

Ningun scurried out of the arroyo and disappeared into a small clump of brush a dozen yards away. In a moment his head appeared, and Travisin followed. They crept more cautiously now from cover to cover. A low, mournful sound cut the stillness. Both stopped dead. Travisin waited for Ningun to move, but he remained stone-still for almost five minutes. No sound followed. Ningun shook his head and whispered, "Night bird."

He led on, not straight up, but almost parallel with the base of the mountain, climbing gradually all the time. They had almost reached the steeper grade when the Apache pointed ahead to a black slash that cut into the mountain. Going closer, Travisin made out a narrow canyon that reached into the mountain on an upgrade. It was gouged sharply into the side of the mountain and extended crookedly down the slight grade to the desert below. Ahead, it made a bend in the darkness and was lost to sight. They climbed along the rim of the canyon for a few minutes while Travisin studied its course and depth, then they doubled back, climbing steadily up the mountain. A hundred yards further on, the Apache gave Travisin a sign and disappeared into the darkness. He waited for almost twenty minutes, toward the end beginning to wonder about the Indian, and then he looked to the side and saw Ningun approaching only a few feet away.

The Apache pressed one finger to his lips, then whispered to the captain. Travisin nodded and followed him, creeping slowly up the rocky incline above. They reached a wide ledge, Ningun leading along it to the left before climbing again over a shoulder-high hump that stretched into a long, flat piece of ground. Two hundred yards to the right, the mountain rose higher to a craggy peak, sharp and jagged. Nothing would be up there. Travisin and Ningun were on the mesa. Not far away they heard a pony sneeze.

On this part of the mesa the grass was tall. They crawled along, a foot at a time, toward the sound of the pony. The grass made a slight, stirring noise as they crawled through it, but at that height it could easily be the wind. Every few feet they would sink to their stomachs and lie flat in the grass for a matter of minutes, and then go on, extending a hand slowly to a firm portion of ground before dragging up the legs just as slowly. In this way they covered a portion of the mesa that extended to a scattered line of small boulders. The occasional snort of a pony seemed to come from less than a stone's throw away.

Travisin raised his head gradually an inch at a time until he could look between two of the rocks. From there the ground dipped slightly into a shallow pocket, descending from four sides to form a natural barricade. As he peered over the rocks, the moon passed behind a cloud and he could make out only the dying embers of a cook fire in the middle of the area. As the cloud moved on, the moon began to reappear gradually, the soft light crawling over slowly from the right, first illuminating the pony herd and then extending toward the center of the pocket. In a few seconds the entire camp area was bathed in the light. Travisin felt a weight drop through his breast as he counted sixty-three Chiricahuas.

The amazement of it held his gaze between the two rocks for a longer time than he realized. He jerked his head back quickly and looked at Ningun who had been spying the camp from a similar concealment. As he looked at Ningun he realized that the Apache understood now, just as he did, why Pillo had left such an obvious trail. But this was not the place to discuss it.

Making their way back to the outer edge of the mesa seemed to take even longer, though actually they snaked through the tall grass at a faster pace than before. They were seasoned enough to retain their calm caution, but now time was even more important, if they were to cope with Pillo. In less than two hours the sun would be present to create new problems. At the edge of the mesa Travisin, still crouched, peered cautiously to the ledge below, and then past it, determining the quickest route that would lead them to their planned rendezvous with Fry and the others.

Without speaking, he nudged Ningun and pointed a direction diagonally down the mountainside. The scout rose to his feet silently and placed himself in position to jump to the ledge below. Travisin turned his head for a last look in the direction of the hostile camp. As he did so, he heard a dull thud and an agonizing grunt escape from the scout. He wheeled, instinctively drawing his pistol, and saw Ningun go backward over the edge, an arrow shaft protruding from his chest.

Travisin was up and hurling himself at the ledge in one motion. It happened so fast that the Apache aiming his bow on the ledge below was just a blur, but he heard the arrow whine overhead as he landed on the sprawled form of Ningun and was projected off balance toward the Apache a few feet away. The Apache hurled his bow aside with a piercing shriek and went for a knife at his waist just as Travisin brought his pistol up. In the closeness, the front sight caught in the Apache's waistband on the upward swing, and the barrel was pressing into his stomach when he pulled the trigger. The Indian screamed again and staggered back off the ledge. Travisin hesitated a second, searching the mountainside for the best escape, but it was too late. He heard the yelp at the same time he felt the heavy blow at the back of his skull. He heard the wind rush through his ears and saw the orange flash sear across his eyes, and then nothing.

6

Pillo waited until the officer opened his eyes and started to prop himself up on his elbows. Then he kicked Travisin in the temple with the side of his moccasined foot. The Indians howled with laughter as Travisin sprawled on his back, shook his head and attempted to rise again. Pillo caught him on the shoulder this time, but still with enough force to slam the officer back against the ground. The other Apaches closed in, a few of them catching Travisin about the head and shoulders with vicious kicks, before Pillo stepped close to Travisin and held his hands in the air. He chattered for some time in Apache, raising and lowering his voice, and at the end they all stepped back; Pillo was still chief, though wizened and scarred with age. Travisin knew enough of the tongue to know that he was being saved for something else. He thought of old Solomon.

Two of the warriors pulled him to his feet and half-dragged him to the center of the rancheria. Most of the Apaches were stripped to breechcloths, streaks of paint on their chests contrasting with the dinginess of their dirt-smudged bodies. They stood about him, silent now, their dark eyes burning with anticipation of what was to come. Asesino, Pillo's son-in-law, walked up to within a foot of the captain, stared at him momentarily and then spat full in his face. Asesino's lips were curling into laughter when Travisin punched him in the mouth and sent him sprawling at the feet of the warriors.

He rose slowly, reaching for his knife, but Pillo again intervened, speaking harshly to his son-in-law. Pillo was the statesman, the general, not a rowdy guerrilla leader. There would be time for blood, but now he must tell this upstart white soldier what the situation was. That it was the Apache's turn.

He began with the usual formality of explaining the Apache position, but went back farther than Cochise and Mangas Coloradas, both in his own lifetime, to list his complaints against the white man. The Apache has no traditional history to fall back on, but Pillo spoke long enough about the last ten years to compare with any plains Indian's war chant covering generations. As he spoke, the other Apaches would grumble or howl, but did not take their eyes from Travisin. The captain stared back at them insolently, his gaze going from one to the next, never dropping his eyes. But he noted more than scowling faces. He saw that though lookouts were posted on the eastern edge of the mesa, the direction from which he and Ningun had come hours before, the western side, was empty of any Apaches.

Pillo was finishing with background now, and becoming more personal. He spoke in a mixture of Spanish and English, relying on Apache when an emphatic point had to be made. He spoke of promises made and broken by the white man. He spoke of Crook, whom the Apache trusted, but who was gone now.

"Look around, white soldier, you see many *Tinneh* here, but you will not live to see the many more that will come. Soon will come Jicarillas, Tontos and many Mescaleros, and the white men will be driven to the north." As he spoke he pushed his open shirt aside and scratched his stomach.

Travisin saw the two animal teeth hanging from his neck by a leather string. It was then that the idea started to form in his mind. It was rash, something he would have laughed at in a cooler moment; but he glanced at the fire that meant torture. He looked across it and saw Gatito. There was the answer! The animal teeth and Gatito.

"Pillo speaks with large mouth, but only wind comes out," Travisin said suddenly, feeling confidence rise at the boldness of his words. "You speak of many things that will happen, but they are all lies, for before any *Tinneh* come I shall drag you and your people back to the reservation, where you will all be punished."

Pillo started to howl with laughter, but was cut short by Travisin. "Hold your tongue, old man! I do not speak with the wind. U-sen Himself sent me. He knows what your medicine is." Travisin paused for emphasis. "And I am that medicine!"

Pillo's lips formed laughter, but the sound was not there. The white soldier spoke of his medicine.

"All your people know that your medicine is the gray wolf who protects you, because U-sen has always made Himself known through the gray wolf to guard you from evil. I tell you, old man, if you or any warrior lays a hand on me as I leave here, you will be struck dead by U-sen's arrow, the lightning stroke. If you do not believe me, touch me!"

Pillo was unnerved. An Apache's medicine is the most important part of his existence. Not something to be tampered with. Travisin addressed Pillo again, turning toward Gatito.

"If Pillo does not believe, let him ask Gatito if I do not have power from U-sen. Ask Gatito, who was the best stalker in the Army, if he was ever able to even touch me, though he tried many times. Ask him if I am not the wolf."

The renegade scout looked at Travisin wide-eyed. He had never thought of this before, but it must be true! He remembered the dozens of times he had tried to win his bet with the captain. Each time he had been but a few feet away, when the captain had laughed and turned on him. The thought swept through his mind and was given support by his primitive superstitions and instincts. Pillo and the others watched him and they saw that he believed. Travisin saw, and exhaled slowly through clenched teeth.

He turned from Pillo and walked toward the western rim of the mesa without another word. It had to be bold or not at all. Apaches in his way fell back quickly as he walked through the circle and out of the rancheria. His strides were long but unhurried as he made his way through the tall grass, looking straight ahead of him and never once behind.

The flesh on the back of his neck tingled and he hunched his shoulders slightly as if expecting at any moment to feel the smash of a bullet or an arrow. For the hundred yards he walked with this uncertainty, the spring in him winding, tightening to catapult him forward into a driving sprint. But he paced off the yards calmly, fighting back the urge to bolt. Nearing the mesa rim his neck muscles uncoiled, and he took a deep breath of the thin air.

There on the western side, the mesa edge slanted, without an abrupt drop, into the irregular fall of the mountainside. A path stretched from the mesa diagonally down the side to be lost among rocks and small rises that twisted the path right and left down the long slope.

Travisin was only a few feet from the path when the Apache loomed in front of him coming up the trail. Though many things raced through his mind, he stopped dead only a split second before throwing himself at the Apache. They closed, chest to chest, and Travisin could smell the rankness of his body as they went over the rim and rolled down the path to land heavily against a tree stump. Travisin lost his hold on the Indian but landed on top clawing for his throat. A saber-sharp pain cut through his back and his nostrils filled with dust and sweat-smell. The Apache's face was a straining blur below him, the neck muscles stretching like steel cords. He pulled one hand from the Apache's throat, clawed up a rock the size of his fist and brought it down in the Indian's face in one sweeping motion, grinding through bone and flesh to drive the Indian's scream back down his throat.

As he rose to run down the path, the carbine shot ricocheted off the mesa rim above him. His medicine was broken.

7

An hour before dawn Fry had finished spotting his scouts along one side of the narrow canyon that gouged into the shoulder of Pillo's mountain stronghold. One scout was a mile behind with the mounts; the others, concealed among the rocks and brush that climbed the canyon wall, were playing their favorite game. An Apache will squat behind a bush motionless all day to take just one shot at an enemy. Here was the promise of a bountiful harvest. Each man was his own troop, his own company, each knowing how to fight the Apache best, for he is an Apache.

They were to meet Travisin and Ningun there at dawn and wait. Wait and watch, under the assumption that sooner or later Pillo would lead his band down from the mountain. The logical trail was through the canyon. And the logical place for a jackpot was here where the canyon narrowed to a defile before erupting out to the base of the mountain.

De Both crouched near Fry, watching him closely, studying his easy calm, hoping that the contagion of his indifference would sweep over him and throttle the gnawing fear in his belly. But de Both was an honest man, and his fear was an honest fear. He was just young. His knees trembled not so much at the thought of the coming engagement, his first, but at the question: Would he do the right thing? What would his reaction be? He knew it would make or break him.

And then, before he could prepare himself, it had begun. Two, three, four carbine shots screamed through the canyon, up beyond their sight. At the same time, there was a blur of motion on the opposite canyon wall not a hundred yards away and the Apache came into sight. He leaped from boulder to rock down the steep wall of the canyon until he was on level ground. He gazed for a few seconds in the direction from which the shots had come, then crossed the canyon floor at a trot and started to scale the other wall from which he would have a better command of the extending defile. He stopped and crouched behind a rock not twenty feet below de Both's position. Then he turned and began to climb again.

Often when you haven't time to think, you're better off, your instinct takes over and your body follows through. De Both pressed against the boulder in front of him feeling the coolness of it on his cheek, pushing his knees tight against the ground. He heard the loose earth crumble under the Apache's moccasins as he neared the rock. He heard the Indian's hand pat against the smooth surface of it as he reached for support. And as his heart hammered in his chest the urge to run made his knees quiver and his boot moved with a spasmodic scrape. It cut the stillness like a knife dragged across an emery stone, and it shot de Both to his feet to look full into the face of the Apache.

Asesino tried to bring his carbine up, but he was too late. De Both's arms shot across the narrow rock between them and his fingers dug into the Apache's neck. Asesino fell back, pushing his carbine lengthwise against the blue jacket with a force that dragged the officer over the rock on top of him, and they writhed on the slope, their heads pointing to the canyon floor. The Indian tried to yell, but fingers, bone-white with pressure, gouged vocal cords and only a gurgling squeak passed agonized lips. His arms thrashed wildly, tore at the back of the blue jacket and a hand crawled downward to unexpectedly clutch the bone handle of the knife. Light flashed on the blade as it rose in the air and plunged into the straining blue cloth.

There was a gasp, an air-sucking moan. De Both rolled from the Apache with his eyes stretched open to see Fry's boot crush against the Indian's cheekbone. His eyes closed then and he felt the burning between his shoulder blades. He felt Fry's hands tighten at his armpits to pull him back up the slope behind the rock. The same hands tore shirt and tunic to the collar and then gently untied the grimy neckerchief to pad it against the wound.

"You ain't bad hurt, mister. You didn't leave enough strength in him to do a good job." And his heavy tobacco breath brushed against the officer's cheek and made him turn his head.

"I feel all right. But . . . what about the blood?"

"I'll fix you up later, mister. No time now. The captain's put in an appearance." He jerked a thumb over his shoulder.

Far down the canyon a lone figure ran, his arms pumping, his head thrown back, mouth sucking in air. It was a long, easy lope paced to last miles without let-up. It was the pace of a man who ran, but knew what he was doing. Death was behind, but the trail was long. As he came nearer to the scouts' positions, Fry raised slightly and gave a low, shrill whistle, then cut it off abruptly. Travisin glanced up the canyon slope without slacking his pace and passed into the shadows of the defile just as the Apaches trickled from the rocks three hundred yards up the canyon. They saw him pass into the narrowness as they swept onto the canyon floor, over fifty strong, screaming down the passage like a cloud of vampires beating from a cavern. Their yells screeched against the canyon walls and whiplashed back and forth in the narrowness.

Fry sighted down his Remington-Hepburn waiting for the hostiles to come abreast. He turned his head slightly and cut a stream of tobacco into the sand. "Captain was sure right about their sign. They was pavin' us a road clean to hell. Have to find out sometime where they all come from." He squinted down the short barrel, his finger taking in the slack on the trigger. "In about one second you can make all the noise you want." The barrel lifted slightly with the explosion and a racing Apache was knocked from his feet. A split second later, nine more carbines blasted into the canyon bottom.

Fry was on his feet after the first shot, pumping bullets into the milling mass of brown bodies as fast as he could squeeze the trigger. The hostiles had floundered at the first shot, tripping, knocking each other down in an effort to reach safety, but they didn't know where to turn. They were caught in their own kind of trap. They screamed, and danced about frantically. A few tried to rush up the slope into the mouth of the murderous fire from the scouts, but they were cut down at once. Others tried to scale the opposite wall, but the steep slope was slow going and they were picked off easily. They dashed about in a circle firing wildly at the canyon wall, wasting their ammunition on small puffs of smoke that rose above the rocks and brush clumps. And they kept dropping, one at a time. Five shots in succession, two, then one. The last bullet scream died away up-canyon. There was the beginning of silence, but almost immediately the air was pierced with a new sound. Throats shrieked again, but with a vigor, with a lust. It was not the agonized scream of the terrified Chiricahua, but the battle yell of the Coyotero scout as he hurled himself down the slope into the enemy. They had earned their army pay; now it was time for personal vengeance.

Half of the hostiles threw their arms into the air as the scouts swarmed into the open, but they came on with knives and gun stocks raised. Savage closed with savage in a grinding melee of thrashing arms and legs in thick dust, the cornered animal, made more ferocious by his fear, battling the hunter who had tasted blood. They came back with their knives dripping, their carbine stocks shattered.

It took two days longer to return to the little subagency on the banks of the Gila, because it is slower travel with wounded men and sixteen Chiricahua hostiles whose legs are roped under the horses' bellies by day and whose hands are lashed to trees by night. Travisin led and was silent.

De Both held himself tense against the searing pain that shot up between his shoulder blades. But oddly enough, he did not really mind the ride home. He looked at the line of sixteen hostiles and felt nothing. No hate. No pity. Slowly it came upon him that it was indifference, and he moved his stained hat to a cockier angle. Boston could be a million miles away and he could be at the end of the earth, but de Both didn't particularly give a damn. He knew he was a man.

Fry chewed tobacco while his listless eyes swept the ground for sign. That's what he was paid for. It kept running through his mind that it was an awful funny thing to go out after sixteen hostiles, meet sixty and still come back with sixteen. Have to tell that one at Lon Scorey's in Globe.

Pillo rode with his chin on his bony chest. He was much older, and the throbbing hole in his thigh didn't help him, either. He was beginning to smell the greenness of decay.

On the afternoon of the fourth day they rode slowly into the quadrangle at Gila. Travisin looked about. Nothing had changed. For a moment he had expected to find something different, and he yearned for something that wasn't there. But he threw aside his longing and slumped back into his role—the role that forced him to be the best Apache campaigner in the Territory.

A cavalry mount stood in front of the agency office and a trooper appeared on the porch as Travisin, Fry and de Both dismounted and walked to the welcome shade of the ramada.

"Compliments of the commanding officer, sir. I've rode from Fort Thomas with this message."

Travisin read the note and turned with a smile to the other two. "Bill, let me tell you one thing if you don't already know it. Never try to figure out the ways of a woman—or the army. This is from Collier. He says the Bureau has decided to return Pillo and his band to his people at Fort Apache. All sixteen of 'em. Certainly is a good thing we've got sixteen to send back."

Fry said, "Yep, you might have got yourself court-martialed. Way it is, if Pillo loses that leg, you'll probably end up back as a looie."

De Both listened and the quizzical look turned to anger. He opened his mouth to speak, but thought better of it and waited until he had cooled off before muttering simply, "Idiots!"

If Travisin was the winking type, he would have looked at

Fry and done so. He glanced at Fry with the hint of a smile, but with eyes that said, "Barney, I think we've got ourselves a lieutenant." Then he walked into the office. There are idiotic Bureau decisions, and there are boots that have been on too long.

And along the Gila, the war drums are silent again. But on frontier station, you don't relax. For though they are less in number, they are still Apaches.

The Rustlers

MOST OF the time there was dead silence. When someone did say something it was never more than a word or two at a time: *More coffee?* Words that were not words because there was no thought behind them and they didn't mean anything. Words like *getting late*, when no one cared. Hardly even noises, because no one heard.

Stillness. Six men sitting together in a pine grove, and yet there was no sound. A boot scraped gravel and a tin cup clanked against rock, but they were like the words, little noises that started and stopped at the same time and were forgotten before they could be remembered.

More coffee? And an answering grunt that meant even less.

Five men scattered around a campfire that was dead, and the sixth man squatting at the edge of the pines looking out into the distance through the dismal reflection of a dying sun that made the grayish flat land look petrified in death and unchanged for a hundred million years.

Emmett Ryan stared across the flats toward the lighter gray outline in the distance that was Anton Chico, but he wasn't seeing the adobe brick of the village. He wasn't watching the black speck that was gradually getting bigger as it approached.

All of us knew that. We sat and watched Emmett Ryan's coat pulled tight across his shoulder blades, not moving body or head. Just a broad smoothness of faded denim. We'd been looking at the same back all the way from Tascosa and in two hundred miles you can learn a lot about a back.

The black speck grew into a horse and rider, and as they moved up the slope toward the pines the horse and rider became Gosh Hall on his roan. Emmett walked over to meet him, but didn't say anything. The question was on his broad, red face and he didn't have to ask it.

Gosh Hall swung down from the saddle and put his hands on the small of his back, arching against the stiffness. "They just rode in," he said, and walked past the big man to the dead fire. "Who's got all the coffee?"

Emmett followed him with his eyes and the question was

still there. It was something to see that big, plain face with the eyes open wide and staring when before they'd always been half-closed from squinting against the glare of twenty-odd years in open country. Now his face looked too big and loose for the small nose and slit of an Irish mouth. You could see the indecision and maybe a little fear in the wide-open eyes, something that had never been there before.

We'd catch ourselves looking at that face and have to look at something else, quick, or Em would see somebody's jaw hanging open and wonder what the hell was wrong with him. We felt sorry for Em—I know I did—and it was a funny feeling to all of a sudden see the big TX ramrod that way.

Gosh looked like he had an apron on, standing over the dead fire with his hip cocked and the worn hide chaps covering his short legs. He held the cup halfway to his face, watching Em, waiting for him to ask the question. I thought Gosh was making it a little extra tough on Em; he could have come right out with it. Both of them just stared at each other.

Finally Emmett said, "Jack with them?"

Gosh took a sip of coffee first. "Him and Joe Anthony rode in together, and another man. Anthony and the other man went into the Senate House and Jack took the horses to the livery and then followed them over to the hotel."

"They see you?"

"Naw, I was down the street under a ramada. All they'd see'd be shadow."

"You sure it was them, Gosh?" I asked him.

"Charlie," Gosh said, "I got a picture in my head, and it's stuck there 'cause I never expected to see one like it. It's a picture of Jack and Joe Anthony riding into Magenta the same way a month ago. When you see something that's different or hadn't ought to be, it sticks in your head. And they was on the same mounts, Charlie."

Emmett went over to his dun mare and tightened the cinch like he wanted to keep busy and show us everything was going the same. But he was just fumbling with the strap, you could see that. His head swung around a few inches. "Jack look all right?"

Gosh turned his cup upside down and a few drops of coffee trickled down to the ashes at his feet. "I don't know, Em. How is a man who's just stole a hundred head of beef supposed to look?"

Emmett jerked his body around and the face was closed again for the first time in a week, tight and redder than usual. Then his jaw eased and his big hands hanging at his sides opened and closed and then went loose. Emmett didn't have anything to grab. Some of the others were looking at Gosh Hall and probably wondering why the little rider was making it so hard for Em.

Emmett asked him, "Did you see Butzy?"

"He didn't ride in. I 'magine he's out with the herd." Gosh looked around. "Neal still out, huh?"

Neal Whaley had gone in earlier with Gosh, then split off over to where they were holding the herd, just north of Anton Chico. Neal was to watch and tell us if they moved them. Emmett figured they were holding the herd until a buyer came along. There were a lot of buyers in New Mexico who didn't particularly care what the brand read, but Emmett said they were waiting for a top bid or they would have sold all the stock before this.

Ned Bristol and Lloyd Cohane got up and stretched and then just stood there awkwardly looking at the dead fire, their boots, and each other. Lloyd pulled a blue bandanna from his coat pocket and wiped his face with it, then folded it and straightened it out thin between his fingers before tilting his chin up to tie it around his neck. Ned pushed his gun belt down lower on his hips and watched Emmett.

Dobie Shaw, the kid in our outfit, went over to his mount and pulled his Winchester from the boot and felt in the bag behind the saddle for a box of cartridges. Dobie had to do something too.

Ben Templin was older; he'd been riding better than thirty years. He eased back to the ground with his hands behind his head tilting his hat over his face and waited. Ben had all the time in the world.

Everybody was going through the motions of being natural, but fidgeting and acting restless and watching Emmett at the same time because we all knew it was time now, and Emmett didn't have any choice. That was what forced Emmett's hand, though we knew he would have done it anyway, sooner or later.

But maybe we looked a little too anxious to him, when it was only restlessness. It was a long ride from Tascosa. A case of let's get it over with or else go on home—one way or the other, regardless of whose brother stole the cows.

Gosh Hall scratched the toe of his boot through the sand, kicking it over the ashes of the dead fire. "About that time, ain't it, Em?"

Emmett exhaled like he was very tired. "Yeah, it's about that time." He looked at every face, slowly, before turning to his mare.

It's roughly a hundred and thirty miles from Tascosa, following the Canadian, to Trementina on the Conchas, then another thirty-five miles south, swinging around Mesa Montosa to Anton Chico, on the Pecos. Counting detours to find water holes and trailing the wrong sign occasionally, that's about two hundred miles of sun, wind, and New Mexico desert—and all to bring back a hundred head of beef owned by a Chicago company that tallied close to a quarter million all over the Panhandle and north-central Texas.

The western section of the TX Company was headquartered at Sudan that year, with most of the herds north of Tascosa and strung out west along the Canadian. Emmett Ryan was ramrod of the home crew at Sudan, but he spent a week or more at a time out on the grass with the herds. That was why he happened to be with us when R. D. Perris, the company man, rode in. We were readying to go into Magenta for a few when Perris came beating his mount into camp. Even in the cool of the evening the horse was flaked white and about to drop and Perris was so excited he could hardly get the words out. And finally when he told his story there was dead silence and all you could hear was R. D. Perris breathing like his chest was about to rip open.

Jack Ryan and Frank Butzinger—Frank, who nobody ever gave credit for having any sand—and over a hundred head of beef hadn't been seen on the west range for three days. R. D. Perris had said, "The tracks follow the river west, but we figured Jack was taking them to new grass. But then the tracks just kept on going. . . ."

Emmett was silent from that time on. He asked a few

questions, but he was pretty sure of the answers before he asked
them. There was that talk for weeks about Jack having been
seen in Tascosa and Magenta with Joe Anthony. And there
weren't many people friendly with Joe Anthony. In his time,
he'd had his picture on wanted dodgers more than once. Two
shootings for sure, and a few holdups, but the holdups were
just talk. Nobody ever pinned anything on him, and with his
gunhand reputation, nobody made any accusations.

Gosh Hall had seen them together in Magenta and he told
Emmett to his face that he didn't like it; but Emmett had
defended him and said Jack was just sowing oats because he
was still young and hadn't got his sense of values yet. But Lloyd
Cohane was there that time at the line camp when Emmett
dropped in and chewed hell out of Jack for palling with Joe
Anthony. Then came the time Emmett walked into the saloon
in Tascosa with his gun out and pushed it into Joe Anthony's
belly before Joe even saw him and told him to ride and keep
riding.

Jack was there, drunk like he usually was in town, but he
sobered quick and followed Anthony out of the saloon when
Emmett prodded him out, and laughed right in Emmett's face
when Em told him to stay where he was. And he was laughing
and weaving in the saddle when he rode out of town with
Anthony.

Until that night Perris came riding in with his story, Em
hadn't seen his brother. So you know what he was thinking;
what all of us were thinking.

Riding the two hundred miles to find the herd was part of
the job, but knowing you were trailing a friend made the job
kind of sour and none of us was sure if we wanted to find the
cattle. Jack Ryan was young and wild and drank too much and
laughed all the time, but he had more friends than any rider
in the Panhandle.

Like Ben Templin said: "Jack's a good boy, but he's got
an idea life's just a big can-can dancer with four fingers of
scootawaboo in each hand." And that was about it.

The splotch of white that was Anton Chico from a distance
gradually got bigger and cleared until finally right in front of
us it was gray adobe brick, blocks of it, dull and lifeless in the

cold late sunlight. Emmett slowed us to a walk the last few hundred feet approaching the town's main street and motioned Ben Templin up next to him.

"Ben," he said, "you take Dobie with you and cut for that back street yonder and come up behind the livery. Don't let anybody see you and hush the stableman if he gets loud about what you're doing. Maybe Butzy'll come along, Ben—if he isn't there already."

I looked at Emmett watching Ben Templin and Dobie Shaw cut off, and there it was. His old face again. All closed and hard with the crow's feet streaking from the corners of his eyes. And his mouth tight like it used to be when he thought and ordered men at the same time, because he always knew what he was doing. You could see Emmett knew what he was doing now, that he'd set his mind. And when Emmett Ryan set his mind his pride saw to it that it stayed set.

Emmett walked his mount down the left side of the narrow main street with the rest of us strung out behind. When he veered over to a hitchrack about halfway down the second block, we veered with him and tied up, straggled along before two store fronts.

Em stepped up on the boardwalk and moved leisurely toward the Senate House hotel almost at the end of the block. He stopped as he crossed the alley next to the hotel and nodded to Lloyd Cohane, then bent his head toward the alley and moved it in a half-circle over his big shoulders. Lloyd moved off down the alley toward the back of the hotel.

"Go on with him, Ned," Em whispered. "Stick near the kitchen door and if anybody but the cook comes out shoot his pants off."

Ned moved off after Lloyd, both carrying carbines. Em looked at Gosh and me, but didn't say anything. He just looked and that meant we were with him and supposed to back up anything he did. Then he turned toward the hotel and slipped his revolver out in the motion. Gosh moved right after him and pointed the barrel of his Winchester out in front of him.

Two idlers sitting in front of the hotel stared at us trying to make out they weren't staring, and as soon as we passed them I heard their chairs scrape and their footsteps hurrying down the boards. A man across the street pushed through the saloon doors without even putting his hands out. A rider slowed up in front of the hotel as if about to turn in and then he kicked his mount into a trot down the street.

In the hotel lobby you could still hear the horse clopping down the street and it made the lobby seem even more quiet and comfortable, feeling the coolness inside and picturing the horse on the dusty street. But there was the clerk with his mouth open watching Emmett walk toward the café entrance, his spurs chinging with each step.

It seemed like, for a show like this, everything was moving too fast. The next thing, we were in the café part and Jack Ryan and Joe Anthony and the other man were looking at us like they couldn't believe their eyes.

None of them moved. Jack's jaw was open with a mouthful of beef, his eyes almost as wide open as his mouth. The other man had a taco in his fingers raised halfway to his mouth and he just held it there. Didn't move it up or down. Joe Anthony's right hand was around a glass of something yellow like mescal. His left hand was below the level of the table. The three of them had their hats on, pushed back, and they looked dirty and tired.

Jack chewed and swallowed hard and then he smiled. "Damn, Em, you must have flown!"

The other man looked at us one at a time slowly, then shrugged his shoulders and said, "What the hell," and shoved the taco in his mouth.

Joe Anthony wiped the back of his hand over his mouth and moved the hand back, smoothing the long mustaches with the knuckle of his index finger. The other hand was still under the table.

Emmett held his revolver pointed square at Joe Anthony and seemed to be unmindful of the other two men. Lloyd and Ned came through the kitchen door and moved around behind Emmett.

"Get up," Em ordered. "And take off your belts."

Somebody's chair scraped, but Joe Anthony said, "Hold it!" and it was quiet.

Anthony was staring back at Emmett. "Do I look like a green kid to you, Ryan?" he said, and half smiled. "You're not telling anybody what to do, cowboy."

"I said get up," Em repeated.

Joe Anthony kept on smiling like he thought Emmett was a fool. He shook his head slowly. "Ryan, the longer you stand there, the shorter your chances are of leaving here on your two feet."

"You're all mouth," Emmett said. "Just mouth."

The outlaw's expression didn't change. His face was good-looking in a swarthy kind of way, but gaunt and hungry-looking with pale, shallow eyes like a man who forgot where his conscience was, or that he ever had one.

His smile sagged a little and he said, "Ryan, let's quit playing. You ride the hell out of here before I shoot you."

"I'm not playing," Emmett said, leveling the revolver. "Get up, quick."

"Ryan," Joe Anthony whispered impatiently, "I've had a Colt leveled on your belly since the second you come through that doorway."

I thought I knew Emmett Ryan, but I didn't know him as well as I supposed. His face didn't change its expression, but his finger moved on the trigger and the room filled with the explosion. His thumb yanked on the hammer and he fired again right on top of the first one.

Joe Anthony went back with his chair, fell hard and lay still. His pistol was still in the holster on his right hip.

Emmett looked down at him. "You're all mouth, Anthony. All mouth."

Nobody said anything after that. We were looking at Em and Em was looking at Joe Anthony stretched out on the floor. I heard steps behind me and there was Dobie Shaw tiptoeing in and looking like he'd dive out the window if anybody said anything.

Emmett waved his gun at the other man and glanced at his brother. "Who's this?"

Jack spoke easily. "Earl Roach. We picked him up for a trail driver. He didn't know it was rustled stock."

Roach was unfastening his gun belt. He shot a look toward Jack. "Boy," he said, "you take care of your troubles and I'll take care of mine."

Dobie Shaw moved up behind Emmett hesitantly and waited for the big foreman to look his way. "Mr. Ryan—Ben's holding

Butzy over to the livery." He went on hurriedly trying to get
the whole story out before Em asked any questions. "Butzy
walked right in and didn't move after Ben throwed down on
him, but there was another one back a ways and he turned and
rode like hell when he saw me and Ben with our guns out. Me
and Ben didn't even get a shot at him 'fore he was round the
corner and gone."

"All right, Dobie. You go on back with Ben." Emmett hesitated and glanced at Jack like he was making up his mind all
over again, but the doubt passed off quickly. He said, "We'll
be over directly. You go on and tell Ben to keep Butzy right
there."

Frank Butzinger was flat against the boards of a stall, though
Ben Templin was standing across the open part of the stable
smoking a cigarette with his carbine propped against the wall.
Ben wasn't paying any attention to him, but even in the dim
light you could see Butzy was about ready to die of fright.

Gosh Hall pushed Jack and Earl Roach toward the stall that
Butzy was in and mumbled something, probably swearing. Jack
looked around at him with a half smile and shook his head like
a father playing Indians with his youngster. Humoring him.

Emmett stood out in the open part with the rest of us spread
around now. He said, "You sell the stock yet?"

"A few," Jack answered. "We got almost a hundred head."

"You got the money?"

"What do you think?"

The foreman motioned to Gosh Hall. "Get some line and
tie their hands behind them."

The little cowboy's face brightened and he moved into the
stall lifting a coil of rope from the side wall. When he pulled
his knife and started to cut it into pieces, the stableman came
running over. He'd been standing in the front doorway, but I
hadn't noticed him there before.

He ran over yelling, "Hey, that's my rope!"

Gosh reached out, laughing, and grabbed one of his braces
and snapped it against his faded red-flannel undershirt. "Get
back, old man, you're interfering with justice." Then he pushed
the man hard against the stall partition.

Emmett took hold of his elbow and pulled him out toward the front of the livery. "You stay out here," he said. "This isn't any of your business." He turned from the man and nodded his head to the stalls where three horses were.

The stable was large, high-ceilinged, with stalls lining both sides. The open area was wide, but longer than it was wide, with heavy timbers overhead reaching from lofts on both sides that ran the length of the stable above the stalls. The stable was empty but for the three horses toward the back.

"Bring those horses up here." Em said it to no one in particular.

When Dobie and Ned and I led the mounts up, I heard Lloyd ask Em if he should go get our horses. Em shook his head, but didn't say anything.

Lloyd said, "Shouldn't we be getting out to the stock, Em?"

"We got time. Neal's watching the cows," Em reminded him. "The man that was with Butzy spread his holler if there were any others out there. They'd be halfway to Santa Fe by now."

He turned on Gosh impatiently. "Come on, get 'em mounted."

I picked up one of their saddles from the rack and walked up behind Gosh, who was pushing the three men toward the horses.

"Look out, Gosh. Let me get the saddles on before you get in the way. You can't throw 'em on with your arms behind your back."

Gosh twisted his mouth into a smile and looked past me at Emmett. There was a wad of tobacco in his cheek that made his thin face lopsided, like a jagged rock with hair on it. He shifted the wad, still smiling, and then spit over to the side.

"You tell him, Em," he said.

Emmett looked at me with his closed-up, leathery face. He stared hard as if afraid his eyes would waver. "They don't need the saddles."

Gosh swatted me playfully with the end of rope in his hand. "Want me to paint you a picture, Charlie?" He laughed and walked out through the wide entrance.

Gosh didn't have to paint a picture. Ben Templin dropped

his cigarette. Lloyd and Ned and Dobie just stared at Emmett, but none of them said anything. Em stood there like a rock and stared back like he was defying anybody to object.

The boys looked away and moved about uncomfortably. They weren't about to go against Emmett Ryan. They were used to doing what they were told because Em was always right, and weren't sure that he wasn't right even now. A hanging isn't an uncommon thing where there is little law. Along the Pecos there was less than little. Still, it didn't rub right—even if Em was following his conscience, it didn't rub right.

I hesitated until the words were in my mouth and I'd have bit my tongue off to hold them back. "You setting yourself up as the law?" It was supposed to have a bite to it, but the words sounded weak and my voice wasn't even.

Emmett said, "You know what the law is." He beckoned to the coil of rope Gosh had hung back on the boards. "That's it right there, Charlie. You know better than that." Emmett was talking to himself as well as me, but you didn't remind that hardheaded Irishman of things like that.

"Look, Em. Let's get the law and handle this right."

"It's black and white, it's two and two, if you steal cows and get caught you hang."

"Maybe. But it's not up to you to decide. Let's get the law."

"I've already decided," was all he said.

The stable hand crept up close to us and waited until there was a pause. "The deputy ain't here," the old man said. "He rode down to Lincoln yesterday morning to join the posse." He waited for someone to show interest, but no one said a word. "They're getting a posse up on account of there's word Bill Bonney's at Fort Sumner."

He stepped back looking proud as could be over his news. I could have kicked his seat flat for what he said.

Gosh came back with two coiled lariats on his arm and a third one in his hands. He was shaping a knot at one end of it.

Earl Roach looked at Gosh, then up to the heavy rafter that crossed above the three horses, then Jack's head went up too.

Gosh spit and grinned at them, forming a loop in the second rope. "What'd you expect'd happen?"

Jack kept his eyes on the rafter. "I didn't expect to get caught."

"Jack's always smiling into the sunshine, ain't he?" Gosh pushed Earl Roach toward his horse. "Mount up, mister."

Roach jerked his shoulder away from him. "I look like a bird to you? You want me up on that horse, you'll have to put me up."

"Earl, I'll put you up and help take you down."

When he got to Butzy and offered him a leg up, Butzy made a funny sound like a whine and started to back away, but Gosh grabbed him by his shirt before he took two steps. Butzy looked over Gosh's bony shoulder, his eyes popping out of his pasty face.

"Em, what you fixin' to do?" His voice went up a notch, and louder. "What you fixin' to do? You just scarin' us, Em?"

If it was a joke, Butzy didn't want to play the fool, but you could tell by his voice what he was thinking. Em didn't answer him.

Gosh finished knotting the third rope and handed it to Dobie, who looked at it like he'd never seen a lariat before.

Gosh said, "Make yourself useful and throw that rope over the rafter."

He went out and brought his horse in and mounted so he could slip the nooses over their heads, but he stood in the stirrups and still couldn't reach the tops of their heads. Emmett told him to get down and ordered Ben Templin to climb up and fix the ropes. Ben did it, but Em had to tell him three times.

Before he jumped down, Ben lighted cigarettes and gave them to Jack and Earl. Butzy was weaving his head around so Ben couldn't get one in his mouth. Just rolling his head around with his eyes closed, moaning.

Gosh looked up at him and laughed out loud. "You praying, Butzy?" he called out. "Better pray hard, you ain't got much time," and kept on laughing.

Ben Templin made a move toward Gosh, but Emmett caught his arm.

"Hold still, Ben." He looked past him at Gosh. "You can do what you're doing with your mouth shut."

Gosh moved behind the horses with the short end of rope in his hand. He edged over behind Earl Roach's horse. "Age before beauty, I always say."

Butzy's eyes opened up wide. "God, Em! Please Em—please—honest to God—I didn't know they was stealing the herd! Swear to God, Em, I thought Perris told Jack to sell the herd. Please, Em—I—let me go and I'll never show my face again. Please—"

"You'll never show it anyway where you're going," Gosh cracked.

Earl Roach was looking at Butzy with a blank expression. His head turned to Jack, holding his chin up to ease his neck away from the chafe of the rope. "Who's your friend?"

Jack Ryan's lips, with the cigarette hanging, formed a small smile at Roach. "Never saw him before in my life." His young face was paler than usual, you could see it through beard and sunburn, but his voice was slow and even with that little edge of sarcasm it usually carried.

Roach shook his head to drop the ash from his cigarette. "Beats me where he come from," he said.

Ben Templin swore in a slow whisper. He mumbled, "It's a damn waste of good guts."

Lloyd and Ned and Dobie were looking at the two of them like they couldn't believe their eyes and then seemed to all drop their heads about the same time. Embarrassed. Like they didn't rate to be in the same room with Jack and Earl. I felt it too, but felt a mad coming on along with it.

"Dammit, Em! You're going to wait for the deputy!" I knew I was talking, but it didn't sound like me. "You're going to wait for the deputy whether you like it or not!"

Emmett just stared back and I felt like running for the door. Emmett stood there alone like a rock you couldn't budge and then Ben Templin was beside him with his hand on Em's arm, but not just resting it there, holding the forearm hard. His other hand was on his pistol butt.

"Charlie's right, Em," Ben said. "I'm not sure how you got us this far, or why, but ain't you or God Almighty going to hang those boys by yourself."

They stood there, those two big men, their faces not a foot apart, not telling a thing by their faces, but you got the feeling if one of them moved the livery would collapse like a twister hit it.

Finally Emmett blinked his eyes, and moved his arm to make Ben let go.

"All right, Ben." It was just above a whisper and sounded tired. "We've all worked together a long time and have always agreed—if it was a case of letting you in on the agreeing. We won't change it now."

Gosh came out from behind the horses. Disappointed and mad. He moved right up close to Emmett. "You going to let this woman—"

That was all he got a chance to say. Emmett swung his fist against that bony tobacco bulge and Gosh flattened against the board wall before sliding down into a heap.

Emmett started to walk out the front and then he turned around. "We're waiting on the deputy until tomorrow morning. If he don't show by then, this party takes up where it left off."

He angled out the door toward the Senate House, still the boss. The hardheaded Irishman's pride had to get the last word in whether he meant it or not.

The deputy got back late that night. You could see by his face that he hadn't gotten what he'd gone for. Emmett stayed in his room at the Senate House, but Ben Templin and I were waiting at the jail when the deputy returned—though I don't know what we would have done if he hadn't—with two bottles of the yellowest mescal you ever saw to ease his saddle sores and dusty throat.

We told him how we'd put three of our boys in his jail—just a scare, you understand—when they'd got drunk and thought it'd be fun to run off with a few head of stock. Just a joke on the owner, you understand. And Emmett Ryan, the ramrod, being one of them's brother, he had to act tougher than usual, else the boys'd think he was playing favorites. Like him always giving poor Jack the wildest broncs and making him ride drag on the trail drives.

Em was always a little too serious, anyway. Of course, he was a good man, but he was a big, red-faced Irishman who thought his pride was a stone god to burn incense in front of. And hell, he had enough troubles bossing the TX crew without getting all worked up over his brother getting drunk and playing a little joke on the owners—you been drunk like that, haven't you, Sheriff? Hell, everybody has. A sheriff with guts enough to work in Bill Bonney's country had more to do than chase after drunk cowpokes who wouldn't harm a fly. And even if they were serious, what's a few cows to an outfit that owns a quarter million?

And along about halfway down the second bottle— So why don't we turn the joke around on old Em and let the boys out tonight? We done you a turn by getting rid of Joe Anthony. Old Em'll wake up in the morning and be madder than hell when he finds out, and that will be some sight to see.

The deputy could hardly wait.

In the morning it was Ben who had to tell Em what happened. I was there in body only, with my head pounding like a pulverizer. The deputy didn't show up at all.

We waited for Emmett to fly into somebody, but he just looked at us, from one to the next. Finally he turned toward the livery.

"Let's go take the cows home," was all he said.

Not an hour later we were looking down at the flats along the Pecos where the herd was. Neal Whaley was riding toward us.

Emmett had been riding next to me all the way out from Anton Chico. When he saw Neal, he broke into a gallop to meet him, and that was when I thought he said, "Thanks, Charlie."

I know his head turned, but there was the beat of his horse when he started the gallop, and that mescal pounding at my brains. Maybe he said it and maybe he didn't.

Knowing that Irishman, I'm not going to ask him.

Three-Ten to Yuma

H<small>E HAD</small> picked up his prisoner at Fort Huachuca shortly after midnight and now, in a silent early morning mist, they approached Contention. The two riders moved slowly, one behind the other.

Entering Stockman Street, Paul Scallen glanced back at the open country with the wet haze blanketing its flatness, thinking of the long night ride from Huachuca, relieved that this much was over. When his body turned again, his hand moved over the sawed-off shotgun that was across his lap and he kept his eyes on the man ahead of him until they were near the end of the second block, opposite the side entrance of the Republic Hotel.

He said just above a whisper, though it was clear in the silence, "End of the line."

The man turned in his saddle, looking at Scallen curiously. "The jail's around on Commercial."

"I want you to be comfortable."

Scallen stepped out of the saddle, lifting a Winchester from the boot, and walked toward the hotel's side door. A figure stood in the gloom of the doorway, behind the screen, and as Scallen reached the steps the screen door opened.

"Are you the marshal?"

"Yes, sir." Scallen's voice was soft and without emotion. "Deputy, from Bisbee."

"We're ready for you. Two-oh-seven. A corner . . . fronts on Commercial." He sounded proud of the accommodation.

"You're Mr. Timpey?"

The man in the doorway looked surprised. "Yeah, Wells Fargo. Who'd you expect?"

"You might have got a back room, Mr. Timpey. One with no windows." He swung the shotgun on the man still mounted. "Step down easy, Jim."

The man, who was in his early twenties, a few years younger than Scallen, sat with one hand over the other on the saddle horn. Now he gripped the horn and swung down. When he was on the ground his hands were still close together, iron

641

manacles holding them three chain lengths apart. Scallen motioned him toward the door with the stubby barrel of the shotgun.

"Anyone in the lobby?"

"The desk clerk," Timpey answered him, "and a man in a chair by the front door."

"Who is he?"

"I don't know. He's asleep . . . got his brim down over his eyes."

"Did you see anyone out on Commercial?"

"No . . . I haven't been out there." At first he had seemed nervous, but now he was irritated, and a frown made his face pout childishly.

Scallen said calmly, "Mr. Timpey, it was your line this man robbed. You want to see him go all the way to Yuma, don't you?"

"Certainly I do." His eyes went to the outlaw, Jim Kidd, then back to Scallen hurriedly. "But why all the melodrama? The man's under arrest—already been sentenced."

"But he's not in jail till he walks through the gates at Yuma," Scallen said. "I'm only one man, Mr. Timpey, and I've got to get him there."

"Well, dammit . . . I'm not the law! Why didn't you bring men with you? All I know is I got a wire from our Bisbee office to get a hotel room and meet you here the morning of November third. There weren't any instructions that I had to get myself deputized a marshal. That's your job."

"I know it is, Mr. Timpey," Scallen said, and smiled, though it was an effort. "But I want to make sure no one knows Jim Kidd's in Contention until after train time this afternoon."

Jim Kidd had been looking from one to the other with a faintly amused grin. Now he said to Timpey, "He means he's afraid somebody's going to jump him." He smiled at Scallen. "That marshal must've really sold you a bill of goods."

"What's he talking about?" Timpey said.

Kidd went on before Scallen could answer. "They hid me in the Huachuca lockup 'cause they knew nobody could get at me there . . . and finally the Bisbee marshal gets a plan. He and some others hopped the train in Benson last night, heading for

Yuma with an army prisoner passed off as me." Kidd laughed, as if the idea were ridiculous.

"Is that right?" Timpey said.

Scallen nodded. "Pretty much right."

"How does he know all about it?"

"He's got ears and ten fingers to add with."

"I don't like it. Why just one man?"

"Every deputy from here down to Bisbee is out trying to scare up the rest of them. Jim here's the only one we caught," Scallen explained—then added, "alive."

Timpey shot a glance at the outlaw. "Is he the one who killed Dick Moons?"

"One of the passengers swears he saw who did it . . . and he didn't identify Kidd at the trial."

Timpey shook his head. "Dick drove for us a long time. You know his brother lives here in Contention. When he heard about it he almost went crazy." He hesitated, and then said again, "I don't like it."

Scallen felt his patience wearing away, but he kept his voice even when he said, "Maybe I don't either . . . but what you like and what I like aren't going to matter a whole lot, with the marshal past Tucson by now. You can grumble about it all you want, Mr. Timpey, as long as you keep it under your breath. Jim's got friends . . . and since I have to haul him clear across the territory, I'd just as soon they didn't know about it."

Timpey fidgeted nervously. "I don't see why I have to get dragged into this. My job's got nothing to do with law enforcement. . . ."

"You have the room key?"

"In the door. All I'm responsible for is the stage run between here and Tucson—"

Scallen shoved the Winchester at him. "If you'll take care of this and the horses till I get back, I'll be obliged to you . . . and I know I don't have to ask you not to mention we're at the hotel."

He waved the shotgun and nodded and Jim Kidd went ahead of him through the side door into the hotel lobby. Scallen was a stride behind him, holding the stubby shotgun close to his leg. "Up the stairs on the right, Jim."

Kidd started up, but Scallen paused to glance at the figure in the armchair near the front. He was sitting on his spine with limp hands folded on his stomach and, as Timpey had described, his hat low over the upper part of his face. You've seen people sleeping in hotel lobbies before, Scallen told himself, and followed Kidd up the stairs. He couldn't stand and wonder about it.

Room 207 was narrow and high-ceilinged, with a single window looking down on Commercial Street. An iron bed was placed the long way against one wall and extended to the right side of the window, and along the opposite wall was a dresser with washbasin and pitcher and next to it a rough-board wardrobe. An unpainted table and two straight chairs took up most of the remaining space.

"Lay down on the bed if you want to," Scallen said.

"Why don't you sleep?" Kidd asked. "I'll hold the shotgun."

The deputy moved one of the straight chairs near to the door and the other to the side of the table opposite the bed. Then he sat down, resting the shotgun on the table so that it pointed directly at Jim Kidd sitting on the edge of the bed near the window.

He gazed vacantly outside. A patch of dismal sky showed above the frame buildings across the way, but he was not sitting close enough to look directly down onto the street. He said, indifferently, "I think it's going to rain."

There was a silence, and then Scallen said, "Jim, I don't have anything against you personally . . . this is what I get paid for, but I just want it understood that if you start across the seven feet between us, I'm going to pull both triggers at once—without first asking you to stop. That clear?"

Kidd looked at the deputy marshal, then his eyes drifted out the window again. "It's kinda cold too." He rubbed his hands together and the three chain links rattled against each other. "The window's open a crack. Can I close it?"

Scallen's grip tightened on the shotgun and he brought the barrel up, though he wasn't aware of it. "If you can reach it from where you're sitting."

Kidd looked at the windowsill and said without reaching toward it, "Too far."

"All right," Scallen said, rising. "Lay back on the bed." He worked his gun belt around so that now the Colt was on his left hip.

Kidd went back slowly, smiling. "You don't take any chances, do you? Where's your sporting blood?"

"Down in Bisbee with my wife and three youngsters," Scallen told him without smiling, and moved around the table.

There were no grips on the window frame. Standing with his side to the window, facing the man on the bed, he put the heel of his hand on the bottom ledge of the frame and shoved down hard. The window banged shut and with the slam he saw Jim Kidd kicking up off of his back, his body straining to rise without his hands to help. Momentarily, Scallen hesitated and his finger tensed on the trigger. Kidd's feet were on the floor, his body swinging up and his head down to lunge from the bed. Scallen took one step and brought his knee up hard against Kidd's face.

The outlaw went back across the bed, his head striking the wall. He lay there with his eyes open looking at Scallen.

"Feel better now, Jim?"

Kidd brought his hands up to his mouth, working the jaw around. "Well, I had to try you out," he said. "I didn't think you'd shoot."

"But you know I will the next time."

For a few minutes Kidd remained motionless. Then he began to pull himself straight. "I just want to sit up."

Behind the table Scallen said, "Help yourself." He watched Kidd stare out the window.

Then, "How much do you make, Marshal?" Kidd asked the question abruptly.

"I don't think it's any of your business."

"What difference does it make?"

Scallen hesitated. "A hundred and fifty a month," he said, finally, "some expenses, and a dollar bounty for every arrest against a Bisbee ordinance in the town limits."

Kidd shook his head sympathetically. "And you got a wife and three kids."

"Well, it's more than a cowhand makes."

"But you're not a cowhand."

"I've worked my share of beef."

"Forty a month and keep, huh?" Kidd laughed.

"That's right, forty a month," Scallen said. He felt awkward. "How much do you make?"

Kidd grinned. When he smiled he looked very young, hardly out of his teens. "Name a month," he said. "It varies."

"But you've made a lot of money."

"Enough. I can buy what I want."

"What are you going to be wanting the next five years?"

"You're pretty sure we're going to Yuma."

"And you're pretty sure we're not," Scallen said. "Well, I've got two train passes and a shotgun that says we are. What've you got?"

Kidd smiled. "You'll see." Then he said right after it, his tone changing, "What made you join the law?"

"The money," Scallen answered, and felt foolish as he said it. But he went on, "I was working for a spread over by the Pantano Wash when Old Nana broke loose and raised hell up the Santa Rosa Valley. The army was going around in circles, so the Pima County marshal got up a bunch to help out and we tracked Apaches almost all spring. The marshal and I got along fine, so he offered me a deputy job if I wanted it." He wanted to say that he started for seventy-five and worked up to the one hundred and fifty, but he didn't.

"And then someday you'll get to be marshal and make two hundred."

"Maybe."

"And then one night a drunk cowhand you've never seen will be tearing up somebody's saloon and you'll go in to arrest him and he'll drill you with a lucky shot before you get your gun out."

"So you're telling me I'm crazy."

"If you don't already know it."

Scallen took his hand off the shotgun and pulled tobacco and paper from his shirt pocket and began rolling a cigarette. "Have you figured out yet what my price is?"

Kidd looked startled, momentarily, but the grin returned. "No, I haven't. Maybe you come higher than I thought."

Scallen scratched a match across the table, lighted the cigarette, then threw it to the floor, between Kidd's boots. "You don't have enough money, Jim."

Kidd shrugged, then reached down for the cigarette. "You've treated me pretty good. I just wanted to make it easy on you."

The sun came into the room after a while. Weakly at first, cold and hazy. Then it warmed and brightened and cast an oblong patch of light between the bed and the table. The morning wore on slowly because there was nothing to do and each man sat restlessly thinking about somewhere else, though it was a restlessness within and it showed on neither of them.

The deputy rolled cigarettes for the outlaw and himself and most of the time they smoked in silence. Once Kidd asked him what time the train left. He told him shortly after three, but Kidd made no comment.

Scallen went to the window and looked out at the narrow rutted road that was Commercial Street. He pulled a watch from his vest pocket and looked at it. It was almost noon, yet there were few people about. He wondered about this and asked himself if it was unnaturally quiet for a Saturday noon in Contention . . . or if it were just his nerves. . . .

He studied the man standing under the wooden awning across the street, leaning idly against a support post with his thumbs hooked in his belt and his flat-crowned hat on the back of his head. There was something familiar about him. And each time Scallen had gone to the window—a few times during the past hour—the man had been there.

He glanced at Jim Kidd lying across the bed, then looked out the window in time to see another man moving up next to the one at the post. They stood together for the space of a minute before the second man turned a horse from the tie rail, swung up, and rode off down the street.

The man at the post watched him go and tilted his hat against the sun glare. And then it registered. With the hat low on his forehead Scallen saw him again as he had that morning. The man lying in the armchair . . . as if asleep.

He saw his wife, then, and the three youngsters and he could almost feel the little girl sitting on his lap where she had climbed up to kiss him good-bye, and he had promised to bring her something from Tucson. He didn't know why they had come to him all of a sudden. And after he had put them out of his mind, since there was no room now, there was an upset feeling inside as if he had swallowed something that would not go down all the way. It made his heart beat a little faster.

Jim Kidd was smiling up at him. "Anybody I know?"

"I didn't think it showed."

"Like the sun going down."

Scallen glanced at the man across the street and then to Jim Kidd. "Come here." He nodded to the window. "Tell me who your friend is over there."

Kidd half rose and leaned over looking out the window, then sat down again. "Charlie Prince."

"Somebody else just went for help."

"Charlie doesn't need help."

"How did you know you were going to be in Contention?"

"You told that Wells Fargo man I had friends . . . and about the posses chasing around in the hills. Figure it out for yourself. You could be looking out a window in Benson and seeing the same thing."

"They're not going to do you any good."

"I don't know any man who'd get himself killed for a hundred and fifty dollars." Kidd paused. "Especially a man with a wife and young ones. . . ."

Men rode into town in something less than an hour later. Scallen heard the horses coming up Commercial, and went to the window to see the six riders pull to a stop and range themselves in a line in the middle of the street facing the hotel. Charlie Prince stood behind them, leaning against the post.

Then he moved away from it, leisurely, and stepped down into the street. He walked between the horses and stopped in front of them just below the window. He cupped his hands to his mouth and shouted, "*Jim!*"

In the quiet street it was like a pistol shot.

Scallen looked at Kidd, seeing the smile that softened his face and was even in his eyes. Confidence. It was all over him. And even with the manacles on, you would believe that it was Jim Kidd who was holding the shotgun.

"What do you want me to tell him?" Kidd said.

"Tell him you'll write every day."

Kidd laughed and went to the window, pushing it up by the top of the frame. It raised a few inches. Then he moved his hands under the window and it slid up all the way.

"Charlie, you go buy the boys a drink. We'll be down shortly."

"Are you all right?"

"Sure I'm all right."

Charlie Prince hesitated. "What if you don't come down? He could kill you and say you tried to break. . . . Jim, you tell him what'll happen if we hear a gun go off."

"He knows," Kidd said, and closed the window. He looked at Scallen standing motionless with the shotgun under his arm. "Your turn, Marshal."

"What do you expect me to say?"

"Something that makes sense. You said before I didn't mean a thing to you personally—what you're doing is just a job. Well, you figure out if it's worth getting killed for. All you have to do is throw your guns on the bed and let me walk out the door and you can go back to Bisbee and arrest all the drunks you want. Nobody's going to blame you with the odds stacked seven to one. You know your wife's not going to complain. . . ."

"You should have been a lawyer, Jim."

The smile began to fade from Kidd's face. "Come on— what's it going to be?"

The door rattled with three knocks in quick succession. Abruptly the room was silent. The two men looked at each other and now the smile disappeared from Kidd's face completely.

Scallen moved to the side of the door, tiptoeing in his high-heeled boots, then pointed his shotgun toward the bed. Kidd sat down.

"Who is it?"

For a moment there was no answer. Then he heard, "Timpey."

He glanced at Kidd, who was watching him. "What do you want?"

"I've got a pot of coffee for you."

Scallen hesitated. "You alone?"

"Of course I am. Hurry up, it's hot!"

He drew the key from his coat pocket, then held the shotgun in the crook of his arm as he inserted the key with one hand and turned the knob with the other. The door opened and slammed against him, knocking him back against the dresser. He went off balance, sliding into the wardrobe, going down on his hands and knees, and the shotgun clattered across the floor to the window. He saw Jim Kidd drop to the floor for the gun. . . .

"Hold it!"

A heavyset man stood in the doorway with a Colt pointing out past the thick bulge of his stomach. "Leave that shotgun where it is." Timpey stood next to him with the coffeepot in his hand. There was coffee down the front of his suit, on the door, and on the flooring. He brushed at the front of his coat feebly, looking from Scallen to the man with the pistol.

"I couldn't help it, Marshal—he made me do it. He threatened to do something to me if I didn't."

"Who is he?"

"Bob Moons . . . you know, Dick's brother. . . ."

The heavyset man glanced at Timpey angrily. "Shut your damn whining." His eyes went to Jim Kidd and held there. "You know who I am, don't you?"

Kidd looked uninterested. "You don't resemble anybody I know."

"You didn't have to know Dick to shoot him!"

"I didn't shoot that messenger."

Scallen got to his feet, looking at Timpey. "What the hell's wrong with you?"

"I couldn't help it. He forced me."

"How did he know we were here?"

"He came in this morning talking about Dick and I felt he needed some cheering up; so I told him Jim Kidd had been tried and was being taken to Yuma and was here in town . . . on his way. Bob didn't say anything and went out, and a little later he came back with the gun."

"You damn fool." Scallen shook his head wearily.

"Never mind all the talk." Moons kept the pistol on Kidd. "I would've found him sooner or later. This way everybody gets saved a long train ride."

"You pull that trigger," Scallen said, "and you'll hang for murder."

"Like he did for killing Dick. . . ."

"A jury said he didn't do it." Scallen took a step toward the big man. "And I'm damned if I'm going to let you pass another sentence."

"You stay put or I'll pass sentence on you!"

Scallen moved a slow step nearer. "Hand me the gun, Bob."

"I'm warning you—get the hell out of the way and let me do what I came for."

"Bob, hand me the gun or I swear I'll beat you through that wall."

Scallen tensed to take another step, another slow one. He saw Moons's eyes dart from him to Kidd and in that instant he knew it would be his only chance. He lunged, swinging his coat aside with his hand, and when the hand came up it was holding a Colt. All in one motion. The pistol went up and chopped an arc across Moons's head before the big man could bring his own gun around. His hat flew off as the barrel swiped his skull and he went back against the wall heavily, then sank to the floor.

Scallen wheeled to face the window, thumbing the hammer back. But Kidd was still sitting on the edge of the bed with the shotgun at his feet.

The deputy relaxed, letting the hammer ease down. "You might have made it, that time."

Kidd shook his head. "I wouldn't have got off the bed." There was a note of surprise in his voice. "You know, you're pretty good. . . ."

At two-fifteen Scallen looked at his watch, then stood up, pushing the chair back. The shotgun was under his arm. In less than an hour they would leave the hotel, walk over Commercial to Stockman, and then up Stockman to the station. Three blocks. He wanted to go all the way. He wanted to get Jim Kidd on that train . . . but he was afraid.

He was afraid of what he might do once they were on the street. Even now his breath was short and occasionally he would inhale and let the air out slowly to calm himself. And he kept asking himself if it was worth it.

People would be in the windows and the doors, though you wouldn't see them. They'd have their own feelings and most of their hearts would be pounding . . . and they'd edge back of the door frames a little more. The man out on the street was something without a human nature or a personality of its own. He was on a stage. The street was another world.

Timpey sat on the chair in front of the door and next to him, squatting on the floor with his back against the wall, was

Moons. Scallen had unloaded Moons's pistol and placed it in the pitcher behind him. Kidd was on the bed.

Most of the time he stared at Scallen. His face bore a puzzled expression, making his eyes frown, and sometimes he would cock his head as if studying the deputy from a different angle.

Scallen stepped to the window now. Charlie Prince and another man were under the awning. The others were not in sight.

"You haven't changed your mind?" Kidd asked him seriously.

Scallen shook his head.

"I don't understand you. You risk your neck to save my life, now you'll risk it again to send me to prison."

Scallen looked at Kidd and suddenly felt closer to him than any man he knew. "Don't ask me, Jim," he said, and sat down again.

After that he looked at his watch every few minutes.

At five minutes to three he walked to the door, motioning Timpey aside, and turned the key in the lock. "Let's go, Jim." When Kidd was next to him he prodded Moons with the gun barrel. "Over on the bed. Mister, if I see or hear about you on the street before train time, you'll face an attempted murder charge." He motioned Kidd past him, then stepped into the hall and locked the door.

They went down the stairs and crossed the lobby to the front door, Scallen a stride behind with the shotgun barrel almost touching Kidd's back. Passing through the doorway he said as calmly as he could, "Turn left on Stockman and keep walking. No matter what you hear, keep walking."

As they stepped out into Commercial, Scallen glanced at the ramada where Charlie Prince had been standing, but now the saloon porch was an empty shadow. Near the corner two horses stood under a sign that said EAT, in red letters; and on the other side of Stockman the signs continued, lining the rutted main street to make it seem narrower. And beneath the signs, in the shadows, nothing moved. There was a whisper of wind along the ramadas. It whipped sand specks from the street and rattled them against clapboard, and the sound was hollow and lifeless. Somewhere a screen door banged, far away.

They passed the café, turning onto Stockman. Ahead, the

deserted street narrowed with distance to a dead end at the rail station—a single-story building standing by itself, low and sprawling, with most of the platform in shadow. The westbound was there, along the platform, but the engine and most of the cars were hidden by the station house. White steam lifted above the roof, to be lost in the sun's glare.

They were almost to the platform when Kidd said over his shoulder, "Run like hell while you're still able."

"Where are they?"

Kidd grinned, because he knew Scallen was afraid. "How should I know?"

"Tell them to come out in the open!"

"Tell them yourself."

"Dammit, *tell* them!" Scallen clenched his jaw and jabbed the short barrel into Kidd's back. "I'm not fooling. If they don't come out, I'll kill you!"

Kidd felt the gun barrel hard against his spine and suddenly he shouted, "Charlie!"

It echoed in the street, but after there was only the silence. Kidd's eyes darted over the shadowed porches. "Dammit, Charlie—hold on!"

Scallen prodded him up the warped plank steps to the shade of the platform and suddenly he could feel them near. "Tell him again!"

"Don't shoot, Charlie!" Kidd screamed the words.

From the other side of the station they heard the trainman's call trailing off, ". . . Gila Bend. Sentinel, Yuma!"

The whistle sounded loud, wailing, as they passed into the shade of the platform, then out again to the naked glare of the open side. Scallen squinted, glancing toward the station office, but the train dispatcher was not in sight. Nor was anyone. "It's the mail car," he said to Kidd. "The second to last one." Steam hissed from the iron cylinder of the engine, clouding that end of the platform. "Hurry it up!" he snapped, pushing Kidd along.

Then, from behind, hurried footsteps sounded on the planking, and, as the hiss of steam died away—"Stand where you are!"

The locomotive's main rods strained back, rising like the

legs of a grotesque grasshopper, and the wheels moved. The connecting rods stopped on an upward swing and couplings clanged down the line of cars.

"Throw the gun away, brother!"

Charlie Prince stood at the corner of the station house with a pistol in each hand. Then he moved around carefully between the two men and the train. "Throw it far away, and unhitch your belt," he said.

"Do what he says," Kidd said. "They've got you."

The others, six of them, were strung out in the dimness of the platform shed. Grim faced, stubbles of beard, hat brims low. The man nearest Prince spat tobacco lazily.

Scallen knew fear at that moment as fear had never gripped him before; but he kept the shotgun hard against Kidd's spine. He said, just above a whisper, "Jim—I'll cut you in half!"

Kidd's body was stiff, his shoulders drawn up tightly. "Wait a minute . . ." he said. He held his palms out to Charlie Prince, though he could have been speaking to Scallen.

Suddenly Prince shouted, "Go down!"

There was a fraction of a moment of dead silence that seemed longer. Kidd hesitated. Scallen was looking at the gunman over Kidd's shoulder, seeing the two pistols. Then Kidd was gone, rolling on the planking, and the pistols were coming up, one ahead of the other. Without moving Scallen squeezed both triggers of the scattergun.

Charlie Prince was going down, holding his hands tight to his chest, as Scallen dropped the shotgun and swung around drawing his Colt. He fired hurriedly. *Wait for a target!* Words in his mind. He saw the men under the platform shed, three of them breaking for the station office, two going full length to the planks . . . one crouched, his pistol up. *That one! Get him quick!* Scallen aimed and squeezed the heavy revolver and the man went down. *Now get the hell out!*

Charlie Prince was facedown. Kidd was crawling, crawling frantically and coming to his feet when Scallen reached him. He grabbed Kidd by the collar savagely, pushing him on, and dug the pistol into his back. "Run, damn you!"

Gunfire erupted from the shed and thudded into the wooden caboose as they ran past it. The train was moving slowly. Just in front of them a bullet smashed a window of the mail car.

Someone screamed, "You'll hit Jim!" There was another shot, then it was too late. Scallen and Kidd leapt up on the car platform and were in the mail car as it rumbled past the end of the station platform.

Kidd was on the floor, stretched out along a row of mail sacks. He rubbed his shoulder awkwardly with his manacled hands and watched Scallen, who stood against the wall next to the open door.

Kidd studied the deputy for some minutes. Finally he said, "You know, you really earn your hundred and a half."

Scallen heard him, though the iron rhythm of the train wheels and his breathing were loud in his temples. He felt as if all his strength had been sapped, but he couldn't help smiling at Jim Kidd. He was thinking pretty much the same thing.

Blood Money

THE YUMA Savings and Loan, Asunción Branch, was held up on a Monday morning, early. By eight o'clock the doctor had dug the bullet out of Elton Goss's middle and said if he lived, then you didn't need doctors anymore—the age of miracles was back. By nine Freehouser, the Asunción marshal, had all the facts—even the identity of the five holdup men—thanks to the Centralia Hotel night clerk's having been awake to see four of them come down from their rooms just after sunup. Then, he had tried to make the faces register in his mind, but even squinting and wrinkling his forehead did no good. The fifth man had been in the hotel lobby most of the night and the clerk knew for sure who he was, but didn't at the time associate him with the others. Later, when Freehouser showed him the WANTED dodgers, then he was dead sure about all of them.

Four were desperadoes. Well known, though with beard bristles and range clothes they looked like anybody else. First, the Harlan brothers, Ford and Eugene. Ford was boss: Eugene was too lazy to work. Then Deke, an old hand whose real name was something Deacon, though no one knew what for sure. And the fourth, Sonny Navarez, wanted in Sonora by the *rurales*; in Arizona, by the marshal's office. He, like the others, had served time in the territorial prison at Yuma.

As far as Freehouser was concerned, they weren't going back to Yuma if he caught them. Not with Elton Goss dying and his dad yelling for blood.

The fifth outlaw was identified as Rich Miller, a rider from down by Four Tanks. Those who knew of him said he was weathered good for his age, though not as tough as he thought he was. A boy going on eighteen and getting funny ideas in his brain because of the changing chemistry in his body. The bartender at the Centralia said Rich had been in and out all day, looking like he was mad at somebody. So they judged Rich had gotten drunk and was talked into something that was way over his head.

A hand from F-T Connected, which was out of Four Tanks, said Rich Miller'd been let go the day before, when the old man caught him drunk up at a line shack and not tending his fences. So what the Centralia bartender said was probably true. Freehouser said it was just too damn bad for him, that's all.

Monday afternoon the marshal's posse was in Four Tanks, then heading east toward the jagged andesite peaks of the Kofas. McKelway, the law at Four Tanks, had joined the posse, bringing five men with him, and offering a neighborly hand. But he became hard-to-hold eager when he found out who they were after. The Harlans, Deke, and Navarez had dead-or-alive money on them. McKelway knew Rich Miller and said he just ought to have his nose wiped and run off home. But Freehouser looked at it differently.

This was armed robbery. Goss, the bank manager, and his son Elton, who clerked for him, were hauled out of bed by two men—they turned out to be Eugene Harlan and Deke. Ford Harlan and Sonny Navarez were waiting at the rear door of the bank. The robbery would have come off without incident if Elton hadn't gone for a gun in a desk drawer. The elder Goss wasn't sure which one shot him. Then they were gone, with twelve thousand dollars.

They rode around front and Rich Miller came out of the Centralia to join them. He'd been sitting at the window, asleep, the clerk thought, wearing off a drunk. He was used to having riders do that. When the rooms were filled up he didn't care. But Rich Miller suddenly came alive and swung onto a mount the Mexican was leading. So all that time he must have been watching the front to see no one sneaked up on them.

McKelway said a boy ought to be allowed one big mistake before he was called hard on something he'd done. Besides, Rich Miller's name didn't bring any reward money.

Tuesday morning, the twenty-man posse was deep in the Kofas. Gray rock towering on all sides, wild country, and now, no trail. Freehouser decided they would split up, climb to higher ground, and wait. Just look around. He sent a man back to Four Tanks to wire Yuma and Aztec in case the outlaws got through the Kofas. But Freehouser was sure they were still in the mountains, somewhere.

Wednesday morning his hunch paid off. One of McKelway's men spotted a rider, and the posse closed in by means of a mirror-flash system they'd planned beforehand. The rider turned out to be Ford Harlan.

Wednesday afternoon Ford Harlan was dead.

He had led them a chase most of the morning, slipping through the man net, but near noon he turned into a dead-end canyon, a deserted mine site that once had been Sweet Mary No. 1. Ford Harlan had been urging his mount up a slope above the mine works, toward an adobe hut perched on a ledge about three hundred yards up, when Freehouser cupped his hands and called for him to halt. He kept on. A moment later Jim Mission, McKelway's deputy, knocked him out of the saddle with a single shot from his Remington.

Then McKelway and Mission volunteered to bring Ford Harlan down. McKelway tied a white neckerchief to the end of his Sharps for a truce flag and they went up. Freehouser had said if you want to get Ford, you might as well go a few more steps and ask the rest if they want to give up. They were almost to the body when the pistol fire broke from above. They scrambled down fast and when they reached the posse, Freehouser was smiling.

They were all up there, Eugene and Deke and the Mexican and Rich Miller. One of them had lost his nerve and opened up. You could see it on Freehouser's face. The self-satisfaction. They were trapped in an old assay shack with a sheer sandstone wall towering behind it—thin shadow lines of crevices reaching to slender pinnacles—and only one way to come down. The original mine opening was on the same shelf; probably they'd hid their horses there.

Freehouser was a contented man; he had all the time in the world to figure how to pry them out of the 'dobe. He even listened to McKelway and admitted that maybe the kid, Rich Miller, shouldn't be hung with the others—if he didn't get shot first.

Some of the posse went back home, because they had jobs to hold down, but the next day, others came out from Asunción and Four Tanks to see the fun.

It seemed natural that Deke should take over as boss. There was no discussing it; no one gave it a thought. Ford was dead.

Eugene was indifferent. Sonny Navarez was Mexican, and Rich Miller was a kid.

The boy had wondered why Deke wasn't the boss even before. Maybe Deke didn't have Ford's nerve, but he had it over him in age and learning. Still, a man gets old and he thinks of too many what-ifs. And sometimes Deke was scary the way he talked about fate and God pulling little strings to steer men around where they didn't want to go.

He was at the window on the right side of the doorway, which was open because there was no door. Eugene and Deke were at the left front window. He could hear Sonny Navarez behind him moving gear around, but the boy did not take his eyes from the slope.

Deke lounged against the wall, his face close to the window frame, his carbine balanced on the sill. Eugene was a step behind him. He was a heavy-boned man, shoulders stretching his shirt tight, and tall, though Deke was taller when he wasn't lounging. Eugene pulled at his shirt, sticking to his body with perspiration. The sun was straight overhead and the heat pushed into the canyon without first being deflected by the rimrock.

The Mexican drew his carbine from his bedroll and moved up next to Rich Miller, and now the four of them were looking down the slope, all thinking pretty much the same thing, though in different ways.

Eugene Harlan broke the silence. "I shouldn't of fired at them."

It could have gone unsaid. Deke shrugged. "That's under the bridge."

"I wasn't thinking."

Deke did not bother to look at him. "Well, you better start."

"It wasn't my fault. Ford led 'em here!"

"Nobody's blaming you for anything. They'd a got us anyway, sooner or later. It was on the wall."

Eugene was silent, and then he said, "What happens if we give ourselves up?"

Deke glanced at him now. "What do you think?"

Sonny Navarez grinned. "I think they would invite us to the rope dance."

"Ford's the one shot that boy in the bank," Eugene protested. "They already got him."

"How would they know he's the one?" Deke said.

"We'll tell them."

Deke shook his head. "Get a drink and you'll be doing your nerves a favor."

Sonny Navarez and Rich Miller looked at Deke and both of them grinned, but they said nothing and after a moment they looked away again, down the slope, which fell smooth and steep. Slightly to the left, beyond an ore tailing, rose the weathered gray scaffolding over the main shaft; below it, the rickety structure of the crushing mill and, past that, six rusted tanks cradled in a framework of decaying timber. These were roughly three hundred yards down the slope. There was another hundred to the clapboard company buildings straggled along the base of the far slope.

A sign hanging from the veranda of the largest building said SWEET MARY NO. 1—EL TESORERO MINING CO.—FOUR TANKS, ARIZONA TERR. Most of the possemen now sat in the shade of this building.

Deke raised his hat again and passed a hand over his bald head, then down over his face, weathered and beard stubbled, contrasting with the delicate whiteness of his skull. Rich Miller's eyes came back up the slope, hesitating on Ford Harlan's facedown body. Then he removed his hat, passed a sleeve across his forehead, and replaced the curled brim low over his eyes.

He heard Eugene say, "You can't tell what they'll do."

"They won't send us back to Yuma," Deke said. "That's one thing you can count on. And it costs money to rig a gallows. They'd just as lief do it here, with a gun—appeals to the sporting blood."

Sonny Navarez said, "I once shot a mountain sheep in this same canyon that weighed as much as a man."

"Right from the start there were signs," Deke said. "I was a fool not to heed them. Now it's too late. Something's brought us to die here all together, and we can't escape it. You can't escape your doom."

Sonny Navarez said, "I think it was twelve thousand dollars that brought us."

"Sure it was the money, in a way," Deke said. "But we're

so busy listening to Ford tell how easy money's restin' in the bank, waitin' to be sent to Yuma, we're not seein' the signs. Things that've never happened before. Like Ford insisting we got to have five—so he picks up this kid—"

Rich Miller said, "Wait a minute!" because it didn't sound right.

Deke held up his hand. "I'm talking about the signs—and Ford all of a sudden gettin' the urge to go on scout when he never done anything like that before. It was all working toward this—and now there's nothing we can do about it."

"I ain't going to get shot up just because you got a crazy notion," Eugene said.

Deke shook his head, wearily. "It's sealed up now. After fate shows how it's going, then it's too late."

"I didn't shoot that man in the bank!"

"You think they'll bother to ask you?"

"Damn it, I'll tell 'em—and they'll have to prove I did it!"

"If you can get close enough to 'em without gettin' shot," Deke said quietly. He brought out field glasses from his saddle-bags, which were below the window, and put the glasses to his face, edging them along the men far below in front of the company buildings.

Rich Miller said to him, "What do you see down there?"

"Same thing you do, only bigger."

"I think," Sonny Navarez said to Deke, "that you are right in what you have said, that they will try hard to kill us—but this boy is not one of us. I think if he would surrender, they would not kill him. Prison, perhaps, but prison is better than dying."

"You worry about yourself," Rich Miller said.

"The time to be brave," the Mexican said, "is when they are handing out medals."

"You heard him," Deke said. "Worry about your own hide. The more people we got, the longer we last. There's nothing that says if you're going to get killed, you got to hurry it up."

Rich Miller watched Eugene move back to the table along the rear wall and pick up the whiskey bottle that was there. The boy passed his tongue over dry lips, watching Eugene drink. It would be good to have a drink, he thought. No, it wouldn't. It would be bad. You drank too much and that's why you're here. That's why you're going to get shot or hung.

But he could not sincerely believe what Deke had said. That one way or the other, this was the end. Down the slope the posse was very far away—dots of men that seemed too small to be a threat. He did not feel sorry about joining the holdup, because he did not let himself think about it. He did feel something resembling sorry for the man in the bank. But he shouldn't have reached for the gun. I wonder if I would have, he thought.

It wasn't so bad up here in the 'dobe. Plenty of water and grub. Maybe we'll have some fun. Look at that crazy Mexican, talking about hunting mountain sheep.

If you were in jail you could say, all right, you made a mistake; but how do you know if you've made a mistake when you're still alive and got two thousand dollars in your pants? My God, a man can do just about anything with two thousand dollars!

Freehouser sat in the shade, not saying anything. McKelway came to him, biting on his pipe idly, and after a while pointed to the mine-shaft scaffolding and said how a man with a good rifle might be able to draw a bead and throw something in that open doorway if he was sitting way up there on top.

Freehouser studied the ore tailings, furrowed and steep, that extended out from the slope on both sides of the hut. If a man was going up to that 'dobe, he'd have to go straight up, right into their guns. Maybe McKelway had something. Soften them up a bit.

Standing by the windows, watching the possemen not moving, became tiresome. So one by one they would go back to the table and take a drink. Rich Miller took his turn and it tasted good. But he did not drink much.

Still, the time dragged on—until Eugene thought of something. He went to his gear and drew a deck of cards.

Sonny Navarez said, "I have not played often."

"Stand by the window awhile," Deke told him. "Then somebody'll spell you. You got enough cash to learn with."

Eugene shook his head, thinking of his brother, who had taken twice as much as the others because the holdup had been his idea. "Damn Ford had four thousand in his bags. . . ."

They started playing, using matches for chips, each one worth a dollar. Rich Miller said the stakes were big . . . he'd never played higher than nickel-dime before; but he began winning right off and he changed his tune. Most of the time they played five-card stud. Deke said it separated the men from the boys and he looked at Rich Miller when he said it. Deke played with a dumb face, but would smile after the last card was dealt—as if the last card always twinned the one he had in the hole. And he lost every hand. Eugene and Rich Miller took turns winning the pots, and after a while Deke stopped smiling.

"We're raising the stakes," he said finally. "Each stick's worth ten dollars." Deke's cut was down to a few hundred dollars.

Eugene took a drink and wiped his mouth and grinned. "Ain't you losing it fast enough?"

Rich Miller grinned with him.

Deke said, "Just deal the cards."

McKelway reached the platform on top of the shaft scaffolding and dropped the line to haul up the rifles—his own Sharps and Jim Mission's roll-block Remington. He was glad Jim Mission was coming up with him. Jim was company and could shoot probably better than he could.

When Jim reached the platform the two men nodded and smiled, then loaded their rifles and practice-sighted on the doorway. McKelway said, Try not to hit the boy, though knocking off any of the others would be doing mankind a good turn, and Jim Mission said it was all right with him.

Eugene got up from the table unsteadily, tipping back his chair; he was grinning and stuffing currency into his pants pockets. In two hours he had won every cent of Deke's and Rich Miller's money. They remained seated, watching him sullenly, thinking it was a damn fool thing to try and win back all your losings in a couple of hands. Eugene took another pull at the bottle and wiped his mouth and looked at them, but he only grinned.

"Sonny!" He called to the Mexican lounging beside the window. "Your turn to get skinned."

The Mexican shook his head. "I could not oppose such luck."

"Come on!"

Sonny Navarez shook his head again and smiled.

Harlan looked at him steadily, frowning. "Are you going to play?"

"Why should I give you my money?"

"You don't come over here, I'll come get you."

The Mexican did not smile now and the room was silent. Rich Miller started to rise, but Deke was up first. "Gene, you want to fight somebody—there's plenty outside."

Eugene ignored him and kept on toward Sonny. The Mexican's hand edged toward his holstered pistol.

"Gene, you sit down now," Deke said tensely.

Eugene stepped into the rectangle of sunlight carpeting in from the doorway. He was stepping out of it when the rifle cracked and sang in the open stillness. Eugene's hands clawed at his face and he dropped without uttering a sound.

McKelway reloaded quickly. He had got one of them, he was sure of that. And it hadn't looked like the boy, else he wouldn't have fired. Jim Mission told him it was good shooting. After that McKelway did some figuring.

From the crest of the ore tailing in front of them, they'd be only about fifty yards from the hut. The only trouble was, they'd be out in the open. He told Jim Mission about it and he said why not go up after dark; then if they didn't see anything they'd still be close enough to shoot at sounds. McKelway said he was just waiting for Jim to say it.

There was no poker the rest of the afternoon. Deke had dragged Eugene by his boots out of the doorway and placed him against a side wall with his hands on his chest, not crossed, but pushed inside his coat. He took the money out of Eugene's pockets—six thousand dollars—and laid it on the table. Then he sat down and looked at it.

Rich Miller pressed close to the wall by the window, studying the slope, wondering where the man with the rifle was. His eyes hung on the weathered shaft scaffolding, and now he wasn't so sure if there'd be any fun.

Once Deke said, "Now it's starting to show itself," but they didn't bother to ask him what.

Sonny Navarez stayed by a window. He would look at

Eugene's body, but most of the time he was watching the dying sun. Rich Miller noticed this, but he figured the Mexican was thinking about God—or heaven or hell—because there was a dead man in the room. Sonny had crossed himself when Eugene was cut down, even though he would have killed him himself a minute before.

The sun was below the canyon rim, though the sky still reflected it red and orange, when Sonny Navarez pulled his pistol.

Deke was raising the bottle. He glanced at the Mexican, but only momentarily. He took a long swallow then and extended the bottle to Rich Miller. But the boy was staring at Sonny Navarez. Deke's head turned abruptly. Sonny's long-barreled .44 was pointing toward them.

Deke took his time putting down the bottle. He looked up again. "What's the idea?"

The Mexican said, "When it is dark I'm leaving."

Deke nodded to the pistol. "You think we're going to try and stop you?"

"You might. I am taking the money."

"You're wasting your time."

Sonny Navarez shrugged. "*Qué va*—it's worth a try. From no matter where you die, it's the same distance to hell."

"You wouldn't have a chance," Rich Miller said. "There's somebody out there close with a rifle dead on this place."

"For this money a man will brave many things," the Mexican said. "And—I am not leaving until dark." Then he told them to face the wall, and when they did, he picked up the bundles of oversize bills and stuffed them inside his jacket.

Rich Miller said, "Do you think you'll get through?"

"Probably no."

Deke said, "You're a damn fool."

"If I get out," Sonny Navarez said, "I will visit a priest and give his church part of the money, and not rob again."

"It's too late for that," Deke said. "It's too late for anything."

No," the Mexican insisted. "I will be very sorry for this crime. With the money that is left after the church I will buy my mother a house in Hermosillo and after that I will recite the rosary every day."

Deke shook his head. "Things are going the way they are for

a reason we don't know. But nothing you can do will change it."

The Mexican shrugged and said, "*Qué va—*"

It was almost full dark when Sonny Navarez moved to the doorway. He stood next to the opening and holstered his pistol and lifted his carbine, which was there against the wall. He levered a shell into the breech and stepped into the opening, crouching slightly. He hesitated, as if listening, then turned to the two men at the table and nodded. As he was turning back, the rifle shot rang in the dim stillness and echoed up-canyon. Sonny Navarez doubled, sinking to his knees, and hung there momentarily, as if in prayer, before falling half through the doorway.

Later, McKelway and Mission climbed down from the ore tailing and reported to Freehouser. The marshal said three out of five men wasn't bad for one day's work. They were sitting on the porch, cigarettes glowing in the darkness, when the rider came in from Asunción. He told them that Elton Goss was going to pull through.

Freehouser laughed and said, well, he guessed the age of miracles was back. A good one on the doctor, eh?

The news made everybody feel pretty good, because Elton was a nice boy. McKelway mentioned that it would also make it a whole lot easier on Rich Miller.

Looking out into the night, the boy could just barely make out the shapes of the mine structures and the cyanide vats, which Deke had told him held 250 tons of ore and had to be hauled all the way across the desert from Yuma. How did he say it? The ore'd pour into the crusher—jaws and rollers that'd beat it almost to powder—then pass into the vats and get leached in cyanide for nine days. Five pounds of cyanide to the ton of water, that was it. He thought, *What's the sense in remembering that?*

It's a strange thing, Rich Miller thought now, *how in two days a man can change from a thirty-a-month rider to an outlaw and not even feel it. Almost like the man has nothing to do with it. Just a rope pulling you into things.*

He remembered earlier in the day, being eager, looking

forward to doing some long-range shooting, but seeing the situation apart from himself. He wondered how he could have thought this. Now there were two dead men in the room—that was the difference.

Later on, he got to thinking about Eugene breaking the poker game and about the Mexican. It occurred to him that both of them, for a short space of time, had all of the money, and now they were dead. Ford had taken the biggest cut, and he was dead. Toward morning he dozed and when he awoke, Deke was sitting, leaning against the wall below the other window.

Deke was silent and Rich Miller said, for something to say, "When they going to try for us?"

"When they get good and damn ready."

Rich Miller was silent and after a while he said, "We could take a chance and give up—you know, not like surrenderin'— with the idea of gettin' away later on when they ain't a hundred of 'em around."

"You know what I told you."

"But you ain't dead sure about that."

"I'd say I'm a little older than you are."

Rich Miller did not answer. Damn, he hated for someone to tell him that. As if old men naturally knew more than young ones. Taking credit for being older when they didn't have anything to do with it.

"What're you thinking about?" Deke said.

"Giving up."

Deke exhaled slowly. "You saw what happens if you go through that door."

"There's other ways."

"Like what?"

"Wavin' a flag."

"You wave anything out that door," Deke said quietly, "I'll kill you."

He's crazy, Rich thought. *He's honest-to-God crazy and doesn't know it.* Deke had butted the table against the wall under the window and now they sat opposite each other, Deke on one side of the window, the boy on the other. Deke had divided the eight thousand dollars between them and said they were going to play poker to keep their minds from blowing away. He placed his pistol on the edge of the table.

They stayed fairly close at first, each winning about the same number of pots, but after a while the boy began to win more often. In the quietness he thought of many things—like not being able to give himself up—and then he remembered something which had occurred to him earlier.

"Deke," the boy said, "you know why Sonny and Eugene got killed?"

"I've been telling you why. 'Cause they were destined to."

"But why?"

"No one knows that."

"I do." The boy watched the older man closely. "Because they had the money." He paused. "Ford had most of it, and he was the first. Eugene had all but Sonny's when he got hit. Then Sonny took all of it and he lasted less than an hour."

Deke said nothing, but his sunken expression seemed more drawn.

They played on in silence and slowly Rich Miller was taking more and more of the money. Deke seemed uncomfortable and he said quietly that he guessed it just wasn't his day. In less than an hour he was down to two hundred and fifty dollars.

"You might clean me out," Deke said.

Rich Miller said nothing and dealt the cards. The first ones down, then a queen to Deke and a jack to himself. He looked at his hole card. A ten of diamonds. Deke bet fifty dollars on the queen.

"You must have twin girls," the boy said.

"You know how to find out."

Rich Miller's next card was a king. Deke's an ace. He bet fifty dollars again. Their fourth cards were low and no help, but Deke pushed in all the money he had.

"That's on a hunch," he said.

Rich Miller dealt the last cards—a queen to Deke, making it an ace, a five, and two queens. He gave himself a second king.

"What you show beats me," Deke said, grinning. He pushed away from the table and stood up. "You got it all, boy. You know what that means."

"It means I'm giving up."

"It's too late. You explained it yourself a while ago—the man who gets the money gets killed!" Deke was grinning deeply. "Now I don't have anything."

"You're dead sure you'll be last."

"As sure as a man can be. It's the handwriting."

"What good'll it do you?"

"Who knows?"

"You're so dead sure, go stand in that doorway."

Deke was silent.

"What about your handwritin'? The pattern says you'll be the last, and even then, who knows? That all the bunk?"

Deke hesitated momentarily, then walked slowly toward the doorway. He stopped next to it, stiffly. Then he moved out.

Rich Miller's eyes stayed on Deke as his hand moved across the table. He lifted Deke's pistol from the table edge and swung it out the window and fired in the direction of the scaffolding.

A high-pitched, whining report answered the shot and hung longer in the air. Deke staggered, turning back into the room, and had time to look at the boy in wide-eyed amazement. Then he was dead.

The boy returned to the window after getting his carbine and, with his bandanna tied to the end of the barrel, waved it in a slow arc back and forth. Once they started up the slope he sat back in the chair and idly turned over his hole card, the ten.

The possemen were drawing closer, up to Ford Harlan's body now. He flipped Deke's hole card. It landed on top of the two queens. Three ladies.

He rose and moved to the doorway as he saw the men nearing the shelf, then glanced down at Deke and shook his head. I sure am crazy, he thought. I never heard before of a man cheating to lose.

He walked through the doorway with his hands above his head.

The Captives

I

H<small>E COULD HEAR</small> the stagecoach, the faraway creaking and the muffled rumble of it, and he was thinking: It's almost an hour early. Why should it be if it left Contention on schedule?

His name was Pat Brennan. He was lean and almost tall, with a deeply tanned, pleasant face beneath the straight hat brim low over his eyes, and he stood next to his saddle, which was on the ground, with the easy, hip-shot slouch of a rider. A Henry rifle was in his right hand and he was squinting into the sun glare, looking up the grade to the rutted road that came curving down through the spidery Joshua trees.

He lowered the Henry rifle, stock down, and let it fall across the saddle, and kept his hand away from the Colt holstered on his right leg. A man could get shot standing next to a stage road out in the middle of nowhere with a rifle in his hand.

Then, seeing the coach suddenly against the sky, billowing dust hanging over it, he felt relief and smiled to himself and raised his arm to wave as the coach passed through the Joshuas.

As the pounding wood, iron, and three-team racket of it came swaying toward him, he raised both arms and felt a sudden helplessness as he saw that the driver was making no effort to stop the teams. Brennan stepped back quickly, and the coach rushed past him, the driver, alone on the boot, bending forward and down to look at him.

Brennan cupped his hands and called, "*Rintoooon!*"

The driver leaned back with the reins high and through his fingers, his boot pushing against the brake lever, and his body half turned to look back over the top of the Concord. Brennan swung the saddle up over his shoulder and started after the coach as it ground to a stop.

He saw the company name, H<small>ATCH & HODGES</small>, and just below it, *Number 42* stenciled on the varnished door; then from a side window, he saw a man staring at him irritably as he approached. Behind the man he caught a glimpse of a woman with soft features and a small, plumed hat and eyes that looked away quickly as Brennan's gaze passed them going up to Ed Rintoon, the driver.

"Ed, for a minute I didn't think you were going to stop."

Rintoon, a leathery, beard-stubbled man in his mid-forties, stood with one knee on the seat and looked down at Brennan with only faint surprise.

"I took you for being up to no good, standing there waving your arms."

"I'm only looking for a lift a ways."

"What happened to you?"

Brennan grinned and his thumb pointed back vaguely over his shoulder. "I was visiting Tenvoorde to see about buying some yearling stock and I lost my horse to him on a bet."

"Driver!"

Brennan turned. The man who had been at the window was now leaning halfway out of the door and looking up at Rintoon.

"I'm not paying you to pass the time of day with"—he glanced at Brennan—"with everybody we meet."

Rintoon leaned over to look down at him. "Willard, you ain't even part right, since you ain't the man that pays me."

"I chartered this coach, and you along with it!" He was a young man, hatless, his long hair mussed from the wind. Strands of it hung over his ears, and his face was flushed as he glared at Rintoon. "When I pay for a coach I expect the service that goes with it."

Rintoon said, "Willard, you calm down now."

"Mr. Mims!"

Rintoon smiled faintly, glancing at Brennan. "Pat, I'd like you to meet Mr. Mims." He paused, adding, "He's a bookkeeper."

Brennan touched the brim of his hat toward the coach, seeing the woman again. She looked to be in her late twenties and her eyes now were wide and frightened and not looking at him.

His glance went to Willard Mims. Mims came out of the doorway and stood pointing a finger up at Rintoon.

"Brother, you're through! I swear to God this is your last run on any line in the Territory!"

Rintoon eased himself down until he was half sitting on the seat. "You wouldn't kid me."

"You'll see if I'm kidding!"

Rintoon shook his head. "After ten years of faithful service the boss will be sorry to see me go."

Willard Mims stared at him in silence. Then he said, his voice calmer, "You won't be so sure of yourself after we get to Bisbee."

Ignoring him, Rintoon turned to Brennan. "Swing that saddle up here."

"You hear what I said?" Willard Mims flared.

Reaching down for the saddle horn as Brennan lifted it, Rintoon answered, "You said I'd be sorry when we got to Bisbee."

"You remember that!"

"I sure will. Now you get back inside, Willard." He glanced at Brennan. "You get in there, too, Pat."

Willard Mims stiffened. "I'll remind you again—this is *not* the passenger coach."

Brennan was momentarily angry, but he saw the way Rintoon was taking this and he said calmly, "You want me to walk? It's only fifteen miles to Sasabe."

"I didn't say that," Mims answered, moving to the coach door. "If you want to come, get up on the boot." He turned to look at Brennan as he pulled himself up on the foot rung. "If we'd wanted company we'd have taken the scheduled run. That clear enough for you?"

Glancing at Rintoon, Brennan swung the Henry rifle up to him and said, "Yes, sir," not looking at Mims; and he winked at Rintoon as he climbed the wheel to the driver's seat.

A moment later they were moving, slowly at first, bumping and swaying; then the road seemed to become smoother as the teams pulled faster.

Brennan leaned toward Rintoon and said, in the noise, close to the driver's grizzled face, "I wondered why the regular stage would be almost an hour early, Ed, I'm obliged to you."

Rintoon glanced at him. "Thank Mr. Mims."

"Who is he, anyway?"

"Old man Gateway's son-in-law. Married the boss's daughter. Married into the biggest copper claim in the country."

"The girl with him his wife?"

"Doretta," Rintoon answered. "That's Gateway's daughter. She was scheduled to be an old maid till Willard come along and saved her from spinsterhood. She's plain as a 'dobe wall."

Brennan said, "But not too plain for Willard, eh?"

Rintoon gave him a side glance. "Patrick, there ain't nothing plain about old man Gateway's holdings. That's the thing. Four years ago he bought a half interest in the Montezuma Copper Mine for two hundred and fifty thousand dollars, and he's got it back triple since then. Can you imagine anyone having that much money?"

Brennan shook his head. "Where'd he get it, to start?"

"They say he come from money and made more by using the brains God gave him, investing it."

Brennan shook his head again. "That's too much money, Ed. Too much to have to worry about."

"Not for Willard, it ain't," Rintoon said. "He started out as a bookkeeper with the company. Now he's general manager—since the wedding. The old man picked Willard because he was the only one around he thought had any polish, and he knew if he waited much longer he'd have an old maid on his hands. And, Pat"—Rintoon leaned closer—"Willard don't talk to the old man like he does to other people."

"She didn't look so bad to me," Brennan said.

"You been down on Sasabe Creek too long," Rintoon glanced at him again. "What were you saying about losing your horse to Tenvoorde?"

"Oh, I went to see him about buying some yearlings—"

"On credit," Rintoon said.

Brennan nodded. "Though I was going to pay him some of it cash. I told him to name a fair interest rate and he'd have it in two years. But he said no. Cash on the line. No cash, no yearlings. I needed three hundred to make the deal, but I only had fifty. Then when I was going he said, 'Patrick'—you know how he talks—'I'll give you a chance to get your yearlings free,' and all the time he's eyeing this claybank mare I had along. He said, 'You bet your mare and your fifty dollars cash, I'll put up what yearlings you need, and we'll race your mare against one of my string for the winner.'"

Ed Rintoon said, "And you lost."

"By a country mile."

"Pat, that don't sound like you. Why didn't you take what your fifty would buy and get on home?"

"Because I needed these yearlings plus a good seed bull. I could've bought the bull, but I wouldn't have had the yearlings to build on. That's what I told Mr. Tenvoorde. I said, 'This deal's as good as the stock you're selling me. If you're taking that kind of money for a seed bull and yearlings, then you know they can produce. You're sure of getting your money.'"

"You got stock down on your Sasabe place," Rintoon said.

"Not like you think. They wintered poorly and I got a lot of building to do."

"Who's tending your herd now?"

"I still got those two Mexican boys."

"You should've known better than to go to Tenvoorde."

"I didn't have a chance. He's the only man close enough with the stock I want."

"But a bet like that—how could you fall into it? You know he'd have a pony to outstrip yours."

"Well, that was the chance I had to take."

They rode along in silence for a few minutes before Brennan asked, "Where they coming from?"

Rintoon grinned at him. "Their honeymoon. Willard made the agent put on a special run just for the two of them. Made a big fuss while Doretta tried to hide her head."

"Then"—Brennan grinned—"I'm obliged to Mr. Mims, else I'd still be waiting back there with my saddle and my Henry."

Later on, topping a rise that was thick with jack pine, they were suddenly in view of the Sasabe station and the creek beyond it, as they came out of the trees and started down the mesquite-dotted sweep of the hillside.

Rintoon checked his timepiece. The regular run was due here at five o'clock. He was surprised to see that it was only ten minutes after four. He remembered then, his mind picturing Willard Mims as he chartered the special coach.

Brennan said, "I'm getting off here at Sasabe."

"How'll you get over to your place?"

"Hank'll lend me a horse."

As they drew nearer, Rintoon was squinting, studying the

three adobe houses and the corral in back. "I don't see any-body," he said. "Hank's usually out in the yard. Him or his boy."

Brennan said, "They don't expect you for an hour. That's it."

"Man, we make enough noise for somebody to come out."

Rintoon swung the teams toward the adobes, slowing them as Brennan pushed his boot against the brake lever, and they came to a stop exactly even with the front of the main adobe.

"Hank!"

Rintoon looked from the door of the adobe out over the yard. He called the name again, but there was no answer. He frowned. "The damn place sounds deserted," he said.

Brennan saw the driver's eyes drop to the sawed-off shotgun and Brennan's Henry on the floor of the boot, and then he was looking over the yard again.

"Where in hell would Hank've gone to?"

A sound came from the adobe. A boot scraping—that or something like it—and the next moment a man was standing in the open doorway. He was bearded, a dark beard faintly streaked with gray and in need of a trim. He was watching them calmly, almost indifferently, and leveling a Colt at them at the same time.

He moved out into the yard and now another man, armed with a shotgun, came out of the adobe. The bearded one held his gun on the door of the coach. The shotgun was leveled at Brennan and Rintoon.

"You-all drop your guns and come on down." He wore range clothes, soiled and sun bleached, and he held the shot-gun calmly as if doing this was not something new. He was younger than the bearded one by at least ten years.

Brennan raised his revolver from its holster and the one with the shotgun said, "Gently, now," and grinned as Brennan dropped it over the wheel.

Rintoon, not wearing a handgun, had not moved.

"If you got something down in that boot," the one with the shotgun said to him, "haul it out."

Rintoon muttered something under his breath. He reached down and took hold of Brennan's Henry rifle lying next to the sawed-off shotgun, his finger slipping through the trigger guard. He came up with it hesitantly, and Brennan whispered, barely moving his lips, "Don't be crazy."

Standing up, turning, Rintoon hesitated again, then let the rifle fall. "That all you got?"

Rintoon nodded. "That's all."

"Then come on down."

Rintoon turned his back. He bent over to climb down, his foot reaching for the wheel below, and his hand closed on the sawed-off shotgun. Brennan whispered, "Don't do it!"

Rintoon mumbled something that came out as a growl. Brennan leaned toward him as if to give him a hand down. "You got two shots. What if there're more than two of them?"

Rintoon grunted, "Look out, Pat!" His hand gripped the shotgun firmly.

Then he was turning, jumping from the wheel, the stubby scattergun flashing head-high—and at the same moment a single revolver shot blasted the stillness. Brennan saw Rintoon crumple to the ground, the shotgun falling next to him, and he was suddenly aware of powder smoke and a man framed in the window of the adobe.

The one with the shotgun said, "Well, that just saves some time," and he glanced around as the third man came out of the adobe. "Chink, I swear you hit him in midair."

"I was waiting for that old man to pull something," said the one called Chink. He wore two low-slung, crossed cartridge belts and his second Colt was still in its holster.

Brennan jumped down and rolled Rintoon over gently, holding his head off the ground. He looked at the motionless form and then at Chink. "He's dead."

Chink stood with his legs apart and looked down at Brennan indifferently. "Sure he is."

"You didn't have to kill him."

Chink shrugged. "I would've, sooner or later."

"Why?"

"That's the way it is."

The man with the beard had not moved. He said now, quietly, "Chink, you shut your mouth." Then he glanced at the man with the shotgun and said, in the same tone, "Billy-Jack, get them out of there," and nodded toward the coach.

2

Kneeling next to Rintoon, Brennan studied them. He watched Billy-Jack open the coach door, saw his mouth soften to a grin as Doretta Mims came out first. Her eyes went to Rintoon, but shifted away quickly. Willard Mims hesitated, then stepped down, stumbling in his haste as Billy-Jack pointed the shotgun at him. He stood next to his wife and stared unblinkingly at Rintoon's body.

That one, Brennan was thinking, looking at the man with the beard—that's the one to watch. He's calling it, and he doesn't look as though he gets excited. . . . And the one called Chink. . . .

Brennan's eyes went to him. He was standing hip-cocked, his hat on the back of his head and the drawstring from it pulled tight beneath his lower lip, his free hand fingering the string idly, the other hand holding the long-barreled .44 Colt, pointed down but cocked.

He wants somebody to try something, Brennan thought. He's itching for it. He wears two guns and he thinks he's good. Well, maybe he is. But he's young, the youngest of the three, and he's anxious. His gaze stayed on Chink and it went through his mind: Don't even reach for a cigarette when he's around.

The one with the beard said, "Billy-Jack, get up on top of the coach."

Brennan's eyes raised, watching the man step from the wheel hub to the boot and then kneel on the driver's seat. He's number-three man, Brennan thought. He keeps looking at the woman. But don't bet him short. He carries a big-gauge gun.

"Frank, there ain't nothing up here but an old saddle."

The one with the beard—Frank Usher—raised his eyes. "Look under it."

"Ain't nothing there either."

Usher's eyes went to Willard Mims, then swung slowly to Brennan. "Where's the mail?"

"I wouldn't know," Brennan said.

Frank Usher looked at Willard Mims again. "You tell me."

"This isn't the stage," Willard Mims said hesitantly. His

face relaxed then, almost to the point of smiling. "You made a mistake. The regular stage isn't due for almost an hour." He went on, excitement rising in his voice, "That's what you want, the stage that's due here at five. This is one I chartered." He smiled now. "See, me and my wife are just coming back from a honeymoon and, you know—"

Frank Usher looked at Brennan. "Is that right?"

"Of course it is!" Mims's voice rose. "Go in and check the schedule."

"I'm asking this man."

Brennan shrugged. "I wouldn't know."

"He don't know anything," Chink said.

Billy-Jack came down off the coach and Usher said to him, "Go in and look for a schedule." He nodded toward Doretta Mims. "Take that woman with you. Have her put some coffee on, and something to eat."

Brennan said, "What did you do with Hank?"

Frank Usher's dull eyes moved to Brennan. "Who's he?"

"The station man here."

Chink grinned and waved his revolver, pointing it off beyond the main adobe. "He's over yonder in the well."

Usher said, "Does that answer it?"

"What about his boy?"

"He's with him," Usher said. "Anything else?"

Brennan shook his head slowly. "That's enough." He knew they were both dead and suddenly he was very much afraid of this dull-eyed, soft-voiced man with the beard; it took an effort to keep himself calm. He watched Billy-Jack take Doretta by the arm. She looked imploringly at her husband, holding back, but he made no move to help her. Billy-Jack jerked her arm roughly and she went with him.

Willard Mims said, "He'll find the schedule. Like I said, it's due at five o'clock. I can see how you made the mistake"—Willard was smiling—"thinking we were the regular stage. Hell, we were just going home . . . down to Bisbee. You'll see, five o'clock sharp that regular passenger-mail run'll pull in."

"He's a talker," Chink said.

Billy-Jack appeared in the doorway of the adobe. "Frank, five o'clock, sure as hell!" He waved a sheet of yellow paper.

"See!" Willard Mims was grinning excitedly. "Listen, you let us go and we'll be on our way"—his voice rose—"and I swear to God we'll never breathe we saw a thing."

Chink shook his head. "He's somethin'."

"Listen, I swear to God we won't tell *anything*!"

"I know you won't," Frank Usher said. He looked at Brennan and nodded toward Mims. "Where'd you find him?"

"We just met."

"Do you go along with what he's saying?"

"If I said yes," Brennan answered, "you wouldn't believe me. And you'd be right."

A smile almost touched Frank Usher's mouth. "Dumb even talking about it, isn't it?"

"I guess it is," Brennan said.

"You know what's going to happen to you?" Usher asked him tonelessly.

Brennan nodded, without answering.

Frank Usher studied him in silence. Then, "Are you scared?"

Brennan nodded again. "Sure I am."

"You're honest about it. I'll say that for you."

"I don't know of a better time to be honest," Brennan said.

Chink said, "That damn well's going to be chock full."

Willard Mims had listened with disbelief, his eyes wide. Now he said hurriedly, "Wait a minute! What're you listening to him for? I told you, I swear to God I won't say one word about this. If you don't trust him, then keep him here! I don't know this man. I'm not speaking for him, anyway."

"I'd be inclined to trust him before I would you," Frank Usher said.

"He's got nothing to do with it! We picked him up out on the desert!"

Chink raised his .44 waist high, looking at Willard Mims, and said, "Start running for that well and see if you can make it."

"Man, be reasonable!"

Frank Usher shook his head. "You aren't leaving, and you're not going to be standing here when that stage pulls in. You can scream and carry on, but that's the way it is."

"What about my wife?"

"I can't help her being a woman."

Willard Mims was about to say something, but stopped. His

eyes went to the adobe, then back to Usher. He lowered his voice and all the excitement was gone from it. "You know who she is?" He moved closer to Usher. "She's the daughter of old man Gateway, who happens to own part of the third richest copper mine in Arizona. You know what that amounts to? To date, three quarters of a million dollars." He said this slowly, looking straight at Frank Usher.

"Make a point out of it," Usher said.

"Man, it's practically staring you right in the face! You got the daughter of a man who's practically a millionaire. His only daughter! What do you think he'll pay to get her back?"

Frank Usher said, "I don't know. What?"

"Whatever you ask! You sit here waiting for a two-bit holdup and you got a gold mine right in your hands!"

"How do I know she's his daughter?"

Willard Mims looked at Brennan. "You were talking to that driver. Didn't he tell you?"

Brennan hesitated. If the man wanted to bargain with his wife, that was his business. It would give them time; that was the main thing. Brennan nodded. "That's right. His wife is Doretta Gateway."

"Where do you come in?" Usher asked Willard Mims.

"I'm Mr. Gateway's general manager on the Montezuma operation."

Frank Usher was silent now, staring at Mims. Finally he said, "I suppose you'd be willing to ride in with a note."

"Certainly," Mims quickly replied.

"And we'd never see you again."

"Would I save my own skin and leave my wife here?"

Usher nodded. "I believe you would."

"Then there's no use talking about it." Mims shrugged and, watching him, Brennan knew he was acting, taking a long chance.

"We can talk about it," Frank Usher said, "because if we do it, we do it my way." He glanced at the house. "Billy-Jack!" Then to Brennan, "You and him go sit over against the wall."

Billy-Jack came out, and from the wall of the adobe Brennan and Willard watched the three outlaws. They stood in close, and Frank Usher was doing the talking. After a few minutes Billy-Jack went into the adobe again and came out with the yellow stage schedule and an envelope. Usher took them and, against the door of the Concord, wrote something on the back of the schedule.

He came toward them folding the paper into the envelope. He sealed the envelope and handed it with the pencil to Willard Mims. "You put Gateway's name on it and where to find him. Mark it personal and urgent."

Willard Mims said, "I can see him myself and tell him."

"You will," Frank Usher said, "but not how you think. You're going to stop on the main road one mile before you get to Bisbee and give that envelope to somebody passing in. The note tells Gateway you have something to tell him about his daughter and to come alone. When he goes out, you'll tell him the story. If he says no, then he never sees his daughter again. If he says yes, he's to bring fifty thousand in U.S. scrip divided in three saddlebags, to a place up back of the Sasabe. And he brings it alone."

Mims said, "What if there isn't that much cash on hand?"

"That's his problem."

"Well, why can't I go right to his house and tell him?"

"Because Billy-Jack's going to be along to bring you back after you tell him. And I don't want him someplace he can get cornered."

"Oh. . . ."

"That's whether he says yes or no," Frank Usher added.

Mims was silent for a moment. "But how'll Mr. Gateway know where to come?"

"If he agrees, Billy-Jack'll give him directions."

Mims said, "Then when he comes out you'll let us go? Is that it?"

"That's it."

"When do we leave?"

"Right this minute."

"Can I say good-bye to my wife?"

"We'll do it for you."

Brennan watched Billy-Jack come around from the corral, leading two horses. Willard Mims moved toward one of them and they both mounted. Billy-Jack reined his horse suddenly, crowding Mims to turn with him, then slapped Mims's horse on the rump and spurred after it as the horse broke to a run.

Watching them, his eyes half closed, Frank Usher said, "That boy puts his wife up on the stake and then he wants to kiss her good-bye." He glanced at Brennan. "You figure that one for me."

Brennan shook his head. "What I'd like to know is why you only asked for fifty thousand."

Frank Usher shrugged. "I'm not greedy."

3

Chink turned as the two horses splashed over the creek and grew gradually smaller down the road. He looked at Brennan and then his eyes went to Frank Usher. "We don't have a need for this one, Frank."

Usher's dull eyes flicked toward him. "You bring around the horses and I'll worry about him."

"We might as well do it now as later," Chink said.

"We're taking him with us."

"What for?"

"Because I say so. That reason enough?"

"Frank, we could run him for the well and both take a crack at him."

"Get the horses," Frank Usher said flatly, and stared at Chink until the gunman turned and walked away.

Brennan said, "I'd like to bury this man before we go."

Usher shook his head. "Put him in the well."

"That's no fit place!"

Usher stared at Brennan for a long moment. "Don't push your luck. He goes in the well, whether you do it or Chink does."

Brennan pulled Rintoon's limp body up over his shoulder and carried him across the yard. When he returned, Chink was coming around the adobe with three horses already saddled. Frank Usher stood near the house and now Doretta Mims appeared in the doorway.

Usher looked at her. "You'll have to fork one of these like the rest of us. There ain't no lady's saddle about."

She came out, neither answering nor looking at him.

Usher called to Brennan, "Cut one out of that team and shoot the rest," nodding to the stagecoach.

Minutes later the Sasabe station was deserted.

They followed the creek west for almost an hour before swinging south toward high country. Leaving the creek, Brennan had thought: Five more miles and I'm home. And his eyes hung on the long shallow cup of the Sasabe valley until they entered a trough that climbed winding ahead of them through the hills, and the valley was no longer in view.

Frank Usher led them single file—Doretta Mims, followed by Brennan, and Chink bringing up the rear. Chink rode slouched, swaying with the movement of his dun mare, chewing idly on the drawstring of his hat, and watching Brennan.

Brennan kept his eyes on the woman much of the time. For almost a mile, as they rode along the creek, he had watched her body shaking silently and he knew that she was crying. She had very nearly cried mounting the horse—pulling her skirts down almost desperately, then sitting, holding on to the saddle horn with both hands, biting her lower lip and not looking at them. Chink had sidestepped his dun close to her and said something, and she had turned her head quickly as the color rose from her throat over her face.

They dipped down into a barranca thick with willow and cottonwood and followed another stream that finally disappeared into the rocks at the far end. And after that they began to climb again. For some time they rode through the soft gloom of timber, following switchbacks as the slope became steeper, then came out into the open and crossed a bare gravelly slope, the sandstone peaks above them cold pink in the fading sunlight.

They were nearing the other side of the open grade when Frank Usher said, "Here we are."

Brennan looked beyond him and now he could make out, through the pines they were approaching, a weather-scarred stone-and-log hut built snugly against the steep wall of sandstone. Against one side of the hut· was a hide-covered lean-to. He heard Frank Usher say, "Chink, you get the man making a fire and I'll get the woman fixing supper."

There had not been time to eat what the woman had prepared at the stage station and now Frank Usher and Chink ate hungrily, hunkered down a dozen yards out from the lean-to where Brennan and the woman stood.

Brennan took a plate of the jerky and day-old pan bread, but Doretta Mims did not touch the food. She stood next to him, half turned from him, and continued to stare through the trees across the bare slope in the direction they had come. Once Brennan said to her, "You better eat something," but she did not answer him.

When they were finished, Frank Usher ordered them into the hut.

"You stay there the night . . . and if either of you comes near the door, we'll let go, no questions asked. That plain?"

The woman went in hurriedly. When Brennan entered he saw her huddled against the back wall near a corner.

The sod-covered hut was windowless, and he could barely make her out in the dimness. He wanted to go and sit next to her, but it went through his mind that most likely she was as afraid of him as she was of Frank Usher and Chink. So he made room for himself against the wall where they had placed the saddles, folding a saddle blanket to rest his elbow on as he eased himself to the dirt floor. Let her try and get hold of herself, he thought; then maybe she will want somebody to talk to.

He made a cigarette and lit it, seeing the mask of her face briefly as the match flared, then he eased himself lower until his head was resting against a saddle, and smoked in the dim silence.

Soon the hut was full dark. Now he could not see the woman, though he imagined that he could feel her presence. Outside, Usher and Chink had added wood to the cook fire in front of the lean-to and the warm glow of it illuminated the doorless opening of the hut.

They'll sit by the fire, Brennan thought, and one of them will always be awake. You'd get about one step through that door and *bam*. Maybe Frank would aim low, but Chink would shoot to kill. He became angry thinking of Chink, but there was nothing he could do about it and he drew on the cigarette slowly to make himself relax, thinking: Take it easy: you've got the woman to consider. He thought of her as his responsibility and not even a doubt entered his mind that she was not. She was a woman, alone. The reason was as simple as that.

He heard her move as he was snubbing out the cigarette. He

lay still and he knew that she was coming toward him. She knelt as she reached his side.

"Do you know what they've done with my husband?"

He could picture her drawn face, eyes staring wide open in the darkness. He raised himself slowly and felt her stiffen as he touched her arm. "Sit down here and you'll be more comfortable." He moved over to let her sit on the saddle blanket. "Your husband's all right," he said.

"Where is he?"

"They didn't tell you?"

"No."

Brennan paused. "One of them took him to Bisbee to see your father."

"My father?"

"To ask him to pay to get you back."

"Then my husband's all right." She was relieved, and it was in the sound of her voice.

Brennan said, after a moment, "Why don't you go to sleep now? You can rest back on one of these saddles."

"I'm not tired."

"Well, you will be if you don't get some sleep."

She said then, "They must have known all the time that we were coming."

Brennan said nothing.

"Didn't they?"

"I don't know, ma'am."

"How else would they know about . . . who my father is?"

"Maybe so."

"One of them must have been in Contention and heard my husband charter the coach. Perhaps he had visited Bisbee and knew that my father . . ." Her voice trailed off because she was speaking more to herself than to Brennan.

After a pause Brennan said, "You sound like you feel a little better."

He heard her exhale slowly and he could imagine she was trying to smile.

"Yes, I believe I do now," she replied.

"Your husband will be back sometime tomorrow morning," Brennan said to her.

She touched his arm lightly. "I *do* feel better, Mr. Brennan."

He was surprised that she remembered his name. Rintoon had mentioned it only once, hours before. "I'm glad you do. Now, why don't you try to sleep?"

She eased back gently until she was lying down and for a few minutes there was silence.

"Mr. Brennan?"

"Yes, ma'am."

"I'm terribly sorry about your friend."

"Who?"

"The driver."

"Oh. Thank you."

"I'll remember him in my prayers," she said, and after this she did not speak again.

Brennan smoked another cigarette, then sat unmoving for what he judged to be at least a half hour, until he was sure Doretta Mims was asleep.

Now he crawled across the dirt floor to the opposite wall. He went down on his stomach and edged toward the door, keeping close to the wall. Pressing his face close to the opening, he could see, off to the right side, the fire, dying down now. The shape of a man wrapped in a blanket was lying full length on the other side of it.

Brennan rose slowly, hugging the wall. He inched his head out to see the side of the fire closest to the lean-to, and as he did he heard the unmistakable click of a revolver being cocked. Abruptly he brought his head in and went back to the saddle next to Doretta Mims.

4

In the morning they brought Doretta Mims out to cook; then sent her back to the hut while they ate. When they had finished they let Brennan and Doretta come out to the lean-to.

Frank Usher said, "That wasn't a head I seen pokin' out the door last night, was it?"

"If it was," Brennan answered, "why didn't you shoot at it?"

"I about did. Lucky thing it disappeared," Usher said. "Whatever it was." And he walked away, through the trees to where the horses were picketed.

Chink sat down on a stump and began making a cigarette.

A few steps from Doretta Mims, Brennan leaned against the hut and began eating. He could see her profile as she turned her head to look out through the trees and across the open slope.

Maybe she *is* a little plain, he thought. Her nose doesn't have the kind of a clean-cut shape that stays in your mind. And her hair—if she didn't have it pulled back so tight she'd look a little younger, and happier. She could do something with her hair. She could do something with her clothes, too, to let you know she's a woman.

He felt sorry for her, seeing her biting her lower lip, still staring off through the trees. And for a reason he did not understand, though he knew it had nothing to do with sympathy, he felt very close to her, as if he had known her for a long time, as if he could look into her eyes—not just now, but anytime—and know what she was thinking. He realized that it was sympathy, in a sense, but not the feeling-sorry kind. He could picture her as a little girl, and self-consciously growing up, and he could imagine vaguely what her father was like. And now—a sensitive girl, afraid of saying the wrong thing; afraid of speaking out of turn even if it meant wondering about instead of knowing what had happened to her husband. Afraid of sounding silly, while men like her husband talked and talked and said nothing. But even having to listen to him, she would not speak against him, because he was her husband.

That's the kind of woman to have, Brennan thought. One that'll stick by you, no matter what. And, he thought, still looking at her, one that's got some insides to her. Not just all on the surface. Probably you would have to lose a woman like that to really appreciate her.

"Mrs. Mims."

She looked at him, her eyes still bearing the anxiety of watching through the trees.

"He'll come, Mrs. Mims. Pretty soon now."

Frank Usher returned and motioned them into the hut again. He talked to Chink for a few minutes and now the gunman walked off through the trees.

Looking out from the doorway of the hut, Brennan said over his shoulder, "One of them's going out now to watch for your husband." He glanced around at Doretta Mims and she answered him with a hesitant smile.

Frank Usher was standing by the lean-to when Chink came back through the trees some time later. He walked out to meet him.

"They coming?"

Chink nodded. "Starting across the slope."

Minutes later two horses came into view crossing the grade. As they came through the trees, Frank Usher called, "Tie up in the shade there!" He and Chink watched the two men dismount, then come across the clearing toward them.

"It's all set!" Willard Mims called.

Frank Usher waited until they reached him. "What'd he say?"

"He said he'd bring the money."

"That right, Billy-Jack?"

Billy-Jack nodded. "That's what he said." He was carrying Rintoon's sawed-off shotgun.

"You didn't suspect any funny business?"

Billy-Jack shook his head.

Usher fingered his beard gently, holding Mims with his gaze. "He can scare up that much money?"

"He said he could, though it will take most of today to do it."

"That means he'll come out tomorrow," Usher said.

Willard Mims nodded. "That's right."

Usher's eyes went to Billy-Jack. "You gave him directions?"

"Like you said, right to the mouth of that barranca, chock full of willow. Then one of us brings him in from there."

"You're sure he can find it?"

"I made him say it twice," Billy-Jack said. "Every turn."

Usher looked at Willard Mims again. "How'd he take it?"

"How do you think he took it?"

Usher was silent, staring at Mims. Then he began to stroke his beard again. "I'm asking you," he said.

Mims shrugged. "Of course, he was mad, but there wasn't anything he could do about it. He's a reasonable man."

Billy-Jack was grinning. "Frank, this time tomorrow we're sitting on top of the world."

Willard Mims nodded. "I think you made yourself a pretty good deal."

Frank Usher's eyes had not left Mims. "You want to stay here or go on back?"

"What?"

"You heard what I said."

"You mean you'd let me go . . . now?"

"We don't need you anymore."

Willard Mims's eyes flicked to the hut, then back to Frank Usher. He said, almost too eagerly, "I could go back now and lead old man Gateway out here in the morning."

"Sure you could," Usher said.

"Listen, I'd rather stay with my wife, but if it means getting the old man out here faster, then I think I better go back."

Usher nodded. "I know what you mean."

"You played square with me. By God, I'll play square with you."

Mims started to turn away.

Usher said, "Don't you want to see your wife first?"

Mims hesitated. "Well, the quicker I start traveling, the better. She'll understand."

"We'll see you tomorrow then, huh?"

Mims smiled. "About the same time." He hesitated. "All right to get going now?"

"Sure."

Mims backed away a few steps, still smiling, then turned and started to walk toward the trees. He looked back once and waved.

Frank Usher watched him, his eyes half closed in the sunlight. When Mims was almost to the trees, Usher said, quietly, "Chink, bust him."

Chink fired, the .44 held halfway between waist and shoulders, the long barrel raising slightly as he fired again and again until Mims went down, lying still as the heavy reports faded into dead silence.

5

Frank Usher waited as Billy-Jack stooped next to Mims. He saw Billy-Jack look up, nodding his head.

"Get rid of him," Usher said, watching now as Billy-Jack dragged Mims's body through the trees to the slope and there let go of it. The lifeless body slid down the grade, raising dust, until it disappeared into the brush far below.

Frank Usher turned and walked back to the hut.

Brennan stepped aside as he reached the low doorway. Usher saw the woman on the floor, her face buried in the crook of her arm resting on one of the saddles, her shoulders moving convulsively as she sobbed.

"What's the matter with her?" he asked.

Brennan said nothing.

"I thought we were doing her a favor," Usher said. He walked over to her, his hand covering the butt of his revolver, and touched her arm with his booted toe. "Woman, don't you realize what you just got out of?"

"She didn't know he did it," Brennan said quietly.

Usher looked at him, momentarily surprised. "No, I don't guess she would, come to think of it." He looked down at Doretta Mims and nudged her again with his boot. "Didn't you know that boy was selling you? This whole idea was his, to save his own skin." Usher paused. "He was ready to leave you again just now . . . when I got awful sick of him way down deep inside."

Doretta Mims was not sobbing now, but still she did not raise her head.

Usher stared down at her. "That was some boy you were married to, would do a thing like that."

Looking from the woman to Frank Usher, Brennan said, almost angrily, "What he did was wrong, but going along with it and then shooting him was all right?"

Usher glanced sharply at Brennan. "If you can't see a difference, I'm not going to explain it to you." He turned and walked out.

Brennan stood looking down at the woman for a few moments, then went over to the door and sat down on the floor just inside it. After a while he could hear Doretta Mims crying again. And for a long time he sat listening to her muffled sobs as he looked out at the sunlit clearing, now and again seeing one of the three outlaws.

He judged it to be about noon when Frank Usher and Billy-Jack rode out, walking their horses across the clearing, then into the trees, with Chink standing looking after them.

They're getting restless, Brennan thought. If they're going to stay here until tomorrow, they've got to be sure nobody's followed their sign. But it would take the best San Carlos tracker to pick up what little sign we made from Sasabe.

He saw Chink walking leisurely back to the lean-to. Chink looked toward the hut and stopped. He stood hip-cocked, with his thumbs in his crossed gun belts.

"How many did that make?" Brennan asked.

"What?" Chink straightened slightly.

Brennan nodded to where Mims had been shot. "This morning."

"That was the seventh," Chink said.

"Were they all like that?" he asked.

"How do you mean?"

"In the back."

"I'll tell you this: Yours will be from the front."

"When?"

"Tomorrow before we leave. You can count on it."

"If your boss gives you the word."

"Don't worry about that," Chink said. Then, "You could make a run for it right now. It wouldn't be like just standing up gettin' it."

"I'll wait till tomorrow," Brennan said.

Chink shrugged and walked away.

After a few minutes Brennan realized that the hut was quiet. He turned to look at Doretta Mims. She was sitting up, staring at the opposite wall with a dazed expression.

Brennan moved to her side and sat down again. "Mrs. Mims, I'm sorry—"

"Why didn't you tell me it was his plan?"

"It wouldn't have helped anything."

She looked at Brennan now pleadingly. "He could have been doing it for all of us."

Brennan nodded. "Sure he could."

"But you don't believe that, do you?"

Brennan looked at her closely, at her eyes puffed from crying. "Mrs. Mims, you know your husband better than I did."

Her eyes lowered and she said quietly, "I feel very foolish sitting here. Terrible things have happened in these two days, yet all I can think of is myself. All I can do is look at myself and feel very foolish." Her eyes raised to his. "Do you know why, Mr. Brennan? Because I know now that my husband never cared for me; because I know that he married me for his own interest." She paused. "I saw an innocent man killed yesterday and I can't even find the decency within me to pray for him."

"Mrs. Mims, try and rest now."

She shook her head wearily. "I don't care what happens to me."

There was a silence before Brennan said, "When you get done feeling sorry for yourself I'll tell you something."

Her eyes came open and she looked at him, more surprised than hurt.

"Look," Brennan said. "You know it and I know it—your husband married you for your money; but you're alive and he's dead and that makes the difference. You can moon about being a fool till they shoot you tomorrow, or you can start thinking about saving your skin right now. But I'll tell you this—it will take both of us working together to stay alive."

"But he said he'd let us—"

"You think they're going to let us go after your dad brings the money? They've killed four people in less than twenty-four hours!"

"I don't care what happens to me!"

He took her shoulders and turned her toward him. "Well, I care about me, and I'm not going to get shot in the belly tomorrow because you feel sorry for yourself."

"But I can't help!" Doretta pleaded.

"You don't know if you can or not. We've got to keep our eyes open and we've got to think, and when the chance comes we've got to take it quick or else forget about it." His face was close to hers and he was still gripping her shoulders. "These men will kill. They've done it before and they have nothing to lose. They're going to kill us. That means we've got nothing to lose. Now, you think about that a while."

He left her and went back to the door.

Brennan was called out of the hut later in the afternoon, as Usher and Billy-Jack rode in. They had shot a mule deer and Billy-Jack carried a hindquarter dangling from his saddle horn. Brennan was told to dress it down, enough for supper, and the rest to be stripped and hung up to dry.

"But you take care of the supper first," Frank Usher said, adding that the woman wasn't in fit condition for cooking. "I don't want burned meat just 'cause she's in a state over her husband."

After they had eaten, Brennan took meat and coffee in to Doretta Mims.

She looked up as he offered it to her. "I don't care for anything."

He was momentarily angry, but it passed off and he said, "Suit yourself." He placed the cup and plate on the floor and went outside to finish preparing the jerky.

By the time he finished, dusk had settled over the clearing and the inside of the hut was dark as he stepped inside.

He moved to her side and his foot kicked over the tin cup. He stooped quickly, picking up the cup and plate, and even in the dimness he could see that she had eaten most of the food.

"Mr. Brennan, I'm sorry for the way I've acted." She hesitated. "I thought you would understand, else I'd never have told you about—about how I felt."

"It's not a question of my understanding," Brennan said.

"I'm sorry I told you," Doretta Mims said.

He moved closer to her and knelt down, sitting back on his heels. "Look. Maybe I know how you feel, better than you think. But that's not important. Right now you don't need sympathy as much as you need a way to stay alive."

"I can't help the way I feel," she said obstinately.

Brennan was momentarily silent. He said then, "Did you love him?"

"I was married to him!"

"That's not what I asked you. While everybody's being honest, just tell me if you loved him."

She hesitated, looking down at her hands. "I'm not sure."

"But you wanted to be in love with him, more than anything."

Her head nodded slowly. "Yes."

"Did you ever think for a minute that he loved you?"

"That's not a fair question!"

"Answer it anyway!"

She hesitated again. "No, I didn't."

He said, almost brutally, "Then what have you lost outside of a little pride?"

"You don't understand," she said.

"You're afraid you can't get another man—is that what it is? Even if he married you for money, at least he married you. He was the first and last chance as far as you were concerned, so you grabbed him."

"What are you trying to do, strip me of what little self-respect I have left?"

"I'm trying to strip you of this foolishness! You think you're too plain to get a man?"

She bit her lower lip and looked away from him.

"You think nobody'll have you because you bite your lip and can't say more than two words at a time?"

"Mr. Brennan—"

"Listen, you're as much woman as any of them. A hell of a lot more than some, but you've got to realize it! You've got to do something about it!"

"I can't help it if—"

"Shut up with that I-can't-help-it talk! If you can't help it, nobody can. All your life you've been sitting around waiting for something to happen to you. Sometimes you have to walk up and take what you want."

Suddenly he brought her to him, his arms circling her shoulders, and he kissed her, holding his lips to hers until he felt her body relax slowly and at the same time he knew that she was kissing him.

His lips brushed her cheek and he said, close to her, "We're going to stay alive. You're going to do exactly what I say when the time comes, and we're going to get out of here." Her hair brushed his cheek softly and he knew that she was nodding yes.

6

During the night he opened his eyes and crawled to the lighter silhouette of the doorway. Keeping close to the front wall, he looked out and across to the low-burning fire. One of them, a shadowy form that he could not recognize, sat facing the hut. He did not move, but by the way he was sitting Brennan knew he was awake. You're running out of time, Brennan thought. But there was nothing he could do.

The sun was not yet above the trees when Frank Usher appeared in the doorway. He saw that Brennan was awake and he said, "Bring the woman out," turning away as he said it.

Her eyes were closed, but they opened as Brennan touched her shoulder, and he knew that she had not been asleep. She looked up at him calmly, her features softly shadowed.

"Stay close to me," he said. "Whatever we do, stay close to me."

They went out to the lean-to and Brennan built the fire as Doretta got the coffee and venison ready to put on.

Brennan moved slowly, as if he were tired, as if he had given up hope; but his eyes were alive and most of the time his gaze stayed with the three men—watching them eat, watching them make cigarettes as they squatted in a half circle, talking, but too far away for their voices to be heard. Finally, Chink rose and went off into the trees. He came back with his horse, mounted, and rode off into the trees again but in the other direction, toward the open grade.

It went through Brennan's mind: He's going off like he did yesterday morning, but this time to wait for Gateway. Yesterday on foot, but today on his horse, which means he's going farther down to wait for him. And Frank went somewhere yesterday morning. Frank went over to where the horses are. He suddenly felt an excitement inside of him, deep within his stomach, and he kept his eyes on Frank Usher.

A moment later Usher stood up and started off toward the trees, calling back something to Billy-Jack about the horses— and Brennan could hardly believe his eyes.

Now. It's now. You know that, don't you? It's now or never. God help me. God help me think of something! And suddenly it was in his mind. It was less than half a chance, but it was something, and it came to him because it was the only thing about Billy-Jack that stood out in his mind, besides the shotgun. *He was always looking at Doretta!*

She was in front of the lean-to, and he moved toward her, turning his back to Billy-Jack sitting with Rintoon's shotgun across his lap.

"Go in the hut and start unbuttoning your dress." He half whispered it and saw her eyes widen as he said it. "Go on! Billy-Jack will come in. Act surprised. Embarrassed. Then smile at him." She hesitated, starting to bite her lip. "Damn it, go on!"

He poured himself a cup of coffee, not looking at her as she walked away. Putting the coffee down, he saw Billy-Jack's eyes following her.

"Want a cup?" Brennan called to him. "There's about one left."

Billy-Jack shook his head and turned the sawed-off shotgun on Brennan as he saw him approaching.

Brennan took a sip of the coffee. "Aren't you going to look in on that?" He nodded toward the hut.

"What do you mean?"

"The woman," Brennan said matter-of-factly. He took another sip of the coffee.

"What about her?" Billy-Jack asked.

Brennan shrugged. "I thought you were taking turns."

"What?"

"Now, look, you can't be so young, I got to draw you a map—" Brennan smiled. "Oh, I see. . . . Frank didn't say anything to you. Or Chink. . . . Keeping her for themselves. . . ."

Billy-Jack's eyes flicked to the hut, then back to Brennan. "They were with her?"

"Well, all I know is Frank went in there yesterday morning and Chink yesterday afternoon while you were gone." He took another sip of the coffee and threw out what was left in the cup. Turning, he said, "No skin off my nose," and walked slowly back to the lean-to.

He began scraping the tin plates, his head down, but watching Billy-Jack. Let it sink through that thick skull of yours. But do it quick! Come on, move, you animal!

There! He watched Billy-Jack walk slowly toward the hut. God, make him move faster! Billy-Jack was out of view then beyond the corner of the hut.

All right. Brennan put down the tin plate he was holding and moved quickly, noiselessly, to the side of the hut and edged along the rough logs until he reached the corner. He listened first before he looked around. Billy-Jack had gone inside.

He wanted to make sure, some way, that Billy-Jack would be

looking at Doretta, but there was not time. And then he was moving again—along the front, and suddenly he was inside the hut, seeing the back of Billy-Jack's head, seeing him turning, and a glimpse of Doretta's face, and the sawed-off shotgun coming around. One of his hands shot out to grip the stubby barrel, pushing it, turning it up and back violently, and the other hand closed over the trigger guard before it jerked down on Billy-Jack's wrist.

Deafeningly, a shot exploded, with the twin barrels jammed under the outlaw's jaw. Smoke and a crimson smear, and Brennan was on top of him wrenching the shotgun from squeezed fingers, clutching Billy-Jack's revolver as he came to his feet.

He heard Doretta gasp, still with the ringing in his ears, and he said, "Don't look at him!" already turning to the doorway as he jammed the Colt into his empty holster.

Frank Usher was running across the clearing, his gun in his hand.

Brennan stepped into the doorway leveling the shotgun. "Frank, hold it there!"

Usher stopped dead, but in the next second he was aiming, his revolver coming up even with his face, and Brennan's hand squeezed the second trigger of the shotgun.

Usher screamed and went down, grabbing his knees, and he rolled to his side as he hit the ground. His right hand came up, still holding the Colt.

"Don't do it, Frank!" Brennan had dropped the scattergun and now Billy-Jack's revolver was in his hand. He saw Usher's gun coming in line, and he fired, aiming dead center at the half-reclined figure, hearing the sharp, heavy report, and seeing Usher's gun hand raise straight up into the air as he slumped over on his back.

Brennan hesitated. Get him out of there, quick. Chink's not deaf.

He ran out to Frank Usher and dragged him back to the hut, laying him next to Billy-Jack. He jammed Usher's pistol into his belt. Then, "Come on!" he told Doretta, and took her hand and ran out of the hut and across the clearing toward the side where the horses were.

They moved into the denser pines, where he stopped and pulled her down next to him in the warm sand. Then he rolled over on his stomach and parted the branches to look back out across the clearing.

The hut was to the right. Straight across were more pines, but they were scattered thinly, and through them he could see the sand-colored expanse of the open grade. Chink would come that way, Brennan knew. There was no other way he could.

7

Close to him, Doretta said, "We could leave before he comes." She was afraid, and it was in the sound of her voice.

"No," Brennan said. "We'll finish this. When Chink comes we'll finish it once and for all."

"But you don't know! How can you be sure you'll—"

"Listen, I'm not sure of anything, but I know what I have to do." She was silent and he said quietly, "Move back and stay close to the ground."

And as he looked across the clearing his eyes caught the dark speck of movement beyond the trees, out on the open slope. There he was. It had to be him. Brennan could feel the sharp knot in his stomach again as he watched, as the figure grew larger.

Now he was sure. Chink was on foot leading his horse, not coming straight across, but angling higher up on the slope. He'll come in where the trees are thicker, Brennan thought. He'll come out beyond the lean-to and you won't see him until he turns the corner of the hut. That's it. He can't climb the slope back of the hut, so he'll have to come around the front way.

He estimated the distance from where he was lying to the front of the hut—seventy or eighty feet—and his thumb eased back the hammer of the revolver in front of him.

There was a dead silence for perhaps ten minutes before he heard, coming from beyond the hut, "Frank?" Silence again. Then, "Where the hell are you?"

Brennan waited, feeling the smooth, heavy, hickory grip of the Colt in his hand, his finger lightly caressing the trigger. It was in his mind to fire as soon as Chink turned the corner. He was ready. But it came and it went.

It went as he saw Chink suddenly, unexpectedly, slip around the corner of the hut and flatten himself against the wall, his gun pointed toward the door. Brennan's front sight was dead on Chink's belt, but he couldn't pull the trigger. Not like this. He watched Chink edge slowly toward the door.

"Throw it down, boy!"

Chink moved and Brennan squeezed the trigger a split second late. He fired again, hearing the bullet thump solidly into the door frame, but it was too late. Chink was inside.

Brennan let his breath out slowly, relaxing somewhat. Well, that's what you get. You wait, and all you do is make it harder for yourself. He could picture Chink now looking at Usher and Billy-Jack. That'll give him something to think about. Look at them good. Then look at the door you've got to come out of sooner or later.

I'm glad he's seeing them like that. And he thought then: How long could you stand something like that? He can cover up Billy-Jack and stand it a little longer. But when dark comes. . . . If he holds out till dark he's got a chance. And now he was sorry he had not pulled the trigger before. You got to make him come out, that's all.

"Chink!"

There was no answer.

"Chink, come on out!"

Suddenly gunfire came from the doorway and Brennan, hugging the ground, could hear the swishing of the bullets through the foliage above him.

Don't throw it away, he thought, looking up again. He backed up and moved over a few yards to take up a new position. He'd be on the left side of the doorway as you look at it, Brennan thought, to shoot on an angle like that.

He sighted on the inside edge of the door frame and called, "Chink, come out and get it!" He saw the powder flash, and he fired on top of it, cocked and fired again. Then silence.

Now you don't know, Brennan thought. He reloaded and called out, "Chink!" but there was no answer, and he thought: You just keep digging your hole deeper.

Maybe you did hit him. No, that's what he wants you to think. Walk in the door and you'll find out. He'll wait now. He'll take it slow and start adding up his chances. Wait till night? That's his best bet—but he can't count on his horse being there then. I could have worked around and run it off. And he knows he wouldn't be worth a damn on foot, even if he did get away. So the longer he waits, the less he can count on his horse.

All right, what would you do? Immediately he thought: I'd count shots. So you hear five shots go off in a row and you make a break out the door, and while you're doing it the one shooting picks up another gun. But even picking up another gun takes time.

He studied the distance from the doorway to the corner of the hut. Three long strides. Out of sight in less than three seconds. That's if he's thinking of it. And if he tried it, you'd have only that long to aim and fire. Unless . . .

Unless Doretta pulls off the five shots. He thought about this for some time before he was sure it could be done without endangering her. But first you have to give him the idea.

He rolled to his side to pull Usher's gun from his belt. Then, holding it in his left hand, he emptied it at the doorway. Silence followed.

I'm reloading now, Chink. Get it through your cat-eyed head. I'm reloading and you've got time to do something.

He explained it to Doretta unhurriedly—how she would wait about ten minutes before firing the first time; she would count to five and fire again, and so on until the gun was empty. She was behind the thick bole of a pine and only the gun would be exposed as she fired.

She said, "And if he doesn't come out?"

"Then we'll think of something else."

Their faces were close. She leaned toward him, closing her eyes, and kissed him softly. "I'll be waiting," she said.

Brennan moved off through the trees, circling wide, well back from the edge of the clearing. He came to the thin section directly across from Doretta's position and went quickly from tree to tree, keeping to the shadows until he was into thicker pines again. He saw Chink's horse off to the left of him. Only a few minutes remained as he came out of the trees to the off side of the lean-to, and there he went down to his knees, keeping his eyes on the corner of the hut.

The first shot rang out and he heard it whump into the front

of the hut. One . . . then the second . . . two . . . he was counting them, not moving his eyes from the front edge of the hut
. . . three . . . four . . . be ready. . . . Five! Now, Chink!

He heard him—hurried steps on the packed sand—and
almost immediately he saw him cutting sharply around the
edge of the hut, stopping, leaning against the wall, breathing
heavily but thinking he was safe. Then Brennan stood up.

"Here's one facing you, Chink."

He saw the look of surprise, the momentary expression of
shock, a full second before Chink's revolver flashed up from his
side and Brennan's finger tightened on the trigger. With the
report Chink lurched back against the wall, a look of bewilder-
ment still on his face, although he was dead even as he slumped
to the ground.

Brennan holstered the revolver and did not look at Chink as
he walked past him around to the front of the hut. He suddenly
felt tired, but it was the kind of tired feeling you enjoyed, like
the bone weariness and sense of accomplishment you felt seeing
your last cow punched through the market chute.

He thought of old man Tenvoorde, and only two days ago
trying to buy the yearlings from him. He still didn't have any
yearlings.

What the hell do you feel so good about?

Still, he couldn't help smiling. Not having money to buy
stock seemed like such a little trouble. He saw Doretta come
out of the trees and he walked on across the clearing.

The Nagual

O FELIO OSO—who had been a vaquero most of his seventy years, but who now mended fences and drove a wagon for John Stam—looked down the slope through the jack pines seeing the man with his arms about the woman. They were in front of the shack which stood near the edge of the deep ravine bordering the west end of the meadow; and now Ofelio watched them separate lingeringly, the woman moving off, looking back as she passed the corral, going diagonally across the pasture to the trees on the far side, where she disappeared.

Now Mrs. Stam goes home, Ofelio thought, to wait for her husband.

The old man had seen them like this before, sometimes in the evening, sometimes at dawn as it was now with the first distant sun streak off beyond the Organ Mountains, and always when John Stam was away. This had been going on for months now, at least since Ofelio first began going up into the hills at night.

It was a strange feeling that caused the old man to do this; more an urgency, for he had come to a realization that there was little time left for him. In the hills at night a man can think clearly, and when a man believes his end is approaching there are things to think about.

In his sixty-ninth year Ofelio Oso broke his leg. In the shock of a pain-stabbing moment it was smashed between horse and corral post as John Stam's cattle rushed the gate opening. He could no longer ride, after having done nothing else for more than fifty years; and with this came the certainty that his end was approaching. Since he was of no use to anyone, then only death remained. In his idleness he could feel its nearness and he thought of many things to prepare himself for the day it would come.

Now he waited until the horsebreaker, Joe Slidell, went into the shack. Ofelio limped down the slope through the pines and was crossing a corner of the pasture when Joe Slidell reappeared, leaning in the doorway with something in his hand, looking absently out at the few mustangs off at the far end of the pasture. His gaze moved to the bay stallion in the corral, then swung slowly until he was looking at Ofelio Oso.

The old man saw this and changed his direction, going toward the shack. He carried a blanket over his shoulder and wore a willow-root Chihuahua hat, and his hand touched the brim of it as he approached the loose figure in the doorway.

"At it again," Joe Slidell said. He lifted the bottle which he held close to his stomach and took a good drink. Then he lowered it, and his face contorted. He grunted, "Yaaaaa!" but after that he seemed relieved. He nodded to the hill and said, "How long you been up there?"

"Through the night," Ofelio answered. Which you well know, he thought. You, standing there drinking the whiskey that the woman brings.

Slidell wiped his mouth with the back of his hand, watching the old man through heavy-lidded eyes. "What do you see up there?"

"Many things."

"Like what?"

Ofelio shrugged. "I have seen devils."

Slidell grinned. "Big ones or little ones?"

"They take many forms."

Joe Slidell took another drink of the whiskey, not offering it to the old man, then said, "Well, I got work to do." He nodded to the corral where the bay stood looking over the rail, lifting and shaking his maned head at the man smell. "That horse," Joe Slidell said, "is going to finish gettin' himself broke today, one way or the other."

Ofelio looked at the stallion admiringly. A fine animal for long rides, for the killing pace, but for cutting stock, no. It would never be trained to swerve inward and break into a dead run at the feel of boot touching stirrup. He said to the horse-breaker, "That bay is much horse."

"Close to seventeen hands," Joe Slidell said, "if you was to get close enough to measure."

"This is the one for Señor Stam's use?"

Slidell nodded. "Maybe. If I don't ride him down to the house before supper, you bring up a mule to haul his carcass to the ravine." He jerked his thumb past his head, indicating the deep draw behind the shack. Ofelio had been made to do this before. The mule dragged the still faintly breathing mustang to the ravine edge. Then Slidell would tell him to push, while he levered with a pole, until finally the mustang went over the side down the steep-slanted seventy feet to the bottom.

Ofelio crossed the pasture, then down into the woods that fell gradually for almost a mile before opening again at the house and outbuildings of John Stam's spread. That *jinete*—that breaker of horses—is very sure of himself, the old man thought, moving through the trees. Both with horses and another man's wife. He must know I have seen them together, but it doesn't bother him. No, the old man thought now, it is something other than being sure of himself. I think it is stupidity. An intelligent man tames a wild horse with a great deal of respect, for he knows the horse is able to kill him. As for Mrs. Stam, considering her husband, one would think he would treat her with even greater respect.

Marion Stam was on the back porch while Ofelio hitched the mules to the flatbed wagon. Her arms were folded across her chest and she watched the old man because his hitching the team was the only activity in the yard. Marion Stam's eyes were listless, darkly shadowed, making her thin face seem transparently frail, and this made her look older than her twenty-five years. But appearance made little difference to Marion. John Stam was nearly twice her age; and Joe Slidell—Joe spent all his time up at the horse camp, anything in a dress looked good to him.

But the boredom. This was the only thing to which Marion Stam could not resign herself. A house miles away from nowhere. Day following day, each one utterly void of anything resembling her estimation of living. John Stam at the table, eyes on his plate, opening his mouth only to put food into it. The picture of John Stam at night, just before blowing out the lamp, standing in his yellowish, musty-smelling long underwear. "Good night," a grunt, then the sound of even, open-mouthed breathing. Joe Slidell relieved some of the boredom. Some. He was young, not bad looking in a coarse way, but, Lord, he smelled like one of his horses!

"Why're you going now?" she called to Ofelio. "The stage's always late."

The old man looked up. "Someday it will be early. Perhaps this morning."

The woman shrugged, leaning in the door frame now, her arms still folded over her thin chest as Ofelio moved the team and wagon creaking out of the yard.

But the stage was not early; nor was it on time. Ofelio urged the mules into the empty station yard and pulled to a slow stop in front of the wagon shed that joined the station adobe. Two horses were in the shed with their muzzles munching at the hay rack. Spainhower, the Butterfield agent, appeared in the doorway for a moment. Seeing Ofelio he said, "Seems you'd learn to leave about thirty minutes later." He turned away.

Ofelio smiled, climbing off the wagon box. He went through the door, following Spainhower into the sudden dimness, feeling the adobe still cool from the night and hearing a voice saying: "If Ofelio drove for Butterfield, nobody'd have to wait for stages." He recognized the voice and the soft laugh that followed and then he saw the man, Billy-Jack Trew, sitting on one end of the pine table with his boots resting on a Douglas chair.

Billy-Jack Trew was a deputy. Val Dodson, his boss, the Doña Ana sheriff, sat a seat away from him with his elbows on the pine boards. They had come down from Tularosa, stopping for a drink before going on to Mesilla.

Billy-Jack Trew said in Spanish, "Ofelio, how does it go?"

The old man nodded. "It passes well," he said, and smiled, because Billy-Jack was a man you smiled at even though you knew him slightly and saw him less than once in a month.

"Up there at that horse pasture," the deputy said, "I hear Joe Slidell's got some mounts of his own."

Ofelio nodded. "I think so. Señor Stam does not own all of them."

"I'm going to take me a ride up there pretty soon," Billy-Jack said, "and see what kind of money Joe's askin'. Way the sheriff keeps me going I need two horses, and that's a fact."

Ofelio could feel Spainhower looking at him, Val Dodson glancing now and then. One or the other would soon ask about his nights in the hills. He could feel this also. Everyone seemed to know about his going into the hills and everyone continued to question him about it, as if it were a foolish thing to do. Only Billy-Jack Trew would talk about it seriously.

At first, Ofelio had tried to explain the things he thought about: life and death and a man's place, the temptations of the devil and man's obligation to God—all those things men begin to think about when there is little time left. And from the beginning Ofelio saw that they were laughing at him. Serious faces straining to hold back smiles. Pseudo-sincere questions that were only to lead him on. So after the first few times he stopped telling them what occurred to him in the loneliness of the night and would tell them whatever entered his mind, though much of it was still fact.

Billy-Jack Trew listened, and in a way he understood the old man. He knew that legends were part of a Mexican peon's life. He knew that Ofelio had been a vaquero for something like fifty years, with lots of lonesome time for imagining things. Anything the old man said was good listening, and a lot of it made sense after you thought about it awhile—so Billy-Jack Trew didn't laugh.

With a cigar stub clamped in the corner of his mouth, Spainhower's puffy face was dead serious looking at the old man. "Ofelio," he said, "this morning there was a mist ring over the gate. Now, I heard what that meant, so I kept my eyes open and sure'n hell here come a gang of elves through the gate dancin' and carryin' on. They marched right in here and hauled themselves up on that table."

Val Dodson said dryly, "Now, that's funny, just this morning coming down from Tularosa me and Billy-Jack looked up to see this be-ootiful she-devil running like hell for a cholla clump." He paused, glancing at Ofelio. "Billy-Jack took one look and was half out his saddle when I grabbed him."

Billy-Jack Trew shook his head. "Ofelio, don't mind that talk."

The old man smiled, saying nothing.

"You seen any more devils?" Spainhower asked him.

Ofelio hesitated, then nodded, saying, "Yes, I saw two devils this morning. Just at dawn."

Spainhower said, "What'd they look like?"

"I know," Val Dodson said quickly.

"Aw, Val," Billy-Jack said. "Leave him alone." He glanced at Ofelio, who was looking at Dodson intently, as if afraid of what he would say next.

"I'll bet," Dodson went on, "they had horns and hairy forked tails like that one me and Billy-Jack saw out on the sands." Spainhower laughed, then Dodson winked at him and laughed too.

Billy-Jack Trew was watching Ofelio and he saw the tense expression on the old man's face relax. He saw the half-frightened look change to a smile of relief, and Billy-Jack was thinking that maybe a man ought to listen even a little closer to what Ofelio said. Like maybe there were double meanings to the things he said.

"Listen," Ofelio said, "I will tell you something else I have seen. A sight few men have ever witnessed." Ofelio was thinking: All right, give them something for their minds to work on.

"What I saw is a very hideous thing to behold, more frightening than elves, more terrible than devils." He paused, then said quietly, "What I saw was a *nagual*."

He waited, certain they had never heard of this, for it was an old Mexican legend. Spainhower was smiling, but half-squinting curiosity was in his eyes. Dodson was watching, waiting for him to go on. Still Ofelio hesitated and finally Spainhower said, "And what's a *nagual* supposed to be?"

"A *nagual*," Ofelio explained carefully, "is a man with strange powers. A man who is able to transform himself into a certain animal."

Spainhower said, too quickly, "What kind of an animal?"

"That," Ofelio answered, "depends upon the man. The animal is usually of his choice."

Spainhower's brow was deep furrowed. "What's so terrible about that?"

Ofelio's face was serious. "One can see you have never beheld a *nagual*. Tell me, what is more hideous, what is more terrible, than a man—who is made in God's image—becoming an animal?"

There was silence. Then Val Dodson said, "Aw—"

Spainhower didn't know what to say; he felt disappointed, cheated.

And into this silence came the faint rumbling sound. Billy-Jack Trew said, "Here she comes." They stood up, moving for the door, and soon the rumble was higher pitched—creaking, screeching, rattling, pounding—and the Butterfield stage was swinging into the yard. Spainhower and Dodson and Billy-Jack Trew went outside, Ofelio and his *nagual* forgotten.

No one had ever seen John Stam smile. Some, smiling themselves, said Marion must have at least once or twice, but most doubted even this. John Stam worked hard, twelve to sixteen hours a day, plus keeping a close eye on some business interests he had in Mesilla, and had been doing it since he'd first visually staked off his range six years before. No one asked where he came from and John Stam didn't volunteer any answers.

Billy-Jack Trew said Stam looked to him like a red-dirt farmer with no business in cattle, but that was once Billy-Jack was wrong and he admitted it himself later. John Stam appeared one day with a crow-bait horse and twelve mavericks including a bull. Now, six years later, he had himself way over a thousand head and a *jinete* to break him all the horses he could ride.

Off the range, though, he let Ofelio Oso drive him wherever he went. Some said he felt sorry for Ofelio because the old Mexican had been a good hand in his day. Others said Marion put him up to it so she wouldn't have Ofelio hanging around the place all the time. There was always some talk about Marion, especially now with the cut-down crew up at the summer range, John Stam gone to tend his business about once a week, and only Ofelio and Joe Slidell there. Joe Slidell wasn't a bad-looking man.

The first five years John Stam allowed himself only two pleasures: he drank whiskey, though no one had ever seen him drinking it, only buying it; and every Sunday afternoon he'd ride to Mesilla for dinner at the hotel. He would always order the same thing, chicken, and always sit at the same table. He had been doing this for some time when Marion started waiting tables there. Two years later, John Stam asked her to marry him as she was setting down his dessert and Marion said yes then and there. Some claimed the only thing he'd said to her before that was bring me the ketchup.

Spainhower said it looked to him like Stam was from a line of hard-headed Dutchmen. Probably his dad had made him work like a mule and never told him about women, Spainhower said, so John Stam never knew what it was like *not* to work and the first woman he looked up long enough to notice, he married. About everybody agreed Spainhower had something.

They were almost to the ranch before John Stam spoke. He had nodded to the men in the station yard, but gotten right up on the wagon seat. Spainhower asked him if he cared for a drink, but he shook his head. When they were in view of the ranch house—John Stam's leathery mask of a face looking straight ahead down the slope—he said, "Mrs. Stam is in the house?"

"I think so," Ofelio said, looking at him quickly, then back to the rumps of the mules.

"All morning?"

"I was not here all morning." Ofelio waited, but John Stam said no more. This was the first time Ofelio had been questioned about Mrs. Stam. Perhaps he overheard talk in Mesilla, he thought.

In the yard John Stam climbed off the wagon and went into the house. Ofelio headed the team for the barn and stopped before the wide door to unhitch. The yard was quiet; he glanced at the house, which seemed deserted, though he knew John Stam was inside. Suddenly Mrs. Stam's voice was coming from the house, high pitched, excited, the words not clear. The sound stopped abruptly and it was quiet again. A few minutes later the screen door slammed and John Stam was coming across the yard, his great gnarled hands hanging empty, threateningly, at his sides.

He stopped before Ofelio and said bluntly, "I'm asking you if you've ever taken any of my whiskey."

"I have never tasted whiskey," Ofelio said and felt a strange guilt come over him in this man's gaze. He tried to smile. "But in the past I've tasted enough mescal to make up for it."

John Stam's gaze held. "That wasn't what I asked you."

"All right," Ofelio said. "I have never taken any."

"I'll ask you once more," John Stam said.

Ofelio was bewildered. "What would you have me say?"

For a long moment John Stam stared. His eyes were hard though there was a weariness in them. He said, "I don't need you around here, you know."

"I have told the truth," Ofelio said simply.

The rancher continued to stare, a muscle in his cheek tightening and untightening. He turned abruptly and went back to the house.

The old man thought of the times he had seen Joe Slidell and the woman together and the times he had seen Joe Slidell drinking the whiskey she brought to him. Ofelio thought: He wasn't asking about whiskey, he was asking about his wife. But he could not come out with it. He knows something is going on behind his back, or else he suspicions it strongly, and he sees a relation between it and the whiskey that's being taken. I think I feel sorry for him; he hasn't learned to keep his woman and he doesn't know what to do.

Before supper Joe Slidell came down out of the woods trail on the bay stallion. He dismounted at the back porch and he and John Stam talked for a few minutes looking over the horse. When Joe Slidell left, John Stam, holding the bridle, watched him disappear into the woods and for a long time after, he stood there staring at the trail that went up through the woods.

Just before dark John Stam rode out of the yard on the bay stallion. Later—it was full dark then—Ofelio heard the screen door again. He rose from his bunk in the end barn stall and opened the big door an inch, in time to see Marion Stam's dim form pass into the trees.

He has left, Ofelio thought, so she goes to the *jinete*. He shook his head thinking: This is none of your business. But it remained in his mind and later, with his blanket over his shoulder, he went into the hills where he could think of these things more clearly.

He moved through the woods hearing the night sounds which seemed far away and his own footsteps in the leaves that were close, but did not seem to belong to him; then he was on the pine slope and high up he felt the breeze. For a time he listened to the soft sound of it in the jack pines. Tomorrow there will be rain, he thought. Sometime in the afternoon.

He stretched out on the ground, rolling the blanket behind his head, and looked up at the dim stars thinking: More and more every day, *viejo*, you must realize you are no longer of any value. The horsebreaker is not afraid of you, the men at the station laugh and take nothing you say seriously, and finally Señor Stam, he made it very clear when he said, "I don't need you around here."

Then why does he keep me—months now since I have been dismounted—except out of charity? He is a strange man. I suppose I owe him something, something more than feeling sorry for him which does him no good. I think we have something in common. I can feel sorry for both of us. He laughed at this and tried to discover other things they might have in common. It relaxed him, his imagination wandering, and soon he dozed off with the cool breeze on his face, not remembering to think about his end approaching.

To the east, above the chimneys of the Organ range, morning light began to gray-streak the day. Ofelio opened his eyes, hearing the horse moving through the trees below him: hooves clicking the small stones and the swish of pine branches. He thought of Joe Slidell's mustangs. One of them has wandered up the slope. But then, the unmistakable squeak of saddle leather and he sat up, tensed. It could be anyone, he thought. Almost anyone.

He rose, folding the blanket over his shoulder, and made his way down the slope silently, following the sound of the horse, and when he reached the pasture he saw the dim shape of it moving toward the shack, a tall shadow gliding away from him in the half light.

The door opened. Joe Slidell came out, closing it quickly behind him. "You're up early," he said, yawning, pulling a suspender over his shoulder. "How's that horse carry you? He learned his manners yesterday . . . won't give you no trouble. If he does, you let me have him back for about an hour." Slidell looked above the horse to the rider. "Mr. Stam, why're you lookin' at me like that?" He squinted up in the dimness. "Mr. Stam, what's the matter? You feelin' all right?"

"Tell her to come out," John Stam said.

"What?"

"I said tell her to come out."

"Now, Mr. Stam—" Slidell's voice trailed off, but slowly a grin formed on his mouth. He said, almost embarrassedly,

"Well, Mr. Stam, I didn't think you'd mind." One man talking to another now. "Hell, it's only a little Mex gal from Mesilla. It gets lonely here and—"

John Stam spurred the stallion violently; the great stallion lunged, rearing, coming down with thrashing hooves on the screaming man. Slidell went down covering his head, falling against the shack boards. He clung there gasping as the stallion backed off; the next moment he was crawling frantically, rising, stumbling, running; he looked back seeing John Stam spurring and he screamed again as the stallion ran him down. John Stam reined in a tight circle and came back over the motionless form. He dismounted before the shack and went inside.

Go away, quickly, Ofelio told himself, and started for the other side of the pasture, running tensed, not wanting to hear what he knew would come. But he could not outrun it, the scream came turning him around when he was almost to the woods.

Marion Stam was in the doorway, then running across the yard, swerving as she saw the corral suddenly in front of her. John Stam was in the saddle spurring the stallion after her, gaining as she followed the rail circle of the corral. Now she was looking back, seeing the stallion almost on top of her. The stallion swerved suddenly as the woman screamed going over the edge of the ravine.

Ofelio ran to the trees before looking back. John Stam had dismounted. He removed bridle and saddle from the bay and put these in the shack. Then he picked up a stone and threw it at the stallion, sending it galloping for the open pasture.

The old man was breathing in short gasps from the running, but he hurried now through the woods and did not stop until he reached the barn. He sat on the bunk listening to his heart, feeling it in his chest. Minutes later John Stam opened the big door. He stood looking down at Ofelio while the old man's mind repeated: Mary, Virgin and Mother, until he heard the rancher say, "You didn't see or hear anything all night. I didn't leave the house, did I?"

Ofelio hesitated, then nodded slowly as if committing this to memory. "You did not leave the house."

John Stam's eyes held threateningly before he turned and

went out. Minutes later Ofelio saw him leave the house with a shotgun under his arm. He crossed the yard and entered the woods. Already he is unsure, Ofelio thought, especially of the woman, though the fall was at least seventy feet.

When he heard the horse come down out of the woods it was barely more than an hour later. Ofelio looked out, expecting to see John Stam on the bay, but it was Billy-Jack Trew walking his horse into the yard. Quickly the old man climbed the ladder to the loft. The deputy went to the house first and called out. When there was no answer he approached the barn and called Ofelio's name.

He's found them! But what brought him? Ah, the old man thought, remembering, he wants to buy a horse. He spoke of that yesterday. But he found them instead. Where is Señor Stam? Why didn't he see him? He heard the deputy call again, but still Ofelio did not come out. He remained crouched in the darkness of the barn loft until he heard the deputy leave.

The door opened and John Stam stood below in the strip of outside light.

Resignedly, Ofelio said, "I am here," looking down, thinking: He was close all the time. He followed the deputy back and if I had called he would have killed both of us. And he is very capable of killing.

John Stam looked up, studying the old man. Finally he said, "You were there last night; I'm sure of it now . . . else you wouldn't be hiding, afraid of admitting something. You were smart not to talk to him. Maybe you're remembering you owe me something for keeping you on, even though you're not good for anything." He added abruptly, "You believe in God?"

Ofelio nodded.

"Then," John Stam said, "swear to God you'll never mention my name in connection with what happened."

Ofelio nodded again, resignedly, thinking of his obligation to this man. "I swear it," he said.

The rain came in the late afternoon, keeping Ofelio inside the barn. He crouched in the doorway, listening to the soft hissing of the rain in the trees, watching the puddles forming in the wagon tracks. His eyes would go to the house, picturing

John Stam inside alone with his thoughts and waiting. They will come. Perhaps the rain will delay them, Ofelio thought, but they will come.

The sheriff will say, Mr. Stam this is a terrible thing we have to tell you. What? Well, you know the stallion Joe Slidell was breaking? Well, it must have got loose. It looks like Joe tried to catch him and . . . Joe got under his hooves. And, Mrs. Stam was there . . . we figured she was up to look at your new horse—saying this with embarrassment. She must have become frightened when it happened and she ran. In the dark she went over the side of the ravine. Billy-Jack found them this morning. . . .

He did not hear them because of the rain. He was staring at a puddle and when he looked up there was Val Dodson and Billy-Jack Trew. It was too late to climb to the loft.

Billy-Jack smiled. "I was around earlier, but I didn't see you." His hat was low, shielding his face from the light rain, as was Dodson's.

Ofelio could feel himself trembling. He is watching now from a window. Mother of God, help me.

Dodson said, "Where's Stam?"

Ofelio hesitated, then nodded toward the house.

"Come on," Dodson said. "Let's get it over with."

Billy-Jack Trew leaned closer, resting his forearm on the saddle horn. He said gently, "Have you seen anything more since yesterday?"

Ofelio looked up, seeing the wet smiling face and another image that was in his mind—a great stallion in the dawn light—and the words came out suddenly, as if forced from his mouth. He said, "I saw a *nagual*!"

Dodson groaned. "Not again," and nudged his horse with his knees.

"Wait a minute," Billy-Jack said quickly. Then to Ofelio, "This *nagual*, you actually saw it?"

The old man bit his lips. "Yes."

"It was an animal you saw, then."

"It was a *nagual*."

Dodson said, "You stand in the rain and talk crazy. I'm getting this over with."

Billy-Jack swung down next to the old man. "Listen a

minute, Val." To Ofelio, gently again, "But it was in the form of an animal?"

Ofelio's head nodded slowly.

"What did the animal look like?"

"It was," the old man said slowly, not looking at the deputy, "a great stallion." He said quickly, "I can tell you no more than that."

Dodson dismounted.

Billy-Jack said, "And where did the *nagual* go?"

Ofelio was looking beyond the deputy toward the house. He saw the back door open and John Stam came out on the porch, the shotgun cradled in his arm. Ofelio continued to stare. He could not speak as it went through his mind: He thinks I have told them!

Seeing the old man's face, Billy-Jack turned, then Dodson.

Stam called, "Ofelio, come here!"

Billy-Jack said, "Stay where you are," and now his voice was not gentle. But the hint of a smile returned as he unfastened the two lower buttons of his slicker and suddenly he called, "Mr. Stam! You know what a *nagual* is?" He opened the slicker all the way and drew a tobacco plug from his pants pocket.

Dodson whispered hoarsely, "What's the matter with you!"

Billy-Jack was smiling. "I'm only askin' a simple question."

John Stam did not answer. He was staring at Ofelio.

"Mr. Stam," Billy-Jack Trew called, "before I tell you what a *nagual* is I want to warn you I can get out a Colt a helluva lot quicker than you can swing a shotgun."

Ofelio Oso died at the age of ninety-three on a ranch outside Tularosa. They said about him he sure told some tall ones— about devils, and about seeing a *nagual* hanged for murder in Mesilla . . . whatever that meant . . . but he was much man. Even at his age the old son relied on no one, wouldn't let a soul do anything for him, and died owing the world not one plugged peso. And wasn't the least bit afraid to die, even though he was so old. He used to say, "Listen, if there is no way to tell when death will come, then why should one be afraid of it?"

The Kid

I REMEMBER looking out the window, hearing the wagon, and saying to Terry McNeil and Delia, "Here comes Repper." And when the wagon came even with the porch, I saw the boy. He was sitting with his legs hanging over the end-gate, but he came forward when Max Repper motioned to him.

That was the first time any of us laid eyes on the boy, and I'll tell you frankly we weren't positive at first it was a boy, even though Max Repper referred to a "him," saying, "Don't let his long hair fool you," and even though up close we could see the features didn't belong to a girl. Still, with the extent of my travel bounded by the Mogollon Rim country, central Sonora, the Pecos River, and the Kofa Mountains—north, south, east, and west respectively—I wasn't going to confine my judgment to this being either just a boy or a girl. There are many things in the world I haven't seen, and the way Terry McNeil was keeping his mouth closed I suspect he was reserving judgment on the same grounds.

Terry was in to buy stores for his prospecting site in the Dragoons. He came in usually about every two weeks, but by the little bit he'd buy it was plain he came for Delia more than for flour and salt-meat.

It was just the three of us in the store when Max Repper came—Terry, taking his time like he was planning to outfit an expedition; Deelie, my girl-child, helping him and hoping he'd take all day; and me. Me being the first line of the sign outside that says PATTERSON GENERAL SUPPLIES. BANDERAS, ARIZONA, TERR.

Now, this Max Repper was a man who saddle-tamed horses on a little place he had a few miles up the creek. He sold them to anybody who needed a horse; sometimes a few to the Cavalry Station at Dos Fuegos, though most often their remounts were all matched and came down from Whipple Barracks. So Max Repper sold mainly to the one hundred and eighty-odd souls who lived in and around Banderas.

He also operated a livery here in the settlement, but even Max admitted it wasn't a paying proposition and ordinarily

716

he wasn't one to come right out and say he was holding a bad guess. Max was a hard-nosed individual, like a man had to be to mustang for a living; but he also had a mile-high opinion of himself, and if any living creature sympathized with him it'd have to have been one of his horse string. Though the way Max broke a horse, the possibility of that was even doubtful.

Repper came in with the boy behind him and he said to me, "Pat, look what the hell I found."

I asked him, "What is it?"

And he said, "Don't let the long hair fool you. It's a boy . . . a *white* boy."

We had to take Max's word for it at first, for that boy cut the strangest figure I ever saw. Maybe twelve years old, he was, with long dark hair hanging to his shoulders Apache style, matted and tangled, but he didn't have on a rag headband and that's why you didn't think of Apache when you looked at him, even though his skin was weathered mahogany and the rest of his getup might have been Indian. His shirt was worn-out cotton and open all the way down, no buttons left; his pants were buckskin, homemade by Indian or Mexican, you couldn't tell which, and he wasn't wearing shoes.

The bare feet made you feel sorry for him even after you looked close and saw something half wild about him. You wondered if the mind was translating what the eyes saw into man-talk or into some kind of gray-shadowed animal understanding.

Terry McNeil was toward the back, leaning on the counter close to Delia. They were just looking. I got up from the desk (it was by the front window and served as "office" for the Hatch & Hodges Line's Banderas station), but I just stood there, not wanting to go up and gawk at the boy like he was P. T. Barnum's ten-cent attraction.

"The good are rewarded," Max Repper said. He grinned showing his crooked yellow teeth, which always took the humor out of anything funny he ever said. "I was thinking about hiring a boy when I found this one." He looked at the boy standing motionless. "He's going to work for me free."

I asked now, "Where'd you find him?"

"Snoopin' around my stores."

"Where's he from?"

"Damn' if I know. He don't even talk."

Max pulled the boy forward by the shoulder right up in front of me and said, "What do you judge his breed to be?" Like the boy was a paint mustang with spots Max hadn't ever seen before.

I asked him again where he'd found the boy and he told how a few nights ago he'd heard something in the lean-to back of his shack, and had eased out there in his sock feet and jabbed a Henry in the boy's back as he was taking down Max's fresh jerky strings.

He kept the boy tied up the rest of the night and fed him in the morning, watched him stuff jerked venison into his mouth, asked him where he came from, and got only grunts for answers.

He put the boy to work watering his corral mounts, and the way the boy roughed the horses told Max maybe there was Apache in his background. But Max didn't know any Apache words and the boy wasn't volunteering any. Max thought of Spanish. The only trouble was he didn't know Spanish either.

The second night the boy tried to run away and Max (grinning as he told it) beat him blue. The third morning Max decided (reluctantly) he'd have to bring the boy in for shoeing. Shoes cost money, but barefooted a boy don't work so good—not on a south Arizona horse ranch.

I realized then Max was honest-to-goodness planning on keeping the boy, but I mentioned, just to make sure, "I suppose you'll take him to Dos Fuegos and turn him over to the Army."

"What for? He don't belong to them."

"He don't belong to you either."

"He sure as hell does. Long as I feed him."

I told Max, "Maybe the Army can trace where this boy came from."

But Repper said he'd tried for two days to get something out of the boy, and if he couldn't, then no lousy Army man could expect to.

"The kid's had his chance to talk," Max said. "If he don't want to, all right, then. I'll draw him pictures of what to do and push him to'ard it."

Max sat the boy down on a stool and I handed the shoes to him and he jammed them on the boy's feet until he thought he'd found the right size. When Max started to button one of them up the boy yanked his foot away and grunted like it hurt him. Max reached up and swatted the boy across the face and he kept still then.

I remember thinking: He handles the boy like he would a wild mustang, not like a human being. And Terry McNeil must have been thinking the same thing. He came up to us, then knelt down next to the boy, ignoring Max Repper, who was ready to put on the other shoe.

The boy looked at Terry and seemed to back off, maybe just a couple of inches on the outside, but the way he tensed you knew an iron door slammed shut inside of him.

Max said, "What in the name of George H. Hell you think you're doing?" Max had no use for Terry—but I'll tell you about that later.

Terry looked up at Repper and said, "I thought I'd just talk to him."

Max most probably wanted to kick Terry in the teeth, especially now, worn out from trying on shoes, and on general principle besides. Terry was the kind of boy who never let anything bother him, never raised his voice, and I know for a fact that burned Max, especially when they had differences of opinion, which was about every other time they ran into each other.

Max was near the end of his short-sized temper, but he held on and forced out a laugh to show Terry what he thought of him and said to me, "Pat, I'm going to buy myself a drink."

I kept just a couple of bottles for customers who didn't have time to get down to the State House. Serving Max, I watched Terry and the boy.

Terry was sitting cross-legged in front of him now slipping off the shoe Max had buttoned up. He took another from the pile of shoes and tried it on, the boy letting him, watching curiously, and I could hear Terry saying something in that slow, quiet way he talked. First, I thought it was Spanish, and maybe it was, but the little bit I could hear after that was a low mumble . . . then bit-off crisp words like *sik-isn* and *nakai*-yes and *pesh-klitso*, though not used together. The kind of talk you hear up at the San Carlos Reservation.

Then Terry leaned close to the boy and for a while I couldn't see the boy's face. Terry leaned back and said something else; then he touched the boy's arm, holding it for a moment, and when he stood up the boy's eyes followed him and they no longer had that locked iron door behind them.

Terry came over to us and said, "The boy was taken from the Mexican village of Sahuaripa something like three years ago. He was out watching the men herd cattle when a Chiricahua raiding party hit them. They killed the others and carried off the boy."

Max didn't speak, so I said, "I thought he was white."

Terry nodded his head. "His Mexican father told him that his real parents had died when he was a small boy. The Mexican had hired out to them as a guide, but they both died of a fever on the way to wherever they were going. So the Mexican went home to Sahuaripa and took the boy with him. He explained to the boy that he and his wife had never had a child, but they had prayed, and he believed the boy to be God's answer. They named the boy Regalo."

Max said, "You expect me to believe that?"

Terry shrugged. "Why shouldn't you?"

Max just looked at Terry, then grinned and shook his head slowly like saying: You think I was born last week? Terry might have told him what he thought, but Repper stomped out, dragging the boy and his new shoes with him.

I said to Terry, "The boy really tell you that?"

"Sure he did."

"What about the past three years?"

"He's been with Chiricahuas. Made blood son of Juh, who's chief of the whole red she-bang." Terry said the boy had wandered off on a lone hunt; his horse lamed and he was cutting back home when he came across Max's place.

"Terry," I said, "I imagine a boy could learn a lot of mean things from Chiricahuas."

And Terry said, "That's why I'm almost tempted to feel sorry for old Max."

Terry went back to outfitting for his expedition, but now he actually put his list down and asked Deelie to fill it. He didn't stay more than ten minutes after that, talking to Deelie, telling her what the boy said. And when he was gone I asked Deelie what his big hurry was.

"I never saw a man so eager to get back to a mine camp," I said.

"Terry's anxious to make this one pay," Deelie said. There was a soft smile on her face and she dropped her eyes quick, which was Deelie's way of telling you she had a secret—though I suspected it was something more akin to wishful thinking. Terry McNeil was never too anxious about anything.

He took everything in long, easy strides, even pretty little seventeen-year-old things like Deelie. I know he was taken with her, ever since the first day he set foot here, which was two years ago. He came through on his way to Dos Fuegos, riding dispatch for General Stoneman, and stopped off to buy a pound of Arbuckle's (he said that ration coffee put him to sleep); Deelie waited on him and I remember he looked at her like she was the only woman between Whipple Barracks and the border. Deelie ate it up and stood by the window after he was gone. Three weeks later he showed up again with a shovel, a pick, and boards for a sluice box; and said he'd once seen a likely placer up in the Dragoons and he'd always wanted to test it and now he was going to.

He must have saved his dispatch-riding money, because the first year and a half he paid his store bill cash and carry though he never struck anything likelier than quartz. Lately, he hadn't been buying so much.

I never have disrespected him for not wanting to work steady. That's his business. Max Repper called him a saddle tramp— not to his face—but whenever he referred to Terry. You see, the big war between those two started over Deelie. Max thought he had priority, even though Deelie practically told him right out she didn't care for him. Then Terry came along and Deelie about strained her back putting on extra charm. Max saw this and blamed Terry for stealing her affections. Max himself, being close to pushing forty and with those yellow snag teeth, couldn't have stole her affections with seven hundred Henry rifles.

Maybe Deelie and Terry were closer now than when they first met, but I didn't judge so close as to make Terry *run* back to his diggings to work on the marriage stake. Right after he left, it dawned on me that he would have to pass Repper's place on the way. So that was probably why he left on the run: to look in there. Repper was burning when he left, and a man of his sour nature was likely to take out his anger even on a boy.

Terry came back about three weeks later. He tied his horse, stood on the porch, and took time to stretch the saddle kinks out of his back while Deelie waited behind the counter dying. And when he came in she gave him a smile brighter than the sun flash of a U.S. Army heliograph. Deelie's smile would come right up from her toes.

"Terry!"

He gave her a nice smile.

I told him, "You look happy enough, but not like you're ready to celebrate pay dirt."

"Getting warmer, Mr. Patterson," he said. Which is what he always said.

"Have you seen the boy?" I asked. And was a little surprised when he nodded right away.

"Saw him this morning."

"How so?"

"Well," Terry said, "I was over to Dos Fuegos last week, and you know that big black-haired lieutenant, the married one with the little boy?" I nodded. "He sold me one of his son's shirts. A red one from St. Louis."

"And you gave it to the boy."

Terry nodded. "Regalo."

"You rode all the way over to Dos Fuegos to buy a shirt for the boy."

"A red one—"

"From St. Louis. How'd he like it?"

"He liked it fine."

"How'd Repper like it?"

"He was in the shack."

Terry asked me if I'd seen the boy and I told him no. Repper had kept to his horse camp since the first time he brought the boy in. Terry said the boy looked all right in body, but not in his eyes.

Later on, after I'd closed up, the three of us were sitting in back having something to eat—Deelie showing off what a good cook she was—when I heard someone at the front door.

Everyone in Banderas knows what time I close; still, it could have been something special, so I walked up front through the dark store and opened the door.

Maybe you've guessed it. I sure didn't. It was the boy, Regalo. He just stood there and I had to take him by the arm and bring him inside. Then, when we reached the light, I saw what was the matter.

He had on the red shirt but the back of it was almost in shreds, and crisscrossing his bare skin were raw welts, ugly red-looking burns like a length of manila had been sanded across his back a couple of dozen times.

Terry was up out of the chair and we eased the boy into it and made him lean forward over the table. Terry knelt down close to him and started to talk in Spanish. Ordinarily I know some, but not the way Terry was running the words together. Then the boy spoke. While he did, Deelie went out and came back with some cocoa butter and she spread it over his back gently without batting an eye. I think right then she advanced seven hundred feet in Terry McNeil's estimation.

The boy said, Terry told us, that Repper had come out of the house and when he saw the new shirt he tried to rip it off the boy, but Regalo ran. That made Repper mad and when he caught him at the barn he reached a hackamore line off a nail and laid it across the boy's back until his arm got tired.

Leaning over the table, the boy didn't cry or whimper, but you knew his back stung like fire.

Terry was saying, let's fix him some eggs, when we heard the door again . . . then heavy footsteps and there was Max Repper in the doorway with his Henry rifle square on us.

"The boy's coming with me." That's all he said. He took Regalo by the arm, yanked him out of the chair, marched him through the front part, and out the door. It happened so fast, I hardly realized Max had been there.

Terry was in the doorway looking up toward the front door. He didn't say a word. Probably he was thinking he should have done something, even if it had happened fast and Max was holding a Henry. Whatever he was thinking, he made up his mind fast. Terry took one last glance at Deelie and was gone.

Of course we knew where he was going. First to the board-inghouse for his gun, then to the livery, then to Repper's place.

We didn't want him to do it . . . but at the same time, we did. The only thing was, someone else should be there. I figured whatever was going to happen ought to have a witness. So I saddled up and rode out about fifteen minutes behind Terry.

I thought I might catch him on the road, but didn't see a soul and finally I cut off to Repper's. There was Terry's clay-bank and just over the rump a cigarette glow where Terry was leaning next to the front door.

"He's not here?"

Terry shook his head.

"But we would have passed him on the road," I said.

"Well," Terry said, "he's got to come sooner or later."

As it turned out, it was just after daybreak when we heard the wagon.

Crossing the yard Max looked at us, but he kept on heading the team for the barn. We walked toward him, approaching broadside, then Max turned the team straight on toward the barn door and we could see the wagon bed. Regalo wasn't in it.

Max stepped off the wagon and waited for us with his hands on his hips.

"He ain't here."

Terry asked him, "What happened?"

"He jumped off the wagon and I lost him in the dark."

"And you've been looking for him."

Max grinned that ugly grin of his. "Sure," he said. "A man don't like to lose his top hand."

Then, glancing at Terry, seeing a look on the boy's face I'd never witnessed before, I knew Max Repper was about to lose his top teeth.

Sure enough. Terry took two steps and a little shuffle dance and hit Max square in the mouth. Max went back, but didn't go down and now he came at Terry. Terry had his right cocked, waiting, and he started to throw it. Max put up his guard and Terry held the right, but his left came around wide and clobbered Max on the ear. Then the right followed through, straightening him up, and the left swung wide again and smacked solid against his cheekbone. Max didn't throw a punch. He wanted to at first, then he was kept too busy trying to cover up. I thought Terry's arms would drop off before Max caved in. Then, there it was, for a split second—Max's chin up like he was posing for a profile—and Terry found it with the best-timed, widest-swung roundhouse I've ever seen.

Max went down and he didn't move. Terry stepped inside the barn and came out with a hackamore. He looked down at Max and started to roll him over with his boot. But then he must have thought, What good will it do— He turned away, dropping the hackamore on top of Repper.

All Terry said was "Long as the boy got away . . . that's the main thing."

After that everything was quiet for a while. Of course what had happened made good conversation, and wherever you'd go somebody would be talking about the half-wild white boy who'd lived with Apaches. And they talked about Max Repper and Terry. Everybody agreed that was a fine thing Terry did, loosening Max's teeth . . . but Terry better watch himself, the way Max holds on to a grudge with both hands and both feet.

Terry went back to his diggings and Deelie wore her tragic look like he was off to the wars. Max would come in about once a week still, but now he didn't talk so much. Ordered what he wanted and got out.

Then one day a man named Jim Hughes came in and told how he'd seen the boy.

Jim had a one-loop outfit a few miles beyond Repper's place. I told him it was probably just a stray reservation buck, but he said no, he came through the willows to the creek off back of his place and there was the boy lying belly down at the side of the creek. The boy jumped up surprised not ten feet away from him, scrambled for his horse, and was gone. And Jim said the boy was wearing a red shirt, the back of it all ripped.

Max heard about it too. The next day he was in asking whether I'd seen the boy. He talked about it like he was just making conversation, but Max wasn't cut out to be an actor. He wanted to find that boy so bad, he could taste it, and it showed through soon as he started talking.

Within the next few days the boy was seen two more times. First by a neighbor of Jim Hughes's who lived this side of him, then a day later by a cavalry patrol out of Dos Fuegos. They gave chase, but the boy ran for high timber and got away. Both times the boy's red shirt was described.

Now there was something to talk about again; everybody speculating what the boy was up to. The cavalry station received orders from the commandant at Fort Huachuca to bring the boy in and be pretty damn quick about it. It didn't look good to have a boy running around who'd been stolen by the Indians. This was something for the authorities. Down at the State House Saloon they were betting five to one the cavalry would never find him, and they had some takers.

Most people figured the boy was out to get Max Repper and was sneaking around waiting for the right time.

I had the hunch the boy was looking for Terry McNeil. And when Terry finally came in again (it had been almost a month), I told him so.

He was surprised to hear the boy had been seen around here and said he couldn't figure it out. Thought the boy would be glad to get away.

"Why would he want to go back to Apaches?" I asked him.

"He lived with them," Terry said.

"That doesn't mean he liked them," I said. "I could see him going back to those Mexican people, but Sahuaripa's an awful long way off and probably he couldn't find his way back."

Terry shook his head. "But why would he be hanging around here?"

"I still say he's looking for you."

"What for?"

"Maybe he likes you."

Terry said, "That doesn't make sense."

"Maybe he likes red shirts."

"Well," Terry said, "I could look for him."

"It would be easier to let him find you," I said.

"If that's what he wants to do."

"Why don't you just sit here for a while," I suggested. "The boy knows you come here. If he wants you, then sooner or later he'll show up."

Terry thought about it, making a cigarette, then agreed finally that he wouldn't lose anything by staying.

Right in front of me Deelie threw her arms around his neck and kissed him about twelve times. I thought: If that's what having him around just a little while will do, what would happen if he agreed to stay on for life?

During the next four days nothing happened. There weren't even claims of seeing the boy. Terry said, well, the boy's probably a hundred miles away now. And I said, Either that or else he's closing in now and playing it more careful. Repper came in once and when he saw Terry he got suspicious and hung around a long time, though acting like Terry wasn't even there.

The night of the sixth day we were sitting out on the porch talking and smoking, like we'd been doing every evening, and I remember saying something about working up energy to go to bed, when Terry's hand touched my arm. He said, "Somebody's standing between those two buildings across the street."

I looked hard, but all I saw was the narrow deep shadow between the two adobes. And I was about to tell Terry he was mistaken when this figure appeared out of the shadows. He stood there for a minute close to one of the adobes, then started across the street, walking slowly.

He came to the steps and hesitated; but when Terry stood up and said, "Regalo," softly, the boy came up on the porch.

Deelie turned the lamp up as we went inside and I heard Terry asking the boy if he was hungry. The boy shook his head. Then we all just stood there not knowing what to say, trying not to stare at the boy. He was wearing the torn red shirt and looking at Terry like he had something to tell him but didn't know the right words.

Then he reached into his shirt, suddenly starting to talk in Spanish. He pulled something out wrapped in buckskin, still talking, and handed it to Terry. Then he stopped and just watched as Terry, looking embarrassed, unwrapped the little square of buckskin.

Terry looked at the boy and then at me, his eyes about to pop out of his head, and I saw what he was holding . . . a raw gold nugget.

It must have been the size of two shot glasses; way, way bigger than any I'd ever had the pleasure of seeing. Terry put it on the counter, stepped back, and looked at it like he was beholding the palace of the king of China.

He just stared, and the boy started talking again in that rapid-fire Spanish like he was trying to say everything at once. Terry looked at the boy and he stared some more until the boy stopped talking.

"What'd he say?" I asked him.

Terry took a minute to look over at me. "He says this is mine and that he'll show me a lot more. A place nobody knows about . . ."

I could believe that. You don't find nuggets that size out in the road. And it made sense the boy might know of a mine. It was common talk that any Apache could be a rich man, the way he knew the country—the whereabouts of mines worked by the Spanish two and three hundred years ago. Sure Indians knew about them, but they weren't going to tell whites and be crowded off their land quicker than it was already happening. In three years with Chiricahuas, Regalo could have learned plenty.

I said, "Terrence, you and that red shirt have made a valuable friendship."

Terry was still about three feet off the ground. He said then, "But he claims he wants to live with me!"

"Well, taking him in is the least you can do, considering—"

"But I can't—"

He stopped there. I turned around to see what Terry was looking at and there was Max Repper in the doorway, with his Henry. Max was grinning, which he hadn't done in a month, and he came forward keeping the barrel trained at Terry.

"I knew he'd show," Repper said, "soon as I saw you hanging around. I came for two things. Him"—he swung the barrel to indicate the boy—"and my nugget."

"Yours?" I said.

"The boy stole it from me."

"You never saw it before you peeked in that window."

"That's your say," Repper answered.

Terry said, "What do you want with the boy?"

"I got work for him till the reservation people take him away."

"He doesn't belong on a reservation," Terry said.

"That's not my worry." Repper shrugged. "That's what they're saying at Dos Fuegos will happen to him."

Terry shook his head slowly, saying, "That wouldn't be right."

Repper lifted the Henry a little higher. "Just hand me the nugget."

Terry hesitated. Then he said, "You come and take it."

"I can do that too," Repper said. He was concentrating on Terry and started to move toward him. His eyes went to the nugget momentarily, two seconds at best, and as they did the boy went for him. He was at Repper's throat in one lunge, dragging him down. Terry moved then, pushing the rifle barrel up and against Repper's face. Repper went down, the boy on top of him, and then a knife was in Regalo's hand.

Deelie screamed and Terry lifted the boy off of Repper, saying, "Wait a minute!" Then, in Spanish, he was talking more quietly, calming the boy.

Repper sat up with his hand to his face. He had a welt across his forehead where the rifle barrel hit, but he was more mad than hurt. He said, "You think I'm going to let you get away with this?"

Terry was himself again. He said, "I don't think you got a choice."

"I haven't?" Max said. "I'll make damn sure he gets put the hell on that reservation."

"If you can prove he's Indian," Terry answered.

Max gave us his sly look. "Either way," he said. "If he ain't Indian then he's white, with white kin, and no authority's going to let him get adopted by a saddle tramp who ain't worked in two years."

It was a good thing Max was sitting down when he said that. Max was through, and he probably knew it, but if Terry wanted the boy, then he'd sure make it plain hell for Terry to keep him.

I told Repper, "That's up to the authorities. The thing is, this boy's got no recollection of white kin and the only other person who knew his parents is dead. And he's said himself he wants to live with Terry."

Max grinned. "And I imagine Terry wants the boy, and his

nugget, to live with him. But like I said, the authorities won't see it that way."

And then Deelie had something to say. She was looking at Max Repper, but I think talking to Terry, and she said, "No, they wouldn't let the boy live with a saddle tramp who hasn't worked in two years . . . but I'm sure they would agree that a successful mining man of Mr. McNeil's character would be more than they could hope for . . . especially since he'll be married within the week."

That was exactly how Deelie did it. I've often wondered if she ever thought Terry married her just so he could raise the boy. I didn't think he did, knowing Terry, and I doubt if Deelie really cared . . . long as she had him.

The Tonto Woman

A TIME WOULD come, within a few years, when Ruben Vega would go to the church in Benson, kneel in the confessional, and say to the priest, "Bless me, Father, for I have sinned. It has been thirty-seven years since my last confession. . . . Since then I have fornicated with many women, maybe eight hundred. No, not that many, considering my work. Maybe six hundred only." And the priest would say, "Do you mean bad women or good women?" And Ruben Vega would say, "They are all good, Father." He would tell the priest he had stolen, in that time, about twenty thousand head of cattle but only maybe fifteen horses. The priest would ask him if he had committed murder. Ruben Vega would say no. "All that stealing you've done," the priest would say, "you've never killed anyone?" And Ruben Vega would say, "Yes, of course, but it was not to commit murder. You understand the distinction? Not to kill someone to take a life, but only to save my own."

Even in this time to come, concerned with dying in a state of sin, he would be confident. Ruben Vega knew himself, when he was right, when he was wrong.

Now, in a time before, with no thought of dying, but with the same confidence and caution that kept him alive, he watched a woman bathe. Watched from a mesquite thicket on the high bank of a wash.

She bathed at the pump that stood in the yard of the adobe, the woman pumping and then stooping to scoop the water from the basin of the irrigation ditch that led off to a vegetable patch of corn and beans. Her dark hair was pinned up in a swirl, piled on top of her head. She was bare to her gray skirt, her upper body pale white, glistening wet in the late afternoon sunlight. Her arms were very thin, her breasts small, but there they were with the rosy blossoms on the tips and Ruben Vega watched them as she bathed, as she raised one arm and her hand rubbed soap under the arm and down over her ribs. Ruben Vega could almost feel those ribs, she was so thin. He felt sorry for her, for all the women like her, stick women drying up in the desert,

731

waiting for a husband to ride in smelling of horse and sweat and leather, lice living in his hair.

There was a stock tank and rickety windmill off in the pasture, but it was empty graze, all dust and scrub. So the man of the house had moved his cows to grass somewhere and would be coming home soon, maybe with his sons. The woman appeared old enough to have young sons. Maybe there was a little girl in the house. The chimney appeared cold. Animals stood in a mesquite-pole corral off to one side of the house, a cow and a calf and a dun-colored horse, that was all. There were a few chickens. No buckboard or wagon. No clothes drying on the line. A lone woman here at day's end.

From fifty yards he watched her. She stood looking this way now, into the red sun, her face raised. There was something strange about her face. Like shadow marks on it, though there was nothing near enough to her to cast shadows.

He waited until she finished bathing and returned to the house before he mounted his bay and came down the wash to the pasture.

Now as he crossed the yard, walking his horse, she would watch him from the darkness of the house and make a judgment about him. When she appeared again it might be with a rifle, depending on how she saw him.

Ruben Vega said to himself, Look, I'm a kind person. I'm not going to hurt nobody.

She would see a bearded man in a cracked straw hat with the brim bent to his eyes. Black beard, with a revolver on his hip and another beneath the leather vest. But look at my eyes, Ruben Vega thought. Let me get close enough so you can see my eyes.

Stepping down from the bay he ignored the house, let the horse drink from the basin of the irrigation ditch as he pumped water and knelt to the wooden platform and put his mouth to the rusted pump spout. Yes, she was watching him. Looking up now at the doorway he could see part of her: a coarse shirt with sleeves too long and the gray skirt. He could see strands of dark hair against the whiteness of the shirt, but could not see her face.

As he rose, straightening, wiping his mouth, he said, "May we use some of your water, please?"

The woman didn't answer him.

He moved away from the pump to the hardpack, hearing the ching of his spurs, removed his hat and gave her a little bow. "Ruben Vega, at your service. Do you know Diego Luz, the horsebreaker?" He pointed off toward a haze of foothills. "He lives up there with his family and delivers horses to the big ranch, the Circle-Eye. Ask Diego Luz, he'll tell you I'm a person of trust." He waited a moment. "May I ask how you're called?" Again he waited.

"You watched me," the woman said.

Ruben Vega stood with his hat in his hand facing the woman, who was half in shadow in the doorway. He said, "I waited. I didn't want to frighten you."

"You watched me," she said again.

"No, I respect your privacy."

She said, "The others look. They come and watch."

He wasn't sure who she meant. Maybe anyone passing by. He said, "You see them watching?"

She said, "What difference does it make?" She said then, "You come from Mexico, don't you?"

"Yes, I was there. I'm here and there, working as a drover." Ruben Vega shrugged. "What else is there to do, uh?" Showing her he was resigned to his station in life.

"You'd better leave," she said.

When he didn't move, the woman came out of the doorway into light and he saw her face clearly for the first time. He felt a shock within him and tried to think of something to say, but could only stare at the blue lines tattooed on her face: three straight lines on each cheek that extended from her cheekbones to her jaw, markings that seemed familiar, though he could not in this moment identify them.

He was conscious of himself standing in the open with nothing to say, the woman staring at him with curiosity, as though wondering if he would hold her gaze and look at her. Like there was nothing unusual about her countenance. Like it was common to see a woman with her face tattooed and you might be expected to comment, if you said anything at all, "Oh, that's a nice design you have there. Where did you have it done?" That would be one way—if you couldn't say something interesting about the weather or about the price of cows in Benson.

Ruben Vega, his mind empty of pleasantries, certain he would never see the woman again, said, "Who did that to you?"

She cocked her head in an easy manner, studying him as he studied her, and said, "Do you know, you're the first person who's come right out and asked."

"Mojave," Ruben Vega said, "but there's something different. Mojaves tattoo their chins only, I believe."

"And look like they were eating berries," the woman said. "I told them if you're going to do it, do it all the way. Not like a blue dribble."

It was in her eyes and in the tone of her voice, a glimpse of the rage she must have felt. No trace of fear in the memory, only cold anger. He could hear her telling the Indians—this skinny woman, probably a girl then—until they did it her way and marked her good for all time. Imprisoned her behind the blue marks on her face.

"How old were you?"

"You've seen me and had your water," the woman said, "now leave."

It was the same type of adobe house as the woman's but with a great difference. There was life here, the warmth of family: children sleeping now, Diego Luz's wife and her mother cleaning up after the meal as the two men sat outside in horsehide chairs and smoked and looked at the night. At one time they had both worked for a man named Sundeen and packed running irons to vent the brands on the cattle they stole. Ruben Vega was still an outlaw, in his fashion, while Diego Luz broke green horses and sold them to cattle companies.

They sat at the edge of the ramada, an awning made of mesquite, and stared at pinpoints of light in the universe. Ruben Vega asked about the extent of graze this season, where the large herds were that belonged to the Maricopa and the Circle-Eye. He had been thinking of cutting out maybe a hundred—he wasn't greedy—and driving them south to sell to the mine companies. He had been scouting the Circle-Eye range, he said, when he came to the strange woman. . . .

The Tonto woman, Diego Luz said. Everyone called her that now.

Yes, she had been living there, married a few years, when she

went to visit her family, who lived on the Gila above Painted
Rock. Well, some Yavapai came looking for food. They clubbed
her parents and two small brothers to death and took the girl
north with them. The Yavapai traded her to the Mojave as a
slave. . . .

"And they marked her," Ruben Vega said.

"Yes, so when she died the spirits would know she was
Mojave and not drag her soul down into a rathole," Diego
Luz said.

"Better to go to heaven with your face tattooed," Ruben
Vega said, "than not at all. Maybe so."

During a drought the Mojave traded her to a band of Tonto
Apaches for two mules and a bag of salt and one day she
appeared at Bowie with the Tontos that were brought in to be
sent to Oklahoma. Among the desert Indians twelve years and
returned home last spring.

"It put age on her," Ruben Vega said. "But what about her
husband?"

"Her husband? He banished her," Diego Luz said, "like
a leper. Unclean from living among the red niggers. No one
speaks of her to him, it isn't allowed."

Ruben Vega frowned. There was something he didn't understand. He said, "Wait a minute—"

And Diego Luz said, "Don't you know who her husband is?
Mr. Isham himself, man, of the Circle-Eye. She comes home
to find her husband a rich man. He don't live in that hut no
more. No, he owns a hundred miles of graze and a house it
took them two years to build, the glass and bricks brought in
by the Southern Pacific. Sure, the railroad comes and he's a rich
cattleman in only a few years."

"He makes her live there alone?"

"She's his wife, he provides for her. But that's all. Once a
month his segundo named Bonnet rides out there with supplies
and has someone shoe her horse and look at the animals."

"But to live in the desert," Ruben Vega said, still frowning,
thoughtful, "with a rusty pump . . ."

"Look at her," Diego Luz said. "What choice does she have?"

It was hot down in this scrub pasture, a place to wither and
die. Ruben Vega loosened the new willow-root straw that did

not yet conform to his head, though he had shaped the brim to curve down on one side and rise slightly on the other so that the brim slanted across the vision of his left eye. He held on his lap a nearly flat cardboard box that bore the name *L. S. Weiss Mercantile Store.*

The woman gazed up at him, shading her eyes with one hand. Finally she said, "You look different."

"The beard began to itch," Ruben Vega said, making no mention of the patches of gray he had studied in the hotel-room mirror. "So I shaved it off." He rubbed a hand over his jaw and smoothed down the tips of his mustache that was still full and seemed to cover his mouth. When he stepped down from the bay and approached the woman standing by the stick-fence corral, she looked off into the distance and back again.

She said, "You shouldn't be here."

Ruben Vega said, "Your husband doesn't want nobody to look at you. Is that it?" He held the store box, waiting for her to answer. "He has a big house with trees and the San Pedro River in his yard. Why doesn't he hide you there?"

She looked off again and said, "If they find you here, they'll shoot you."

"They," Ruben Vega said. "The ones who watch you bathe? Work for your husband and keep more than a close eye on you, and you'd like to hit them with something, wipe the grins from their faces."

"You better leave," the woman said.

The blue lines on her face were like claw marks, though not as wide as fingers: indelible lines of dye etched into her flesh with a cactus needle, the color worn and faded but still vivid against her skin, the blue matching her eyes.

He stepped close to her, raised his hand to her face, and touched the markings gently with the tips of his fingers, feeling nothing. He raised his eyes to hers. She was staring at him. He said, "You're in there, aren't you? Behind these little bars. They don't seem like much. Not enough to hold you."

She said nothing, but seemed to be waiting.

He said to her, "You should brush your hair. Brush it every day. . . ."

"Why?" the woman said.

"To feel good. You need to wear a dress. A little parasol to match."

"I'm asking you to leave," the woman said. But didn't move from his hand, with its yellowed, stained nails, that was like a fist made of old leather.

"I'll tell you something if I can," Ruben Vega said. "I know women all my life, all kinds of women in the way they look and dress, the way they adorn themselves according to custom. Women are always a wonder to me. When I'm not with a woman I think of them as all the same because I'm thinking of one thing. You understand?"

"Put a sack over their head," the woman said.

"Well, I'm not thinking of what she looks like then, when I'm out in the mountains or somewhere," Ruben Vega said. "That part of her doesn't matter. But when I'm *with* the woman, ah, then I realize how they are all different. You say, of course. This isn't a revelation to you. But maybe it is when you think about it some more."

The woman's eyes changed, turned cold. "You want to go to bed with me? Is that what you're saying, why you bring a gift?"

He looked at her with disappointment, an expression of weariness. But then he dropped the store box and took her to him gently, placing his hands on her shoulders, feeling her small bones in his grasp as he brought her in against him and his arms went around her.

He said, "You're gonna die here. Dry up and blow away."

She said, "Please . . ." Her voice hushed against him.

"They wanted only to mark your chin," Ruben Vega said, "in the custom of those people. But you wanted your own marks, didn't you? *Your* marks, not like anyone else. . . . Well, you got them." After a moment he said to her, very quietly, "Tell me what you want."

The hushed voice close to him said, "I don't know."

He said, "Think about it and remember something. There is no one else in the world like you."

He reined the bay to move out and saw the dust trail rising out of the old pasture, three riders coming, and heard the woman say, "I told you. Now it's too late."

A man on a claybank and two young riders eating his dust, finally separating to come in abreast, reined to a walk as they reached the pump and the irrigation ditch. The woman, walking from the corral to the house, said to them, "What do you want? I don't need anything, Mr. Bonnet."

So this would be the Circle-Eye foreman on the claybank. The man ignored her, his gaze holding on Ruben Vega with a solemn expression, showing he was going to be dead serious. A chew formed a lump in his jaw. He wore army suspenders and sleeve garters, his shirt buttoned up at the neck. As old as you are, Ruben Vega thought, a man who likes a tight feel of security and is serious about his business.

Bonnet said to him finally, "You made a mistake."

"I don't know the rules," Ruben Vega said.

"She told you to leave her be. That's the only rule there is. But you bought yourself a dandy new hat and come back here."

"That's some hat," one of the young riders said. This one held a single-shot Springfield across his pommel. The foreman, Bonnet, turned in his saddle and said something to the other rider, who unhitched his rope and began shaking out a loop, hanging it nearly to the ground.

It's a show, Ruben Vega thought. He said to Bonnet, "I was leaving."

Bonnet said, "Yes, indeed, you are. On the off end of a rope. We're gonna drag you so you'll know the ground and never cross this land again."

The rider with the Springfield said, "Gimme your hat, mister, so's you don't get it dirty."

At this point Ruben Vega nudged his bay and began moving in on the foreman, who straightened, looking over at the roper, and said, "Well, tie on to him."

But Ruben Vega was close to the foreman now, the bay taller than the claybank, and would move the claybank if the man on his back told him to. Ruben Vega watched the foreman's eyes moving and knew the roper was coming around behind him. Now the foreman turned his head to spit and let go a stream that spattered the hard-pack close to the bay's forelegs.

"Stand still," Bonnet said, "and we'll get her done easy. Or you can run and get snubbed out of your chair. Either way."

Ruben Vega was thinking that he could drink with this

ramrod and they'd tell each other stories until they were drunk. The man had thought it would be easy: chase off a Mexican gunnysacker who'd come sniffing the boss's wife. A kid who was good with a rope and another one who could shoot cans off the fence with an old Springfield should be enough.

Ruben Vega said to Bonnet, "Do you know who I am?"

"Tell us," Bonnet said, "so we'll know what the cat drug in and we drug out."

And Ruben Vega said, because he had no choice, "I hear the rope in the air, the one with the rifle is dead. Then you. Then the roper."

His words drew silence because there was nothing more to be said. In the moments that Ruben Vega and the one named Bonnet stared at each other, the woman came out to them holding a revolver, an old Navy Colt, which she raised and laid the barrel against the muzzle of the foreman's claybank.

She said, "Leave now, Mr. Bonnet, or you'll walk nine miles to shade."

There was no argument, little discussion, a few grumbling words. The Tonto woman was still Mrs. Isham. Bonnet rode away with his young hands and a new silence came over the yard.

Ruben Vega said, "He believes you'd shoot his horse." The woman said, "He believes I'd cut steaks, and eat it too. It's how I'm seen after twelve years of that other life."

Ruben Vega began to smile. The woman looked at him and in a few moments she began to smile with him. She shook her head then, but continued to smile. He said to her, "You could have a good time if you want to."

She said, "How, scaring people?"

He said, "If you feel like it." He said, "Get the present I brought you and open it."

He came back for her the next day in a Concord buggy, wearing his new willow-root straw and a cutaway coat over his revolvers, the coat he'd rented at a funeral parlor. Mrs. Isham wore the pale blue-and-white lace-trimmed dress he'd bought at Weiss's store, sat primly on the bustle, and held the parasol against the afternoon sun all the way to Benson, ten miles, and up the main street to the Charles Crooker Hotel where the drummers and cattlemen and railroad men sitting in their front-porch rockers stared and stared.

They walked past the manager and into the dining room before Ruben Vega removed his hat and pointed to the table he liked, one against the wall between two windows. The waitress in her starched uniform was wide-eyed taking them over and getting them seated. It was early and the dining room was not half filled.

"The place for a quiet dinner," Ruben Vega said. "You see how quiet it is?"

"Everybody's looking at me," Sarah Isham said to the menu in front of her.

Ruben Vega said, "I thought they were looking at me. All right, soon they'll be used to it."

She glanced up and said, "People are leaving."

He said, "That's what you do when you finish eating, you leave."

She looked at him, staring, and said, "Who are you?"

"I told you."

"Only your name."

"You want me to tell you the truth, why I came here?"

"Please."

"To steal some of your husband's cattle."

She began to smile and he smiled. She began to laugh and he laughed, looking openly at the people looking at them, but not bothered by them. Of course they'd look. How could they help it? A Mexican rider and a woman with blue stripes on her face sitting at a table in the hotel dining room, laughing. He said, "Do you like fish? I know your Indian brothers didn't serve you none. It's against their religion. Some things are for religion, as you know, and some things are against it. We spend all our lives learning customs. Then they change them. I'll tell you something else if you promise not to be angry or point your pistol at me. Something else I could do the rest of my life. I could look at you and touch you and love you."

Her hand moved across the linen tablecloth to his with the cracked, yellowed nails and took hold of it, clutched it.

She said, "You're going to leave."

He said, "When it's time."

She said, "I know you. I don't know anyone else."

He said, "You're the loveliest woman I've ever met. And the strongest. Are you ready? I think the man coming now is your husband."

It seemed strange to Ruben Vega that the man stood looking at him and not at his wife. The man seemed not too old for her, as he had expected, but too self-important. A man with a very serious demeanor, as though his business had failed or someone in his family had passed away. The man's wife was still clutching the hand with the gnarled fingers. Maybe that was it. Ruben Vega was going to lift her hand from his, but then thought, Why? He said as pleasantly as he was able, "Yes, can I help you?"

Mr. Isham said, "You have one minute to mount up and ride out of town."

"Why don't you sit down," Ruben Vega said, "have a glass of wine with us?" He paused and said, "I'll introduce you to your wife."

Sarah Isham laughed; not loud but with a warmth to it and Ruben Vega had to look at her and smile. It seemed all right to release her hand now. As he did he said, "Do you know this gentleman?"

"I'm not sure I've had the pleasure," Sarah Isham said. "Why does he stand there?"

"I don't know," Ruben Vega said. "He seems worried about something."

"I've warned you," Mr. Isham said. "You can walk out or be dragged out."

Ruben Vega said, "He has something about wanting to drag people. Why is that?" And again heard Sarah's laugh, a giggle now that she covered with her hand. Then she looked up at her husband, her face with its blue tribal lines raised to the soft light of the dining room.

She said, "John, look at me. . . . Won't you please sit with us?"

Now it was as if the man had to make a moral decision, first consult his conscience, then consider the manner in which he would pull the chair out—the center of attention. When finally he was seated, upright on the chair and somewhat away from the table, Ruben Vega thought, All that to sit down. He felt sorry for the man now, because the man was not the kind who could say what he felt.

Sarah said, "John, can you look at me?"

He said, "Of course I can."

"Then do it. I'm right here."

"We'll talk later," her husband said.

She said, "When? Is there a visitor's day?"

"You'll be coming to the house, soon."

"You mean to see it?"

"To live there."

She looked at Ruben Vega with just the trace of a smile, a sad one. Then said to her husband, "I don't know if I want to. I don't know you. So I don't know if I want to be married to you. Can you understand that?"

Ruben Vega was nodding as she spoke. He could understand it. He heard the man say, "But we *are* married. I have an obligation to you and I respect it. Don't I provide for you?"

Sarah said, "Oh, my God—" and looked at Ruben Vega. "Did you hear that? He provides for me." She smiled again, not able to hide it, while her husband began to frown, confused.

"He's a generous man," Ruben Vega said, pushing up from the table. He saw her smile fade, though something warm remained in her eyes. "I'm sorry. I have to leave. I'm going on a trip tonight, south, and first I have to pick up a few things." He moved around the table to take one of her hands in his, not caring what the husband thought. He said, "You'll do all right, whatever you decide. Just keep in mind there's no one else in the world like you."

She said, "I can always charge admission. Do you think ten cents a look is too high?"

"At least that," Ruben Vega said. "But you'll think of something better."

He left her there in the dining room of the Charles Crooker Hotel in Benson, Arizona—maybe to see her again sometime, maybe not—and went out with a good conscience to take some of her husband's cattle.

CHRONOLOGY

NOTE ON THE TEXTS

NOTES

Chronology

BY GREGG SUTTER

1925   Born Elmore John Leonard Jr. on October 11 in New Orleans, Louisiana, son of Elmore John Leonard and Amelia Flora Rivé. (Parents were both born in Orleans Parish, New Orleans; mother on July 14, 1895, father on November 30, 1893. Parents married in Texas in 1918, where father was serving in the army. Sister Flora Margaret born September 29, 1919. At the time of Leonard's birth, father is an accountant with Ernst & Ernst.)

1927–29   Father works as office manager for the Chevrolet Motor Co., a division of General Motors. In 1929, the family begins a series of moves around the South, starting in Dallas, where they live at 5147 Miller Avenue.

1930–32   Family moves to 1715 N. Linn Avenue in Oklahoma City. Father works on General Motors dealership planning and development, making frequent out-of-town trips for General Motors. Leonard acquires an early love of books, encouraged by his sister reading to him: "My sister . . . instilled in me a love of books. I'm sure that it got me into writing." Reads "everything from *Cinderella* and *Little Goody Two-Shoes* to *Treasure Island* and *The Adventures of Huckleberry Finn*. Then, Raphael Sabatini's *The Sea Hawk* and *Scaramouche*; and the Don Sturdy series of adventure novels." In 1932, the family relocates to Detroit for six months; father continues to work for General Motors. Leonard receives first communion at Visitation Church on 12th Street in Detroit.

1933   Family moves to Memphis, where father is now regional accounting manager for Buick Motor Co. They live at 2388 Poplar Boulevard. Leonard is inspired by newspaper photo of Bonnie Parker smoking a cigar and holding a handgun; imitates the pose in a photo with his mother and sister in front of a 1928 Oakland automobile.

1934   Family moves to Detroit, where they will settle for the next nine years, living initially at the Abington Hotel & Apartments, 700 Seward Avenue. Leonard is enrolled in Blessed Sacrament School, 82 Belmont, behind the Cathedral of the Most Blessed Sacrament.

1935–39   Leonard and his friends play football and baseball on a lot at the corner of Boston Boulevard and John R Street. Later recalls taking the Woodward Avenue streetcar to go to the J. L. Hudson Department Store toy department, and on summer Sundays boarding the Windsor Ontario Ferry for a nickel ride across the river to Canada. Leonard entertains friends by "telling movies," like *Captain Blood* and *Mutiny on the Bounty.* In Sister Estelle's fourth and fifth grade classroom, Leonard—fascinated by World War I trench warfare—stages a dramatized version of Erich Maria Remarque's *All Quiet on the Western Front.* Older sister Margaret, "Mickey," joins the Book of the Month Club in 1937; Leonard reads Isak Dinesen's *Out of Africa*, Marjorie Kinnan Rawlings's *The Yearling*, Carl Van Doren's *Benjamin Franklin*, and C. S. Forester's Captain Horatio Hornblower novels.

1940–42   The family moves to 70 Highland, in Highland Park. Leonard enrolls at Catholic Central High School for freshman year; plays football and baseball, and is elected freshman class president. The yearbook states that Leonard is "at home both with books and on the field." Reads Book of the Month Club selections such as Richard Wright's *Native Son*, Arthur Koestler's *Darkness at Noon*, and John Steinbeck's *The Moon Is Down.* Decides that some Club books use too many words and not enough dialogue; later says that reading Ernest Hemingway's *For Whom the Bell Tolls*, the selection for November 1940, got him started as a writer. Transfers to the Jesuit-run University of Detroit High School in his sophomore year. The family rents a house at 18900 Northlawn, near the school. A classmate gives him the nickname "Dutch," after the Washington Senators "knuckleballer" Emil "Dutch" Leonard. Goes on summer trip to Missoula, Montana, with baseball coach and three classmates.

1943   In senior year lives with coach when parents relocate to Washington, D.C. Continues to focus on sports; yearbook states, "Elmore Leonard . . . three years ago stepped into football and baseball fame, consistently merited honors." Graduates from the University of Detroit High School in June. Frequently attends jazz concerts at Eastwood Gardens on Eight Mile Road and Gratiot Avenue, where he does quite a bit of underage drinking. Reading includes Jesse

Stuart's *Taps for Private Tussie*, Ted Lawson's *Thirty Seconds over Tokyo*, and Richard Tregaskis's *Guadalcanal Diary*. Tries to join the Marines, but is rejected because of poor eyesight. After graduation travels to Los Angeles with two friends; they hang around Hollywood and Vine looking for movie stars, attend one premiere, and see Tyrone Power in his Marine uniform. Leonard is drafted on October 11, his 18th birthday, and assigned to the Seabees, the fighting construction battalion of the U.S. Navy.

1944   Leonard is sent to the U.S. Naval Training Center in Newport, Rhode Island, where he spends six months in service school and learns general storekeeping, accounting, disbursing, storing, ships services, and small stores, which, he later says, "all adds up to exactly nothing." Graduates as Seaman First Class. Begins corresponding with Ruthann Finneren, sister of a high school classmate; writes that he's leading a very "liquid existence . . . you'd be surprised at little Dutchy and at the amount of beer and liquor he can consume now." Tells her he plans to attend the Jesuit institution Georgetown University after war; credits the Jesuits with teaching him how to think. In May writes, "having a lovely time sightseeing in Boston through the window of every saloon in town." In June, ships out to the Shoemaker Navy Training and Distribution Center on Treasure Island near San Francisco. Sails from San Francisco to New Guinea aboard the SS *Azalea City*. After a week or two in New Guinea, sails to Los Negros in the Admiralty Islands aboard an Australian troop carrier. ("They gave everyone a quart of beer and the Aussies reminded you of pirates, wearing bandannas round their heads and singing 'Waltzing Matilda.' I thought, 'This is a fun ship to be on.'") He is stationed on the Admiralty Islands, where the Seabees maintain an airstrip for fighter planes launching attacks on Truk and Rabaul; works in the ship store. He does not see combat.

1945   Entertained by Max Shulman's *The Feather Merchants*. Begins to outline fictional stories to amuse Ruthann: "Someday I'm going to get good and drunk and write a book. Would you take notes for me? You're the only gal who would know how to spell all the dirty words." Sails to the Philippines on the HMAS *Kanimbla*. Spends a month in Sangley Pointe, Cavite, Luzon. Falls for Estella, a seventeen-year-old Filipina hostess at the Sunset bar. On December 17 begins voyage home on the USS *Tazewell*.

1946   The *Tazewell* transport arrives at Treasure Island on January 5. Given leave, races to a ballroom in Oakland to see bandleader Stan Kenton: "The high point was standing close to the stage and staring up at June Christy doing 'Buzz Me Baby.'" Received on board the USS *Towner*, which arrives at Seattle on January 25 and enters the Bremerton Navy Yard for voyage repairs. In Seattle, gets "Dutch" tattooed on his right shoulder: "You'd drink whiskey and get tattooed. It was a lot of fun." The *Towner* sails through the Panama Canal; Leonard, on guard duty, lets a prisoner out to see the canal. *Towner* arrives at Norfolk, Virginia, on April 10. Discharged from the Navy in June, returns to Detroit and enrolls in the University of Detroit, majoring in English and philosophy.

1947   Goes to jazz clubs on Hastings Street in the segregated black area of Detroit, often alone, since the neighborhood makes girlfriends nervous; his favorite clubs are The Flame Show Bar and Sportree's. At the Paradise Theater, sees bands including Jimmy Lunceford, Fletcher Henderson, and Andy Kirk and his Clouds of Joy with Mary Lou Williams. In July vacations in Florida and Bay St. Louis, Mississippi; writes Ruthann, "We arrived here at the Bay . . . last Saturday—a week ago—We fish, drink, swim, crab, drink, play cards, go to the movies, and drink. It keeps us busy."

1948   On the university campus, meets future wife Beverly Cline (born January 9, 1927). Joins university writers' club, the Manuscribblers, and enters annual writing contest. "Our English instructor told us [that] anybody who enters this contest will get an automatic B for the course." Writes a story about a chef: "I think it was called 'The Kitchen Inquisition,'" he later recalls. "And I came in among the top 10. So then the next year, I entered the contest again, and I came in second." In September, father becomes manager of his own General Motors dealership, Rio Grande Motors in Las Cruces, New Mexico. Leonard plans to join his father in New Mexico, and announces intention, after graduating, to go to General Motors Dealers' Son School in Detroit, established to prepare dealers' heirs for operating family franchise.

1949   Father dies of a cerebral hemorrhage on March 24 in Las Cruces. Leonard briefly tries to save the dealership with brother-in-law Joe Madey, but Motors Holding, which holds the mortgage, will not back them. A GM executive gives Leonard a referral to Campbell-Ewald Advertising Agency in Detroit. On July 30 Leonard marries Beverly Cline. For six months they will live with her aunt in Dearborn. Leonard goes to work in October for Campbell-Ewald as "the youngest married office boy."

1950   Finishes college at night and graduates midyear with a major in English and a minor in philosophy. Leonard and Beverly live for six months in a small apartment near Blessed Sacrament Cathedral. Writes short story "One, Horizontal," set in Detroit and written in a hard-boiled, first-person style. He and Beverly move to 17460 Redwood Avenue, Lathrup Village, Michigan. Daughter Jane Clare Leonard is born on August 11.

1951   Decides to write Western fiction because of his fondness for Western movies such as *The Plainsman* (1936), *My Darling Clementine* (1946), and *Red River* (1948), and because the market for Westerns is thriving in hardcover books, slick magazines including *The Saturday Evening Post* and *Colliers*, pulp magazines like *Dime Western* and *Zane Grey's Western*, and Hollywood adaptations. In April, submits first Western short story, "Tizwin," to *Argosy*; it is rejected, but editor John Bender encourages him to send more. Decides to focus on Apache tribes and the U.S. Cavalry in 1880s Arizona and New Mexico; reads *On the Border with Crook*, *The Truth About Geronimo*, and *The Look of the West*, and also subscribes to magazine *Arizona Highways* for descriptions of terrain: "When I needed a canyon or a desert, whatever the scene called for, I would find one in *Arizona Highways*." His first sale, the third story he writes, is a novelette called "Trail of the Apache," to *Argosy*, appearing in the December issue, for which he is paid $1,000. Argosy uses the byline "E. J. Leonard" instead of his own preference "Dutch Leonard." *Argosy* fiction editor James B. O'Connell cautions him not to give up his job: "You ought to know right at the beginning that writing for a living is a most hazardous occupation." Son Peter Anthony Leonard is born on October 7. The *Argosy* story attracts the attention of agent Marguerite Harper, whose clients include Luke Short and Peter Dawson; she offers to take Leonard as a client, with a goal of getting him published in *The Saturday Evening Post.*

1952   Writes for Western pulps at a steady pace, publishing six stories in 1952. When Hemingway's novel *The Old Man and the Sea* is published in the September 1, 1952, issue of *Life* magazine, Leonard studies it carefully.

1953   Writes ten stories, including "Three-Ten to Yuma," a 4,500-word story which he sells to *Dime Western* for ninety dollars. ("I had to rewrite one of the scenes and do two revisions on my description of the train. The editor insisted on it. This guy made me work. 'You can do it better. You're not using all your senses. It's not just a walk by the locomotive. What's the train doing? How does it smell? Is there steam?' He made me work for my ninety bucks. Which was good.") Completes his first novel, *The Bounty Hunters,* earning a $3,000 advance plus royalties.

1954   *The Bounty Hunters* is published in April by Houghton Mifflin in hardcover, and simultaneously by Ballantine in paperback; the *New York Times* calls it "a first novel and a good one." The *Pasadena Independent* writes: "Leonard is a new writer but already he has moved into company with such Western story greats as James Warner Bellah and Ernest Haycox." The book's publication earns Leonard a spread in *The Detroit Free Press Magazine* where he talks about how to become an author. Submits second novel, initially called *The Devil at Randado,* to Houghton Mifflin; editor Austin Olney, declaring Leonard to be a "natural" writer, responds: "I think it's an even better book than *The Bounty Hunters* and I have great faith in your future as a novelist." Son Christopher Conway Leonard is born May 12. Leaves Campbell-Ewald temporarily for a smaller advertising agency; returns ten months later as a writer on the Chevrolet account. Discovers the writing of Richard Bissell (*High Water, 7½ Cents*), who becomes a major influence. ("With Bissell I felt a rapport, as though we shared much the same attitude about life. That's why his influence was so profound—because style comes out of attitude. It's the *sound* of the writer's temperament, of how he thinks and feels. I learned from Bissell to be myself, have a pretty good time writing and not think of it as work.")

1955 Develops a writing routine, getting up at 5 A.M. and writing for two hours before making breakfast for his kids and getting ready for work: "I had a rule that I had to write a page before I put the water on for the coffee." Once at work, whenever he has time, opens middle desk drawer and continues writing in longhand on a yellow legal pad until he sees someone coming through the frosted glass of his office. Second novel, retitled *The Law at Randado*, is published in June. Publishes four short stories. After meeting cornet player Wild Bill Davison at a New York jazz club, buys a used cornet but does not master it. Listens to jazz musicians including Marian McPartland, Chico Hamilton, Ahmad Jamal, and the Modern Jazz Quartet with Milt Jackson. Marguerite Harper sells story "The Waiting Man" to *The Saturday Evening Post* for $850. She uses legendary Hollywood agent H. N. Swanson, who in the past has represented writers including F. Scott Fitzgerald, John O'Hara, and Raymond Chandler, to negotiate deal with Columbia Pictures for "Three-Ten to Yuma."

1956 Novel *Escape from Five Shadows* is published by Houghton Mifflin in June. *The Bounty Hunters* is published in England by Robert Hale. "The Waiting Man," retitled "Moment of Vengeance," appears in *The Saturday Evening Post* (April 21); Swanson closes deal for the story with Meridian Productions and it is adapted as an episode of the CBS program *Schlitz Playhouse of the Stars* on September 28, with Ward Bond, Angie Dickinson, and Gene Nelson. Tries to develop a new story called *Saber River* as a *Post* serial; does research and a treatment for non-Western screenplay *Malaya*, set in a resettlement camp on the Malay Peninsula, but abandons project. At the agency, gets in the habit of drinking before meeting with clients he considers boring: "I felt that I would have to drink in order to sit and listen to them." Writes Chevrolet ads, although he dislikes the banality of copywriting, which he finds "cute, alliterative, full of similes and metaphors." He is featured in a full-page *New Yorker* ad for Campbell-Ewald, sitting at his typewriter with a cow skull, two six-shooters, and a rifle on the wall behind him, with the headline "Meanwhile back at the agency." The ad describes him as "a rising young writer of Western novels" whose "gunsights never become entangled in fancy verbal foliage."

1957   *The Law at Randado* and *Escape from Five Shadows* pub-
        lished in England by Robert Hale. Son William Rivé
        Leonard is born on July 20. Columbia Pictures releases
        two successful films based on Leonard stories: *The Tall
        T* (released April), based on "The Captives," directed by
        Budd Boetticher and starring Randolph Scott, and *3:10 to
        Yuma* (August), directed by Delmer Daves, starring Glenn
        Ford and Van Heflin. (Walter Winchell writes that "*3:10 to
        Yuma* is three hours and ten minutes past *High Noon*.")
        Donald Fine, Leonard's editor at Dell, praises his new
        book *Last Stand at Saber River* as "some of the best and
        most affecting writing I've ever read in a Western . . . at
        times its quality goes beyond the confines of many more
        pretentious books."

1958–59 Publishes two stories in 1958 and 1959 but, at Harper's
        strong urging, thinks about switching genres because of
        the declining market for Western fiction. The *Post* turns
        down *Saber River* as a serial, calling it too grim. *Last Stand
        at Saber River* is published in 1959 as a paperback original
        by Dell. Observing changes in Leonard, Fine writes to
        him: "I got the feeling that writing was becoming a big
        damned chore to you when I talked to you and that you'd
        tightened up considerably. It shouldn't be (a chore). You've
        got a house, a job . . . and you've got talent. What the hell
        more do you need?" Through a former classmate, William
        Deneen, Leonard writes his first film script, *The Man
        Who Had Everything*, a half-hour film to be shown at
        Catholic high schools to recruit priests for the Francis-
        can Order. Completes *Hombre* in late 1959, his sole novel
        written in the first person. Leonard writes his only fan
        letter to sportswriter W. C. Heinz, after reading his boxing
        novel *The Professional* (1958); Heinz informs him that the
        only other fan letter he has received came from Ernest
        Hemingway.

1960   Attempts to sell five of his previously published Western
        stories to television show *Laramie*, but fails to attract
        interest. Harper encourages Leonard to write a suspense
        novel.

1961   Ballantine buys *Hombre* in January and publishes it in
        September. In March, Leonard quits Campbell-Ewald
        to write fiction full-time; intends to live off his profit-
        sharing check of eleven and a half thousand dollars for six

months while he writes another book. The money is used instead to buy a house at 420 Suffield in Birmingham, a suburb of Detroit. With added financial pressure of family and house, Leonard temporarily abandons fiction writing for freelance advertising work; clients include Hurst Performance Products and Eaton Chemical. Deneen hires Leonard to write short educational films on geography and history for Encyclopædia Britannica Films. The films, produced over the next several years, include such titles as *The French and Indian War*, *Settlers of the Old Northwest Territory*, *Frontier Boy of the Early Midwest*, *Puerto Rico: Its Past, Present and Promise*, and *The Danube Valley*. A story, "Only Good Ones," is published in Macmillan anthology *Western Roundup*, edited by Nelson Nye.

1962   In late January, Marguerite Harper writes: "What happened to all those grandiose promises of some fiction writing? Or some saleable articles?" Swanson sends *Hombre* and "Only Good Ones" to David Dortort, producer of the television series *Bonanza*; nothing comes of this initiative.

1963–65   For Britannica films, Leonard goes to Madrid with Deneen; they are given permission to use the set for Samuel Bronston's epic production *The Fall of the Roman Empire* for the films *Claudius, Boy of Ancient Rome*, *Julius Caesar: The Rise of the Roman Empire*, and *Life in Ancient Rome*.

1966   *Hombre* is sold to Twentieth Century-Fox, with Leonard receiving $9,000, enough to live on while he writes a book. After five years away from writing fiction, Leonard finishes his first non-Western novel, *Mother, This Is Jack Ryan* (later *The Big Bounce*). Leonard writes to Fine: "The new book got me going again and I've got a couple more ideas now I want to develop. The new one has a resort area background (Lake Huron) with migrant Mexican cucumber pickers down the road. I can't get away from Mexicans." Swanson reads it and tells him, "Kiddo, I'm going to make you rich." *The Big Bounce* gets eighty-four rejections from publishers and movie studios. Daughter Katherine Mary Leonard is born February 19. Still thinking about Westerns, Leonard inquires about doing a script for the Western TV series *Shenandoah*; Swanson informs him the show has not been renewed. In September, Swanson takes over from Marguerite Harper, who is very ill.

1967   Sends his 1961 story, "Only Good Ones" (retitled "Santos"),
        to Swanson, who calls it "one of the best Western short sto-
        ries ever written" and approves Leonard's plan to expand
        it into a book, while suggesting he add a subplot to make
        it more substantial. Leonard takes his advice and finishes
        the book (now titled *Valdez Is Coming*) in seven weeks.
        Marguerite Harper dies, April 1, at age 72. For a short time
        Leonard is represented by New York agent Max Wilkinson
        for books and foreign sales, before Swanson takes over as his
        exclusive agent. *Hombre*, directed by Martin Ritt and star-
        ring Paul Newman, is released by Twentieth Century-Fox
        in March. Movie rights to *Valdez Is Coming* are acquired by
        Burt Lancaster and producer Ira Steiner. Leonard lobbies
        to write the screenplay. Signs deal for *The Big Bounce* with
        Greenway Productions, who agree to pay a bonus if the
        novel comes out in hardcover. Reads *Night Comes to the
        Cumberlands: A Biography of a Depressed Area* by Harry
        M. Caudill, and gets the idea for screenplay *The Broke-
        Leg War* (later *The Moonshine War*). In December, writes
        Swanson: "I've got a good story, one that comes out of
        the characters and that I can tell effectively. I feel that I'm
        in my element, so I'm not worried about over-writing or
        over-doing the hillbilly sound of it." Continues to work
        on a few industrial film jobs and script revisions for Ency-
        clopædia Britannica.

1968   Continues to revise *The Big Bounce* and works on *The
        Moonshine War*, traveling to Kentucky for research.
        Swanson is impressed with Leonard's screenplay: "I can
        tell you right now this script is as excellent a job as any
        of our screenwriters could turn out. At any time you
        decide you want a career as a screenwriter, I'm ready to
        run with you." In March, producer Martin Ransohoff
        asks Leonard to come out to Hollywood to discuss
        The Moonshine War. Swanson writes: "It's nice to be
        wanted, isn't it?" Leonard and Wilkinson give up trying
        to sell *The Big Bounce* in hardcover in the U.S. Leonard
        reacts negatively to Robert Dozier's screenplay for *The
        Big Bounce*: "It's a 1957 situation TV script with dirty
        words . . . I think they're missing an opportunity to do
        something interesting and different." In November, buys
        his mother The Coconut Palms, a small motel at 3221 NE
        9th Street in Pompano Beach, Florida.

1969   *The Big Bounce,* directed by Alex March and starring Ryan
        O'Neal, is released by Warner Brothers in March. Leonard
        walks out of a screening in New York: "It's the second
        worst movie ever made. There has to be one that's worse."
        The film receives poor notices. *The Big Bounce* is published
        as a Fawcett Gold Medal paperback in April; Robert Hale
        publishes it in hardcover in England. While in Hollywood,
        Leonard sees his favorite bandleader, Count Basie, at the
        Whisky a Go Go accompanied by jazz singer Carmen
        McRae. In July, starts screenplay for *Forty Lashes Less One*
        for National General Pictures, but the film is never made.
        Doubleday publishes *The Moonshine War* in hardcover in
        August. Leonard becomes a member of Writers Guild of
        America, West.

1970   In February, Swanson informs Leonard that Howard Jaffe
        and Edward Lewis, a producing team at Columbia, want to
        do a film about Mexican-American migrant fruit pickers;
        after meeting with Jaffe, Leonard writes treatment called
        Picket Line. The Moonshine War is published in England
        by Robert Hale. In June, sends Swanson a treatment for
        Jesus Saves, centered on a television evangelist and a born-
        again rock musician. Swanson responds: "It has all the ear-
        marks of a successful screen story and book . . . I had a few
        reservations . . . thinking that it would be compared with
        Elmer Gantry. However, you have ducked that very neatly
        and the injection of the religious rock music makes it very
        palatable." In May, the Leonards and three other couples
        vacation in England, Greece, and Paris; they rent a yacht and
        tour the Greek islands. MGM releases *The Moonshine
        War,* directed by Richard Quine and starring Patrick
        McGoohan, in July; film is poorly received by critics. In
        August, Jaffe decides not to go forward with *Picket Line.*
        Valdez Is Coming published by Fawcett Publications in
        October. Leonard's drinking begins to affect his health:
        "I came back from California throwing up blood," he
        later recounts. "I was in the emergency room and they
        couldn't stop the bleeding." He turns out to be suffering
        from acute gastritis, which the examining doctor has told
        him is usually found only "in skid-row bums." Leonard
        undergoes surgery.

1971   Swanson advises Leonard to turn *Picket Line* into a novel
        that can be sold as a film for television. Swanson closes

deal on *Sinola* (later *Joe Kidd*) with producer Sidney Beckerman in February, with Clint Eastwood slated to star. United Artists releases *Valdez Is Coming*, directed by Edwin Sherin and starring Burt Lancaster, in April. Leonard is pleased with the film: "It amazed me that the film version ended exactly the way the book did, with the bad guy choosing to back down rather than go for the gun." In October, Leonard sends treatment of *American Flag*, a mining story set in 1910, to Swanson, who comments: "It captured our fancy very quickly. . . . The character is strong and the locale really different. No cowboys and Indians." In December, Swanson delivers first draft of *American Flag* screenplay to First Artists, with Steve McQueen intended to star.

1972   In February, Swanson advises Leonard to read George V. Higgins's newly published novel *The Friends of Eddie Coyle*, noting its "fine dialogue and underworld characters. Very heavy, as they say on the Strip." The book will be a major influence on Leonard, who credits Higgins with showing him how to "loosen up" his writing and "get into scenes quicker." Before *Joe Kidd* is released, Eastwood calls Leonard and asks him to show him something like *Dirty Harry* only different: "A guy with a big gun—he doesn't have to be in law enforcement." Leonard tells Eastwood the rough idea of what becomes *Mr. Majestyk* and sends a treatment; Eastwood passes on it. Novel *Forty Lashes Less One* is published by Bantam in October. Universal releases *Joe Kidd*, directed by John Sturges, in July. Leonard is not happy with the film, contending that Sturges changed the motivation of the main character from a glory-seeking egomaniac to a good guy, forcing minor characters into the antagonist role. (*Joe Kidd* is not novelized because, according to Leonard, "nobody offered enough money.")

1973   Writes original screenplay *Mr. Majestyk* for Walter Mirisch, using much of the material from *Picket Line*. Revisions are held up because of a writers' strike. In June, accepts an offer from Dell to novelize *Mr. Majestyk*. Leonard completes *Fifty-Two Pickup*, his first crime novel set in Detroit, and sends it to Ross Claiborne at Delacorte Press, where his editor will be Jackie Farber. In December, Swanson is prodding Leonard to come out to Hollywood to meet with willing producers and "get a little larceny going."

1974   *Fifty-Two Pickup* is published by Delacorte in April, and by Secker and Warburg in England. Leonard defines his new approach in notes for a speech: "My crime stories are set in the present and usually within a relatively short time frame: a few days or weeks and with a certain urgency, something about to happen. I don't care for novels that go on and on for years." *Mr. Majestyk*, Leonard's novelization of his screenplay, is published in June; the movie, directed by Richard Fleischer and starring Charles Bronson, is released a month later. Leonard goes to his first AA meeting: "I was getting more noticeably drunk. I wasn't handling it the way I used to be able to. In fact, I was two different people . . . It was inevitable that if I had any intelligence at all, I had to stop. I realized that I had to quit or go all the way and forget about it, the hell with it. Good-bye brains." The same month, separates from Beverly. "We always drank. We always drank together . . . Every single night, we would get into arguments, with me drunk and her part of the way, with me saying vicious things, which I couldn't believe the next day. I'd be filled with remorse." Moves to apartment 609 at the Merrillwood Apartments, 225 E. Merrill Street, in downtown Birmingham, where he will live alone until 1979. Begins affair with Joan Shepard, who with her husband has been part of Leonard's circle of acquaintances at Pine Lake Country Club. Sees her at his second-story office at 199 Pierce Street, around the corner from his apartment; puts a copy of *Arizona Highways* in the window to signal the coast is clear. Finishes new novel *The Frank and Ernest Method*. Swanson is critical: "My main comment can be summed up by saying I think the reader and the audience must like one of the two men, and be rooting for him to get out of the armed robbery even at the cost of strong measures against his partner. If the interest is perfectly balanced between them, I don't think it will be a successful piece."

1975   Swanson shops *The Frank and Ernest Method* with mixed results; Mirisch says it has "too many familiar elements." Producer Menahem Golan hires Leonard to adapt *Fifty-Two Pickup* and set it in Tel Aviv; he writes two drafts and is happy with them, but "Golan wanted me to add more intrigue, more secret papers. I told him, you don't want me, get another writer." During stay in Israel begins drinking again: "I drank as soon as I got on the plane. I drank in

Tel Aviv, where there are only two honest-to-God saloons in the whole town . . . I picked a country where nobody drinks to do my drinking." For Universal and Walter Mirisch, writes screenplay based on the novel *Wild Card* by Raymond Hawkey and Roger Bingham, his first adaptation. Begins novel *Unknown Man No. 89*. For John Foreman, Paul Newman's partner, who has asked for an original screenplay for Sean Connery and Michael Caine, Leonard writes a fifty-page treatment called *Swag* (later *The Hawkbill Gang*), a caper story set in England, Spain, and North Africa against the backdrop of the Spanish Civil War. Foreman asks Leonard to come to Morocco to meet with Connery and Caine, who are making *The Man Who Would Be King*, but subsequently declines to go forward with the project because of the cost of shooting in England. Leonard asks Delacorte if they see a book in the treatment and they pass, but decide to use the title *Swag* for his next novel, instead of *The Frank and Ernest Method*.

1976   *Swag* is published by Delacorte in March. Begins work on *Hat Trick* (*The Hunted*), a novel set in Israel, and makes several more trips to Israel for research. Putnam president Walter J. Minton passes on it, doubting that he can sell enough copies to make it worthwhile. In November, Leonard begins to explore the possibilities of a crime story called *Backfire*, featuring as principal character a Detroit cop named Dick Speed who has already appeared in *Swag* and *Unknown Man No. 89*.

1977   On January 24, at 9:30 in the morning, Leonard has what he determines will be his last drink, Scotch and Vernor's Ginger Ale. He later writes: "I never wrote when I was drinking or drunk—I knew better than to do that—though I did work hung-over at times. So I didn't think it had much of any effect on my writing until I quit . . . By then I was in AA and perhaps not taking myself so seriously. I do think my writing began to improve at this time, mainly because I wasn't taking the writing so seriously, either. I had learned to relax and not think of it as writing." Leonard and Beverly are divorced in May. *Unknown Man No. 89* published by Delacorte in June. The novel, which reprises the character Jack Ryan from *The Big Bounce*, contains a subplot that parallels Leonard's struggle with alcohol. *Unknown Man No. 89* receives

a major review from *The New York Times*: "Leonard bows
to no one in plot construction. Yet there is never the
feeling of gimmickry in his plots . . . He has a wonderful
ear, and his dialogue never has a false note. . . . He can
write circles around almost anybody active in the crime
novel today." Pleased by the book's reception, but chafes
at comparisons in some reviews to Raymond Chandler
and Dashiell Hammett, neither of whom he claims as an
influence. (Cites James M. Cain as the only hard-boiled
writer he has read.) *Hombre* voted one of the top twenty-
five Westerns of all time by Western Writers of America. In
a radical departure from the crime genre, Leonard writes
Juvenal (later *The Juvenal Touch* and eventually published
as *Touch*), whose central character works in an alcoholic
rehabilitation center across the street from the Stroh Brew-
ery Company in Detroit. Juvenal, who has the Stigmata
(the wounds of Christ) and a gift of healing, is modeled
on his friend Father Juvenal Carlson, a Franciscan friar
based in the Amazon: "He is such a giving, accepting,
easygoing person, he's made a lasting impression on me."
Leonard later says of the book: "*Touch* is about accepting what is. Abiding by the facts, nothing more." *The
Hunted* is published by Dell in September. By October,
Swanson reports an "alarming number of rejections" on
Juvenal. He concludes: "Consensus of opinion; probably best writing you have done to date, but unfortunate
choice of subject." Reconnects with University of Detroit
classmate William C. Marshall, now a private detective in
Miami; his father-in-law is Joe "Scarface" Bommarito, a
high-ranking member of the Detroit Mafia. Marshall helps
with research on *Seascape* (later *Gold Coast*), a novel with
characters from Detroit but set in Fort Lauderdale and
Miami. He introduces Leonard to Ernesto "Chili" Palmer,
a former associate of crime boss Joe Colombo, who works
with Marshall on collections. Leonard writes novel *Mickey
Free*.

1978   Bantam changes the title of *Mickey Free* (to be published
as a paperback original) to *The Switch*, a change to which
Leonard strongly objects. He is also unhappy with the
painting of the three central characters on the book's cover:
"It looks like the result of an art director who hasn't read
the book, having given a few facts to an illustrator who
hasn't read it either. The two guys are slobs and the woman

is an over-age groupie." *The Switch* is published in June. Kathy Werbelow, reviewing it for *The Detroit Free Press,* praises Leonard's work but takes him to task for his portrayal of women in *The Switch*: "Leonard's sexual attitudes are about as liberated as Mickey Spillane's. Even in a book that purports to be partly about a woman's self-discovery, the women are defined mostly in terms of their physical attributes." Leonard determines to take a closer look at his women characters and begins to give them more important roles. Dell releases *Swag* in paperback under the title *Ryan's Rules.* Joan Shepard is divorced from her husband, H. Clare Shepard. Leonard toys with the idea of using a pseudonym, Emmett Long, for his new Western *Legends* (later *Gunsights*). Universal buys the movie rights to *Unknown Man No. 89* for Alfred Hitchcock, one of the last properties optioned by him before his death in 1980. With a Birmingham, Michigan, producer, Tom Brank, plans to produce *The Hunted*; writes screenplay under title *Hat Trick. The Detroit News* asks Leonard to write a profile of the Detroit Police Department Felony Homicide Section, known as Squad 7. He later recalls it as "the kind of assignment a professional journalist would spend three or four days on. I spent weeks with the cops before I wrote a word. This was all new to me and I saw no end to the possibilities. As a result I spent most of the next three months with the homicide cops." "Impressions of Murder" is published in *The Detroit News Sunday Magazine* on November 12. Considers writing "a murder mystery from the police point of view entitled *Your Body, Your Case*; this evolves into the novel *Hang Tough* (later *City Primeval*).

1979   In March, *The Switch* is nominated for the Edgar Award for Best Paperback Mystery of 1978. *Gunsights* is published by Bantam in August. Leonard works on *City Primeval.* In the summer, Gregg Sutter and hard-boiled fiction expert Russell Rein visit Leonard at the Merrillwood Apartments in Birmingham; Sutter offers to do library research for Leonard. Leonard marries Joan Shepard in September and they move to a corner house at 476 Fairfax in Birmingham. Joan assumes an even greater role in his writing. Leonard tells an interviewer: "She has been called my truth index. She senses immediately when my people are acting out of character, taking on a slightly different sound, or when I'm repeating myself or using too many words."

1980   *City Primeval: High Noon in Detroit* is published in October
        by Arbor House, a company founded by Leonard's previ-
        ous editor at Dell, Donald Fine, who is now again his
        editor. United Artists buys the film rights, with Leon-
        ard writing the screenplay, under his original title *Hang
        Tough*. Writes original screenplay for *High Noon, Part II:
        The Return of Will Kane*, directed by Jerry Jameson and
        starring Lee Majors, a sequel to Fred Zinnemann's 1952
        movie. It is broadcast on CBS November 15. *Gold Coast* is
        published in December by Bantam.

1981   Hires Sutter in January to work for him as a researcher.
        Writes *Split Images* with Raymond Cruz (the protagonist
        of *City Primeval*) as hero, but Swanson warns that they
        won't be able to sell movie rights because United Artists
        owns the rights to the character; decides to change Ray-
        mond Cruz to Bryan Hurd and "lighten his mustache"
        without otherwise altering character. Begins a correspon-
        dence with crime novelist John D. MacDonald, who has
        written a glowing blurb for *Split Images*: "He doesn't
        cheat the reader. He gives true value." Director Sam Peck-
        inpah comes to Detroit in the spring to scout locations for
        Hang Tough. Due in part to the writers' strike, the film is
        not made. Leonard begins writing novel *Cat Chaser*. *Split
        Images* is published by Arbor House.

1982   *Cat Chaser* appears from Arbor House in June. A Western
        short story, "The Tonto Woman," is published by Double-
        day in anthology *Roundup*, edited by Stephen Overholser.
        For his next novel, *Stick*, reprises the character Ernest
        "Stick" Stickley, from *Swag*, saying he "wants to see what
        he's doing now."

1983   *Stick* published in February by Arbor House. Golan films
        Fifty-Two Pickup as *The Ambassador*, which Leonard notes
        has little resemblance to the novel: "It has none of my
        characters, none of my situations, nothing"; collects what
        he is owed but has his name removed from credits. In
        August, Swanson conducts an auction for Leonard's new
        novel *LaBrava* with a floor of $350,000 for the book plus
        $150,000 for the screenplay. *Stick* begins shooting in Octo-
        ber from Leonard's screenplay, directed by and starring
        Burt Reynolds. *LaBrava* is published by Arbor House in
        November.

1984   Discusses an original screenplay with Sidney Poitier, a sequel to *In the Heat of the Night*, set in Philadelphia; project goes nowhere, but some elements are transferred to new novel *Boardwalk* (later *Glitz*), set in Atlantic City; makes research trip there with Sutter in March. *LaBrava* receives Edgar Allan Poe Award from Mystery Writers of America for Best Novel. Swanson invites Leonard to his house. When Leonard remarks, "Do you realize you've represented me for thirty years, and this is the first time you've invited me into your house?" Swanson replies, "Well, kiddo, you weren't making any money to speak of, until recently." Swanson takes out an ad in the trade papers: "Not since I represented John O'Hara has a writer defined so well what happens between a man and a woman. Not since Damon Runyon has any fellow done dialogue that rings so true and is as entertaining at the same time. Not since James M. Cain has a writer shown how the lives of everyday people can turn into explosive melodrama. Not since Raymond Chandler have I had a man who knows so well the hills and valleys of plotting." Sees the movie *Stick* in June, and writes disappointed letter to Burt Reynolds: "When I'm writing I see real people and hear real people talking. But when I view the picture I see too often actors acting, actors hitting the wrong word, mugging, overstating or elaborating on a punch line, ad-libbing clichés, setting a record for the frequent use of 'asshole.' I hear what seem to me too many beats between exchanges, pauses for reactions, smiles for the benefit of the audience—like saying, get it?—or sneers or wide-eyed looks that I don't see in real life." Novelist Donald Westlake, aware of the situation, writes Leonard: "Dutch, why do you keep hoping to make a good movie . . . The books are ours; everything else is virgins thrown in the volcano. Be happy if the check is good."

1985   *Glitz* is published in February and appears on *The New York Times* Best Sellers list, a first for Leonard, who is now being touted as "the greatest living crime writer" and "an overnight success after 23 books." The book is enthusiastically reviewed in the *Times* by Stephen King. J. D. Reed, writing in *Time*, labels Leonard "the Dickens of Detroit." Leonard appears on the cover of *Newsweek* in April. Universal releases *Stick* on April 26; the film is unsuccessful. Arbor House publishes *Elmore Leonard's Dutch Treat* in

December, an omnibus containing *The Hunted*, *Swag*, and *Mr. Majestyk,* with an introduction by George Will. During this period begins to correspond with many other writers, including Charles Willeford, Lawrence Block, Evan Hunter, Tony Hillerman, Pete Hamill, Russell Banks, Ross Thomas, Jim Harrison, James W. Hall, Andre Dubus, Dean Koontz, and Walker Percy.

1986   Contributes chapter ("Quitting") to Dennis Wholey's *The Courage to Change: Personal Conversations About Alcoholism*, published in January by Houghton Mifflin; credits Joan for helping him to stop drinking: "She was so supportive, without pushing or nagging, but with sympathy—the right kind of sympathy. She'd say, 'You are absolutely out of your mind.' Maybe it was the way she said it." Leonard says that quitting drinking has helped his writing: "I have so much more confidence in my work. I can try different things. I can experiment in different styles. I look forward to working in the morning, something I didn't use to do. It was always a chore." He also acknowledges a spiritual dimension: "Today I realize I have complete trust in God. I'm in His hands. Now what I'm going to do is try to live according to His will. God's will, I think, is misinterpreted. God's will to me means one thing—love. . . . The key is getting out of yourself." After reading his screenplay for *Glitz*, a studio executive, according to Leonard, "says, 'All you've done is adapt the book, scene for scene.' I said, yes. He said, 'You don't have to be a screenwriter to do that.' I think what he was saying, the screenwriter is obliged to revise scenes and dialogue, change things around, whether he feels the need to or not." John D. MacDonald writes to Leonard: "I don't see how you endure those people, and endure group effort, and endure conferences and stupid revision requests and kindred bullshit. Please write the Hollywood book and kill them off in ugly ways." Writes *Bandits*, a novel in which the Nicaraguan Contras are cast as the bad guys. "I didn't go into it with the idea of making it political," Leonard says. "A producer had told me he would love to do the big caper kind of movie, where the old pros get together and plan a heist, like *The Asphalt Jungle*. I said, 'Yeah, I'd like to try that. It's been done before, but I haven't done it.'" Arbor House publishes *Elmore Leonard's Double Dutch Treat* in April, a second omnibus containing *The Moonshine War*, *Gold Coast*, and *City Primeval*. The Cannon Group releases *52 Pick-Up* on November 7, directed by John Frankenheimer and starring Roy Scheider. The location has been changed from Detroit to Los Angeles. Although the story line has been considerably changed, Frankenheimer tells Leonard: "We used so much dialogue out of the book that I think you deserve a screen credit." Leonard later recalls: "All I did was add commas where proper names are used in the dialogue, and spell 'all right' with two words." The script is credited to Leonard and John Steppling.

1987   *Bandits* is published in January by Arbor House. Universal pilot *Desperado*, written by Leonard, premieres on NBC in April; it is produced by Walter Mirisch, directed by Virgil W. Vogel, and stars Alex McArthur. Adapts *The Rosary Murders*, a novel by fellow Detroiter and former priest William X. Kienzle. Leonard finds the story line unsatisfying: "There's no way to show who the murderer might be, so you don't see him until the last act. It's not unlike that Eastwood movie *Tightrope*, where they finally pull a ski mask off the killer and the audience thinks, Yeah? So who's that?" *Touch*, written in 1977, is published in September by Arbor House. To research a new novel, *Get Shorty*, sends Sutter to Florida to talk to Bill Marshall and Chili Palmer about collections, shylocking, and Chili's mob-related experiences.

1988   *Freaky Deaky* is published by Arbor House in May. It marks a return to a Detroit setting, and is later cited by Leonard as his favorite among his books. Leonard contributes essay "On Richard Bissell" to *Rediscoveries II*, published by Carroll & Graf.

1989   Moves to a much larger home less than a mile away, with swimming pool and tennis court, at 2192 Yarmouth in Bloomfield Village. *Killshot* is published by Arbor House in April. *The Rosary Murders*, directed by Fred Walton and starring Donald Sutherland, is released in August.

1990   Mother, who has been living at the home of her daughter Margaret Madey in Little Rock, Arkansas, dies on February 9 at age 95. *Get Shorty* is published by Delacorte in August, marking Leonard's return to Delacorte and editor

Jackie Farber. Buys condo at Old Port Cove Harbor Village Condominiums: 1133 Marine Way East, No. I-1L, North Palm Beach, Florida. Turner Pictures releases *Border Shootout*, based on *The Law at Randado*, directed by Chris McIntyre and starring Cody Glenn and Glenn Ford, directly to video.

1991   H. N. Swanson dies on May 31 at age 91. In June, Leonard is guest speaker at convention sponsored by Western Merchandisers in Amarillo, Texas; meets Raylan Davis, loves his first name, and asks him: "How would you like to be the star of my next book?" *Maximum Bob* is published by Delacorte in August. Makes research trip for *Pronto* with Joan to Rapallo, Italy. *Cat Chaser,* directed by Abel Ferrara and with a screenplay by Leonard, is released by Vestron Pictures. Leonard is the subject of a BBC documentary, *Elmore Leonard's Criminal Records*, produced and directed by Mike Dibb and Rosana Horsley. The filmmakers follow Leonard on visits to locations from his work, and to meet people who influenced his books and characters. Filming took place in Detroit, Birmingham, Algonac, Walpole Island (Canada), West Palm Beach, Belle Glade, and Hollywood. Interviewees include Joan, Sutter, Detroit homicide detectives, Judge Marvin Mounts, a Palm Beach County, Florida, judge who helped Leonard shape the title character of *Maximum Bob*, and Walter Mirisch.

1992   The International Association of Crime Writers awards Leonard the North American Hammett Prize for *Maximum Bob*. Receives the Grand Master Edgar Award from the Mystery Writers of America. *Rum Punch* is published by Delacorte in August. Buys a bigger condo at Old Port Cove on the Intercoastal Waterway. An independent production of *Split Images*, directed by Sheldon Larry and starring Gregory Harrison, is released directly to video. Director William Friedkin, whose wife, Sherry Lansing, is the head of Paramount, commissions Leonard to write an original screenplay, *Stinger*, set in Palm Beach County. In December, Joan is diagnosed with lymphoma.

1993   Joan Leonard dies of lymphoma on January 13. Leonard makes research trip with Sutter for his next novel, *Riding the Rap*, traveling to Cassadaga, Florida. In the spring, hires gardener Christine Kent (born April 4, 1949) to supervise care for the property. In August, after a brief courtship, Leonard marries Christine. *Pronto* is published by Delacorte in October; it introduces the character Deputy U.S. Marshal Raylan Givens. Michael Siegel of the Swanson agency becomes Leonard's agent and then manager. Friedkin and Leonard give up on *Stinger*. Leonard has lost his enthusiasm for writing scripts: "This is the last one," he says.

1994   An excerpt from *Riding the Rap* is published in *The New Yorker* in June. Travels with Christine to Australia for Adelaide Festival. In November receives first John D. MacDonald Award for Excellence in Florida Fiction at the fifth John D. MacDonald conference in Fort Lauderdale. Short story "Hurrah for Captain Early" is published in Doubleday anthology *New Trails: 23 Original Stories from Western Writers of America*, edited by John Jakes and Martin H. Greenberg.

1995   In March, Christine's daughter, Geraldine Regal, is killed in a car accident on Woodward Avenue after visiting her mother and Leonard. Miramax options *Bandits*, *Freaky Deaky*, *Killshot*, and *Rum Punch* for Quentin Tarantino; Tarantino initially envisions adapting, producing, and costarring in *Killshot* opposite Robert De Niro, with Tony Scott directing, before deciding to adapt *Rum Punch*. Elmore's Olympia SG3 manual typewriter breaks and he replaces it with an IBM Wheelwriter 1000. When Sutter sends Leonard a ten-year-old newspaper clipping of a female U.S. Marshal in front of the Federal Courthouse in Fort Lauderdale, holding a shotgun during a pretrial hearing for three Colombian nationals on cocaine charges, Leonard reacts: "She's a book!" While in Florida, Leonard and Sutter connect with their friend Special Agent James O. Born and meet with a Florida Department of Law Enforcement task force hunting down six inmates from Glades Correctional Institution in Belle Glade who escaped through a tunnel they dug beneath a chapel under construction on the compound. *Riding the Rap* is published by Delacorte in June. Accepting post of president of the Mystery Writers of America, Leonard says: "When I was told I had been named your president for this year I thought, Wait a minute, the only club I've ever belonged to is AA and I haven't been to a meeting in about five years. I'm not exactly a joiner." MGM releases *Get Shorty*, directed by Barry Sonnenfeld and starring John Travolta and Gene Hackman, in October. The film is a critical and box office success, ending a run of disappointing adaptations. Leonard is pleased by *Get Shorty*, commenting: "I . . . was surprised to see the film had become a comedy. I told Barry Sonnenfeld after I saw it, 'I don't write comedy.' He said, 'No, but it's a funny book.' . . . The lines were delivered the way they were written, seriously, the way I heard the characters when I was writing." At the premiere, MGM president Frank Mancuso asks Leonard to write a sequel. Along with Dave Barry, Carl Hiaasen, Edna Buchanan, and nine other writers, contributes a chapter to *Naked Came the Manatee*, a compilation novel set in Miami, published as a serial in the *Miami Herald*.

1996   Considers writing a Chili Palmer novel set in the New York fashion business, but changes his mind and tells Sutter: "Let's do Cuba a hundred years ago." Receives honorary Doctor of Humane Letters degree from Florida Atlantic University. *Out of Sight* is published by Delacorte in September. Receives the Michigan Author Award.

1997   *Naked Came the Manatee* is published by Putnam in January. In the summer, goes to Los Angeles with Sutter to research *Be Cool*, the sequel to *Get Shorty*, reprising the character Chili Palmer and set in the music business; meets music industry figures including Guy Oseary (Madonna's manager) and producer Rick Rubin; sits in on a Red Hot Chili Peppers rehearsal and a mixing session with Don Was and Richie Sambora for Sambora's newest CD. Receives Literary Lion award from the New York Public Library. During the course of the year five television and theatrical films based on Leonard's work appear: *Last Stand at Saber River*, directed by Dick Lowry and starring Tom Selleck, broadcast in January on Turner Network Television; *Touch*, directed by Paul Schrader and starring Skeet Ulrich, released by Lumiere International/United Artists in February; a TV movie of *Pronto*, directed by Jim McBride, starring Peter Falk, and featuring the first appearance on screen of Raylan Givens (James LeGros), broadcast in June on Showtime; *Elmore Leonard's Gold Coast*, directed by Peter Weller and starring David Caruso, broadcast on Showtime in September; and Quentin Tarantino's *Jackie Brown*, based on *Rum Punch* and starring Pam Grier, Samuel L. Jackson, Robert Forster, and Robert De Niro. Leonard considers *Jackie Brown* his favorite among adaptations of his work.

1998   Michigan governor John Engler decrees that January 16, 1998, is Elmore Leonard Day; presentation takes place at Borders Books in Birmingham. At a Writers Bloc event held at the Writers Guild Theatre in Beverly Hills on January 23, he is interviewed by novelist Martin Amis, who says of Leonard: "He is as close as anything you have here in America to a national novelist, a concept that almost seemed to die with Charles Dickens." *Cuba Libre*, novel set in the period of the Spanish-American War, is published by Delacorte in February. Michael Siegel brings in Andrew Wylie as Leonard's new literary agent; Wylie combines works from two publishers, William Morrow and Dell, in uniform editions designed by Chip Kidd. In June, Universal releases *Out of Sight*, directed by Steven Soderbergh, with a screenplay by Scott Frank and starring George Clooney. Despite good reviews the movie does not do well at the box office because of an unfavorable release date. Becomes member of the Academy of Motion Picture Arts and Sciences. Warner Brothers Television broadcasts six episodes of *Maximum Bob*, a series produced by Barry Sonnenfeld, written by Alex Gansa and starring Beau Bridges, on ABC in the summer. Leonard dismisses it as "Heehaw, The Movie." The first collection of Leonard's Western stories is published by Delacorte as *The Tonto Woman and Other Western Stories* in September. Photographed by Annie Leibovitz for an American Express ad, part of their "Portraits" campaign.

1999   *Be Cool* is published by Delacorte Press in February. On the book tour, Leonard makes appearances in Los Angeles, New York, Boston, and Detroit with Massachusetts-based band The Stone Coyotes, who are featured in the book; he reads from *Be Cool* and they play songs, including "Odessa," written specifically for the book. Short story "Sparks" is published in Delacorte anthology *Murder and Obsession*, edited by Otto Penzler. Short story "Hanging Out at the Buena Vista" is published in *USA Weekend* summer fiction issue in June.

2000 Receives Doctor of Humane Letters, University of Michigan, and gives the commencement address for the winter graduating class. *Pagan Babies* is published in September by Delacorte. As guest of honor at Bouchercon (The World Mystery Convention) in Denver in September, Leonard delivers his "Ten Rules of Writing," written on two unruled yellow pages that afternoon at the Adam's Mark Hotel. The rules (including the famous "Try to leave out the part that readers tend to skip") will be reprinted many times. Writes introduction to a new edition of *The Friends of Eddie Coyle*, published by Owl Books in September.

2001 "Ten Rules of Writing" is published in *The New York Times* (July 16) as part of their Writers on Writing Series, under the title "Easy on the Adverbs, Exclamation Points and Especially Hooptedoodle." Short story "Chickasaw Charlie Hoke" (whose title character is later incorporated in *Tishomingo Blues*) is published in New Millennium Press anthology *Murderers' Row*, edited by Otto Penzler. Writes introduction to new edition of W. C. Heinz's boxing novel *The Professional*, published by Da Capo Press. "Fire in the Hole," a Raylan Givens novella, is published by Contentville Press as an e-book. Leonard, an avowed technophobe, remarks: "I wrote a story for Contentville on the Internet, a novella that I won't be able to read because I don't have a computer." Researching *Tishomingo Blues*, Leonard and Sutter go to Miracle Strip Amusement Park in Panama City Beach, Florida, to watch high divers set up diving towers; also make trips to Civil War reenactments in Michigan and battle sites in Mississippi, including Corinth and Brices Cross Roads.

2002 Signs new publishing contract with HarperCollins. *Tishomingo Blues* is published by their William Morrow imprint in February. In April, presents appreciation of John Steinbeck at ceremony in New York to celebrate the twentieth anniversary of The Library of America. Short story collection *When the Women Come Out to Dance* is published in November; the title story is performed as a one-act play by Food For Thought Productions in New York, with Judith Light and Rosie Perez reading. Also in the collection is "Fire in the Hole," in which Raylan Givens returns to his native Harlan County, Kentucky. Researches novel *Mr. Paradise*, returning to a Detroit setting, and featuring the

Detroit Police Homicide Squad. HarperCollins, under the HarperTorch imprint, begins releasing mass market editions of nearly all Leonard's novels.

2003   A film of *Tishomingo Blues*, with Don Cheadle intended to star and direct, is scrapped by producer Bob Yari. ABC Television broadcasts *Karen Sisco* (October 1–December 11), series produced by Bob Brush and starring Carla Gugino and Robert Forster, based on characters from *Out of Sight* and the short story "Karen Makes Out." ABC cancels the series, in Leonard's estimation, "just when it was starting to settle down."

2004   Three books published by William Morrow: novel *Mr. Paradise* (January), children's story *A Coyote's in the House* (May), and *The Complete Western Stories of Elmore Leonard* (November). Warner Brothers releases remake of *The Big Bounce*, directed by George Armitage and starring Owen Wilson. Leonard comments: "Now I have seen the worst movie ever made." His main complaint is the transposition of the story from the "Thumb" area of Michigan to the North Shore of Oahu: "Every time there was a break in the action, they'd cut away to surfers."

2005   MGM releases *Be Cool*, directed by F. Gary Gray and starring John Travolta, in March; the film is poorly received critically and is a commercial disappointment. *The Hot Kid* is published by William Morrow in May, introducing another U.S. Marshal character, Carl Webster; the antagonist, Jack Belmont, is named for Leonard's first great-grandson. In September, Leonard begins writing *Comfort to the Enemy*, a Carl Webster story to be serialized in fourteen parts in *The New York Times Sunday Magazine*. Feels constrained by *Times* editorial rules not designed for fiction, especially prohibitions on foul language: "They rendered my bad guys nearly mute."

2006   Proclamation by the State of Oklahoma and the city of Tulsa names May 12, 2006, as Elmore Leonard Day. Receives Cartier Diamond Dagger Award from the UK Crime Writers Association, the Louisiana Writer of the Year for 2006 at the Louisiana Book Festival, and the Raymond Chandler Award at the Noir in Festival in Courmayeur, Italy.

2007   On January 13, Elmore's sister Margaret Leonard Madey dies in Little Rock at age 87. *Up in Honey's Room*, the third Carl Webster novel, set in Detroit in the 1940s, is published by William Morrow in May. *Elmore Leonard's 10 Rules of Writing* published as a book, with illustrations by Joe Ciardiello, by William Morrow. Lionsgate releases a remake of *3:10 to Yuma*, directed by James Mangold and starring Russell Crowe and Christian Bale. Leonard has no connection with production. The radically altered final scene bemuses him: "It was a dumb ending."

2008   Son Peter Leonard publishes first novel, *Quiver*, in May; he and his father begin appearing together at festivals and libraries. Receives the 2008 F. Scott Fitzgerald Award at the F. Scott Fitzgerald Conference in Rockville, Maryland. Two short films are made from Leonard stories: *The Tonto Woman*, directed by Daniel Barber with a screenplay by Joe Shrapnel, and *Sparks*, written and directed by Joseph Gordon-Levitt; *The Tonto Woman* is nominated for an Academy Award. Leonard writes foreword to Walter Mirisch's autobiography, *I Thought We Were Making Movies, Not History*.

2009   Receives Owen Wister Award from the Western Writers of America. The Weinstein Company releases *Killshot*, directed by John Madden, starring Mickey Rourke and Diane Lane, in January. Plagued with rewrites and interference, the film has only a token theatrical release. *Comfort to the Enemy* is published by Weidenfeld & Nicolson in April. *Road Dogs* is published by William Morrow in May. In December, receives Lifetime Achievement Award from PEN USA. Visits set of FX cable television series *Justified* (based on *Fire in the Hole*) in Santa Clarita, California. Timothy Olyphant, who plays Raylan Givens, and the show's creator, Graham Yost, encourage him to write a Raylan story. Credited as an executive producer on the show, Leonard says: "I felt I ought to do something." Is impressed with Yost's devotion to Leonard's work, indicated by Yost's giving each of the show's writers a blue wristband with the initials "W.W.E.D." (What Would Elmore Do?).

2010   *Justified* premieres on March 16. *Djibouti* is published by William Morrow in October. Christine is spending much time apart from Leonard at the condo in North Palm Beach.

2011   Leonard receives a Peabody Award as executive producer on *Justified*. Short story "Chick Killer," featuring Deputy U.S. Marshal Karen Sisco, is published in *McSweeney's* Issue #39. Writes foreword to Julia Reyes Taubman's book *Detroit: 138 Square Miles.* In April, Christine returns from Florida and informs Leonard that she wants a divorce; the marriage has been in trouble for some time, and she has become increasingly alienated from Leonard and his family.

2012   Final novel *Raylan*—combining three separate Raylan stories—published in January; spends five weeks on *The New York Times* Best Sellers list. Film of *Freaky Deaky*, directed by Charles Matthau, is released in April, and is poorly received. Short story "Ice Man"—the first chapter of his novel in progress—is published in the June issue of *The Atlantic.* In November, receives National Book Foundation Award for Distinguished Contribution to American Letters; he is introduced at the ceremony by Martin Amis. Divorce becomes final in December.

2013   In February, writes whimsical op-ed piece for *The New York Times* during selection of new pope entitled "For Pope: A Dude Like Dad." In May, receives the Thomas Cooper Award at the University of South Carolina. Tours the special collections library, examining the original typescript of *The Friends of Eddie Coyle* as well as many rare Hemingway editions. Has trouble getting new novel *Blue Dreams* going; decides to bring Raylan in one more time ("He's always there when I need him"). On July 29 Sutter calls to ask if he wants to accept yet another writing prize, the Scripter award from the University of Southern California; Leonard turns it down, saying, "I have to write my book." At a little after nine o'clock that evening, suffers a massive stroke. After three weeks in the Intensive Care Unit and Hospital hospice at William Beaumont Hospital, Leonard arrives home. A hospital bed is placed in his office, and he is surrounded by his children and grandchildren. He dies at 7:15 the following morning, August 20. Funeral is held at Holy Name Catholic Church at 630 Harmon Street in Birmingham, Michigan. It is attended by many friends and family; Timothy Olyphant, Graham

Yost, Scott Frank, James W. Hall, and close friend Mike Lupica are among those in attendance. Navy officers in white dress uniforms conduct a "farewell to arms" flag presentation and play "Taps" on a bugle for Leonard, as a Navy veteran of World War II. His ashes were interred at Greenwood Cemetery in Birmingham, Michigan, on October 11, 2016, on what would have been his ninety-first birthday. The headstone bears the inscription "The Dickens of Detroit."

This volume contains four novels—*Last Stand at Saber River* (1959), *Hombre* (1961), *Valdez Is Coming* (1970), and *Forty Lashes Less One* (1972)—and a selection of eight short stories by Elmore Leonard.

Leonard's earliest published writing was in the Western genre, beginning with the short story "Trail of the Apache" (1951), included in this volume; he published twenty-nine other Western short stories, all but three from 1952 to 1959. He published eight Western novels from *The Bounty Hunters* (1954) to *Gunsights* (1979).

The original publishers of the four novels in this volume were as follows:

Last Stand at Saber River (New York: Dell Publishing Co., April 1959). This was published as a Dell First Edition.

Hombre (New York: Ballantine Books, September 1961).

Valdez Is Coming (Greenwich, Connecticut: Fawcett Gold Medal Books, October 1970).

Forty Lashes Less One (New York: Bantam Books, April 1972).

All of these were originally published as paperback originals. Leonard did not revise them after their initial publication. The texts in this volume are those of the first editions.

The stories in this volume originally appeared in the following periodicals:

Trail of the Apache: *Argosy*, December 1951. Leonard's original title was "Apache Agent."

The Rustlers: *Zane Grey's Western*, February 1953. Leonard's original title was "Along the Pecos."

Three-Ten to Yuma: *Dime Western Magazine*, March 1953.

Blood Money: *Western Story Magazine*, October 1953. Leonard's original title was "Rich Miller's Hand."

The Captives: *Argosy*, February 1955.

The Nagual: *2-Gun Western*, November 1956. Leonard's original title was "The Accident at John Stam's."

The Kid: *Western Short Stories*, December 1956. Leonard's original title was "The Gift of Regalo."

The Tonto Woman: Stephen Overholser, ed., *Roundup: A Western Writers of America Anthology* (Garden City, New York: Doubleday, 1982).

In 2004 *The Complete Western Stories of Elmore Leonard* (New York: William Morrow/HarperCollins) was published under the editorship of Leonard's longtime associate Gregg Sutter. While surviving typescripts of Leonard's stories sometimes indicate minor differences from the periodical texts, the Morrow anthology in general conforms to the published versions but establishes a consistent format for stories that first appeared in a wide variety of periodicals. There is no indication that Leonard wished to make any changes to these stories following their original publication. The texts included in this volume are those of *The Complete Western Stories of Elmore Leonard*.

This volume presents the texts of the original printings chosen for inclusion here, but it does not attempt to reproduce features of their typographic design. The texts are presented without change, except for the correction of typographical errors. Spelling, punctuation, and capitalization are often expressive features, and they are not altered, even when inconsistent or irregular. The following is a list of typographical errors corrected, cited by page and line number: 98.4, on his; 146.8, Colt's,; 161.35, coming, into; 186.36–37, everyone; 188.26, this." The; 189.38, it."; 257.25, to?; 283.21, Hauchuca; 362.10, answered; 415.26, woman Tell; 417.2, Remmington; 423,6, neither.; 428.22, words.'; 437.9, named; 453.24, year's; 462.19, said.; 469.5, persevernce.; 480.1, tailer; 483.8, Shelly; 492.12, or your; 495.6, awkardly; 498.3, tempation; 507.25, her, twisted; 507.31, glow.; 513.9, said.; 536.8, lizzards; 536.34, tatoos; 540.19, nose.; 541.23, telling telling; 546.7, anytime; 546.10, starting; 558.18, Sentinel".; 566.11, sight of of; 571.29, him; 572.7, "Dancy; 575.8, shouder; 580.11, creeking; 592.10, Cook's; 610.1, Commanches; 610.2, Commanche; 636.12, have had bit; 657.10, The Fords,; 662.2, way of.

Notes

In the notes below, the reference numbers denote page and line of this volume (the line count includes titles and headings but not blank lines). No note is made for material found in standard desk-reference books. References to the Bible have been keyed to the King James version. For further information on Elmore Leonard's life and works, and references to other studies, see Gregg Sutter, "Research and the Elmore Leonard Novel: Parts One and Two," *The Armchair Detective* (Winter and Spring 1986); Gregg Sutter, "A Conversation with Elmore Leonard," in *The Complete Western Stories of Elmore Leonard* (New York: William Morrow/HarperCollins, 2004); David Geherin, *Elmore Leonard* (New York: Continuum, 1989); James E. Devlin, *Elmore Leonard* (New York: Twayne Publishers, 1999); Paul Challen, *Get Dutch!: A Biography of Elmore Leonard* (Toronto: ECW Press, 2000); and Charles J. Rzepka, *Being Cool: The Work of Elmore Leonard* (Baltimore: Johns Hopkins University Press, 2013).

LAST STAND AT SABER RIVER

6.11–12 J. A. Wharton . . . Nathan Bedford Forrest] John Austin Wharton (1828–1865), colonel of the 8th Texas Cavalry, later promoted to major general; Brigadier General Forrest (1821–1877), Confederate cavalry commander, later promoted to lieutenant general.

6.14 Murfreesboro] Forrest raided the Union base at Murfreesboro, Tennessee, on July 13, 1862.

6.21 Wilson's Union Cavalry] Brigadier General James H. Wilson (1837–1925) commanded the cavalry corps of the Army of the Ohio during the Franklin campaign.

6.26–27 General Hood . . . Nashville.] Lieutenant General John Bell Hood (1831–1879) commanded the Confederate Army of Tennessee, July 1864–January 1865. Hood's attempt to capture Nashville failed, and his army was defeated in the battle of Nashville, December 15–16, 1864.

6.33–34 Chickamauga . . . Fort Pillow, Bryce's Crossroads, Thompson's Station] Battle of Chickamauga, Chickamauga Creek, Georgia, September 18–20, 1863; the Confederate capture of Fort Pillow, Henning, Tennessee, April 12, 1864, ended with the massacre of hundreds of African American Union soldiers; Battle of Brice's Crossroads, Mississippi, June 10, 1864; Battle of Thompson's Station, Tennessee, March 5, 1863. All these battles were Confederate victories.

10.14   Rochester lamps] Improved kerosene lamp originally manufactured in Rochester, New York, and patented in 1884.

10.33–36   Kirby Smith . . . Bull Nelson] Confederate Major General Edmund Kirby Smith (1824–1893) defeated Union troops under Major General William "Bull" Nelson (1824–1862) at the battle of Richmond, Kentucky (August 29–30, 1862).

11.38   Fort Buchanan] U.S. Army post near present-day Sonoita, Arizona, 1856–65.

17.22–23   Sherrod Hunter's Texas Brigade] Sherod Hunter (b. 1834) served as a Confederate captain in Arizona Territory, Texas, and Louisiana; his activities subsequent to the war's end are unknown.

40.26   Tishomingo Creek] The battle of Brice's Crossroads (see note 6.33–34) was fought along the eastern side of Tishomingo Creek.

40.31   Gatrel's Georgia Company] Cavalry unit commanded by Henry Gartrell.

41.23   Kossuth army hat] Slouch hat; wide-brimmed military hat so called in the U.S. after Hungarian revolutionary Lajos Kossuth (1802–1894).

62.40   remuda] Herd of horses available for selection by ranch hands.

64.32–34   Chancellorsville . . . Von Gilsa's exposed flank] The Union brigade commanded by Prussian-born Colonel Leopold von Gilsa (1824–1870) was routed on May 2, 1863, by the Confederate attack led by Thomas J. (Stonewall) Jackson against the exposed Union flank near Chancellorsville.

65.12   J. H. Carleton] Union Brigadier General James Henry Carleton (1815–1873) commanded the Department of New Mexico (including Arizona), 1862–65.

89.23   second Seminole war] The second war between the United States and the Seminoles was fought in Florida, 1835–42.

89.29–30   Fort Marion] U.S. Army fort and prison established in 1821 at Spanish fortress Castillo de San Marcos in St. Augustine, Florida.

90.7   Dick Taylor] Confederate Lieutenant General Richard Taylor (1826–1879), son of President Zachary Taylor.

92.34   Abel Streight] Union army colonel (1828–1892) who led a brigade in an unsuccessful raid through northern Alabama, April–May 1863.

HOMBRE

169.16   Fort Thomas] U.S. Army fort in Graham County, Arizona, established in 1876 and given the name Fort Thomas in 1882; used by the Department of the Interior since 1891.

173.30 *tizwin*] Or tiswin; fermented beverage made from mescal plants.

186.4   Rochester lamp] See note 10.14.

186.8   Concord] Coach manufactured in Concord, New Hampshire, beginning in 1826, and known for its leather suspension braces, which made for a
more comfortable ride.

196.31 Chato and Chihuahua] Chato (c. 1860–1934), Apache warrior who
led raids in 1882 and was captured two years later; he later served as a scout
for the U.S. Army. Chihuahua (c. 1825–1901), Chiricahua Apache chief who
led raids in Arizona and Mexico in the 1870s and 1880s.

196.36 *mozos*] Male servants.

204.31 *palo verdes*] Flowering plants (*Parkinsonia*) of the pea family, native
to semidesert regions.

209.30 Yuma] Yuma Territorial Prison in Yuma, Arizona, operated from
1876 until 1909, when prisoners were transferred to the new prison in Florence, Arizona.

VALDEZ IS COMING

283.21 Fort Huachuca Tenth fuzzhead Cavalry] Fort Huachuca, U.S. Army
installation in Arizona established in 1877; 10th Cavalry, one of two African
American cavalry regiments established in 1866.

288.12 tulapai] Apache beverage made from fermented corn along with roots
and herbs.

294.28 when General Crook chased Geronimo] Brigadier General George
Crook (1828–1890), as commander of the Department of Arizona, pursued
Chiricahua Apache leader Geronimo (c. 1829–1909) after the latter broke out
of the San Carlos Reservation in 1881, and again when, after surrendering in
1884, Geronimo broke out again the following year. Geronimo's final surrender was negotiated in September 1886.

294.29–30 Whipple Barracks] Fort Whipple was established in December
1863 and moved in March 1864 to a location near the site of Prescott, Arizona,
the capital of Arizona Territory founded at the same time.

315.6–8 Porfirio Díaz and Carmelita at Niagara Falls, and the Prince of
Wales on his visit to Washington.] Mexican president Díaz (1830–1915) and
his second wife Carmen Romero Rubio (1864–1944) visited Niagara Falls
during their honeymoon travels in the United States in 1883. In 1860, the
future Edward VII (1841–1910) made an extended trip to the United States,
the first by an heir to the British throne.

316.10 Fort Apache] Established in 1870 on the White Mountain River in
Arizona.

316.32–33   "Peaches," . . . Tso-ay] Tso-ay (or Tzoe) was a Cibecue Apache who after fighting with Chato's band was captured by the U.S. Army in 1883.

316.40   Fort Sill, Oklahoma] Established 1869 by the 10th Cavalry, the fort was also the site of the Kiowa-Comanche Agency.

321.32   *rurales*] The Guardia Rural, Mexican police force founded in 1861, deployed against bandits and later as an instrument of political repression.

336.19   The Canticle of the Sun] Hymn of praise written in the Umbrian dialect of Italian by St. Francis of Assisi around 1224.

344.2   *chivarra*] Goatskin.

399.12   *atole*] Hot beverage made from corn and *masa* (cooked maize flour).

FORTY LASHES LESS ONE

419.1–2   FORTY LASHES LESS ONE] 2 Corinthians 11:24: Five times I received at the hands of the Jews the forty lashes less one.

422.12   Yuma Territorial Prison] See note 209.30.

427.37   Fort Leavenworth] The military prison at Fort Leavenworth, Kansas, was established in 1874.

433.5   Siboney] Village near Santiago de Cuba where U.S. forces landed in 1898 during the Spanish-American War.

459.9   24th Infantry Regiment] African American U.S. Army unit established in 1869.

469.3   what St. Paul said about being in prison] Four books of the New Testament—Ephesians, Philippians, Colossians, and Philemon—are said to have been written by the apostle Paul while in prison.

487.12   *Ephesians* 4:1–6.] I, therefore, the prisoner of the Lord, beseech you to walk worthy of the calling with which you were called, with all lowliness and gentleness, with long suffering, bearing with one another in love, endeavoring to keep the unity of the Spirit in the bond of peace. *There is* one body and one Spirit, just as you were called in one hope of your calling; one Lord, one faith, one baptism; one God and Father of all, who *is* above all, and through all, and in you all.

494.2   that woman at the well.] See John 4:6–29.

494.5   the time they're stoning the whore] See John 7:53–8:11.

495.23–24   knocked to the ground the way St. Paul did.] See Acts 9:4.

497.5–15   'Brethren, gladly . . . cold and nakedness.'] See 2 Corinthians 11:19–27.

497.19–20   'My grace . . . in weakness.'] See 2 Corinthians 12:9.

498.10–13   'whoever brings . . . multitude of sins.'] See James 5:20.

498.36–37   'We know . . . abiding in him.'] See 1 John 3:15.

500.2–3   Ham made some dirty remark] See Genesis 9:22.

502.29   Geronimo] See note 294.28. Geronimo died February 17, 1909, at the hospital of Fort Sill, Oklahoma, where he continued to be held as a prisoner of war.

STORIES

591.12   wickiups] Apache dwellings made of brush, often covered with animal hides or blankets.

591.22   Fort Thomas] See note 169.16.

592.10–11   Cooke's "Cavalry Tactics"] *Cavalry Tactics* (1861), manual by Colonel Philip St. George Cooke (1809–1895), who served as a Union brigadier general during the Civil War.

594.5   "Dandy 5th,"] The 5th U.S. Cavalry Regiment.

597.17   Crook] See note 294.28.

598.39   Arivaipa] A band of the San Carlos Apaches.

601.22   tizwin] See note 173.30.

609.38   Quana Parker at Adobe Walls] Quahadi Comanche war chief Quanah Parker (c. 1845–1911) led a large party of Comanches and Cheyennes against buffalo hunters at the trading post Adobe Walls in Hutchinson County, Texas, in 1874; their attack was repelled after three days of fighting.

618.2–3   Cochise . . . Mangas Coloradas] Cochise (c. 1824–1874), Central Chiricahua Apache leader, who conducted raids against U.S. troops and civilians, 1861–72, before agreeing to live on a reservation; Mangas Coloradas (1795–1863), chief of the Eastern Chiricahua Apaches, allied himself with his son-in-law Cochise in an attack on U.S. Army troop; ultimately captured and taken to Fort McLane, New Mexico, where he was killed and decapitated while in custody.

618.21   *Tinneh*] Or Tineh. Apache: the people.

619.1   U-sen] Apache: God.

624.32   Fort Apache] See note 316.10.

636.29–30   Bill Bonney's at Fort Sumner] William H. Bonney, putative identity of the outlaw known as Billy the Kid (1859?–1881). Fort Sumner, military fort and prison in southwestern New Mexico, 1863–69; the property, which was purchased by a private owner, was the scene of Billy the Kid's shooting by Sheriff Pat Garrett on July 14, 1881.

641.2   Fort Huachuca] See note 283.21.

646.16   Nana] Leader of the Warm Springs Apache (1815?–1895). In 1877, he fled the San Carlos reservation in Arizona to which the tribe had been relocated, and, assuming leadership after the death of Victorio in 1880, waged a long struggle against the U.S. Army and American settlers before surrendering to General George Crook in 1883.

656.22   *rurales*] See note 321.32.

702.2   vaquero] Cowboy; herdsman.

721.12   General Stoneman] George Stoneman, Jr. (1822–1894), Union cavalry officer in the Civil War; later military commander of the Department of Arizona, 1869–71.

721.13   Arbuckle's] Brothers John and Charles Arbuckle of Allegheny, Pennsylvania, patented a process of roasting coffee in 1865; their product, sold in one-pound bags and obviating the need for consumers to roast the beans themselves, became a staple in the American West.

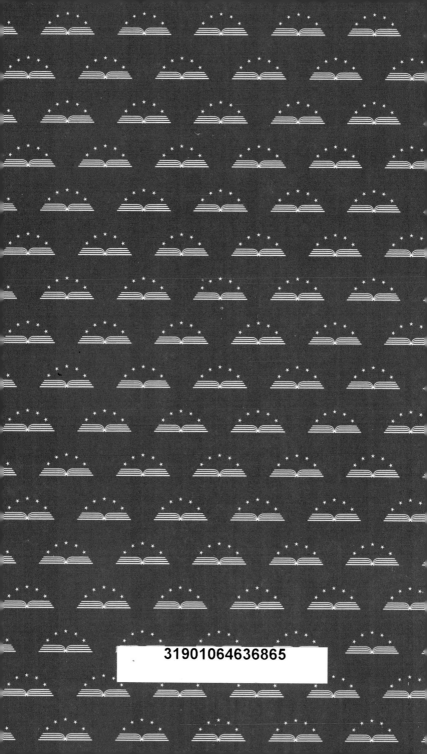